Jonathan Kellerman's series of detective novels featuring Alex Delaware have made him an internationally best-selling author. He lives with his wife, the novelist Faye Kellerman, and their four children in California.

Books by Jonathan Kellerman

WHEN THE BOUGH BREAKS

BLOOD TEST

OVER THE EDGE

THE BUTCHER'S THEATRE

SILENT PARTNER

TIME BOMB

PRIVATE EYES

DEVIL'S WALTZ

BAD LOVE

SELF-DEFENCE

THE WEB

THE CLINIC

SURVIVAL OF THE FITTEST

BILLY STRAIGHT

MONSTER

DOCTOR DEATH

Jonathan Kellerman

TIME WARNER PAPERBACKS

A *Time Warner* Book

First published in the United States in 2000
by Random House, Inc.

First published in Great Britain in 2000
by Little, Brown and Company

This edition published by Warner Books in 2002

Copyright © 2000 by Jonathan Kellerman

The moral right of the author has been asserted.

A CIP catalogue record for this book
is available from the British Library

ISBN 0 7515 2532 4

Printed and bound in Great Britain by
Clays Ltd, St Ives plc

Time Warner Paperbacks
An imprint of
Time Warner Books UK
Brettenham House
Lancaster Place
London WC2E 7EN

www.TimeWarnerBooks.co.uk

THIS ONE'S FOR
DR. JERRY DASH

1

Irony can be a rich dessert, so when the contents of the van were publicized, some people gorged. The ones who'd believed Eldon H. Mate to be the Angel of Death.

Those who'd considered him Mercy Personified grieved.

I viewed it through a different lens, had my own worries.

Mate was murdered in the very early hours of a sour-smelling, fog-laden Monday in September. No earth-quakes or wars interceded by sundown, so the death merited a lead story on the evening news. Newspaper headlines in the *Times* and the *Daily News* followed on Tuesday. TV dropped the story within twenty-four hours, but recaps ran in the Wednesday papers. In total, four days of coverage, the maximum in short-attention-span

L.A. unless the corpse is that of a princess or the killer can afford lawyers who yearn for Oscars.

No easy solve on this one; no breaks of any kind. Milo had been doing his job long enough not to expect otherwise.

He'd had an easy summer, catching a quartet of lovingly stupid homicides during July and August—one domestic violence taken to the horrible extreme and three brain-dead drunks shooting other inebriates in squalid Westside bars. Four murderers hanging around long enough to be caught. It kept his solve rate high, made it a bit—but not much—easier to be the only openly gay detective in LAPD.

"Knew I was due," he said. It was the Sunday after the murder when he phoned me at the house. Mate's corpse had been cold for six days and the press had moved on.

That suited Milo just fine. Like any artist, he craved solitude. He'd played his part by not giving the press anything to work with. Orders from the brass. One thing he and the brass could agree on: reporters were almost always the enemy.

What the papers *had* printed was squeezed out of clip-file biographies, the inevitable ethical debates, old photos, old quotes. Beyond the fact that Mate had been hooked up to his own killing machine, only the sketchiest details had been released:

Van parked on a remote section of Mulholland Drive, discovery by hikers just after dawn.

DR. DEATH MURDERED.

I knew more because Milo told me.

The call came in at eight P.M., just as Robin and I had

finished dinner. I was out the door, holding on to the straining leash of Spike, our little French bulldog. Pooch and I both looking forward to a night walk up the glen. Spike loved the dark because pointing at scurrying sounds let him pretend he was a noble hunter. I enjoyed getting out because I worked with people all day and solitude was always welcome.

Robin answered the phone, caught me in time, ended up doing dog-duty as I returned to my study.

"Mate's yours?" I said, surprised because he hadn't told me sooner. Suddenly edgy because that added a whole new layer of complexity to my week.

"Who else merits such blessing?"

I laughed softly, feeling my shoulders humping, rings of tension around my neck. The moment I'd heard about Mate I'd worried. Deliberated for a long time, finally made a call that hadn't been returned. I'd dropped the issue because there'd been no good reason not to. It really *wasn't* any of my business. Now, with Milo involved, all that had changed.

I kept the worries to myself. His call had nothing to do with my problem. Coincidence—one of those nasty little overlaps. Or maybe there really are only a hundred people in the world.

His reason for getting in touch was simple: the dreaded W word: whodunit. A case with enough psychopathology to make me potentially useful.

Also, I was his friend, one of the few people left in whom he could confide.

The psychopathology part was fine with me. What bothered me was the friendship component. Things I knew but didn't tell him. *Couldn't* tell him.

CHAPTER

2

I agreed to meet him at the crime scene the following Monday at 7:45 A.M. When he's at the West L.A. station, we usually travel together, but he was already scheduled for a 6:15 meeting downtown at Parker Center, so I drove myself.

"Sunrise prayer session?" I said. "Milking the cows with guys in suits?"

"Cleaning the stable while guys in suits rate my performance. Gonna have to find a clean tie."

"Is the topic Mate?"

"What else. They'll demand to know why I haven't accomplished squat, I'll nod a lot, say 'Yassuh, yassuh,' shuffle off."

Mate had been butchered fairly close to my home, and I set out at seven-thirty. The first leg of the trip was ten minutes north on Beverly Glen, the Seville fairly sailing because I was going against traffic, ignoring the angry faces of commuters incarcerated by the southbound crush.

Economic recovery and the customary graft had spurred unremitting roadworks in L.A., and hellish traffic was the result. This month it was the bottom of the glen: smug men in orange CalTrans vests installing new storm drains just in time for the next drought, the usual municipal division of labor: one guy working for every five standing around. Feeling like a pre-Bastille Royalist, I sped past the queue of Porsches and Jaguars forced to idle with clunkers and pickups. Democracy by oppression, everyone coerced into bumper-nudging intimacy.

At Mulholland, I turned left and drove four miles west, past seismically strained dream houses and empty lots that said optimism wasn't for everyone. The road coiled, scything through weeds, brush, saplings, other kindling, twisted upward sharply and changed to packed, ocher soil as the asphalt continued east and was renamed Encino Hills Drive.

Up here, at the top of the city, Mulholland had become a dirt road. I'd hiked here as a grad student, thrilling at the sight of antlered bucks, foxes, falcons, catching my breath at the furtive shifting of high grass that could be cougars. But that had been years ago, and the suddenness of the transformation from highway to impasse caught me by surprise. I hit the brakes hard, steered onto the rise, parked below the table of sallow dirt.

Milo was already there, his copper-colored unmarked pulled up in front of a warning sign posted by the county: seven miles of unfinished road followed, no vehicles permitted. A locked gate said that L.A. motorists couldn't be trusted.

He hitched his pants, loped forward, took my hand in both of his giant mitts.

"Alex."

"Big guy."

He had on a fuzzy-looking green tweed jacket, brown twill pants, white shirt with a twisted collar, string tie with a big, misshapen turquoise clasp. The tie looked like tourist junk. A new fashion statement; I knew he'd put it on to needle the brass at this morning's meeting.

"Going cowboy?"

"My Georgia O'Keeffe period."

"Natty."

He gave a low, rumbling laugh, pushed a lick of dry black hair off his brow, squinted off to the right. Focusing on a spot that told me exactly where the van had been found.

Not up the dirt road, where untrimmed live oaks would have provided cover. Right here, on the turnoff, out in the open.

I said, "No attempt to conceal."

He shrugged and jammed his hands in his pockets. He looked tired, washed-out, worn down by violence and small print.

Or maybe it was just the time of year. September can be a rotten month in L.A., throat-constrictingly hot or clammy cold, shadowed by a grimy marine layer that turns the city into a pile of soiled laundry. When September mornings start out dreary they ooze into sooty afternoons and sickly nights. Sometimes blue peeks through the clouds for a nanosecond. Sometimes the sky sweats and a leaky-roof drizzle glazes windshields. For the past few years resident experts have been blaming it on El Niño, but I don't recall it ever being any different.

September light is bad for the complexion. Milo's didn't need any further erosion. The gray morning light fed his pallor and deepened the pockmarks that peppered his cheeks and ran down his neck. White sideburns below still-thick black hair turned his temples into a zebra-striped stunt. He'd gone back to drinking moderately and his weight had stabilized—240 was my guess—much of it settling around his middle. His legs remained skinny stilts, comprising a good share of his seventy-five inches. His jowls, always monumental, had given way around the edges. We were about the same age—he was nine months older—so I supposed my jawline had surrendered a bit, too. I didn't spend much time looking in the mirror.

He walked to the kill-spot and I followed. Faint chevrons of tire tracks corrugated the yellow soil. Nearby lay a scrap of yellow cordon tape, dusty, utterly still. A week of dead air, nothing had moved.

"We took casts of the tracks," he said, flicking a hand at them. "Not that it matters. We knew where the van came from. Rental sticker. Avis, Tarzana branch. Brown Ford Econoline with a nice big cargo area. Mate rented it last Friday, got the weekend rate."

"Preparing for another mercy mission?" I said.

"That's what he uses vans for. But so far no beneficiary's come forth claiming Mate stood him up."

"I'm surprised the companies still rent to him."

"They probably don't. The paperwork was made out to someone else. Woman named Alice Zoghbie, president of the Socrates Club—right-to-die outfit headquartered in Glendale. She's out of the country, attending some sort of humanist convention in Amsterdam—left Saturday."

"She rented the van and split the next day?" I said.

"Apparently. Called her home, which also doubles as the Socrates office, got voice mail. Had Glendale PD drive by. No one home. Zoghbie's message says she's due back in a week. She's on my to-do list." He tapped the pocket where his notepad nestled.

"I wonder why Mate never bought a van," I said.

"From what I've seen so far, he was cheap. I tossed his apartment the day after the murder, not much in the way of creature comforts. His personal car's an old Chevy that has seen better days. Before he went automotive he used budget motels."

I nodded. "Bodies left on the bed for the cleaning crew to find next morning. Too many traumatized maids turned into bad publicity. I saw him on TV once, getting defensive about it. Saying Christ had been born in a barn full of goat dung, so setting doesn't matter. But it does, doesn't it?"

He looked at me. "You've been following Mate's career?"

"Didn't have to," I said, keeping my voice even. "He wasn't exactly media-shy. Any tracks of other cars nearby?"

He shook his head.

"So," I said, "you're wondering if the killer drove up with Mate."

"Or parked farther down the road than we checked. Or left no tracks—that happens plenty, you know how seldom forensic stuff actually helps. No one's reported seeing any other vehicles. Then again, no one noticed the damned *van*, and it sat here for hours."

"What about shoe prints?"

"Just the people who found the van."

"What's the time-of-death estimate?" I said.

"Early morning, one to four A.M." He shot his cuff and looked at his Timex. The watch crystal was scarred and filmed. "Mate was discovered just after sunrise—six-fifteen or so."

"The papers said the people who found him were hikers," I said. "Must've been early risers."

"Coupla yuppies walking with their dog, came up from the Valley for a constitutional before hitting the office. They were headed up the dirt road and noticed the van."

"Any other passersby?" I pointed down the road, toward Encino Hills Drive. "I used to come up here, remember a housing development being built. By now it's probably well-populated. That hour, you'd think a car or two would drive by."

"Yeah, it's populated," he said. "High-priced development. Guess the affluent get to sleep in."

"Some of the affluent got that way by working. What about a broker up early to catch the market, a surgeon ready to operate?"

"It's conceivable someone drove past and saw something, but if they did they're not admitting it. Our initial canvass produced zip by way of neighborly help. How many cars have you seen while we stood here?"

The road had been silent.

"I got here ten minutes before you," he said. "One truck. Period. A gardener. And even if someone did drive by, there'd be no reason to notice the van. No street-lights, so before sunrise it would've been pure black. And if someone did happen to spot it, no reason to give it a thought, let alone stop. There was county construction going on up here till a few months ago, some kind of drain line. CalTrans crews left trucks overnight all the time. Another parked vehicle wouldn't stand out."

"It stood out to the yuppies," I said.

"Stood out to their *dog*. One of those attentive retrievers. They were ready to walk right past the van but the dog kept nosing around, barking, wouldn't leave it alone. Finally, they had a look inside. So much for walking for health, huh? That kind of thing could put you off exercise for a long time."

"Bad?"

"Not what *I'd* want as an aerobic stimulant. Dr. Mate was trussed up to his own machine."

"The Humanitron," I said. Mate's label for his death apparatus. Silent passage for Happy Travelers.

Milo's smile was crooked, hard to read. "You hear about that thing, all the people he used it on, you expect it to be some high-tech gizmo. It's a piece of junk, Alex. Looks like a loser in a junior-high science fair. Mismatched screws, all wobbly. Like Mate cobbled it from spare parts."

"It worked," I said.

"Oh yeah. It worked fine. Fifty times. Which is a good place to start, right? Fifty families. Maybe someone didn't approve of Mate's brand of travel agency. Potentially, we're talking hundreds of suspects. Problem one is we've been having a hard time reaching them. Seems lots of Mate's chosen were from out-of-state—good luck locating the survivors. The department's lent me two brand-new Detective-I's to do phone work and other scut. So far people don't want to talk to them about old Eldon, and the few who do think the guy was a saint— 'Grandma's doctors watched her writhe in agony and wouldn't do a damn thing. Dr. Mate was the only one willing to help.' Alibi-talk or true belief? I'd need face-to-faces with all of them, maybe you there to psycho-analyze, and so far it's been telephonic. We're making our way through the list."

"Trussed to the machine," I said. "What makes you think homicide? Maybe it was voluntary. Mate decided it was his own time to skid off the mortal coil, and practiced what he preached."

"Wait, there's more. He was hooked up, all right— I.V. in each arm, one bottle full of the tranquilizer he uses—thiopental—the other with the potassium chloride for the heart attack. And his thumb was touching this little trip-wire doohickey that gets the flow going. Coroner said the potassium had kicked in for at least a few minutes, so Mate would've been dead from that, if he wasn't dead already. But he was. The gizmo was all for *show*, Alex. What *dispatched* him was no mercy killing: he got slammed on the head hard enough to crack his skull and cause a subdural hematoma, then someone cut him up, none too neatly. 'Ensanguination due to exten-sive genital mutilation.' "

"He was castrated?" I said.

"And more. Bled out. Coroner says the head wound was serious, nice columnar indentation, meaning a length of pipe or something like that. It would've caused big-time damage if Mate had lived—maybe even killed him.

But it wasn't immediately fatal. The rear of the van was soaked with blood, and the spatter says arterial spurts, meaning Mate's heart was pumping away when the killer worked on him."

He rubbed his face. "He was vivisected, Alex."

"Lord," I said.

"Some other wounds, too. Deliberate cuts, eight of them, deep. Abdomen, groin and thighs. Squares, like the killer was playing around."

"Proud of himself," I said.

He pulled out his notepad but didn't write.

"Any other wounds?" I said.

"Just some superficial cuts the coroner says were probably accidental—the blade slipping. All that blood had to make it a slippery job. Weapon was very sharp and single-edged—scalpel or a straight razor, probably with scissors for backup."

"Anesthesia, scalpel, scissors," I said. "Surgery. The killer must have been drenched. No blood outside the van?"

"Not one speck. It looked like the ground had been swept. This guy took *extreme* care. We're talking wet work in a confined space in the dead of night. He had to use some kind of portable light. The front seat was full of blood, too, especially the passenger seat. I'm thinking this bad boy did his thing, got out of the van, reentered on the passenger side—easier than the driver's seat because no steering wheel to get in the way. That's where he cleaned most of the mess off. Then he got out again, stripped naked, wiped off the rest of the blood, bundled the soiled stuff up, probably in plastic bags. Maybe the same plastic he'd used to store a change of clean clothes.

He got into his new duds, checked to cover any prints or tracks, swept around the van and was gone."

"Naked in full view of the road," I said. "That would be risky even in the dark, because he'd have to use a flashlight to check himself and the dirt. On top of operating in the van using light. *Someone* could've driven by, seen it shining through the van windows, gone to check, or reported it."

"The light in the van might not have been that big a problem. There were sheets of thick cardboard cut to the right size for blocking the windows on the driver's seat. Also streaked with arterial blood, so they'd been used during the cutting. Cardboard's just the kind of home-made thing Mate would've used in lieu of curtains, so my bet is Dr. Death brought them himself. Thinking he was gonna be the trusser, not the trussee. Same for the mattress he was lying on. I think Mate came ready to play Angel of Death for the fifty-first time and someone said, 'Tag, you're it.'

"The killer used the cardboard, then removed it from the windows," I said. "*Wanting* the body to be discovered. Display, just like the geometrical wounds—like leaving the van in full sight. Look what *I* did. Look who I *did* it to."

He stared down at the soil, grim, exhausted. I pictured the slaughter. Vicious blitz assault, then deliberate surgery on the side of an ink-black road. The killer silent, intent, constructing an impromptu operatory within the confines of the van's rear compartment. Picking his spot, knowing few cars drove by. Working quickly, efficiently, taking the time to do what he'd come to do—what he'd fantasized about.

Taking the time to insert two I.V. lines. Positioning Mate's finger on the trigger.

Swimming in blood, yet managing to escape without leaving behind a dot of scarlet. Sweeping the dirt . . . I'd never encountered anything more premeditated.

"What was the body position?"

"Lying on his back, head near the front seat."

"On the mattress he provided," I said. "Mate prepares the van, the killer uses it. Talk about a power trip. Co-optation."

He thought about that for a long time. "There's something that needs to be kept quiet: the killer left a note. Plain white paper, eight by eleven, tacked to Mate's chest. Nailed into the sternum, actually, with a stainless-steel brad. Computer-typed: *Happy Traveling, You Sick Bastard.*"

Vehicle noise caused us both to turn. A car appeared from the west, on the swell that led down Encino Hills. Big white Mercedes sedan. The middle-aged woman at the wheel kept to forty miles per while touching up her makeup, sped past without glancing at us.

"Happy Traveling," I said. "Mate's euphemism. The whole thing stinks of mockery, Milo. Which could also be why the killer coldcocked Mate before cutting him up. He set up a two-act play in order to parody Mate's technique. Sedate first, then kill. Piece of pipe instead of thiopental. Brutal travesty of Mate's ritual."

He blinked. The morning gloom dulled his leaf-green eyes, turned them into a pair of cocktail olives. "You're saying this guy is playing doctor? Or he *hates* doctors? Wants to make some sort of *philosophical* statement?"

"The note may have been left to get you to *think* he's taking on Mate philosophically. He might even be telling *himself* that's the reason he did it. But it ain't so. Sure, there are plenty of people who don't approve of what Mate did. I can even see some zealot taking a potshot at him, or trying to blow him up. But what you just described goes way beyond a difference of opinion. This guy enjoyed the *process*. Staging, playing around, enacting the *theater* of death. And at this level of brutality and calculation, it wouldn't surprise me if he's done it before."

"If he has, it's the first time he's gone public. I called VICAP, nothing in their files matches. The agent I spoke to said it had elements of both organized and disorganized serials, thank you very much."

"You said the amputation was clumsy," I said.

"That's the coroner's opinion."

"So maybe our boy's got some medical aspirations. Someone with a grudge, like a med-school reject, wanting to show the world how clever he is."

"Maybe," he said. "Then again, Mate *was* a legit doc and *he* was no master craftsman. Last year he removed a liver from one of his travelers, dropped it off at County Hospital. Packed with ice, in a picnic cooler. Not that anyone would've accepted it, given the source, but the liver was garbage. Mate took it out all wrong, hacked-up blood vessels, made a mess."

"Doctors who don't do surgery often forget the little they learned in med school," I said. "Mate spent most of his professional life as a bureaucrat, bouncing from public health department to public health department. When did this liver thing happen? Never heard about it."

"Last December. You never heard about it because it was never made public. 'Cause who'd want it to get out? Not Mate, because he looked like a clown, but not the D.A.'s office, either. They'd given up on prosecuting Mate, were sick of giving him free publicity. I found out because the coroner doing the post on Mate had seen the paperwork on the disposal of the liver, had heard people talking about it at the morgue."

"Maybe I wasn't giving the killer enough credit," I said. "Given the tight space, darkness, the time pressure, it couldn't have been easy. Perhaps those error wounds weren't the only time he slipped. If he nicked himself he could've left behind some of his own biochemistry."

"From your mouth to God's ears. The lab rats have been going over every square inch of that van, but so far the only blood they've been able to pull up is Mate's. O positive."

"The only common thing about him." I was thinking of the one time I'd seen Eldon Mate on TV. Because I had followed his career, had watched a press conference after a "voyage." The death doctor had left the stiffening corpse of a woman—almost all of them were women—in a motel near downtown, then showed up at the D.A.'s office to "inform the authorities." My take: to brag. The man had looked jubilant. That's when a reporter had brought up the use of budget lodgings. Mate had turned livid and spat back the line about Jesus.

Despite the public taunt, the D.A. had done nothing about the death, because five acquittals had shown that bringing Mate up on charges was a certain loser. Mate's triumphalism had grated. He'd gloated like a spoiled child.

A small, round, bald man in his sixties with the constipated face and the high, strident voice of a petty functionary, mocking the justice system that couldn't touch him, lashing out against those "enslaved to the hypocritic oath." Proclaiming his victory with rambling sentences armored with obscure words ("My partnership with my travelers has been an exemplar of mutual fructification"). Pausing only to purse slit lips that, when they weren't moving, seemed on the verge of spitting. Microphones shoved in his face made him smile. He had hot eyes, a tendency to screech. A hit-and-run patter had made me think *vaudeville*.

"Yeah, he was a piece of work, wasn't he?" said Milo. "I always thought when you peeled away all the medico-legal crap, he was just a homicidal nut with a medical degree. Now he's the victim of a psycho."

"And that made you think of me," I said.

"Well," he said, "who else? Also, there's the fact that one week later I'm no closer to anything. Any profound, behavioral-science insights would be welcome, Doctor."

"Just the mockery angle, so far," I said. "A killer going for glory, an ego out of control."

"Sounds like Mate himself."

"All the more reason to get rid of Mate. Think about it: if you were a frustrated loser who saw yourself as genius, wanted to play God publicly, what better than dispatching the Angel of Death? You're very likely right about it being a travel gone wrong. If the killer did make a date with Mate, maybe Mate logged it."

"No log in his apartment," Milo said. "No work records of any kind. I'm figuring Mate kept the paperwork with that lawyer of his, Roy Haiselden. Mouthy fellow, you'd think he'd be blabbing nonstop, but nada. He's gone, too."

Haiselden had been at the conference with Mate. Big man in his fifties, florid complexion, too-bushy auburn toupee. "Amsterdam, also?" I said. "Another humanist?"

"Don't know where yet, just that he doesn't answer calls . . . Yeah, everyone's a humanist. Our *bad* boy probably thinks he's a humanist."

"No, I don't think so," I said. "I think he likes being bad."

Another car drove by. Gray Toyota Cressida. Another female driver, this one a teenage girl. Once again, no sideward glance.

"See what you mean," I said. "Perfect place for a nighttime killing. Also for a travel jaunt, so maybe Mate chose it. And after all the flack about tacky settings, perhaps he decided to go for scenic—final passage in a serene spot. If so, he made the killer's job easier. Or the killer picked the spot and Mate approved. A killer familiar with the area—maybe even someone living within walking distance—could explain the lack of tire tracks. It would also be a kick—murder so close to home and he gets away with it. Either way, the confluence between his goals and Mate's would've been fun."

"Yeah," Milo said, without enthusiasm. "Gonna have my D-I's canvass the locals, see if any psychos with records turn up." Another glance at his watch. "Alex, if the killer set up an appointment with Mate by faking terminal illness, that implies theater on another level: acting skills good enough to convince Mate he was dying."

"Not necessarily," I said. "Mate had relaxed his standards. When he started out, he insisted on terminal illness. But recently he'd been talking about a dignified death being anyone's right."

No formal diagnosis necessary. I kept my face blank.

Maybe not blank enough. Milo was staring at me. "Something the matter?"

"Beyond a tide of gore in the morning?"

"Oh," he said. "Sometimes I forget you're a civilian. Guess you don't wanna see the crime-scene photos."

"Do they add anything?"

"Not to me, but . . ."

"Sure."

He retrieved a manila packet from the unmarked. "These are copies—the originals are in the murder book."

Loose photos, full-color, too much color, the van's interior shot from every angle. Eldon Mate's body was pathetic and small in death. His round white face bore *the look*—dull, flat, the assault of stupid surprise. Every murdered face I'd seen wore it. The democracy of extinction.

The flashbulb had turned the blood splatter greenish around the edges. The arterial spurts were a bad abstract painting. All of Mate's smugness was gone. The Humanitron behind him. The photo reduced his machine to a few bowed slats of metal, sickeningly delicate, like a baby cobra. From the top frame dangled the pair of glass I.V. bottles, also blood-washed.

Just another obscenity, human flesh turned to trash. I never got used to it. Each time I encountered it, I craved faith in the immortality of the soul.

Included with the death photos were some shots of the brown Econoline, up close and from a distance. The rental sticker was conspicuous on the rear window. No attempt had been made to obscure the front plates. The van's front end so ordinary . . . the front.

"Interesting."

"What is?" said Milo.

"The van was backed in, not headed in the easy way." I handed him a picture. He studied it, said nothing.

"Turning around took some effort," I said. "Only reason I can think of is, it would've made escape easier. It probably wasn't the killer's decision. He knew the van wouldn't be leaving. Although I suppose he might have considered the possibility of being interrupted and having to take off quickly. . . . No, when they arrived, Mate was in charge. Or thought he was. In the driver's seat literally and psychologically. Maybe he sensed something was off."

"It didn't stop him from going through with it."

"Could be he put his reservations aside because he also enjoyed a bit of danger. Vans, motels, sneaking around at night say to me he got off on the whole cloak-and-dagger thing."

I handed him the rest of the photos and he slipped them in the packet.

"All that blood," I said. "Hard to imagine not a single print was left anywhere."

"Lots of smooth surfaces in the van. The coroner did find smears, like finger-painting whirls, says it might mean rubber gloves. We found an open box in the front. Mate was a dream victim, brought all the fixings for the final feast." He checked his watch again.

"If the killer had access to a surgical kit, he could've also brought sponges—nice and absorbent, perfect for cleanup. Any traces of sponge material in the van?"

He shook his head.

I said, "What else did you find, in terms of medical supplies?"

"Empty hypodermic syringe, the thiopental and the potassium chloride, alcohol swabs—that's a kicker, ain't it? You're about to kill someone, you bother to swab them with alcohol to prevent infection?"

"They do it up in San Quentin when they execute someone. Maybe it makes them feel like health-care professionals. The killer would've liked feeling legitimate. What about a bag to carry all that equipment?"

"No, nothing like that."

"No carrying case of any kind?"

"No."

"There had to be some kind of case," I said. "Even if the equipment was Mate's, he wouldn't have left it rolling around loose in the van. Also, Mate had lost his license but he still fancied himself a doctor, and doctors carry black bags. Even if he was too cheap to invest in leather, and used something like a paper sack, you'd expect to find it. Why would the killer leave the Humanitron and everything else behind and take the case?"

"Snuff the doctor, steal his bag?"

"Taking over the doctor's practice."

"*He* wants to be Dr. Death?"

"Makes sense, doesn't it? He's murdered Mate, can't exactly come out into the open and start soliciting terminally ill people. But he could have something in mind."

Milo rubbed his face furiously, as if scrubbing without water. "More wet work?"

"It's just theory," I said.

Milo gazed up at the dismal sky, slapped the packet of death photos against his leg again, chewed his cheek. "A sequel. Oh that would be peachy. Extremely *pleasant*. And this theory occurs to you because *maybe* there was a bag and *maybe* someone took it."

"If you don't think it has merit, disregard it."

"How the hell should *I* know if it has merit?" He stuffed the photos in his jacket pocket, yanked out his pad, opened it and stabbed at the paper with a chewed-down pencil. Then he slammed the pad shut. The cover was filled with scrawl. "The bag coulda been left behind and ended up in the morgue without being logged."

"Sure," I said. "Absolutely."

"Great," he said. "That would be great."

"Well, folks," I said, in a W. C. Fields voice, "in terms of theory, I think that's about it for today."

His laughter was sudden. I thought of a mastiff's warning bark. He fanned himself with the notepad. The air was cool, stale, still inert. He was sweating. "Forgive the peckishness. I need sleep." Yet another glance at the Timex.

"Expecting company?" I said.

"The yuppie hikers. Mr. Paul Ulrich and Ms. Tanya Stratton. Interviewed them the day of the murder, but they didn't give me much. Too upset—especially the girl. The boyfriend spent his time trying to calm her down. Given what she saw, can't blame her, but she seemed . . . delicate. Like if I pressed too hard she'd disintegrate. I've been trying all week to arrange the reinterview. Phone tag, excuses. Finally reached them last night, figured I'd go to their house, but they said they'd rather meet up here, which I thought was gutsy. But maybe they're thinking some kind of self-therapy—whatchamacallit—working it *through*." He grinned. "See, it *does* rub off, all those years with you."

"A few more and you'll be ready to see patients."

"People tell *me* their troubles, they get locked up."

"When are they due to show up?"

"Fifteen minutes ago. Stopping by on their way to work—both have jobs in Century City." He kicked dust. "Maybe they chickened out. Even if they do show, I'm not sure what I'm hoping to get out of them. But got to be thorough, right? So what's your take on Mate? Do-gooder or serial killer?"

"Maybe both," I said. "He came across as arrogant, with a low view of humanity, so it's hard to believe his altruism was pure. Nothing else in his life points to exceptional compassion. Just the opposite: instead of taking care of patients, he spent his medical career as a paper pusher. And he never amounted to much as a doctor until he started helping people die. If I had to bet on a primary motive, I'd say he craved attention. On the other hand, there's a reason the families you've talked to support him. He alleviated a lot of suffering. Most of the people who pulled the trigger of that machine were in torment."

"So you condone what he did even if his reasons for doing it were less than pure."

"I haven't decided how I feel about what he did," I said.

"Ah." He fiddled with the turquoise clasp.

There was plenty more I could've said and I felt low,

evasive. Another burst of engine hum rescued me from self-examination. This time, the car approached from the east and Milo turned.

Dark-blue BMW sedan, 300 model, a few years old. Two people inside. The car stopped, the driver's window lowered and a man with a huge, spreading mustache looked out at us. Next to him sat a young woman, gazing straight ahead.

"The yuppies show up," said Milo. "Finally, someone respects the rule of law."

3

Milo waved the BMW up, the mustachioed man turned the wheel and parked behind the Seville. "Here okay, Detective?"

"Sure—anywhere," said Milo.

The man smiled uncomfortably. "Didn't want to mess something up."

"No problem, Mr. Ulrich. Thanks for coming."

Paul Ulrich turned off the engine and he and the woman got out. He was medium-size, late thirties to forty, solidly built, with a well-cured beach tan and a nubby, sunburned nose. His crew cut was dun-colored, soft-looking to the point of fuzziness, with lots of pinkish scalp glowing through. As if all his hair-growing energy had been focused on the mustache, an extravagance as wide as his face, parted into two flaring red-brown wings, stiff with wax, luxuriant as an old-time grenadier's. His sole burst of flamboyance, and it clashed with haberdashery that seemed chosen for inconspicuousness on Century Park East: charcoal suit, white button-down shirt, navy and silver rep tie, black wing-tips.

He held the woman's elbow as they made their way toward us. She was younger, late twenties, as tall as he, thin and narrow-shouldered, with a stiff, tentative walk that belied any hiking experience. Her skin tone said indoors, too. More than that: indoor pallor. Chalky-white edged with translucent blue, so pale she made Milo look ruddy. Her hair was dark brown, almost black, boy-short, wispy. She wore big, black-framed sunglasses, a mocha silk blazer over a long brown print dress, flat-soled, basket-weave sandals.

Milo said, "Ms. Stratton," and she took his hand reluctantly. Up close, I saw rouge on her cheeks, clear gloss on chapped lips. She turned to me.

"This is Dr. Delaware, Ms. Stratton. Our psychological consultant."

"Uh-huh," she said. Unimpressed.

"Doctor, these are our witnesses—Ms. Tanya Stratton and Mr. Paul Ulrich. Thanks again for showing up, folks. I really appreciate it."

"Sure, no prob," said Ulrich, glancing at his girlfriend. "I don't know what else we can tell you."

The shades blocked Stratton's eyes and her expression. Ulrich had started to smile, but he stopped midway. The mustache straightened.

He, trying to fake calm after what they'd been through. She, not bothering. The typical male-female mambo. I tried to imagine what it had been like, peering into that van.

She touched a sidepiece of her sunglasses. "Can we get this over quickly?"

"Sure, ma'am," Milo said. "The first time we talked, you didn't notice anything out of the ordinary, but sometimes people remember things afterward—"

"Unfortunately, we don't," said Tanya Stratton. Her voice was soft, nasal, inflected with that syllable-stretching California female twang. "We went over it last night because we were coming here to meet you. But there's nothing."

She hugged herself and looked to the right. Over at the spot. Ulrich put his arm around her. She didn't resist him, but she didn't give herself over to the embrace.

Ulrich said, "So far our names haven't been in the paper. We're going to be able to keep it that way, aren't we, Detective Sturgis?"

"Most likely," said Milo.

"Likely but not definitely?"

"I can't say for sure, sir. Frankly, with a case like this, you never know. And if we ever catch who did it, your testimony might be required. I certainly won't give your names out, if that's what you mean. As far as the department's concerned, the less we reveal the better."

Ulrich touched the slit of flesh between his mustaches. "Why's that?"

"Control of the data, sir."

"I see . . . sure, makes sense." He looked at Tanya Stratton again. She licked her lips, said, "At least you're honest about not being able to protect us. Have you learned anything about who did it?"

"Not yet, ma'am."

"Not that you'd tell us, right?"

Milo smiled.

Paul Ulrich said, "Fifteen minutes of fame. Andy

Warhol coined that phrase and look what happened to him."

"What happened?" said Milo.

"Checked into a hospital for routine surgery, went out in a bag."

Stratton's black glasses flashed as she turned her head sharply.

"All I meant, honey, is celebrity stinks. The sooner we're through with this the better. Look at Princess Di— look at Dr. Mate, for that matter."

"We're not celebrities, Paul."

"And that's good, hon."

Milo said, "So you think Dr. Mate's notoriety had something to do with his death, Mr. Ulrich?"

"I don't know—I mean, I'm no expert. But wouldn't you say so? It does seem logical, given who he was. Not that *we* recognized him when we saw him—not in the condition he was in." He shook his head. "Whatever. You didn't even tell us who he was when you were questioning us last week. We found out by watching the news—"

Tanya Stratton's hand took hold of his biceps.

He said, "That's about it. We need to get to work."

"Speaking of which, do you always hike before work?" said Milo.

"We walk four, five times a week," said Stratton.

"Keeping healthy," said Ulrich.

She dropped her hand and turned away from him.

"We're both early risers," he said, as if pressed to explain. "We both have long workdays, so if we don't get our exercise in the morning, forget it." He flexed his fingers.

Milo pointed up the dirt road. "Come here often?"

"Not really," said Stratton. "It's just one of the places we go. In fact, we rarely come up here, except on Sundays. Because it's far and we need to drive back, shower off, change. Mostly we stick closer to home."

"Encino," said Milo.

"Right over the hill," said Ulrich. "That morning we were up early. I suggested Mulholland because it's so pretty." He edged closer to Stratton, put his hand back on her shoulder.

Milo said, "You were here, when—six, six-fifteen?"

"We usually start out by six," said Stratton. "I'd say we were here by six-twenty, maybe later by the time we parked. The sun was up already. You could see it over that peak." Pointing east, toward foothills beyond the gate.

Ulrich said, "We like to catch at least part of the sunrise. Once you get past there"—hooking a thumb at the gate—"it's like being in another world. Birds, deer, chipmunks. Duchess goes crazy 'cause she gets to run around without a leash. Tanya's had her for ten years and she still runs like a puppy. Great nose, thinks she's a drug dog."

"Too good," said Stratton, grimacing.

"If Duchess hadn't run to the van," said Milo, "would you have approached it?"

"What do you mean?" she said.

"Was there anything different about it? Was it conspicuous in any way?"

"No," she said. "Not really."

"Duchess must've sensed something off," said Ulrich. "Her instincts are terrific."

Stratton said, "She's always bringing me *presents.* Dead squirrels, birds. Now *this.* Every time I think about it I get sick to my stomach. I really need to go, have a pile of work to go through."

"What kind of work do you do?" said Milo.

"Executive secretary to a vice president at Unity Bank. Mr. Gerald Van Armstren."

Milo checked his notes. "And you're a financial planner, Mr. Ulrich?"

"Financial consultant. Mostly real-estate work."

Stratton turned abruptly and walked back to the BMW.

Ulrich called out "Honey?" but he didn't go after her. "Sorry, guys. She's been really traumatized, says she'll never get the image out of her head. I thought coming up here might actually help—not a good idea at all." He shook his head, gazed at Stratton. Her back was to him. "Really *bad* idea."

Milo strode over to the car. Tanya Stratton stood with her hand on the handle of the passenger door, facing west. He said something to her. She shook her head, turned away, revealing a tight white profile.

Ulrich rocked on his heels and exhaled. A strand of mustache hair that had eluded wax vibrated.

I said, "Have you two been together long?"

"A while. She's sensitive . . ."

Over by the car, Stratton's face was a white mask as Milo talked. The two of them looked like kabuki players.

"How long have you been into hiking?" I said.

"Years. I've always exercised. It took a while to get Tanya into it. She's not—let's just say this'll probably be the conclusion of that." He looked over at the BMW.

"She's a great gal, just needs . . . special handling. Actually, there *was* one thing I remembered. Came to me last night, isn't that bizarre? Can I tell you or do I have to wait for him?"

"It's fine to tell me."

Ulrich smoothed his left mustache. "I didn't want to say this in front of Tanya. Not because it's anything significant, but she thinks anything we say will get us more deeply involved. But I don't see how this could. It was just another car. Parked on the side of the road. The south side. We passed it as we drove up. Not particularly close, maybe a quarter mile down that way." Indicating east. "Couldn't be relevant, right? Because by the time we arrived Mate had been dead for a while, right? So why would anyone stick around?"

"What kind of car?" I said.

"BMW. Like ours. That's why I noticed it. Darker than ours. Maybe black. Or dark gray."

"Same model?"

"Can't say, all I remember is the grille. No big deal, there've got to be lots of Beemers up here, right? I just thought I should mention it."

"You didn't happen to notice the license plate?"

He laughed. "Yeah, right. And the facial features of some psychotic killer drooling at the wheel. No, that's all I can tell you—a dark Beemer. The only reason I even remembered it was that when Detective Sturgis called last night, he asked us to search our minds for any other details, and I really gave it a go. I can't even swear it was that dark. Maybe it was medium-gray. Brown, whatever. Amazing I remembered it at all. After seeing what was inside that van, it's hard to think about anything else.

Whoever did that to Mate must have really hated him."

I said, "Rough. Which window did you look through?"

"First the front windshield. Saw blood on the seats and I said, 'Oh shit.' Then Duchess ran around the back so we followed her. That's where we caught a full view."

Milo backed away and Stratton got in the car.

Ulrich said, "Better hustle. Nice to meet you, Dr. Delaware."

He jogged toward the blue car, saluted Milo as he got in. Starting up, he shifted into gear, hooked a U-turn and sped down the rise.

I told Milo about the dark BMW.

"Well, it's something," he said. Then he laughed coldly. "No, it's not. He's right. Why would the killer stick around for three, four hours?" He stashed the notepad back in his pocket. "Okay, one reinterview heard from."

"She's a tense one," I said.

"Blame her? Why? She set off some buzzers?"

"No. But I see what you meant about delicacy. What did she tell you when you spoke to her alone?"

"It was *Paul's* idea to come up here. *Paul's* idea to hike. *Paul's* a superjock, would live in a tree if he could. They probably weren't in the throes of love when they found Mate. Guess it didn't spice up their relationship."

"Murder as aphrodisiac."

"For some folks it is . . . Now that I know about the second BMW I'm gonna have to log and do *some* kind of follow-up . . . hopefully a basic DMV will sync with some neighbor's vehicle and that'll be it." He rubbed his ear, as if dreading phone work. "First things first. Follow up with my junior D's to see how the family list is going. If you're so inclined, you could do some research on Mate."

"Any particular *theories* you want checked out?"

"Just the basic one: someone hated him bad enough to slaughter him. Not necessarily a news item. Maybe someone popping off about Mate in cyberspace."

"Our killer's a careful fellow. Why would he go public?"

"It's beyond long shot, but you never know. Last year we had a case, father who molested and murdered his five-year-old daughter. We suspected him, couldn't get a damn bit of evidence. Then a half year later, the asshole goes and brags about it to another pedophile in a chat room. Even then it was only a lucky accident that we heard about it. One of our vice guys was monitoring the kiddie-rapers, thought the details sounded familiar."

"You never told me about that one."

"I'm not out to introduce *pollution* into your life, Alex. Unless I need help."

"Sure," I said. "I'll do what I can."

He slapped a hand on my shoulder. "Thank you, sir. The suits are right miffed about a high-profile case popping up right now, just when the crime rate was allegedly dropping. Just when they thought they'd get some *good* publicity before funding time. So if you produce, I might even be able to get you some money fairly soon."

I panted like a dog. "Oh, Master, how wonderful."

"Hey," he said, "hasn't the department always treated you well?"

"Like royalty."

"Royalty . . . you and old Duchess . . . Maybe it's *her* I should be interviewing. Maybe it'll come to that."

CHAPTER

4

I drove down Mulholland and eased into the traffic at Beverly Glen. The jazz station had gotten talky of late so the radio was tuned to KUSC. Something easy on the ears was playing. Debussy was my guess. Too pretty for this morning. I switched it off and used the time to think about the way Eldon Mate had died.

The phone call I'd made when I'd first heard about it.

No answer, and trying again was a much worse idea than it had been last week. But how long could I work with Milo without clearing things up?

As I tossed it back and forth, the ethical ramifications spiraled. Some of the answers were covered in the rule books, but others weren't. Real life always transcends the rule books.

I arrived home hyped by indecision.

The house was quiet, cooled by the surrounding pines, oak floors gleaming, white walls bleached metallic by eastern light. Robin had left toast and coffee out. No sign of her, no panting canine welcome. The morning paper remained folded on the kitchen counter.

She and Spike were out back in the studio. She had several big jobs backordered. With obligation on both our minds, we hadn't talked much since rising.

I filled a cup and drank. The silence was annoying. Once, the house had been smaller, darker, far less comfortable, considerably less practical. A psychopath had burned it down a few years ago and we'd rebuilt. Everyone agreed it was an improvement. Sometimes, when I was alone, there seemed to be too much space.

It's been a long time since I've pretended to be emotionally independent. When you love someone for a long time, when that love is cemented in routine as well as thrill, her very presence fills too much space to be ignored. I knew Robin would interrupt her work if I dropped in, but I was in no mood to be sociable, so instead of continuing out the back door, I reached for the kitchen phone and checked with my service. And the problem of the unanswered call solved itself.

"Morning, Dr. Delaware," said the operator. "Only one message, just a few minutes ago. A Mr. Richard Doss, here's the number."

An 805 exchange, not Doss's Santa Monica office. Ventura or Santa Barbara County. I punched it in and a woman answered, "RTD Properties."

"Dr. Delaware returning Mr. Doss's call."

"This is his phone-routing service, one moment."

Several clicks cricketed in my ear, followed by a rub of static and then a familiar voice. "Dr. Delaware. Long time."

Reedy tone, staccato delivery, that hint of sarcasm. Richard Doss always sounded as if he was mocking someone or something. I'd never decided if it was intentional or just a vocal quirk.

"Morning, Richard."

More static. Fade-out on his reply. Several seconds passed before he returned. "We may get cut off again, I'm out in the boonies, Carpinteria. Looking at some land. Avocado orchard that'll do just fine as a minimall if my cold-blooded capitalist claws get hold of it. If we lose each other again, don't phone me, I'll phone you. The usual number?"

Taking charge, as always. "Same one, Richard." Not *Mr. Doss,* because he'd always insisted I use his first name. One of the many rules he'd laid down. The illusion of informality, just a regular guy. From what I'd seen, Richard T. Doss never really let down his guard.

"I know why you called," he said. "And why you think I called back."

"Mate's death."

"Festive times. The sonofabitch finally got what he deserved."

I didn't reply.

He laughed. "Come on, Doctor, be a sport. I'm dealing with life's challenges with humor. Wouldn't a psychologist recommend that? Isn't humor a good coping skill?"

"Is Dr. Mate's death something you need to cope with?"

"Well . . ." He laughed again. "Even positive change is a challenge, right?"

"Right."

"You're thinking how vindictive I'm being—by the way, when it happened I was out of town. San Francisco. Looking over a hotel. Trailed by ten clinically depressed Tokyo bankers. They paid thirty million five years ago, are itching to unload for considerably less."

"Great," I said.

"It certainly is. Do you recall all that yellow-peril nonsense a while back: death rays from the Rising Sun, soon our kids will be eating sushi for school lunch? About as realistic as Godzilla. Everything cycles, the key to feeling smart is to live long enough." Another laugh. "Guess the *sonofabitch* won't feel smart anymore. So . . . that's my alibi."

"Do you feel you need an alibi?" The first thing I'd wondered when I'd heard about Mate.

Silence. Not a phone problem this time; I could hear him breathing. When he spoke again, his tone was subdued and tight.

"I wasn't being literal, Doctor. Though the police *have* tried to talk to me, probably have some kind of list they're running down. If they're proceeding sequentially, I'd be at the bottom or close to it. The sonofabitch murdered another two women after Joanne. Anyway, enough of that. *My* call wasn't about him, it's about Stacy."

"How's Stacy doing?"

"Essentially fine. If you're asking did the sonofa-bitch's death flash her back to her mother, I haven't noticed any untoward reactions. Not that we've talked about it. Joanne hasn't been a topic since Stacy stopped seeing you. And Mate's never been of interest to her, which is good. Dirt like that doesn't deserve her time.

Essentially, we've all been fine. Eric's back at Stanford, finished up the year with terrific grades, working with an econ professor on his honors paper. I'm flying up to see him this weekend, may take Stacy with me, give her another look at the campus."

"She's decided on Stanford?"

"Not yet, that's why I want her to see it again. She's in good shape application-wise. Her grades really picked up after she saw you. This semester she's going the whole nine yards. Full load, A.P. courses, honors track. We're still trying to decide whether she should apply for early admission or play the field. Stanford and the Ivys are taking most of their students early. Her being a legacy won't hurt, but it's always competitive. That's why I'm calling. She still has problems with decision-making, and the early-admit deadlines are in November, so there's some time pressure. I assume you'll be able to find time for her this week."

"I can do that," I said. "But—"

"Payment will be the same, correct? Unless you've raised your fee."

"Payment's the same—"

"No surprise," he said. "With the HMOs closing in, you'd be hard-pressed to raise. We've still got you on computer, just bill through the office."

I took a single deep breath. "Richard, I'd be happy to see Stacy, but before I do you need to know that the police have consulted me on Mate's murder."

"I see . . . Actually, I don't. Why would they do that?"

"I've consulted to the department in the past and the primary detective is someone I've worked with. He hasn't made a specific request, just wants open-ended psychological consultation."

"Because the sonofabitch was crazy?"

"Because the detective thinks I might be helpful—"

"Dr. Delaware, that's ambiguous to the point of meaninglessness."

"But true," I said, inhaling again. "I've said nothing about having seen your family, but there may be conflict. Because they *are* running down the list of Mate's—"

"Victims," he broke in. "Please don't give me that 'travelers' bullshit."

"The point I'm trying to make, Richard, is that the police *will* try to reach you. Before I go any further, I wanted to discuss it with you. I don't want you to feel there's a conflict of interest, so I called—"

"So you've found yourself in a conflictual situation and now you're trying to establish your position."

"It's not a matter of position. It's—"

"Your sincere attempt to do the right thing. Fine, I accept that. In my business we call it due diligence. What's your plan?"

"Now that you've called and asked me to see Stacy again, I'll bow off Mate."

"Why?"

"She's an ongoing patient, continuing as consultant is not an option."

"What reason will you give the police?"

"There'll be no need to explain, Richard. One thing, though: the police may learn about our relationship anyway. These things have a way of getting out."

"Well, that's fine," he said. "Don't keep any secrets on my account. In fact, when they do get hold of me, I'll inform them myself that Stacy's seen you. What's to hide? Caring father obtains help for suffering children? Even better, go ahead and tell them yourself."

He chuckled. "Guess it's fortunate that I do have an alibi—you know what, Doctor? Bring the police on. I'll be happy to tell them how I feel about the sonofabitch. Tell them there's nothing I'd like better than to dance on the sonofabitch's grave. And don't even think about giving up your consultant money, Dr. Delaware. Far be it from me to reduce your income in the HMO age. Keep right on working with the cops. In fact, I'd *prefer* that."

"Why?"

"Who knows, maybe you'll be able to dig around in the sonofabitch's life, uncover some dirt that tells the world what he really was."

"Richard—"

"I know. You'll be discreet about anything you find, discretion's your middle name and all that. But everything goes into the police file and the police have big mouths. So it'll come out . . . I like it, Dr. Delaware. By working for them you'll be doing double duty for *me*. Now, when can I bring Stacy by?"

I made an appointment for the next morning and hung up feeling as if I'd stood on the bow of a small boat during a typhoon.

Half a year had passed since I'd spoken to Richard Doss, but nothing had changed about the way we interacted. No reason for it to be any different. Richard hadn't changed, that had never been his goal.

One of the first things he'd let me know was that he despised Mate. When Mate's murder had flashed on the tube, my initial thought had been: *Richard went after him.*

After hearing the details of the murder, I felt better. The butchery didn't seem like Richard's style. Though how sure of that could I be? Richard hadn't disclosed any more about himself than he'd wanted to.

In control, always in control. One of those people who crowds every room he enters. Maybe that had been part of what led his wife to seek out Eldon Mate.

The referral had come from a family-court judge I'd worked with named Judy Manitow. The message her clerk left was brief: a neighbor had died, leaving behind a seventeen-year-old daughter who could use some counseling.

I called back, hesitant. I take very few therapy cases, stay away from long-termers, and this didn't sound like a quickie. But I'd worked well with Judy Manitow. She was smart, if authoritarian, seemed to care about kids. I phoned her chambers and she picked up herself.

"Can't promise you it'll be brief," she admitted. "Though Stacy's always impressed me as a solid kid, no obvious problems. At least until now."

"How did her mother die?"

"Horribly. Lingering illness—severe deterioration. She was only forty-three."

"What kind of illness?"

"She was never really diagnosed, Alex. The actual cause of death was suicide. Her name was Joanne Doss. Maybe you read about her? It happened three months ago. She was one of Dr. Mate's . . . I guess you couldn't call her a patient. Whatever he calls them."

"Travelers," I said. "No, I didn't read about it."

"It wasn't much of a story," she said. "Back of the

Westside supplement. Now that they don't prosecute Mate, guess he doesn't get prime coverage. I knew Joanne for a long time. Since we had our first babies. We did Mommy and Me together, preschool, the works. Went through it twice, had kids the same years. My Allison and her Eric, then Becky and Stacy. Becky and Stacy used to hang out. Sweet kid, she always seemed . . . grounded. So maybe she won't need long-term therapy, just a few sessions of grief work. You used to do that, right? Working on the cancer wards at Western Pediatrics?"

"Years ago," I said. "What I did there was mostly the reverse. Trying to help parents who'd lost kids. But sure, I've worked with all kinds of bereavement."

"Good," she said. "I just felt it was my duty because I know the family and Stacy seems to be a little depressed—how *couldn't* she be? I know you'll like her. And I do think you'll find the family interesting."

"Interesting," I said. "Scariest word in the English language."

She laughed. "Like someone trying to fix you up with an ugly blind date. 'Is he cute?' 'Well, he's *interesting*.' That's not what I meant, Alex. The Dosses are smart, just about the brightest bunch I've ever met. *Individuals,* each of them—one thing I promise you, you won't be bored. Joanne earned two PhDs. First in English from Stanford, she'd already gotten an appointment as a lecturer at the U. when they moved to L.A. She switched gears suddenly, enrolled as a *student*, took science courses when she was pregnant with Eric. She ended up getting a doctorate in microbiology, was hired by the U. to do research. Before she got sick, she ran her own lab.

Richard's a self-made millionaire. Stanford undergrad and MBA. He and Bob were in the same fraternity. He buys distressed properties, fixes them up, develops. Bob says he's amassed a fortune. Eric's one of those extreme geniuses, won awards in everything—academics, sports, you name it, a fireball. Stacy never seemed to have his confidence. More . . . internal. So it makes sense she'd be the one hit hardest by Joanne's death. Being a daughter, too. Mothers and daughters have something special."

She paused. "I've gone on a bit, haven't I? I guess it's because I really like the family. Also, to be honest, I've put myself in a spot. Because Richard was resistant to the idea of therapy. I had to work on him a bit to get him to agree. It was Bob who finally got through. He and Richard play tennis at the Cliffside; last week Richard mentioned to Bob that Stacy's grades had slipped, she seemed more tired than usual, did he have a recommendation for vitamins. Bob told him he was being a damn fool, Stacy didn't need vitamins, she needed counseling, he'd better get his own act in gear."

"Tough love," I said. "Must have been some tennis game."

"I'm sure it was testosterone at its finest. I love my guy, but he's not a master of subtlety. Anyway, it worked. Richard agreed. So, if you *could* see Stacy, it would help me not look like a complete idiot."

"Sure, Judy."

"Thank you, Alex. There'll certainly be no problem paying the bills. Richard's doing great financially."

"What about emotionally?"

"To tell the truth, he seems fine there, too. Not that he'd ever show it. He did have time to adjust, because

Joanne was sick for over a year . . . Alex, I've never seen such a negative transformation. She gave up her career, withdrew, stopped taking care of herself. Gained weight— I'm talking a tremendous amount, really huge, maybe seventy, a hundred pounds. She became this . . . inert lump. Stayed in bed, eating and sleeping, complaining of pain. Her skin broke out in rashes—it was a horror."

"And there was never any diagnosis?"

"None. Several doctors saw her, including Bob. He wasn't her internist—Bob likes to stay away from people he knows socially, but he worked up Joanne as a favor to Richard. Found nothing, referred her to an immunologist who did his thing and sent her to someone else. And so on and so on."

"Whose decision was it to go to Mate?"

"Definitely Joanne's—not Richard's, Joanne never told him, just disappeared one night and was found the next morning out in Lancaster. Maybe that's why Richard *hates* Mate so much. Being left out. He found out when the police called him. Tried to get in touch with Mate but Mate never returned his calls. Enough, I'm digressing."

"On the contrary," I said. "Anything you know could be helpful."

"That's all I know, Alex. A woman destroyed herself and now her kids are left behind. I can only imagine what poor Stacy's going through."

"Does she look depressed to you?"

"She's not the kind of kid to bleed all over, but I'd say yes. She *has* gained some weight. Nothing like Joanne, maybe ten pounds. But she's not a tall girl. I know how my girls watch themselves, at that age they all do. That and she seems quieter, preoccupied."

"Are she and Becky friends?"

"They used to be really close," she said. "But Becky doesn't know anything, you know kids. We're all very fond of Stacy, Alex. Please help her."

The morning after that conversation, a secretary from RTD Properties called and asked me to hold for Mr. Doss. Pop music played for several minutes and then Richard came on sounding alert, almost cheerful, not at all like a man whose wife had killed herself three months before. Then again, as Judy had said, he'd had time to prepare.

No hint of the resistance Judy had described. He sounded eager, as if readying himself for a new challenge.

Then he began laying out the rules.

No more of that "Mr. Doss," Doctor. Call me Richard.

Services to be billed monthly through my corporate office, here's the number.

Stacy can't afford to miss school, so late-afternoon appointments are essential.

I expect some definition of the process you foresee, specifically what kind of treatment is called for and how long it will take.

Once you've completed your preliminary findings, please submit them to me in writing and we'll take it from there.

"How old is Stacy?" I said.

"She turned seventeen last month."

"There's something you should know, then. Legally, she has no rights to confidentiality. But I can't work with a teen unless the parent agrees to respect confidentiality."

"Meaning I'm shut out of the process."

"Not necessarily . . ."

"Fine. When can I bring her in?"

"One more thing," I said. "I'll need to see you first."

"Why?"

"Before I see a patient, I take a complete history from the parent."

"I don't know about that. I'm extraordinarily busy, right in the middle of some complex deals. What would be the point, Doctor? We're focusing on a rather discrete topic: Stacy's grief. Not her infancy. I could see her development being relevant if it was a learning disability or some kind of immaturity, but any school problems she's experiencing have got to be a reaction to her mother's death. Don't get me wrong, I understand all about family therapy, but that's not what's called for here.

"I consulted a family therapist when my wife's illness intensified. Some quack referred by a doctor I no longer employ, because he felt someone should inquire about Stacy and Eric. I was reluctant, but I complied. The quack kept pressuring me to get the entire family involved, including Joanne. One of those New Agey types, miniature fountain in the waiting room, patronizing voice. I thought it was absolute nonsense. Judy Manitow claims you're quite good."

His tone implied Judy was well-meaning but far from infallible.

I said, "Whatever form treatment takes, Mr. Doss—"

"Richard."

"I'll need to see you first."

"Can't we do history-taking over the phone? Isn't that what we're doing right now? Look, if payment's the issue, just bill me for telephonic services. God knows my lawyers do."

"It's not that," I said. "I need to meet you face-to-face."

"Why?"

"It's the way I work, Richard."

"Well," he said. "That sounds rather dogmatic. The quack insisted on family therapy and you insist upon face-to-face."

"I've found it to be the best way."

"And if I don't agree?"

"Then I'm sorry, but I won't be able to see your daughter."

His chuckle was flat, percussive. I thought of a mechanical noisemaker. "You must be busy to afford to be that cavalier, Doctor. Congratulations."

Neither of us talked for several seconds and I wondered if I'd erred. The man had been through hell, why not be flexible? But something in his manner had gotten to me—the truth was, he'd pushed, so I'd pushed back. Amateur hour, Delaware. I should've known better.

I was about to back off when he said, "All right, I admire a man with spine. I'll see you once. But not this week, I'm out of town . . . Let me check my calendar . . . hold on."

Click. On hold again. More pop music, belch-tone synthesizer syrup in waltz-time. "Tuesday at six is my only window this week, Doctor."

"Fine."

"Not *that* busy, eh? Give me your address."

I did.

"That's residential," he said.

"I work out of my house."

"Makes sense, keep the overhead down. Okay, see you Tuesday. In the meantime, you can begin with Stacy on Monday. She'll be available anytime after school—"

"I'll see her after we've spoken, Richard."

"What a *tough* sonofabitch you are, Doctor. Should've gone into *my* business. The money's a helluva lot better and you could still work out of your house."

5

An alibi.

Richard's call made me want to get out of the house. I filled a cup for Robin and carried it, along with mine, out through the house and into the garden. Passing the perennial bed Robin had laid down last winter, crossing the footbridge to the pond, the rock waterfall. Placing the coffee on a stone bench, I paused to toss pellets to the koi. The fish darted toward me before the food hit the water, coalescing in a frothy swirl at the rim. Iron skies bore down, dyeing the water charcoal, playing on metallic scales. The air was cool, odorless, just as stagnant as up at the murder site, but greenery and water burble blunted the sense of lifelessness.

Up in the hills, September haze can be romanticized as fog. Our property's not large, but it's secluded because of an unbuildable western border, and surrounded by old-growth pines and lemon gums that create the illusion of solitude. This morning the treetops were capped with gray.

I crouched, allowing one of the larger carp to nibble my fingers. Reminding myself, as I sometimes did, that life was transitory and I was lucky to be living amid beauty and relative quiet. My father destroyed himself with alcohol and my mother was heroic but habitually sad. No whining, the past isn't a straitjacket. But for people breast-fed on misery, it can be an awfully tight sweater.

No sounds from the studio, then the chip-chip of Robin's chisel. The building's a single-story miniature of the house, with high windows and an old, burnished pine door rescued by Robin from a downtown demolition. I pushed the door open, heard music playing softly—Ry Cooder on slide. Robin was at her workbench, hair tied up in a red silk scarf, wearing gray denim overalls over a black T-shirt. Hunched in a way that would cause her shoulders to ache by nightfall. She didn't hear me enter. Smooth, slender arms worked the chisel on a guitar-shaped piece of Alaskan spruce. Wood shavings curled at her feet, creating a cozy bed for Spike. His bulldog bulk had sunk into the scrap, and he snored away, flews flapping.

I watched for a while as Robin continued to tune the soundboard, tapping, chiseling, tapping again, running her fingers along the inner edges, pausing to reflect before resuming. Her wrists were child-size, seemed too fragile to manipulate steel, but she handled the tool as if it was a chopstick.

Biting her lower lip, then licking it, as her back humped more acutely. A stray bit of auburn curl sprang loose from the kerchief and she tucked it back impatiently. Oblivious to my presence though I stood ten, fifteen feet away. As with most creative people, time and space have no meaning for her when her mind's engaged.

I came closer, stopped at the far end of the bench. Mahogany eyes widened, she placed the chisel on the workbench and the ivory flash of those two oversize incisors appeared between full, soft lips. I smiled back and held out a cup, enjoying the contours of her face, heart-shaped, olive-tinted, decorated by a few more lines than ages ago when we'd met, but still smooth. Usually, she wore earrings. Not this morning. No watch, no jewelry or makeup. She'd rushed out too quickly to bother.

I felt a nudge at my ankle, heard a wheeze and a snort. Spike grumbled and butted my shin. We'd both adopted him, but he'd adopted her.

"Call off your beast," I said.

Robin laughed and took the coffee. "Thanks, baby." She touched my face. Spike growled louder. She told him, "Don't worry, you're still my handsome."

Setting the cup down, she wrapped both her arms around my neck. Spike produced a poor excuse for a bark, raspy and attenuated by his stubby bulldog larynx.

"Oh, Spikey," she told him, snaring her fingers in my hair.

"If you stop to pet him," I said, "*I'll* start snorting."

"Stop what?"

"This." I kissed her, ran my hands over her back, down to her rear, then up again, grazing her shoulder blades. Starting at the top and kneading the knobs of her spine.

"Oh that's good. I'm a little sore."

"Bad posture," I said. "Not that I'd ever preach."

"No, nothing like that."

We kissed again, more deeply. She relaxed, allowing her body—all 110 pounds of it—to depend upon mine. I felt the warmth of her breath at my ear as I undid the straps of her overalls. The denim fell to her waist but no farther, blocked by the rim of the workbench. I stroked her left arm, luxuriating in the feel of firm muscle under soft skin. Slipping my fingers under her T-shirt, I aimed for the spot that tended to pain her—two spots, really, a pair of knots just above her gluteal cleft. Robin's by no means skeletal; she's a curvy woman, blessed with hips and thighs and breasts and that sheath of body fat that is so wonderfully female. But a small frame meant a back narrow enough for one of my hands to cover both tendernesses simultaneously.

She arched toward me. "Oh . . . you're bad."

"Thought it felt good."

"That's why you're bad. I should be working."

"I should be, too." I took her chin in one hand. Reached down with my other hand and cupped her bottom. No jewelry or makeup, but she had taken the time for perfume, and the fragrance radiated at the juncture of jawline and jugular.

Back to the sore spots.

"Fine, go ahead," she whispered. "Now that you've corrupted me and I'm completely distracted." Her fingers fumbled at my zipper.

"Corruption?" I said. "This is nothing."

I touched her. She moaned. Spike went nuts.

She said, "I feel like an abusive parent." Then she put him outside.

When we finished, the coffee was long cold but we drank it anyway. The red scarf was on the floor and the wood shavings were no longer in a neat pile. I was sitting in an old leather chair, naked, with Robin on my lap. Still breathing hard, still wanting to kiss her. Finally, she pulled away, stood, got dressed, returned to the guitar top. A private-joke smile graced her lips.

"What?"

"We moved around a bit. Just want to make sure we didn't get anything on my masterpiece."

"Like what?"

"Like sweat."

"Maybe that would be a good thing," I said. "Truly organic luthiery."

"Orgasmic luthiery."

"That, too." I got up and stood behind her, smelling her hair. "I love you."

"Love you, too." She laughed. "You are such a *guy*."

"Is that a compliment?"

"Depends on my mood. At this moment, it's a whimsical observation. Every time we make love you tell me you love me."

"That's good, right? A guy who expresses his feelings."

"It's great," she said quickly. "And you're very consistent."

"I tell you other times, don't I?"

"Of course you do, but this is . . ."

"Predictable."

"One hundred percent."

"So," I said, "Professor Castagna has been keeping a record?"

"Don't have to. Not that I'm complaining, sweetie. You can always tell me you love me. I just think it's cute."

"My predictability."

"Better that than instability."

"Well," I said, "I can vary it—say it in another language—how about Hungarian? Should I call Berlitz?"

She pecked my cheek, picked up her chisel.

"Pure guy," she said.

Spike began scratching at the door. I let him in and he raced past me, came to a short stop at Robin's feet, rolled over and presented his abdomen. She kneeled and rubbed him, and his short legs flailed ecstatically.

I said, "Oh you Jezebel. Okay, back to the sawmill."

"No saw today. Just this." Indicating the chisel.

"I meant me."

She looked at me over her shoulder. "Tough day ahead?"

"The usual," I said. "Other people's problems. Which is what I get paid for, right?"

"How'd your meeting with Milo go? Has he learned anything about Dr. Mate?"

"Not so far. He asked me to do some research on Mate, thought I'd try the computer first."

"Shouldn't be hard to produce hits on Mate."

"No doubt," I said. "But finding something valuable in the slag heap's another story. If I dead-end, I'll try the research library, maybe Bio-Med."

"I'll be here all day," she said. "If you don't interrupt me, I'll push my hands too far. How about an early dinner?"

"Sure."

"I mean, baby, don't stay away. I want to hear you say you love me."

Pure guy.

Often, especially after a day when I'd seen more patients than usual, we spent evenings where I did very little talking. Despite all my training, sometimes getting the words out got lost on the highway between Head and Mouth. Sometimes I thought about the nice things I'd tell her, but never followed through.

But when we made love . . . for me, the physical released the emotional and I supposed that put me in some sort of Y-chromosome file box.

There's a common belief that men use love to get sex and women do just the opposite. Like most alleged wisdom about human beings, it's anything but absolute; I've known women who turned thoughtless promiscuity into a fine art and men so bound by affection that the idea of stranger-sex repulsed them to the point of impotence.

I'd never been sure where Richard Doss fell along that continuum. By the time I met him, he hadn't made love to his wife for over three years.

He told me so within minutes of entering the office. As if it was important for me to know of his deprivation. He'd resisted any notion of anyone but his daughter being my patient, yet began by talking about himself. If he was trying to clarify something, I never figured out what it was.

He'd met Joanne Heckler in college, termed the match "ideal," offered the fact that he'd stayed married to her over twenty years as proof. When I met him, she'd been dead for ninety-three days, but he spoke of her as having existed in a very distant past. When he professed to have loved her deeply, I had no reason to doubt him, other than the absence of feeling in his voice, eyes, body posture.

Not that he was incapable of emotion. When I opened the side door that leads to my office, he burst into the house talking on a tiny silver cell phone, continuing to talk in an animated tone after we'd entered the office and I'd sat behind my desk. Wagging an index finger to let me know it would be a minute.

Finally, he said, "Okay, gotta go, Scott. Work the spread, at this point that's the key. If they give us the rate they promised, we're in like Flynn. Otherwise it's a deal-killer. Get them to commit now, not later, Scott. You know the drill."

Eyes flashing, free hand waving.

Enjoying it.

He said, "We'll chat later," clicked off the phone, sat, crossed his legs.

"Negotiations?" I said.

"The usual. Okay, first Joanne." At his mention of his wife's name, his voice went dead.

Physically, he wasn't what I'd expected. My training is supposed to endow me with an open mind, but everyone develops preconceptions, and my mental picture of Richard Doss had been based upon what Judy Manitow had told me and five minutes of phone-sparring.

Aggressive, articulate, dominant. Ex–frat boy, tennis-playing country-club member. Tennis partner of Bob Manitow, who was a physician but about as corporate-looking as you could get. For no good reason, I'd guessed someone who looked like Bob: tall, imposing, a bit beefy, the basic CEO hairstyle: short and side-parted, silver at the temples. A well-cut suit in a somber shade, white or blue shirt, power tie, shiny wing-tips.

Richard Doss was five-five, tops, with a weathered leprechaun face—wide at the brow tapering to an almost womanish point at the chin. A dancer's build, very lean, with square shoulders, a narrow waist. Oversize hands sporting manicured nails coated with clear polish. Palm Springs tan, the kind you rarely saw anymore because of the melanoma scare. The fibrous complexion of one who ignores melanoma warnings.

His hair was black, kinky, and he wore it long enough to evoke another decade. White man's afro. Thin gold chain around his neck. His black silk shirt had flap pockets and buccaneer sleeves and he'd left the top two buttons undone, advertising a hairless chest and extension of the tan. Baggy, tailored gray tweed slacks were held in place by a lizard-skin belt with a silver buckle. Matching loafers, no socks. He carried a smallish black purselike thing in one hand, the silver phone in the other.

I would've pegged him as Joe Hollywood. One of those producer wanna-bes you see hanging out at Sunset Plaza cafés. The type with cheap apartments on month-to-month, poorly maintained leased Corniches, too much leisure time, schemes masquerading as ideas.

Richard Doss had made his way south from Palo Alto and embraced the L.A. image almost to the point of parody.

He said, "My wife was a testament to the failure of

modern medicine." The silver phone rang. He jammed it to his ear. "Hi. What? Okay. Good . . . No, not now. Bye." Click. "Where was I—modern medicine. We saw dozens of doctors. They put her through every test in the book. CAT scans, MRIs, serologic, toxicologic. She had two lumbar punctures. No real reason, I found out later. The neurologist was just 'fishing around.'"

"What were her symptoms?" I said.

"Joint pain, headaches, skin sensitivity, fatigue. It started out as fatigue. She'd always been a ball of energy. Five-two, a hundred and ten pounds. She used to dance, play tennis, powerwalk. The change was gradual—at first I figured a flu, or one of those crazy viruses that's going around. I figured the best thing was stay out of her face, give her time to rest. By the time I realized something serious was going on, she was hard to reach. On another planet." He hooked a finger under the gold chain. "Joanne's parents didn't live long, maybe her constitution . . . She'd always been into the mom thing, that went, too. I suppose *that* was her main symptom. Disengagement. From me, the kids, everything."

"Judy told me she was a microbiologist. What kinds of things did she work on?"

He shook his head. "You're hypothesizing the obvious: she was infected by some pathogen from her lab. Logical but wrong. That was looked into right away, from every angle—some sort of rogue microbe, allergies, hypersensitivity to a chemical. She worked with germs, all right, but they were *plant* germs—vegetable pathogens—molds and funguses that affect food crops. Broccoli, specifically. She had a USDA grant to study broccoli. Do you like broccoli?"

"Sure."

"I don't. As it turns out, there *are* cross-sensitivities between plants and animals, but nothing Joanne worked with fit that category—her equipment, her reagents. She went through every blood test known to medicine." He thumbed black silk cuff. His watch was black-faced with a gold band, so skinny it looked like a tattoo.

"Let's not get distracted," he said. "The precise reason for what happened to Joanne will never be known. Back to the core issue: her disengagement. The first thing to go was entertaining and socializing. She refused to go out with anyone. No more business dinners—too tired, not hungry. Even though all she did in bed was eat. We're members of the Cliffside Country Club and she'd played tennis and a little golf, used the gym. No more. Soon, she was going to bed earlier and rising later. Eventually, she started spending all her time in bed, saying the pain had gotten worse. I told her she might be aching because of inactivity—her muscles were contracting, stiffening up. She didn't answer me. That's when I started taking her to doctors."

He recrossed his legs. "Then there was the weight gain. The only thing she *didn't* withdraw from was food. Cookies, cake, potato chips, anything sweet or greasy." His lips curled, as if he'd tasted something bad. "By the end she weighed two hundred ten pounds. Had more than doubled her weight in less than a year. A hundred and ten extra pounds of pure fat—isn't that incredible, Doctor? It was hard to keep seeing her as the girl I married. She used to be lithe. Athletic. All of a sudden I was married to a stranger—some asexual alien. You're with someone for twenty-five years you just don't stop liking them, but I won't deny it, my feelings for her changed—for all practical purposes she was no longer my wife. I tried to help her with the food. Suggesting maybe she'd be just as satisfied with fruit as with Oreos. But she wouldn't hear of it and she arranged the grocery deliveries when I was at work. I suppose I could've taken drastic measures—gotten her on fen-phen, bolted the refrigerator, but food seemed to be the only thing that kept her going. I felt it was cruel to withdraw it from her."

"I assume every metabolic link was checked out."

"Thyroid, pituitary, adrenal, you name it. I know enough to be an endocrinologist. The weight gain was simply Joanne drowning herself in food. When I made suggestions about cutting back, she responded the same way she did to any opinion I offered. By turning off completely—here, look."

Out of the purse came a pair of plastic-encased snap-shots. He made no effort to hand them to me, merely stretched out his arm so I had to get up from my chair to retrieve them.

"Before and after," he said.

The left photo was a color shot of a young couple. Green lawn, big trees, imposing beige buildings. I'd collaborated with a Stanford professor on a research project years ago, recognized the campus.

"I was a senior, she was a sophomore," said Doss. "That was taken right after we got engaged."

For many students, the seventies had meant long coifs, facial hair, torn jeans and sandals. Counterculture giving way to Brooks Brothers only when the realities of making a living sank in.

It was as if Richard Doss had reversed the process. His college 'do had been a dense black crew cut. In the picture he wore a white shirt, pressed gray slacks, horn-rimmed glasses. And here were the shiny black wing-tips. Study-pallor on the elfin face, no tan.

Youthful progenitor of the corporate type I'd expected him to be.

Distracted expression. No celebration of the engage-ment that I could detect.

The girl under his arm was smiling. Joanne Heckler, petite as described, had been pretty in a well-scrubbed way. Fair-skinned and narrow-faced, she wore her brown hair long and straight, topped by a white band. Glasses for her, too. Smaller than Richard's, and gold-framed. A diamond glinted on her ring finger. Her sleeveless dress was bright blue, modest for that era.

Another elf. Marriage of the leprechauns.

They say couples who live together long enough start to look like each other. Richard and Joanne had begun that way but diverged.

I turned to the second photo, a washed-out Polaroid. A subject who resembled no one.

Long-view of a king-size bed, shot from the foot. Rumpled gold comforter strewn across a tapestry-covered bed bench. High mound of beige pillows propped against the headboard. In their midst, a head floated.

White face. Round. So porcine and bloated the features were compressed to a smear. Bladder-cheeks. Eyes buried in folds. Just a hint of brown hair tied back tight from a pasty forehead. Pucker-mouth devoid of expression.

Below the head, beige sheets rose like a bell-curved, tented bulk. To the right was an elegant carved night-stand in some kind of dark, glossy wood, with gold pulls. Behind the headboard was peach wallpaper printed with teal flowers. A length of gilded frame and linen mat hinted at artwork cropped out of the photo.

For one shocking moment, I wondered if Richard Doss had a postmortem shot. But no, the eyes were open . . . something in them . . . despair? No, worse. A living death.

"Eric took it," said Doss. "My son. He wanted a record."

"Of his mom?" I said. Hoarse, I cleared my throat.

"Of what had happened to his mom. Frankly put, it pissed him off."

"He was angry at her?"

"No," he said, as if I were an idiot. "At the situation. That's how my son deals with his anger."

"By documenting?"

"By organizing. Putting things in their place. Person-ally, I think it's a great way to handle stress. Lets you wade through the emotional garbage, analyze the factual content of events, get in touch with how you feel, then move on. Because what choice is there? Wallow in other people's misery? Allow yourself to be destroyed?"

He pointed a finger at me, as if I'd accused him of something.

"If that sounds callous," he said, "so be it, Doctor. You haven't lived in my house, never went through what I did. Joanne took over a year to leave us. We had time to figure things out. Eric's a brilliant boy—the smartest person I've ever met. Even so, it affected him. He was in his second semester at Stanford, came home to be with Joanne. He devoted himself to her, so if taking that picture seems callous, bear that in mind. And it's not as if his mother minded. She just lay there—that picture captures exactly what she was like at the end. How she ever mobilized the energy to contact the sonofabitch who killed her I'll never know."

"Dr. Mate."

He ignored me, fingered the silver phone. Finally our eyes met. I smiled, trying to let him know I wasn't judging. His lids were slightly lowered. Beneath them, dark eyes shone like nuggets of coal.

"I'll take those back." He leaned forward, holding out his hand for the pictures. Again, I had to stand to return them.

"How did Stacy cope?" I said.

He took his time zipping open the purse and placing the snapshots within. Crossing his legs yet again. Massaging the phone, as if hoping a call would rescue him from having to answer.

"Stacy," he said, "is another story."

6

I booted up the computer. Eldon Mate's name pulled up over a hundred sites.

Most of the references were reprints of newspaper columns covering Mate's career as a one-way travel agent. Pros, cons, no shortage of strong opinions from experts on both sides. Everyone responding on an intellectual level. Nothing psychopathic, none of the cold cruelty that had flavored the murder.

A "Dr. Death Home Page" featured a flattering photo of Mate, recaps of his acquittals and a brief biography. Mate had been born in San Diego sixty-three years ago, received a degree in chemistry from San Diego State and worked as a chemist for an oil company before entering medical school in Guadalajara, Mexico, at the age of forty. He'd served an internship at a hospital in Oakland, gotten licensed as a general practitioner at forty-six.

No specialty training. The only jobs the news pieces had mentioned were civil service positions at health departments all over the Southwest, where Mate had overseen immunization programs and pushed paper. No indication he'd ever treated a patient.

Beginning a new career as a doctor in middle age but avoiding contact with the living. Had he been drawn to medicine in order to get closer to death?

The name and phone number at the bottom of the page was Attorney Roy Haiselden's. He'd listed no e-mail address.

Next came several euthanasia stories:

The first few covered the case of Roger Damon Sharveneau, a respiratory therapist at a hospital in Rochester, New York, who'd confessed eighteen months earlier to snuffing out three dozen intensive-care patients by injecting potassium chloride into their I.V. lines—wanting to "ease their journey." Sharveneau's lawyer claimed his client was insane, had him examined by a psychiatrist who diagnosed borderline personality and prescribed the anti-depressant imipramine. A few days later, Sharveneau recanted. Without his confession, the only evidence against him was proximity to the ICU every night a questionable death had occurred. The same applied to three other techs, so the police released Sharveneau, terming the case "still under investigation." Sharveneau filed for disability benefits, granted an interview to a local newspaper and claimed he'd been under the influence of a shadowy figure named Dr. Burke, whom no one had ever seen. Soon after, he overdosed fatally on imipramine.

The case prompted an investigation of other respiratory techs living in the Rochester area. Several with criminal backgrounds were found working at hospitals and convalescent homes around the state. The health commissioner vowed to institute tighter controls.

I plugged Sharveneau's name into the system, found only one follow-up article that cited lack of progress on the original investigation and doubts as to whether the thirty-six deaths had been unnatural.

The next link was a decade-old case: four nurses in Vienna had killed as many as three hundred people using overdoses of morphine and insulin. Arrest, conviction, sentences ranging from fifteen years to life. Eldon Mate was quoted as suggesting the killers might have been acting out of compassion.

A similar case from Chicago: two years later, a pair of nurses' aides who'd smothered elderly terminal patients to death as part of a lesbian romance. Plea bargain for the one who talked, life without parole for the other. Once again, Mate had offered a contrarian opinion.

Onward. A Cleveland piece dated only two months earlier. Kevin Arthur Haupt, an emergency medical tech working the night shift on a city ambulance, had decided to shortcut the treatment of twelve drunks he'd picked up on heart-attack calls by clamping his hand over their noses and mouths during transport to the hospital. Discovery came when one of the intended victims turned out to be healthier than expected, awoke to find himself being smothered and fought back. Arrest, multiple murder charge, guilty plea, thirty-year sentence. Mate wondered in print if spending money to resuscitate habitual alcoholics was a wise use of tax dollars.

An old wire-service piece about the Netherlands, where assisted suicide was no longer prosecuted, claimed that doctor-initiated killings had grown to 2 percent of all recorded Dutch deaths, with 25 percent of physicians admitting they'd euthanized patients deemed unfit to live, without the patients' consent.

Years ago, while working Western Pediatrics Medical Center, I'd served on something called the Ad Hoc Life Support Committee—six physicians and myself, drafted by the hospital board to come up with guidelines for ending the treatment of children in final-stage illness. We'd been a fractious group, producing debate and very little else. But each of us knew that scarcely a month went by when a slightly-larger-than-usual dose of morphine didn't find its way into the mesh of tubes attached to a tiny arm. Kids suffering from bone or brain cancer, atrophied livers, ravaged lungs, who just happened to "stop breathing," once their parents had said good-bye.

Some caring soul ending the pain of a child who would've died anyway, sparing the family the agony of a protracted deathwatch.

The same motivation claimed by Eldon H. Mate.

Why did it feel different to me from Mate's gloating use of the Humanitron?

Because I believed the doctors and nurses on cancer wards had been acting out of compassion, but I suspected Mate's motivations?

Because Mate came across obnoxious and publicity-seeking?

Was that the worst type of hypocrisy on my part, accepting covert god-play from those I greeted in the hall while allowing myself to be repelled by Mate's in-your-face approach to death? So what if the screeching little man with the homemade killing machine wouldn't have

won any charm contests. Did the *psyche* of the travel
agent matter when the final *destination* was always the
same?

My father had died quietly, fading away from
cirrhosis and kidney failure and general breakdown of his
body after a lifetime of bad habits. Muscles reabsorbing,
skin bagging as he devolved into a wizened, yellowed
gnome I hardly recognized.

As the poisons in his system accumulated, it took
only a few weeks for Harry Delaware to sink from
lethargy to torpor to coma. If he'd gone out screaming in
agony, would I now harbor any reservations about the
Humanitron?

And what about people like Joanne Doss, suffering
but undiagnosed?

If you accepted death as a civil rights issue, did a
medical label matter? Whose life *was* it, anyway?

Religion supplied answers, but when you took God
out of the equation, things got complicated. That was as
good a reason as any for God, I supposed. I wished I'd
been blessed with a greater capacity for faith and obedi-
ence. What would happen if one day I found myself
being devoured by cancer, or deadened by paralysis?

Sitting there, hand poised to strike the ENTER key, I
found that my thoughts kept flying back to my father's
last days. Strange—he rarely came to mind.

Then I pictured Dad as a healthy man. Big bald
head, creased bull neck, sandpaper hands from all those
years turning wood on the lathe. Alcohol breath and
tobacco laughter. One-handed push-ups, the too-hard
slap on the back. He'd been well into his fifties by the
time I could hold my own against him in the arm wrestles

he demanded as a greeting ritual during my increasingly rare trips back to Missouri.

I found myself edging forward on the chair. Positioning myself for combat, just as I'd done as Dad's forearm and mine pressed against each other, hot and sticky. Elbows slipping on the Formica of the kitchen table as we purpled and strained, muscles quivering with tetany. Mom leaving the room, looking pained.

By the time Dad hit fifty-five, the pattern was set: mostly I'd win, occasionally we'd tie. He'd laugh at first.

Alexander-er, when I was young I could climb walls!

Then he'd light up a Chesterfield, frown and mutter, leave the room. My visits thinned to once a year. The ten days I spent sitting silently holding my mother's hand as he died was my longest stay since leaving home for college.

I shuttered the memories, tried to relax, punched a key. The computer—perfect, silent companion that it was—obliged by flashing a new image.

A site posted by a Washington, D.C.–based handicapped-rights group named Still Alive. A position statement: all human life was precious, no one should judge anyone else's quality of life. Then a section on Mate—to this group, Hitler incarnate. Archival photo of Still Alive members picketing a motel where Mate had left a traveler. Men and women in wheelchairs, lofting banners. Mate's reaction to the protest: "You're a bunch of whiners who should examine your own selfish motivations."

Quotes from Mate and Roy Haiselden followed:

"The storm troopers came for me, but I wouldn't play passive Jew" (Mate, 1991).

"Darwin would have loved to meet [District

Attorney] Clarkson. The idiot's living proof of the missing link between pond slime and mammalian organisms" (Haiselden, 1993).

"A needle in a vein is a hell of a lot more humane than a nuclear bomb, but you don't hear much outrage from the morality mongoloids about atomic testing, do you?" (Mate, 1995).

"Any pioneer, anyone with a vision, inevitably suffers. Jesus, Buddha, Copernicus, the Wright brothers. Hell, the guy who invented stickum on envelopes probably got abused by the idiots who manufactured sealing wax" (Mate, 1995).

"Sure, I'd go on *The Tonight Show,* but it ain't gonna happen, folks! Too many stupid rules imposed by the network. Hell, I'd help someone *travel* on *The Tonight Show* if the fools who made the rules would let me. I'd do it live—so to speak. It would be their highest-rated show, I can promise you that. They could play it during sweeps week. I'd play some music in the background—something classical. Use some poor soul with a totally compromised nervous system—maybe an advanced muscular dystrophy case—limbs out of control, tongue flapping, copious salivation, no bladder or bowel control—let them leak all over the soundstage, show the world how pretty decay and disease are. If I could do that, you'd see all that sanctimonious drivel about the nobility of life fade away pronto. I could pull off the whole thing in minutes, safe, clean, silent. Let the camera focus on the traveler's face, show how peaceful they were once the thiopental kicked in. Teach the world that the true nature of compassion isn't some priest or rabbi claiming to be God's holy messenger or some government mongoloid lackey who couldn't pass a basic biology course trying to tell me what's life and what isn't. 'Cause it's not that complex, amigos: when the brain ain't workin', you ain't livin'. *The Tonight Show* . . . yeah, that would be educational. If they let me set it up the right way, sure, I'd do it" (Mate, 1997, in response to a press question about why he liked publicity).

"Dr. Mate should get the Nobel Prize. Double payment. For medicine *and* peace. I wouldn't mind a piece of that, myself. Being his lawyer, I deserve it" (Haiselden, 1998).

Other assorted oddities, ranked lower for relevance:

A three-year-old Denver news item about a Colorado "outsider" artist with the improbable name of Zero Tollrance who'd created a series of paintings inspired by Mate and his machine. Using an abandoned building in a run-down section of Denver, Tollrance, previously unknown, had exhibited thirty canvases. A freelance writer had covered the show for *The Denver Post*, citing "several portraits of the controversial 'death doctor' in a wide range of familiar poses: Gilbert Stuart's George Washington, Thomas Gainsborough's Blue Boy, Vincent van Gogh's bandaged-ear self-portrait, Andy Warhol's Marilyn Monroe. Non-Mate works included collages of coffins, cadavers, skulls and maggot-infested meat. But perhaps the most ambitious of Tollrance's productions is a faithfully rendered re-creation of Rembrandt's *Anatomy Lesson*, a graphic portrayal of human dissection, with Dr. Mate serving a dual role, as scalpel-wielding lecturer as well as flayed cadaver."

When asked how many paintings had sold, Tollrance "walked away without comment."

Mate as cutter and victim. Be interesting to talk to Mr. Tollrance. Save. Print.

Two citations from a health-issues academic bulletin board posted by Harvard University: a geriatric study found that while 59.3 percent of the relatives of elderly patients favored legalizing physician-assisted suicide, only 39.9 percent of the old people agreed. And a study done at a cancer treatment center found that two thirds of the American public endorsed assisted death but 88 percent of cancer patients suffering from constant pain had no interest in exploring the topic and felt that a doctor's bringing it up would erode their trust.

In a feminist resource site I found an article in a journal called *S(Hero)* entitled "Mercy or Misogyny: Does Dr. Mate Have a Problem with Women?" The author wondered why 80 percent of Mate's "travelers" had been female. Mate, she claimed, had never been known to have a relationship with a woman and had refused to answer questions about his personal life. Freudian speculation followed.

Milo hadn't mentioned any family. I made a note to follow up on that.

The final item: four years ago, in San Francisco, a group calling itself the Secular Humanist Infantry had granted Mate its highest award, the Heretic. Prior to the ceremony, a syringe Mate had used on a recent "travel venture" had been auctioned off for two hundred dollars, only to be confiscated immediately by an undercover police officer citing violation of state health regulations. Commotion and protest as the cop dropped the needle into an evidence bag and exited. During his acceptance speech, Mate donated his windbreaker as a consolation prize and termed the officer a "mental gnat with all the morals of a rotavirus."

The name of the winning bidder caught my eye.

Alice Zoghbie. Treasurer of the Secular Humanist Infantry, now president of the Socrates Club. The same woman who'd leased the death van and left that day for Amsterdam.

I ran a search on the club, found the home page, topped by a logo of the Greek philosopher's sculpted head surrounded by a wreath that I assumed was hemlock. As Milo'd said, headquarters on Glenmont Circle in Glendale, California.

The Socrates mission statement emphasized the "personal ownership of life, unfettered by the outmoded and barbaric conventions foisted upon society by organized religion." Signed, Alice Zoghbie, MPA. A hundred-dollar fee entitled the fortunate to notification of events and all other benefits of membership. AMEX, VISA, MC, and DISC accepted.

Zoghbie's master's in public administration didn't tell me much about her professional background. Searching her name produced a long article in *The San Jose Mercury News* that filled in the blanks.

Entitled "Right-to-Die Group's Leader's Comments Cause Controversy," the piece described Zoghbie as

> fiftyish, pencil-thin and tall. The former hospital personnel director is now engaged full-time running the Socrates Club, an organization devoted to legalizing assisted suicide. Until recently, members have maintained a low profile, concentrating upon filing

friend-of-court briefs in right-to-die cases. However, recent remarks by Zoghbie at last Sunday's brunch at the Western Sun Inn here in San Jose have cast the club into the limelight and raised questions about its true goals.

During the meeting, attended by an estimated fifty people, Zoghbie delivered a speech calling for the "humane dispatch of patients with Alzheimer's disease and other types of 'thought impairment,' " as well as disabled children and others who are legally incapable of making "the decision they'd clearly form if they were in their right minds."

"I worked at a hospital for twenty years," the tan, white-haired woman said, "and I witnessed firsthand the abuses that took place in the name of treatment. Real compassion isn't creating vegetables. Real compassion is scientists putting their heads together to create a measurement scale that would quantify suffering. Those who score above a predetermined criterion could then be helped in a timely manner even if they lacked the capacity to liberate them-selves."

Reaction to Zoghbie's proposal by local religious leaders was swift and negative. Catholic Bishop Armand Rodriguez termed the plan "a call to geno-cide," and Dr. Archie Van Sandt of the Mount Zion Baptist Church accused Zoghbie of being "an instru-ment of cancerous secularism." Rabbi Eugene Brandner of Temple Emanu-El said that Zoghbie's ideas were "certainly not in line with Jewish thought at any point along the spectrum."

An unattributed statement by the Socrates Club issued two days later attempted to qualify Zoghbie's remarks, terming them "an impetus to discussion rather than a policy statement."

Dr. J. Randolph Smith, director of the Western Medical Association's Committee on Medical Ethics, viewed the disavowal with some skepticism. "A simple reading of the transcript shows this was a perfectly clear expression of philosophy and intent. The slippery slope yawns before us, and groups such as the Socrates Club seem intent on shoving us down into the abyss of amorality. Given further acceptance of views such as Ms. Zoghbie's, it's only a matter of time before the legalization of murder of those who say they want to die gives way to the murder of those who have never asked to die, as is now the case in the Netherlands."

I logged off, called Milo at the station. A young man answered his phone, asked me who I was with some suspicion and put me on hold.

A few seconds later, Milo said, "Hi."

"New secretary?"

"Detective Stephen Korn. One of my little helpers. What's up?"

"Got some stuff for you, but nothing profound." Got a resolved ethical issue, too, but I'll save that for later.

"What kind of stuff?" he said.

"Mostly biography and the expected controversy, but Alice Zoghbie's name came up—"

"Alice Zoghbie just called me," he said. "Back in L.A. and willing to talk."

"Thought she wasn't due for two days."

"She cut her trip short. Distraught about Mate."

"Delayed grief reaction?" I said. "Mate's been dead for a week."

"She claims she didn't hear about it till yesterday. Was up in Nepal somewhere—climbing mountains, the Amsterdam thing was the tail end of her trip, big confab of death freaks from all over the world. Not the place to choke on your chicken salad, huh? Anyway, Zoghbie says she had no access to news in Nepal, got to Amsterdam three days ago, her hosts met her at the airport and gave her the news. She slept over one day, booked a return flight."

"So she arrived two days ago," I said. "Still a bit of delay before she called you. Giving herself time to think?"

"Composing herself. Her quote."

"When are you meeting her?"

"Three hours at her place." He recited the Glenmont address.

"Socrates Club headquarters," I said. "Found their website. Hundred bucks to join, credit-card friendly. Wonder how many of her bills that pays."

"You don't trust this lady's intentions?"

"Her views don't inspire trust. She thinks senile old folks and handicapped kids should be put out of their misery, whether they want to be or not. Got the quotes for you—part of today's work product. Along with assorted other goodies, including some other death-freak stuff and more weirdness."

I told him about Roger Sharveneau and the other hospital ghouls, finished with Zero Tollrance's exhibition.

"Cute," he said. "The art world's always been a warm and fuzzy place."

"One thing about Tollrance I found particularly interesting: he posed Mate in *The Anatomy Lesson* as wielding the scalpel *and* getting flayed."

"So?"

"It implies a certain ambivalence—wanting to play doctor *on* the doctor."

"You're saying I should take this guy seriously?"

"Might be interesting to talk to him."

"Tollrance, like that's a real name . . . Denver . . . I'll see what I can find."

"How far down the family list have your little helpers gotten?" I said.

"All the way down in terms of locating phone numbers and first attempts at contact," he said. "They've talked to about half the sample. Everyone loves Mate."

Not everyone. "Want me to come along to meet Alice in Deathland?"

"Sure," he said. "Look how cruel life can be. Climbing mountains in Nepal one day, enduring the police the next . . . She's probably one of those fit types, body image *über alles*."

"Depends on whose body you're talking about."

7

We agreed to meet at the station in two hours and I hung up. I'd intended to bring up the Doss family but hadn't. My excuse: some topics didn't lend themselves to phone chat.

I wanted to know more about Eldon Mate the physician, so I drove over to the Bio-Med library at the U., found myself a terminal. The periodicals index gave me a few more magazine articles but nothing new. I scanned scientific databases for any technical articles Mate might have published, not expecting anything in view of his lackluster career, but I found two citations: a Chemical Abstracts reference that led me to a thirty-year-old letter to the editor Mate had written in response to an article about polymerization—something about small molecules combining to create large molecules and the potential for better gasoline. Mate disagreed crankily. The author of the article, a professor at MIT, had dismissed Mate's comments as irrelevant. Mate's title, back then, had been assistant research chemist, ITEG Petroleum.

The second reference appeared in MEDLINE, sixteen years old, also a letter, this time in a Swedish pathology journal. Mate had his MD by then, cited his affiliation at Oxford Hill Hospital in Oakland, California. No title. No mention that he was a lowly intern.

The second letter didn't argue with anyone. Titled "Precise Measurement of Time of Death: A Social Boon," it began with a quote by Sir Thomas Browne:

"We all labour against our own cure, for death is the cure of all diseases."

Mate went on to bemoan the

stigma associated with cellular cessation, and subsequent moral cowardice exhibited by physicians when dealing with parathanatological phenomena. As the ultimate caretakers of body and that fiction known as "soul," we must do everything in our power to demystify the process of life termination, utilizing the scientific tools at our disposal to avoid needless prolongation of "life" that is the fruit of theology-based myths.

In this regard, quantification of precise time of death will be useful in robbing the myth mongers of their fictions and save costs that accrue from the needless employment of so-called heroic measures that create nothing more than respirating corpses.

Along these lines, I have attempted to discern which outward physical manifestations advertise the precise shutoff of vital systems. The central nervous system often continues to fire synaptically well after the heart stops beating and vice versa. Even a high-school biology student can keep a pithed frog's heart beating for a substantial "postmortem" period through the use of stimulant drugs. Furthermore, brain death is not a discrete event, and this fact leads to confusion and uncertainty.

I have thus looked for other changes, specifically ocular and muscular alterations, that correlate with our best judgment of thanatological progress. I have sat at the bedside of numerous premortem patients, gazing into their eyes and studying minute movements of their faces. Though this research is in the formative stage, I am encouraged by what appears to be a dual manifestation of cardiac and neurological shutoff typified by simultaneous twitchlike movement of the eyes combined with a measurable slackening of the lips. In some patients, I have also discerned an audible noise that appears to manifest sublaryngitically—perhaps the "death rattle" commonly cited in popular fiction. However, this does not occur in all patients and is best dispensed with in favor of the aforementioned ocular-muscular phenomenon I label the "lights-out" syndrome. I suggest that this event be studied in great detail for its potential in serving as a simple yet precise indicator of cellular surrender.

Interns back then worked hundred-hour weeks. This intern had found the time to indulge his extracurricular interest.

Sitting and staring into the eyes of the dying, trying to capture the precise moment.

My hunch about his intentions confirmed. Early in the game, Mate's obsession had been with the minutiae of death, not the quality of life.

No comments from the Swedish journal editor. I wondered how Mate's side activities had been received at Oxford Hill Hospital.

Leaving the reading room, I found a pay phone in

the hallway, got Oakland Information and asked for the number. No listing.

Returning to the computers, I looked up the call number of the Joint Commission on Accreditation of Healthcare Organizations rosters, found the bound volumes in the stacks, and beginning with the year of Mate's internship, looked up Oxford Hill. In business and accredited fully. Same for the following five years, then nothing.

The place had been legitimate, but it had closed down. Good luck finding someone who remembered the middle-aged intern with the ghoulish hobby.

What use was there excavating Mate's past, anyway? He'd become the victim, and it was the butcher I needed to understand, not the slab of meat in the back of the rented van.

I left the library and drove to the West L.A. station.

When I pulled up, Milo was standing in front with two men in their late twenties. Both wore gray sport coats and dark slacks and held notepads against their thighs. Both were tall as Milo, each was forty pounds lighter. Neither looked happy.

The man to the left had a puffy face, squashed features and wheat-colored blow-dried hair. The other D-I was dark, balding, bespectacled.

Milo said something to them and they returned inside.

"Your little elves?" I said, when he came over.

"Korn and Demetri. They don't like working for me, and my opinion of them ain't too grand. I put them back on the phones, recontacting families. They whined about

scut work—oh this younger generation. Ready for
Zoghbie? Let's take my Ferrari, in case we need a police
presence."

He crossed the street to the police lot and I followed
in the Seville, waiting till he backed out, then sliding into
his parking space. Signs all over said POLICE PERSONNEL
ONLY, ALL OTHERS WILL BE TOWED.

I got in the unmarked and handed him the material
I'd printed from the Internet. He put it on the backseat,
wedged between two of the file boxes that filled the
space. The car smelled of old breakfast. The police radio
was stuttering and Milo snapped it off.

"What if?" I said, pointing to the warning signs.

"I'll go your bail." Stretching his neck to one side, he
winced, cleared his throat, pressed down on the gas and
sped to Santa Monica Boulevard, then over to the 405
North, toward the Valley. I knew what I had to do and my
body responded by tightening up. When we passed the
mammoth white boxes that the Getty Museum comprised, I told him about Joanne Doss.

He didn't say anything for a while. Opened his
window, spit, rolled it up.

Another minute passed. "You were waiting for the
right moment to inform me?"

"As a matter of fact, I was. Till a few hours ago, I
couldn't tell you anything, because even the fact that I'd
seen them was confidential. Then Mr. Doss called and
asked me to see his daughter and I figured I'd have to
bow off Mate. But he wants me to continue."

"First things first, huh?" His jaw worked.

I kept quiet.

"And if he'd said *not* to mention it?"

"I'd have bowed off, told you I couldn't explain why."

Half mile of silence. He stretched his neck again. "Doss . . . yeah, local family—the Palisades. Toward the end of the list—the missus was in her early forties."

"Traveler number forty-eight," I said.

"You knew her?"

"No, she was already dead when I saw Stacy—the daughter."

"Mr. Doss is one of those who has not returned our repeated calls."

"He travels a lot."

"That so . . . Anything about him I should worry about?"

"Such as?"

He shrugged. "You tell me. He said you could blab, right?"

He kept his eyes on the freeway, but I felt surveilled.

"Sorry if this is rubbing you the wrong way," I said. "Maybe I should've begged off the case right from the beginning."

Pause. Long pause, as if he was considering that. Finally, he said, "Nah, I'm just being a hard-ass. We've all got our rule books . . . So what was the matter with Mrs. Doss that led her to consult Dr. Mate?"

"She was one of the undiagnosed ones I mentioned. Had been deteriorating for a while. Fatigue, chronic pain, she withdrew socially, took to bed. Gained a hundred pounds."

He whistled, touched his own gut. "And no clue as to why all this happened?"

"She saw a lot of doctors, but no formal diagnosis," I said.

"Maybe a head case?"

"Like I said, I never knew her, Milo."

He smiled. "Meaning you're also thinking she might've been a head case . . . and Mate killed her anyway—'scuse me, assisted her *passage*. That could irritate a family member, if they didn't think she was really sick."

He waited.

I said nothing.

"How long after she died did you see the daughter?"

"Three months."

"Why're you seeing her again? Something to do with Mate's murder?"

"That I can't get into," I said. "Let's just say it's nothing you have to worry about."

"Something that just happens to come up now, after Mate's killed?"

"College," I said. "Now's when kids get serious about applying to college."

He didn't answer. The freeway was uncommonly clear and we sped toward the 101 interchange. Milo pumped the unmarked up the eastbound ramp and we merged into slightly heavier traffic. Orange signs on the turnoff announced impending construction for one and a half years. Everyone was going fifteen miles over the limit, as if getting in some last speed licks.

He said, "So you're telling me Mr. Doss is like all the others—big fan of Mate?"

"I'll leave it to him to express his opinion on that."

He smiled again. Not a nice smile at all. "The guy didn't like Mate."

"I didn't say that."

"No, you didn't." He eased up on the gas pedal. We cruised past the Van Nuys exits, Sherman Oaks, North Hollywood. The freeway turned into the 134.

I said, "I found a feminist journal that claimed Mate hated women. Because eighty percent of his travelers were female and he'd never been seen with a woman. Know anything about his personal life?"

Graceless change of subject. He knew what I was doing but let it ride. "Not so far. He lived alone and his landlady said she'd never seen him go out with anyone. I haven't checked marriage licenses yet, but no one's turned up claiming insurance benefits."

"Wonder if a guy like that would carry life insurance," I said.

"Why not?"

"I don't think he valued life."

"Well, maybe you're right, 'cause I didn't find any policies at his apartment. Then again, all his papers might be with that goddamn attorney, Haiselden, who is still incommunicado. Maybe Ms. Zoghbie can direct us to him."

"Find out anything else about her?"

"No criminal record, not even parking tickets. Guess she just gets off on people dying. There seems to be a lot of that going around, doesn't there? Or maybe it's just my unique perspective."

Any attraction Alice Zoghbie had to the culture of death wasn't reflected by her landscaping.

She lived in a vanilla stucco English country house centered on a modest lot in the northern hills of Glendale. Cute house. The spotless shake roof over the entry turret was topped by a copper rooster weather vane. White pullback drapes framed immaculate mullion windows. A flagstone path twisted its way toward an iron canopy over a carved oak door. Banks of flowers rimmed the house, arranged by descending height: the crinkled foliage and purple bloom of statice, then billowing clouds of multicolored impatiens fringed by a low border of some sort of creeping white blossom.

A white Audi sat in the cobblestoned driveway, shaded by a young, carefully shaped podocarpus tree, still staked. On the other side of the flagstone stood an equally tonsured, much larger sycamore. Where the sun hit, the sloping lawn was so green it appeared spray-painted. The big tree had started to release its leaves, and the sprinkle of rusty-brown on grass and stone was the sole suggestion that not everything could be controlled.

Milo and I parked on the street and climbed the pathway. The door knocker was a large brass goat's head, and he lifted the front part of the animal's face, causing it to leer, allowed the jaw piece to fall, setting off oak vibrations. The door opened before the sound died.

"Detectives?" said the woman in the doorway. Thrust of hand, firm dry handshake for both of us. "Please! Come on in!"

Alice Zoghbie was indeed fiftyish—early fifties was my guess. But despite sun-worn skin and a cap of white-hot hair, she seemed more youthful than middle-aged.

Tall, slim, full-busted, strong square shoulders, long limbs, rosy overlay on the outdoorsy dermis, wide sapphire eyes. As she led us through the round entry hall created by the turret into a small, elegant living room, her stride took on a dancer's bounce—speedy, well-lubricated, arms swinging, hips swaying.

The room was set up as carefully as the flower beds. Yellow walls, white moldings, a red damask sofa, various floral-print chairs. Little tables placed strategically by someone with an eye. California oil paintings hung on the walls, all in period gilt frames. Nothing that looked expensive, but each picture was right for its place.

Alice Zoghbie stood in front of a blue brocade chair and cocked a hip, indicating the red couch for us. After we sat, she folded herself on the chair, tucked one leg under the other and smoothed back a feather of white bangs. Down cushions on the sofa made us sink low. Milo's weight plunged him below me and I noticed him shifting uncomfortably.

Alice Zoghbie laced her fingers in her lap. Her face was round, taut around the mandible, seamed at the eyes. She wore a bulky baby-blue cashmere turtleneck, pressed blue jeans, white socks, white suede loafers. Big silver pearls covered her earlobes, and a gold chain interspersed with multicolored cabochons followed the swell of her chest. Bare fingers. Between us was a tile-inlaid coffee table set with a Japanese Imari bowl full of hard candy. Gold and green nuggets; butterscotch and mint.

"Please," she said, pointing to the candy. Managing to sound lighthearted while wearing a grave expression.

"No, thanks," Milo said. "Appreciate your seeing us, ma'am."

"This is all so hideous. Do you have any idea who sacrificed Eldon?"

"Sacrificed?"

"That's what it was," she said. "Some fanatic asshole

making a point." One hand clenched. She stared down at her fist, opened the fingers.

"Eldon and I talked about the risk—some lunatic deciding to make headlines. He said it wouldn't happen and I believed him, but it did, didn't it?"

"So Dr. Mate wasn't afraid."

"Eldon didn't function from fear. He was his own man. Knew the only way to dictate your own passage was to dictate the terms. And Eldon was committed—vital. He intended to be around for a long, long time."

Milo moved his bulk again, as if trying to remain afloat in a sea of red silk. The movement served only to plunge him lower and he edged forward on the couch. "But you and he did discuss danger."

"I brought it up. In general terms, so no, there's no specific asshole I can direct you toward. Maybe it was one of those pathetic cripples who used to carp at him."

"Still Alive," I said.

"Them, their ilk."

Milo said, "You spoke in general terms, but did something happen to make you worry, ma'am?"

"No, I simply wanted Eldon to be more careful. He didn't want to hear it. He just didn't believe anyone would hurt him."

"What kind of precautions did you want him to take?"

"Simple security. Have you seen his apartment?"

"Yes, ma'am."

"Then you know. It's a joke, anyone could just walk in. It wasn't that Eldon was reckless. He simply wasn't attuned to his surroundings. Most brilliant people aren't. Look at Einstein. Some foundation sent him a ten-thousand-dollar check and he never cashed it."

"Dr. Mate was brilliant," said Milo.

Alice Zoghbie stared at him. "Dr. Mate was one of the great minds of our generation."

That didn't jibe with med school in Mexico, internship at an obscure hospital, the bureaucratic jobs. Alice Zoghbie might have known what I was thinking, because now she turned to me and said, "Einstein worked as a clerk until the world discovered him. The world wasn't smart enough to understand him. Eldon had a mind that just never stopped working. Thinking all the time. Science, history, you name it. And unlike most people, he wasn't blinded by personal circumstance."

"Because he lived alone?" I said.

"No, no, that's not what I *mean*. He didn't get distracted by irrelevancies. I'll bet you assume his own parents died in pain and that's why he decided to dedicate his life to relieving pain." Her hand drew an invisible X. "*Wrong*. Both his mother and his father lived to ripe old ages and passed on peacefully."

"Maybe *that* impressed him," said Milo. "Seeing the way it should be."

Alice Zoghbie uncrossed a long leg. "What I'm trying to get across to you people is that Eldon had a worldview perspective."

"Seeing the big picture."

Zoghbie shot him a disgusted look. "Talking about him is making me very *sad*."

Stating it calmly, almost boastfully. Milo remained expressionless and I did the same.

She gazed back at both of us, as if waiting for further response. Suddenly, the lower lids of the sapphire eyes pooled and twin rivulets flowed down her cheeks.

Tears flowing perfectly parallel to her slender nose. She sat there, immobile, allowing the tracks to reach the corners of her mouth before reaching up and dabbing with spidery fingers. Pink glossy nail polish. From somewhere in the house, a clock chimed.

She said, "I sure as hell hope you find the vicious fuck who did this. They just can't get away with this. That would be the worst thing."

"They?"

"They, he, whoever."

"What would be the worst thing, ma'am?"

"No consequences. Everything should have consequences."

"Well," said Milo, "my job is catching vicious fucks."

Zoghbie's expression went flat.

"Ma'am, is there anything you can tell us that might help the process along?"

"Enough with the ma'am, *okay*?" she said. "It's coming across patronizing. Is there anything I can tell you? Sure, look for a fanatic—probably a religious extremist. My bet would be a Catholic, they seem to be the worst. Though I was married to a Muslim, and they're no great shakes." Her head bobbed forward as she studied Milo's face. "What's your background?"

"Actually, I was raised Catholic, ma'am."

"So was I," said Zoghbie. "Down on my knees confessing my sins. What rubbish. The pity for both of us. Candles and guilt and bullshit spewed by impotent old men in funny hats—yes, I'd definitely look for a Catholic. Or a born-again Christian. Anyone fundamentalist for that matter. Orthodox Jews are just as bad, but they don't seem as predisposed to violence as the Catholics, probably because there's not enough of them to get cocky. Fanatics are all cut out of the same mold: God's on my side, I can do whatever the fuck I please. As if the Pope or Imam Whatever is going to be around when your loved one is writhing in agony and choking on their own vomit. The whole right-to-life thing is obscene. Life's sacred but it's okay to set off bombs at abortion clinics, pick off doctors. Eldon was made an example of. Look for a religious fanatic."

She smiled. It didn't fit the diatribe. Her eyes were dry again.

"Talk about sin," she said. "Hypocrisy's the worst sin. Why the hell can't we get past the bullshit they feed us in childhood and learn to think independently?"

"Conditioning," I said.

"That's for lower animals. We're supposed to be better."

Milo pulled out his pad. "Do you know of any actual threats against Dr. Mate?"

The specificity of the question—the police routine—seemed to bore her. "If there were, Eldon never told me."

"What about his attorney, Roy Haiselden. Do you know him, as well?"

"Roy and I have met."

"Any idea where he is, ma'am? Can't seem to locate him."

"Roy's all over the place," she said. "He owns laundromats up and down the state."

"Laundromats?"

"Coin-ops in strip malls. That's how he makes his money. What he does for Eldon doesn't pay the bills. It basically killed the rest of his law practice."

"Have you known him and Dr. Mate for a long time?"

"I've known Eldon for five years, Roy a little less."

"Any reason Mr. Haiselden wouldn't return our calls?"

"You'd have to ask him that."

Milo smiled. "Five years. How'd you get to know Dr. Mate?"

"I'd been following his career for a while." Her turn to smile. "Hearing about him was like a giant lightbulb going on: someone was finally shaking things up, doing what needed to be done. I wrote him a letter. I guess you could call it a fan letter, though that sounds so adolescent. I told him how much I admired his courage. I'd been working with a humanist group, had retired from my job—got retired, actually. I decided to find some meaning in all of it."

"You were fired because of your views?" I said.

Her shoulders shifted toward me. "Big surprise?" she snapped. "I was working in a hospital and had the nerve to talk about things that needed talking about. That chafed the hides of the assholes in charge."

"Which hospital?"

"Pasadena Mercy."

Catholic hospital.

She said, "Leaving that dump was the best thing that ever happened to me. I founded the Socrates Club, kept with the SHI—my first group. We were having a convention in San Francisco and Eldon had just won another victory in court, so I thought, Who better to deliver the keynote? He answered my invitation with a charming note, accepting." Blink. "After that, Eldon and I began to see each other—socially but not sexually, since you're obviously going to ask. Life of the mind; I'd have him over for dinner, we'd discuss things, I'd cook for him. Probably the only decent meals he had."

"Dr. Mate didn't care about food?" said Milo.

"Like most geniuses, Eldon tended to ignore his personal needs. I'm a great cook, felt it was the least I could do for a mentor."

"A mentor," said Milo. "He was training you?"

"A philosophical guide!" She jabbed a finger at us. "Stop wasting your time with me and catch this fuck-head."

Milo sat back, sank in, surrendered to gravity. "So the two of you became friends. You seem to be the only female friend he had—"

"He wasn't *gay,* if that's what you're getting at. Just *choosy.* He was married and divorced a long time ago. Not an edifying experience."

"Why not?"

"Eldon didn't say. I could see he didn't want to talk about it and I respected his wishes. Now, is there anything else?"

"Let's talk about the weekend Dr. Mate was murdered. You—"

"Rented the van? Yes, I did. I'd done it before because when Eldon showed up at the rental company, sometimes there were troubles."

"They didn't want to rent to him."

Zoghbie nodded.

"So," said Milo, "the night he was murdered, Dr. Mate was planning to help another traveler."

"I assume."

"He didn't tell you who?"

"Of course not. Eldon never discussed his clinical activities. He called and said, 'Alice, I'll be needing a van tomorrow.'"

"Why didn't he discuss his work?" said Milo.

"Ethics, Detective," Zoghbie said with exaggerated patience. "Patient confidentiality. He was a doctor."

The phone rang, distant as the clock chime.

"Better get that," she said, standing. "Could be the press."

"They've been in touch?"

"No, but they might be, once they find out I'm back."

"How would they know that, ma'am?"

"Please," she said. "Don't be naïve. They have their ways." She dance-walked through the dining room and out of sight.

Milo rubbed his face and turned to me. "Think Mate was boffing her?"

"She did take the time to mention that their relationship was social but not sexual. Because we were obviously going to ask. So maybe."

Alice Zoghbie returned, looking grim.

"The press?" said Milo.

"A nuisance call—my accountant. The IRS wants to audit me—big surprise, huh? I've got to go gather my tax records, so if there's nothing else . . ." She pointed to the door.

We stood.

"You climb mountains for fun?" said Milo.

"I hike, Detective. Long-distance walks on the lower slopes, no pitons or any of that stuff." She gave Milo's gut a long appraisal. "Stop moving and you might as well die."

That reminded me of something Richard Doss had told me six months ago:

I'll rest when I'm dead.

Milo said, "Did Dr. Mate stay active?"

"Mentally, only. Never could get him to exercise. But what does that have to do with—"

"So you have no idea who Dr. Mate was going to help the weekend he died?"

"No. I told you, we never discussed patient issues."

"The reason I'm asking is—"

"You think a traveler killed him? That's absurd."

"Why, ma'am?"

"These are sick people we're talking about, Detective. Weak people, quadriplegics, Lou Gehrig's disease, terminal cancer. How could they have the strength? And why would they? Now, please."

Her foot tapped. She looked jumpy. I supposed an audit could do that to you.

"Just a few more details," said Milo. "Why'd you choose the Avis in Tarzana? Far from here and from Dr. Mate's place."

"That was the *point,* Detective."

"What was?"

"Covering our tracks. Just in case someone got suspicious and refused to rent to us. That's also why I chose Avis. We alternated. Last time was Hertz; before that, Budget."

She hurried to the door, opened it, stood tapping her foot. "Forget about it being a traveler. None of Eldon's people would hurt him. Most of the time they required help just to get over to the travel site—"

"Help from who?"

Long silence. She smiled, folded her arms. "No. We're not going there."

"Other people have been involved?" said Milo. "Dr. Mate had assistants?"

"Unh-unh, no way. Couldn't tell you even if I wanted to, because I don't know. Didn't want to know."

"Because Dr. Mate never discussed clinical details with you."

"Now please leave."

"Let's say Dr. Mate did have confederates—"

"Say whatever you please."

"What makes you so sure one of them couldn't have turned on him?"

"Because why *would* they?" She laughed. Harshly. Too loudly. "I can't get you to see: Eldon was brilliant. He wouldn't have trusted just anyone." She put a foot out onto her front porch, jabbed a manicured fingernail. "Look. For. A. Fanatic."

"What about a fanatic passing himself off as a confederate?"

"Oh please." Another loud laugh. Zoghbie's hands flew upward, fingers fluttering. She dropped them quickly. A series of clumsy movements, at odds with the dancer's grace. "I can't answer any more stupid questions! This is a very hard *time* for me!"

The tears returned. No more symmetrical trickle. A gush.

This time she wiped them hastily.

She slammed the door behind us.

8

Back in the unmarked, Milo looked up at the vanilla cottage. "What a harpy."

"Her attitude changed after that phone call," I said. "Maybe it was the IRS. Or she was let down that it wasn't the press. But maybe it was someone who'd worked with Mate, telling her to be discreet."

"Dr. Death had his own little elves, huh?"

"She did everything but confirm their existence. Which leads me to an interesting question: this morning we talked about the killer luring Mate to Mulholland by posing as a traveler. What if he was someone Mate already knew and trusted?"

"Elf goes bad?"

"Elf gets next to Mate because he likes killing people. Then he decides he's finished his apprenticeship. Time to co-opt. It would fit with playing doctor, taking Mate's black bag."

"So I shouldn't start rounding up Catholics and Orthodox Jews, huh? Old Alice would have been an asset to the Third Reich. Too bad her alibi checks out—flights confirmed by the airlines." He punched the dashboard lightly. "A confederate gone bad . . . I've gotta get hold of Haiselden, see what kind of paper he's been stashing."

"What about storage lockers in Mate's name?" I said.

"Nothing, so far. No POBs either. It's like he was covering his tracks all the time—the same kind of crap you get with a vic who's a criminal."

"All part of the intrigue. Plus, he did have enemies."

"Then why *wasn't* he more careful? She's right about the way he lived. No security at all."

"Monumental ego," I said. "Play God long enough, you can start to believe your own publicity. Mate was out for notoriety right from the beginning. Fooled around on the edge of medical ethics long before he built the machine." I told him about the letter to the pathology journal, Mate's death-side vigils, staring into the faces of dying people.

He said, "Cellular cessation, huh? Goddamn ghoul. Can you imagine being one of those poor patients? Here you are, stuck in the ICU, fading in and out of consciousness, you wake up, see some schmuck in a white coat just sitting there, *staring* at you. Not doing a damn thing to help, just trying to figure out exactly when you're gonna croak? And how could he look in their eyes if they were that sick?"

"Maybe he lifted the lids and peeked," I said.

"Or used toothpicks to prop them up." He slapped the dash again. "Some childhood *he* must've had." Another glance at the vanilla house. "An ex-wife. First

I've heard of it. Don't want her popping up in the press and making me look like the fool I feel." Smile. "And some of my best sources have been exes. They *love* to talk."

He got on the cell phone: "Steve, it's me . . . No, nothing earthshaking. Listen, call County Records and see if you can find any marriage certificate or divorce papers on old Eldon. If not, try other counties . . . Orange, Ventura, Berdoo, try 'em all."

"Before med school, he worked in San Diego," I said.

"Try San Diego first, Steve. Just found out he was based there before he became a doc . . . Why? Because it might be important . . . What? Hold on." He turned to me: "Where'd Mate go to med school?"

"Guadalajara."

That made him frown. "Mexico, Steve. Forget trying to pry anything out of there."

I said, "He interned in Oakland. Oxford Hills Hospital, seventeen years ago. It's out of business, but there might be some kind of record."

"That's Dr. Delaware," said Milo. "He's been doing some independent research . . . Yeah, he does that . . . What? I'll ask him. If none of what I told you pans out, try our buds at Social Security. No one's filed for insurance benefits, but maybe there're some kind of federal payments going out to dependents . . . I know it's an hour of voice mail and brain death, Steve, but that's the job. If you get nothing with SS, go back to the counties, Kern, Riverside, whatever, just keep working your way through the state . . . Yeah, yeah, yeah . . . Any callback from Haiselden? Okay, stay on him, too . . . Leave *fifty* goddamn messages at his house and his office if you have to. Zoghbie said he runs laundromats . . . yeah, as in clean clothes. Check that out. If that doesn't lead anywhere, bug his neighbors, be a pest— What's that? Which one?" Tiny smile. "Interesting . . . yeah, I know the name. I definitely know the name."

He hung up. "Poor baby is getting bored . . . he wanted me to ask you if working with me will turn him psychotic."

"There's always that chance. What made you smile?"

"Your man, Doss, finally called back. Korn and Demetri are gonna talk to him tomorrow."

"Progress," I said.

"Mrs. Doss," he said. "Was she able to move around on her own?"

"As far as I know. She may have driven herself to meet Mate."

"May have?"

"No one knows."

"She just walked out on hubbie?"

I shrugged. But she had. Middle of the night, no note, no warning.

No good-bye.

The deepest wound she'd inflicted on Stacy . . .

"Not very considerate," he said.

"Pain will do that to you."

"Time to call in Dr. Mate . . . Take two aspirins, hook yourself up to the machine and *don't* call me in the morning."

He started up the car, then swiveled toward me again, wedging his bulk against the steering wheel. "Seeing as we'll be face-to-face with Mr. Doss soon, are there any blanks you want to fill in?"

"He didn't like Mate," I said. "Wanted me to tell you."

"Bragging?"

"More like nothing to hide."

"What was his beef with Mate?"

"Don't know."

"Maybe the fact that Mate killed his wife and he never knew it was going to happen?"

"Could be."

He leaned across the seat, moved his big face inches from mine. I smelled aftershave and tobacco. The wheel dug into his sport coat, bunching the tweed around his neck, highlighting love handles. "What's going on here, Alex? The guy said you could talk. Why're you parceling info out to me?"

"I guess I'm still not comfortable talking about patients. Because sometimes patients feel really communicative, then they change their minds. And what's the big deal, Milo? Doss's feelings about Mate aren't relevant. He has an alibi as tight as Zoghbie's. Out of town, just like Zoghbie. The day Mate was killed he was in San Francisco looking at a hotel."

"To buy?"

I nodded. "He was in the company of a group of Japanese businessmen. Has the receipts to prove it."

"He told you all that?"

"Yes."

"Well, ain't that fascinating." He knuckled his right eye with his left hand. "In my experience, it's mostly criminals who come prepared with an alibi."

"He wasn't prepared," I said. "It came up in the course of the conversation."

"What, like 'How's it going, Richard?' 'Peachy, Doc—and by the way I have an alibi'?"

I didn't answer.

He said, "Buying a hotel. Guy like that, rich honcho, gotta be used to delegating. Why would he do his own dirty work? So what the hell's an *alibi* worth?"

"The job done on Mate, all that anger. All that personal viciousness. Did it smell like hired help to you?"

"Depends upon what the help was hired to do. And who got hired." He reached out, placed a heavy hand on my shoulder. I felt like a suspect and I didn't like it. "Do you see Doss as capable of setting it up?"

"I've never seen any signs of that," I said in a tight voice.

He released his hand. "That sounds like a maybe."

"This is exactly why I didn't want to get into it. There's absolutely nothing I know about Richard Doss that tells me he's capable of contracting that level of brutality. Okay?"

"That," he said, "sounds like expert-witness talk."

"Then count yourself lucky. 'Cause when I go to court I get paid well."

We stared at each other. He shifted away, looked past me, up at Zoghbie's house. Two California jays danced among the branches of the sycamore.

"This is something," he said.

"What is?"

"You and me, all the cases we've been through, and now we're having a wee bit of *tension*."

Veneering the last few words in an Irish brogue. I wanted to laugh, tried to, more to fill time and space than out of any glee. The movement started at my diaphragm but died, a soundless ripple, as my mouth refused to obey.

"Hey," I said, "can this friendship be saved?"

"Okay, then," he said, as if he hadn't heard. "Here's a direct question for you: is there anything else you know that I should know? About Doss or anything else?"

"Here's a direct answer: no."

"You want to drop the case?"

"Want me to?"

"Not unless you want to."

"I don't want to, but—"

"Why would you want to stay on it?" he said.

"Curious."

"About what?"

"Whodunit, whydunit. And riding around with the police makes me feel oh-so-safe. You want me off, though, just say so."

"Oh Christ," he said. "Nyah-nyah-nyah-nyah-*nyah*-nyah."

Now we both laughed. He was sweating again and my head hurt.

"So," he said. "Onward? You do your job, I do mine—"

"And I'll get to Scotland afore ye."

"It ain't Scotland I care about," he said. "It's Mulholland Drive—gonna be interesting hearing what Mr. Doss has to say. Maybe I'll interview him myself. When are you seeing the daughter—what's her name?"

"Stacy. Tomorrow."

He wrote it down. "How many other kids in the family?"

"A brother two years older. Eric. He's up at Stanford."

"Tomorrow," he said. "College stuff." ·

"You got it."

"I may be talking to her, too, Alex."

"She didn't carve up Mate."

"Long as you've got a good rapport with her, why don't you ask her if her daddy had it done."

"Oh sure."

He shifted into drive.

I said, "I wouldn't mind getting a look at Mate's apartment."

"Why?"

"To see how the genius lived. Where is it?"

"Hollywood, where else? Ain't no bidness like *shooow* bidness. C'mon, I'll *shooow* you—fasten your seat belt."

9

Mate's building was on North Vista, between Sunset and Hollywood, the upper level of a seventy-year-old duplex. The landlady lived below, a tiny ancient named Mrs. Ednalynn Krohnfeld, who walked stiffly and wore twin hearing aids. A sixty-inch Mitsubishi TV ruled her front room, and after she let us in she returned to her chair, folded a crocheted brown throw over her knees and fastened her attention upon a talk show. The skin tones on the screen were off, flesh dyed the carotene orange of a nuclear sunburn. Trash talk show, a pair of poorly kept women cursing at each other, setting off a storm of bleeps. The host, a feloniously coiffed blonde with lizard eyes behind oversize eyeglasses, pretended to represent the voice of reason.

Milo said, "We're here to take another look at Dr. Mate's apartment, Mrs. Krohnfeld."

No answer. The image of a hollow-eyed man flashed

in the right-hand corner of the screen. Gap-toothed fellow leering smugly. A written legend said, *Duane. Denesha's husband but Jeanine's lover.*

"Mrs. Krohnfeld?"

The old woman quarter-turned but kept watching.

"Have you thought of anything since last week that you want to tell me, Mrs. Krohnfeld?"

The landlady squinted. The room was curtained to gloom and barricaded with old but cheap mahogany pieces.

Milo repeated the question.

"Tell you about what?" she said.

"Anything about Dr. Mate?"

Head shake. "He's dead."

"Has anyone been by recently, Mrs. Krohnfeld?"

"What?"

Another repeat.

"By for what?"

"Asking about Dr. Mate? Snooping around the apartment?"

No reply. She continued to squint. Her hands tightened and gathered the comforter.

Duane swaggering onstage. Taking a seat between the harridans. Giving a so-what shrug and spreading his legs wide, wide, wide.

Mrs. Krohnfeld muttered something.

Milo kneeled down next to her recliner. "What's that, ma'am?"

"Just a bum." Fixed on the screen.

"That guy up there?" said Milo.

"No, no, no. Here. Out there. Climbing up the stairs." She jabbed an impatient finger at the front window, slapped both hands to her cheeks and plucked. "A bum—lotsa hair—dirty, you know, street trash."

"Climbing the stairs to Dr. Mate's apartment? When?"

"No, no—just tried to get up there, I shooed him away." Glued to the orange melodrama.

"When was this?"

"Few days ago—maybe Thursday."

"What did he want?" said Milo.

"How would I know? You think I let him in?" One of the feuding women had jumped to her feet, pointing and cursing at her rival. Duane was positioned between them, relishing every strutting-rooster moment of it.

Bleep bleep bleep. Mrs. Krohnfeld read lips and her own mouth slackened. "Such talk!"

Milo said, "The bum, what else can you tell me about him?"

No answer. He asked the same question, louder. Mrs. Krohnfeld jerked toward us. "Yeah, a bum. He went . . ." Jabbing over her shoulder. "Tried to go up. I saw him, yelled out the window to get the hell outa there, and he skedaddled."

"On foot?"

Grunt. "That type don't drive no Mercedes. What a louse." This time, directing the epithet at Duane. "Stupid idjits, wasting their time on a louse like *that.*"

"Thursday."

"Yup—or Friday . . . look at that." The women had raced toward each other and collided, alloying into a clawing, hair-pulling cyclone. "Idjits."

Milo sighed and rose. "We're going upstairs now, Mrs. Krohnfeld."

"When can I put the place up for rent?"

"Soon."

"Sooner the better—*idjits.*"

The steps to Mate's unit were on the right side of the duplex, and before I climbed I had a look at the rear yard. Not much more than a strip of concrete, barely space for the double carport. An old Chevy that Milo identified as Mate's was parked next to an even older Chrysler New Yorker. Unused laundry lines sketched crosshatch shadows across the cement. Low block fencing revealed neighbors on all sides, mostly multiple-unit apartment buildings, higher than the duplex. Throw a barbecue down here and lots of people would know the menu.

Mate had chased headlines, desired no privacy in his off-hours.

An exhibitionist, or had Alice Zoghbie been right? Not cued into his surroundings.

Either way, easy victim.

I mentioned that to Milo. He sucked his teeth and took me back to the entrance.

Mate's front door was capped by a small overhang. Ads from fast-food joints littered the floor. Milo picked them up, glanced at a few, dropped them. Yellow tape banded the plain wood door. Milo yanked it loose. One key twist and we were in. A single lock, not a dead bolt. Anyone could've kicked it in.

Mold, must, rot, the nose-tweaking snap of decaying paper. Air so heavy with dust it felt granular.

Milo opened the ancient venetian blinds. Where light penetrated the apartment it highlighted the particulate storms that we set off as we moved through tight, shadowed spaces.

Tight because virtually the entire front of the flat was filled with bookshelves. Plywood cases, separated by narrow aisles. Unfinished wood, warped shelves suffering under the weight of scholarship.

Life of the mind. Eldon Mate had turned his entire domicile into a library.

Even the kitchen counters were piled high with books. Inside the fridge were bottles of water, a moldering slab of hoop cheese, a few softening vegetables.

I walked around reading titles as dust settled on my shoulders. Chemistry, physics, mathematics, biology, toxicology. Two entire cases of pathology, forensics, another wall of law—civil liability, jurisprudence, the criminal codes of what appeared to be every state of the union.

Mostly crumbling paperbacks and cold shabby texts with torn spines and flaking pages, the kind of treasures that can be found at any thrift shop.

No fiction.

I moved to the tiny back room where Mate had slept. Ten feet square, low-ceilinged, lit by a bare bulb screwed to a white porcelain ceiling fixture. Bare gray walls jaundiced by western light seeping through parchment-colored window shades. The cheap cot and nightstand took up most of the space, leaving barely enough room for a raw-looking three-drawer pine dresser. Ten-inch Zenith TV atop the dresser—as if Mate had had to make up for Mrs. Krohnfeld's video excess.

A door led to the adjoining bathroom, and I went in there because bathrooms can sometimes tell you more about a person than any other space. This one didn't.

Razor, shaving cream, laxative, antigas tablets and aspirin in the medicine cabinet. Amber ring around the tub. Bar of green soap bottomed by slime, sitting like a dead frog in a brown plastic dish.

The closet was skinny and crammed full, sharp with the reek of camphor. A dozen wash-and-wear white shirts, half that many pairs of gray twill slacks, all Sears label; one heavy charcoal suit from Zachary All, wide lapels testifying to a long-ago fashion cycle; three pairs of black cap-toe oxfords stretched by cedar shoe trees; two beige windbreakers, also Sears; a pair of narrow black ties hanging from a hook—polyester, made in Korea.

"What was his financial situation?" I said. "Doesn't look like he spent much on clothes."

"He spent on food, gas, car repairs, books, phone and utilities. I haven't gotten his tax forms yet, but there were some bankbooks in there." Indicating the dresser. "His basic income seems to have been his U.S. Public Health Service pension. Two and a half grand a month deposited directly into the savings account, plus occasional cash payments, two hundred to a thou each, irregularly spaced. Those I figure were donations. They add up to another fifteen a year."

"Donations from who?"

"My guess would be satisfied travelers—or those who survived them. None of the families we've talked to admit paying Mate a dime, but they'd want to avoid looking like they hired someone to kill Grandma, wouldn't they? So he was pulling in around fifty grand a year, and in terms of assets he was no pauper. The three other passbooks were for jumbo CDs of a hundred grand each. Dinky interest, doesn't look as if he cared about investing. I figure three hundred would be about a decade of income minus expenses and taxes. Looks like he's just about held on to every penny he's earned since going into the death business."

"Three hundred thousand," I said. "An MD in practice could put away a lot more than that over ten years. So he wasn't in the travel business to get rich. Notoriety was the prize, or he really was operating idealistically. Or both."

"You could say the same for Mengele." Flipping the skimpy mattress, he peered underneath. "Not that I haven't done this already." His back must have twinged, because he sucked in breath as he straightened.

"Okay?" he said.

Suddenly the room felt oppressive. Some of the book aroma had made its way in here, along with a riper smell, more human—male. That and the mothballs added up to the sad, sedate aroma of old man. As if nothing here was expected to ever change. That same sense of staleness and stasis that I'd experienced up on Mulholland. I was probably getting overimaginative.

"Anything interesting on his phone bills?" I said.

"Nope. Despite his publicity-seeking, once he got home, he wasn't Mr. Chatty. There were days at a time when he never phoned anyone. The few calls we did find were to Haiselden, Zoghbie, and boring stuff: local market, Thrifty Drugs, couple of used-book stores, shoemaker, Sears, hardware store."

"No cell phone account?"

He laughed. "The TV's black-and-white. Guy didn't own a computer or a stereo. We're talking manual typewriter—I found blank sheets of *carbon* paper in the dresser."

"No sheets with any impressions for a hot clue? Like in the movies?"

"Yeah, right. And I'm Dirty Harry."

"Old-fashioned guy," I said, "but he pushed the envelope ethically."

I opened the top drawer of the dresser on mounds of folded underwear, white and rounded like giant marshmallows. Stuffed on each side were cylinders of rolled black socks. The middle drawer contained stacks of cardigans, all brown and gray. I ran my hand below them, came up empty. The next drawer was full of medical books.

He said, "Same with the bottom. Guess next to killing people, reading was his favorite thing."

I crouched and opened the lowest drawer. Four hardbacks, the first three with warped bindings and foxed edges. I inspected one. *Principles of Surgery*.

"Copyright 1934," I said.

"Maybe if he'd kept up, that liver would've fared better."

The fourth book caught my eye. Smaller than the others. Ruby-red leather binding. Shiny new . . . gold-tooled decorations on the ribbed spine. Ornate gilt lettering, but a crude, orange-peel texture to the leather—leatherette.

Collector's edition of *Beowulf* published by some outfit called the Literary Gem Society.

I picked it up. It rattled. Too light to be a book. I lifted the cover. No pages within, just hollow, Masonite space. MADE IN TAIWAN label affixed to the underside of the lid.

A box. Novelty-shop gag. Inside, the source of the rattle:

Miniature stethoscope. Child-size. Pink plastic tubing, silvered plastic earpieces and disc. Broken earpieces—snapped off cleanly. Silvery grit in the box.

Milo's eyes slitted. "Why don't you put that down."

I complied. "What's wrong?"

"I checked that damned drawer the first time I tossed the place and that wasn't in there. The other books were, but not that. I remember reading each of the copyrights, thinking Mate was relying on antiques."

He stared into the red box.

"A visitor?" I said. "Our van-boy commemorating what he'd done? Broken stethoscope delivering a message? 'Mate's out of business, *I'm* the doctor now'?"

He bent, wincing again. "Looks like someone clipped the plastic clean. From the dust, maybe he did it right here . . . very clean."

"No problem if you had bone shears. One very nasty little elf."

He rubbed his face. "He came back to celebrate?"

"And to leave his mark."

He walked to the door, looked out at the bookcases in the front room, scowled. "I've been here twice since the murder and nothing else looks messed with . . ."

Talking to himself more than to me. Knowing full well that with thousands of volumes, there was no way to be sure. Knowing the yellow tape across the door was meaningless, anyone could've pried the lock.

I said, "The bum Mrs. Krohnfeld saw—"

"The bum walked up the stairs in plain sight and ran away when Mrs. Krohnfeld screamed at him. She said he was a mess. Wouldn't you expect our boy to be a little better organized?"

"Like you said, some people delegate."

"What, the killer hires a schizo to break in and stick a box in a drawer?"

"Why not?"

"If it was an attempt to piss on Mate's grave, wouldn't delegating lessen the thrill?"

"Probably, but at this point he's being careful," I said. "And delegating could offer its own thrill: being the boss, wielding power. It could've happened this way: the killer knows the neighborhood because he stalked Mate for a while. He cruises Hollywood, finds a street guy, gives him cash to deliver a package. Half up front, the rest upon completion. He could've even positioned himself up the street. To watch and get off and to make sure the street guy followed through. He picked someone disorganized *specifically*, because it added another layer of safety: if the bum gets caught there's very little he can tell you. The killer used some sort of disguise for extra insurance."

His cheeks bubbled as he filled them with air, bounced it around, blew it out silently. Out of his pocket came a sealed package of surgical gloves and an evidence bag.

"Dr. Milo's in the house," he said, working his hands into the latex. "You touched it, but I'll vouch for you." Fully gloved, he lifted the box, examined it on all sides.

"Someone who knows the neighborhood," he said. "Hollywood Boulevard's full of novelty shops, maybe I can find someone who remembers selling this recently."

I said, "Maybe the choice of titles wasn't a coincidence."

"*Beowulf*?"

"Valiant hero slays the monster."

• • •

We spent another hour in the apartment, going over the kitchen and the front rooms, searching cupboards, scanning the bookcases for other false volumes, coming up with nothing. In some of the books, I found bills of sale going back decades. Thrift shops in San Diego, Oakland, a few in L.A.

Outside on the landing, Milo retaped the door, locked up and brushed dust from his lapels. He looked shrunken. Across the street, a middle-aged Hispanic woman stood in the paltry shade of a wretched-looking magnolia, purse in hand, newspaper folded under her arm. No one else around, and like any midday pedestrian in L.A. she stood out. No bus stop; probably waiting for a ride. She saw me looking at her, stared back for a second, shifted the purse to the other shoulder, removed the paper and began to read.

"If the box is a 'gift,'" I said, "it's another point in favor of the confederate angle. Someone wanting to put himself in Mate's place. Literally. Choosing the bedroom's consistent with that: the most personal space in the apartment. Think of it as a rape of sorts. Which is consistent with the violation of Mate's genitalia. Someone into power, domination. Playing God—a psychopathic monotheist, there can only be one deity, so he needs to eliminate any competition. On the competition's home base. I can see him walking around, exhilarated by triumph. Enjoying the extra bit of thrill of sneaking into an official crime scene. Maybe he came at night to minimize the chance of discovery, but still he couldn't be sure. If you or anyone else from the department had shown up, he'd have been trapped. The bedroom's at the back of the apartment and there's no rear exit. No place to hide except that bedroom closet, so to escape he'd have had to cross the front room, hide in that maze of bookshelves. I think he's jazzed by the danger element. It's the same first impression I had of the murder itself. Choosing an open road to perform surgery on Mate. Removing the cardboard so Mate's body would be discovered. Cleaning up carefully but leaving the scene naked. The note. Extreme meticulousness combined with recklessness. A psychopath with an above-average IQ. He's bright enough to plan precisely in the short term, but vulnerable in the long run because he gets off on danger."

"Is that supposed to comfort me?"

"He ain't Superman, Milo."

"Good. 'Cause I ain't got no kryptonite."

He stood there thinking and swinging the bag. The woman across the street looked up. Our eyes met. She returned to her paper.

"If the guy walked around," said Milo, "maybe he touched stuff. After the apartment was printed. Now you and I just mauled it . . . Asking for new prints is gonna be fun."

"I doubt he left any. That careful, he is."

"I'll ask anyway." He began trudging down the stairs. Stopped midway. "If this is a message, who's it aimed at? Not the public. Unlike the body and the note, there was no way he could be sure it would be found."

"At this point," I said, "he's talking to himself. Doing anything he can to enhance the kick, evoke memories of the kill. He may very well want to return to the scene of the murder but views that as too dangerous, so breaking into Mate's home, directly or by surrogate, would be the next-best thing."

I thought of something Richard Doss had told me . . . *dancing on Mate's grave.*

"Broken stethoscope," I said. "If I'm right about his taking the black bag, the message is clear: '*I* get the real tools, *you* get broken garbage.'"

We resumed our descent. At the bottom of the stairs, Milo said, "The idea of a confederate gets me thinking. About Attorney Haiselden, who should be in town but isn't. Because who spent more time with Mate? Who'd be more familiar with the apartment, maybe even have a key? The guy's behavior is *wrong*, Alex. Here we are, Mate's cold for a week, Haiselden should be throwing *press* conferences. But not a peep out of him. Just the opposite—he rabbits. Collecting coins from laundro-mats? Gimme a break, this asshole's *hiding* from some-thing. Zoghbie said representing Mate was the only thing Haiselden did as a lawyer. That says overinvolvement. Mate was *Haiselden's* ticket to celebrity. Maybe Haiselden got hooked on it, wanted more, no more second fiddle. He watches Mate I.V. enough travelers, figures it qualifies him as a death doc. Hell, maybe Haiselden's one of those guys who went to law school because he couldn't get into *med* school."

"Interesting," I said. "Something else I pulled off the computer fits that. Newspaper account of a press confer-ence Haiselden *did* call after one of the trials. He said Mate deserved the Nobel Prize, then he added that as Mate's lawyer, *he* deserved part of the money."

His free hand balled. "I've been delegating finding him to Korn and Demetri, but now I'm handling it person-ally. Going over to his house, right now. South Westwood. I can drop you at the station or you can come along."

I looked at my watch. Nearly five. It had been a long day. "I'll call Robin and come along."

We crossed the street to the unmarked. Milo locked the evidence bag in the trunk, circled to the driver's side, stopped. Glancing to his left.

The Hispanic woman hadn't moved. Milo turned. Her head flipped away, quick as a shuffled card, and I knew she'd been watching us.

Eyes back on the newspaper. Concentrating. The paper waved. No breeze, her hands had tightened. Her bag was a macramé sack that she'd placed on the grass.

Milo studied her. She ignored him. Licked her lips. Buried her nose deeper in newsprint.

He began to turn away from her, and her eyes flicked—just for a second—toward Mate's apartment.

He said, "Hold on."

I followed him as he strode toward her. Her hands were clenching the paper, causing it to shimmy. She folded her lips inward and drew the newsprint closer to her face. I got near enough to read the date. Yesterday's paper. The classifieds. Employment opportunities . . .

Milo said, "Ma'am?"

The woman looked up. Her lips unfolded. Thin purplish lips, chapped and puckered, bleached white around the edges. The rest of her complexion was nutmeg brown. Bags under the eyes.

She was somewhere between fifty and sixty, short and heavy with a plump face and big, gorgeous black eyes. She wore a navy polyester bomber jacket over a blue-and-white flowered dress that reached to midcalf. The dress material looked flimsy, riding up her stocky frame, adhering to bulges. Thick ankles swelled over the top seams of old but clean Nike running shoes. White socks rolled low exposed chafed shins. Her nails were square-cut. Her black hair was threaded with gray and braided past her waist. Her skin was slack around neck, jaw and chipmunk cheeks, but stretched tight over a wide brow. No makeup, no jewelry. A rural look.

While working at Western Peds, I'd known several Latin women who'd chosen that same unadorned appearance. Long hair, always a braid, dresses, never pants. Devout women, Pentecostal Christians.

"Something I can do for you, ma'am?"

"Are you . . . you're police, right?" The old mouth emitted a young voice, breathy and tentative. No accent; the merest softening at the end of each syllable. She could've found employment giving phone sex.

"Yes, ma'am." Milo flashed the badge. "And you are . . . ?"

She reached into the macramé bag and brought out a red plastic alligator-print wallet. Producing her own I.D., as if it had been demanded of her many times.

Social Security card. She thrust it at Milo.

He read, "Guillerma Salcido."

"Guillerma Salcido *Mate*," said the woman defiantly. "I don't use his name anymore, but that doesn't change a thing. I'm still Dr. Mate's wife—his widow."

uillerma Mate stood straighter, as if fortified by the claim. Took the Social Security card from Milo's fingers and slipped it back into her purse.

"You're married to Dr. Mate?" He sounded doubtful.

Another dip into the bag, another thrust of paper.

Marriage license, fold marks grubby, photocopied lettering faded to the color of raw plywood. Date of issue, twenty-seven years ago, City of San Diego, County of San Diego. Guillerma Salcido de Vega and Eldon Howard Mate wagering on nuptial bliss.

"There," she said.

"Yes, ma'am. Do you live here in L.A.?"

"Oakland. When I heard—it's been a long time, I didn't know if I should come. I'm busy, got a job taking care of the elderly at a convalescent home. But I figured I should come. Eldon was sending me money, this pension he had. Now that he's gone, I should know what's going on. I took the Greyhound. When I got here I couldn't believe it. What a mess this place is, all the streets dug up. I got lost on the city bus. I've never been here."

"To L.A.?"

"I been to L.A. Never been *here*." Jabbing a stubby finger at the duplex. "Maybe the whole thing was a sign."

"A sign?"

"What happened to Eldon. I don't mean I'm some prophet. But when things happen that aren't natural, sometimes it means you have to take a big step. I thought I should find out. Like who's burying him? He had no faith, but everyone should be buried—he didn't want to be cremated, did he?"

"Not that I know."

"Okay. Then maybe I should do it. My church would help."

"How long exactly has it been since you saw Dr. Mate?"

She touched her finger to her upper lip. "Twenty-five years and . . . four months. Since right after my son was born—his son. Eldon Junior, he goes by Donny. Eldon didn't like Donny—didn't like kids. He was honest about that, told me right at the beginning, but I figured he was just talking, once he had his own he'd change his mind. So I got pregnant anyway. And what do you think? Eldon left me."

"But he supported you financially."

"Not really," she said. "You can't call five hundred a month support—I always worked. But he did send it every month, money order, right on the dot, I'll give him that. Only, this month I didn't get it. It was due five days ago, I have to figure out who to talk to at the army. It was an army reserve pension, they need to send it directly to me now. You have any idea how to contact them?"

"I might be able to get you a number," said Milo. "During the twenty-five years, how often did you and Dr. Mate communicate?"

"We didn't. He just sent the money. I used to think it was because he felt guilty. About walking out. But now I know he probably didn't. For guilt you got to have faith, and Eldon didn't believe in nothing. So maybe he did it out of habit, I don't know. When his mother was alive he used to send *her* money. Instead of visiting. He was always one for habits—doing things the same exact way, every single time. One color shirt, one color pants. He said it left time for important things."

"Like what?"

She shrugged. Her eyes fluttered and she began to sway. Began to fall. Both Milo and I took hold of her shoulders.

"I'm okay," she said, shrugging us off angrily. Smoothing her dress, as if we'd messed it. "Got a little low blood sugar, that's all, no big deal, I just got to eat. I brought food from home, but in the bus station someone stole my Tupperware." The black eyes lifted to Milo. "I want to eat something."

We drove her to a coffee shop on Santa Monica near La Brea. Dulled gold booths, streaked windows, fried-bacon air, the clash and clatter of silverware scooped into gray plastic tubs by sleepy busboys who looked underage. Milo chose the usual cop's vantage point at the back of the restaurant. The nearest patrons were a pair of CalTrans workers inhaling the daily steak-and-eggs special heralded by a front-door banner. Loss leader; the price belonged to the fifties. Unlikely to cover the cost of slaughter.

Guillerma Mate ordered a double cheeseburger, fries and a Diet Dr Pepper. Milo told the waitress, "Ham on rye, potato salad, coffee."

The ambience was doing nothing for my appetite, but I'd put nothing in my stomach since the morning coffee and I asked for a roast-beef dip on French roll, wondering if the meat had been carved from the budget cows.

The food came quickly. My beef dip was lukewarm and rubbery, and from the way Milo picked, his order was no better. Guillerma Mate ate lustily while trying to maintain dignity, cutting her burger up into small pieces and forking morsels into her mouth with an assembly-line pace. Finishing the sandwich, she forked french fries one at a time, consuming every greasy stick.

She wiped her mouth. Sipped Dr Pepper through two straws. "I feel better. Thanks."

"Pleasure, ma'am."

"So who killed Eldon?" she said.

"I wish I knew. This pension—"

"He had two, but I only get one—the five hundred from the reserves. The big one for a couple thousand from the Public Health Service he kept for himself. I don't think I coulda gotten more out of him. We weren't even divorced and he was giving me money." She edged closer across the table. "Did he *make* more?"

"Ma'am?"

"You know, from all the killing he did?"

"What do you think of all the killing he did?"

"What do I think? Disgusting. Mortal sin—that's why I don't go by his name. Had everything changed back to

Salcido—he wasn't even a *doctor* when we were married.
Went to medical school *after* he walked out. Went down
in Mexico, because he was too old for anyplace else. I
have friends up in Oakland who know we were married.
At my church. But I keep it quiet. It's embarrassing.
Some of them used to tell me to go get a lawyer, Eldon's
rich now, I could get more out of him. I told them it
would be sin money. They said I should take it anyway,
give it to the church. I don't know about that—did he
leave a will?"

"We haven't found one yet."

"So that means I have to go through that thing—
probate."

Milo didn't answer.

"Actually," she said, "we did talk in the beginning,
Eldon and me. Right after he walked out. But just a few
times. Donny and me were in San Diego, and Eldon
wasn't that far, down in Mexico. Then, after he became a
doctor, he went up to Oakland to work in a hospital and I
did a real stupid thing: I took Donny and we went there,
too. I don't know what I coulda been thinking, maybe
now that he was a doctor—it was stupid, but there I was
with a boy who didn't even know his father."

"Oakland didn't work out?" I said.

"Oakland worked out, I'm still there. But Eldon
didn't work out. He wouldn't talk to Donny, wouldn't even
pick him up, look at him. I remember it like yesterday,
Eldon in his white coat—that scared Donny and he
started screaming, Eldon got mad and yelled at me to get
the brat out of there—the whole thing just fell apart."

She picked at a scrap of lettuce. "I called him a
couple more times after that. He wasn't interested.

Refused to visit. Donny's being born just turned him off like a faucet. So I moved across the bridge to San Francisco, got a job. Funny thing is, a few years later I was back to Oakland 'cause the rent was cheaper, but by that time Eldon was gone and the checks were coming from Arizona, he had some kind of government job doing I don't know what. Back *then's* when I thought of getting a lawyer."

"Any reason you didn't file for divorce?" I said.

"Why bother?" she said. "There was no other man I wanted to know, and Eldon was sending me his army pension. You know how it is."

"How is it?" said Milo.

"You don't make a move in the beginning, nothing happens. He sent the check every month, that was enough for me. Then when he started in on that killing business, I knew I was lucky he'd left. Who'd want to live with *that*? I mean, when I heard about that I got sick, really *sick*. I remember the first time. I saw it on TV. Eldon standing there—I hadn't seen him in years and now he was on the TV. Looking older, balder but the same face, the same voice. *Bragging* about what he did. I thought, He's finally gone a hundred percent crazy. The next day I was on the phone, changing my name on the Social Security and everything else I could find."

"So you never talked to him about his new career?"

"Didn't talk to him about anything," she said. "Didn't I just say that?" She shoved her plate away. Pulled more soda through the straws, let the brown liquid drop like the bubble in a carpenter's level before it reached her lips.

"Even if it *was* making him real rich, how would it look if suddenly I showed up wanting more?" She touched the handle of her butter knife. "That was filthy money. I been working my whole life, doing just fine—tell me, *did* he get rich from the killing?"

"Doesn't look like it," said Milo.

"So what was the point?"

"He claimed he was helping people."

"The devil claims he's an *angel*. Back when I knew Eldon, he wasn't interested in helping anyone but himself."

"Selfish?" I said.

"You bet. Always in his own world, doing what he wanted. Which was reading, always reading."

"Why'd you come down here, ma'am?" said Milo.

She held her hands out, as if expecting a gift. Her palms were scrubbed pale, crisscrossed by brown hatch marks. "I told you. I just thought I should—I guess I was curious."

"About what?"

She moved back in the booth. "About Eldon. Where he lived—what had happened to him. I never *could* figure him out."

"How'd the two of you meet?" I said.

She smiled. Smoothed her dress. Sucked soda up the straw. "What? Because he was a doctor and I'm some brown lady?"

"No—"

"It's okay, I'm used to it. When we were married and I used to walk Donny in the stroller, people thought I was the maid. 'Cause Donny's light like Eldon—spitting *image* of Eldon, in fact, and Eldon *still* didn't like him. Go figure. But stuff like that don't bother me anymore, the only thing that matters is doing right for Jesus—that's the real reason I'd never put a claim on Eldon's killing money. Jesus would weep. And I know you're gonna think I'm some kind of religious nut for saying this, but my faith is strong, and when you live for Jesus your soul is full of riches."

She laughed. "Of course, a nice meal once in a while don't hurt, right?"

"How about dessert?" said Milo.

She pretended to contemplate the offer. "If you're having."

He waved for the waitress, "Apple pie. Hot, à la mode. And for the lady . . ."

Guillerma Mate said, "As long as we're talking pie, honey, you got any chocolate cream?"

The waitress said, "Sure," copied down the order, turned to me. I shook my head and she left.

"Eldon didn't believe in Jesus, that was the problem," said Guillerma, dabbing at her lips again. "Didn't believe in nothing. You wanna know how we met? It was just one of those *things*. Eldon was living at this apartment complex where my mother did the cleaning—she wasn't legal so she couldn't get a decent job. My dad was a hundred percent legal, had a work permit, did landscaping for Luckett Construction, they were the biggest back then. My dad got citizenship, brought my mom over from El Salvador, but she never bothered to get papers. I was born here, pure American. My friends call me Willy. Anyway, Eldon was living in the complex and I used to run into him when I was washing down the walkways or trimming the flowers. We'd talk."

"This was in San Diego?"

"That's right. I was out of high school only a few

years, helping my mom out, taking classes part time at the JC, planning to be a nurse. Eldon was a lot older— thirty-six and he looked in his forties, had lost most of his hair already. I wasn't attracted to him at first, but then I started to like him. 'Cause he was polite. Not just for show, all the time. Quiet, too. That was good, I'd had enough of noisy men. Also, back then I thought he was a genius. He had a job as a chemist, kept science books and all kinds of other books everywhere, reading all the time. Back then, that impressed me. Back then I thought education was the way to get saved."

"No more, huh?"

"Wise man, fool—we're all weak mortals. The only genius is the one up there." Pointing to the ceiling. "Proof is, would a genius go around killing other people? Even those who asked for it? Does that sound like a smart thing to do when we're all gonna answer for our deeds in the next world?"

She shook her head and spoke to the ceiling tiles. "Eldon, I wouldn't want to be in your shoes right now."

The dessert came. She waited until Milo'd taken a forkful before attacking her pie.

I said, "But at the beginning you were impressed with his education."

"I used to think education was everything. I was gonna be a registered nurse—when I moved up to Oakland, I had these . . . fantasies, I guess you'd call 'em. Eldon would open up a doctor's office, I'd work with him. But then he wouldn't have nothing to do with Donny and me, so I had to keep working and never got to finish school." She licked her lips. "I'm not complaining. I take care of the elderly, do what nurses do, anyway. And now

I know there's no shortcut to happiness, doesn't matter what your job is in this world. The main world is the one *afterward*, and the only way to get *there* is Jesus. It's exactly what my mother taught me, only back then I wasn't listening to her. No one listened to her, that was the burden she carried around. My father was *godless*. She never turned him around till he was dying, and even then, not till the pain came on real bad, so what else could he do but pray?"

The back of her spoon skated over the chocolate cream pie, picking up a coating of whipped cream. She licked it, said, "My dad smoked all his life, got lung cancer, it spread to his bones, all over his spine. He died in bad pain, choking and screaming. It was horrible. Made a big impression on Eldon."

"Eldon saw your father die?" I said.

"You bet. Dad died right after we were married. We'd go visit Dad in the hospital and he'd be coughing up blood and screaming from the pain and Eldon would turn white as a ghost and have to leave. Who'da figured he'd be a doctor? You know what *I* think? Seeing Dad die could be part of what started out Eldon on this killing business. 'Cause it really *was* horrible, Mom and me got through it by praying. But Eldon didn't pray. Refused to, even when Mom begged him. Said he wouldn't be a hypocrite. If you don't have no faith, seeing something like that is gonna scare you."

She finished her pie.

Milo said, "Is there anything you can tell us that might help us learn who killed your husband?"

"I'd say someone didn't like what Eldon was doing."

"Anyone in particular?"

"No," she said. "I'm just talking . . . logical. There's got to be lots of people who didn't approve of Eldon. Not God-fearing people, God-fearing people don't go running around killing. But maybe someone . . ." Smile. "You know, it could be someone *like* Eldon. Got no faith and a big hate grew inside him *about* Eldon. 'Cause Eldon had a difficult personality—didn't care what he said or how he said it. Least, that's the way he was back when we were married. Always getting into it with people—bring him into a place like this and he'd be complaining about the food, marching up to the manager and starting an argument. Maybe he got the wrong person mad and this person said, Look what he does and gets away with it, sure, it's okay to kill, it's no different from tying my shoes. 'Cause let's face it, if you don't believe in the world hereafter, what's to stop you from killing or raping or robbing or doing whatever it is your lust tells you to do?"

Milo sat there, probing the rim of his piecrust with his fork. I wondered if he was thinking what I was: a lot of insight in one little speech.

"So," she said, "who do I talk to about that pension? And the will?"

Back in the car, Milo made a series of calls and got her the number of the army pension office.

"As far as the will is concerned," he told her, "we're still trying to contact Dr. Mate's lawyer. A man named Roy Haiselden. Has he ever called you?"

"That big fat guy always with Eldon on TV? Nope— you think *he* has the will?"

"If there is one, he might. Nothing's been filed with County Records. If I learn anything, I'll let you know."

"Thanks. I guess I'll be staying in town for a few days, see what I can find out. Know of any clean, cheap places?"

"Hollywood's a tough area, ma'am. And nothing decent's gonna be that cheap."

"Well," she said, "I'm not saying I don't have any money. I work, I brought two hundred dollars with me. I just don't want to spend more than I have to."

We drove her to a West Coast Inn on Fairfax near Beverly and checked her in. She paid with a hundred-dollar bill, and as we walked her to her first-floor room, Milo warned her about flashing cash on the street and she said, "I'm not stupid."

The room was small, clean, noisy, with a view across Fairfax: cars whizzing by, the sleek, modern lines of the CBS studios a black-and-white subpanel to the horizon.

"Maybe I'll see a game show," she said, parting the drapes. She removed another floral dress from the macramé bag and headed for the closet. "Okay, thanks for everything."

Milo handed her his card. "Call me if you think of anything, ma'am—by the way, where's your son?"

Her back was to us. She opened the closet door. Took a long time to hang the dress. On the top shelf was an extra pillow that she removed. Fluffing, compressing, fluffing.

"Ma'am?"

"Don't know where Donny is," she said.

Punching the pillow. All at once, she looked tiny and bowed. "Donny's real smart, just like Eldon. Did a year at San Francisco State. I used to think he'd be a doctor, too. He got good grades, he liked science."

She stood there, hugging the pillow.

"What happened?" I said.

Her shoulders heaved.

I went over and stood next to her. She edged away, placed the pillow atop a dresser. "They said it was drugs—my friends at church said it had to be that. But I never saw him take any drugs."

"He changed," I said.

She bent, cupped a hand over her eyes. I risked taking her by the elbow. Her skin was soft, gelatinous. I guided her onto a chair, handed her a tissue that she grabbed, crushed, finally used to wipe her face.

"Donny changed totally," she said. "Stopped taking care of himself. Grew long hair, a beard, got filthy. Like one of those homeless people. Only he's *got* a home, if he'd ever come back there."

"How long has it been since you've seen him?"

"Two years."

She sprang up, marched into the bathroom, closed the door. Water ran for a while, then she emerged announcing she was tired. "When I'm ready to eat, where can I get some dinner around here?"

"Do you like Chinese, ma'am?" said Milo.

"Sure, anything."

He phoned up a takeout place and asked them to deliver in two hours. When we left, she was consulting the cable TV channel guide.

Out in the car, Milo sat back in his seat and frowned. "One happy family. And Junior's a homeless guy with mental problems, maybe a druggie. Someone with a reason to kill Mate—who might still want to *be* Mate.

Maybe I was wrong to dismiss the street bum so quickly."

"If Donny was intelligent to begin with, even with some sort of mental breakdown, he might've held on to enough smarts to be able to plan. Mate abandoned and rejected him in the worst kind of way. Exactly the kind of primal anger that leads to violence. Mate's getting famous wouldn't have helped things. Maybe Donny smoldered, seethed, decided to come back, take over the family business . . . Oedipus wrecks. Maybe Mate finally agreed to see him, arranged a talk up in Mulholland because he didn't want Donny in his apartment. He could've even had concerns about his safety, that's why he backed the van in. But he went through with it—guilt, or he enjoyed the danger."

He made no comment, got on the phone, hooked up with NCIC, asked for a felony search on Eldon S. Mate. Nothing. But plugging in Eldon *Salcido* pulled up three convictions. All in California, and the vital statistics fit.

Driving under the influence six years ago, larceny two years after that, assault eighteen months ago. Jail time in Marin County. Release six months ago.

"A year and a half in jail and he doesn't call his mother," I said. "Socially isolated. And he progressed from DUI to assault. Getting more aggressive."

"Family values," he said. "Be interesting to see what the grieving widow does when she finds out Mate left over three hundred grand in the bank. Wonder if Alice or anyone else will press a claim—that's really why old Willy came down here. It always boils down to anger and money—okay, I'll look into Donny, but in the meantime let's try to ferret out that goddamn lawyer."

11

Roy Haiselden was living better than his prime client, but he was no sultan.

His house was a peach-colored, one-story plain-wrap on Camden Avenue, west of Westwood, south of Wilshire. Mown lawn but no shrubs, empty driveway. Alarm-company sign staked in the grass. Milo rang the bell, knocked on the door—dead-bolted with a sturdy Quikset—pushed open the mail slot and sighted down.

"Just some throwaway flyers," he said. "No mail. So he left recently."

He rang and knocked again. Tried to peer through the white drapes that sheathed the front windows, muttered that it just looked like a goddamn house. A check in back of the house revealed more grass and a small oval swimming pool set in a brick deck, the water starting to green, the gunite spotted with algae.

"If he had a pool man," I said, "looks like he canceled

a while back. Maybe he's been gone for a while and put on a mail stop."

"Korn and Demetri checked for that. And the gardener's been here."

The garage was a double, locked. Milo managed to pry the door upward several inches and he peered in. "No car, old bicycle, hoses, the usual junk."

He inspected every side of the house. Most of the windows were barred and bolted and the back door was secured by an identical dead bolt. The kitchen window was undraped but narrow and high, and he boosted me up for a look.

"Dishes in the sink, but they look clean . . . no food . . . another alarm sticker high on the window, but I don't see any alarm leads."

"Probably a fake-out job," he said. "One of those clever boys who thinks appearance is everything."

"Overconfident," I said. "Just like Mate."

He let me down. "Okay, let's see what the neighbors have to offer."

Both of the adjacent houses were empty. Milo scrawled requests to call on the back of his business cards and left them in the mailboxes. In the second house to the south, a young black man answered. Clean-shaven, full-faced, barefoot, wearing a gray athletic shirt with the U. logo and red cotton shorts. Under his arm was a book. A yellow underlining pen was clenched between his teeth. He removed it, shifted the book so I could see the title: *Organizational Structure: An Advanced Text*. The room behind him was set up with two bright-blue beanbag chairs and not much else. Soda cans, potato chip bags, an extra-large pizza box mottled with grease on the thin khaki rug.

He greeted Milo pleasantly, but the sight of the badge caused his face to tighten.

"Yes?" The unspoken overtone: *What now?* I wondered how many times he'd been stopped for driving in Westwood.

Milo stepped back, bent his knee in a relaxed pose. "I was wondering, sir, if you've seen your neighbor Mr. Haiselden recently."

"Who—oh him. No, not for a few days."

"Could you say how many days, Mr . . ."

"Chambers," said the young man. "Curtis Chambers. I think I saw him drive away five, six days ago. Whether he's been back since, I can't say, 'cause I've been holed up here studying. Why?"

"Do you recall what time of day it was when you saw him, Mr. Chambers?"

"Morning. Before nine. I was going to meet with a prof and he needed to do it by nine. I think it was Tuesday. What's going on?"

Milo smiled and held up a delaying finger. "What kind of car was Mr. Haiselden driving?"

"Some kind of van. Silver, with a blue stripe down the side."

"That his only vehicle?"

"Only one I've seen him in."

"Anyone else live there with him?"

"Not that I know," said Curtis Chambers. "Could you please tell me what's up?"

"We're trying to contact Mr. Haiselden about a case—"

"Dr. Death's murder?"

"You've seen him with Dr. Mate?"

"No, but everyone knew he was Dr. Death's lawyer. People in the neighborhood talk about it. He's a jerk, Haiselden. Last year, we had a party—there are four of us living here, grad students. Nothing wild, we're all grinds, all we had was that single party the entire year to celebrate semester-end. We tried to be considerate, even sent notes around to the neighbors. One woman—Mrs. Kaplan next door—sent us a bottle of wine. No one had a problem with it except Haiselden. *He* called the cops on us. Twenty after eleven and believe me, it was nothing wild, just some music, maybe it got a little loud. What an uptight hypocrite. After all the disruption he brought to the neighborhood."

"What kind of disruption?"

"Reporters, media, all that garbage."

"Recently?"

"No, a few years ago," said Chambers. "I never saw it, wasn't living here back then, but one of my room-mates was—he said the whole street was a zoo. This was back when Mate was still getting arrested. He and Haiselden threw press conferences right here. TV crews would show up—lights, cameras, the works. Blocked driveways, cigarettes and garbage left on the lawns. Some of the neighbors finally complained to Haiselden, but he ignored them. So after all that, he goes and calls the cops on *us*. A jerk, always had this irritated look on his face. So why do you want him? Did he kill his buddy?"

"Why would you say that, Mr. Chambers?"

Chambers grinned. "Because I don't like the man . . . and the fact that he split. You'd think, his being Mate's mouthpiece, that he'd stick around, grab some more PR.

'Cause that's what it was all about, right? That's the only problem I have with what Mate did."

"What do you mean?" said Milo.

"The tackiness, making a spectacle out of other people's pain. You want to put a sick person out of their misery, fine. But shouldn't it be private? From what my roommate told me about the way Haiselden used to behave, he loved playing for the cameras. So you'd think he'd be doing the same thing now. Though I guess there's nothing for him to comment on anymore, with Mate gone."

"Guess not," said Milo. "Is there anything else you want to tell me about him?"

"Nope—listen, if you leave me your number and I see him, I'll call you. Siccing the cops on our party. What a jerk."

Driving back to the station, Milo said, "First Mrs. Mate, now him. Insights from the man on the street. Everyone seems to have figured things out except me."

"A lawyer who drives a van."

"Yeah, yeah, psycho killer's transport of choice. Wouldn't that be something? One serial killer representing another in court. And winning."

"Only thing he did win," I said. "He couldn't make a living practicing law, so he turned to coin-ops. Zoghbie said it was because of Mate, but maybe he was struggling before and Mate was his salvation. He latches on to the whole travel thing, rides the coattails, enjoys the glory. Then he and Mate have some kind of rift. Or, as you said, Haiselden starts yearning for more."

"Up the suspect ladder he goes. Time for a pass by his office."

"Where's that?"

"Miracle Mile, the old part, east of Museum Row. He leases some space over a Persian restaurant. Him and some other low-rent outfits. The place has a moldy feel to it, like out of an old movie."

"No secretary?"

"I've been there twice, Korn and Demetri another two times. The door's always locked and no one answers. Time to find the landlord. No sense wasting *your* time. Go home to Robin and Fido."

I didn't argue. I was tired. And Stacy Doss was coming in tomorrow; I needed to review her file.

"So who're you concentrating on?" I said. "Haiselden or Donny Mate?"

"Do I have to choose between Door Number One and Door Number Two, Monty? Can I take Number Three? Better yet, I'll concentrate on both of them. If Donny's our street wacko, it may take a while to find him. I wanna find out if he was released clean or placed on parole. Maybe he's got a P.O. I can talk to. If he was the bum Mrs. Krohnfeld saw, maybe he's still hanging in Hollywood. That would also fit with your idea about stalking Mate."

"Stalking Daddy."

"Who's off in his own world and thinks he's immortal . . . I think I'll touch base with Petra, she's as clued in to the streets as anyone."

Petra Connor was a Hollywood Division homicide detective, young, bright, intense, recently promoted to D-II because of some help she'd given Milo on a series of killings of handicapped people. Just after that, she and her partner had solved the Lisa Ramsey case—ex-wife of a TV actor, found hacked up in Griffith Park. She'd referred me a case, a twelve-year-old boy who'd witnessed the crime while living in the park, a brilliant, complex child, one of the most fascinating patients I'd ever encountered. Rumors were that her partner, Stu Bishop, was in line for a major administrative job and that she'd be a D-III by year's end, then groomed by the new chief for something conspicuous.

"Give her my best," I said.

"Sure," he said, but his tone was detached and his eyes were somewhere off in the distance.

Staring into *his* own world. At that moment, I was happy not to be sharing.

CHAPTER

12

Monday, nine-thirty P.M., nearing the end of a very long day.

Robin was soaking in the bath and I was in bed, reviewing Stacy Doss's chart.

Tomorrow morning, Stacy and I would be talking, ostensibly about college.

She'd used college as a cover the first time.

March, a warm Friday afternoon. I'd seen two other kids before her, sad children caught up in the poison of a custody dispute. The next hour was spent writing reports. Then waiting for Stacy. Curious about Stacy.

Despite my preconceptions about Richard Doss—*because* of them—I'd labored to keep an open mind about his daughter. Still, I wondered. What kind of girl would result from the union of Richard and Joanne? I really had no clue.

The red light signaling someone at the side door lit up precisely on time and I went to fetch her. A small girl—five-two in brown loafers. Perfect genetic logic; no reason for the Dosses to produce a basketball player. A bright-green oversize book was sandwiched between her right arm and her chest, the title obscured by her sleeve. She wore a white cotton mock turtle, snug blue jeans, white socks with the loafers.

Normal teenage curves, a bit of flesh on her face, but certainly not overweight. If she'd gained ten pounds, as Judy Manitow had claimed, she'd have been extremely thin before. That made me wonder about Judy—her own tendency toward sharp angles, snapshots of her daughters in her chambers. A pair of bright-eyed blondes in very short, very tight party dresses . . . also skinny. The younger one—Becky—veering too close to skeletal?

No matter, Stacy was the patient. She had full cheeks but a long face that evoked her mother's college picture. Richard's high, broad brow, stippled by a few tiny pimples. Pixie features; another endowment from both parents.

She smiled nervously. I introduced myself and held out my hand. She took it readily, maintained eye contact, flashed a half-second smile that burned lots of calories.

Making an effort.

Prettier than Joanne, with dark, almond eyes and the kind of small-boned good looks that would attract the boys. During my high-school days, she'd have been labeled a Gidget. In any generation, she'd be termed cute.

Another paternal donation: her hair—thick, black, very curly. She wore it long and loose, glossed with some kind of product that relaxed the helixes to dancing corkscrews. Lighter complexion than Richard's—skin the color of clotted cream. Thin skin; traces of blue surfaced at jawline and temple. A cuticle picked raw on her left middle finger had turned red and swollen to a silky sheen.

She hugged the book tighter and followed me in. "That's a pretty pond I passed. Koi, right?"

"Right."

"The Manitows have a koi pond, a big one."

"Really." I'd been in Judy Manitow's chambers several dozen times, never visited her home.

"Dr. Manitow put in an incredible waterfall. You could swim in there. Yours is actually more . . . accessible. You have a beautiful garden."

"Thanks."

We entered the office and she sat down with the green book across her lap. Yellow lettering shouted: *Choosing the Right College for You!*

"No problem finding the place?" I said, settling opposite her.

"Not at all. Thanks for seeing me, Dr. Delaware."

I wasn't used to being thanked by adolescents. "My pleasure, Stacy."

She blushed and turned away.

"Recreational reading?" I said.

Another strained smile. "Not exactly."

She began to look around the office.

"So," I said, "do you have any questions?"

"No, thanks." As if I'd offered her something.

I smiled. Waited.

She said, "I guess I should talk about my mother."

"If you want to."

"I don't know if I want to." Her right index finger curled and moved toward her left hand, located the inflamed cuticle. Stroking. Picking. A dot of blood stretched to a scarlet comma. She covered it with her right hand.

"Dad says he's worried about my future, but I suppose I should talk about Mom." She angled her face so that it was shielded by black curls. "I mean, it's probably the right thing for me. That's what my friend says—she wants to be a psychologist. Becky Manitow, Judge Manitow's daughter."

"Becky's been doing some amateur therapy?"

She shook her head as if thinking about that made her tired. Her eyes were the same dark brown as her father's, yet a whole different flavor. "Becky's been in counseling herself, thinks it's the cure for everything. She lost a lot of weight, even more than her mother wanted her to, so they shipped her off to some therapist and now she wants to be one."

"You two friends?"

"We used to be. Actually, Becky's not . . . I don't want to be cruel, let's just say she's not into school."

"Not an intellectual."

She let out a small, soft laugh. "Not exactly. My mom used to tutor her in math."

Judy had never mentioned her daughter's problem. No reason to. Still, I wondered why Judy hadn't referred Stacy to Becky's therapist. Maybe too close to home, keeping everything in neat little boxes.

"Well," I said, "no matter what Becky or anyone says, you know what's best for you."

"Think so?"

"I do."

"You don't even know me."

"Competent till proven otherwise, Stacy."

"Okay." Another weak smile. So much effort to smile. I wrote a mental note: *poss. depress. as noted by J. Manitow.*

Her hand lifted. The blood on her finger had dried and she rubbed the sore spot. "I don't think I really do. Want to talk about my mother, that is. I mean, what can I say? When I think about it I get down for days, and I've already had enough of those. And it's not as if it was a shock—her . . . what happened. I mean it *was*, when it actually happened, but she'd been sick for so long."

Same thing her father had said. Her own little speech, or his?

"This," she said, smiling again, "is starting to sound like one of those gross movies of the week. Lindsay Wagner as everyone's mom . . . What I'm saying is that what happened to my mother took so long . . . It wasn't like another friend of mine, *her* mother died in a skiing accident. Crashed into a tree and she was gone, just like that." Snap of the inflamed finger. "The whole family watching it happen. *That's* traumatic. My mother . . . I knew it was going to happen. I spent a long time wondering *when*, but . . ." Her bosom rose and fell. One foot tapped. The right index finger sought the sore spot again, curled to strike, scratched, retracted.

"Maybe we *should* talk about my so-called future," she said, lifting the green book. "First could I use the bathroom, please?"

• • •

She was gone ten minutes. After seven I started to wonder, was ready to get up to check if she'd left the house, but she returned, hair tied back in a bushy ponytail, mouth shiny with freshly applied lip gloss.

"Okay," she said. "College. The process. My lack of direction."

"That sounds like something someone told you."

"Dad, my school counselor, my brother, everyone. I'm almost eighteen, nearly a senior, so I'm supposed to be into it—career aspirations, compiling lists of extracurricular activities, composing brag sheets. Ready to sell myself. It feels so . . . phony. I go to Pali Prep, freak-city when it comes to college. Everyone in my class is freaking out daily. I'm not, so I'm the space alien." Her free hand flipped the edges of the green book's pages.

"Can't get into it?" I said.

"Don't *want* to get into it. I honestly don't care, Dr. Delaware. I mean, I know I'm going to end up somewhere. Does it really make a difference *where*?"

"Does it?"

"Not to me."

"But everyone's telling you you should care."

"Either explicitly or, you know—it's in the air. The atmosphere. At school everything's been split down the middle—sociologically. Either you're a goof and you know you'll end up at a party school, or you're a grind and expected to obsess on Stanford or the Ivy League. I *should* be a grind, because my grades are okay. I should have my nose glued to the SAT prep book, be filling out practice applications."

"When do you take the SAT?"

"I already took it. In December. We all did, just for

practice. But I did okay enough, don't see why I should go through it again."

"What'd you get?"

She blushed again. "Fifteen-twenty."

"That's a fantastic score," I said.

"You'd be surprised. At PP, kids who get fifteen-eighty take it again. One kid had his parents write that he was American Indian so he'd get some kind of minority edge. I don't see the point."

"Neither do I."

"I honestly think that if you offered most of the senior class a deal to murder someone in order to be guaranteed admission to Harvard, Stanford or Yale, they'd take it."

"Pretty brutal," I said, fascinated by her choice of example.

"It's a brutal world out there," she said. "At least that's what my father keeps telling me."

"Does he want you to take the SAT again?"

"He pretends he's not pressuring me, but he lets me know he'll pay for it if I want to."

"Which is a kind of pressure."

"I suppose. You met him . . . What was that like?"

"What do you mean?"

"Did you get along? He told me you were smart, but there was something in his voice—like he wasn't sure about you." She cracked up. "I've got a big mouth . . . Dad's super-active, always needs to keep moving, thinking, doing something. Mom's illness drove him crazy. Before she got sick, they were totally active together— jogging, dancing, tennis, traveling. When she stopped living, he was left on his own. It's made him cranky."

That sounded detached, a clinical assessment. The family observer? Sometimes kids assume that role because it's easier than participating.

"Tough adjustment for him," I said.

"Yes, but he finally caught on."

"About what?"

"About having to do things for himself. He always finds a way to adjust."

That sounded accusatory. My raised eyebrow was my next question.

She said, "His main way of handling stress is by staying on the go. Business trips. You know what he does, right?"

"Real-estate development."

She shook her head as if I'd gotten it wrong, but said, "Yes. Distressed properties. He makes money off other people's failures."

"I can see why he'd view the world as brutal."

"Oh yes. The brutal world of distressed *properties*." She laughed and sighed and her hands loosened. Placing the big green book on an end table, she pushed it away. Her hands returned to her lap. Loose. Defenseless. Suddenly she was slumping like a teenager. Suddenly she seemed truly happy to be here.

"He calls himself a heartless capitalist," she said. "Probably because he knows that's what everyone else says. Actually, he's quite proud of himself."

Undertone of contempt, low and steady as a monk's drone. Deriding her father to a virtual stranger but doing it charmingly. That kind of easy seepage often means the lid's rising on a long-boiling pot.

I sat there, waiting for more. She crossed her legs,

slumped lower, fluffed her hair, as if aiming for nonchalance.

Her shrug said, Your turn.

I said, "I get the feeling real estate isn't a strong interest of yours."

"Who knows? I'm thinking of becoming an architect, so I can't hate it that much. Actually, I don't hate business at all, not like some other kids do. It's just that I'd rather build something than be a . . . I'd rather be productive."

"Rather than be a what?"

"I was going to say scavenger. But that's not fair to my father. He doesn't cause anyone else to fail. He's just there to seek opportunities. Nothing wrong with that, it's just not what *I'd* like to do—actually, I have no *idea* what I'd like to do." She rang an imaginary bell. "Dah-*dah*, big insight. I have no *goals*."

"What about architecture?"

"I probably just say that to tell people something when they ask me. For all I know, I might end up despising architecture."

"Do any subjects in school interest you?" I said.

"I used to like science. For a while, I thought medicine might be a good choice. I took all the A.P. science courses, got fives on the exams. Now I don't know."

"What changed your mind?" *The death of your scientist mother?*

"It just seems . . . well, for one, medicine's not what it used to be, is it? Becky told me her father can't stand his job anymore. All the HMOs telling him what he can and can't do. Dr. Manitow calls it *mis*managed care. After all that school, it would be nice to have some occupational freedom. Do you like *your* job?"

"Very much."

"Psychology," she said, as if the word was new. "I was more interested in real science—oh, sorry, that was rude! What I meant was hard science . . ."

"No offense taken." I smiled.

"I mean, I do respect psychology. I was just thinking more in terms of chemistry and biology. For myself. I'm good with organic things."

"Psychology *is* a soft science," I said. "That's part of what I like about it."

"What do you mean?" she said.

"The unpredictability of human nature," I said. "Keeps life interesting. Keeps me on my toes."

She thought about that. "I had one psych course, in my junior year. Non–honor track, actually a Mickey Mouse. But it ended up being interesting . . . Becky went nuts with it, picking out every symptom we learned about and pinning it on someone. Then she got real cold to me—don't ask me why, I don't know. Don't care, either, we haven't shared common interests since the Barbies got stored in the closet . . . No, I don't think any kind of medicine's for me. Frankly, none of it seems too scientific. My mother saw every species of doctor known to mankind and no one could do a thing for her. If I ever decide to do anything with my life, I think I'd like it to be more productive."

"Something with quick results?"

"Not necessarily quick," she said. "Just valid." She pulled the ponytail forward, played with the crimped edges. "So what if I'm unfocused. I'm the second child, isn't that normal? My brother has enough focus for both of us, knows exactly what he wants: to win the Nobel

Prize in economics, then make billions. One day you'll read about him in *Fortune*."

"That is pretty specific."

"Eric's always known what he wants. He's a genius— picked up *The Wall Street Journal* when he was five, read an article on supply and demand in the soybean market and gave his kindergarten class a lecture the next day."

"Is that a family tale?" I said.

"What do you mean?"

"It sounds like something you might've heard from your parents. Unless you remember it yourself. But you were only three."

"Right," she said. Confused. "I think I heard it from my father. Could've been my mother. Either of them. My father still tells the story. It probably *was* him."

Mental note: *What stories does Dad tell about Stacy?*

"Does that mean something?" she said.

"No," I said. "I'm just interested in family tales. So Eric's focused."

"Focused and a genius. I mean that literally. He's the smartest person I've ever met. Not a nerd, either. Aggressive, tenacious. Once he sets his mind on something, he won't let go."

"Does he like Stanford?"

"He likes it, it likes him."

"Your parents went there?"

"Family tradition."

"Does that put pressure on you to go there, as well?"

"I'm sure Dad would be thrilled. Assuming I'd get in."

"You don't think you would?"

"I don't know—don't really care."

I'd put some space between our chairs, careful not to crowd her. But now her body arched forward, as if yearning for touch. "I'm not putting myself down, Dr. Delaware. I know I'm smart enough. Not like Eric, but smart enough. Yes, I probably could get in, if for no other reason than I'm a multiple legacy. But the truth is, all that is wasted on me—*smarts* are wasted on me. I really couldn't care less about intellectual goals or tackling challenges or changing the world or making big bucks. Maybe that sounds airheady, but that's the way it is."

She sat back. "How much time do we have left, please? I forgot my watch at home."

"Twenty minutes."

"Ah. Well . . ." She began studying the office walls.

"Busy day?" I said.

"No, easy day, as a matter of fact. It's just that I told my friends I'd meet them at the Beverly Center. Lots of good sales on, perfect time to do some airhead shopping."

I said, "Sounds like fun."

"Sounds mindless."

"Nothing wrong with leisure."

"I should just enjoy my life?"

"Exactly."

"Exactly," she repeated. "Just have fun." Tears welled in her eyes. I handed her a tissue. She took it, crushed the paper, enveloping it with a fine-boned, ivory fist.

"Let's," she said, "talk about my mother."

I saw her thirteen times. Twice a week for four weeks, then five weekly sessions. She was punctual, cooperative, filled the first half of each session with edgy fast-talk about movies she'd seen, books she'd read, school, friends. Keeping the inevitable at bay, then finally relenting. Her decision, no prodding from me.

The final twenty minutes of each session reserved for her mother.

No more tears, just soft-spoken monologues, heavy with obligation. She'd been sixteen when Joanne Doss began falling apart, remembered the decline, as had her father, as gradual, insidious, ending in grotesquerie.

"I'd look at her and she'd be lying there. Passive— even before, she was always kind of passive. Letting my father make all the decisions—she'd cook dinner but *he'd* determine the menu. She was a pretty good cook, as a matter of fact, but what she made never seemed to matter to her. Like it was her job and she was going to do it and do it well, but she wouldn't pretend to be . . . inspired. Once, years ago, I found this little menu box and she'd put in all these dinner plans, stuff she cut out of magazines. So once upon a time, I guess she cared. But not when I was around."

"So your dad had all the opinions in the family," I said.

"Dad and Eric."

"Not you?"

Smile. "Oh, I have a few, too, but I tend to keep them to myself."

"Why's that?"

"I've found that a good strategy."

"For what?"

"A pleasant life."

"Do Eric and your father exclude you?"

"No, not at all—not consciously, anyway. It's just that

the two of them have this . . . let's just call it a big male thing. Two major brains speeding along. Jumping in would be like hopping on a moving train—good metaphor, huh? Maybe I should use it in English class. My teacher's a real pretentious snot, loves metaphors."

"So joining in's dangerous," I said.

She pressed a finger to her lower lip. "It's not that they put me down . . . I guess I don't want them to think I'm stupid . . . They're just . . . they're a *pair,* Dr. Delaware. When Eric's home, sometimes it's like having Dad in duplicate."

"And when Eric's not home?"

"What do you mean?"

"Do you and your father interact?"

"We get along, it's just that he travels and we have different interests. He's into collecting, I couldn't care less about accumulating stuff."

"Collecting what?"

"First it was paintings—California art. Then he sold those for a giant profit and got into Chinese porcelain. The house is filled with walls and walls of the stuff. Han dynasty, Sung dynasty, Ming dynasty, whatever. I appreciate it. It's beautiful. I just can't get into accumulating. I guess he's an optimist, buying porcelain in earthquake country. He putties it down with this wax the museums use, but still. If the Big One comes, our house will be one big crockery disaster zone."

"How did it fare during the last quake?"

"He didn't have it back then. He got into it when Mom started to get sick."

"Do you think there's a connection?" I said.

"Between what?"

"Getting into porcelain and your mother becoming ill."

"Why should there be—oh I see. She couldn't do things with him anymore, so he learned to amuse himself. Yes, maybe. Like I said, he knows how to adapt."

"What did your mom think about the porcelain?"

"She didn't think anything, that I saw. She didn't think much about anything—Eric likes the porcelain. He can inherit it, I couldn't care less." Sudden smile. "I'm the Queen of Apathy."

At the end of the sixth session, she said, "Sometimes I wonder what kind of guy I'll marry. I mean, will it be someone dominant like Dad or Eric, because that's what I'm used to, or will I go in a totally opposite direction—not that I'm thinking about that. It's just that Eric was down for the weekend and the two of them went off to some Asian art auction and I watched them leave the house—like twins. That's basically what I know of men."

She shook her head. "Dad keeps buying stuff. Sometimes I think that's what he's all about—expansion. As if one world's not big enough for him—Eric was thinking of coming with me today to meet you."

"Why?"

"He doesn't have classes till tomorrow, asked me if I wanted to hang out before he flies up tonight. Kind of sweet, don't you think? He really is a good brother. I told him I had to see you first. He didn't know about you, Dad makes a big thing about confidentiality. Gave me this whole big speech about even though I was under eighteen, as far as he was concerned I had full rights. Like he was giving me a big gift, but I think he's kind of embarrassed about it. Once, when I brought up Becky's therapy, he changed the subject really fast . . . Anyway, Eric hadn't known about you and it surprised him. He started asking me all these questions, wanting to know if you were smart, where you got your degree. I realized I didn't know."

I pointed to my diplomas.

She said, "The good old U. Not Stanford or the Ivys, but it'll probably satisfy him."

"Do you feel you need to satisfy Eric?"

"Sure, he's the smart one . . . No, he's entitled to his opinion, but they don't influence mine. He decided not to come, took a bike ride instead. Maybe one day you'll get to meet him."

"If I behave myself?"

She laughed. "Yes, absolutely. Meeting Eric is a reward of the highest order."

I'd thought a lot about Eric. About the hellish Polaroids he'd shot of his mother. Standing at the foot of the bed, highlighting her misery in cold, unforgiving light. His father considered them trophies, carried them around in that little purse.

How badly had Richard Doss hated his wife?

I said, "How did Eric react to your mother's death?"

"Silence. Silent anger. He'd already dropped out of school to be with her, maybe that did it for him. Because right after, he returned to Stanford." Sudden chill in her voice. She picked at her cuticles, stared down into her lap.

Bad move, bringing up her brother. Keep the focus on her, always on her.

But I wondered if she'd ever seen the snapshots.

"So," I said.

"So." She looked at her watch.

Ten minutes to go. She frowned. I tried to reel her back in: "A couple of weeks ago, we were discussing how expressing opinions can be tricky in your family. How did your mother—"

"By having none. By turning herself into a nothing."

"A nothing," I said.

"Exactly. That's why I wasn't surprised when I found out what she did—with Mate. I mean I was, when I heard about it on the news. But after the shock wore off, I realized it made sense: the ultimate passivity."

"So you had no warning—"

"None. She never said a word to me. Never said good-bye. That morning she had called me in to say hi before I went to school. Told me I looked pretty. She did that sometimes, there was nothing different. She looked the way she always did. Erased—the truth is she'd already rubbed herself out by the time Mate got involved. The media always make it out like he's doing something but he isn't. Not if the other people were like my mom. He didn't do a damn thing. There was nothing left for him to do. She didn't want to *be*."

I readied my hand for a dive toward the tissue box. Stacy straightened, placed her feet on the floor, sat up straight.

"The whole thing's an incredible pity, Dr. Delaware."

Back to the clinical detachment of the first session.

"Yes, it is."

"She was brilliant, *two* PhDs, she could've won the Nobel Prize if she'd wanted to. *That's* where Eric got his smarts. My father's a bright man, but she was a *genius*.

Her parents were brilliant, too. Librarians, they never made much money, but they were brilliant. Both died young. Cancer. Maybe my mother was afraid of dying young. Of cancer, I don't know. She brought Becky Manitow from a D to a B in algebra. When Becky stopped seeing her, she dropped down to a D again."

"Becky stopped because your mother was ill?"

"I suppose."

Long silence. A minute to go.

She said, "Our time's up, isn't it."

"In a moment," I said.

"No. Rules are rules. Thanks for all your help, I'm dealing with stuff pretty well. All things considered." She picked up her books.

"All things considered?"

"One never knows," she said. Then she laughed. "Oh, don't worry about me. I'm fine. What's the choice?"

During the last few sessions, she entered ready to talk about her grief. Dry-eyed, solemn, no changes of subject or digressions to trivia or laughing dance-aways.

Trying.

Yearning to understand why her mother had left her without saying good-bye. Knowing some questions could never be answered.

Asking them anyway. Why her family? Why *her*?

Had her mother even been sick? Had it all been psychosomatic, the way Dr. Manitow said it was—she'd heard him say so to Judge Manitow when the two of them didn't know she was in earshot. Judge Manitow saying, *Oh, I don't know, Bob.* He replying, *Trust me, Judy, there's nothing physically wrong with her—it's slow suicide.*

Stacy, listening from the bathroom next to the kitchen, had been angry at him, really furious, what a bastard, how could he say something like that.

But then she started wondering herself. Because the doctors never did find anything. Her father kept saying doctors don't know everything, they're not as smart as they think. Then he stopped taking her for tests, so didn't that prove that even *he* thought it might be in Mom's head? You'd think *something* would show up on *some* test . . .

During the eleventh session, she talked about Mate.

Not angry at him, the way Dad was. The way Eric was. That's all the two of them could do when faced with something they couldn't control. Get angry at it. Big male thing, get pissed off, want to crush it.

I said, "Your father wants to crush Mate?"

"Rhetorically. He says that about anything he doesn't like—some guy trying to cheat him in a business deal, he jokes about pulverizing him, wiping him off the planet, that kind of macho BS."

"What do you think of Mate?"

"Pathetic. A loser. With or without him, Mom would have stopped being."

At the beginning of the twelfth session she announced that there was nothing left to say about her mother, she'd better start paying attention to her future. Because she'd finally decided she just might want one.

"Maybe architecture, still." Smile. "I've eliminated everything else. I'm forging straight ahead, Dr. Delaware. Setting my sights on architecture at Stanford. Everyone will be happy."

"Including you?"

"Definitely including me. No point doing anything if it doesn't bring me satisfaction. Thanks for getting me to see that."

She was ready to terminate, but I encouraged her to make another appointment. She came in the next week with brochures and the course catalog from Stanford. Going over the architecture curriculum with me. Telling me she was pretty sure she'd made the right choice.

"If you don't mind," she said, "I'd like to come in when I apply next year. Maybe you can give me some pointers—if you do that kind of thing."

"Sure. My pleasure. And call any time something's on your mind."

"You're very nice," she said. "It was instructive to meet you."

I didn't have to ask what she meant. I was a male who wasn't her father, wasn't her brother.

CHAPTER

13

It was nearly ten P.M. when I closed the file.

Stacy had left therapy claiming she'd found direction. This morning her father had implied the transformation had been temporary. She'd promised to call but never followed through. Normal teenage flakiness? Not wanting me to view her as a failure?

Despite her declaration of independence, I'd never considered her a therapeutic triumph. You couldn't deal with what she'd been through in thirteen sessions. I suppose I'd known all along that she'd held back.

Would we really talk about college tomorrow morning?

I paged through the file again, found something in my notes of the eleventh session. My deliberately sketchy shorthand, born of too many subpoenas.

Pt. disc. fath. hostility to Mate.

That's all the two of them could do when faced with something they couldn't control. Get angry at it. Big male thing, get pissed off, want to crush it.

The phone rang.

"Dr. Delaware, this came in an hour ago," said the operator. "A Mr. Fusco, he said you can call him back anytime."

The name wasn't familiar. I asked her to spell it.

"Leimert Fusco. I thought it was Leonard but it's Leimert." She recited a Westwood exchange. "Guess what, Doctor—he says he's with the FBI."

The Federal Building, where the FBI was headquartered, was in Westwood, on Wilshire and Veteran. Only blocks, as a matter of fact, from Roy Haiselden's house. Something to do with that? Then why call me, not Milo?

Better to check with Milo. I figured the frustrations of the day would push him to keep going, so I tried his desk at the station. No answer there or at his home, and his cell phone didn't connect.

Unsure I was doing the right thing, I punched in Fusco's number. A deep, harsh voice—heavy shoes being dragged over rough cement—recited the usual speech: "This is Special Agent Leimert Fusco. Leave a message."

"This is Dr. Alex Delaware returning your—"

"Doctor," the same voice broke in. "Thanks for getting back so quickly."

"What can I do for you?"

"I've been assigned to look into a police case you're currently working on."

"Which case is that?"

Laughter. "How many police cases are you working on? Don't worry, Doctor, I'm aware of your allegiance to Detective Sturgis, have cleared it with him. He and I will be meeting soon, he wasn't sure whether or not you'd be able to make it. So I thought I'd touch base with you personally, just to see if you've got any information you'd like to share with the Bureau. Psychological insights. By the way, I'm trained as a psychologist."

"I see." I didn't. "The little I know I've told Detective Sturgis."

"Yes," said Fusco. "He as much as said so."

Silence.

He said, "Well, thanks anyway. It's a tough one, isn't it?"

"Looks to be."

"Guess we've all got our work cut out for us. Thanks for calling back."

"Sure," I said.

"You know, Doctor, we do have some expertise in this area. The Bureau."

"What area, specifically?"

"Psychopathic killings. Homicides with psychosexual overtones. Our data banks are pretty impressive."

"Great," I said. "Hope you come up with something."

"Hope so, too. Bye now."

Click.

I sat there feeling like an unwitting character in a candid video.

Something about him . . . I called information and asked for the FBI number. Same prefix Fusco had given, so his number was probably an extension. A female recorded voice said no one was in this late. Rust never sleeps, but the government does.

I tried Milo, again, no success.

Fusco's call bothered me. Too brief. Pointless. As if he'd been checking me out.

Knowing I was being paranoid, I got up, checked all the doors and windows, set the alarm. When I got to the bedroom, Robin was in bed reading, and I slid in beside her. She had on one of my T-shirts and nothing else and I stroked her flank.

"You've been industrious," she said.

"Midwestern work ethic." I reached up under the T-shirt, felt the orange peel of goose bumps between her shoulder blades.

She yawned. "Ready to sleep?"

"I don't know."

She mussed my hair. "Another rough night in store?"

"Hope not."

"You're sure you don't want to try to sleep?"

"In a while," I said. "I promise."

"Well, I've got to nighty-night."

She turned off the light, we kissed, and she rolled away. I got up, closed the bedroom door after me, padded to the kitchen and made some green tea. From his bed in the service porch, Spike played a prolonged snore solo.

I sipped the tea and tried to forget everything. Normally, I like the stuff. Tonight it reminded me of sushi bars minus the food, which is kind of like a concert hall without the music. I reminded myself that it was the only herbal substance proven to the satisfaction of whizbang white-coats to be good for you, crammed as it is with antioxidants. And with all life throws at you, why oxidize needlessly?

When I finished the cup, I gave Milo one last try, reversing the order: cell phone first, then home, then the station. Superstition paid off; he picked up in the detective's room.

"Where've you been?" I said, realizing I sounded like a peeved parent.

"Right here. Why? What's wrong?"

"I just called a few minutes ago and they said you were gone."

"Gone upstairs. The lieutenant's office. Not Mate, bureaucratic BS, seems my poor little baby detectives are unhappy. Insufficiently challenged by their assignment to Homicide. Like I'm running a kindergarten."

"No success finding Haiselden?"

"Rub it in," he said. "Some therapist you are. Locked office, the landlord's some Chinese guy, barely speaks English, Haiselden's rent isn't due for another two weeks, so what does he care? I guess I should go back to his house, try to find out who does his gardening . . . Normally, I'd send Korn and Demetri to do it, but all their bitching means I have to be careful."

"You're on the defensive? Thought LAPD was para-military."

"More like day care, nowadays. Did you know you can get into the Academy now with prior drug arrests as long as they're not *too* serious. Cokehead cops. Reassuring, huh? Anyway, what's up?"

I told him about Fusco's call.

"Yeah, the grand voice of the federal government. He's got a PhD, I figured he might call you."

"I didn't want to talk to him without clearing it with you. Not that I have anything to tell him."

"Oh," he said. "Yeah, of course. Sorry I didn't tell you it was okay. He's originally from Virginia, big-time poohbah from their Behavioral Science Unit. Looks like my call to VICAP triggered something."

"What's he offering?"

"A powwow. I figure what he really wants is to pick my brain—little does he know what a waste that'll be. If the case is hopeless, he bugs out. If I'm onto something, he jumps aboard, sees if he can claim some credit . . . He faxed a charming note: *Anything I can do, blah blah blah . . . Lem. Assistant Deputy Director, Behavioral Science,* hoo-ha."

"He said you'd be meeting with him soon."

"He wanted tomorrow, I put him off, said I'd be in touch. Gonna keep putting him off, unless the bosses order me to waste time. Or do you think I should be open-minded?"

"Not so open your brain falls out."

"That's already happened . . . If we do meet, it's gonna be at his expense. Two-pound steaks, hyperthyroid potatoes at the Dining Car or The Palm—I'm making myself hungry. I work three months out of the year to pay the IRS. Let the Bureau pick up the tab for my cholesterol. Anything else?"

"Still planning on seeing Mr. Doss tomorrow?"

"Eleven A.M., his office. Why?"

"How 'bout that," I said. "Eleven's when I'm due to see Stacy."

"There you go," he said. "Synchronicity—something you want to tell me about Daddy?"

"Nope."

"Okay, then, happy therapy, I'm heading home. If I fall asleep at the wheel, you can have my pencil box."

"Take care of yourself," I said.

"Sure, I always do. Sweet dreams, Professor."

"Same to you."

"I don't dream, Alex. Against department regulations."

14

Eleven A.M. Tuesday. Sun and heat and clarity, an unseasonably beautiful morning. The weather didn't matter much. I waited in my office for half an hour, no sign of Stacy.

I cleared some paperwork, phoned Pali Prep. The secretary knew my name because I'd treated other students. Yes, Stacy had been excused from class. Two hours ago. I tried the Doss home, no answer. No cancellation message left at my service. I wanted to call Richard's office, but with teenagers you had to be careful not to breach trust, especially when dealing with a parent like Richard.

Also, Milo was with Richard, and that complicated matters.

Ten more minutes and now the session time was gone. Your basic no-show. Happened all the time. It had never happened with Stacy. But I hadn't seen Stacy in half a year, and six months was a long stretch of adolescence. Maybe seeing me had been her father's idea and she'd finally stood up to him.

Or perhaps Mate's death had something to do with it, churning up memories that reminded her what could happen to a woman who allowed herself not to *be*.

I filed the chart, expecting a phone call from one Doss or the other by day's end.

But it was Milo who cleared things up.

He showed up at my house just after one P.M.

"Had a quiet morning, huh?" He walked past me and entered the kitchen. My fridge is an old friend of his, and he greeted it with a small smile, removing a half-gallon of milk and a ripe peach. Looking inside the carton, he muttered, "Not much left, why bother with a glass."

He brought the milk to the table, upended the carton, gulped, wiped his mouth, assaulted the peach as if exacting revenge on all fruit.

"No session with little Ms. Doss," he said. "Swami Milo knows because Ms. Doss came over to Daddy's office right around the time she was supposed to be with you. Right when I'd started talking to Daddy. Something about her brother. Looks like he's run away."

"From Stanford?"

"From Stanford. Doss moved my eleven up to ten and I'd just gotten into his sanctum sanctorum—ever been there?"

I shook my head.

"Penthouse suite with an ocean view, executive trappings plus your basic private museum. Antiques, paintings, but mostly walls of Oriental breakables—hundreds of bowls, vases, statues, little incense burners, whatever.

These glass shelves that make it look as if everything's floating. Had me worried about breathing too hard, but maybe that's the point. Maybe throwing me off balance is why he changed the time. He left the message at midnight, it was only by luck that I got it. I figure the plan was I wouldn't, would show up at eleven, and he'd tell me aw shucks. Anyway, I made it, waited, finally got ushered in, Doss is sitting behind this ultrawide desk, so big that I've got to reach over and kill my back to shake his hand—the guy thinks everything out, doesn't he, Alex?"

I remembered my stretch for the photos. "So what happened?"

"My butt's just hitting the chair and his intercom burps. 'Stacy's here.' *That* throws *Doss*. Before he puts down the phone, the kid runs in, like she's about to blurt something to Daddy. Then she sees me, gives Daddy one of those we-have-to-talk-in-private looks, Doss asks me to please leave for a second. I head back for the waiting room, but the secretary's on the phone, has her back to me, so I keep the door open a crack, I know it's naughty, but . . ."

Detective's grin, ripe with suspicion and worst-case glee.

"Mostly what I heard was a helluva lot of anxiety. A few 'Stanford's, bunch of 'Eric's, so I knew it had something to do with her brother. Then Doss starts asking her questions—'When?' 'How?' 'You're sure?' Like what's going on is her fault. At that point, the secretary gets off the phone, turns around, shoots me a murderous look and closes the door. I wait out there another ten minutes."

He chomped the peach, ripping golden flesh away

from the pit. Went for the milk, holding the spout inches from his mouth. White liquid arced down his gullet. His throat muscles pulsed. Lowering the empty carton, he crushed it, said, "Ahhh, does a body good."

"What else?" I said.

"A few minutes later, Stacy comes out looking very uptight and leaves. Then Doss emerges, tells me he can't talk, family emergency. I do the old protect-and-serve: Any way I can be of service, sir? Doss looks at me like, Who are you kidding, moron. Then he tells me to make another appointment with the secretary, goes back inside the Porcelain Palace. The secretary looks at her book, says, Nothing tomorrow, how about Thursday? I say fine. When I'm back down in the parking garage, I ask the attendant to show me Doss's car. Black-on-black BMW 850i, chrome wheels, illegally tinted windows, custom spoiler. Shiniest damn thing I've ever seen, like he dipped it in glass. There's only one exit from the garage, so I wait down the block. But Doss never comes out, so whatever the problem is, he's handling it by phone. One thing I did think of, though: a dark BMW. What Paul Ulrich saw parked on the road the morning of Mate's murder."

"Lots of those on the Westside."

"True." Jumping up, he made it back to the fridge with two giant steps, grabbed a new quart of orange juice, popped the seal, began gulping. "But I'm still curious, so I call Stanford, locate Eric's dorm, talk to his roommate, some kid named Chad Soo. What I manage to get out of him is that Eric was looking real depressed for a few days, then he didn't come back to his room for a couple of days after that."

"When?"

"Yesterday, but Chad didn't call till this morning. Didn't want to get Eric in trouble, but Eric had a big test he didn't show up for and that wasn't like Eric, so after the second day he thought maybe he should tell someone. He called the house, talked to Stacy."

"He told you all this?"

"He was under the misconception that I was Palo Alto PD. So how come the kid gets depressed now, Alex? Nine months since his mother dies, but a week after Mate gets killed?"

"Mate's death could've brought up memories," I said.

"Yeah, well . . . that's how I knew your morning was gonna be quiet. So Stacy never called?"

"I'm sure she will when things settle down."

He drank more juice. I said, "Regarding the BMW, Ulrich said he saw a smaller model, like his."

"Yes, he did."

I got up. "I'm going to try to reach Stacy. From my office."

"Meaning I'm kicked out."

"Meaning feel free to stay in the kitchen."

"Fine," he said. "I'll wait."

"Why?"

"Something about this family bugs me."

"What?"

"Too secretive, too evasive. Doss has no reason to play games with me unless he's got something to hide."

I headed for the office. He called out, "Make sure you close the door all the way."

Richard's secretary used her boss's very busy schedule as a weapon: the chance of talking to him today was less probable than the sudden achievement of world peace.

"I'm calling about Stacy," I said. "Any idea where she might be?"

"Is there a problem, sir?"

"She didn't show up for her appointment at eleven," I said.

"Oh?" But she didn't sound surprised. "Well, I'm sure there's an explanation . . . May I assume you'll be billing us anyway, Doctor?"

"That's not the issue. I want to make sure everything's okay."

"Oh . . . I see. Well, as I said, Mr. D.'s not here now. But I did see Stacy a while back and she's fine. She didn't mention the appointment."

"Richard made it. Perhaps he forgot to tell her. Please have him call me."

"I'll give him the message, sir, but he's traveling on business."

"Business as usual?" I said.

Pause. "We will honor your bill, Dr. Delaware. Bye now."

Returning to the kitchen, I found myself hoping something—a sudden lead, anything—had spirited Milo away and I wouldn't have to wear my calm mask. But he was still sitting at the table, finishing the juice, looking too damn smug for someone working a whodunit with no clues.

"Bellyful of double-talk?" he said.

I shrugged. "So what's next?"

"More of the same, I guess . . . Doss is an interesting one. Little man behind a gigantic desk, his chair's elevated on some kind of pedestal. I'll bet he's one of those guys who believes intimidation is the ultimate orgasm. The power of positive domination. Yeah, I've definitely got to take a closer look at him."

"What about Roy Haiselden and Donny Mate?"

"Still looking for them, too. I lucked out and found Haiselden's gardener mowing the lawn. Haiselden didn't tell him to stop showing up."

"Keeping up appearances," I said.

"The utilities are also still on. Only the mail's been cut off. Waiting in the Westwood branch, general delivery. And Alice Z. was telling the truth about Haiselden being into laundromats. He's the registered owner of six, mostly on the Eastside—El Monte, Artesia, Pasadena."

"Collecting coins can be a dangerous business. Did he do it himself?"

"Don't know yet. All I've got is his business registration. Roy Haiselden d.b.a. Kleen-U-Up, Inc. As far as Donny Mate goes, there was no parole, he served his full sentence, was let straight out. Petra's asking about him. Thanks for brunch."

His hand landed on my shoulder. Lightly, very lightly, then he began to leave.

"Happy hunting," I said.

"I'm always happy when hunting."

15

Stacy's call came at four P.M. The connection was grainy and I wondered where she was. Had Richard given her her own little silver phone?

"Sorry for the inconvenience," she said, not sounding apologetic at all. Cool. The detachment was back.

"What happened, Stacy?"

"Don't you already know?" From cool to cold.

"Eric," I said.

"So my father was right."

"About what?"

"The cop who was here to talk to him. My father said he's your friend. He informs you, you inform him. Didn't you think that would be a *problem,* Dr. Delaware?"

"Stacy, I spoke to your father about that and he—"

"You didn't speak to *me* about it."

"We haven't spoken at all. I was planning to bring it up when you arrived."

"And if I told you I didn't like it?"

"Then I'd drop off the Mate investigation. That's exactly what I planned to do until your father asked me not to. He wanted me to continue."

"Why would he want that?"

"You'd have to ask him, Stacy."

"He told you to continue?"

"In no uncertain terms. Stacy, if it's a matter of trust—"

"I don't get it," she said. "When he told me about the cop, he seemed angry."

"At something Detective Sturgis did?"

"At being questioned like a criminal. And he's right. After all we went through with my mother, to be harassed by the police. And now I find out *you're* working *with* them. It just seems . . . wrong."

"Then I'm off the investigation."

"No," she said. "Don't bother."

"You're my patient, you come first."

Pause. "That's the other thing. I'm not sure I want to be your patient—nothing to do with you. I just don't see why I need therapy again."

"So the appointment was all your father's idea?"

"Same as all the other appointments—no, I don't mean that. Before, once I got into it, it was good. Great. You helped me. I'm coming across so rude, I'm sorry. I just don't see that I need any more help."

"Maybe not," I said. "But can we at least sit down once to discuss it? I've got time right now if you can make it over."

"I—I don't know. Things are pretty intense—what exactly did your cop friend tell you about Eric?"

"That Eric hadn't returned to his dorm for a couple of days. That he'd missed a test."

"More like a day and a half," she said. "It's probably no big deal, he was always going off on his own."

"Back when he was living at home?"

"Back to ninth or tenth grade. He'd cut school without explanation, take his bike somewhere, disappear all day. Later, he told me he used to check out used-book stores, play pool on the pier, or go over to the Santa Monica courts and listen to trials. The school used to phone, but Eric always got away with it because his grades were so much higher than anyone else's. Once he got his driver's license, he'd go away overnight, not come home till morning. *That* got to my father. Waking up in the morning and finding Eric's bed still made and Eric gone. Then Eric would drive up at breakfast time, start toasting Pop-Tarts, and the two of them would get into hassles, my father demanding to know where Eric had been, Eric refusing to say."

"Did your mother get involved?"

"When she was still healthy, she'd take my father's side. But Dad's always been the main one."

"Was Eric ever punished?"

"Dad made threats—kept warning he'd take away Eric's car keys, but Eric shined him on. Everyone knew he wouldn't follow through."

"Why not?"

"Because Eric's his golden boy. Any time Dad complains about him, all Eric has to say is, 'What? Aren't straight A's good enough? Want me to get higher than sixteen hundred on the SAT?' Same for Pali Prep. He was their big advertisement. Perfect GPA, Bank of America

Award winner, National Merit Scholar, Prudential Life Scholar, Science Achievement winner, hockey team, fencing team, baseball team. When he interviewed for Stanford, the interviewer called our headmaster and told him he'd just encountered one of the great minds of the century. So why would they want to tick him off?"

"So you're not worried about him," I said.

"Not really . . . The only thing that does bother me is his missing an exam. Eric always took care of business, academically speaking . . . Maybe he just decided to hike."

"Hike?"

"Back when he was living at home and stayed out all night, he'd sometimes come home with mud on his shoes, looking pretty dusty. At least one time I'm sure he was out camping. This was maybe a year ago, when he was home taking care of Mom. Our rooms are next to each other, and when he came in I woke up, went to see what was going on. He was folding up this nylon tent, had this backpack, bag of potato chips and candy, pepperoni sticks, whatever. I said, 'What's all this, some kind of loner-loser picnic?' He got angry and kicked me out of his room. So maybe that's what he did last night—went out hiking. There are lots of nice places around Palo Alto. Maybe he just wanted to get away from the city lights so he could look up at the stars. He used to love astronomy, had his own telescope, all these expensive filters, the works."

I heard her breath catch.

"What is it, Stacy?"

"I was just thinking . . . We had a dog, this yellow mutt named Helen that we got from the pound. Eric would take her with him on long walks, then she got old and lost the use of her legs and he built her a little wagon thingie and pulled her around—pretty funny-looking, but he took it seriously. She died—a short while before Mom. Eric stayed out all night with her. That's got to be what happened. When I asked him about it, he said he did his best thinking late at night, up in the mountains. So that's probably it, he's a little stressed, decided to try that. As far as the test, he probably figured he could talk his professor into a makeup—Eric can talk his way into anything."

"Why's he stressed?"

"I don't know." Long silence. "Okay, to be honest, Eric's having a *real* hard time. With Mom. He had a terrible time with it right from the beginning. Took it much worse than I did. Bet that's not what my father told you, though. Right?"

My son deals with his anger by organizing . . . I think it's a great way of handling stress . . . Get in touch with how you feel, then move on.

"We didn't discuss Eric in detail," I said.

"But I know," she said. "Dad thinks I'm the screwed-up one. Because I get low, while Eric does a great job of looking okay on the surface—keeping up his grades, staying achievement-oriented, saying the right things to my father. But I can see through that. *He's* the one who took it really hard. By the time my mother died, I'd already done my years of crying, but Eric kept trying to pretend nothing was wrong. Saying she'd get better. Sitting with Mom, playing cards with her. Acting happy, like nothing was any big deal. Like she just had a cold. I don't think he ever dealt with it. Maybe hearing about Dr. Mate brought the memories back."

"Did Eric talk about Mate?"

"No. We haven't talked at all, not for weeks. Sometimes he e-mails me, but I haven't heard from him in a while . . . One time—toward the end of my mother's . . . a few days before she died, Eric came into my room and found me crying, asked what was the matter. I said I was sad about Mom and he just *lost* it, started screaming that I was stupid, a wimp and a loser, that falling apart would accomplish nothing, I shouldn't be so selfish, thinking about my own feelings—*wallowing* in my feelings was the phrase he used. It was Mom's feelings I should be concentrating on. We all needed to be positive. To never give up."

"He was tough on you," I said.

"No big deal. He yells at me all the time, that's his style. Basically, he's this big huge brain machine with the emotions of a little kid. So maybe he's having some sort of delayed reaction, doing what he used to do when he got uptight. Do you think I *should* be worried about him?"

"No, but I think you did exactly the right thing by calling your father."

"Walking in on that detective . . . Guess what my father did? Chartered a plane and flew up to Palo Alto. He looked worried. And *that* bothers me."

"He doesn't get worried too often?"

"Never. He says anxiety is the province of fools."

I thought: The lack of anxiety is the province of psychopaths. Said, "So you're alone in the house."

"Just for a couple of days. I'm used to it, my father travels all the time. And Gisella—the maid—comes every day."

The phone cut in and out during the last sentence.

"Where are you, Stacy?"

"At the beach, some big parking lot on PCH. I must have driven here from Dad's office." She laughed. "Don't even remember. *That's* weird."

"Which beach?" I said.

"Um, let's see . . . There's a sign over there, says . . . Topanga . . . Topanga Beach. Kind of pretty out here, Dr. Delaware. Plenty of traffic on the highway, but no one on the sand—except for one guy walking around near the tide line . . . seems to be looking for something . . . he's holding some kind of a machine . . . looks like a metal detector . . . I know this place, you can see it from Dad's office."

Her voice had softened, turned dreamy.

"Stay right there, Stacy. I can be there in twenty, twenty-five minutes."

"There's no need," she said. It sounded like a policy statement.

"Humor me, Stacy."

Silence. Crackle. For a moment I thought I'd lost her. Then: "Sure. Why not? Got nowhere else to go."

I drove too fast, thinking about Eric. A brilliant, impetuous loner, used to getting his way. The one person who seemed able to elude Richard's dominance. Working hard at maintaining control, but powerless over what had mattered most: his mother's survival.

Close to his father, and his father despised Mate, expressed his hatred openly.

Eric. A hiker who disappeared when he wanted to, liked the mountains, knew the terrain. Dark, hidden places, like the dirt road stretch of Mulholland.

Impetuous enough to get violent? Smart enough to clean up thoroughly?

How far had filial devotion taken him?

After Joanne's death, Richard had tried to contact Mate, but the death doctor hadn't called back. Had Joanne warned Mate about Richard? Knowing Richard would fight her decision—that's why she'd kept it from him. From her children, as well.

But what if Mate *had* answered a call from Eric?

Poor, distraught kid wanting to talk about his mother's final passage. Had there been enough of the physician left in Mate to respond to a cry for help?

Dark BMW parked down the road.

Borrowing Daddy's car . . .

I kept racing west on Sunset, turning it over and over. Pure speculation, I'd never breathe a word to Milo or anyone else, but there was nothing that *didn't* fit.

A red light at Mandeville Canyon stopped the Seville, but my mind kept revving.

Stacy had offered a sibling's eloquence: a big brain machine combined with emotional immaturity.

Combined with boiling, adolescent rage. Perfect for the meld of compulsive planning and reckless daring that had transformed the brown van into a charnel house on wheels.

Broken stethoscope . . . *Beowulf. Happy Traveling, You Sick Bastard.*

Slaying the monster, as if it were just another myth— just another video game.

There was an adolescent feel to the phony book. To sneaking into Mate's flat and leaving a note. The message itself. Primitive gamesmanship, but backed up by an intellect that was starting to scare the hell out of me.

Where had Eric been last Sunday? The trip from Stanford to L.A. was no big deal, shuttles from San Francisco ran all day. Easy enough for a college student with a credit card. Do your business, jet back to school, show up for class as if nothing had happened.

But now the perfect student had missed a test for the first time. Unable to run from what he'd done? Or had some other stress worked apart the fissures that had spidered their way across the perfect porcelain image of the Doss family?

Richard jetting up to Stanford, leaving Stacy alone, sitting at the beach, oblivious . . . I sensed she'd always been alone. Squeakless wheel not getting any grease.

A car horn honked. The light had turned green but I'd sat there—obliviousness was contagious.

I shot forward, warning myself not to get caught up in it. Not good for the soul, all this hypothesizing. Besides, Milo had other suspects.

Roy Haiselden. Donny Mate.

Richard Doss.

None of the above? None of my business. Time to concentrate on what the state said I was qualified to do.

Stacy was easy to spot. Little white Mustang coupe facing the water, one of the few cars stationed in the city lot that paralleled the beach. Low tide, miles of beige kissing Wedgwood-blue water, all of it topped by the same clear sky as inland. The ocean was pretty but roiling. As I hooked across the highway and pulled onto the asphalt beside her, I saw the man with the metal detector, a hundred feet past Stacy's car, knees bent, hunched over a find.

Stacy's windows were closed. As I got out of the Seville, the driver's panel rolled down. She glanced at me, both hands on the steering wheel. Her face was thinner than six months ago. Deepened hollows around the cheeks, darkened flesh beneath the eyes, a few more pimples. No makeup. Her black hair was tied back in a ponytail, bound by a red rubber band.

"Didn't know doctors still did house calls." Weak smile. "Beach calls. I must have sounded pretty screwed up for you to drive all the way here. I'm sorry."

The man with the metal detector straightened, turned and faced us. As if he could hear our conversation. But of course he couldn't. Too far away and the ocean was roaring.

Before I could answer, Stacy said, "Why'd you come, Dr. Delaware? Especially after I snotted off to you like that."

"I wanted to make sure you were okay."

"You thought I'd do something stupid?"

"No," I said. "You sounded worried about Eric. You're by yourself. If there's some way I can help, I want to."

Her eyes faced forward and her hands whitened around the wheel. "That's . . . very sweet, but I'm fine . . . No, I'm not. I'm screwed up, aren't I? Even our dog was screwed up."

"Helen."

She nodded. "Two legs that couldn't move, and Eric pulled her around. That's why you drove all the way—you think I'm cracking up."

"No," I said. "I think you've got good insights."

She whipped around, stared at me. Laughed. "Maybe I should be a psychologist, then. Like Becky— not that she'd ever get to be one. Talk is, she's barely passing. That's got to be making Dr. Manitow and the judge real happy . . ."

"You sound angry at them," I said.

"I do? No, not at all. I'm a little resentful of *Becky*, turning into a total snob, never even saying hello. Maybe she's getting back at me for Eric. He and Allison Manitow were dating and Eric dumped her . . . but that was a long time ago . . . Why am I talking about this?"

"Maybe it's on your mind."

"No it's not. Helen is. After I told you about her on the phone, I started thinking about her." Laughter. "She had to be the dumbest mutt ever put on this earth, Dr. Delaware. Thirteen years old and she was never completely housebroken. When you gave her a command, she just sat there and stared at you with her tongue hanging out. Eric called her the Ultimate Canine Moron Alien from the Vortex of Idiocy. She used to jump on him and paw him and lick him and he'd say, Get a brain, bitch. But he ended up feeding her, walking her, cleaning up her poop. 'Cause Dad was too busy and Mom was too passive . . . That stupid little wagon he rigged up, it kept her alive. My father wanted to put her to sleep, but Eric wouldn't hear of it. Eventually, even with the wagon, she started failing. Toward the end, he was carrying her outside to poop, cursing the whole time. Then one night, he took her with him on one of his overnights. She looked awful—rotting gums, her hair was falling out in clumps. Even so, when Eric wheeled her out she looked thrilled—like, Oh boy, another adventure. They were out all night. The next morning Eric came home by himself."

She turned to me. "No one talked about it. A few weeks later, Mom died."

Her fingers snapped away from the steering wheel, as if shoved by an unseen demon, flew to her face, grabbing, concealing. She bent forward, touched her brow to the steering wheel. The ponytail bounced, black curls fibrillating. She shook like a wet puppy, and when she cried out the ocean blocked nearly all the sound. The man with the metal detector had moved fifty yards up the beach, back in his own world, hunched, probing.

When I reached through the window and placed a hand on Stacy's shoulder, she shivered, as if repulsed, and I withdrew.

All those years listening to people in pain and I can do it like a pro, but I've never stopped hating it. I stood there and waited as she sobbed and shuddered, voice tightening and rising in pitch until she was letting out the raw keen of a startled gull.

Then she stopped shaking, went silent. Her hands flipped upward, like visors, exposing her face, but she kept her head low, mumbled at the steering wheel.

I bent forward, heard her say, "Disappearing."

"What is?"

She shut her eyes, opened them, turned toward me. Heavy, labored movements.

"What?" she said sleepily.

"What's disappearing, Stacy?"

She gave a casual shrug. "Everything."

I didn't like the sound of her laughter.

Eventually, I convinced her to get out of the car and we strolled north on the asphalt, following the shoreline, not talking. The man with the metal detector was a pulsating speck.

"Buried treasure," she said. "That guy believes in it. I saw him up close, he's got to be seventy, but he's digging for nickels— Listen, I'm sorry for making you come all the way out here. Sorry for being bratty over the phone. For hassling you because you're working with the cops. You're entitled to do whatever work you want."

"It had to be confusing," I said. "Your father okayed it, but he didn't tell you. If he changed his mind, he didn't tell me."

"I don't know that he did. He was just getting peevy because the cop came to question him and he doesn't like not being in charge."

"Still," I said, "I think it's best that I drop off the—"

"No," she said. "Don't do it on my account. I don't care—it really doesn't matter. Who am I to take away your income?"

"It's no big deal, Stacy—"

"No. I insist. Someone killed that man and we should be doing everything we can to find out who it was."

We.

"For justice," she said. "For society's sake. No matter who he was. People can't get away with that kind of thing."

"How do you feel about Dr. Mate?"

"Don't feel much, one way or the other. Dr. Delaware, all those other times we talked, I was never really honest with you. Never talked about how screwed up our family is. But we are—no one really communicates. It's like we live together—exist together. But we don't . . . connect."

"Since your mother got sick?"

"Even before then. When I was young and she was healthy, we must have had fun together, but I don't remember. I'm not saying she wasn't a good mother. She did all the right things. But I never felt she . . . I don't know, it's hard to express. It's like she was made of air— you couldn't get hold of it . . . I just can't resolve what she did, Dr. Delaware. My dad and Eric blamed Mate, it was this big topic in our house, what a monster he was. But that's not true, they just can't deal with the truth: it was *her* decision, wasn't it?"

Turning to me. Wanting a real answer, not therapeutic reflection.

"Ultimately it was," I said.

"Mate was just the vehicle—she could have chosen anyone. She left because she just didn't care enough to keep trying. She made a *decision* to leave us, without saying good-bye."

Snapping her arms across her bust, she drew her shoulders forward, as if bound by the straps on a straitjacket.

"Of course," she said, "there was the pain, but . . . ." She chewed her lip. Shook her head.

"But what?" I said.

"With all that pain, she kept eating—she used to have such a good figure. That was always a big thing in the house—her figure, my father's physique. They both used to wear the skimpiest bathing suits. It was embarrassing. I remember once, the Manitows were over for a swim party and Mom and Dad were in the pool . . . groping each other. And Dr. Manitow was just staring.

Like, how tasteless—I guess that was good, though. Right? The fact that they were attracted to each other. My father would always talk about how they didn't age as quickly as everyone else, they'd always be kids. And then Mom just . . . *inflated* herself."

She took a step, put her foot down heavily, stopped again, fought back tears. "What's the use of going on and on about it? She did it, it's over, whatever . . . I have to keep thinking of the good memories, don't I? Because she *was* a good mother . . . I know that."

She edged closer to me. "Everyone talks about getting closure, moving on. But where do I go *to*, Dr. Delaware?"

"That's what we need to find out. That's why I'm here."

"Yes. You are." She surged forward, threw her arms around me. Her hands dug into my coat. Curly, shampooed hair—too-sweet shampoo, heavy with apricots—tickled my nose.

Someone watching from a distance would have thought, Romance on the beach.

The professional thing would be to pull away. I compromised, avoiding a full embrace by keeping one arm at my side. Patting her back lightly with the other.

What used to be called therapeutic touch, before the lawyers got involved.

I held her for the shortest possible period, then gently drew away.

She smiled. We resumed walking. Walked in step. I kept enough distance between us to avoid the accidental graze of hand against hand.

"College," she said, laughing. "That's what we were

supposed to be talking about this morning."

"College isn't all of your future, but it's part of it," I said. "Part of where to *go*."

"A small part. So no big deal, I'll make Dad happy, apply to Stanford. If I get in, I'll go. Why not? One place is the same as another. I'm not some spoiled brat. I know I'm lucky my dad can afford a place like that. But there are other things we need to talk about, right? If you trust me not to flake out, I can come in tomorrow—if you've got time."

"I've got time. How about after school—five P.M."

"Yes," she said. "Thank you so, so much . . . I'd better get back home, see if Dad called, maybe he found Eric—he'll probably just blow into the dorm and scream at my father for flying up."

We turned around.

Back at the Mustang, she said, "And I meant what I said—please don't stop working with the cops. Take care of *yourself*."

Nice kid.

I watched her drive away, eased onto PCH feeling pretty good.

16

When I got home, Robin was in the kitchen stirring a pot—one of those big blue things flecked with white. Spike was off in a corner, making rapturous overtures to a delicious-looking bone.

"You look tired," she said.

"Bad traffic." I kissed her cheek and looked inside the pot. Chunks of lamb, carrots, prunes, onions. My nose filled with cumin and cinnamon and heat, and my eyes watered.

"Something new," she said. "A tajine. Got the recipe from the guy who sells me maple."

I dipped the spoon, blew, tasted. "Fantastic, thank you, thank you, thank you."

"Hungry?"

"Starving."

"No sleep, no food." She sighed. "Bad traffic, where?"

I told her about having to meet a patient at the beach.

"Emergency?"

"Potentially, but it resolved." I placed my arms under her rear, lifted her, deposited her on the counter.

"What is this?" she said. "Passion amid the pots and pans, one of those male-fantasy things?"

"Maybe later. If you behave yourself." I went to the fridge, found some leftover white wine, sniffed the bottle, poured two glasses. "First we celebrate."

"What's the occasion?"

"No occasion," I said. "That's the point."

The rest of the evening passed quietly. No calls from Milo or anyone else. I tried to imagine what life would be like without a phone. We ate too much lamb, drank enough wine to get silly. The idea of making love seemed remote, more of a scripted segment than passion; both of us seemed content just to be.

So we just sat on the couch, holding hands, not moving, not talking. Would it be like this when we grew old? That prospect seemed suddenly glorious.

Eventually, something changed in the air, and we began touching each other, stroking, kissing, risking exploration. Eventually, we were naked, intertwined, moving from the couch to the floor, enduring chafed knees and elbows, strained muscles, ridiculous postures.

We ended up in bed. Afterward, Robin showered off, then announced she was going to do a bit of carving, did I mind?

After she left for the studio, I slouched in my big leather chair reading journals, Hawaiian slack-key guitar music droning in the background. For a while I did a pretty good job of forgetting. Then I was thinking about

Stacy again. Eric. Richard. The deterioration of Joanne Doss.

I considered calling Judy Manitow, tomorrow, to find out if she'd come up with any new insights since the original referral. Bad idea. Stacy might find that intrusive. And Stacy had told me enough for me to see that the Dosses and the Manitows had been entangled beyond mere neighborliness. Joanne tutoring Becky, Eric dumping Allison, Becky and Stacy drifting apart.

Bob regarding Richard and Joanne's displays of affection with distaste.

Judy and Bob, dealing with Becky's problems. Yet they'd cared enough about Stacy to pressure Richard to contact me.

Me, not Becky's therapist, because they'd been guarding their privacy—keeping Stacy's issues at arm's length from Becky's? Or had it been Becky's choice—Stacy had just told me Becky had distanced herself, barely spoke to her. Whatever the details, it was best to avoid further complications.

I got up and poured a finger of Chivas. Added to the wine, that put me way past my usual alcohol consumption. Some Hawaiian virtuoso let forth a glissando in C-wahine tuning and I thought about palm trees.

I finished the scotch and had another.

On Wednesday morning, I woke up with a well-deserved headache, an agreeably moldy tongue, sandpaper eyes. Robin was already out in back. I couldn't smell the coffee she'd put on.

I took a one-minute shower and got dressed without falling over, looked for the morning paper. Robin had been so eager to work that she hadn't taken it in. I went outside and retrieved it.

The front page screamed at me.

The Mysterious Portrait of Dr. Death

Sudden Appearance of Painting Raises
New Questions About Eldon Mate's Murder

SANTA MONICA. When Grant Kugler, owner of the Primal Images art gallery on Colorado Avenue, showed up last night to unpack an installation, he found a surprise donation propped against the rear door. A package, wrapped in brown paper, containing an original, unsigned oil painting described as a copy of Rembrandt's "The Anatomy Lesson." Only this version deviated from the original in that it depicted murdered "death doctor" Eldon Mate in a double role, as dissector and cadaver.

"Not the work of a master," opined Kugler. "I'd rate it competent. Why it ended up at my door, I can't say. I'm not one for representational art, though I can be amused by social commentary."

The article went on to quote "police sources who spoke on condition of not being named," and attested to "intriguing similarities between the painting and details of the Eldon Mate crime scene, raising questions about the identity of the artist and the motivations for abandoning the portrait. The picture has been taken into custody."

That conjured images of burly men trying to figure out a way of handcuffing the frame. I wondered how long it would take Milo to get in touch. I'd finished half a cup of coffee when the phone screeched.

"I assume you read," he said.

"Sounds like Zero Tollrance is in town."

"Tried to do some follow-up on that Colorado article you gave me. No one knows Tollrance, there was no lease on the building he used for his show because he was squatting in it, one of those big industrial shells full of lowlifes. I don't know if Tollrance was even living there. Denver PD never heard of him, and the critic who wrote up the show doesn't remember much other than Tollrance looked like a bum and didn't answer his questions—didn't talk at all, just pointed to his canvases and stomped away. He figured him for a nut. That's why he called it 'outsider art.' "

"A bum."

"Long hair and a beard. Mr. Critic said he had some 'primitive talent.' Said the same thing the gallery owner did—representation's not his thing. Which I guess means in the art world, if you know how to draw, you suck."

"So why'd he go to Tollrance's show?"

"Cuuuuurious. *Intriiiiigued.* Couldn't even get out of him how he found out about the show. Maybe Tollrance faxed him an announcement, maybe not. He said there hadn't been much of a crowd, no one buying. He never heard from Tollrance again, has no idea what happened to the paintings."

"Well, we know where one is," I said. "A bearded bum could be the same guy Mrs. Krohnfeld chased away. Could be Donny Salcido Mate."

"It crossed my mind," he said.

"Any idea where Donny was at the time of the show?"

"No, but it wasn't prison. He didn't get busted till four months later."

"His mother said by then he was living on the street,"
I said. "He could've drifted east, ended up in Colorado,
found himself a vacant building to pursue his art. Funny,
his mother never mentioned any talent. Then again, she
didn't want to talk about him at all."

"I called her at the motel. She checked out yesterday.
You're thinking Donny painted Daddy getting sliced up,
then maybe decided to act it out?"

"The paintings could've been yet another attempt to
establish a bond with Daddy. Selling *himself*. Maybe he
tried to show off to Mate and got rebuffed again."

"Why deliver the painting to the gallery?"

"He's an artist. He wants recognition. And look at the
painting he delivered. All the others were straight
portraits of Mate. *The Anatomy Lesson* put Mate on the
dissecting table."

"*Look what I did to Daddy.* Showing off."

"Just like the note. And the broken stethoscope."

"On the other hand," he said, "Tollrance could just
be another starving artist, and this is a pure publicity
stunt—taking advantage of Mate's murder to breathe
some life into a dead career. If so, it worked—here he is
on the front page, making my life difficult. If he shows up
tomorrow on TV with an agent and a publicist, scratch
the whole psychological scenario."

"Maybe," I said. "This *is* L.A. But if he doesn't
surface, that says something, too."

Three beats of silence. "Meanwhile, the painting's
resting comfortably in our evidence room. Care to see it?"

"Sure," I said. "Representation *is* my thing."

17

N ot half bad, but no Rembrandt," I said.

Milo ran his finger along the top of the canvas. We were in the Robbery-Homicide room, second story at West L.A. Half a dozen detectives hunched at their desks, a few sidelong stares as Milo propped the painting on his chair.

Zero Tollrance's masterpiece was all browns and blacks and muted light, just the merest wash of pink where the left arm of the man on the dissecting table had been reduced to tendons and ligaments.

Cadaver with the fussy, soft face of Eldon Mate. Even Tollrance's middling talent made that clear. Seven men, extravagantly robed and ruffed and goateed, surrounded the dissecting table, gazing down at the corpse with academic detachment. The dissector—another Mate—was clad in a black robe, white lace collar, tall black hat, probing the shredded arm with a scalpel, wearing a look of boredom.

In the original, the artist's genius had distracted from the cruelty of the scene. Tollrance's cartoon drove it home. Angry swirling brushstrokes, pigments laid on thickly to the point of impasto, sharp peaks of paint stabbing up from the surface of the canvas.

A smallish canvas—twenty-four by eighteen inches. I'd expected something far more grand.

Reducing Mate to size?

Milo lifted a stack of message slips, let them fall to the desk in disarray. "Kugler, the art dealer, has been bugging me all day. All of a sudden, he likes realism."

"Probably got an offer," I said. "Same guy who'll pay big bucks for a stained blue dress."

Phones rang, keys clicked, someone laughed. The room smelled of scorched coffee and gym sweat. "Got sleazeball talk shows wanting to interview me, too. And a six A.M. memo from the brass reminding me to keep my mouth shut."

"Tollrance has bought himself some celebrity, too," I said. "I wonder how long that'll satisfy him."

"Meaning he'll want true realism?"

I shrugged.

"Well," he said, "so far, he hasn't made any slipups." He tapped the upper edge of the painting. "Not a single print. Maybe you're right, a careful head case." He angled the painting toward me. "Does seeing this give you any other ideas?"

"Not really," I said. "Rage toward Mate. Ambivalence about Mate. You don't need me to tell you that."

His phone rang. "Sturgis— Oh yeah, hi." His expression brightened, as if an internal filament had ignited.

"Really? Thanks. When? . . . Sure, that would be better than convenient. I've got Dr. D. with me— Yeah, sure, great."

"Talk about karma," he said, hanging up. "That was Petra. Seems she came up with some stuff on Donny. She's on her way to a trial at the Santa Monica courthouse, will stop by in ten minutes. We'll meet her out in front."

We waited by the curb. Milo paced and smoked a Tiparillo and I thought about the Doss family. A few moments later, Petra Connor drove up in a black Accord, parked in the red zone, and got out with her usual economy of movement. I'd never seen her when she wasn't wearing a black pantsuit. This time it was a slim-cut thing with indigo overtones, some kind of slinky wool that flattered her long, lean frame and looked beyond a D-II's budget. On her feet were medium-heeled black lace-ups. Her black hair was cropped in the usual no-nonsense wedge cut, and slung across her shoulder was a black leather bag the texture of a wind-whipped motorcycle jacket. No gun visible beneath the tailored jacket, so she was probably toting it in the bag.

The bad September light was somehow kind to her ivory skin, setting off her tight jaw, pointed chin, ski-slope nose. Pretty, in a taut way, but something about her always warned, Keep Your Distance. The dedication with which she'd followed Billy Straight's recovery told me there was warmth tucked behind the searching brown eyes. But that was inference on my part; she was all business, never talked about herself. I figured she'd jumped high hurdles to get where she was.

"Hi," she said, flashing a cool smile, and I knew what I was supposed to ask.

"How's our guy?"

"Doing great from what I can tell. Straight A's, and he tested out a full grade ahead—amazing, considering most of what he knows is self-taught. A true intellectual, just like you said at the beginning."

"What about his ulcer?" I said.

"Clearing up slowly. He fusses about taking his medicine, but for the most part he's compliant. He's also making some friends. Finally. Other 'creative' types, quoth the principal. Mrs. Adamson's big worry is he doesn't want to do much other than study and read and play with his computer."

"What would she prefer him to do?"

"I'm not sure there's anything specific—she just seems to be nervous. About doing everything right. I think she feels she needs to report to me. She calls me once a week."

"Hey, you're the long arm of the law," I said.

Small smile. "I know she really cares about him. I tell her not to worry, he'll be fine."

She blinked, wanting confirmation.

"Good advice," I said.

Rosy coins appeared on her cheeks. "All in all he's getting plenty of attention. Maybe too much, considering that he's basically a loner? Sam shows up like clockwork on Friday, takes him to Venice on weekends. San Marino all week, then the freak scene. How's that for contrast?"

"Multicultural experience. I'm sure he can handle it."

"Yes—good. If any problems come up, I assume it's okay to call you."

"Anytime."

"Thanks." She turned to Milo. "Sorry, I know you're waiting for this." Out of the leather bag came a folder. "Here's the info on your Mr. Salcido. Turns out he's a known quantity to us. Because of the Hollywood redevelopment thing, Councilwoman Goldstein's office ordered us to keep tabs on transients—the Bum Squad, we called it, lasted a month. Salcido's name came up in one Bum Squad file. No arrest, all they did was canvass squats, find out what the squatters were up to. If they saw drugs or any other crime, they could make an arrest, but basically it was to appease Councilwoman Goldstein."

Milo flipped the chart open. Petra said, "Salcido was living in an abandoned building near Western and Hollywood—the one with the big frieze in front, I think Louis B. Mayer or some other film type built it. Later, the Bummers found out he had a felony record and noted it accordingly."

"Our tax dollars at work." Milo thumbed the pages of the file. "Was he living alone?"

"Unless a known associate is noted, he probably was."

"Says they found him in 'a room full of garbage.'"

"As you see, he claimed to be gainfully employed but couldn't produce backup. The squad pegged him as mentally ill, probably a dope fiend, suggested he seek some help at a community MH center. He refused."

"Why didn't the squad evict him?"

"Without a complaint from the owner, no grounds. I stopped off at the building this morning but he's gone, everyone is. Just construction workers, big remodeling project. Sorry it's not more."

"Hey, it's something—thanks for taking the time," said Milo. "Squatting by himself . . ."

I knew he was thinking about the abandoned building in Denver. He turned a page. "No mug shot?"

"The Bummers didn't carry cameras. But look at the back page, I got a booking photo faxed down from Marin County Jail, not terrific quality."

Milo found the shot, studied it, showed it to me.

Eldon Salcido Mate, freshly inducted to penal custody, numbered plaque dangling from a chain around his neck, the mandatory sullen stare leavened by a hard, hot light in the eyes that might've been madness, or just the glare of the room.

Long, stringy hair but clean-shaven. Light-complected, as Guillerma Salcido had said. Round face, weak around the jowls. Small, prissy features that could've made incarceration a greater-than-usual challenge. Premature wrinkles. A young man aging too fast.

Striking resemblance to a face on a dissecting table; Guillerma Salcido Mate had been right. Donny was his father's son.

Milo read some more. "Says here he claimed to be working in a tattoo parlor on the Boulevard, didn't remember which one."

"I tried a few places, no one knows him. But the jailer up in Marin said Salcido had done some skin work on other inmates, that was probably what kept him safe."

"Safe from what?" I said.

"The jail's organized along gang lines," she said. "Someone without affiliation is fair prey unless they've got something to offer. Salcido sold his art, but the jailer said no one wanted him in their group because he was seen as a mental case."

"Tattoos," said Milo. "The boy likes to draw."

Petra nodded. "I read about the painting. You're thinking it's him?"

"Seems like a good bet."

"What's the painting like?"

"Not what I'd want in my dining room." Milo shut the file. "You're an artist, aren't you?"

"Not hardly."

"Come on, I've seen your stuff."

"My past life," she insisted.

"Want to see it?"

She looked at her watch. "Sure, why not?"

She held it at arm's length. Squinted. Turned it around, inspected the sides. Placed it on the floor and backed away ten feet before returning to get another close look.

"He really slapped on the paint," she said. "Looks like he worked quickly here—probably a palette knife as well as a brush . . . here, too . . . fast but not sloppy, the composition's actually pretty good—he got the proportions just about right."

She turned away from the painting. "This is only a guess, but what I see here is someone alternating between careful draftsmanship and abandon—at some point he planned meticulously, but once he got into the groove he gave himself over to it."

Milo frowned, then glanced at me.

"Anyway," said Petra. "So much for art criticism."

"What does that mean?" Milo asked her. "Being careful and then cutting loose."

"That he's like most artists."

"You see any talent here?"

"Oh sure. Nothing staggering, but he can render. Plenty of ambition, too—redoing Rembrandt."

"Rembrandt and tattoos," said Milo.

"If Salcido did tattoos well enough to keep himself out of trouble in prison, he's got to be pretty good. Skin work's challenging, you have to get a feel for the changing density of the epidermis, movement, resistance to the needle."

Now she was flushed pink.

Milo smiled. "I'm not even going to ask."

She smiled back. "High school. Anyway, got to run. Hope it helps."

"I owe you, Petra."

"I'm sure I'll find a way to collect." Shifting her bag to her other shoulder, she moved toward the stairs. "I wish I could tell you we'll have our eyes peeled for Salcido, Milo, but you know how it is—sorry to run."

"Good luck in court," said Milo.

"Hopefully I won't need luck. No-brainer shooting that got transferred to SM because downtown's back-logged with potential three-strikers. Unattractive defendant, inexperienced public defender with a caseload as long as *The English Patient*. Today I will triumph! Nice to see you, Doctor—let's keep rooting for Billy."

Back to Milo's desk. During the time we'd spent with Petra, a new message slip had been added to the stack.

"Special Agent Fusco again. The painting probably heated up *his* attention-seeking blood." He tossed the slip, looked across the room.

Detectives Korn and Demetri were headed our way. They stopped at the desk, glaring, as if it was a barrier to freedom. Milo made the introductions. They nodded stiffly, didn't offer their hands. Demetri's eyeglasses were slightly askew and his bald head was sunburned and peeling.

"What's up, gentlemen?"

"Nothing," said Demetri. He had one of those voices so low it sounded electronically manipulated. "That's the problem."

Korn ran his finger under his collar. His blow-dried hair seemed an affront to his partner's tonsure. "Nothing with *whipped* cream and a cherry," he said. "We spent all morning at Haiselden's neighborhood. Found the gardener, big deal. Haiselden's paid up for the month, guy has no idea where señor is, couldn't give a *shit* where señor *went*. Haiselden's mail is piling up at the Westwood post office, but we can't get hold of it without a warrant. You want us to do that?"

"Yes," said Milo.

"Figures."

"Problem, Steve?"

"No. No problem at all." Korn played with his collar again. Demetri removed his glasses and wiped them on a corner of his sport coat.

"Don't lose heart, boys," said Milo. "Haiselden's mail stop shows he definitely rabbited. So keep on him—who knows, you might solve this one."

A glance passed between the two detectives. Demetri shifted his weight to his left leg. "That's assuming Haiselden has anything to do with Mate. We discussed it and we're not convinced he does."

"Why's that, Brad?"

"There's sure no evidence in that direction. Besides,

it doesn't make sense. Haiselden made money from Mate. Why would he off his meal ticket? We figure he just went on a vacation—probably got depressed *because* he lost his meal ticket."

"Taking some time off to reflect," said Milo.

"Right."

"Diagnosis of depression, he decided to deal with his feelings on some sunny beach."

Demetri looked at Korn for support. Korn said, "Makes sense to me." His jaw tightened. "With all the publicity over Mate, maybe Haiselden wants time to sort things out. Face it, you've got nothing on his being dirty."

"Nothing at all," said Milo. "Except for the fact that he was a damn publicity hound who rabbited during what has to be the most public moment of his life."

Neither of the younger men spoke.

"Okay then," said Milo. "So how about you write up that warrant for his mail, see if you can get hold of his credit card bills, too. Maybe there'll be a travel agent charge somewhere in there and you can verify your vacation hypothesis."

Another passed glance. Demetri said, "Yeah, sure, whatever you say. We figured we'd hit the gym first. All the hours we've been puttin' in, we haven't had a chance to work out."

"Sure. Get yourselves a coupla Jamba Juices afterward—make sure they put plenty of enzymes in them."

"Something else," said Demetri. "That painting, we just saw it. Real piece of shit, if you ask me."

"Everyone's a critic," said Milo.

CHAPTER

18

hat now?" I said.

"If those two manage to write a decent warrant application, I'll have a look at Haiselden's mail. More likely, I'll be correcting their grammar. Meantime, I'm gonna check out art galleries, tattoo parlors, see if anyone else knows Donny, as himself or Tollrance. The fact that he chose a Santa Monica gallery might mean he left Hollywood and is squatting somewhere on the Westside. There are a few abandoned buildings in Venice I want to take a look at."

"Are you liking him better than Haiselden because of the painting?"

"That, his felony record, and what Petra said about the combination of cleverness and psychosis—your hypothesis. With Haiselden, all I've got is his rabbiting, for all I know those two La-Z-Boys could be right and it's one big goose chase, but let them prove it to me." He stood. "As good a time as any to heed the call of nature. 'Scuse me."

He loped toward the men's room and I used his phone to call in for messages.

Two requests for consults from judges that had come in during my ride to the station, and Richard Doss's office wanting me to call—that one was less than five minutes old.

Richard's secretary—the same woman who'd treated me like hired help yesterday—thanked me for getting back *so* soon and asked me to *please* hold for just *one* second. Before her words had faded, Richard came on.

"Thank you," he said, in a tone I'd never heard. Hoarse, faltering, tentative. Both volume and tone controls switched to low.

"What's up, Richard?"

"I found Eric. This morning, four A.M., on campus, he never left, was sitting in an out-of-the-way spot, under a tree. He'd been there for a long time, just sitting, won't say why. He refuses to talk to me at all. I did manage to get him back on the plane, brought him back to L.A. He's missing all kinds of exams, but I don't give a goddamn about that. I'd like you to see him. *Please*."

"Does Stacy know about this?"

"I knew you'd be concerned about sibling rivalry, or whatever, so I asked her if you could see Eric and she said sure—if you want to verify that, I'll get her on another line."

Voice straining—a man racing against something inexorable.

"No, that's all right, Richard," I said. "Have you had Eric examined medically?"

"No, there wasn't a scratch on him. It's his psychological status I'm worried about. Let's do it sooner rather than later, okay? This isn't Eric. He's always been the— Never lost his productivity. Whatever the hell's going on, I don't like it. When should we set it up?"

"Bring him by this afternoon. But please have a physician check him out first. Just to make sure we're not missing something."

Silence. "Sure. Whatever you say. Are there any particular tests you want?"

"Check for head trauma, fever, acute infection."

"Fine, fine—what time?"

"Let's plan on four."

"That's nearly four hours from now."

"If the doctor finishes sooner, call me. I'll stay close. Where's Eric now?"

"Right here, in my office. I've got him in the conference room. One of my girls is keeping him company."

"He hasn't said anything since you found him?"

"Not a word, just sitting there—this is so damned neurotic, but I can't help thinking this is what Joanne did. The way she started. Pulling away."

"When you touch Eric or move him, how's his muscle tone?"

"Fine, it's not like he's catatonic or anything. He looks me in the eye, I can tell he's all there. He just won't talk to me. Shutting me out. I don't like this one damn bit. One more thing: I don't want Stanford to know about this, see him as damaged goods. The only one who knows so far is that Chinese kid, the roommate, and I let *him* know it would be in all our interests to keep this close to the vest."

Click.

Milo entered the room. Before he reached the desk, another detective pulled a sheet out of the fax machine and handed it to him.

"Look at this," he said, bringing it over. "Further communication from Agent Fusco. Persistent little civil servant, ain't he?"

He placed the fax on the desk. Reprint of a news item, dated fifteen months earlier, datelined Buffalo, New York.

Doctor Suspected in Attempted Murder

An emergency room physician who allegedly laced the drink of a former supervisor with poison is being sought by police. Michael Ferris Burke, 38, is suspected of concocting a lethal combination of toxic materials in an attempt to murder Selwyn Rabinowitz, chairman of the Department of Emergency Medicine at Unitas Critical Care Center in Rochester. Burke had recently been placed on suspension by Rabinowitz due to "questionable medical practices" and had made veiled threats to his superior. Rabinowitz drank one sip of the doctored coffee and grew ill almost immediately. Suspicion fell on Burke because of the threats and due to the fact that the suspended doctor had left town. Several syringes and vials were recovered from a locker in the physicians' lounge at Unitas, but police refuse to say if they belonged to Burke. Rabinowitz remains hospitalized in stable condition.

Below the article, a few lines of neat, upright handwriting:

Detective Sturgis:
You might want to know more about this.
Lem Fusco

"So what's he saying?" said Milo. "This has something to do with Mate?"

"Burke," I said. "Why's that name familiar?"

"Hell if I know. I'm getting to the point where everything sounds familiar."

I gave the clipping another read. Something came into focus. "Where's the material I pulled off the Internet?"

He opened a drawer, searched for a while, pulled out more papers, produced the printouts. I found what I was looking for right away. "Here you go. Another upstate New York story. Rochester. Roger Sharveneau, the respiratory tech who confessed to poisoning ICU patients, then recanted. Months later, he claimed to have been under the influence of a Dr. Burke, whom no one had ever seen. No sign anyone followed up on that, probably because Sharveneau's pattern of confessing and recanting led them to believe he'd made it all up. But *this* Dr. Burke was working in Buffalo, sixty, seventy miles away, and getting into mischief. Poison mischief, and Sharveneau died of an overdose."

Milo exhaled. "Okay," he said. "I give in. S.A. Fusco gets his meeting. Want to come?"

"If it's soon," I said. "I've got an appointment at four."

"Appointment for what?"

"What they sent me to school for."

"Oh yeah, you do that occasionally, don't you." He punched the number Fusco'd listed on the fax, got through, listened.

"Taped message," he said. "Hey, personalized for me . . . If I'm interested, meet him at Mort's Deli on Wilshire and Wellesley in Santa Monica. He'll be the one with the boring tie."

"What time?"

"He didn't specify. He knew I'd call after I got the fax, is confident I'll show up. I just love being played." He put on his jacket.

"What key?" I said.

"D minor. As in detective. As in dumb. But why the hell not, the deli's not far from those squats in Venice. How about you?"

"I'll take my own car."

"Sure," he said. "That's how it starts. Soon you'll be wanting your own dish and spoon."

CHAPTER

19

The exterior of Mort's Deli was a single cloudy window over a swath of brown board below red-painted letters proclaiming lunch for $5.99. The interior was all yellows and scarlets, narrow black leatherette booths, wallpaper that looked inspired by parrot plumage, the uneasily coexisting odors of fried fish, pickle brine and overripe potatoes.

Leimert Fusco was easy to spot, with or without neckwear. The only other patron was an ancient woman up in front spooning soup into a palsying mouth. The FBI man was three booths back. The tie was gray tweed—same fabric and shade as his sport coat, as if the jacket had given birth to a nursing pup.

"Welcome," he said, pointing to the sandwich on his plate. "The brisket's not bad for L.A." In his fifties, the same gravel voice.

"Where's the brisket better?" said Milo.

Fusco smiled, showed lots of gum. His teeth were huge, equine, white as hotel sheeting. Short, bristly white hair rode low on his brow. Long, heavily wrinkled face, aggressive jaw, big bulbous nose. The tail end of his fifties. The saddest brown eyes I'd ever seen, nearly hidden by crepey folds. He had broad shoulders and wide hands. Seated, he gave the impression of bulk and frustrated movement.

"Meaning, where am I from?" he said. "Most recently Quantico. Before that, all kinds of places. I learned about brisket in New York—where else? Spent five years at the main Manhattan office. Those qualifications good enough for you to sit down?"

Milo slid into the booth and I followed.

Fusco looked me over. "Dr. Delaware? Excellent. My doctorate's not in clinical. Personality theory." He twisted the tweed tie. "Thanks for coming. I won't insult your intelligence by asking how you're doing on Mate. You're here because even though you think it's a waste of time, you're not in a position to refuse data. Want to order something, or is this going to remain at the level of testosterone-laden watchfulness?"

"So how do you really feel about life?" said Milo.

Fusco gave another toothy grin.

"Nothing for me," Milo said. "What's with this Burke?"

A waitress approached. Fusco motioned her away. Next to his sandwich was a tall glass of cola. He sipped, put the glass down silently.

"Michael Ferris Burke," he said, as if delivering the title of a poem. "He's like the AIDS virus: I know *what* he is, know what he *does*, but I can't get hold of him."

Gazing pleasantly at Milo. I wondered if the AIDS reference went beyond general metaphor.

Milo's expression said he thought it did. "We've all got our problems. Want to fill me in, or just bitch?"

Fusco kept smiling as he reached down to his left and produced a brick-red accordion file folder, two inches thick and fastened with string.

"Copy of the Burke file for your perusal. More accurately, the Rushton file. He went to med school as Michael Ferris Burke, but he was born Grant Huie Rushton. There are a few other monikers in between. He likes to reinvent himself."

"So now he can get a job in Hollywood," said Milo.

Fusco pushed the file closer. Milo hesitated, then pulled it over and placed it on the seat between us.

Fusco said, "If you want a capsule summary, I'll give you one."

"Go ahead."

The muscles of Fusco's left eyelid twitched before settling. "Grant Huie Rushton was born forty years ago in Queens, New York. Flushing, to be exact. Full-term birth, no complications, only child. The parents were Philip Walter Rushton, a tool-and-die maker, age twenty-nine, and Lorraine Margaret Huie, twenty-seven, a housewife. When the boy was two, both parents were killed in an accident on the Pennsylvania Turnpike. Little Grant was shipped off to Syracuse to be raised by his maternal grandmother, Irma Huie, a widow with a history of alcoholism."

Fusco's hands rubbed together. "Logic and psychology tell me Rushton's problems had to begin early, but getting hold of childhood records that document his pathology has been difficult because he never received professional help. I located some grade-school reports that note 'disciplinary problems.' He wasn't a sociable child, so locating peers who remember him clearly has been a problem. A trip I made to his Syracuse neighborhood several years ago unearthed some people who remember the boy as bright and talented and major-league mean—'malicious' is the word that keeps cropping up."

He ticked his left index finger with its right-hand counterpart. "Cruelty to animals, bullying other kids, suspicions of neighborhood pranks and thefts and burglaries. The grandmother was an inept parent, and Grant had free rein. He was smart enough to avoid getting caught, has no juvenile record that I can find. His high-school yearbook entry—a copy's in there—lists no extracurricular activities or honors. He graduated with a B average, which for him was no challenge, he could've done that in his sleep. A few Unsatisfactories in conduct but no suspensions or expulsions." To me: "You know the data on psychopaths, Doctor. High IQ can be protective. Grant Rushton knew how to keep his impulses under control, even back then. Precisely when he went all the way is unclear, but when he was eighteen, a fourteen-year-old girl—a neighbor—disappeared. Her body was found two months later in a forested area on the outskirts of town. Decomposition was advanced and precise cause of death was never determined, but the autopsy did reveal head trauma and neck wounds and sexual exploration without actual rape. The investigation never got very far and no suspects were ever named."

"Was Rushton questioned?" said Milo.

"No. After the girl—Jennifer Chapelle—was found, Rushton graduated and joined the navy. Basic training in California—Oceanside. Honorable discharge after only two months. Military records have proven to be less than precise. All I've been able to learn is that he went AWOL once and they let him go."

"That merits honorable?" I said.

"In a volunteer military, sometimes it does. During the time he was stationed at Oceanside, a prostitute named Kristen Strunk was chopped up and dumped a mile from the base. Another unsolved."

"Same question," said Milo. "Was Rushton ever considered a suspect?"

Fusco shook his head. "Bear with me. After his discharge, Grant Rushton died: single-car crash off the old Route 66 in Nevada. Burned-up auto, charred corpse."

"Same death as his parents," I said.

Fusco's sad eyes glowed.

Milo said, "What are you saying? A body switch?"

"The corpse was never examined closely—we're talking french fry. It wasn't till years later, when I matched Rushton's navy prints to those of Michael Burke, that I came across the switch. By that time, it was too late to learn anything about who really got burned. The owner was an accountant from Tucson, driving to Vegas with his wife. The car was hot-wired while they sat at a truckstop eating burgers."

"Any idea who got burned?" said Milo.

Fusco shook his head and looked over his shoulder again. "No sign of Rushton for a year and a half. I figure he copped one or more false identities and traveled

around for a while. The next time I can tag him he was
living in Denver and going by the name of Mitchell Lee
Sartin, a student at Rocky Mountain Community College,
majoring in biology. The print backtrack verifies Sartin as
Rushton. He applied for a job as a security guard, got his
fingers inked. The Sartin I.D. was one of those graveyard
switcheroos—the real Mitchell was buried twenty-two
years before, in Boulder. Sudden infant death, three
months old."

"And no reason for the security firm to cross-
reference with the navy," said Milo.

"Not hardly. Those guys have been known to hire
schizophrenics. The prints were checked with local
felony files, where, of course, they didn't show up. Sartin
got a job patrolling a pharmaceutical company at night.
By day, he attended classes. He lasted one semester—
straight A's. Life sciences and a course in human figure
drawing."

"Drawing," I said. "Is that what you meant by
talented?"

Fusco nodded. "A couple of his former schoolmates
remember him as a great doodler—cartoons, mostly.
Obscene stuff, making fun of teachers, other authority
figures. He never worked for the school paper. Never
chose to *affiliate*."

He took a long drink of cola. "During Sartin's enrollment at Rocky Mountain CC, two female students went
missing. One was eventually found up in the mountains,
dead, sexually abused and mutilated. The other girl's
whereabouts remain unknown. This was the first time
Grant Rushton/Mitchell Sartin attracted any attention
from law enforcement. He was among several individuals

questioned by the Denver police because he'd been seen talking to one of the girls in the college cafeteria the day before she disappeared. But it was just a routine interview, no reason to check further. Sartin didn't re-enroll, left town. Disappeared."

"All this within two years of high-school graduation?" I said. "He was only twenty?"

"Correct," said Fusco. "Precocious lad. The next few years are another cloudy area. I can't prove it, but I know he returned to Syracuse to visit Grandma a year later. Though no one remembers seeing him."

"Something happened to Grandma," said Milo.

Fusco's lips curled inward. He ran a hand over the white bush atop his head. "One of those Syracuse winters, late at night, Grandma drove her car into a tree on a rural road and went through the windshield. Her blood alcohol was just over the limit and an empty brandy bottle was found on the front seat. By the time they found her body, it was frozen stiff. No reason to think it was anything other than a single-driver DUI thing, except for the fact that Grandma was a stay-at-home drinker, never went out at night. Rarely drove, period. No one could explain why she'd taken the car out in a freezing storm or why she was out in the sticks, a good fifteen miles from her house. No one also thought to question why, with that kind of impact, the bottle would be right there on the seat. Irma Huie didn't leave much of an estate—her place was rented, she kept no bank accounts. The police didn't find any money, not a penny in the cookie jar. Which I find curious because she'd lived on pension money from her husband and Social Security income, and her landlord said she kept cash around, he'd seen wads of bills bound by rubber bands. A year later, Mitchell Sartin surfaced as Michael Ferris Burke and enrolled in City University of New York as a sophomore pre-med major. He presented a transcript—later shown to be forged—from Michigan State University, claiming a year of courses, GPA of 3.8. CUNY bought it. Burke gave his age as twenty-six—to match the stats on another I.D. he'd cribbed, this time from a dead baby in Connecticut. But he was only twenty-two."

"He bought himself some time with Grandma's money?" I said. "But he made no attempt to claim the pension or the Social Security payments."

"He knows how to be careful," said Fusco. "That's why there are periods in his life I just can't tag, and a lot of what I'm going to tell you won't go beyond theory and guesses. But have I said anything, so far, that doesn't make sense from a psychological standpoint, Doctor?"

"Go on," I said.

"Let me backtrack. During the year between Irma Huie's death in Syracuse and Michael Burke's enrollment at CUNY, two clusters of mutilation murders occurred that bear marked similarities to the particulars of the Denver victim. The first popped up in Michigan. Beginning four months after Mitchell Sartin left Colorado, three coeds were attacked in Ann Arbor. All were jogging at night on pathways near the University of Michigan campus. Two were ambushed from behind by a man wearing a ski mask, knocked to the ground, punched in the face till semiconscious, then raped, stabbed and slashed with a sharp knife—probably a surgical scalpel. Both escaped with their lives when other joggers happened upon the scene, and the assailant fled into the bushes. The third girl wasn't so lucky. She was taken three months later, by the time some of the campus panic generated by the first two attacks had died down. Her body was found near a reservoir, badly mutilated."

"Mutilated in what way?" I said.

"Extensive abdominal and pelvic cutting. Wrists and ankles bound to a tree with a thick hemp rope. Breasts removed, skin peeled from the inner thighs—your basic sadistic sexual surgery. Subdural hematomas from head wounds that might've eventually proven fatal. But arterial spurts on the tree said she'd been alive while being cut. The official cause of death was bleeding out from a jugular slash. Shreds of blue paper were found nearby and the Ann Arbor investigators matched it, eventually, to disposable surgical scrub suits used at that time at the University of Michigan Medical Center. That led to numerous interviews with med-school staff and students, but no serious leads developed. The surviving girls could only give a sketchy description of the attacker: male Caucasian, medium-size, very strong. He never spoke or showed his face, but one of them remembers seeing white skin between his sleeve and his glove. His modus was to throw a choke hold on them as he hit them from behind, then flip them over and punch them in the face. Three very hard blows in rapid succession." Fusco's fist smacked into an open hand. Three loud, hollow reports. The old woman drinking soup didn't turn around.

"'Calculated,' one of the surviving victims called it. A girl named Shelly Spreen. I had the chance to interview her four years ago—fourteen years after the attack. Married, two kids, a husband who loves her like crazy. Reconstructive facial surgery restored most of her looks, but if you see pre-attack pictures, you know it didn't do the trick completely. Gutsy girl, she's been one of the few people willing to talk to me. I'd like to think talking about it helped her out a little."

"Calculated," I said.

"The way he hit her—silently, mechanically, methodically. She never felt he was doing it out of anger, he always seemed to be in control. 'Like someone going about his business,' she told me. Ann Arbor did a competent job, but once again, no leads. I had the luxury of working backward—focusing on young men in their twenties, possibly security guards, or university employees who'd left town shortly after, then dropped completely out of sight. The only individual who fit the bill was a fellow named Huey Grant Mitchell. He'd worked at the U. Mich medical school, as an orderly on the cardiac unit."

I said, "Grant Huie Rushton plus Mitchell Sartin equals Huey Grant Mitchell—wordplay instead of a graveyard switch."

"Exactly, Doctor. He loves to play. The Mitchell I.D. was created out of whole cloth. The job reference he gave—a hospital in Phoenix, Arizona—turned out to be bogus, and the Social Security number listed on his employment application was brand-new. He paid for his Ann Arbor single with cash, left behind no credit card receipts—no paper trail of any kind, except for a single employment rating: he'd been an excellent orderly. I think the switch from graveyard hoax to brand-new I.D. represents a psychological shift. Heightened confidence."

Fusco pushed his Coke glass away, then the half-eaten sandwich. "Something else leads me to think he was stretching. Craving a new game. During the time he worked the cardiac floor, several patients died suddenly and inexplicably. Sick but not terminally ill patients who could've gone either way. No one suspected anything—no one realizes anything, to this day. It's just something that turned up when I was digging."

"He cuts up girls and snuffs ICU patients?" said Milo. "Versatile."

Any trace of amiability left Fusco's face. "You have no idea," he said.

"You're talking nearly two decades of bad stuff and it's never come out? What, one of those covert federal things? Or are you out to write a book?"

"Look," said Fusco, jawbones flexing. Then he smiled, sat back. Let his eyes disappear in a mass of folds. "It's covert because I've got nothing to go overt. Air-sandwich time. I've only been on it for three years."

"You said two clusters. Where and when was the second?"

"Back here, in your Golden State. Fresno. A month after Huey Mitchell left Ann Arbor, two more girls were snagged off hiking trails, two weeks apart. Both were found tied to trees, cut up nearly identically to the Colorado and the Michigan vics. A hospital orderly named Hank Spreen left town five weeks after the second body turned up."

"Spreen," I said. "Shelly Spreen. He took his *victim's* name?"

Fusco grinned horribly. "Mr. Irony. Once again, he got away with it. Hank Spreen had worked at a private hospital in Bakersfield specializing in cosmetic work, cyst removals, that kind of thing. It was a big surprise when three post-op patients had sudden reversals and died in the middle of the night. Official cause: heart attacks, idiopathic reactions to anesthesia. That happens, but not usually three times in a row over a six-month period. The publicity helped close the hospital down, but by then Hank Spreen was long gone. The following summer, Michael Burke showed up at CUNY."

"Long body list for a twenty-two-year-old," I said.

"A twenty-two-year-old smart enough to make it through pre-med and med school. He worked his way through by holding down a job as a lab assistant to a biology professor—basically a nighttime bottle washer, but he didn't need much income, lived in student housing. Had Grandma's dough. Pulled a 3.85 GPA—from what I can tell, he really earned those grades. Summers, he worked as an orderly at three public hospitals—New York Medical, Middle State General and Long Island General. He applied to ten med schools, got into four, chose the University of Washington in Seattle."

"Any coed murders during his pre-med period?" said Milo.

Fusco licked his lips. "No, I can't find any definite matches during that time. But there was no shortage of missing girls. All over the country, bodies that never showed up. I believe Rushton/Burke kept on killing but hid his handiwork better."

"You believe? This joker's a homicidal psychopath and he just changes his ways?"

"Not his ways," said Fusco. "His mode of expression. That's what sets him apart. He can let loose his impulses along with the bloodiest of them, but he also knows how to be careful. Exquisitely careful. Think about the patience it took to actually become a doctor. There's something else to consider. During his New York period, he may have diverted his attention from rape/murder to the parallel interest he'd developed in Michigan and continued in Bakersfield: putting hospital patients out of their misery. I know they seem like different patterns, but what they've got in common is a lust for power. Playing God. Once he learned all about hospital systems, playing ward games would've been a snap."

"How is he supposed to have killed all those patients?" said Milo.

"There are any number of ways that make detection nearly impossible. Pinching off the nose, smothering, fooling with med lines, injecting succinyl, insulin, potassium."

"Any funny stuff go down at the three hospitals where Burke spent his summers?"

"New York's the worst place to obtain information. Large institutions, lots of regulations. Let's just say I have learned of several questionable deaths that occurred on wards where Burke was assigned. Thirteen, to be exact."

Milo pointed down at the file folder. "All this is in here?"

Fusco shook his head. "I've limited my written material to data, no supposition. Police reports, autopsies, et cetera."

"Meaning some of your stuff was obtained illegally, so it can never be used in court."

Fusco didn't reply.

"Pretty dedicated, Agent Fusco," said Milo. "Cowboy stuff's not exactly what I'm used to when dealing with Quantico."

Fusco flashed those big teeth of his. "Pleased to bust your stereotype, Detective Sturgis."

"I didn't say *that*."

The agent leaned forward. "I can't stop you from being hostile and distrustful. But, really, what's the point of playing uptight-local-besieged-by-the-big-bad-Fed? How many times does someone offer you this level of information?"

"Exactly," said Milo. "When something seems to be too good to be true, it usually is."

"Fine," said Fusco. "If you don't want the file, give it back. Good luck chipping away at Dr. Mate. Who, by the way, began his own little death trip around the same time Michael Burke/Grant Rushton decided to seriously pursue a career in medicine. I believe Burke took note of Mate. I believe Mate's escapades and the resulting publicity played a role in Michael Burke's evolution as a ward killer. Though, of course, Michael had begun snuffing out patients earlier. Michael's main objective *was* killing people." To me: "Wouldn't you say that applied to Dr. Mate, as well?"

Calling Burke by his first name. The hateful intimacy born of futile investigation.

Milo said, "You see Mate as a serial killer?"

Fusco's face went pleasantly bland. "You don't?"

"Some people consider Mate an angel of mercy."

"I'm sure Michael Burke could manipulate some people to say the same of him. But we all know what was really going on. Mate loved the ultimate power. So does Burke. You know all the jokes about doctors playing God. Here're a couple who put it into practice."

Milo rubbed the side of the table as if cleaning off his

fingertips. "So Mate inspires Burke, and Burke goes up to Seattle for med school. He moves around a lot."

"He does nothing *but* move," said Fusco. "Funny thing, though: until he showed up in Seattle and purchased a used VW van, he'd never officially owned a car. Like I said, a retrovirus—keeps changing, can't be grabbed hold of."

"Who died in Seattle?"

"The University of Washington hasn't been forthcoming with its records. Au contraire, officially none of their wards have experienced a pattern of unusual patient deaths. But would you take that to the bank? There's certainly no shortage of serials up there."

"So now Burke's back to girls? What, he's the Green River Killer?"

Fusco smiled. "None of the Green River scenes match his previous work, but I know of at least four cases that do bear further study. Girls cut up and left tied to trees in semirural spots, all within a hundred miles of Seattle, all unsolved."

"Burke's fooling with I.V. lines by day, cutting up girls in his spare time, somehow working in med school."

"Bundy killed and worked while in law school. Burke's a lot smarter, though like most psychopaths he tends to slack off. That almost cost him his MD. He had to spend a summer making up poor basic-science grades, received low marks for his clinical skills, graduated near the bottom of his class. Still, he finished, got an internship at a V.A. clinic in Bellingham. Once again, I can't get hold of hospital records, but if someone finds an unusual number of old soldiers expiring under his watch, I'm not going to faint from shock. He finished an emergency medicine residency at the same place, got a six-figure job with Unitas, moved back to New York, and added another car to his auto arsenal."

"He held on to the van?" I said.

"Most definitely."

"What kind of car?" said Milo. I knew he was wondering: BMW?

"Three-year-old Lexus," said Fusco. "The way I see it, emergency medicine's perfect for a twisted loner— plenty of blood and suffering, you get to make life-and-death decisions, cut and stitch, the hours are flexible— work a twenty-four-hour shift, take days off. And important: no follow-up of patients, no long-term relationships, office or staff. Burke could've gone on for years, but he's still a psychopath, has that tendency to screw up. Finally did."

Milo smiled. He'd been living with an E.R. doctor for fifteen years. I'd heard Rick praise the freedom that resulted from no long-term entanglements.

"Poisoning the boss," Milo said. "The article said he'd been suspended for bad medicine. Meaning?"

"He had a habit of not showing up at the E.R. when he was supposed to. Plus poor doctor-patient relations. The boss—Dr. Rabinowitz—said sometimes Burke could be terrific with patients. Charming, empathetic, taking extra time with kids. But other times he'd turn—lose his temper, accuse someone of overdramatizing or faking, get really nasty. He actually tried to kick a few patients out of the E.R., told them to stop taking up bed space that belonged to sick people. Toward the end, that was happening more and more. Burke was warned repeatedly, but he simply denied any of it had ever happened."

"Sounds like he was losing it," said Milo. He looked at me.

"Maybe heightened tension," I said. "The pressure of working a tough job when his qualifications were marginal. Being scrutinized by people who were smarter. Or some kind of emotional trauma. Has he ever had an outwardly normal relationship with a woman?"

"No long-term girlfriend, and he's a nice-looking guy." Fusco's eyes drooped lower. His hands balled. "That brings me to another pattern. A more recent one, as far as I can tell. He developed a friendship with one of his patients up in Seattle. Former cheerleader with bone cancer. Burke was circulating through as an intern, ended up spending a lot of time with her."

"Thought you couldn't get hospital records," said Milo.

"I couldn't. But I did find some nurses who remembered Michael. Nothing dramatic, they just thought he'd spent too much time with the cheerleader. It ended when the girl died. A couple of weeks later, the first of the four unsolved cutting vics was found. Next year, in Rochester, Burke got close to another sick woman. Divorcée in her early fifties, onetime beauty queen with brain cancer. She came into the E.R. in some sort of crisis, Burke revived her, visited her during the four months she spent as an inpatient, saw her at home after she was discharged. He was at her side when she died. Pronounced her dead."

"Died of what?" said Milo.

"Respiratory failure," said Fusco. "Not inconsistent with the spread of her disease."

"Any mutilation clusters after that?"

"Not in Rochester, per se, but five girls within a two-hundred-mile radius have gone missing during Burke's two years at Unitas Hospital. Three of them after Burke's lady friend died. I agree with Dr. Delaware's point about loss and tension."

"Two hundred miles," said Milo.

Fusco said, "As I've pointed out, Burke has the means to travel. And plenty of privacy. In Rochester, he lived in a rented house in a semirural area. His neighbors said he kept to himself, tended to disappear for days at a time. Sometimes he took along skis or camping equipment—both the van and the Lexus had roof racks. He's in good shape, likes the outdoors."

"These five cases are missing only, no bodies?"

"So far," said Fusco. "Detective, you know that two hundred miles is no big deal if you've got decent wheels. Burke kept his vehicles in beautiful shape, clean as a whistle. Same for his house. He's a lad of impeccable habits. The house reeked of disinfectant, and his bed was made tight enough to bounce a hubcap."

"How'd he get tagged for poisoning Rabinowitz?"

"Circumstantial. Burke kept screwing up, and Rabinowitz finally put him on suspension. Rabinowitz said the look in Burke's eyes gave him the creeps. A week later, Rabinowitz got sick. It turned out to be cyanide. Burke was the last person to be seen in the vicinity of Rabinowitz's coffee cup other than Rabinowitz's secretary, and she passed the polygraph. When the locals tried to question Burke and put him on the machine, he was gone. Later, they found needles and a penicillin ampule in a locker in the physicians' lounge, traces of cyanide in the ampule. Rabinowitz is lucky he took a small sip. Even with that, he was hospitalized for a month."

"Burke left cyanide in his locker?"

"In another doctor's locker. A colleague Burke had had words with. Fortunately for him, he was alibied. Home sick with the stomach flu, never left his house, lots of witnesses. There was some suspicion he'd been poisoned, too, but it turned out to just be the flu."

"So all you've really got on the poisoning is Burke's rabbit."

"That's all Rochester's got. I've got *that*." Pointing toward the still-unopened file folder. "I've also got Roger Sharveneau, certified respiratory tech. Buffalo police never checked out his Burke story, but Sharveneau worked at Unitas for three months, same time Burke was there. Sharveneau mentions Burke, and a week later *he's* dead."

"Why didn't Buffalo check out the Burke lead?" said Milo.

"To be charitable," said Fusco, "Sharveneau came across highly disturbed and lacking credibility. My guess would be severe borderline personality, maybe even a full-blown schizophrenic. He jerked Buffalo PD around for a month—confessing, recanting, then hinting that maybe he'd killed some of the patients but not all of them, calling press conferences, changing lawyers, acting goofier and goofier. During the time he was locked up he went on a hunger strike, went mute, refused to talk to the court-appointed psychiatrists. By the time he gave them the Burke story, they were fed up with him. But I believe he did know Michael Burke. And that Burke had some kind of influence on him."

I said, "Why would Burke put himself in jeopardy by confiding in someone as unstable as Sharveneau?"

"I'm not saying he confided in Sharveneau, or gave Sharveneau direct orders. I'm saying he exerted some kind of influence. It could very well have been subtle—a remark here, a nudge there. Sharveneau was unstable, passive, highly suggestible. Michael Burke's the peg that fits that hole: dominant, manipulative, in his own way charismatic. I believe Burke knew what buttons to push."

Milo said, "Dominant, manipulative, and he gets away with bad stuff. So what's next, he runs for public office?"

"You don't want to see the profiles of the people who run the country."

"The Bureau's still doing that J. Edgar stuff, huh?"

Fusco smiled.

Milo said, "Even if your boy really is the ultimate purveyor of evil, what's the connection to Mate?"

"Tell me about Mate's wounds."

Milo laughed. "How about you tell me what you think they might be."

Fusco shifted in the booth, leaned to his left, stretched his left arm across the top of the seat. "Fair enough. I'd guess that Mate was rendered semiconscious or totally unconscious, probably with a strong blow to the head that came from behind. Or a choke hold. The papers said he was found in the van. If that's true, that's at odds with Burke's tree-propping signature. But the wooded site fits Burke's kills. More public than Burke's previous dumps, but that fits the pattern of increased confidence. And Mate was a public figure. I suspect Burke conned Mate into arranging a meeting, possibly by feigning interest in Mate's work. From what I've seen of Mate, an appeal to his ego would be most effective."

He stopped.

Milo said nothing. His hand had come to rest atop the file folder. Touching the string. Unfurling it slowly.

Fusco said, "However the meeting was arranged, I see Burke familiarizing himself with the site beforehand, learning the traffic patterns, leaving a getaway vehicle within walking distance of the kill-spot. Which in his case, could be miles. Probably to the east of the kill-spot, because the east affords multiple avenues of escape. Living in L.A., Burke needs wheels, so I'm sure he's obtained registration under a new identity, but whether he used his own car or a stolen vehicle, I couldn't say."

"I assume you've combed DMV, done all the combinations of Burke, Rushton, Sartin, Spreen, whatever."

"You assume correctly. No good hits."

"You were going to speculate about the wounds."

" 'Speculate.' " Fusco smiled. "Brutal but precise, carved with a surgical-grade blade or something equally sharp. There may also have been some geometry involved."

"What do you mean by geometry?" said Milo, sounding casual.

"Geometrical shapes incised into the skin. He began that in Ann Arbor, the last victim, diamonds snipped out of her upper pubic region. When I first saw it, I thought: his idea of a joke—the irony again, diamonds are a girl's best friend. But then he changed shapes with one of the Fresno vics. Circles. So I won't tell you I know exactly what it means, just that he likes to play around."

"There were two Fresno victims," I said. "Was only one incised geometrically?"

Fusco nodded. "Maybe Burke had to hurry away from the other kill."

"Or maybe," said Milo, "both victims weren't his."

"Read the file and decide for yourself." Fusco drew his glass nearer, touched the corner of his sandwich.

"Anything more you want to say?"

"Just that you probably didn't find much trace evidence, if any. Burke loves to clean up. And killing Mate would represent a special achievement for him: synthesis of his two previous modes: bloody knife work and pseudo-euthanasia. The papers said Mate was hooked up to his own machine. That true?"

"Pseudo-euthanasia?"

"It's never real," said Fusco with sudden heat. "All that talk about right to die, putting people out of their misery. Until we can crawl into a dying person's head and read their thoughts, it'll never be real." Forced smile, more of a snarl, really: "When I heard about the painting, I knew I had to be more assertive with you. Burke loves to draw. His house in Rochester was full of art books and sketch pads."

"How good is he?" I said.

"Better than average. I took some photos. It's all in there. But don't hold me to any specific guess, look at the overall picture. I've done hundreds of profiles, most of the time I miss something."

"What you've done with Burke goes beyond profiling," I said.

He stared at me. "Meaning what?"

"Sounds as if you've made him your project."

"Part of my current job description is depth research on cold cases." To Milo: "You'd know something about that."

Milo uncoiled the string and opened the file. Inside

were three black folders, labeled I, II, and III. He
removed the first, opened it to a page containing five
photocopied head shots.

In the upper left: a color school photo of ten-year-old
T-shirted Grant Huie Rushton. Button nose, blond crew
cut, Norman Rockwell cute, except this kid hadn't smiled
for the camera. Had looked away from it, set his mouth in
a horizontal line that should've been merely noncom-
mittal, but wasn't.

Anger. Cool anger, backed by . . . wariness? Emotional
unsteadiness? Furtive, wounded eyes. Norman Rockwell
meets Diane Arbus. Or was I interpreting because of
what Fusco had told me?

Next: a high-school graduation shot. At eighteen,
Grant Rushton looked more relaxed. Pleasant-looking
young man wearing a plaid shirt, face broadened by
puberty, the features symmetrical, tending a bit toward
pug. Clear complexion but for sprinkles of pimples in the
folds between nostril and cheek. Strong, square chin,
mouth shut tight but uplifted at the corners. Teenage
Grant's hair was several shades darker but still fair, worn
to his shoulders with thick bangs. This time, he
confronted the lens, full-face—confident—more than
that: brash. By then, Fusco claimed, Rushton had
murdered and gotten away with it.

Below the childhood shots was Huey Mitchell's
bearded face on a Great Lakes Security badge. The beard
was thick, spade-shaped, a mink brown that contrasted
with Mitchell's dirty-blond head hair. Running from atop
the cheekbones to his first shirt button in an uninter-
rupted swath broken only by a mouth slit, it rendered any
comparison to the other photos useless. Mitchell wore his

hair even longer, drawn back tight into a ponytail that dangled over his right shoulder.

The pale eyes narrower, harder. My flash impression would have been blue-collar resentment. Vital statistics: five-ten, one eighty, blond hair, blue eyes.

The bottom row featured two pictures of Michael Burke, MD. In the first, taken from a New York driver's license, the beard remained, this time clipped and barbered to an inch of dark pelt that served the now powerful-looking head well. So did Burke's haircut— razor-layered, blow-dried, worn just above the ears. By his early thirties, Burke's face had begun to reveal the advent of middle age: thinner hair, wrinkles around the mouth, puffiness under the eyes. Overall, a pleasant-looking man, wholly unremarkable.

This time the stats said five-nine, one sixty-five.

"He shrank an inch and lost fifteen pounds?" I said.

"Or lied about it to Motor Vehicles," said Fusco. "Doesn't everyone?"

"People reduce their weight, but they don't generally claim to be shorter."

"Michael isn't people," said Fusco. "You'll also notice that the license says brown eyes. His true color's green-blue. Obviously, Burke jerked them around—either because he was hiding something or just having fun. On his Unitas I.D., he's back to blue."

I examined the last photo.

Michael F. Burke, MD, Dept. of Emergency Medicine.

Clean-shaven. Square-jawed, even fuller, the hair thinner but worn slightly longer, flatter. Burke had been content with a decent comb-over.

I compared the last shot with Grant Rushton's high-school photo, searching for some commonality. Similar bone structure, I supposed. The eyes were the same shape, but even there, gravity had tugged sufficiently to prevent immediate identification. Huey Mitchell's beard obscured everything. Rushton's bang-shadowed brow and Burke's clear forehead gave the rest of their faces entirely different appearances.

Five faces. I'd never have linked any of them.

Milo shut the folder and placed it back in the file. Fusco had been waiting for some kind of response and now he looked unhappy, curled his fingers around his glass.

"Anything else?" said Milo.

Fusco shook his head. Unfolding a paper napkin, he wrapped the half-eaten brisket sandwich and stashed it in a pocket of his sport coat.

"You bunked down at the Federal Building?" said Milo.

"Officially," said Fusco, "but mostly I'm on the road. I wrote down a number in there that routes automatically to my beeper. My fax runs twenty-four hours a day. Feel free, anytime."

"On the road where?"

"Wherever the job takes me. As I said, I've got projects other than Michael Burke, though Michael does tend to occupy my thoughts. Tonight, I'll be flying up to Seattle, see if I can get U. Wash to be a bit more forth-coming. Also, to look into those unsolveds, which is a mite touchy. With all the publicity about the Pacific Northwest being the serial-killer capital of the world and no resolution on Green River, they don't like being reminded of loose ends."

Milo said, "Bon voyage."

Fusco slid out of the booth. No briefcase. His jacket bulged where he'd stuffed the sandwich. Not a tall man, after all. Five-eight, tops, with a big torso riding stumpy, bowed legs. His jacket hung open and I saw several black pens lined up in his shirt pocket, the beeper and a cell phone hitched to his belt. No visible weapon. Fingering his white hair, he left the restaurant, limping. Looking like a tired old salesman who'd just failed to make his quota.

20

Milo and I stayed in the booth.

The waitress was leaning protectively over the old woman. He waved for her. She held up a finger.

He said, "Just like the Feds—we get stuck for the check."

"He liked the brisket, but didn't eat much of it," I said. "Maybe his gut's full of something else."

"Like what?"

"Frustration. He's been on this for a while—got a bit touchy when I called Burke his project. Sometimes that can lead to tunnel vision. On the other hand, there's a lot that seems to match."

"What—'geometry'?"

"A killer with a medical background and artistic interests, the combination of 'euthanasia' and lust-murder. And he was awfully close when he described the details of Mate's murder, down to the blitz attack and the cleanup."

"That he could've gotten from a departmental leak."

The waitress came over. "It's been taken care of, sir. The white-haired gentleman."

"And a gentleman he is." Milo handed her a ten.

"The tip's also been taken care of," she said.

"Now it's been taken care of twice."

She beamed. "Thanks."

When she was gone, I said, "See, you judged him too harshly."

"Force of habit . . . Okay, so some of my income tax came back to me . . . Yeah, there are similarities, there often are with psycho killers, right? Limited repertoire: you bludgeon, you shoot, you cut. But it's far from a perfect match. Starting with the basics: Mate's not a young girl and he wasn't tied against a tree. Fusco can fudge all he wants, but, PhD or not, in the end it comes down to his *feelings*. And where does making Burke a suspect lead *me*? Trying to chase down some phantom the Bureau hasn't been able to snag for three years? I've already got prospects close to home."

His hand grazed the file folder. "If I don't cooperate eventually, he'll call the brass and I'll be stuck with task-force bullshit. For the moment, he's trying cop-to-cop."

A couple of multiple-pierced kids dressed in black entered the deli and took a booth at the front. Lots of laughter. I heard the word "pastrami" used as if it was a punch line.

"Nitrites for the night crawlers," Milo muttered. "Wanna do me a big favor? One that won't put you in conflict of interest?" Tapping the file. "Go over this for me. You come up with something juicy, I take it more seriously . . . Artistic. Burke draws, he doesn't paint.

We've already got a good idea who did that masterpiece.
. . . So, you mind?"

"Not at all."

"Thanks. That frees me up for the fun stuff."

"Which is?"

"Scrounging through putrid squats in Venice. Cop's day at the beach."

He hoisted himself out of the booth.

"Feds with PhDs," he said. "Bad guys with MDs. And *moi* with a lowly master's—it's not pretty, being outclassed."

I brought the file home just after three. Robin's truck was gone and the day's mail was still in the box. I collected the stack, made coffee, drank a cup and a half, brought the file to my office and called my service.

Richard Doss's secretary had phoned to let me know Eric would be a half hour early for his four o'clock appointment. The boy had been examined by Dr. Robert Manitow; if I had time, please call the doctor.

She'd left Manitow's number and I punched it. His receptionist sounded harried and my name evoked no recognition. She put me on hold for a long time. No music. Good.

I'd never met Bob or talked to him, knew him only from silver-framed family photos on a carved credenza in Judy's chambers.

A clipped voice said, "Dr. Manitow. Who's this?"

"Dr. Delaware."

"What can I do for you?" Curt. Had his wife never mentioned working with me?

"I'm a psychologist—"

"I know who you are. Eric's on his way over to see you."

"How's he doing physically?"

"He's doing fine. It was your idea to have me check him out, wasn't it?" Each word sounded as if it had been dragged over broken glass. No mistaking the accusatory tone.

I said, "I thought it would be a good idea, seeing what he's gone through."

"What exactly is he supposed to have gone through?"

"Beyond the long-term effects of losing his mom, his behavior was unusual, according to his father. Disappearing without explanation, refusing to talk—"

"He talks fine," said Manitow. "He just talked to me. Told me this whole thing was bullshit, and I heartily concur. He's a *college* student, for God's sake. They leave home and do all kinds of crazy things—didn't you?"

"His roommate was concerned enough to—"

"So the kid decided not to be perfect, for once. Of all people, I thought you'd evaluate the source before getting sucked into all this hysteria."

"The source?"

"Richard," he said. "Everything in Richard's life is one big goddamn production. The whole family's like that—nothing's casual, everything's a big goddamn deal."

"You're saying they overdramatize—"

"Don't do that," he said. "Don't bounce my words back to me like I'm on the couch. Hell yes, they overdramatize. When they built that house of theirs, they should've included an amphitheater."

"I'm sure you know them well," I said, "but given what happened to Joanne—"

"What happened to Joanne was hell for those poor kids. But the truth is, she was screwed up psychologically. Pure and simple. Not a damn thing wrong with her other than she chose to drop out of life and eat herself to death. She discarded her good sense. That's why she called that quack to finish the job. Nothing more than depression. I'm no shrink, and *I* could diagnose it. I told her to get psychiatric help, she refused. If Richard had listened to me in the first place and had her committed, they could've put her on a good tricyclic and she might be alive today and the kids could've been spared all the shit they went through."

He wasn't talking loud but I found myself holding the phone away from my ear.

He said, "Good luck with the kid. *I've* got to run."

Click. His anger hung in the air, bitter as September smog.

Yesterday, after viewing Stacy's pain as we walked along the beach, I'd decided not to call Judy, wondering about entanglements between the Manitows and the Dosses, something that went beyond Mommy and Me, country-club tennis, Laura Ashley bedrooms. Now my curiosity took off in a whole new direction.

Her Eric, my Allison, then Stacy and Becky . . .

Becky having trouble in school—tutored by Joanne, then dropping back down to D's when Joanne could no longer see her . . . Was Bob's anger a reaction to perceived rejection?

Becky getting too skinny, entering therapy, trying to play therapist with Stacy, then cooling off.

Eric dumping Allison. Yet another rejection?

Bob Manitow smarting at his daughter's broken

heart? No, it had to be more than that. And his resentment of the Dosses' problems wasn't shared by his wife.
Judy had referred Stacy to me because she cared about
the girl . . . Just another case of male impatience versus
female empathy? Or had Bob's empathy been trashed by
his inability to rouse Joanne from what he saw as
"nothing more than depression"? Sometimes physicians
get angry at psychosomatic illness . . . or maybe this
physician was just having a really bad day.

I thought of something else: Stacy's tale of how Bob
had stared with distaste as Richard and Joanne groped
each other in the pool.

A prudish man, offended? Perhaps his resentment at
having to confront the Dosses' tribulations was *emotional*
prudishness. I'd seen that most often in those running
from their own despair, what a professor of mine had
called baloney fleeing the slicer.

No sense speculating, the Manitows weren't the
issue; I'd allowed Bob Manitow's anger to take me too far
afield. Still, his reaction had been so intense—so out of
proportion—that I had trouble letting go of it, and as I
waited for Eric my thoughts kept drifting back to Judy.

Pencil-thin Judy in her chambers. Impeccable office,
impeccable occupant. Tanned, tight-skinned, strong-
boned good looks. Hanging her robe on a walnut valet,
revealing the body-hugging St. John Knits suit underneath.

The room perpetually ready for a photo shoot:
polished furniture, fresh flowers in crystal vases, soft
lights, gelid convexities. No hint that the fury and
tedium of Superior Court waited just beyond the door.

Those family photos. Two lithe blond girls with that

same strong-boned beauty. Thin, very thin. Dad in the background . . . Had any of them smiled for the camera? I couldn't remember, was pretty sure Bob hadn't.

Stick-mom and a pair of stick-daughters, Becky carrying it too far. Did Judy's attention to detail manifest as pressure upon her kids to look, sound, act, *be* faultless? Had the Dosses and their problems somehow become enmeshed with their neighbors?

Maybe I was indulging myself in speculation because the family was far less unpleasant than the file I'd taken from the deli. *Geometry.*

Finally, the red light flashed.

Richard and Stacy at the side door. Eric between them.

Richard in his usual black shirt and slacks, the little silver phone in one hand. Looking a bit haggard. Stacy's hair was loose and she wore a sleeveless white dress and white flats. I thought of a little girl in church.

Eric gave a disgusted look. His father and his sister had spoken about him in a way that connoted a huge presence. But when it came to physical stature, Doss DNA hadn't faltered. He was no taller than Richard, and a good ten pounds lighter. A dejected slump bowed his back. Small hands, small feet.

A frail-looking boy with enormous black eyes, a delicate nose, and a soft, curling mouth. Rounder face than Stacy's, but that same leprechaun cast. Copper skin, black hair clipped so short the curls had diminished to fuzz. His chambray shirt was oversize, and it bagged over the sagging waistband of dirt-stained baggy khakis wrinkled to used-Kleenex consistency. The cuffs accordioned atop running shoes encrusted with gray dried mud. Skimpy beard stubble dotted his chin and cheeks.

He looked everywhere but at me, his fingers flexed against his thighs. Delicate hands. Blackened, cracked nails, as if he'd been clawing in the dirt. His father hadn't tried to clean him up. Or maybe he'd tried and Eric had resisted.

I said, "Eric? Dr. Delaware," and extended my hand. He ignored the gesture, stared at the ground. The fingers kept flexing.

Good-looking kid. On a certain kind of sweet, convincing, college night, girls attracted to the brooding, sensitive type would be drawn to him.

Just as I began to retract my hand, he gripped it. His skin was cold, moist. Turning to his father, he grimaced, as if bracing for pain.

I said, "Richard, you and Stacy can wait out here or walk around in the garden. Check back in an hour or so."

"You don't need to talk to me?" said Richard.

"Later."

His lips seemed on the verge of a retort—making a point—but he thought better of it. "Okay then, how about we get coffee or something, Stace? We can make it into Westwood and back in an hour."

"Sure, Daddy."

I caught Stacy's eye. She gave a tiny nod, letting me know seeing her brother was okay. I nodded back, the two of them left, and I closed the door behind Eric and myself and said, "This way."

He followed me into the office, stood in the center of the room.

"Make yourself comfortable," I said. "Or at least as comfortable as you can be."

He moved to the nearest chair and lowered himself slowly.

"I can understand your not wanting to be here, Eric. So if—"

"No, I want to be here." A big man's voice flowed out of the cupid's mouth. Richard's baritone, even more incongruous. He flexed his neck. "I deserve to be here. I'm fucked up." He fingered a shirt button. "That's absurd, isn't it?" he said. "The way I just phrased that. The way we use 'fuck' as a pejorative. Supposedly the most beautiful act in the world and we use it that way." Sickly smile. "Scroll back and edit: I'm *dysfunctional*. Now you're supposed to ask in what way."

"In what way?"

"Isn't your job finding out?"

"Yup," I said.

"Good deal, your job," he said, looking around the office. "No need for any equipment, just your psyche and the patient's encountering each other in the great affective void, hoping for a collision of insight." The briefest smile. "As you can see, I've had intro psych."

"Did you enjoy it?"

"Nice relief from the cold, cruel world of supply and demand. One thing did bother me, though. You people put so much emphasis upon function and dysfunction but pay no attention to guilt and expiation."

"Too value-free for you?" I said.

"Too *incomplete*. Guilt's a virtue—maybe the *cardinal* virtue. Think about it: what else is going to motivate us bipeds to behave with proper restraint? What else prevents society from sinking into mass, entropic fuck-upedness?"

His left leg crossed over his right and his shoulders loosened. Using big words relaxed him. I imagined his first, precocious utterances, met with astonishment, then cheers. Achievements piling up, expectations exceeded.

I said, "Guilt as a virtue."

"What other virtue *is* there? What else keeps us civilized? Assuming we *are* civilized. Highly open to debate."

"There are degrees of civilization," I said.

He smiled. "You probably believe in altruism for its own sake. Good deeds carried out for the intrinsic satisfaction. I think life's essentially an avoidance paradigm: people do things to avoid being punished."

"Does that come from personal experience?"

He shifted back in the chair. "Well, well, well. Isn't that a bit *directive*, considering I've been here all of five minutes and it's not exactly a voluntary transaction?"

I said nothing.

He said, "Get too pushy and I could revert to the treatment I gave my father when he chanced upon my meditation spot."

"Which is?"

"Total freeze-out—what you guys call elective mutism."

"At least it's 'elective.' "

He stared at me. "Meaning?"

"Meaning you're in control," I said.

"Am I? Is there really any such thing as volition?"

"Without volition, why the need for guilt, Eric?"

He frowned for less than a second. Wiped away consternation with a smile. "Aha!" Fingering a button of his wrinkled shirt. "A philosopher. Probably an Ivy League guy—let's take a look at those diplomas . . . Oh. Sorry, the U. Native son?"

"Midwesterner."

"Corn and cows and yet you're philosophical—this could start sounding like *My Dinner with Andre.*"

"Favorite movie of yours?" I said.

"I liked it, considering the chattiness level. *Lethal Weapon*'s more to my taste."

"Oh?"

"The comfort of simplicity."

"Because life's complicated."

He began to reply, checked himself, scanned my diplomas again, resumed studying the carpet. Neither of us spoke for a minute or so, then he looked up. "Waiting me out? Technique Number Thirty-six B?"

"It's your time," I said.

"Your job requires patience. I'd be lousy at it. I've been told I don't suffer fools well."

"Told by whom?"

"Everyone. Dad. He meant it as a compliment. He's rather proud of me and displays it with ostentatious shows of support—there's a case of constructive guilt for you."

"What's your father guilty about?" I said.

"Losing control. Raising his kiddies by himself when all three of us know what he'd really rather be doing is flying all over the country amassing real estate."

"It's not as if it was his decision."

"Well"—the curling lips twisted upward—"Dad's not always rational. But then, who is? To understand the root of his guilt, you'd need to know something about his background—do you?"

"Why don't you fill me in."

"He's your basic self-made man, the cream of immigrant stock. His father's Greek, his mother's Sicilian. They ran a grocery in Bayonne, New Jersey, can't you just smell the Kalamata olives? In that world, family means mama, papa, kiddies, grape leaves, farting after too much soup, the usual Mediterranean accoutrements. But poor Dad's stuck with no mama in *his* family—he didn't save his wife."

"Was that within his power?"

His face flushed and his hands rolled into fists. "How the fuck should *I* know? Why even ask that kind of question when it's structurally *unanswerable*? Why should I have to answer *any* of your questions?"

He looked at the door, as if considering escape, muttered, "What's the use?" and slumped lower.

"The question bothered you," I said. "Have you been asked it by someone else?"

"No," he said. "And why would I give a *fuck* about anyone else? Why the *fuck* would I give a *fuck* about the fucking *past,* period? It's what's happening now that's . . . Forget it, there's clearly no point discussing this. Don't start feeling all triumphant because the first time I meet you I exhibit emotion. If you knew me, you'd know that's no big deal. I'm *Mr.* Emotion. I think it, I say it, in the brain, out the mouth. I'll emote to a fucking *stranger* if the mood strikes me, so this isn't progress."

More sotto voce swearing.

"The only reason I let Dad get me into this is . . ."

Silence.

"Is what, Eric?"

"He caught me in a weak moment. The moon was

full and I was full of shit. Believe me, it won't happen again. First item of business: back to Palo Alto tonight. Second item: get a new roommate who won't rat me out if I decide to deviate from routine. This is *bullshit,* understand? I know it, Dr. Manitow knows it and if you earned all that paper on the wall, you should know it."

"Much ado about nothing," I said.

"It sure isn't *A Midsummer Night's Dream*—no comedy in my life, *dottore,* I'm a po', po' child of tragedy. My mother came to a horrible end, I'm entitled to be obnoxious, right? Her death bought me *leeway.*" His hands pressed together prayerfully. "Thank you, Mom, for miles of leeway."

He slid down so that he was nearly lying in the chair. Smiled. "Okay then, let's talk about something a bit cheerier—how about them Dodgers?"

I said, "Seeing as you're going back to Stanford and I'll probably never talk to you again, I'm going to incur your wrath by suggesting you find someone there to talk to— Hear me out, Eric. I'm not saying you're dysfunctional. But you have been through something terrible and—"

"You are so full of shit," he broke in. Discomfortingly mild tone. "How can you sit there and judge my experience?"

"I'm not judging, I'm empathizing. I was older than you when my father died, but not much older. He brought on his own death, too. I was a good deal older when my mother died, but the loss was more profound because I was closer to her and now I was an orphan. There's something about that—the aloneness. My father's death was a big blow to my sense of trust. The fact that something so important can be taken away from you, just like that. The powerlessness. You view the world differently. I think that's worth talking about to someone who'll really listen."

The black eyes hadn't moved from mine. A vein in his neck pulsed. He smiled. Slouched. "Nice speech, bro. What's that called? Constructive self-disclosure? Technique Number Fifty-five C?"

I shrugged. "Enough said."

"Sorry," he said in a small, hurried voice. "You're a nice guy. Problem is, *I'm* not. So don't waste your time."

"You seem heavily invested in that," I said.

"In what?"

"Being the quirky, obnoxious genius. My guess is that somewhere along the line you were taught to associate smarts with having an edge. But I've met some really bad people and you don't qualify for that club."

His face went scarlet. "I apologized, man. No need to twist the fucking *knife*."

"No need for apologies, Eric. This is about you, not me. And yes, you're right, that was constructive self-disclosure. I chose to expose part of myself in the hope it might spur you to get some help."

He turned away from me. "This *is* bullshit. If Dad hadn't been a fucking old maid and freaked out, none of this would be happening."

"That wouldn't change the reality."

"Give me a break."

"Forget philosophy, Eric. Forget intro psych. *Your* reality is what you're experiencing. Most people your age don't have to endure what you've endured. Most aren't concerned with guilt and expiation."

His shoulders jerked as if I'd shaken him. "I. Was. Talking. Abstractly."

"Were you?"

He seemed poised to leap from the chair. Settled back down. Laughed. "So you've met a lot of bad guys, have you?"

"More than I'd care to."

"Killers?"

"Among others."

"Serial killers?"

"That, too."

Another laugh. "And you don't think I'd qualify?"

"Let's call it an educated guess, Eric. Though you're right: I don't really know you. I'm also guessing guilt's more than an abstraction for you. Your father and your sister both told me how much time you spent with your mother during her illness. Taking the semester off—"

"So, now I get punished for it? Have to listen to all this fucking *shit*?"

"Being here's not punishment."

"It is if it's against your will."

"Could your father really have forced you?" I said.

He didn't answer.

"It's your choice," I said. "Your volition. And since this is a one-shot deal, the best I can do is give you some advice and let you run with it."

"*My* advice is forget it—don't waste your midwestern time. I shouldn't be here in the first place. I shouldn't be horning in on Stacy's therapy."

"Stacy's okay with it—"

"That's what she says. That's the way she always starts out, path of least resistance, everything's fine. But, believe me, she'll get pissed about it, it's just a matter of time. Basically, she hates me. I'm a shadow in her life, the best thing that ever happened to her was my going away. Stanford's the last place she should go, but with Dad leaning on her, she'll comply once again—the path of least resistance. She'll come up there, want to hang out with me, start hating me again."

"She stops hating you when you're apart?"

"Absence makes the heart grow fonder."

"Sometimes absence makes the heart grow hollow."

"Profound," he said. "All this fucking profundity so early in the day."

"You really think Stacy hates you."

"Ah *knows* she duz. Not that I can do anything about it. Birth order's birth order, she'll just have to deal with being number two."

"And you have to deal with being number one."

"The burdens of primacy." He peeled back a sleeve. "Oh man, left my watch back in my dorm room . . . Hopefully no one swiped it—I've really got to get back, take care of business. How much more time do we have?"

"Ten more minutes."

He examined the room some more, saw the play corner, the bookcase stacked with board games. "Hey, let's play Candy Land. See who gets to the top of that big rock-candy mountain first."

"Nothing wrong," I said, "with having a sweet life."

He wheeled, gaped at me. I never saw the tears in his eyes but the frantic way he swiped at them told me they were there. "Everything's a punch line with you—making your fucking point. Well, thanks for all the fucking *insight,* Doc."

The bell rang. Eight minutes early. Richard, overeager?

I picked up the phone, punched the intercom button for the side door.

"It's me," said Richard. "Sorry for interrupting, but we've got a bit of a problem out here."

Eric and I hurried over. Richard stood on the porch along with Stacy. Two tall men behind them.

Detectives Korn and Demetri.

Richard said, "These gentlemen want me to accompany them to the police station."

Korn said, "Hey, Doc. Nice place."

Richard said, "You *know* them?"

"What's going on?" I said.

Korn said, "Like Mr. Doss said, his presence is requested at the station."

"For what?"

"Questioning."

"In regard to?"

Demetri stepped forward. "That's not your business, Doctor. We allowed Mr. Doss to call you because his children are present and one of them's a minor. The boy's twenty, right? So he can drive both of them home in Mr. Doss's car."

He and Korn moved closer to Richard. Richard looked scared.

Stacy said, "Daddy?" Her eyes were wide with terror.

Richard didn't answer her. Nor did he ask what it was all about. Not wanting his children to hear the answer?

"You ride with us, sir," said Demetri.

"First I'm calling my lawyer."

"You're not being arrested, sir," said Korn. "You can call from the station."

"I'm going to call my lawyer." Richard brandished the silver phone.

Korn and Demetri looked at each other. Korn said, "Fine. Tell him to meet you at the West L.A. station, but you're coming with us."

"What the fuck," said Eric, moving toward the detectives.

Demetri said, "Stand back, son."

"I'm not your fucking son. If I was, my knuckles would be scraping the ground."

Demetri reached inside his jacket and touched his gun. Stacy gasped and Eric's eyes got wide.

I placed my hand on his shoulder, bore down. He was trembling.

Richard stabbed the keypad of the silver phone. Eric got next to Stacy, put his arm around her. She threw her arm across his chest. Her lips quivered. Eric's were still but the neck vein was racing. Both of them watched their father as he held the phone to his ear.

Richard's foot tapped impatiently. No more fear in his eyes. Calm under fire, or not totally surprised?

"Saundra? Richard Doss. Please get Max on the phone . . . What's that? When? . . . Okay, listen, it's really important that I talk to him . . . I'm in a bit of a jam . . . no, something different, I can't get into it right now. Just reach him in Aspen. ASAP. I'll be at the West L.A. police station—with some detectives . . . What're your names?"

"Korn."

"Demetri."

Richard repeated that. "Reach him, Saundra. If he

can't jet back, at the very least I need the name of someone who can help me. I'm on cellular. I'm counting on you. Bye." He clicked off the phone.

"On our way," said Demetri.

Richard said, "Demetri. Greek?"

"American," said Demetri, too quickly. Then: "Lithuanian. A long time ago. Let's get going, sir."

No one can make "sir" sound like an insult the way a cop can.

Stacy started to cry. Eric held her tight.

Richard said, "I'll be okay, kids, you just hold on—I'll see you for dinner. Promise."

"Daddy," said Stacy.

"It'll be fine."

"Sir," said Korn, taking hold of Richard's arm.

"Hold on," I said. "I'm going to call Milo."

Both detectives grinned, as if on cue. I was the perfect shill.

Demetri moved behind Richard as Korn kept his grip. The two of them shadowing the much smaller man.

"*Milo,*" Demetri said, "knows."

CHAPTER

21

The big, pale palm of a hand hung inches from my face, a fleshy cloud.

"Don't," said Milo, barely audible. "Don't say a thing."

It was 5:23. I was in the front reception area of the West L.A. station and he'd just come down the stairs.

I wanted to knock his hand away, waited as it lowered. His jacket was off but his tie was tight—too tight, reddening his neck and face. What did *he* have to be angry about?

I'd been waiting in the lobby for over an hour, most of it alone with the civilian clerk behind the desk, a pasty, overly enunciative man named Dwight Moore. I knew some of the clerks. Not Moore. The first time I'd approached, he'd looked wary, as if I had something to sell. When I asked him to reach Milo upstairs, he took a long time to put the call through.

For the next sixty-three minutes I used every anger-reduction trick I knew while warming a hard plastic chair as Moore answered the phone and moved paper around. Twenty minutes into the wait, I stepped up to the desk and Moore said, "Why don't you just go home, sir? If he really does know you, he's got your number."

My hands clenched below the counter. "No, I'll wait."

"Suit yourself." Moore got up, walked into a back room, returned with a large cup of coffee and a glazed bear claw. He ate with his back to me, taking very small bites and wiping his chin several times. Minutes dripped by. A few blues came and went, some of them greeting Moore, none with enthusiasm. I thought of Stacy and Eric watching their father taken away by LAPD's finest.

At five-fifteen, an elderly couple in matching green cardigans walked into the station and asked Moore what could be done about their lost dog. Moore adopted a skeptical look and gave them the number for Animal Control. When the woman asked another question, Moore said, "I'm not Animal Control," and turned his back.

"What you are," said the old man, "is a little prick."

"Herb," said his wife, easing him toward the door.

As they left, he told her, "And they wonder why no one likes them."

Five-twenty. Eric and Stacy were nowhere in sight. If they'd made it, I assumed they'd been allowed upstairs, but Moore wouldn't confirm it.

I'd sped over in the Seville, following Richard's black BMW as Eric gunned it down from the glen and wove through Westwood traffic. Easy to follow: the car was a blade of onyx cutting through dirty air. The car that I'd wondered about as the match to the vehicle Paul Ulrich had spotted on Mulholland. Richard, Eric . . .

The boy drove much too fast, took foolish chances. At Sepulveda and Wilshire, he ran a red light, nearly collided with a gardener's truck, swerved into the center lane, sped away from a chorus of honks. I was two cars back, got caught at the light, lost sight of him. By the time I reached the station, I couldn't find the BMW on the street. No parking space for me in the police lot this time. I circled several times, finally grabbed a spot two blocks away. Jogging the distance, I arrived huffing.

Remembering the fear in Stacy's eyes as Korn and Demetri placed their father in the back of a dung-brown unmarked. Tears striping her face. As Korn slammed the door of the police car, she mouthed, "Daddy." Eric dragged her to the BMW, opened her door, nearly shoved her into the passenger seat. Flashing me one furious look, he ran to the driver's side, started the car up hard, shoved the RPMs to a defiant whine. Fishtailing and burning rubber, he took off.

"Where are the kids?" I asked Milo.

Something in my voice made him wince. "Let's talk upstairs, Alex."

The use of my name made Moore look up. "Hey there, Detective Sturgis," he said. "This gent's been waiting for you."

Milo grunted and led me to the stairs. We climbed quickly to the second floor, but instead of exiting, he stopped at the fire door and leaned against it. "Hear me out. This was not my decision—"

"You didn't send those two—"

"The command to pick up and question Doss came from downtown. *Command*, not request. Downtown claims they tried to reach me. I was out in Venice, and instead of trying harder they went around me and gave the order to Korn."

"Demetri said you knew."

"Demetri's an asshole." Neck bulging against the collar. Unhealthy flush. I was three steps below him and he probably didn't mean to glare down at me. But the effect was there—looming bulk, volcanic rage. The stairwell was hot, gray, soupy with the steel-and-sweat pungence of a high-school corridor.

"Would I have done the same thing?" he said. "Yes, it was a command. But not at your house. So please. I've got plenty to deal with."

"Fine," I said, not sounding fine at all. "But cut me some slack, too. I saw the looks on those kids' faces. What the hell's the emergency? What's Richard done?"

He exhaled. "Upsetting his kids is the least of his problems. He's in serious trouble, Alex."

My stomach lurched. "On Mate?"

"Oh yeah."

"What the hell changed in two hours?" I said.

"What changed is we've got *evidence* on Doss."

"What kind of evidence?"

He ran a finger under his collar. "If you breathe a word of it, you're essentially decapitating me."

"Heaven forbid," I said. "Without a head, you couldn't eat. Come on, what do you have?"

He stretched a leg, sat on the top step. "What I have is a pleasant fellow named Quentin Goad, locked up at County, waiting trial on an armed robbery beef."

He fished a mug shot out of his pocket. Heavyset white man with a shaved head and black goatee.

"Looks like an overweight Satan," I said.

"When Quentin's not holding up 7-Elevens, he works construction—roofing and sheet-metal work. He's done a lot of work for Mr. Doss—apparently Mr. Doss likes to hire cons, pays them under the table to avoid taxes, which tells you something about *his* character. The way Goad tells it, two months ago he was roofing a project out in San Bernardino—some big shopping center Doss bought cheap and was refurbishing—when Doss approached him and offered him five thousand bucks to kill Mate. Told him to make it nasty and bloody so everyone would think it was a serial killer. Gave Goad a thousand up front, promised four when the job was finished. Goad says he took the dough but never intended to follow through, saw it as a perfect way to con Doss and cut town with a grand. He'd been wanting to move to Nevada anyway, because he had two strikes against him in California and it made him nervous."

"Don't tell me," I said. "Before he left, he decided to give himself a going-away party."

"A month ago, hamburger joint in San Fernando, late at night, just before closing time. Mr. Goad, a .22, a paper bag. Eight-hundred-buck haul. Goad already had the counter boy facedown on the floor and the money in the bag when the security guard appeared out of nowhere and took him down. Gunshot to the leg. Flesh wound. Goad spent two weeks at County Gen getting free medical care, and then they moved him to the Twin Towers. The .22 wasn't even loaded."

"So now he's facing three strikes and he's trying to

deal by selling out Richard. He's claiming Richard gave him money two months ago and didn't mind no follow-through. The Richard I know isn't high on patience."

"Richard bugged him, all right. About three weeks in, wanting a progress report. Goad told him he needed to plan it just right, was watching Mate, waiting for the perfect opportunity."

"Was he?"

"He says no. The whole thing was a scam."

"Come on, Milo, however you look at it, this guy's a liar and a—"

"Low-life moke. And if it was only Goad's story, your pal would be facing a much brighter future. Unfortunately, witnesses saw Doss and Goad meet at one of Goad's hangouts—ex-con bar in San Fernando, only a block from the hamburger joint he tried to rip off, which tells you how smart Goad is. The thing is, Doss didn't act too smart, either. We've got three drinkers and the bartender who saw the two of them having a serious head-to-head. They remember Doss because of the way he dressed. Fancy black duds, he didn't fit in. The waitress saw Doss pass an envelope to Goad. Nice, fat envelope. And she's got no reason to lie."

"But she never actually saw money changing hands."

"What?" he said. "Doss was passing him Halloween candy?"

"Goad claims Richard passed him cash, right out in the open?"

"The bar's a con hangout, Alex. Dark dive. Maybe Doss figured no one was watching. Or that it wouldn't come back to haunt him. For all I know, this isn't the first time Doss paid a con to do dirty work for him. We've also recovered some of the money. Doss paid Goad ten hundreds, Goad spent eight but two bills are left. We just printed Doss, should know soon if anything shows up. Want to take bets on that?"

"A dumb psychopath like Goad actually held on to loose cash?"

"He says it was Greyhound money. Something to tide him over until he pulled off the hamburger heist. What's the alternative explanation, Alex? Everyone in the bar's lying? Some grand conspiracy to frame poor Richard because maybe one time he played golf with O.J.? Come on, this is crime as I know it: tawdry, predictable, stupid. Doss may be a hotshot businessman but he was out of his element and he screwed up. He's been on my list, along with Haiselden and Donny. Now he's moved up to number one man."

"Does Goad claim Richard gave him a reason to kill Mate?"

"Goad says Richard told him Mate had murdered his wife. That she wasn't really sick, that as a doctor Mate should have known that, should have tried to talk her out of it. He told Goad he'd be doing a public service by getting rid of the guy. As if Goad cared about doing good—your boy thinks he's street-smart but that shows how out of his element he was. Mr. Brentwood slumming with the lowlife . . . It sounds damn real to me, Alex."

"Even if you do find Richard's prints on the money, what would that prove?" I said. "Goad worked for Richard and you just said he paid his workers under the table."

He looked up at me wearily. "All of a sudden you're a defense attorney? In my humble opinion, your time would be better spent dealing with those two kids than constructing excuses for their daddy. I'm sorry for you that it worked out this way, but as the guy who's been slogging this case, I'm happy as hell to have a real lead."

He didn't look happy.

I said, "Once more with feeling: where are the kids now?"

He hooked a thumb at the door. "I put them in a victim's family room. Assigned them a nice, sensitive female D to keep them company."

"How're they doing?"

"Don't know. Frankly, I've been spending my time on the phone with my alleged superiors and trying to talk to Daddy—who's clammed till his attorney gets here. I can't promise you the kids won't be interviewed eventually, but right now they're just waiting. Want to see them?"

"If they'll see me," I said. "Having the gruesome twosome show up at my door didn't do much for my credibility."

"I'm *sorry*, Alex. Goad's PD called Parker Center direct, ready to deal, and a big brass hard-on developed. Try to forget the kids for a second and see this for what it is: major unsolved homicide going nowhere and along comes credible evidence of a prior threat against the victim from someone with means and motive. At the very least, we've got Doss on conspiracy to solicit murder, which might be enough to hold him while we go looking for goodies."

"How'd Korn and Demetri figure out where he was?"

"Dropped in on his secretary." He chewed his cheek. "Saw your name in the appointment book."

"Great."

"You of all people should know it's not a pretty job, Alex."

"When's Richard's lawyer due?"

"Soon. Big-time mouthpiece named Safer, specializes in getting the upper crust out of scrapes. He'll advise Doss to stay clammed, we'll try to hold your boy on conspiracy. Either way, it'll take a long time clearing the paperwork, so figure on his being here overnight, at least."

He stood, stretched his arms, said, "I'm stiff, too much sitting around."

"Poor baby."

"You want me to apologize again? Fine, mea culpa, culpa mea."

I said, "What about Fusco's file? What about the painting? What does Doss have to do with that?"

"Who's to say the painting has anything to do with the murder? And no, nothing's forgotten, just deferred. If you can still bring yourself to do it, read the damn file. If not, I understand."

He shoved at the door and walked out into the hall.

The victim's family room was a few doors up. A young, honey-haired woman in a powder-blue pantsuit stood a few feet away.

"Detective Marchesi, Dr. Delaware," said Milo.

"Hi," she said. "I offered them Cokes but they refused, Milo."

"How're they doing?"

"Can't really say, because I've been out here the whole time. They insisted—the boy insisted—that they be by themselves. He seems to be the boss."

"Thanks, Sheila," said Milo. "Take a break."

"Sure. I'll be at my desk if you need me."

Marchesi made her way to the detective's room. Milo said, "All yours," and I turned the handle.

The room wasn't much different from an interrogation cell, had probably been converted from one. Tiny, windowless, hemmed by high-gloss mustard walls. Three chairs upholstered in mismatched floral cotton prints instead of county-issue metal. In place of the steel table with the cuff bolts was a low wooden slatted thing that resembled a picnic bench with the legs cut off. Magazines: *People, Ladies' Home Journal, Modern Computer.*

Eric and Stacy sat in two of the chairs.

Stacy stared at me.

Eric said, "Get out."

Stacy said, "Eric—"

"He's the fuck out of here—don't argue, Stace. He's obviously part of this, we can't trust him."

I said, "Eric, I can understand your thinking—"

"No more bullshit! The fat cop's your pal, you set my dad up, you fuck!"

I said, "Just give me—"

"I'll give you dick!" he shouted. Then he rushed me as Stacy cried out. Suffused blood darkened his skin to chocolate. His eyes were wild and his arms were churning and I knew he'd try to hit me. I backed away, got ready to protect myself without hurting him. Stacy was still shouting, her voice high and feline and frightened. I'd made it out the door when Eric stopped, stood there, waved his fist. Spittle foamed at the corners of his mouth.

"Get out of our lives! We'll take care of *ourselves*!"

Over his shoulder, I saw Stacy, bent low, face buried in her hands.

Eric said, "You're off the case, you fucking loser."

22

I drove home, cold hands strangling the steering wheel, heart punching against my chest wall.

Try to forget the kids, they were no longer my affair. Concentrate on facts.

Milo was right. The facts fit. His instincts had aimed him at Richard. Time to be honest: so had mine. The first time I'd heard about Mate's death, Richard had popped into my head. I'd run from the truth, hidden behind the complexities of ethical conflict, but now reality was spitting in my face.

I recalled Richard's gloating after bringing up Mate's death: *Festive times. The sonofabitch finally got what he deserved.*

Finally. Did that mean he'd turned to someone else when Goad had failed to follow through?

Means, motive. Vicarious opportunity. Ready with an alibi. Milo had pegged it right away. People like

Richard didn't do their own dirty work.

For all my theories about co-optation and irony, did the van butchery boil down to stupid, bloody revenge?

But why? What could lead someone as bright as Richard to risk so much over a man who'd been no more than an accomplice to his wife's last wishes? Was he one of those skillful psychopaths bright enough to channel his drives into high finance?

Distressed properties. A man who profited from the distress of others. Had Richard been running from a truth of his own? The fact that Joanne had frozen him out of her life, shut him out completely, chosen death in a cheap motel room over a life with him in the Palisades?

Dying in the company of another man . . . the intimacy of death. The feminist journal—*S(Hero)*—wondered about the preponderance of female travelers, speculated about the sexual overtones of assisted suicide. Had Richard seen Joanne's last night as the worst kind of adultery? I supposed it was possible, but it still seemed so . . . clumsy.

Was Richard behind the phony book and the broken stethoscope? *You're out of business, Doc?*

A sick uneasiness slithered over me. *Happy Traveling, You Sick Bastard* . . . Why had Richard contacted me within a week of the murder? Stacy's college future, as he'd claimed, or, knowing that Quentin Goad had been arrested, was he preparing himself for exactly what had happened?

Asking me to see Eric, too.

Take care of the kids while I'm gone . . . Look how *that* had turned out.

Then I thought of something much worse. Eric, all that talk of guilt and expiation.

The *directed* child, the gifted firstborn who'd dropped out to tend to his mother, had seemed to be adjusting. Suddenly leaving his dorm room, sitting up all night . . . obsessed with guilt because guilt was all he felt?

Involved. Had his father been cruel enough, crazy enough to get him *involved*?

I'd allowed myself to wonder if Eric had been Mate's slayer. Now that I'd seen his anger at work, those speculations took on weight.

Richard's deal with Goad peters out, so he keeps it in the family.

Dad in San Francisco, son down in L.A. for a couple of days with the keys to Dad's car.

I wanted to think Richard was—if nothing else—too smart for that, but if he'd been willing to risk his family by passing cash in a con bar, was there any reason to trust his judgment?

Something—a fissure—had forced its way through this family. Something to do with Joanne's death—the how, the why. Bob Manitow claimed her deterioration was all due to depression, and maybe he was right. Even so, that kind of emotional collapse didn't manifest overnight. What had led a woman with two PhDs to destroy herself slowly?

Something long-standing . . . something *Richard* had reason to feel guilty about? A guilt so crushing it had caused him to displace his feelings onto Mate?

Kill the messenger.

Make it bloody.

Father and son. And daughter.

Stacy sitting alone at the beach. Eric sitting alone under a tree. Everyone isolated. Driven apart . . . something that Mate's murder had brought to a head? Here I was again, guessing. Obsessing.

Once, when I was nine, I went through a compulsive phase, labeling my drawers, lining my shoes up in the closet. Unable to sleep unless I pulled the covers over my head in a very special way. Or maybe I'd just been trying to shut out the sound of my father's rage.

I turned off Veteran onto Sunset, raced up the glen, was still groping and supposing when the road to my house appeared so suddenly I nearly missed it. Hooking onto the bridle path, I sped up the hill, drove through the gateposts, parked in front of my little chunk of the American dream.

Home sweet home. Richard's was being torn down, brick by brick.

Robin was in the living room, straightening up. No sign of Spike.

"Out in back," she said. "Doing his business, if you must know."

"A businessman."

She laughed, kissed me, saw my face. Looked at the file. "Looks like you've got business, too."

"Things you don't want to know about," I said.

"More on Mate? The news said they arrested someone."

"Did they." I told her about Korn and Demetri's drop-in.

"*Here?* Oh my God."

"Rang the bell and took him away in front of his kids."

"That's horrible—how could Milo *do* that?"

"Not his decision. The brass went around him."

"That's just horrible—must have been hell for *you*."

"A lot worse for the kids."

"Poor things . . . The father, Alex, is he capable of that? Sorry, they're still your patients, I shouldn't be asking."

I said, "I'm not sure they are. And I don't have a good answer to that."

But I'd answered her as clearly as if I'd spelled it out. *Sure, he's capable.*

"Honey?" she said, cupping her hand around the back of my neck. She stood on her tiptoes, pressed her nose to mine. I realized I'd been standing there for a long time, silent, oblivious. The file felt leaden. I hoisted it higher.

She put her arm around my waist and we entered the kitchen. She poured iced tea for both of us and I sat at the table, placing Fusco's opus out of my field of vision. Fighting the urge to walk away from her, throw myself into the FBI man's crusade. Wanting to build up faith in Fusco's project, discover some grand, forensic *aha!* that would exonerate Richard, make me a hero in Stacy's eyes. Eric's, too.

Instead, I sat there, reached for the remote control, flicked on TV news. A red UPDATE! banner filled a corner of the screen. A very happy reporter clutched his microphone and warbled, ". . . in the murder of death doctor Eldon Mate. Police sources tell us that the man being questioned is Richard Theodore Doss, forty-six, a wealthy Pacific Palisades businessman and former husband of Joanne Doss, a woman whose suicide Dr. Mate assisted nearly a year ago. Reports of a possible murder-for-hire scheme have not been confirmed. A few minutes ago Doss's attorney arrived at the West Los Angeles police station. We'll update you on this story as it unfolds. Brian Frobush for On-the-Scene News."

In the background was the building I'd just left. The news crew must have showed up moments after I drove away.

I pressed OFF. Robin sat down next to me.

We touched glasses. I said, "Cheers."

I endured ten more minutes of togetherness. Then I told her I was sorry, picked up the file, and left.

Wounds.

Fissures. Real ones.

It was well after midnight. Robin had been asleep for over an hour and I was pretty sure she hadn't heard when I'd left the bed and made my way to the office.

I'd started with the file, but she'd come after me. Convincing me to bathe with her, take a walk, a long walk. Drive into Santa Monica for an Italian dinner. Come home and play Scrabble, then gin, then sit side by side in bed collaborating on the crossword puzzle.

"Like normal folks," I said, when she said she was sleepy.

"Acting. Genius."

"I love you—and see, I said it without making love first."

"Hey, a new pattern."

"What do you mean?"

"Saying it before. How nice." She reached for me.

Now here I was, throwing on a robe, making my way through the dark house, feeling like a burglar.

Back in the office. Switching on the green-shaded desk lamp and casting a hazy beam on the file.

The room was cold. The house was cold. The robe was old terry cloth, worn to gauze in spots. No socks. The chill took hold in the soles of my feet and worked its way up to my thighs. Telling myself that was appropriate for the task at hand, I drew the file close and untied the string.

Fusco had spared no detail in his study of Grant Rushton/Michael Burke.

Everything neat, organized, subheaded, three-hole-punched. The detached precision of postmortem reports, the weights and measures of degradation.

Page after page of crime-scene description—Fusco's summaries and analyses as well as some of the original police reports. The agent's prose was more erudite than the typically stilted cop-write, but still far from Shake-speare. He seemed to like dwelling on the nasty stuff, or maybe that was my fatigue and the cold talking.

I stuck with it, found myself entering a state of hyperawareness as I sucked up page after page of small print, photographs, crime-scene Polaroids. Autopsy shots. The beautiful, hideous, lurid hues of the human body imploded, debased, exploited like a rain forest. Sternum-cracking, face-peeling, skin-flaying, all in the name of truth. The framing of flesh-tunnels in three-by-five universes, blossoming orchids of ruptured viscera, rivers of hemoglobin syrup.

Dead faces. *The look.* Extraction of the soul.

A realization strobed my brain: Mate would've liked this.

Had he sensed what was happening to him?

I returned my eyes to the pictures. Women—things that had once been women—propped up against trees. A page of abdominal close-ups, gashes and gapes on skin transmuted to plum-colored shapes sketched on gray paper. Precisely excised wounds. The geometry.

The chill found my chest. Inhaling and letting the breath out slowly, I studied the shapes and tried to recall the death shots of Mate that Milo had showed me up on Mulholland.

Craving equivalence between all of this and the concentric squares engraved in Mate's flabby white belly.

Some concordance, I supposed, but once again Milo was right. Lots of killers like to carve.

Skin art . . .

Where was Donny Salcido Mate, self-proclaimed Rembrandt of the flesh? *The Anatomy Lesson.* Let us carve and learn.

Let us carve Daddy? 'Cause we hate Daddy but want to be him? The art of death . . . Why couldn't it be him? It *should* be him.

Then I thought of Guillerma Mate, the way she'd stood at the closet of that dingy little motel room, frozen, as I asked about her only child. Maybe faith was its own reward, but still, hers had to be a lonely life: a single mom, abandoned by her husband, disappointed by her only child.

She prayed regularly, offered thanks.

Casting her eye upon some grand world to come, or had she truly found peace? Her bus trip to L.A. said she hadn't.

Richard and his kids, Guillerma and her boy.

Alone, everyone alone.

23

Three hours into Thursday.

Three twenty-two A.M. and I'd finished every word in Fusco's omnibus. No thunderous conclusions. Then I went over the photos a second time and saw it.

Crime-scene shot from a Washington State unsolved—one of the four victims murdered during Michael Burke's term as a medical student. Four killings Fusco saw as consistent with Burke's technique because the victims had been left propped against or near trees.

The girl was a twenty-year-old waitress named Marissa Bonpaine, last seen serving shrimp cocktail at a stand in the Pike Place Market in Seattle, found a week later splayed in front of a fir in a remote part of the Olympic National Forest. No footprints near the scene; the buildup of pine needles and decaying leaves on the forest floor was a potentially fertile nest for forensic data, but nothing had been found. Add eleven days of rain to that, and the scene was as clean as the operating room the killer had intended it to be.

Marissa Bonpaine had been savaged in a manner I now found uncomfortably familiar: throat slash, abdominal mutilations, sexual posturing. A single, deep trapezoidal wound just above the pubic bone could be considered geometrical, though the edges were rough. Death from shock and blood loss.

No blunt-force head wound. I supposed Fusco would attribute that to the killer's escalating confidence and the seclusion of the spot: wanting Bonpaine conscious, wanting her to watch, to suffer. Taking his time.

I checked the girl's physical dimensions. Four-eleven, one hundred one. Tiny, easy to subdue without knocking her out.

What caught my eye wasn't any of that; after three hours of wading in gore and sadism, I'd grown sadly habituated.

I'd noticed something glinting against the brown cushion of forest detritus, several feet to the right of Marissa Bonpaine's frail left hand. Something shiny enough to catch the miserly light filtering through the dense conifer ceiling and bounce it back. I flipped pages till I found the police report.

A hiker had found the body. Forest rangers and law enforcement personnel from three departments had conducted a two-hundred-yard grid search and listed their findings under "Crime Scene Inventory." One hundred eighty-three retrieved items, mostly trash— empty cans and bottles, broken sunglasses, a can opener, rotted paper, cigarette butts—tobacco and cannabis— animal skeletons, solid lead buckshot, two copper-jacketed bullets ballistically analyzed but deemed unimportant because Marissa Bonpaine's body bore no gunshot wounds. Three pairs of insect-infested hiking boots and other discarded clothing had been studied by the crime lab and dated well before the murder.

Halfway down the list, there it was:

C.S.I. Item #76: Child's toy hypodermic, manu. TommiToy, Taiwan, orig. component of U-Be-the-Doctor Kit, imported 1989–95. Location: ground, 1.4 m from victim's l. hand, no prints, no organic residue.

No residue might have indicated recent placement, but the rain might have just washed any residue away. I read the rest of the Bonpaine documents. No sign anyone had considered the toy. A review of all the other Washington cases revealed no other medical toys.

Marissa Bonpaine was the last of the Washington victims. Her body had been found July 2, but the abduction was believed to have occurred around June 17. More page-flipping. Michael Burke had received his MD on June 12.

Graduation party?

I'm a doctor, here's my needle!

I'm *the* doctor!

Stethoscope, hypodermic. One broken, the other intact. I knew what Milo would say. Cute, but so what?

Maybe he was right—he'd been too damn right, so far—and the injector was nothing more than a piece of trash left by some kid who'd hiked through the forest with his parents.

Still, it made me wonder.

A message . . . always messages.

To Marissa: I'm the doctor.

To Mate: I'm the doctor and you're not.

I reread Fusco's notes. No mention of the toy.

Maybe I'd mention it to Milo. If he and I had the chance to talk soon.

I flipped back to the front of the first volume, the various incarnations of Michael Burke, studied every feature of every photo. A song danced through my head—*Getting to know you, getting to know all about you*—but Burke remained a stranger.

High-IQ psychopath, lust-killer, master euthanist. Comforter of terminally ill women, brutalizer of healthy females. Compartmentalizing. It helped in murder as well as politics.

Maybe in real estate, as well. The world of distressed properties.

Milo had his prime witness and I had two toys. Still, the wounds fit. And Milo had asked me to study the files.

You're out of business, I'm in.

When we'd questioned Alice Zoghbie, we'd asked her about confederates, and she'd just about admitted they existed but refused to go further, pooh-poohed the chance anyone close to Mate could have savaged him.

Eldon was brilliant. He wouldn't have trusted just anyone.

But Mate would've *loved* the idea of the MD side-kick. Another boost to his respectability—supervising an internship in cellular cessation.

Zoghbie was worth another try. She'd worshiped Mate, would want to punish his murderer. Now I had a name to throw her, a general physical description, could observe her reaction. What risk was there? I'd call her later this morning. Worst case, she'd tell me to go to hell.

Best case, I'd learn something, maybe make some progress revealing a new suspect.

Someone other than Richard. *Anyone* but Richard.

Stretching out on the old leather sofa, I covered myself with a woolen throw, stared up at the ceiling, knowing I'd never fall back asleep.

When I awoke, it was just after seven and Robin was standing over me.

"What a guy," she said, "moves out to the couch even when he hasn't misbehaved." She sat perched on the edge of the cushion, smoothed my hair.

"Morning," I said.

She looked at the file. "Cramming for the big test?"

"What can I say? Always been a grind."

"And look where it's gotten you."

"Where?"

"Fame, fortune. Me. Rise and shine. Fix yourself up so I can take care of you—I seem to be doing that a lot, lately, don't I?"

Showering and shaving provided a veneer of humanness, but my stomach recoiled at the idea of breakfast and I sat watching as Robin ate toast and eggs and grapefruit. We shared a pleasant half hour and I thought I pulled off amiable pretty well. When she left for the studio, it was eight and I turned on the morning news. Recap of the Doss story but no new facts.

At 8:20, I phoned Alice Zoghbie and heard the taped

greeting from her machine. Just as I hung up, my service rang in.

"Morning, Dr. Delaware. I have a Joseph Safer on the phone."

Richard's lawyer. "Put him on."

"Doctor? Joe Safer. I'm a criminal-defense attorney representing your patient Richard Doss."

Mellow baritone. Slow pace but no faltering. The voice of an older man—deliberate, grandfatherly, comforting.

"How's Richard doing?" I said.

"We-ell," said Safer, "he's still incarcerated, so I don't imagine he's doing too well. But that should be resolved by this afternoon."

"Paperwork?"

"Not to be paranoid, Doctor, but I do wonder if the boys in blue haven't slowed things down a bit."

"God forbid."

"Are you a religious man, Doctor?"

"Doesn't everyone invoke God when times get rough?"

He chuckled. "How true. Anyway, the reason I'm calling is once Richard does get out, he would like to speak with you about his children. How to best get them through this."

"Of course," I said.

"Terrific. We'll be in touch." Cheerful. As if planning a picnic.

"What's in store for him, Mr. Safer?"

"Call me Joe . . . We-ell, that's hard to say . . . we both enjoy the privilege of confidentiality here, so I'll be a bit forthcoming. I don't believe the police have anything one might judge as seriously incriminating. Unless something turns up during the search, and I don't expect it will . . . Doctor, you've got more latitude than I in terms of your confidentiality."

"What do you mean?"

"Unless your patient poses a Tarasoff risk, you're not obligated to divulge anything. I, on the other hand . . . There are questions I don't ask."

Letting me know he didn't want to know if his client was guilty. That I should keep my mouth shut if I knew.

"I understand," I said.

"Splendid . . . Well, then talk about Stacy and Eric for a moment. They seem like nice children. Bright, extremely bright, that's evident even under the circumstances. But troubled—they'd have to be. I'm glad you're on board if therapy's called for."

"There may be a problem with that. Eric's furious with me, convinced I'm aligned with the police. I can understand that because I am friends with one of the—"

"Milo Sturgis," said Safer. "A very effective investigator—I'm well aware of your friendship with Mr. Sturgis. Commendable."

"What is?"

"A heterosexual man enjoying a friendship with a homosexual man. One of my sons was gay. He taught me a lot about having an open mind. I didn't learn quickly enough."

Past tense. His voice had dropped in pitch and volume. "Impetuous youth," he continued. "I'm referring to Eric. I have five of my own, thirteen grandchildren. Four of my own, to be truthful. My boy Daniel passed on last year. His diagnosis sped up my learning curve."

"I'm sorry."

"Oh it was terrible, Doctor, your life's never the same . . . but enough of that. In terms of Eric's recalcitrance, I'll have a talk with the boy. As will Richard. What about Stacy? I don't have as much of a feel for her. She sits there while Eric does all the talking. Reminds me of my Daniel. He was my firstborn, always a peacemaker—his siblings' ambassador to their mother and me when things got rough."

I heard him sigh.

"Stacy's a good kid," I said. "My primary patient in the family. I had only one session with Eric, and not a complete one. The police showed up before we were through and took Richard away."

"Yes. Dreadful. Rather cossack-like behavior . . . We-ell, thank you for your time, Dr. Delaware. Take care of yourself. You're needed here."

24

Thursday at 8:45 A.M. I called Alice Zoghbie, got the same taped message. Fifteen minutes later, I caught a newsbreak. Different reporter, same I've-got-a-scoop smile. Another backdrop that I recognized.

". . . the woman, Amber Breckenham, claims that in addition, Haiselden regularly abused her and her daughter during their relationship. We're here at Haiselden's house, where neighbors say he hasn't been seen for well over a week. At the moment this remains a civil case, and no word has come down from LAPD as to whether a criminal investigation will be pursued. From Westwood, with another bizarre twist on the murder of death doctor Eldon Mate, I'm Dana Almodovar, On-the-Spot News."

Shift to the weather report. Hazy skies, low sixties to mid-seventies, for the fortieth day in a row. I played with the remote, finally found a complete story on one of the networks specializing in lurid.

Amber Breckenham, thirty-four, the manager of one of Roy Haiselden's laundromats, in Baldwin Park, had filed a civil suit against her former boss. A shot of Breckenham walking into court with her attorney showed a tall, thickly built bleached blonde. Holding her hand was a dark-haired girl, eleven or twelve. The child kept her head down, but someone called her name— "Laurette!"—and she looked up just long enough for the camera to capture a glimpse of pretty African features and straightened hair brushed back from a high, smooth brow.

Breckenham's story was that she'd had a seven-year affair with Haiselden, during which time he'd claimed to be investing her money but had, in fact, embezzled. Furthermore, he'd abused her physically and intimidated Laurette psychologically. The suit was for five million dollars, most of it punitive damages.

Haiselden's reason for cutting town? Scratch one murder suspect?

But if Amber Breckenham's charges were true, it indicated Mate had been less than a sterling judge of character. Had he misjudged fatally?

Or had choosing Joanne Doss been his big mistake?

And what had been *Joanne's* mistake—the sin, if there was one, that had caused her to turn herself into the creature in Eric's Polaroid?

I left the house, drove to the U. for my second trip to the research library in as many days.

Only one reference to Joanne's death, a page-20 story in the *Times*:

Body Found in Desert Motel

Attributed to Dr. Mate's Machine

LANCASTER. A motel maid entering to clean a room at the Happy Trails Motel on the outskirts of this high desert community discovered the fully clothed body of a Pacific Palisades woman early yesterday morning. While no sightings of "death doctor" Eldon Mate's van in the vicinity have been reported, toxicologic analysis of the blood of Joanne Doss, 43, indicating the presence of two drugs used consistently by the self-styled euthanist, as well as puncture marks suggesting intravenous injection, and the absence of forced entry or struggle, have led Sheriff's detectives to suspect assisted suicide.

Lead investigator David Graham stated, "She looked peaceful. Classical music was playing on the radio and she'd eaten a last meal. From what I understand, Dr. Mate encourages his patients to listen to music."

Ms. Doss, married to a businessman and the mother of two, was reported to have suffered from deteriorating health, and would be the forty-eighth person whose death Mate has facilitated. Given Mate's success in avoiding conviction, and most recently, his indictment, authorities say it is unlikely criminal charges will be filed.

No follow-up, not even an obituary for Joanne.

No attempt by Mate to claim credit. Maybe I'd missed something. I spent another half hour combing the data banks. Not a single additional line on Joanne Doss's final night. Because by victim number forty-eight, Mate and the Humanitron were no longer news?

Mate had hooked two additional travelers to his machine before ending up in the van himself.

The van. When had he stopped using motels?

Using Mate's name as a keyword and limiting my search to three months before and after Joanne's death, I pulled up three references.

Traveler forty-seven, seven weeks before Joanne: Maria Quillen, sixty-three, terminal ovarian cancer, her body deposited at the front door of the County Morgue wrapped in a frilly pink comforter. Mate's business card tucked into the folds. Driven in the rented van where Mate had helped her die.

Mate informed the press of the details.

Number forty-nine, one month after Joanne. Alberta Jo Johnson, fifty-four, muscular dystrophy. A black woman, the papers specified. Mate's first African American. As if her death represented a new variant of affirmative action. Her corpse had been left at the Charles Drew Medical Center in South L.A., similarly wrapped.

Another van job. Another statement by Dr. Mate.

Now my pulse was racing. I found the fiftieth traveler, a man named Brenton Spear. Lou Gehrig's. Van. Press conference.

Three people with definitive diagnoses. Three van jobs, three public statements—Mate chasing the press because, I was right, he loved the attention.

No word out of him on Joanne. No van.

Joanne's death didn't fit.

I kept searching till I found the last time he'd used a motel.

Number thirty-nine, a full two years before Joanne. Another Lou Gehrig's patient, Reynolds Dobson, dispatched in a Cowboy Inn up near Fresno.

I reread the account of Joanne's final night. No

sightings of Mate in the vicinity. *Attribution* to Mate because circumstances had pointed to him.

Cheap motel, the risk of a traumatized maid. After nearly a year's success with motor vehicles, it didn't make sense.

Mate hadn't taken credit for Joanne, because he knew he didn't deserve it.

Then why hadn't he come out and denied his involvement?

Because that would have made him look foolish. *Displaced.*

Someone horning in, a new Dr. Death, just as I'd guessed.

Broken stethoscope. Someone—Michael Burke?—making his grand entry by bathing himself in the blood of his predecessor. Hacking off Mate's manhood—you could deny Freud had ever existed and still understand *that.*

But how had Joanne gotten in contact with the person who'd accompanied her to the Happy Trails Motel?

Maybe I had it all wrong and Mate *had* known. Had allowed his apprentice to strike out on his own.

I considered that. Joanne, ready to die, calling Mate and talking instead to an underling—let's say Burke. Mate supervising, judging Burke's readiness. Unaware Burke was already an expert in the fine art of cellular cessation.

Then I remembered Michael Burke's affinity for older, seriously ill women—patients he met in hospitals—and a whole different scenario flashed.

Joanne, shuffled from doctor to doctor, enduring

batteries of medical tests. MRIs, CAT scans, lumbar punctures. Procedures carried out in hospitals.

I pictured her, bloated, pain-racked, regressed to silence, waiting in yet another antiseptic waiting room for the next round of indignities, as people in white coats hurried by, no one noticing her.

Then someone did. A charming, helpful young man. MD on his badge, but he took the time to talk. How wonderful to finally encounter a doctor who actually *talked*!

Or perhaps Burke had been more than a drop-in. Maybe he'd actually carried out some of the tests. Working as a *technician,* because he hadn't figured out a way, yet, to bogus a new medical diploma but was well-qualified to obtain a paramedical job.

Either way, I needed to learn where Joanne had been evaluated. Richard could tell me, but Richard was indisposed. Bob Manitow would also know, but there was no reason to think he'd even take my call. Whatever the reason for his antipathy, his wife didn't share it.

I'd phone Judy, find some pretense for asking about Joanne's hospital experiences—wanting to know more so I could help the kids. Especially now that Richard was in jail. I'd also try to learn more about the stress fractures that had worked their way through the Doss family. Maybe her family, as well. About why *her* husband was so angry.

Better a face-to-face, a chance to read nonverbal cues. Could I get Judy out of chambers long enough? She and I had always been cordial, and I'd come through for her on lots of tough cases. Now she'd landed me in the toughest one of all and I was ready to tell her so.

I called her number at Superior Court, expecting someone to tell me the judge was in trial. Instead, she picked up herself. "You're calling about Richard."

"The police took him away at my house. Eric and Stacy were there."

"You're kidding. Why would they do that?"

"Orders from above," I said. "They see Richard as a prime suspect for Mate. Have you heard anything around the courthouse?"

"No," she said, "just what was on the news. Bob and I were in Newport for the evening, never looked at the TV, didn't find out about it till last night when we drove home and saw the police cars at Richard's house. I just can't believe this, Alex. It makes no sense."

"Richard as a murderer."

Pause. "Richard doing something so stupid."

"On the other hand," I said, "he did despise Mate. Wasn't shy about expressing it."

"You think he's *guilty*?"

"Just playing devil's advocate."

"I don't allow those in my court— Seriously, Alex, if Richard was up to no good, why would he advertise it? All that tough talk was just Richard being Richard. Spouting off, attributing blame. He's always been a big blamer."

"Who else did he blame besides Mate?"

"No one in particular—it's just his overall style. Being dominant. The truth is, Richard's always been a difficult person—and yes, he does have a vindictive streak. You should hear him talk about how he destroys business rivals. But this? No, it just doesn't make sense. He has too much to lose— Hold on . . ." Fifteen-second hold. "Alex, they're waiting for me, got to go."

"Could we talk more, Judy?"

"What about?"

"Eric and Stacy. With all this going on, I really need all the data I can get. If you could spare me an hour, I'd greatly appreciate it."

"I . . . I just don't know what I can tell you that hasn't already been said." Brittle laughter. "Some referral, huh? I'll bet from now on you're not going to return my calls quite so quickly."

"I'll always take your referrals, Judy."

"Why's that?"

"Because you give a damn."

"Oh come on," she said. "Don't get all sugary on me. I'm just a judicial hack, putting in my time."

"I don't think so."

"That's very kind of you." Now she sounded sad. "Just an hour?"

"Use that egg timer you pull out when attorneys go on too long."

She laughed again. "You've heard about that."

"I've seen it. The Jenkins case."

"Oh yeah, good old Mr. and Mrs. Jenkins. That one deserved an egg timer with a sonic alarm— Okay, let me check my calendar, here . . . there's so much scrawl I can barely make it out."

"Sooner rather than later if possible, Judy."

"Hold again . . ." Another female voice in the background. Her clerk Doris's contralto. Judy's soprano reply. "The husband's lawyer is trying to pull shtick, time to whip him into shape . . . Okay, how about dinner tonight? I've got a ton of reports to do, will be working late,

anyway. Bob's taking Becky to the Cliffside, so I'm flexible. How about someplace on my way home—Grun!, in
Westwood. That's not far from you—eight-thirty
tonight."

"Grun! it is. Thanks, Judy. I really appreciate it."

"Oh yes," she said, "I'm quite the saint."

25

Westwood Village, as those who live nearby are quick to point out, used to be a nice place.

Once a high-end shopping district for a high-end residential area, a twist of charmingly curving streets lined with single-story brick buildings, the Village has devolved into a confused tangle of neon and chrome, weekends pulsating with noise, fast-food joints ejaculating gusts of grease and sugar.

Some of that was inevitable. Dominating the north end of the Village is the land-grant sprawl of the U., perched like a hungry bear. The encroachment stretches beyond campus borders, as the university pounces on vacant offices and builds parking lots. Student sensibilities means multiplex theaters, U-print T-shirt shops, discount record stores, jeans emporiums. Student budgets means burgers, not beluga. When a grizzly lolls near a trout stream, guess who gets eaten?

But there are other beasts at work. Developers, aiming to squeeze every dollar out of dirt. Building up, up, up, beyond, beyond, beyond. Lunching and boozing and bribing their way past zoning restrictions. People like Richard.

As token appeasements to the neighbors, some of the high-rise barons bring in pricey restaurants. Grun! was one of those, set on the top floor of a heartless black glass rhomboid on the north end of Glendon. The latest creation of a German celebrity chef with his own brand of frozen dinners.

I'd been there once, the lunch guest of an overeager personal-injury lawyer. Allegedly healthful dining formed of unlikely ethnic melds, prices that kept out the middle class. Waiters in pink shirts and khakis who launched into a world-weary, robotic recitation of the daily specials as if it was another audition. What happened to all the kids who didn't break into pictures?

I drove down Hilgard, passing sorority houses to the west, the U.'s botanical garden to the east, made it to the restaurant in ten minutes. I live close to the Village, but I rarely venture into the cacophony.

A red-jacketed valet lounged by the curb. I squeezed in between two Porsche Boxsters, and the attendant examined the Seville as if it was a museum piece.

I was inside by eight-thirty on the nose. The hostess was a hollow-cheeked, lank-haired brunette working hard on a Morticia Addams act. Judy Manitow hadn't arrived. It took a while to get Tish's attention and figure out that the JTJ in the reservation book stood for Judy the Judge. Tish directed me to the bar. I looked over her shoulder at the half-empty dining room and gave my best boyish grin. She sighed and fluttered her lashes and allowed me to trail her to a corner table.

Half-empty but noisy, sound waves caroming against bleached wood walls, ostentatiously distressed plank floors and mock-wormwood ceiling beams. Where plaster had been applied, it was an unhealthy sunburn pink. Iron tables covered in rose linen, chairs sheathed in dark green suedette.

Tish stopped midway in our trek. Sighed again. Turned. Rotated her neck, as if warming up for a workout. "I just love the way the light hits the room from this spot."

"Fantastic." Lights, camera, action. *Cut.*

The table was barely big enough for solitaire. A couple of waiters loitered nearby but neither made a move toward me. Finally, a Hispanic busboy came over and asked if I wanted something to drink. I said I'd wait and he thanked me and brought water.

Ten minutes later, Judy breezed in looking harried. She wore a formfitting, plum-colored knit suit, the skirt ending two inches above her knees, and matching pumps with precarious heels. Her cream-colored handbag had a sparkly clasp that functioned like a headlight, and as she approached at power-walk speed I thought of a little hot rod.

She looked even thinner than I remembered, facial bones expressing themselves sharply under an ash-blond, tennis-friendly cap of hair. Sparkles flashed at her neck, too, and on both hands. As she got closer, she saw me, wiggled two fingers, and picked up speed, playing a castanet solo on the plank floor, hips swiveling, calves defined. The waiters exchanged appreciative glances as they followed her and I wondered if they thought they had her figured out.

Good-looking, wealthy woman out for a night on the town. Little chance she'd be pegged as a presiding Superior Court judge.

I stood to greet her and she pecked my cheek. When I held her chair, she acted as if she was used to it.

"Good to see you again, Alex. Though I'm sure we'd both rather it be under different circumstances."

One of the loitering waiters came over, smiled at Judy, opened his mouth. Before he could speak, she said, "Gin and tonic. Sapphire gin. And no bruising. Please."

He pouted and his eyes found their way over to me. "Sir?"

"Iced tea."

"Very good."

As he walked away, Judy said, "Veddy *good.* I'm so glad the children approve." She laughed. Too loud, too much edge. "I don't know why I suggested this place, Bob and I never come anymore . . . Pardon me, Alex, I'm feeling mean, need time to wind down and get human. That's one good thing about the drive from downtown. If you don't succumb to road rage, there's plenty of time to decompress."

"Rough day in court?" I said.

"Is it ever sweetness and light? No, nothing extra-ordinary, just the usual parade of people with unsolvable problems. When things are fairly calm on the outside, I have no problem with any of it. But today . . ." She fingered a diamond ring on her left hand. Big, round solitaire in a platinum setting. Her right hand sported a cocktail piece—yellow diamonds and sapphires formed into a marigold. "I still can't believe this mess with Richard. Did you have a chance to see Eric and Stacy after they took him away?"

"I saw them briefly at the station but didn't have a chance to talk to them. Richard's lawyer—Joseph Safer— called me this morning and told me he expected to get Richard out by today and that Richard would be calling me to talk. I'm still waiting."

It had been a day for waiting. And guesswork. If a hypothesis is formed in the forest and no one's there to . . . After returning from the library, I'd gone over Fusco's file again, no new insights. No new messages from anyone. I hadn't run for a couple of days, forced myself to do it, ended up in the mountains for a long time, got home still wired, did some push-ups, showered, drank water.

At six, despite the dinner appointment with Judy, I broiled two steaks and baked a couple of Idahos. Steak with Robin. I figured on a salad with Judy. Light and healthful me, what a social butterfly.

The drinks came. Judy raised her glass, inspected the contents and sipped. "Joe Safer is a prince—I'm not being sarcastic. The ideal defense attorney: kindly demeanor combined with the single-mindedness of a psychopath. If I were in trouble, I'd want him to talk for me." Her blue eyes clouded for a moment. She drank some more and they seemed to clear.

"Ah," she said. "This hits the spot. I don't ingest enough poison."

"Too temperate?"

"Too weight-conscious."

"You?"

She smiled. "When I was sixteen I weighed a hundred and ninety-seven pounds. In high school, I was a total slug. To be accurate, I was *repugnant*. Walking two steps exhausted me." Another sip. "I guess that's why I could empathize with Joanne . . . up to a point."

"Up to a point?" I said.

"Only up to a point." Angry squint. "Let's just say that where she ended up was a whole different planet." She drank more, licked her lips.

"It's hard to imagine someone deciding to eat herself into a stupor."

"Oh," she said, "Joanne was full of surprises."

"Such as?"

Another squint. "Just that. And unlike me, she started off thin."

Her voice had filled with anger and I decided to veer away. When in doubt, show personal interest.

"How'd you take off the weight?" I said.

"The old-fashioned way: deprivation. Self-denial has become my lifestyle, Alex." She ran her finger around the rim of the glass. "There's no other way, is there?"

"Self-denial?"

"Fighting," she said. "Most people lack the will. That's why we spend gazillions on the so-called war on drugs, preach about smoking and eating too much fat, but never make any progress. People will never stop getting high. People will take comfort where they find it." Another laugh. "Some talk for a judge, huh? Anyway, I take care of myself. For health, not cosmetics. I keep my family healthy."

"Your girls are pretty athletic, aren't they?"

"What makes you say that?"

"I seem to recall pictures in your office—outdoor sports?"

"My, what a memory," she said. "Yes, Ali and Becky like to sail and ski and they're trim now, but both of them have a tendency to pudge. Lousy genetics: Bob and I were both lumpy kids. I stay on them. It's easier now that they've discovered boys." She sat back. "They both have, thank goodness. Does that sound terrible? Perfectionistic mom?"

"I'm sure you care about them."

"That was shamelessly nonjudgmental, Alex. We're diametric opposites, aren't we? I get paid to do precisely what you avoid."

The waiter approached and asked if she wanted a refill.

"Not at this point," she said. "The doctor here will have a look at the menu, but I know what I want. The Tender Greens Salad, everything chopped very fine, no dried apricots or olives or nuts, dressing on the side."

"I'll have the same," I said, "but leave in the nuts."

The waiter glanced at his list of specials and walked away looking miffed. Judy said, "Leave in the nuts? Funny . . . So—you have no idea how Eric and Stacy are coping?"

"I'm sure it's rough for them. Any further thoughts about Richard?"

"Do I think he's capable of soliciting murder? Alex, you know as well as I do that no one can ever really fathom what goes on in someone's head. So yes, I suppose it's theoretically possible that Richard tried to have Mate killed. But the way they said he did it sounds so damn stupid, and Richard's anything but."

"Joanne was brilliant, too."

Her face tightened. Tiny lines, softened by makeup and indirect lighting, appeared all over the surface of her skin. A woman cracking.

"Yes, she was. I won't profess to understand why she did the things she did."

I waited for the stress lines to fade. They didn't. She was gazing into her gin and tonic, playing with the stirrer.

"I guess we never really understand anyone, do we?"

I said, "Let's assume—for argument's sake—that Richard did pay Quentin Goad. Why would he hate Mate that much?"

She touched a finger to her upper lip, massaged, looked up at the ceiling. "Perhaps he saw Mate as taking away something that belonged to him. Richard likes his possessions."

"Was he especially possessive when it came to Joanne?"

"More than any other alpha male? He's a middle-aged *man,* Alex. He's from a certain generation."

"So he saw Joanne as his."

"Bob sees me as his. If you're asking was Richard pathologically jealous, I never saw it."

"And Joanne chose to exclude him from the most important decision of her life."

She swiped her lips with her napkin. "Meaning?"

"Meaning I don't understand much about this family, Judy."

"Neither do I," she said, very softly. "Neither do I." The restaurant din nearly blocked out the sound and I realized I was reading her lips.

"Have you ever met Richard's parents?"

"No," she said. "They never visited, as far as I know, and Richard never talked about them. Why?"

"Grabbing any fact I can. Eric told me he's Greek-Sicilian."

"I suppose I was aware of that—Joanne must've said something, or one of the kids did. But I can't recall Richard ever making a thing about it. I never saw grape leaves in the house, or anything like that."

She looked and sounded tired, as if talking about the Doss family drained her.

I said, "As friends and neighbors, they must have been a challenge."

"What do you mean?" she said, in the same sharp tone I'd heard her use on an errant lawyer.

"They're the kind of people to whom things happen. When I spoke to Bob about Joanne's diagnosis, he sounded pretty frustrated about Joanne's condition—"

"Did he?" she said absently. She gazed around the room. A few more tables had filled. "That's just Bob being Bob. He prides himself on being analytic: identify the problem, cut it out."

"Which he couldn't do with Joanne."

"No, he couldn't." She stirred the drink. Eyes down again. Stress lines deeper.

"Bob seems to feel her illness was all emotional depression," I said.

She looked over at a table to the right. Two couples seated a few minutes ago, laughing, drinking. She summoned the waiter over, ordered another gin and tonic.

"Do you agree?" I said.

"With what?"

"That it was all emotional."

"I'm not a doctor, Alex. I couldn't begin to fathom Joanne's motivation." Another glance at the happiness nearby.

"In terms of Eric and Stacy—"

"Eric and Stacy are going to cope and move on, right? That's why I sent Stacy to you."

Her second drink came. We traded courtroom stories and I listened to her go on about municipal politics, the D.A.'s inability to collect child support. That enabled me to steer the conversation back where I wanted it.

"They couldn't get Mate, either."

She stirred gin, nodded.

"I'm not sure Mate was happy about that," I said. "No more prime time."

"Yes, he was a grandstander, wasn't he?"

"The interesting thing is, Judy, he never took credit for Joanne's death. Never even tried, and it's the only case I could find where that was true."

She'd been holding the glass in midair, lowered it slowly. "You've been researching?"

"The police assumed Mate had assisted Joanne, but they never confirmed it."

"I'd say it's a pretty good assumption, Alex. Her body was full of those chemicals Mate used."

Our salads arrived. Big plate of what looked like lawn shavings. A few cashews on mine. My belly was still filled with steak and nothing had transpired to spark my appetite. I pushed leaves around. Judy aimed her fork at a cherry tomato, tried to stab it, but it rolled out from under the tines. For a split second, fury darkened her face. Talking about the Dosses had been an ordeal.

She speared a speck of lettuce. "Even if Richard was

stupid enough to give money to that loser, the loser backed out. I'm hoping he didn't try again. After we spoke, I asked around. So far, nothing beyond solicitation. Have you heard anything to the contrary?"

"No," I said.

"Passion, Alex. It makes people do crazy things."

"Richard was passionate about Joanne?"

"I suppose he was." Peeling back her sleeve, she glanced at the Lady Rolex.

"Here comes the egg timer," I said.

She smiled. "I'm sorry, Alex. I'm very tired—not hungry, either. Is there anything else?"

"I'd like to know more about Eric."

"Just what I told you the first time. A genius, perfectionistic. Dominant personality."

"Stacy said he and Ali dated."

Pause. "Yes, they did. Year ago. Ali said he was a bit of a control freak—nothing weird, he just proved too intense for her. She broke it off."

Stacy had said Eric had severed the relationship. Teenage soap opera. Did it matter?

I said, "He sounds a lot like Richard."

"He's Richard's boy all the way. Like a little nuclear weapon with legs."

"And Stacy?"

"You're Stacy's therapist. What do you think?"

"Was she distant from Joanne?"

"Why do you ask that?"

"Because it was Eric who spent time with Joanne during her last days."

She pushed her plate away. "Alex, I think you've gotten the wrong idea about the Dosses and us. We were friends, neighbors, lunched at the Cliffside. But for the most part they kept their problems to themselves and we lived our own life. Richard told Bob that Stacy seemed to be drifting. From the little I saw, she seemed a bit depressed, so I sent her to you. That's all there is. I can't carry any more on my shoulders. I'm sorry I haven't been more helpful, but that's all there is."

She got up, marched to our waiter, who was talking with a colleague, stood there for a few seconds, then said something that caused his head to retract, as if he'd been bitten. He stalked away and she returned, finished her drink while standing. "Snotty little bastard. I'm waiting to tell him we're ready for the check, he's discussing his latest *audition*."

Looking off to one side, the object of her wrath raced over, flung the check at the table and fled. Judy reached for it, but I got there first.

"What?" she said. "Bribing the judge?"

"Thanking the judge for her time," I said.

"That's all I've given you," she said. "Time. Heat, no light."

Her Lexus had been left at the curb and I waited for her to drive away. As I waited for the Seville, I tried to make sense out of the last half hour.

She'd arrived at the restaurant looking strained—more tense than I'd ever seen her—and each of my questions seemed to yank her psyche's drawstring tighter. Before she left, she warned off further inquiry. So I'd opened some kind of wound but had no idea what it was.

No chance to get to the topic of hospitals, no way to work it into the conversation.

I'd watched her in court, seen her handle the toughest of cases with aplomb, so this was something personal . . . The closest she'd gotten to autobiography was self-loathing about her teenage obesity.

I was repugnant . . . But if that related to the Dosses, I was missing the connection.

I can't carry any more on my shoulders.

Burdened by the Dosses, as was her husband? Bob expressing it as anger because he was a man of a certain generation?

Some kind of intimacy gone terribly bad? Bob jealous of Richard and Joanne in the pool—did it all reduce to another sleazy suburban couples' swap?

And had that related, in some way, to Joanne's decline? Something Richard couldn't forgive her for?

Guilt and expiation. Had *Eric* found out?

Eric and Allison breaking up, Becky in therapy, eating disorders, poor grades, Joanne quitting as tutor, Stacy losing focus, Eric dropping out. Bob enraged, Judy on the edge . . . Joanne dead.

Put together a certain way, I could make it sound like a psychopathology stew.

Even so, what did it have to do with Mate's corpse stretched out in the back of a van, geometry on flesh?

Why hadn't Mate taken credit for Joanne?

The Seville screeched to a halt and the attendant held my door with an expression that said I didn't deserve it. Driving away, I went over it again, finally decided I'd wasted my time and Judy's, most certainly damaged my relationship with the presiding judge of family court.

Another day, another triumph. The car was low on gas and I filled up at a station on Wilshire, used the pay phone near the men's room to call my service. Joseph Safer had phoned five minutes earlier from the Dosses' home number.

Richard answered, hoarse, quieter than usual. "Doctor—hold on." A second later, Safer's melodious voice flowed through the receiver.

"Doctor, thanks so much for getting back promptly."

"What's up?"

"Richard and the children are home. Richard arrived four hours ago, but I waited until the hubbub died down before I called you."

"Press hubbub?"

"Press, police, what you'd expect. As far as I can tell, everyone's departed with the exception of a single unmarked police car parked down the block. Occupied by the two gentlemen who accosted Richard at your home, as a matter of fact."

Korn and Demetri on butt-numbing duty. So Milo had regained at least some of the upper hand.

"Not too subtle," I said.

"We-ell." Safer chuckled. "Cossacks aren't generally known for subtlety."

"Did they search the house?"

"They threatened to," said Safer. "We're disputing their contentions, urging the judge to exercise some restraint. I realize it's an imposition at this hour— however, if you could find time to come over to chat with Richard and the children, that would be marvelous."

"At the house?"

"I could bring them to your office, but with all they've been through . . ."

"No, that's fine," I said. "I'll be right over."

CHAPTER

26

Safer gave me directions to the house: west on Sunset, past the Pacific Palisades shopping district, a mile beyond the old Will Rogers estate, then a quick turn north.

Twenty minutes or so from the Village, just as close to my home. In all the time I'd spent with the Dosses, I'd never seen them in their natural surroundings. Back when I was an intern at Western Peds, I found time to make house calls, school visits. After I got licensed, I rarely ventured from the comfort of my own furniture. Was I nothing more than a primatologist deluding himself that he understood chimps because he'd observed them scratching and swinging behind the bars of zoo cages?

House calls were impractical.

Practicality could be confining. Now I'd have the chance to stretch.

• • •

I found the turnoff easily enough and sped up a very dark street that climbed into the Palisades. No sidewalks, front lawns the size of small parks, walls and gates and talkboxes, night-black shrubbery, towering cascades of old-growth trees.

Close enough to the ocean to feel the breeze and smell the brine. Were ugly September mornings better up here? I caught glimmers of moon-blanched water between the bulk of big houses. As I continued, the properties got wider, offered broader glimpses of Pacific. Now I was high enough to see all of the moon, gravid and low. The sky was a cloudless indigo comforter.

Very few cars were parked on the street, and the unmarked, fifty yards up, was as inconspicuous as a roach on a fridge. I sped by, vaguely aware of two heads in front, not bothering to notice if Korn or Demetri made me. Assuming they had. Now I was a notation in the murder book.

I cruised, looked for the address Safer had given me, wondered which neighboring structure housed the Manitows' dreams and nightmares.

Richard's monument to success turned out to be a two-story Monterey colonial, pale and ambitious above a hillock of ryegrass spacious enough to host several clusters of trees. Coconut palms, Canary Island pines, lemon eucalyptus, pittosporum, all prettified by clean white lighting that created herbal sculpture. Meticulous flower beds kissed the front of the house. Lights from within turned curtained windows amber. The lack of wall and gate implied openness, welcome. So much for architectural cues.

Stacy's Mustang sat in the driveway, in front of a

silver Cadillac Fleetwood of a size no longer manufactured. No sign of Richard's black BMW. Perhaps the auto
warrant had gone through and the vehicle was being
raked and combed and vacuumed and luminoled in some
forensic garage.

I pulled in behind the Caddy. Its plates read
SHYSTER.

A Bouquet Canyon rock pathway snaked to a heavy
door banded with hand-forged iron. Before I got to the
entrance, the door opened and a rabbi gazed out at me. A
tall, rangy, black-suited, yarmulked, gray-bearded rabbi
in his sixties. The beard was clipped square and blocked
the knot of his silver-gray tie. The suit was double-
breasted and tailored. He stood with his hands behind his
back and rocked. His presence threw me. The Dosses
were Greek-Sicilian, not Jewish.

The rabbi said, "Doctor? Joe Safer."

One hand appeared. We shook, and Safer motioned
me into a chandeliered entry hall guarded by a pair of
blue-and-white vases as high as my shoulder. An iron-
railed staircase swept upward to the second story. Safer
and I walked under it and continued to another vestibule
bottomed by a crimson Persian runner that fed into a
wide, bright hallway. To the left was a dining room
papered in blue and set up with plum-colored rosewood
furniture that looked old. Across the foyer was a high-
ceilinged living room. Ivory ceiling, cream silk sofas,
cherrywood floors. If the neutral tones had been
designed to show off what was on the walls, they worked.

Case after case of brass-framed, mirror-backed,
glassed-in étagères, custom-fit to the crown molding.
Glass shelves so clear they were rendered nearly

invisible. What rested upon them appeared suspended in midair, just as Milo had described.

Hundreds of bowls, chargers, ewers, jars, shapes I couldn't identify, each piece spotlit and gleaming. One side wall of more blue and white, the other filled with simple-looking gray-green pieces, the widest expanse populated by a porcelain bestiary: horses and camels and dogs and fantastic, bat-eared creatures that resembled the spawn of a dragon with a monkey, all dappled in beautifully dripping mixtures of blue, green and chartreuse. Human figurines rode some of the horses. On a seven-foot coffee table sat what looked like a miniature temple glazed with the same multicolored splotch.

"Something, eh?" said Safer. "Richard informs me that those animals are all Tang dynasty. Over a thousand years old. They pull them up out of graves in China, beautifully preserved. Quite remarkable, wouldn't you say?"

"Quite brave keeping them here," I said, "given the seismic risks."

Safer stroked his beard and pushed his yarmulke back on his head. His hair was an iron-gray crew cut specked with red. I still couldn't get rid of the rabbinical image. Remembered his comment about the death of his gay son. *His diagnosis sped my learning curve.* His eyes were gray-green, borderline warm. Like many tall men, he stooped.

"Richard's a courageous man," he said. "The children are courageous. Let's go see them."

We continued through the center hallway. Black carpeting muffled our steps as we passed more brass cases. Monochrome bowls of every color, the mirror backs reflecting Chinese inscriptions on white bases, tiny mud-colored figurines, shelves of potters' creations in white and cream and gray, more of that pale, clean green that I decided I liked best. A row of closed doors, two more at the rear. Safer beckoned me through the one that was open.

Cathedral ceiling, black leather sofas and chairs, black grand piano filling a corner. Through a wall of french doors, an aqua pool and green-lit foliage. Beyond the chlorinated water, palm fringes and the hint of ocean. The seating faced rosewood bookshelves filled with hard-covers, a Bang & Olufsen stereo system, a seventy-inch TV, laser-disc machine, other amusements. On an upper shelf, four family photos. Three of Richard and the kids, a single portrait of Joanne as a smiling young woman.

Richard sat upright on the largest of the sofas, unshaven, sleeves rolled to the elbows, kinky hair ragged—pulled-at, as if birds had attacked, seeking nesting material. He wore the usual all-black and blended so thoroughly with the couch that his body contours were obscured. It made him seem very small— like a growth that had sprouted from the upholstery.

"You're here," he said, sounding half asleep. "Thanks."

I took an armchair and Richard gazed up at Joe Safer.

Safer said, "I'll go see how the kids are doing," and left. Richard picked something out of the corner of his mouth. Sweat beads ringed his hairline.

When Safer's footsteps had faded completely, he said, "They say he's the best." Staring past me. "This is our family room."

"Beautiful house," I said.

"So I've been told."

"What happened?" I said. Any way he took that would be fine.

He didn't answer, kept his gaze above me—focused on the blank TV. As if waiting for the set to come on by itself and feed him some form of enlightenment.

"So," he said, finally. "Here we are."

"What can I do for you, Richard?"

"Safer says anything I tell you is confidential, unless you think I'm a direct threat to someone else."

"That's true."

"I'm no threat to anyone."

"Good."

He jammed his fingers in his hair, tugged at the wiry strands. "Still, let's keep it hypothetical. For the sake of all concerned."

"Keep what hypothetical?" I said.

"The situation. Say a person—a man, by no means a stupid man but not infallible—say he falls prey to an impulse and does something stupid."

"What impulse?"

"The drive to attain closure. Not a smart move, in fact it's the single stupidest, most insane thing he's ever done in his life, but he's not in his right mind because events have . . . changed him. In the past, he's lived a life full of expectations. That's not to say he's wedded to optimism. Of all people, he knows things don't always work out according to plan. He's earned a *living* understanding that. But still, after all these years of building, establishing, he's done very well, gotten sucked in by the trap of rising expectations. Feels he has a right to some degree of comfort. Then he learns differently."

He shrugged. "What's done is done."

"His acting on impulse," I said.

He sucked in breath, gave a sick smile. "He's not in his right mind, let's leave it at that."

Crossing his legs, he sat back, as if giving me time to digest. I had a pretty good idea what he was up to. Working on a diminished-capacity defense. Safer's advice or his own idea?

"Temporary insanity," I said.

"If it comes to that. The only problem is, because he's so screwed up, in the process he may have upset his kids. His own peccadilloes, he can deal with. But his kids, he needs help with that."

Murder-for-hire as a peccadillo.

I said, "Do the kids know what he's done?"

"He hasn't told them, but they're smart kids, they may have figured it out."

"May have."

He nodded.

I said, "Does he intend to tell them?"

"He doesn't see the point of that."

"So he wants someone else to tell them."

"No," he said, suddenly raising his voice. A splash of rose seeped from under his shirt collar and climbed to his earlobes, vivid as a port-wine stain. "He definitely does *not* want that, that is *not* the issue. Helping them through the process *is*. I—he needs someone to tide them over until things settle down."

"He expects things to settle down," I said.

He smiled. "Circumstances dictate optimism. So, do we have an understanding of the issues at hand?"

"No knowledge provided to the kids, holding their

hands until their father is out of trouble. Sounds like high-priced baby-sitting."

The flush darkened his entire face, his chest heaved and his eyes began to bulge. The surge of color made me draw back defensively. It's the kind of thing you see in people who have a serious problem with anger. I thought of Eric's outburst in the victims' room at the station.

New side of Richard. Before this, he'd been unfailingly contentious, sometimes irritable, but always cool.

He worked at cooling off now, placing one hand on the arm of the sofa, cupping a knee with the other, as if hastening self-restraint. Ticking off the seconds with his index finger. Ten ticks later, he said, "All right," in the tone you'd use with a slow learner. "We'll call it baby-sitting. Well-trained, well-*paid* baby-sitting. The main thing is the kids get what they need."

"Until things settle down."

"Don't worry," he said. "They will. The funny thing is, despite his poor judgment, he didn't actually *do* anything."

"Soliciting murder's not nothing—hypothetically speaking."

His eyelids drooped. He got up, stepped closer to my chair. I smelled mint on his breath, cologne, putrid sweat. "Nothing *happened*."

"Okay," I said.

"*Nothing.* This person learned from his mistake."

"And didn't try again."

He aimed a finger gun down at me. "Bingo." Easy tone, but the flush had lingered. He stood there, finally returned to the sofa. "Okay then, we have a meeting of the minds."

"What exactly do you want me to tell your kids, Richard?"

"That everything's going to be fine." Making no attempt to steer it back to third-person theoretical. "That I may be . . . indisposed for a while. But only temporarily. They need to know that. I'm the only parent they have left. *They* need *me*, and *I* need *you* to facilitate."

"All right," I said. "But we should also be looking for other sources of support. Are there any family members who could—"

"No," he said. "No one. My mother's dead, and my father's ninety-two and living in a home in New Jersey."

"What about Joanne's side—"

"Nothing," he said. "Both of her parents are gone and she was an only child. Besides, I don't need meddling laymen, I need a professional. Not a bad deal for you. I'll start paying you the way I pay Safer—driving time, thinking time, every billable second."

I didn't answer.

He said, "Why do we have this thing, you and I, everything turns into a push-and-pull?"

Lots of answers to that one, none good. I said, "Richard, we have a meeting of the minds on one point: my role is helping Stacy and Eric. But I need to be honest with you: I have no magic to offer them. Information's my armament. I need to be equipped."

"Oh for God's sake," he said, "what do you want from me, confession? Expiation?"

"Expiation," I said. "Eric used that word, too."

His mouth opened. Shut. The flush drained from his face. Now he'd paled. "Eric has a good vocabulary."

"It's not a topic you and he have discussed?"

"Why the hell *would* it be?"

"I was just wondering if Eric had some reason to feel guilty."

"What the hell about?"

"That's what I'm asking," I said, feeling more like a lawyer cross-examining than a therapist easing pain. He was right, this was our script, and I was as much a player as he.

"No," he said, "Eric's fine. Eric's a great kid." He slumped, rubbed his eyes, half disappeared into the couch, and I began to feel sorry for him. Then I thought of him passing cash to Quentin Goad. In the name of closure.

"So there's nothing particular on Eric's mind."

"His mother destroyed herself, his father got hauled in by the gestapo. Now, what could be on his *mind*?"

He resumed staring at the TV screen. "What's the problem here? Do you resent us because we've made it? Did you grow up poor? Do you resent rich kids? Does having to deal with them day in and day out because they're the ones who pay your bills piss you off? Is that the reason you won't help us?"

My sigh was involuntary.

He said, "Okay, okay, sorry, that was out of line, it's been a . . . rough time. All I'm asking for is some help with Eric and Stacy. If I wasn't so close to the situation, I could deal with it myself. At least I have the insight to know my limitations, right? How many parents can you say that of?"

Footsteps sounded from above. Someone walking. Pacing. Stopping. The kids on the second floor . . .

I said, "No stonewall, Richard. I'm here for Eric and Stacy. Are you in any state to answer a few questions about Joanne?"

"What about Joanne?"

"Basic history. At what hospital did she take her medical tests?"

"St. Michael's. Why?"

"I may want to look at her medical records."

"Same question."

"I'm still trying to understand what was wrong with her."

"Her medical records won't tell you a damn thing," he said. "That's the point, the doctors didn't know. And what does Joanne's illness have to do with the current situation?"

"It may have something to do with Eric and Stacy," I said. "As I said, I run on information. May I have a release from you to look at her records?"

"Sure, sure, Safer can give it to you, I signed over power of attorney to him while I was indisposed. Now, how about going up to talk to my kids?"

"Please bear with me," I said. "After Joanne died, you called Mate, but he never called you back—"

"Did I tell you that?"

"No, Judy did when she made the referral."

"Judy." He swiped at his brow with the back of his hand. "Well, Judy's correct. I did try. Not once, several times. The bastard never gave me the courtesy."

"He didn't throw a press conference regarding Joanne, either."

His eyes slitted. "So?"

"Publicity seemed to be a motive for him—"

"You've got that right," he said. "He was a scum-sucking publicity hound. But don't ask me to explain what he did and didn't do. To me he was a name in the papers."

Easy to erase?

I said, "One other discrepancy: by the time Joanne contacted Mate, he'd already shifted from motels to vans. Yet Joanne died in a motel. Would there have been some reason for her to insist upon that? Some reason for her to travel to Lancaster—"

"She was *never* there," he said.

"Never at the motel?"

"Never in Lancaster." He laughed. Sudden, bitter, incongruous laughter. "Not till that night. It was a thing between us. I was out there all the time, did several projects there, building shopping centers, turning shit into gold. Used to copter from the Municipal Bank Building to Palmdale, drive the rest of the way. Spent so many goddamn hours there I used to feel I was *made* of sand. Joanne never saw *any* of it. I used to ask her—*beg* her—to drive out, just once in a while. Join me for lunch, see what we were accomplishing. I told her the desert could be beautiful when you looked at it a certain way, we could find some good, cheap eats, go casual—goddamn Pizza Hut or something, like when we were broke and dating. No way. She always turned me down, said it was too far to drive. Too much traffic, too dry, too hot, too busy, there was always a reason."

He laughed again. "But she ended up there." Turning to stare at me. For once, not a combative glare. Sad, pitiful, seeking an answer.

"Oh Jesus," he said. An abrupt, suppressed sob made

him choke. He bounced once on the sofa, as if levitated by pain and slammed back down by fate.

"Goddamn her," he whispered. Then he lost the fight and the tears gushed. He punched air, punched his knees, attacked his own chest, his shoulder, knuckled his eyes. Hid his face from me.

"Fuckin' *Lancaster*! For *that* she goes out there! Oh *Jesus*! Oh Jesus. *Christ*!"

He lowered his head between his legs, as if about to vomit, found no comfort in that position and sprang up, running to the wall of French doors, where he turned his back on me and cried silently while facing his swimming pool and his land and the faraway ocean.

"She must've really hated me," he said.

"Why would she hate you, Richard?"

"For not forgiving her."

"What did she do?"

"No," he said. "No more of this, don't strip off my *skin*, just let me get through this with my *skin* on, okay? I won't try to tell you how to do your job, just let it be. Help my kids. *Please*."

"Sure," I said. "Of course."

27

The footsteps from above resumed. Moments later Joe Safer knocked on the doorjamb. Richard was still staring through the glass. He turned.

Safer said, "Everything all right?"

"Joe, I'm really bushed, think I'll lie down." Trudging to the sofa, Richard removed his shoes, lined them up at the base of the couch, stretched out.

"Why don't you go upstairs to bed?" said Safer.

"Nah, I'll just sack out here. This is my relaxation spot." Richard reached for a remote control, clicked on seventy inches of the Home & Garden channel. Someone wearing a plaid shirt and a massive tool belt building a redwood deck. Making it look as easy as licking an envelope, the way those types always do.

Within seconds, Richard seemed hypnotized.

"Ready for the children?" Safer asked me.

"Ready."

I followed him up a rear staircase, arranging the file cards in my head.

Guilt, expiation. *I didn't forgive her.*

Joanne transgressing—probably exactly what I'd guessed: an affair.

Eric, close to his father, aligned with his father. Had Joanne's transgression led her son to despise her? Spending time with her as she destroyed herself, loving her but also *hating* her? Could that explain the Polaroids? Documenting her descent—her punishment—then passing the pictures to Richard . . .

That level of filial contempt was hard to imagine, but Eric was explosive and impulsive and he had the genes for it. Now, months later, was he coming to grips with what he'd done? Seeking his own expiation?

Richard had just admitted paying Quentin Goad to murder the death doctor.

Make it look bloody . . . the wrong guy to cheat on. With Richard's need for control, how could Joanne have expected anything but rejection and retribution?

Attempted murder as closure . . . and, if Mate hadn't helped Joanne die, a grand mistake.

If he hadn't, who *had*?

Do-it-yourself job? As a microbiologist, Joanne had access to lethal chemicals, the skills for self-injection. But given her physical condition I couldn't see her driving to Lancaster by herself . . .

She hated me. Now I had a reason she'd died in the Happy Trails Motel.

So maybe Mate *had* been there, agreeing to revert back to rented rooms in order to respect Joanne's wishes. Same for the lack of publicity: perhaps Joanne had requested he keep it quiet. For the sake of the kids? No, that made no sense. If she'd wanted to shield Eric, why choose such a conspicuous suicide?

Why kill herself by *any* means?

One thing seemed clear: Mr. and Mrs. Doss had suffered through a troubled relationship. Mrs. had sinned and Mr. had refused to forgive her.

Joanne had bought into Richard's rage. Hating herself enough to self-destruct.

But she hadn't gone out without a parting shot.

Taking control of the last day of her life. Contacting Mate—or someone else—on the sly. Dying on her own terms.

Lancaster. The ultimate screw-you to Richard.

Because she knew Richard well, knew he'd try to direct his anger everywhere else and a corpse in a cheap motel would be something he couldn't escape.

Or so she'd hoped. If funneling Richard toward crushing introspection had been Joanne's goal, she'd failed miserably. As Judy had said, Richard was a blamer.

And Richard liked to crush his adversaries.

A few minutes before, spinning his "hypothetical" tale, he'd brushed off the deal with Quentin Goad as an act of folly, denied he'd made a second attempt.

Yet he'd come prepared with an alibi, was already talking about temporary insanity. Milo would laugh all that off. You didn't have to be a *detective* to laugh it off. Because Richard was a ruthless, self-centered control freak who'd believed himself aggrieved. And as I'd just seen, Richard had a *very* bad temper.

Now here I was in his house, on his terms.

Safer reached the top of the stairs and paused at a small back landing that faced a closed door. "They're both in Eric's room," he said. "Would you like to see them together or separately?"

"Let's see how it goes."

"But together would be okay?"

"Why?"

He frowned. "To be frank, Doctor, neither of them wants to be alone with you."

"They still think I betrayed them?"

Safer righted his yarmulke. "I'm sorry. Richard talked to them and so did I, but you know adolescents. I hope this doesn't turn out to be a complete waste of your time."

Or worse, I thought.

Safer touched the doorknob but didn't turn it. "So how did it go with Richard?"

"Richard seems to feel rosy about the future," I said.

Rosy. The moment I said it I realized it was the same word I'd thought of upon seeing Richard's anger-flush. Poor old Dr. Freud wasn't getting enough respect in the age of Prozac.

"We-ell," said Safer, "a positive attitude is a good thing, wouldn't you say?"

"In Richard's case, is it justified?"

One big, gnarled hand came forward and smoothed the beard. "Let's put it this way, Doctor. I can't promise to bring everything to a close immediately, but I'm feeling positive, as well. Because when you get down to it, what do the police have? The Johnny-come-lately accusations of a habitual felon facing a three-strikes life sentence? Allegedly corroborative eyewitness testimony about some sort of envelope being handed over to someone by someone else in a poorly lit bar for who knows what purpose?"

I smiled. "Richard just happened to be there?"

Safer shrugged. "Richard has no specific memory of that particular meeting, but he says if it did occur, it was to pay Mr. Goad. It's customary for him to pay his workers in cash when they're short of funds—"

"Altruism?" I said. "Or good commerce when you deal with ex-cons?"

Safer smiled. "Richard employs people no one else wants to hire, sometimes helps them out when they're down. I have a long list of other employees who'll testify to his goodwill."

"So the eyewitnesses are a wash," I said.

"Eyewitnesses," he said, as if it was a diagnosis. "I'm sure you're familiar with the psychological research on the unreliability of eyewitness testimony. I wouldn't be surprised if a careful check into the backgrounds of these particular eyewitnesses reveals histories of alcoholism, drug abuse, criminal behavior."

"And poor lighting."

"That, as well."

"Sounds open-and-shut," I said.

"Overconfidence is dangerous, Doctor, but unless I receive an unpleasant surprise . . ." Safer's green eyes narrowed. "Are there any contingencies I should be aware of?"

"None that I know of."

"Good, that's very good. Now, I'll continue to do my job and I'll let you do yours."

. . .

The door opened to a long, central hallway that mirrored the corridor downstairs. Bare beige walls, outlet to the front steps at the far end, closets and alcoves to the left, bedrooms to the right, the tinge of dirty laundry in the air. Safer led me past double doors that framed a huge, white-carpeted chamber. Gold-upholstered chairs. Arboreal wallpaper—the paper I'd seen in Eric's snapshots of Joanne . . . I peeked in, saw the sleigh bed, made up with a silk comforter. Had no trouble picturing a disembodied head, bloated body swaddled to the neck . . .

The other bedroom doors were shut. Safer skipped the first and knocked on the second. No answer, he opened the door a crack, then all the way. The dirty-laundry smell intensified.

Faded blue paper—repeating print of tiny athletes in combative poses. A poster on the facing wall said, WELCOME TO THE COMFORT OF CHAOS. Other posters on two other walls, mostly concert mementos: Pearl Jam, Third Eye Blind, Everclear, Barenaked Ladies. A cartoon of Albert Einstein with his pants down and his genitals dangling, looking confused. The caption: WHO THE FUCK SAYS YOU'RE SO SMART?

Academic certificates hung crookedly. National Merit Scholarship, Bank of America Award, General Studies Award, Science Achievement Award, valedictorian. Two curtained windows, doors to a private bathroom and a closet, a chrome-and-glass storage unit stuffed with paperbacks, spiral notebooks, three-ring binders, loose paper, a cheap Tijuana plaster statue of a bull. On a top shelf, a collection of gold plastic men proclaimed the joys of athletic accomplishment.

Double bed, its sheet tangled, wrinkled, half off the mattress. Behind the sleeping platform, stereo equipment, computers, printers. The floor was littered with wadded underwear, shirts, jeans, socks, a pair of dirty sneakers. Empty blue nylon backpack, food wrappers, Snapple bottles, crushed cans of Surge.

Eric sat near the headboard, Stacy was perched at the foot. Their backs to each other. She had on a yellow T-shirt over white capris. He wore black jeans and a black sweatshirt. Like father . . .

Both of them barefoot. Both of them red-eyed.

Eric slid one fingernail under another, flicked something. "Here it comes," he said.

"Son," said Joe Safer.

Eric's upper lip curled. "Yes, *Dad*?"

Stacy shuddered and hugged herself. Raw cuticles on her fingers. Her hair was unbound, wild and ragged, like her father's.

Safer said, "Dr. Delaware was kind enough to come here at this hour. Your father would like you to talk to him."

"Talk talk talk," said Eric. "Hap-hap-*happy* talk."

Stacy shuddered again. She managed to look at me, aiming but pulling off scared.

"Eric," said Safer, "I'm asking you to be courteous. Your father and I are both asking you."

"How is Dad?" said Stacy. "Where is he? What's he doing?"

"He's downstairs resting, dear."

"Does he want something to eat?"

"No, he's fine, dear," said Safer. "I made him a sandwich a while back."

"Was it *kosher*?" said Eric.

Silence in the stale room.

Safer stroked his beard and smiled sadly.

"Nice kosher pickle," said Eric. "Nize leetle piece of corned *beef*—"

Stacy said, "Stop it, Eric—"

"Nize little matzo ball—"

"*Shut up, Eric!*"

"Stop *what*? What the fuck am I *doing*?"

"You know what you're doing. Stop being *rude*!"

They glared at each other. Stacy turned away first. Gave a small, furious wave, showed Eric her back. Stood up. "Enough of this, I'm out of here—I'm sorry, Dr. Delaware, I just can't talk to you or anyone else right now. If I need you, I'll call you—I really will, Mr. Safer."

"Safer," muttered Eric. "Dad's writing him huge checks, and are any of us any *safer*?"

Stacy shouted, "*You are so . . .*"

"I'm what?"

Another dismissive wave. Stacy moved toward the door.

Eric said, "I'm *what*, smart-girl?"

Stacy kept going.

"Go ahead, leave, but don't think you're out of it," Eric called after her. "We're never really out of our misery unless we *put* ourselves out of it."

Stacy stopped. Another shudder took hold of her body. Her face convulsed and white foam bubbled at the corners of her mouth. Turning, she canted forward, tiny hands compressed into hard little fists. For a moment, I thought she'd charge him. Flushed, herself. The Doss flush.

"You!" she said. "You . . . are . . . evil."

She ran out, I followed, caught up with her at the door to the last bedroom.

"No! *Please!* I know you want to help but . . ."

"Stacy—"

She rushed into the bedroom but left the door open. I walked in.

Smaller room than Eric's. Pink and baby-blue paper, ribbons and leaves and flowers. White iron bed with brass accents, pink comforter, stuffed animals piled into an upholstered armchair. Clothes and books strewn about, but not the calculated entropy of Eric's personal space.

She walked to a window, touched shuttered blinds. "This is so humiliating, you seeing us like this."

"These are tough times," I said. *House calls.* How much *didn't* I know about thousands of other patients?

"There's no excuse," she said. "We're just . . ."

She trailed off. Hunched her back like an old woman and tore at a cuticle.

"I'm here to help, Stacy."

No answer. Then: "It's secret, right? Whatever we talk about? Nothing changes that?"

"Nothing," I said. *Unless you're planning to kill someone.*

I waited for her to talk. She didn't.

"What's on your mind, Stacy?"

"*He* is."

"Eric?"

Nod. "He *scares* me."

"How does he scare you, Stacy?"

"By—he—the way he talks—the things he says . . .

No, no, forget it, forget I just said that. Please. Just forget it. He's fine, everything's fine."

She slipped a finger between the blades of the blinds and peered out at the night.

I said, "What did Eric say that scared you?"

She spun around. "*Nothing!* I said *forget* it!"

I stood there.

"What?" she said.

"If you're scared, let me help."

"You can't—there's nothing you can—it's—I just—he—Helen—we were sitting there. After we got back from the police station and he started talking about Helen."

"Your dog."

"What's the difference? Please! Please don't make me get into it!"

"I can't make you do anything, Stacy. But if Eric's in some kind of danger—"

"No, no, that's not what I mean—he—you remember what I told you about *Helen* . . ."

"She was sick. Eric took her up to the mountains and you never saw her again. What's he saying about her?"

"Nothing," she said. "Nothing, really . . . Besides, what's the big deal? It was the right thing to do—she was sick, she was a *dog,* for God's sake, people do that all the time, it's the *humane* thing to do."

"Putting her out of her misery. Eric told you he did it?"

"Yes—never before, not till now. I mean I knew, but he never mentioned before, not once. Then tonight, after we got back. Dad and Mr. Safer were downstairs and we were up here and all of a sudden he starts getting *into* it. *Laughing* about it."

She sat down on the edge of the armchair, crushing stuffed animals. Reaching behind, she took one in her arms—a small, frayed elephant.

"He laughed about Helen," I said. "And now he's talking about people being put out of their misery."

"No—just forget it." Weak voice, lacking conviction.

"You're worried," I went on. "If Eric could do that to Helen, maybe he could do it to a human being. Maybe he had something to do with your mother's death."

"No!" she shouted. "Yes! That's what—he basically told me! I mean, he didn't come out and say it but he kept hinting around at it. Talking about Helen, how her eyes looked—how she was okay with it, peaceful. She looked up at him and licked his face and he hit her over the head with a rock. One time, he said. That's all it took. Then he buried her—it was brave of him, right? I couldn't have done it, it needed to be done, she was so sick."

She rocked in the chair, held the elephant to her breast.

"Then he got a *creepy* smile. Said sometimes you have to take matters into your own hands, how no one knows what's right or wrong unless they're in your shoes. How maybe there really is no right or wrong, just rules that people take on because they're too scared to make their own decisions. He said helping Helen was the noblest thing he'd ever done."

She squeezed the elephant harder and its tiny face compressed to something grotesque. "I'm so *scared*. What if he did another Helen?"

"No reason to believe that," I said, lying because now

I had an explanation for why Mate hadn't claimed Joanne. I went on in my best therapist voice: "He's upset, just as you are. Things will settle down, Eric will settle down."

My voice and my brain diverged as I continued to comfort, thinking all the while: mother and son, guilt, expiation. Joanne and Eric planning . . . Eric taking pictures because he knew she'd be leaving soon, wanted to grasp every opportunity for memorial.

Too sickening to contemplate, but I couldn't *stop* contemplating. I hoped the revulsion hadn't found its way into my voice. Must have faked it okay because Stacy stopped crying.

"Everything will be fine?" she said in a little girl's voice.

"Just hang in there."

She smiled. Then the smile turned into something fearful and ugly. "No, it won't. It will never be fine."

"I know it seems like that right now—"

"Hey," she said, "Eric's right. Nothing's complicated. You're born, life sucks, you die." She ripped a cuticle bloody, licked the wound, picked some more.

"Stacy—"

"Words," she said. "They sound nice."

"They're true, Stacy."

"I wish . . . Things will be better?" More need than challenge.

"Yes," I said. Lord help me.

New kind of smile. "I'm definitely *not* going to Stanford. I have to find my own place . . . Thank you, Dr. Delaware, this has been—"

Her words were cut off by sounds from below.

From the front of the house, loud enough to filter upstairs and through the door to her bedroom. Screams and percussion, frantic footsteps, more screams—bellows.

The pretty music of shattering glass.

28

I ran out, rushed down the stairs, followed the noise.

The living room. Figures in black.

Two figures, crouched combatively.

Richard shouted, "What the fuck have you done?" and advanced on his son.

Eric waved a baseball bat.

Behind the boy stood what remained of the display cases. Ravaged, the brass dented, glass doors splintered and ragged. Glass spikes and shards on the carpet, glittery dust like raw diamonds. Broken pottery within the cases and on the floor. Horses and camels and little human figurines turned to rubble.

Richard got closer. His mouth was open. His breath rasped.

Eric panted also. He gripped the bat with both hands. "Don't even think about it."

"Put it down!" Richard commanded.

Eric didn't move.

"Put it the fuck *down!*"

Eric laughed and took another swing at the porce-lain. Richard rushed forward, threw himself at the bat, managed to get hold of it as Eric grunted and struggled to wrestle control.

The two of them fell to the floor, entwined black clothes coating with glass and dust. I dived in, mindful of the bat, aiming for the bat. Reaching it, feeling hardwood, sweaty and gritty, the crunch underneath as fragments bit into my knees. I tugged at the bat. Some give, then resist-ance. A fist landed on my jaw but I kept my grip.

Eric and Richard kept growling and spitting, flailing at each other, me, anyone, anything.

Another pair of hands entered the fray.

"Stop!"

I extricated myself. Joe Safer stood there, hands pressed to his cheeks, eyes aflame. Eric and Richard were concentrating on ownership of the bat. "Stop, you idiots, or I'm walking out permanently and leaving you all to your misery!"

Richard stopped first. Eric kept growling but his hands loosened, and Safer and I both rushed forward and pulled the bat away from him.

Richard sat down on the floor, letting the ruins of his collection fall through his fingers. He looked stunned—anesthetized. Tiny cuts flecked his face and his hands, one eye was swollen. A few feet away, Eric was down on his knees, looking out at nothing. Other than a split lip, he showed no obvious injury. My jaw was throbbing and I touched it. Hot, starting to swell, but I could move it, nothing broken.

"For God's sake," said Safer. "Look what you've done to the doctor. What's the *matter* with you people? Are you *savages*?"

Eric smiled. "We're the elite. Pathetic, huh?"

Safer pointed a finger at him. "You be quiet, my friend. You keep that mouth of yours shut—don't you dare interrupt me—"

"Why should—"

"Eh-eh, don't test me, young man. One more problem and I'm calling the police and having you hauled into jail. And I can keep you there, you'd better believe I can."

"Who ca—"

"You'll care. Within an hour you'll be anally raped and worse. Now zip the lip!"

Eric's hands began to shake. He glanced at the havoc he'd created. Smiled. Started to cry.

No one talked. Safer took in the ruin and shook his head.

"I'm so sorry," he said to me. "Are you all right?"

"I'll be fine."

"Eric," Richard pleaded. "Why? What have I done to you?"

Eric looked at Safer, requesting permission to talk. Safer said, "Why, indeed, Eric?"

Eric faced Richard. Mumbled something.

"What?" said Richard.

"Sorry."

"Sorry," Richard echoed. "That's *it*?"

Louder mumble.

"Speak up, for God's sake," said Richard. "What the hell led you to . . ." He shook his head, let it drop.

"Sorry, Daddy," said Eric. "Sorry, sorry, sorry."

"*Why*, Eric?"

Eric began to sob. Richard moved to comfort him, thought better of it, plopped back down.

"Why, son?" he said.

"Forgiveness," said Eric. "Forgiveness is all."

Richard had turned pale again. A bad-looking pale, green around the edges. He picked up a pottery fragment. Green and blue and chartreuse. Part of a horse's face.

"Oh my God," said a voice from behind us.

Stacy stood at the entrance to the living room. Hands at her side, eyes so bugged they seemed ready to take off in orbit.

Just moments ago, hearing talk about finding her own way, I'd allowed myself a small hit of self-congratulation. Now, any victory was a joke, demolished as surely as thousand-year-old pottery drawn from the grave.

"No," said Stacy.

"Dear?" said Safer.

When she didn't answer, he said, "No what?"

She didn't seem to hear him, had turned to me.

"No," she said. "I don't want any more of this."

"And you don't have to take any more, dear," said Safer. "You're certain that jaw's okay, Doctor?"

"I'll survive."

"Richard," he said, "is your maid in the house?"

"No," muttered Richard. "Night off."

"Stacy, please get the doctor an ice pack."

Stacy said, "Absolutely," and left.

Safer faced Richard and Eric: "Now the two of *you*

will clean up this terrible mess and I'll figure out if you deserve my further involvement in your case, Richard."

"Please," said Richard.

"Just clean it up," ordered Safer. "Do something useful. Do something together."

He shepherded me out of the room, through the dining room and into the kitchen. One of those vast white lacquer and black granite setups—what realtors call catering kitchens. Another L.A. pretense: upscale isolates staking claim to sociability.

Stacy was wrapping ice cubes in a towel. "One second."

"Thank you, dear," said Safer, as she brought it over. I pressed the cloth to my face.

"I'm so sorry," she told me. "So, so sorry."

"No big deal," I said. "It's really nothing."

The three of us stood there. Listening. No sound through the kitchen door.

Safer said, "Please go up to your room, Stacy. I need to confer with the doctor."

She complied.

Safer said, "At least one of them seems normal."

He pushed back his yarmulke, removed his suit jacket and folded it over a chair, sat down at the kitchen table.

"What just happened out there?" he said.

"I wouldn't even guess."

"Not that that's going to change my strategy vis-à-vis Richard. I'll get him past the immediate threat . . . but that *boy*. He's seriously disturbed, isn't he?"

"Very angry," I said. *You'd be angry, too, if you'd*

helped your mother die, couldn't talk about it to anyone.

"Do you see him as a danger to himself and others? Because if he is, I'll get a seventy-two-hour hold."

"Possibly, but don't ask me to go there. Get someone else for that."

He massaged the tabletop. "I understand, conflict of interest."

Yet another.

"Speaking of which," he said, "let's discuss Detective Sturgis. I know we've talked about this and please don't be offended, but I believe in an ounce of prevention. What you saw tonight—nothing gets repeated."

"Of course."

"Good," he said. "Taken care of. And again I apologize. Now as far as Stacy's concerned, you do agree she needs to be out of here? At least for tonight."

"Do you have a place for her to go?"

"My house. I live in Hancock Park, have plenty of room, and my wife won't be put out. She's used to entertaining."

"Entertaining clients?"

"Clients, guests, she's a very social person. Tomorrow night's our Sabbath, Stacy can have a multicultural experience. Shall I call Mrs. Safer?"

"If you can get Stacy to agree."

"I think I can," he said. "Stacy impresses me as a very reasonable young woman. Quite possibly the one sane person in this . . . museum of psychopathology."

He went upstairs and I sat in the kitchen nursing my jaw. Thinking about Eric's rage.

Forgiveness is all.

And Richard hadn't forgiven, so now he was paying for it.

He and Eric, two kegs of explosives . . . not my concern. Not unless it affected Stacy, I had to focus on Stacy.

Safer was right, she needed to be out of here. A night or two at his house might work out, but after that . . .

Safer returned. "I convinced her, she's packing a bag. Let me go tell Richard."

I accompanied him into the living room. The mess was partially cleaned—dust and fragments swept into piles, brooms leaning against the shattered cases.

Richard and Eric sat on the floor, their backs to a sofa. Richard's arm around Eric's shoulder, Eric's head against Richard's chest, his eyes closed, his face tear-streaked.

Pietà in the Palisades.

Richard looked different. Not flushed, not pale. Expressionless. Crushed. Dragged to the edge and dropped off.

He didn't seem to notice as Safer and I approached, but when we got within two feet of the case, he turned slowly and held Eric tighter. Eric's body flopped. The boy's eyes remained shut.

"He's tired," said Richard. "I need to put him to bed. I used to do that when he was little. Tell him stories and put him to bed."

Safer gave a start. Remembering his own son?

"Do that," he said. "Take care of him. I'm bringing Stacy to my house."

Richard's eyebrows arched. "Your house? Why?"

"To keep things simple, Richard. I promise to take

good care of her. I'll get her to school on time tomorrow and she'll spend the weekend with us. Or with friends, if she so prefers."

Not the Manitows, I thought.

Richard said, "She wants to go?"

"My idea," said Safer. "She agreed."

Richard licked his lips, turned to me.

I nodded.

"Okay," he said. "I guess. Tell her to come in before she leaves. Let me give her a kiss."

29

I climbed the stairs, nursing my jaw. Stacy sat on her bed. Her voice came out small and wounded. "I'm tired, please don't make me talk."

I stayed with her for a while. When I returned to the kitchen, Joe Safer was talking on the phone, elbow resting on the counter near a black-and-chrome coffee machine from Germany. I found a jar of espresso in one of the refrigerators, packed enough for six cups, and sat listening to the drip and thinking about what guilt and expiation really meant to Eric. Safer left the room and kept talking. I drank by myself. A while later, the doorbell rang and Safer came back in to the kitchen accompanied by a tall, husky young man with wavy blond hair and a briefcase.

"This is Byron. He'll be staying here tonight."

Byron winked and inspected the appliances. He wore a blue oxford shirt, khakis and penny loafers, had hyphens for eyes and facial muscles that looked para-lyzed. When we shook hands, his felt like a bone carving. Safer went upstairs. Byron and I didn't talk.

No sound from the living room. The entire house was too damn quiet. Then I heard footsteps from above and a few seconds later Stacy entered, followed by the lawyer. Safer was carrying a small floral overnight bag. Stacy looked tiny, shriveled, much too old.

I followed the two of them outside and watched him help her into his Cadillac. Byron remained in the doorway, hands on hips.

"What is he, exactly?" I said.

"Someone who helps me. Richard and Eric seem calm, but just in case."

"Were you an oldest child, Joe?"

"Oldest of seven. Why?"

"You like to take care of things."

His smile was weary. "Don't think I'm paying for that bit of analysis."

He drove away and I watched the Cadillac's taillights disappear. Down the block, the unmarked hadn't moved. The night had turned dank, redolent of fermenting seaweed. My jaw ached and my clothes had sweated through. I trudged to the Seville. Instead of turning around and heading south, I drove farther north till I found it.

Six houses up. Big Tudor thing behind brick walls and iron gates, vines encircling the brick, the tip-off: Judy's white Lexus visible through the rails. Another vanity plate: HCDJ.

Here Come Da Judge. The first time I'd seen it was when I'd accompanied her from her courtroom to her parking space. One of the many times we'd worked together.

All those referrals. This would be the last, wouldn't it?

I stopped in front of her house, looking for . . . what?

Light glowed behind a couple of curtained mullioned windows. Movement flashed on the second story— central window. Just a smudge of a silhouette, shifting, then freezing, then moving again. Human, but that's about all I could say.

Hooking a three-pointer, my headlights aimed through the Manitow gate, I paused, half hoping someone would notice and show themselves. No one did and I headed back toward Sunset, passing the unmarked. Movement there, too, but the drab sedan remained in place.

I drove east, trying not to think about anything. On the way home I stopped at a twenty-four-hour drugstore in Brentwood and bought the strongest Advil I could find.

Friday morning, I woke up before Robin, just as the sun whitened the curtains. My jaw felt tender, but the swelling wasn't too bad. I drew the covers over my face, pretended to sleep, waited till Robin had risen, show-ered and left. Not wanting to explain. Eventually, I'd have to.

Using the bedroom phone, I called Safer's office.

"Good morning, Doctor. How's your battle wound?"

"Healing. How's Stacy?"

"She slept soundly," he said. "I had to wake her to get her to school on time. Lovely girl. She even tried to make breakfast for my wife and me. I hope she survives her family. Psychologically speaking."

I thought about Stacy's little speech about self-determination, wondered if it would stick.

"What she needs," I said, "is to separate from her family. Achieve her own identity. Richard expects her to go to Stanford because he and Joanne did. She should go anywhere but there."

"And Eric's at Stanford," he said.

"Exactly."

"The boy hasn't separated adequately?"

"Don't know," I said. "Don't know enough about him to pontificate." Don't *want* to know if he sat by a bed in a cheap motel and inserted a needle into his mother's vein. "If you have any influence with Richard, you might guide him toward allowing Stacy some choice."

"Makes sense," he said, but he sounded distracted. "I understand the boy's not your primary patient, but he continues to bother me. That level of anger. Any new thoughts on why he'd explode like that?"

"None. How was he last night?"

"Byron reports that father and son cleaned up, then went to sleep. Eric's still sleeping."

"And Richard?"

"Richard's up. Richard's full of ideas."

"I'll bet he is. Listen, Joe, I need to take a look at Joanne Doss's medical records."

"Why's that?"

"To try to understand her death. If I'm going to help Stacy, I need as much information as possible. The medical tests were conducted at St. Michael's. Richard said you've got power of attorney, so please sign a release and fax it over to their Medical Records office."

"Done. Of course, you'll notify me if you learn something I should know."

"Such as?" I said.

"Such as anything I should know." His voice had hardened. "Agreed?"

I thought of all I hadn't told him. Knew there was plenty he hadn't told me.

"Sure, Joe," I said. "No problem."

Popping more Advil, I iced my jaw, took a short run, cleaned up, walked over to Robin's studio, stuck my head in and got an earful of noise. My beloved, suited and goggled, standing behind the plastic walls of the spray booth as she wielded a lacquer gun. Knowing she couldn't be interrupted and doubting she could see me, I waved and left for St. Michael's Medical Center.

Sunset to Barrington, Barrington to Wilshire. Driving too fast to Santa Monica. No reason to hurry. My reason for checking out the hospital was to look for Michael Ferris Burke, or whatever he was calling himself now. But my fresh suspicions about Eric dimmed any prospects of finding a Michael Burke connection to Joanne's final trip.

Not an evil stranger. Family.

But what else was there for me to do?

And maybe I *would* find something.

That made me laugh out loud. Shrink's denial. I wanted anyone in that motel room other than Eric.

The boy's rage came back to me in a bitter surge, and the facts spat in my face.

Helen, the dog. Guilt and expiation.

That level of anger.

The noblest thing he'd ever done.

Mate's death had stirred up Eric's guilt. Richard's attempt at vengeance had fueled it further.

Eric knowing an innocent man had been targeted, because Mate hadn't brought about Joanne's death.

Wondering what his father would have done to *him*, had he known. Then reversing the anger—turning it on his father. Because Richard had caused it all by not forgiving.

Blaming. Like father . . .

I thought about the way the death plan might've gone down. Weeks, maybe months, of planning between Eric and Joanne. Easy collusion, or had Eric tried to talk his mother out of it? Finally given up and settled for immortalizing her with Polaroids?

How had she convinced him? Telling him it was *noble*?

Or had he needed little convincing—enraged at her, too. One of those terrifying kids who are missing that little, secret shred of brain tissue that inhibits evil?

The scheme, then the night of judgment . . . surreptitious mother–son outing on one of the many nights when Richard was out of town. Eric driving, Joanne riding along.

The long, dark trip to the edge of the desert. Lancaster, because Mom was adamant about that.

Obscene. How could a mother do that to a son? What transgression had she committed that could've been worse than *that*?

I was unlikely to find the answer in her hospital chart. But one did what one could.

One did what was right. And hoped for some final day of judgment.

Transcendence.

Absolution.

St. Michael's limestone and mirrored mass filled several square blocks on Wilshire, in Santa Monica, half a mile east of the beach. I'd lectured there a few years earlier, teaching family-practice residents about divorce and child abuse and bed-wetting, but I had no idea how to find Medical Records and the personnel office.

I got directions from a kid with a skimpy blond beard and a badge alleging he was an MD. North side of the complex, adjoining buildings.

I hit personnel first—Human Resources. Most companies call it that now—warm fuzzy twist on the lexicon. Does it ease the pain when they fire you?

The office was small, stark, sterile, occupied by an imperious-looking black woman in an orange suit who sat entering columns of data into a PC. I was wearing my Western Pediatrics badge, had my I.D. card from the med school crosstown ready as backup. But she smiled when I told her I was in charge of arranging a faculty party and needed some office addresses, and handed over a phone-book-size volume marked Staff Roster. Her openness felt fresh and clean and odd. I'd been hanging around too long with cops, lawyers, psychopaths, other evasive creatures.

She returned to her desk and I thumbed through the book. The professional staff was listed at the front. Pages of doctors. Names, office addresses, photos. No personal data. No one who resembled the various faces of the man

Leimert Fusco claimed was the real Dr. Death. The same went for the rear sections listing social workers, physical therapists, occupational therapists, respiratory therapists.

When I brought the book back, the woman in orange said, "Hope it's a good party."

Medical Records was a bit more complicated. The receptionist was one of those pucker-mouthed types weaned on skepticism, and she hadn't seen Joe Safer's faxed authorization. Finally the paperwork materialized and she produced Joanne Doss's inch-thick chart.

"You need to read it here. That fax doesn't authorize photocopying."

"No problem."

"That's what they all say."

"Who?"

"Doctors who work for lawyers."

I took the file across the room. Multicolored pages of lab reports. Numbers in boxes. Motley samples of physician scrawl. Bob Manitow's name appeared only on the referral form. Fifteen other doctors had attempted to discern the cause of Joanne's misery.

Blood work, urinalysis, X rays, CAT scans, PET scans, MRIs, the lumbar punctures Richard had told me about because nothing else had turned up.

The operative word: "negative."

Clear spinal fluid. *Normal BUN, creatinine, calcium, phosphorus, iron, T-protein, albumin, globulin . . .*

Morbidly obese white female . . .

Complains of joint pain, lethargy, fatigue . . .

Onset of symptoms 23 mo. ago, steady weight gain of nearly 50 kg . . .

Thyroid function normal . . .

All endocrine systems normal, except for glucose of 123. Glucose tolerance borderline, possible prediabetic condition, probably secondary to obesity.

BP: 149/96. Borderline hypertension, probably secondary to obesity.

Repeat of blood work, urinalysis, X rays, CAT scans . . .

No MD's name that matched any of Grant Rushton's incarnations.

The last notation read: *Psychiatric consultation suggested, but patient refused . . .*

Of course she had.

Too late for confession.

On the way out, I stopped at a pay phone and checked in with my service.

Last guy in L.A. with no cell phone. It had taken me years to buy a VCR, a good deal longer to get cable hookup. I'd stalled at getting a computer even after the libraries at the U. abandoned their card catalogs. Then my electric typewriter broke and I couldn't find replacement parts.

My father had been a machinist. I stayed away from machines. Lived with a woman who loved them. No sense introspecting.

The operator said, "Only one, it just came in. A Detective Connor. That's not the one who usually calls you, is it?"

"No," I said. "What did she want?"

"No message, just to call."

Petra had left her number at Hollywood Division.

Another detective answered and said, "She's out, want her mobile?"

I got through. Petra said, "Milo asked me to let you know that we found Eldon Salcido. He thought you might want to take a look at him."

Milo sending a message through her, rather than calling himself. Knowing he and I were firmly planted on opposite sides of the Doss investigation.

Had Safer warned him off, or was he opting for discretion on his own? Either way, it felt weird.

"Did he say why I should take a look?"

"No," she said. "I assumed you'd know. It was a short conversation. Milo sounded pretty hassled, still fighting to get warrants on that fat cat."

"Where'd Salcido show up?"

"On the street. Literally. Messed up—beat up. Looks like he ran into the wrong bunch of butt-kickers. A resident coming out to collect the morning paper found him. Salcido was lying in the gutter. His pockets were empty, but that doesn't mean he was robbed, he might not have carried a wallet. One of our cars got the call, recognized him from a picture I hung up in the squad room. He's at Hollywood Mercy."

"Conscious?" I said.

"Yes, but uncooperative. I left your name with the nurses." She gave me a room number.

"Thanks," I said.

"If you have any problems, call me. If you learn anything interesting from Salcido, you can call me, too."

"Because Milo's busy."

"Seems to be. Isn't everyone?"

"Better than the alternative," I said.

"You said it. By the way, I'm seeing Billy tomorrow. We're going over to see the new science center at Exposition Park. Anything you want to pass along?"

"Best regards and continue doing what he's doing. And keep busy. Not that he needs me to tell him that."

She laughed. "Yes, he's a wonder, isn't he?"

30

It took forty minutes on the 10 East and surface streets to get to the shabby section of East Hollywood where Beverly meets Temple.

Second hospital of the day.

Hollywood Mercy was five stories of earthquake-stressed, putty-colored stucco teetering atop a scrubby knoll that overlooked downtown. The building had an inadequate parking lot, a cracked tile roof, some nice ornate moldings from the days when labor was cheap, most with chunks missing. City ambulances ringed the entry. The front vestibule was crowded with long lines of sad-looking people waiting for approval from clerks in glass cages. CAT scans, PET scans, MRIs; the same high-tech alphabet I'd seen at St. Michael's, but this place looked like something out of a black-and-white movie and it smelled like an old man's bedroom.

Mate's bedroom.

His son was recuperating on the fourth floor, in
something called the Special Care Unit. An unarmed
security guard was posted at the swinging doors that led
to the ward, and my I.D. badge got me waved through.
On the other side was a chunky corridor five doors long
with a nurses' station at the end. A black man with a
shaved head sat near a stack of charts, writing, and a
lantern-jawed, straw-haired woman in her sixties tapped
her finger to soft reggae thumping from an unseen radio.
I announced myself.

"In there," said the female nurse.

"How's he doing?"

"He'll survive." She pulled out a chart. A lot thinner
than Joanne Doss's encyclopedia of confusion. A Hollywood Division police report was stapled to the inside
front cover.

Eldon Salcido had been found beaten and semiconscious at 6:12 A.M. in the gutter of a residential block of
Poinsettia Place, north of Sunset.

Three blocks from his father's apartment on Vista.

Paramedics had transported him, and an E.R. resident had admitted him for repair and observation.
Contusions, abrasions, possible concussion later ruled
absent. No broken bones. Extreme mental agitation and
confusion, possibly related to preexisting alcoholism,
drug abuse, mental illness or some combination of all
three. The patient had refused to identify himself, but
police at the scene had supplied the vitals. The fact that
Salcido was an ex-con with a felony record was duly
noted.

Restraints ordered after the patient assaulted staff.

"Who'd he hit?" I said.

"One of our predecessors, last shift," said the male nurse. "Her big crime was offering him orange juice. He knocked it out of her hand, tried to punch her. She managed to lock him in and called security."

"Another day in paradise," said the woman. "Probably a candidate for detox, but our detox unit shut down last month. You here to evaluate him for transfer?"

"Just to see him," I said. "Basic consult."

"Well, you might end up doing it for free. We can't find a Medi-Cal card on him and he isn't talking."

"That's okay."

"Hey, if you don't care, I sure don't. Room 405."

She came out from behind the counter and unlocked the door. The room was cell-size and green, with a lone, grilled window that framed an air shaft, a single bed and an I.V. bottle on a stand, not hooked up. The vital-signs monitor above the headboard was switched off and so was the tiny TV bracketed to the far wall. A low industrial buzz seeped through the window.

Donny Salcido Mate lay on his back, bare-chested, shackled with leather cuffs, staring at the ceiling. A tight, sweat-stained top sheet bound him from the waist down. His trunk was hairless, undernourished, off-white where it wasn't blue-black.

Blue coils squirmed all over him. Skin art, continuing around his back and down both arms. Pictorial arms striped by bandages. Dried blood crusted the edges of the dressings. A swatch of gauze banded his forehead, a smaller square bottomed his chin. Purpling bruises cupped both eyes and his lower lip was a slab of liver. Other dermal images peeked out from within the coils: the leering face of a nightmarishly fanged cobra, a flabby,

naked woman with a sad mouth, one wide-open eye
emitting a single tear. Gothic lettering spelling out
"Donny, Mamacita, Big Boy."

Technically well-done tattoos, but the jumble made
me want to rearrange his skin.

"A walking canvas," opined the straw-haired nurse.
"Like that book by the *Martian Chronicles* guy. Visitor,
Mr. Salcido. Ain't that grand?"

She walked out and the door hissed shut. Donny
Salcido Mate didn't budge. His hair was long, stringy, the
burnt bronze of old motor oil. An untrimmed beard, two
shades darker, blanketed his face from cheekbone to
jowl.

No resemblance to the mug shot I'd seen. That made
me think of the beard Michael Burke had grown when
adopting his Huey Mitchell persona in Ann Arbor. In
fact, *Donny's* hirsute face bore a resemblance to
Mitchell's. But not the same man. None of that cold,
blank stagnancy in the eyes. These rheumy browns were
bouncy, heated, hyperactive. Hundred percent scared
prey, not predator.

I stepped closer to the bed. Donny Salcido moaned
and twisted away from me. A tattoo tendril climbed up
his carotid, disappearing into the beard thatch like a
vining rose. Yellowing crust flecked the edges of his
mustache. His lips were cracked, his nose had been
broken, but not recently, probably more than once; the
cartilage between his eyes was sunken, as if scooped by a
dull blade, the flesh below a nest of gaping black pores.
Orange splotches remained on his skin where he'd been
disinfected with Betadine, but whoever had cleaned him
up hadn't gotten rid of the street stink.

"Mr. Salcido, I'm Dr. Delaware."

His eyes jammed shut.

"How're you doing?"

"Let me out of here." Clear enunciation, no slur. I waited, got caught up in the skin mural. Subtle shadings, good composition. I got past that, searched for an image that would tie in with his father. Nothing obvious. The tattoos seemed to encroach on one another. This was the junction of talent and chaos.

Bumps in the crook of his arm caught my eye. Fibrosed needle marks.

His eyes opened. "Get these things off," he said, rattling the cuffs.

"The nurses got a little upset when you tried to hit one of them."

"Never happened."

"You didn't try to hit a nurse?"

Headshake. "She aggressed on me. Tried to force juice down my windpipe. Not my esophagus, my windpipe, *get* it? Nasopharynx, epiglottis—know what happens when you do *that*?"

"You choke."

"You aspirate. Fluid straight into the lungs. Even if you don't suffocate, it creates a pleural cesspool, perfect culture for bacteria. She was out to drown me—if she couldn't accomplish that, infect me." A tongue, gray and fuzzed, caressed his lips. He gulped.

"Thirsty?" I said.

"Strangling. Get these things off of me."

"How'd you get hurt?"

"You tell me."

"How would I know?"

"You're the doctor."

"The police say someone hit you."

"Not some*one*. *Ones*. I got jumped."

"Right there on Poinsettia?"

"No, San Francisco. I walked all the way here because this glorious place is where I wanted to be treated." His head rolled toward me. "Better get me outta here or give me my Tegretol. When I'm out of my Tegretol, I get interesting."

"You suffer from seizures?"

"No, stupid. Cognitive dysfunction, affective scrambling, inability to regulate emotional outbursts. I'm prone to a mood disorder, get too unhappy, everything gets scrambled, no telling what I'll do." His wrists shot upward. The cuffs rattled louder.

"Who prescribed the Tegretol for you?"

"I did. Got a hoard at my place, but you supposed healers won't let me get to it."

"Where's your place?"

"Me to know, you to find out."

"What dosage do you take?"

"Depends," he said, grinning. His gums were swollen, inflamed, rotted black at the tooth line. "Three hundred migs on a good day, more if I'm feeling baaad— better be careful, I'm getting that *baaad* feeling right now. The old prodrome: everything turning glassy, circular, convex, pistons pumping, heart jumping. Soon I'm going to be all scrambled, who knows, maybe I could break free of these, eat you *up*—where's your white coat, what kind of doctor are you, anyway?"

"Psychologist."

"Fuck. Useless. Get me someone who can prescribe. Or let me outta here. I'm the victim, once this story gets out you and everyone else associated with it are not going to look good. Assuming the publishers print it. But they won't. They're part of it, too."

"Part of what?"

"The great conspiracy to denude my brain." Smile. "Nah, that's bullshit. I'm not paranoid, I've got a mood disorder."

"Who attacked you?" I said.

"Mexicans. Gangbangers. Punks. Illegal aliens, refuse of society."

"Did they try to rob you?"

"They tried and they succeeded. I'm walking down the street, minding my own, they drive up to the curb, get out, beat the shit out of me, go through my pockets."

"What did they get?"

"Everything in my pockets." He shook his head. "You're useless, I'm terminating this interview."

"Were you carrying a weapon?" I said.

He began to hum.

"Poinsettia is three blocks from your father's place."

The humming got louder. His eyelids twitched. He started breathing faster.

"Planning a visit to your father's place?" I said, talking over it. "Last time you tried, the lady downstairs interrupted you. How many times have you gotten inside?"

His head snapped toward me. "I *am* going to bite off your nose. Eye for an eye—avenge what that other psychologist did—Lecter. No, he was a psychiatrist, that was a great movie. I watched it and ate fava beans for weeks afterward."

"Did you kill your father?" I said.

"Sure," he said. "Bit off *his* nose, too. Had it with *pinto* beans and . . . some kind of wine . . . why am I thinking Chablis? Get me my fucking Tegretol."

"I'll see what I can do," I said.

"Don't lie to me, degree-boy."

"I'll do what I can."

"No, you won't."

I left him, returned to the station, paged the doctor who'd written the last note—early this morning. A woman named Greenbaum, first-year resident. Meaning she'd only been in training for a few months. She called back, saying she was at County General, wouldn't be rotating back in Hollywood until tomorrow. I told her why I was with Salcido and asked her about the medication.

"Yes," she said, "he claims he needs it to maintain 'internal stability.' He played that tune for me, too. I'm waiting to talk to the attending."

"He's self-medicating for assaultiveness and mood swings. If he's already on Tegretol, he's probably gone through lithium and the neuroleptics. Maybe in prison."

"Maybe, but I can't get anything out of him resembling a clinical history. Tegretol's okay, but there's the issue of side effects. I need blood levels on him."

"Did you have a chance to talk to him?"

"He didn't talk."

"He's a bit more verbal now," I said. "There's some IQ there. He knows how it feels before the assaultiveness comes on, is fighting to maintain control."

"So what're you saying?"

"I'm suggesting that at least in one respect he may know what's best for him."

"Did you see that skin of his?" she said.

"Hard to miss."

"Pretty disorganized for someone who knows what's best for him."

"True, but—"

"I get it," she said. "The police sent you to see him and you want him coherent so he'll talk to you."

"That's part of it. The other part is he's already been assaultive and if something works for him, maybe it should be considered. I'm not trying to tell you how to do your job—"

"No, actually you are." She laughed. "But sure, why not? Everyone else does. Okay, no sense having him freak out and me getting a three A.M. call. I'll try to get hold of the attending again. If she okays it, he gets dosed."

"He says he's been taking three hundred milligrams daily."

"He says? The lunatics run the asylum?"

"Look at Washington, D.C."

She laughed harder. "What do the police want with him?"

"Information."

"On what?"

"A homicide."

"Oh. Great. A murderer. Can't wait to see him again."

"He's not a suspect," I said. "He's a potential witness."

"A witness? Guy like that, what kind of witness could he be?"

"Hard to say. Right now, I'm trying to get some rapport. We're talking about his family."

"His family? What, good old-fashioned psychoanalysis? The stuff you read about in books?"

I returned to Donny's room. He was facing the door. Waiting.

"No promises," I said, "but the resident's calling the supervising doctor."

"How long till I get my Tegretol?"

"If she gets the okay, soon."

"An eternity. What bullshit."

"You're welcome, Mr. Salcido."

He drew back his lips. Half his teeth were missing. The stragglers were cracked and discolored.

I pulled a chair next to the bed and sat down. "Why were you on your way to your father's place?"

"He never came to my place, why should I go to *his* place?"

"But you did."

"I know that, stupid! It's rhetorical—Ciceronian. I'm questioning my own motives—engaging in introspection. Isn't that good? A sign of progress?" He spat and I had to move away to avoid being the target.

"I don't know *why* I do what I do," he said. "If I did, would I be *here*?"

I said nothing.

"I hope this happens to *you* one day," he said. "Feeling this passive. Weak. You think my skin's so weird? What's weird about it? Every shrink I talked to told me skin wasn't important, the thing was to look within. Get past the surface."

"How many shrinks have you talked to?"

"Too many. All assholes like you." He closed his eyes. "Talking faces, little crushing rooms just like this . . . Get past the skin, the skin, look inside. Man, I *like* the skin. The skin is all. The skin holds it all in."

The eyes opened. "C'mon, man, get these things off, let me touch my skin. When I can't touch it I feel like I'm not there."

"In time, Donny."

He moaned and rolled his head away from me.

"Your skin," I said. "Did you do all that yourself?"

"Idiot. How could I do the back?"

"What about the rest of it?"

"What do you think?"

"I think you did. It's good work. You're talented. I've seen your other artwork."

Silence.

"*The Anatomy Lesson*," I said. "All those other masterpieces. Zero Tollrance."

His body jerked. I waited for him to speak.

Nothing.

"I think I understand why you chose that name, Donny. You have zero tolerance for stupidity. You don't suffer fools." Like father . . .

He whispered something.

"What's that?" I said.

"Patience . . . is not a virtue."

"Why not, Donny?"

"You wait, nothing happens. You wait long enough, you choke. Rot. Time dies."

"People die, time goes on."

"You don't get it," he said, a bit louder. "People dying is nothing—worm food. Time dies, everything freezes."

"When you paint," I said, "what happens to time?"

A tiny smile showed itself amid the beard. "Eternity."

"And when you're not painting?"

"I'm too late."

"Too late for what?"

"Responses, being there, everything—my timing's off. I've got a sick brain, maybe the limbic system, maybe the prefrontal lobes, the temporals, the thalamus. Nothing moves at the right pace."

"Do you have a place where you can paint now?"

He stared at me. "Screw you. Get me out of here."

"You offered your art to your father, but he wouldn't accept it," I said. "After he was gone, you tried to give it to the world. To show them what you were capable of."

His lips folded inward and he chewed on them.

"Did you kill him, Donny?"

I bent closer. Close enough for him to bite my nose.

He didn't. Just stayed in place, prone, staring at the ceiling.

"Did you?" I said.

"No," he finally said. "Too late. As usual."

After that, he shut up tight. Ten minutes into the impasse, the straw-haired nurse came in carrying a metal tray that held a plastic cup of water and two pills, one oblong and pink, the other white disc.

"Breakfast in bed," she announced. "Two-hundred-milligram morsel with a one-hundred chaser."

Donny was panting. He forgot his restraints, tried to

sit up. The cuffs snapped against his wrists and he slammed back down, breathing even faster.

"No water," he said. "I won't be drowned."

The nurse frowned at me as if I was to blame. "Suit yourself, Señor Salcido. But if you can't swallow it dry, I'm not going back to the doctor to authorize an injection."

"Dry is good. Dry is safe."

She handed me the tray. "Here, you give it to him, I'm not getting my fingers bit off."

She watched as I took the pink pill and brought it close to Donny's face. His mouth was already wide open. His molars and most of his bicuspids were missing. Putrid breath streamed up at me. I dropped in the pink lozenge. He caught it on his gray tongue, flipped it backward, gulped, said, "Delicious."

In went the white pill. He grinned. Burped. The nurse snatched the tray and left, looking disgusted.

I sat back down.

"There you go," I said.

"Now you go," he said. "I had enough of you."

I tried awhile longer, asking him if he'd ever actually gotten into the apartment, what did he think of his father's library, had he read *Beowulf*. Mention of the book drew no response from him.

The closest I got to conversation was when I let him know I'd met his mother.

"Yeah? How's she doing?"

"She's concerned about you."

"Go fuck yourself."

I pressed him about novelty shop gags, phony books. Broken stethoscopes.

He said, "What in the ripe rotten fuck are you talking about?"

"You don't know?"

"Hell no, but go ahead, talk all you want, I'm coasting now. Getting smooth."

Then he closed his eyes, curled as fetally as the cuffs allowed, and went to sleep.

Not faking; real slumber, chest rising and falling in a slow, easy beat. The rhythmic snores of one at peace.

I left Hollywood Mercy trying to classify him. Assaultive and deeply disturbed, but bright and manipulative.

Combative and pigheaded, too. Eldon Mate had rejected his son unceasingly, but genetics couldn't be denied.

Zero Tollrance. He'd turned himself into a walking canvas, drifting from squat to squat, numbed his pain with dope and anticonvulsants and anger and art.

Painting his father's portrait, over and over.

Offering his *best* to his father, getting *rejected* over and over.

As good a motive for patricide as any. And Donny had considered it, he'd definitely considered it.

Did you kill him?

Too late. As usual.

Denying he'd followed through. As did Richard. Brilliant, bloody production, and no one was willing to take credit.

Despite Donny's slyness, I found myself believing him. The mental impairment was real. Tegretol was powerful stuff, end-stage medication for mood disorders when lithium failed. No fun, not an addict's choice. If Donny craved it, he'd suffered.

He'd dissected his father on canvas, but the real-life murder reeked of a mix of calculation and brutality that seemed beyond him. I tried to picture him organizing what had happened up on Mulholland. Stalking, enticing, writing a mocking note, hiding a broken stethoscope in a box. Cleaning up perfectly, sufficiently meticulous not to leave a speck of DNA.

This was a guy who got mugged and left in the gutter. Who got yelled at by an elderly landlady and fled.

My mention of the book and the scope had elicited nothing from him. His clumsy attempt to enter his father's apartment in full view of Mrs. Krohnfeld was miles from that degree of sophistication. His entire life pattern was a series of failed attempts. I doubted he'd ever gotten past Eldon Mate's front door.

No, someone a lot more intact than Donny Salcido Mate had planted that toy. The personality combination I'd suggested at the beginning—the same mixture suggested by Fusco.

Smarts and rage. Outwardly coherent but with a bad temper problem.

Someone like Richard.

And his son. I thought of how the boy had pulverized six figures' worth of treasure.

It kept coming back to Eric.

Dispirited, I headed west on Beverly and considered how Eric might've lured Mate to Mulholland. Wanting to talk about his mother? To talk about what *he'd* done to his mother—*for* his mother. Claiming to

Mate that he'd been *inspired* by the death doctor. The appeal to Mate's vanity might have worked.

But if Eric had been the one in that motel room, why butcher Mate? Covering for himself? Thin. So perhaps Mate *had* been involved. And Eric, knowing of his father's hatred for the death doctor, perhaps even knowing about the failed contract with Quentin Goad, had taken it upon himself to act.

Blood orgy to please the old man.

Happy Traveling, You Sick Bastard. The phrasing had an adolescent flavor to it. I could hear the sentence tumbling from Eric's lips.

But if Eric had slaughtered Mate, why was he now striking out against his father? Had he finally come to grips with what he'd done? Turned his anger on Richard—blaming, just as the old man was wont to do?

Father and son rolling, wrestling, snorting on the floor. Tearing at each other, only to embrace. Ambivalence. Apparent reconciliation.

But if what I suspected was true, the boy was unpredictable and dangerous. Joe Safer had sensed that, asked my opinion. I'd avoided an answer, claiming I needed to focus upon Stacy, but also wanting to avoid additional complications. Now I had to wonder if Eric's presence in the house put Stacy—and Richard—in danger.

I'd call Safer as soon as I got home. Hold back my suspicions and keep my comments general—Eric's bad temper, the effects of stress, the need to be careful.

The afternoon traffic had sludged to chrome cholesterol, cars lurching forward in fits and starts, tempers flaring. I allowed myself to be drawn into it, oblivious to petty resentments, thinking about real rage: Eric and

Mate on Mulholland. Blunt-force injury to Mate's head. As in baseball bat.

Perhaps the boy had gotten Mate up there with a simple lie: misrepresenting himself as a terminally ill patient pining for the love bite of the Humanitron.

A young, male traveler. Mate, defensive about too many females, those nasty feminist jibes about his sexuality, would have liked that.

The meet, the kill, then weeks later Eric sneaks into Mate's apartment and hides the stethoscope.

Out of business, Doc.

High intelligence, savage anger. The boy had plenty of both.

And sneaking out in the middle of the night was Eric's habit, he'd done it for years.

Helen, the dog . . .

A look at the boy's phone records and credit-card log would be instructive. Had he booked a flight from Palo Alto to L.A. on or around the day of Mate's murder? Made a second trip to pull off the break-in?

Taking all those risks simply to taunt Mate's ghosts.

Or was it the cops he was out to humiliate? Because, after shedding blood, he learned that he *liked* it?

The juxtaposition of blood and pleasure. That's the way it had started for Michael Burke. That's the way it always started.

Someone that young and smart warping so severely. Terrifying.

I wanted to bounce it all off Milo. *Intriguing,* he'd say, *but all theory.*

And theory was where it would freeze because I couldn't—didn't *want* to—probe further.

A horn honked. Someone screeched to a stop. Someone cursed. The air outside looked heavy and milky and poisonous. I sat in my steel box, one among thousands, pretending to navigate.

31

Four P.M. Corned-beef sandwiches and beer in the fridge, a note from Robin pinned to a carton of coleslaw. She and Spike had gone to A&M Studios to sit in on a recording session. The bassist was debuting an eight-string she'd created. Rhythm-and-blues tracks; Spike loved that kind of thing.

The studio was on La Brea near Sunset; I'd been only a few blocks away. Ships passing . . .

Mail was piled up on the dining room table; from the looks of it, mostly bills, and hucksters promising immortality. I phoned Safer. He was in court, unavailable, so I tried the Dosses.

Richard answered. "Doctor. So you got the packet."

"What packet?"

Pause. "Doesn't matter . . . What can I do for you?"

"I was calling to see how you're doing."

"Stacy's fine. Went to school. She's staying away for

the weekend." His voice dropped. "I suppose that's best."

"And Eric?"

"On his way back to Stanford. I got him a plane out of Van Nuys."

"You think he's ready for that?"

"Why not?"

"Last night—"

"Last night was an aberration, Doctor. With all he's gone through, he should've blown a long time ago. Tell the truth, I'm glad he finally did. It's just pottery, I'm fully insured. We'll tell the carrier it was an accident—the bolts on the cases came loose."

"Is he going to get some help at Stanford?"

"We discussed that," he said. "He's considering it."

"I think you should be more directive—"

"Look, Doctor, I appreciate all you've done, but frankly Eric doesn't . . . he doesn't feel comfortable with you. Not your fault, everyone relates differently, you're fine for Stacy, not Eric. Probably all for the best, avoiding sibling rivalry. So why don't you concentrate on Stacy and I'll handle Eric."

"I think he needs help, Richard."

"Your opinion has been duly noted."

"What about you, Richard? How are you doing?"

"I'm alone. Guess I'd better get used to that."

"Anything I can do?"

"No, I'm fine—no thanks to your buddy the detective. He keeps trying to search every square inch I own. And hounding Safer, asking for an 'interview.' Talk about euphemism. But that's okay, everyone has to do their job. Safer tells me I'll be free of all this crap soon enough.

Gotta go, Doctor, call coming in on the other line. If Stacy needs you, I'll be in touch."

"She doesn't want an appointment?"

"I'll ask her. Thanks. Bye."

I found "the packet" in the middle of the mail stack. Courier-delivered envelope, the return address, RTD Properties. Folded into a sheet of RTD stationery was a check written on RTD business account IV. Fifteen thousand dollars. A typed note:

> *Mr. D. thanks you for your time. He trusts this will cover everything to date.*
>
> *Terri, Accounting*
>
> *I'll be in touch.*

Not likely. I knew severance pay when I saw it.

I couldn't talk to Milo, so I called Petra to let her know my impressions of Donny Salcido Mate. She was at her desk, courteous enough, but she sounded busy and I asked her if it was a bad time.

"It's fine," she said. "I just have to run over to Hollywood Pres in a few minutes, start some paper on a new one. Boy meets girl, boy beds girl, boy kills girl, then tries to kill himself. Guy's hooked up to life support, some people can't do anything right. What's up?"

I summarized my bedside chat with Donny.

She said, "Is this guy dangerous?"

"If he doesn't get medicated, maybe. I can't promise you he didn't kill his father, but I wouldn't bet on it."

I explained my reasoning.

She said, "Makes sense. I'll pass it on, see if Milo wants me to hold him on anything . . . Listen, I know I'm a pest about Billy, but kid care isn't my thing, I'm the youngest in my family. Tomorrow when I see him, I was thinking of bringing him some books. Anything in particular you'd suggest?"

"He's always liked history."

"I've already gotten him plenty of history books. I thought fiction might be a nice switch—maybe the classics? Do you see him as able to handle *Les Misérables*? Or *The Count of Monte Cristo,* something like that?"

"Sure," I said. "Either."

"Good, I wasn't sure. Because of the themes—abandonment, poverty. You don't think it's too close to home?"

"No, he'll be fine with it, Petra. I can see books like that appealing to his moral core."

"He's sure got one of *those*, doesn't he?" she said. "I'm still trying to figure out where it came from."

"If you knew, you could sell it."

"And do something else for a living."

"Such as?" I said.

She laughed. "Such as nothing. I love my job."

Saturday morning I awoke thinking about Eric as a murderer. It stayed on my mind during the breakfast that Robin and I shared out near the pond. Then I looked around, saw how beautiful the world was and wondered if I was just letting my imagination run wild because I couldn't stand nice. After all, not a shred of evidence pointed to the boy—or his mother—even talking to Mate.

Mate's records might shed some light on that. And I

was certain that records existed, because Mate had regarded his work as historically significant, would have wanted every detail recorded for posterity.

Milo had guessed Roy Haiselden had them, and he might be right. Now that he had Richard as a suspect, and Haiselden's motive for disappearing had become clear, he was unlikely to pursue the attorney.

No criminal charges had been lodged against Haiselden yet, but domestic violence and child-abuse allegations meant that other detectives would be looking for him, meaning someone might get a warrant. But the Breckenham civil suit had been filed in Baldwin Park, sheriffs jurisdiction. My only sheriffs contact was Ron Banks, a downtown homicide investigator and Petra Connor's boyfriend. I'd met him once, not exactly foundation for a favor.

After we cleaned up, Robin and I went shopping for groceries, then walked in the hills with the pooch. Then she retired for a nap and I went into my office, ignited the computer and gave the Internet another try. Nothing new on Mate except for a couple of cybergossips in a right-to-die chat room exercising their constitutional right to be paranoid.

Am I being too imaginative, wondered whiteknight, *to suggest that following the death of Dr. Mate further attempts are being made to silence those with the courage to face off against The Powers That Be?*

Not at all, responded funnigirl. *I've heard the police from various cities have gotten together to create a taskforce on euthanasia. The plan is to kill people then make it look as if the right-to-die folks are behind it. Shades of Grassy Knoll.*

Screenplays were everywhere. I logged off.

Mate's records . . . Time to give the ever-amiable Alice Zoghbie another try? For all I knew, Haiselden had never had the files, they'd been stored at the pretty little vanilla house on Glenmont.

No reason for her to be any more forthcoming.

Unless I pointed out the discrepancies between Joanne's assisted suicide and Mate's other travelers. Suggested Mate *hadn't* helped Joanne, that Richard had killed Zoghbie's mentor for nothing—had turned Mate into the sacrificial lamb she'd claimed.

If she knew that already, hearing about Richard's arrest would have sent her reeling, she might even be contemplating coming forth. If so, maybe I could tip the scales—turn her grief to my advantage.

Manipulative, but she was someone who believed the infirm should be encouraged not to exist.

At worst, she'd slam the door in my face. Nothing lost; as things stood, I was pretty useless.

I made the drive to Glendale in thirty-five minutes. In the morning light, Alice Zoghbie's house was even cuter, flower beds crayon bright, the copper rooster weather vane vibrating in a breeze I couldn't feel. The same white Audi sat in the cobblestone driveway. Dust on the windshield.

A bit more humanity on the street this time. An old man sweeping his front porch, a young couple pulling out of their carport.

I tapped the goat's-head knocker lightly. No answer. My second attempt, more energetic, was also met with silence.

Making my way back to the driveway, I walked past the Audi to a green wooden gate. Bees buzzed, butterflies fluttered. I called out, "Hello?" then Alice Zoghbie's name, got no reply. Flowers kissed the side of the house. Lights on in the kitchen.

The gate was latched but not locked. I reached around, popped it open, continued along a cobblestone path shaded by the arthritic boughs of an old, scarred sycamore. A small stoop led up to the kitchen door. Four panes of glass gave me something to look through. Lights on, but unoccupied. Dishes in the sink. A carton of milk and half an orange on the counter. The fruit, slightly withered. I knocked. Nothing. Climbing down the stoop, I moved along the side of the house, peeking in windows, listening. Just the bee buzz.

The backyard was small, charmingly landscaped, with hedges of Italian cypress on two sides that blocked the neighbors' views, and a tall wooden fence at the back. Victorian lawn furniture, more flower beds. The kind of flowers that bloom in shade. A dark yard, shrouded by a second sycamore, even larger, stout branches supporting a macramé hammock.

Trunk as thick as two people.

Two people propped against the trunk.

The buzzing, louder—not bees, flies, a storm of flies.

Both of the bodies were tied to the tree with thick rope, fastened tight at chest level and around the waist. The hemp was crusted maroon and brown and black.

Barefoot corpses, insects reconnoitering between fingers and toes. The woman slumped to the right. She had on a blue floral housedress with an elastic neckband. The elastic had allowed the garment to be yanked down without ripping, exposing what had once been her breasts. The killer had hiked it above her waist, too, raised her knees, spread her legs. Wounds everywhere, that same red-black splotching her skin and her clothing, running down her thighs, filthying the grass. Her flesh was green-tinged where the blood hadn't settled.

Triangles sliced into her abdomen, three of them. Her head drooped to her chest, so that I couldn't see her face. A black gaping necklace was visible along her jawline. A helmet of white hair, sparkling where it wasn't fly-crowded, said she'd once been Alice Zoghbie.

The man's khaki shorts had been removed and folded next to his left thigh. His blue polo shirt remained on but had been rolled up to his nipples. Big man, heavy, flabby. Stiff, reddish toupee—a hairpiece I'd seen on TV.

Triangles danced along the swell of Roy Haiselden's abdomen, too, distorted by his paunch. His head lolled to the right. Toward Alice Zoghbie, as if straining to listen to some secret she was imparting.

Not much remained of his face. His genitals had been removed and placed on the grass between his legs. They'd shriveled and shrunk and bugs congregated there with special enthusiasm.

The fingers of his left hand were entwined with Alice Zoghbie's.

The two of them, holding hands.

I'd broken into frosty sweat, wasn't breathing, but my brain was racing. My eyes shifted from the bodies to something else, off to the left, a few feet away. A wicker picnic basket. Propped against it, a tall green bottle, foil-topped. Champagne. Atop the basket, a pair of tiny, gold-lidded jars.

Too far for me to read the labels and I knew better than to disturb the crime scene.

Red jar, black jar. Caviar?

Champagne and caviar, an upscale picnic. Bare feet and her housedress said Alice and the man had no intention of going anywhere.

Posed.

The irony.

A bluebottle fly alighted on Alice Zoghbie's left breast, scuttled, paused, explored some more before taking off in flight—heading toward me.

I backed away. Retreated through the gate, knowing my prints were on the handle, it wouldn't be long before someone would want to talk to me. Leaving it open, I retraced my steps down the driveway, past the Audi, to the curb.

The old man had gone inside. The street had reverted to torpor. So many perfect lawns. Sparrows skittered. How long before the vultures arrived?

Inside the Seville, I breathed.

Last guy in L.A. without a damned cell phone.

I got out of there, drove to a gas station on Verdugo Road, sweat-drenched, collar tight. I parked near the pay phone, composed myself, got out. Other people pumped gas as I tried to look any way other than how I felt.

The killings were in Glendale PD jurisdiction, but to hell with that, I called Milo.

32

Any idea when he'll be back?"

"I think he went downtown to do some paper-work," said the clerk, a woman, one I didn't know. "I can transfer you to Detective Korn. He works with Detective Sturgis. Your name, sir?"

"No thanks," I said.

"You're sure?"

She sounded nice so I gave her the ugly details and hung up before she could respond.

I drove back to L.A., hoping for an empty house. Wanting time to breathe, to sort things out.

Repulsed, still shaken. Sweat came gushing out of my pores as the image of the bodies kept smacking me across the brain.

Milo and I had visited Alice Zoghbie five days ago.

No skin sloughing, no maggots, the beginnings of the

green tinge . . . I was no forensic pathologist, but I'd seen enough corpses to guess that not more than a couple of days had passed since the murder. Alice's mail and phone records could clear that up . . .

Propped, holding hands, a picnic.

Someone canny enough to overpower a big man like Haiselden and a woman who hiked the Himalayas.

Someone they knew. A confederate. Had to be.

The feelings of disgust didn't subside, but a new sensation joined them—strange, juvenile glee.

Not Eric, not Richard. No motive and both their whereabouts were well accounted for during the past two or three days. Same for Donny Salcido.

Propped against a tree. Geometry. Michael Burke's trademarks. Time to give Leimert Fusco's big black book another review.

Time to call Fusco—but Milo deserved to know first.

I was on the 134, driving much too fast, hoping for an empty house, thinking about Haiselden hiding from the civil suit only to encounter something much worse.

He'd probably been hiding out with Alice all along— I recalled the phone call she'd taken when Milo and I had visited. Afterward, she couldn't wait to get rid of us. Probably from her pal, wanting to know if the coast was clear.

The two of them waylaid right there in Alice's house. Someone they knew . . . someone respectable, trusted. A bright young doctor who'd apprenticed to Mate.

No doubt Glendale police had already been dispatched to the scene. Soon my prints on the gate would be lifted and within days they'd be matched to the Medical Board files in Sacramento.

Milo needed to know soon.

If I couldn't reach him, should I go straight to Fusco? The FBI man had said he was flying up to Seattle. Wanting to check on the unsolveds—something specific about the Seattle unsolveds?

The last Seattle victim—Marissa Bonpaine. Plastic hypodermic found on the forest floor. Cataloged and forgotten.

Not a coincidence. Couldn't be a coincidence.

Fusco had left me his beeper number and his local exchange, but both were back home in the Burke file.

I pushed the Seville up to ninety.

I unlocked my front door. Robin's truck was gone—prayers answered. I raced to my office, feeling guilty about being quite so pleased.

I tried Milo again, got no answer, decided sooner was better than later and phoned Fusco's beeper and routing number. No callback from him, either. I was starting to feel like the last man on Earth. After another futile attempt to reach Milo, I punched in FBI headquarters at the Federal Building in Westwood and asked for Special Agent Fusco. The receptionist put me on hold, then transferred me to another woman with the throaty voice of a lounge singer who took my name and number.

"May I tell him what this is about, sir?"

"He'll know."

"He's out of the office. I'll give him the message."

I pulled out the big black accordion file, flung it open, stared at pictures of corpses against trees, geometrical wounds, the parallels inescapable.

All my theories about family breakdown, the Dosses,

the Manitows, and it had come down to just another psychopath. I paged through police reports, found the Seattle cases, the data on Marissa Bonpaine, was halfway through the small print when the doorbell rang.

Leaving the file on the desk, I trotted to the front door. The peephole offered a fish-eye view of two people—a man and a woman, white, early thirties, expressionless.

Clean-cut duo. Missionaries? I could use some faith but was in no mood to be preached to.

"Yes?" I said, through the door.

I watched the woman's mouth move. "Dr. Delaware? FBI. May we please speak with you."

Throaty voice of a lounge singer.

Before I could answer, a badge filled the peephole. I opened the door.

The woman's lips were turned upward, but the smile appeared painful. Her badge was still out. "Special Agent Mary Donovan. This is Special Agent Mark Bratz. May we please come in, Dr. Delaware?"

Donovan was five-six or so with short light-brown hair, a strong jaw and a firm, busty, low-waisted body packed into a charcoal-gray suit. Rosy complexion, an aura of confidence. Bratz was a half head taller with dark hair starting to thin, sleepy eyes and a round, vulnerable face. The skin around his jowls was raw, and a small Band-Aid was stuck under one ear. He wore a navy-blue suit, white shirt, gray and navy tie.

I stepped back to let them enter. They stood in the entry hall, checking out the house, until I invited them to sit.

"Thanks for your time, Doctor," said Donovan, still

smiling as she took the most comfortable chair. She carried a huge black cloth purse, which she placed on the floor.

Bratz waited until I'd settled, then positioned himself so the two of them flanked me. I tried to look casual, thinking about the open file on the desk, trying *not* to think about what I'd just seen in Glendale.

"Nice house," said Bratz. "Bright."

"Thanks. May I ask what this is about?"

"Very nice," said Donovan. "Care to guess, Doctor?"

"Something to do with Agent Fusco."

"Something to do with *Mr.* Fusco."

"He's not with the FBI?"

"Not any longer," said Bratz. His voice was high, tentative, like that of a bashful kid asking for a date. "Mr. Fusco retired from the Bureau a while back—was asked to retire."

"Because of personal issues," said Donovan. She took a pad and a Sony minirecorder out of her bag, set them on the coffee table. "Mind if I record?"

"Record what?"

"Your impressions of Mr. Fusco, sir."

"You're saying he was mustered out because of personal issues?" I said. "Are we talking criminal issues? Is he dangerous?"

Donovan glanced at Bratz. "May I record, sir?"

"After you tell me what's going on, maybe."

Donovan's fingernails tapped the Sony. Surprisingly long nails. French tips. Her lipstick was subtle. Her expression wasn't. She had no use for civilians who didn't fall in line.

"Sir," she said. "It's in your best interests—"

"I need to know. Is Fusco a criminal suspect?" As in multiple murder.

"At this point, sir, we're simply trying to find him. To help him." Her index finger touched the Sony's REC button.

I shook my head.

"Sir, we could arrange for you to be questioned at Bureau headquarters."

"That would take time, paperwork, and something tells me time's of the essence," I said. "On the other hand, you could tell me what's going on and I could co-operate and we could all try to have something of a weekend."

She looked at Bratz. No signal from him that I saw, but she turned back to me and her expression had softened.

"Here's a summary, Doctor. All you need to know and more: Leimert Fusco was a highly admired member of the Bureau—I assume you've heard of the BSU? The original Behavioral Science Unit at Quantico? Mr. Fusco was a member of the freshman class. Actually, he's Dr. Fusco. Has a PhD in psychology, same as you."

"So he informed me. Why was he asked to leave the Bureau?"

Bratz leaned across and clicked on the recorder, said, "How'd you meet him, sir?"

"Sorry, I'm not comfortable with this," I said, sorry about a lot more. Moments ago, I'd been ready to focus on Michael Burke as the real Dr. Death. If Fusco had lied, what happened to that scenario?

"What's the problem, sir?" said Donovan.

"Talking to you, going on record, without knowing

the full picture. I spent time with Fusco. I need to know who I was dealing with."

Another look passed between them. Donovan's mouth turned up again and she crossed her legs, setting off little scratchy sounds. Short legs, but shapely. Runner's calves in sheer stockings. Bratz snuck a peek at them, as if they were still a novelty. I wondered how long they'd been partnered.

"Fair enough, sir," she said, suddenly sunny. She tossed her hair, but it didn't move much. Leg recross. She inched closer to me. I could imagine some FBI seminar. *Achieve rapport with the subject by any appropriate means.* "But first, let me take a stab at how you met him: he contacted Detective Sturgis and asked to meet with you to discuss a homicide—most likely that of Dr. Mate—because you're the psychological consultant on the case. He told you he knows who the murderer is." Lots of teeth. "How'm I doing so far?"

"Very well," I said.

"Michael Burke," said Bratz. "He wanted you to believe in Dr. Michael Burke."

"Is Burke fiction?"

Bratz shrugged. "Let's just say Dr. Fusco's obsessed."

"With Burke."

"With the *idea* of Burke," said Donovan.

"Are you telling me he made Burke up?"

She glanced at the recorder. Switched it off. "Okay, here's the whole story, but we insist you keep it confidential. Agent Fusco had an honorable career with the Bureau. For several years, he was assigned to the Midtown Manhattan office as director of behavioral sciences. Five years ago, his wife died—breast cancer—

and he was left sole parent of his child. A daughter, four-teen years old, named Victoria. What made Mrs. Fusco's death especially traumatic for Agent Fusco was that Victoria had also been diagnosed with cancer. Several years before, as a toddler. A bone tumor, she was treated at Sloan-Kettering, apparently cured. Shortly after his wife passed away, Fusco requested a transfer, said he wanted to raise Victoria in a quieter environment. An administrative position was found for him in the Buffalo office and he purchased a home near Lake Erie."

"Not a career move," I said. "He was devoted to the girl."

Donovan nodded. "Everything seemed fine for a couple of years, then the girl got sick again, at sixteen. Leukemia. Apparently the radiation she'd received for her bone tumor years ago had caused it."

"Secondary tumor," I said. Rare but tragic; I'd seen it at Western Peds.

"Exactly. Agent Fusco began bringing Victoria down to New York to be re-treated at Sloan-Kettering. She went into one remission, relapsed, received more chemo, achieved only a partial remission, started to weaken, tried some experimental drugs and got better but even weaker. Agent Fusco decided to continue her treatment closer to home, at a hospital in Buffalo. The goal was to increase her strength until she was able to tolerate a bone-marrow transplant back in New York. She improved for a while, then came down with pneu-monia because chemotherapy had weakened her immune system. Her doctors hospitalized her and, unfortunately, she passed away."

"Was that expected?"

"From what we can gather, it wasn't unexpected but neither was it inevitable."

"One of those fifty-fifty situations," said Bratz.

"A hospital in Buffalo," I said. "Was she cared for by a respiratory tech named Roger Sharveneau?"

Donovan frowned. Looked at Bratz. He shook his head, but she said, "Possibly."

"Possibly?"

"Roger Sharveneau was on duty during Victoria's final hospitalization. Whether he was ever her therapist is unclear."

"Missing records?" I said.

"What's the difference?" said Bratz.

"Was Michael Burke also working there during that period?"

Bratz's eyes narrowed. Donovan said, "There's no record of Burke caring for her."

"But he was circulating through at the time— probably freelancing at the E.R.," I said.

Silence from both of them.

I went on: "When did Fusco become convinced that someone—Sharveneau or Burke, or both of them—had murdered his daughter?"

"Months later," said Donovan. "After Sharveneau began confessing. Fusco claimed he recognized him from the ward, had seen him in Victoria's room when he had no good reason to be there. He tried to interview Sharveneau in jail, was refused permission by the Buffalo police because the Bureau had no standing in the case and *he* certainly didn't—it was obviously a personal issue. Agent Fusco didn't react well to that. After Sharveneau was released, he persisted, harassing Sharveneau's lawyer. He became increasingly . . . irate. Even after Sharveneau committed suicide, he didn't cease."

"Was Fusco considered a suspect in Sharveneau's supposed suicide?" I said.

Second's hesitation. "No, never. Sharveneau had been in hiding, there's no evidence Fusco ever found him. Meanwhile, Agent Fusco's work product deteriorated and the Bureau sent him back to Quantico for several months. Had him teach seminars to beginning profilers. As a cooling-off measure. It seemed to be working, Fusco looked calm, more content. But that turned out to be a ruse. He was utilizing the bulk of his energies researching Burke, accessing data banks without permission. He was brought back to New York for a meeting with his superiors, during which he was let go on disability pension."

"*Emotional* disability," said Bratz.

"You see him as seriously disturbed?" I said. "Out of touch with reality?"

Bratz exhaled, looked uncomfortable.

"You've met him," said Donovan. "What do you think, Doctor?"

"To me he seemed pretty focused."

"That's the problem, Doctor. Too much focus. He's already committed a score of felonies."

"Violent felonies?"

"Mostly multiple thefts."

"Of what?"

"Data—official police records from various jurisdictions. And he continues to represent himself as a special agent. If all that got out . . . Doctor, the Bureau has sympathy for his misfortune. The Bureau respects him—

respects what he once was. No one wants to see him end up in jail."

"Is he off base on Burke?" I said.

"Burke's not the issue," said Bratz.

"Why not?"

"Burke's not the issue for *us*," Donovan clarified. "We handle only internal investigations, not external criminal matters. S.A. Fusco's been identified as an internal issue."

"Is anyone in the Bureau looking into Michael Burke?"

"We wouldn't have access to that information, sir. Our goal is simple: take custody of Leimert Fusco, for his own good."

"What happens to him if you find him?" I said.

"He'll be cared for."

"Committed?"

Donovan frowned. "Cared for. Humanely. Forget all the movies you've seen. Dr. Fusco's a private citizen now, due the same rights as anyone else. He'll be cared for until such a time as he's judged competent—it's for his own good, Doctor. No one wants to see a man of his . . . fortitude and experience end up in jail."

Bratz said, "We've been looking for him for a while, finally traced him to L.A. He covers his tracks pretty well, got himself a cell phone account under another name, but we found it and it led us to an apartment in Culver City. By the time we got there, he was gone. Packed up. Then an hour ago, you called and we just happened to be there."

"Lucky break for you," I said.

"Where is he, Doctor?"

"Don't know."

His hand clenched. "Why were you attempting to call him, sir?"

"To discuss Michael Burke. I'm sure you know I'm a psychological consultant to LAPD. I've been asked to interface with S.A. Fusco." I shrugged. "That's it."

"Come on, Doctor," said Bratz. "You don't want to be putting yourself in an awkward position. We'll be contacting Detective Sturgis soon enough, he'll tell us the truth."

"Be my guests."

Bratz hemmed me closer and I sniffed mentholated cologne. His jaw was set. No more vulnerability. "Why would you care about Dr. Burke? A suspect's already in custody on Mate."

"Being thorough," I said.

"Thorough," Bratz repeated. "Just like Fusco."

"You know, Doctor," said Donovan, "some people say you're kind of obsessive."

I smiled. How long before the prints on Alice Zoghbie's gate got decoded and they found out about it? "Sounds like you've been researching me."

"We can be thorough, too."

"If only everyone was," I said. "Better world. The trains would run on time."

Bratz rubbed a patch of raw skin and looked at the recorder. Nothing of substance had been recorded. "You think this is a joke, my friend? You think we want to sit around with you, bullshitting?"

I turned and looked into his eyes. "I doubt you're enjoying this any more than I am, but that doesn't change the facts. You asked me if I knew where Fusco was, I told you the truth. I don't. He said he'd be out of town, left the cell-phone number. I tried it and he didn't answer, so I phoned the Federal Building. Obviously that's something he didn't instruct me to do, so we're *obviously* not colluding on anything."

"What cell number did he give you?"

"Hold on and I'll get it for you."

"You do that," said Bratz, barely opening his mouth.

I went into my office, stashed the accordion file in a drawer, copied down the number and returned. Bratz was on his feet, studying prints on the wall. Donovan's nylon-glossed knees were pressed together. I handed her the slip.

"Same one we've got, Mark," she said.

Bratz said, "Let's get out of here."

I said, "Even if Fusco had left me a detailed itinerary, why would it be any more credible than anything else he told me?"

"You're saying Fusco just told you about Burke, then dropped out of sight."

"Told Detective Sturgis and myself. We met with him, together, just as you said."

"Where?"

"Mort's Deli. Sturgis didn't buy the Burke theory, basically shunted it to me. As you said, he's got a suspect."

"And your opinion?"

"About what?"

"Burke."

"I need more data. That's exactly why I tried to reach Fusco. If I'd known it was going to get this complicated . . ."

Bratz turned toward me. "Understand this: if Fusco keeps improvising, it could get real complicated."

"Makes sense," I said. "Rogue agent running wild,

psychological expert goes haywire. Public relations night-mare for you guys."

"Something wrong with that? Protecting the Bureau's integrity so it can do its job?"

"Not at all. Nothing wrong with integrity."

"True, Doctor," said Donovan. "Just make sure you're holding on to yours."

I watched them drive away in a dark blue sedan.

They'd labeled Fusco obsessive but hadn't dismissed the core of his investigation. *An internal issue.* Not their problem.

Meaning someone else in the Bureau might very well be looking into Michael Burke. Or they weren't.

When news of the Zoghbie-Haiselden murder broke, Fusco's nose would twitch harder. He'd probably try to contact Milo, even fly back down to L.A. Get snagged by his former comrades, taken into custody. For his own good.

He'd had a tragic life, but right now worrying about his welfare wasn't my job either. I went back inside, gave Milo yet another try. Daring another attempt at the West L.A. station, ready to disguise my voice if the same clerk answered.

This time it was a bored-sounding man who patched me up to the Robbery-Homicide room.

A familiar voice picked up Milo's extension. Del Hardy. A long time ago the veteran detective and Milo had worked together. Del was black, which hadn't mattered much, and married to a second wife who was a devout Baptist, which had—she'd kiboshed the partner-ship. I knew Del was a year from retirement, planning something down in Florida.

"Working Saturday, Del?"

"Long as it's not Sunday, Doc. How's the guitar-playing?"

"Not doing enough of it. Seen the big guy recently?"

"Happened to see him about an hour ago. He said he was going over to Judge MacIntyre's house, try for some warrants. Pasadena—I can give you the number if it's important. But Judge MacIntyre gets cranky about being bugged on the weekend, so why don't you try Milo's mobile."

"I did. He didn't answer."

"Maybe he shut it off, didn't want to annoy Judge MacIntyre."

"Scary guy, huh?"

"MacIntyre? Yeah, but law and order. If he thinks you're righteous he'll give all sorts of leeway—okay, here it is."

A frosty-voiced woman said, "What's this about?"

"I'm a police consultant, working on a homicide case. It's important that I reach Detective Sturgis. Is he there?"

"One minute."

Four minutes later, she came back on. "He's on his way out, said *he'll* call *you*."

It took another quarter hour for Milo to ring in.

"What's so important, Alex? How the hell did you get MacIntyre's number—you almost messed me up, I was in the middle of getting paper on Doss. Got some, too."

"Sorry, but you were wasting your time." I told him what I'd seen in Alice Zoghbie's backyard. The way I'd reported it to the police clerk, my prints on the gate.

"This is a joke, right?" he said.

"Ha ha ha."

Long silence. "Why'd you go out there in the first place, Alex?"

"Boredom, overachievement—what's the difference? This changes everything."

"Where are you right now?"

"Home. Just finished with some visitors." I began to tell him about Donovan and Bratz.

"Stop," he said. "I'm coming over—no, better if we meet somewhere, just in case they're still watching you. I just got on the 110—let's make it somewhere central . . . Pico-Robertson, the parking lot behind the Miller's Outpost, southeast corner. If I'm late, buy yourself some jeans. And try to figure out if the feebies are tailing you. If they are, I doubt they'll be using more than one car, which will make it damn near impossible for them to pull it off if you're looking out for them. Did you happen to notice what kind of car they were driving?"

"Blue sedan."

"Check for it three, four car lengths behind you. If you see it, drive back home and wait."

"High intrigue."

"Low intrigue," he said. "Bureaucracy's big toes getting stepped on. Zoghbie and Haiselden—did you notice any overt putrefaction?"

"Green tinge, no maggots, lots of flies."

"Probably a day or two at most . . . and you're saying the positioning was similar to the stuff in Fusco's file?"

"Identical. Geometrical wounds, as well."

"Oh my," he said. "Every day brings new thrills."

• • •

I wrote a note to Robin and left, drove more slowly than usual, looked out for the blue sedan or anything else that spelled government-issue. No sign of a tail, as far as I could tell. I reached the Miller's Outpost lot before Milo, parked where he'd instructed, got out of the car and stood against the driver's door. Still, no blue car. The lot was half full. Shoppers streamed in and out of the store, business at a nearby newsstand was brisk, cars roared by on Robertson. I waited and thought about putrefaction.

Milo showed up ten minutes later, surprisingly well-put-together in a gray suit, white shirt, maroon tie. Warrant-begging duds. No string tie for Judge MacIntyre.

He motioned me into the unmarked, lit up the cold stub of a Panatela as I eased into the passenger seat.

He scanned the lot, fondled his cell phone, let his eyes drift to the jeans store. "Time to get myself some easy-fit . . . Glendale's at the scene—they've pegged it to an anonymous caller. How does it feel to be an archetype?"

"Glorious. But I won't be anonymous long. The gate."

"Yeah, terrific. I'm waiting to hear back from their detectives. News jackals picked it up, too, it's only a matter of time before they tie Zoghbie and Haiselden to Mate and we're back on page one."

"That's exactly what Burke wants," I said. "But maybe he had another motive for killing Zoghbie and Haiselden: to get hold of any records that incriminated him. He might very well have been planning it for a while, but Richard's arrest might have sped things up: he wouldn't like someone else getting credit for his handiwork. Like

Mate, he's after the attention, is eliminating the old guard, telling the world he's the new Dr. Death."

He chewed the cigar's wooden tip, blew out acrid smoke. "You buy the whole Burke thing even though Fusco misrepresented himself?"

"When will you be going over to the Zoghbie crime scene?"

"Soon."

"Wait till you see it. Everything fits. And Donovan and Bratz never dismissed Fusco's findings, they're just worried he'll do something that makes the Bureau look bad. Fusco's convinced Sharveneau and/or Burke murdered his daughter. Personal motivation can get in the way, but sometimes it's potent fuel."

He sucked in smoke, held it in his lungs for a long time, drew a lazy circle on the windshield fog. "So I've been spinning my wheels on Doss . . . who, from what I've been told by business associates, has very complicated financial records—maybe I'll send my files to the Fraud boys."

He faced me. "Alex, you know damn well he solicited Goad to kill Mate, we're not talking Mother Teresa. Just because Goad didn't go all the way doesn't put Doss in the clear."

"I realize that. But it doesn't change what I saw in Glendale."

"Right," he said. "Back to square goddamn one . . . Burke, or whatever the hell he's calling himself . . . you're saying he craves center stage. But he can't go public the way Mate did . . . so what does that mean? More nasties against trees?" His laugh was thick with affliction and anger. "Gee, *that's* a terrific lead. Let's go check out every

bit of bark in the goddamn county—where the hell do I
go with this, Alex?"

"Back to Fusco's files?" I said.

"You've already been through them. Okay, I'll accept
the fact that Burke is evil personified. Now, where the
hell do I find him?"

"I'll go over them again. You never know—"

"You're right about that," he said. "I never *do* know.
Spend half my damn life in blissless ignorance . . . Okay,
let's handle some short-term matters. Like keeping you
out of jail once those prints cross-reference to the
Medical Board. Did you touch anything but the gate?"

"The front door knocker. I also knocked on the side
door, but just with my knuckles."

"The old goat's head," he said. "When I first saw it I
wondered if Alice was into witchcraft or something. That,
combined with all her talk of Mate being a sacrifice. So
she ends up tied up— All right, look, I'm going to run
interference for you with Glendale PD, but at some point
you'll have to talk to them. It'll take days for the prints to
be analyzed, maybe a good week for the cross-reference,
even longer if the med files aren't on Printrak. But I need
to work with them, so I'm telling them about you
sooner—figure on tomorrow. I'll try to have them interview you on friendly territory."

"Thanks."

"Yeah. Thanks, too." He inhaled, made the cigar tip
glow, created another quarter inch of ash.

"For what?"

"Being such a persistent bastard."

"What's next?" I said.

"For you? Keeping out of trouble. For me, anguish."

"Want Fusco's file?"

"Later," he said. "There's still Doss's paper to deal with. I can't let warrants lapse on an attempted murder case. I do that and Judge MacIntyre puts me on his naughty list. I'll sic Korn and Demetri on Doss's office, have them shlep the financial records to the station so I can get moving at Glendale. Maybe the scene will tell me something. Maybe Burke/whatever missed something in Alice's house and we can get a lead on him." He crushed the cigar in the ashtray. "Fat chance of that, right?"

"Anything's possible."

"Everything's possible," he said. "That's the problem."

By the time I got back, Robin was home. We had a takeout Chinese dinner and I fed slivers of Peking duck to Spike, acting like a regular, domestic guy with nothing heavier on my mind than taxes and prostate problems. This time I went to sleep when Robin did and drifted off easily. At 4:43 A.M., I woke up with a stiff neck and a stubborn brain. Cold air had settled in during the night and my hands felt like freezer-burned steaks. I put on sweats, athletic socks and slippers, shuffled to my office, removed Fusco's file from the drawer where I'd concealed it from Donovan and Bratz.

Starting again, with Marissa Bonpaine, finding nothing out of the ordinary but the plastic hypodermic. An hour in, I got drowsy. The smart decision would have been to crawl back in bed. Instead, I lurched to the kitchen. Spike was curled up on his mattress in the adjacent laundry room, flat little bulldog face compressed against the foam. Movement beneath his eyelids said he was dreaming. His expression said they were sweet dreams—a beautiful woman drives you around in her truck and feeds you kibble, why not?

I headed for the pantry. Generally, that's a stimulus for him to hurry over, assume the squat, wait for food. This time, he raised an eyelid, shot me a "you've got to be kidding" look, and resumed snoring.

I chewed on some dry cereal, made a tall mug of strong instant coffee, drank half trying to dispel the chill. The kitchen windows were blue with night. The suggestion of foliage was a distant black haze. I checked the clock. Forty minutes before daybreak. I carried the mug back to my office.

Time for more tilting, Mr. Quixote.

I returned to my desk. Ten minutes later I saw it, wondered why I hadn't seen it before.

A notation made by the first Seattle officer on the Bonpaine murder scene—a detective named Robert Elias, called in by the forest rangers who'd actually found the body.

Very small print, bottom of the page, cross-referenced to a footnote.

Easy to miss—no excuses, Delaware. Now it screamed at me.

The victim, wrote Elias, *was discovered by a hiker, walking with his dog (see ref, 45).*

That led me to the rear of the Bonpaine file, a listing of over three hundred events enumerated by the meticulous Detective Elias.

Number 45 read: *Hiker: tourist from Michigan. Mr. Ferris Grant.*

Number 46 was an address and phone number in Flint, Michigan.

Number 47: *Dog: black labr. retriev. Mr. F. Grant states "she has great nose, thinks she's a drug dog."*

I'd heard that before, word for word. Paul Ulrich describing Duchess, the golden retriever.

Ferris Grant.

Michael Ferris Burke. *Grant* Rushton.

Flint, Michigan. Huey Grant Mitchell had worked in Michigan—Ann Arbor.

I phoned the number Ferris Grant had left as his home exchange, got a recorded message from the Flint Museum of Art.

No sign Elias had followed up. Why would he bother? Ferris Grant had been nothing more than a helpful citizen who'd aided a major investigation by "discovering" the body.

Just as Paul Ulrich had discovered Mate.

How Burke must have loved that. Orchestrating. Providing himself with a legitimate reason to show up at the crime scene. Proud of his handiwork, watching the cops stumble.

Psychopath's private joke. Games, always games. His internal laughter must have been deafening.

Hiker with a dog.

Paul Ulrich, Tanya Stratton.

I paged hurriedly to the photo gallery Leimert Fusco had assembled, tried to reconcile any of the more recent portraits of Burke with my memory of Ulrich. But Ulrich's face wouldn't take shape in my head, all I recalled was the handlebar mustache.

Which was exactly the point.

Facial hair changed things. I'd been struck by that when trying to reconcile the various photos of Burke.

The beard Burke had grown as Huey Mitchell, hospital security guard, as effective as any mask.

He'd gone on to use another Michigan identity. Ferris Grant . . . the Flint Museum. Another ha ha: *I'm an artist!* Reverting to Michigan—to familiar patterns—because at heart, psychopaths were rigid, there always had to be a script of sorts.

I studied Mitchell's picture, the dead eyes, the flat expression. Luxuriant mask of a beard. Heavy enough to nurture a giant mustache.

When I tried to picture Ulrich's face, all I *saw* was the mustache.

I strained to recall his other physical characteristics.

Medium-size man, late thirties to forty. Perfect match to Burke on both counts.

Shorter, thinner hair than any of Burke's pictures—balding to a fuzzy crew cut. Each picture of Burke revealed a steady, sequential loss, so that fit, too.

The mustache . . . stretching wider than Ulrich's face. As good a mask as any. I'd thought it an unusual flamboyance, contrasting especially with Ulrich's conservative dress.

Financial consultant, Mr. Respectable . . . Something else Ulrich had said—one of the *first* things he'd said—came back to me: *So far our names haven't been in the paper. We're going to be able to keep it that way, aren't we, Detective Sturgis?*

Concerned about publicity. Craving publicity.

Milo had answered that the two of them would probably be safe from media scrutiny, but Ulrich had stuck with the topic, talked about fifteen minutes of fame.

Andy Warhol coined that phrase and look what happened to him . . . checked into a hospital . . . went out in a bag . . . celebrity stinks . . . look at Princess Di, look at Dr. Mate.

Letting Milo know that fame was what he was after. Playing with Milo, the way he'd toyed with the Seattle cops.

Getting as close as he could to criminal celebrity without confessing outright.

It had been no coincidence that he and Tanya Stratton had chosen Mulholland for a morning walk that Monday.

Stratton had come out and said so: *We rarely come up here, except on Sundays.* Resentful about the change in routine. About *Paul's* insistence.

She'd complained to Milo that *everything* had been Paul's idea. Including the decision to talk to Milo up at the site, rather than at home. Ulrich had claimed to be attempting a kind of therapy for Tanya, but his real motive—multiple motives—had been something quite different: keep Milo off Ulrich's home territory, and get another chance at déjà vu.

Ulrich had talked about the horror of discovering Mate, but I realized now that emotion had been lacking.

Not so, Tanya Stratton. She'd been clearly upset, eager to leave. But Ulrich had come across amiable, helpful, relaxed. *Too* relaxed for someone who'd encountered a bloodbath.

An outdoorsy guy—Fusco had said Michael Burke skied, fancied himself an outdoorsman—Ulrich had chatted about staying fit, the beauty of the site.

Once you get past the gate, it's like being in another world.

Oh yeah.

His world.

Amiable guy, but the charm was wearing thin with Stratton. Was she edgy because she'd begun to sense something about her boyfriend? Or just a relationship gone stagnant?

I recalled her pallor, the unsteady gait. Wispy hair. Dark glasses—hiding something?

A fragile girl.

Not a well girl?

Then I understood and my heart beat faster: one of Michael Burke's patterns was to hook up with sick women, befriend them, nurture them.

Then guide them out of this world.

He enjoyed killing on so many levels. The consummate Dr. Death, and one way or the other the world was going to know it. How Eldon Mate's fame—the legitimacy Mate had obtained while dispatching fifty lives—must have eaten at Burke. All those years in medical school, and Burke still couldn't practice openly the way Mate did, had to serve as Mate's apprentice.

Had to masquerade as a *layman.*

Because since arriving in L.A., he hadn't found a way to bogus his medical credentials, had to represent himself as a financial consultant.

Mostly real-estate work . . . Century City address. Nice and ambiguous.

Home base, Encino. *Just over the hill.* Respectable neighborhood for an upstanding guy.

In L.A. you could live off a smile and a zip code.

The business card Ulrich had given Milo was sitting in a drawer at the West L.A. station. I phoned information and asked for Ulrich's Century City business listing, was only half surprised when I got one. But when I tried the number, a recording told me the line had been disconnected. No Encino exchange for either him or Tanya Stratton, nothing anywhere in the Valley or the city.

Tanya. Not a well girl.

A relationship on the wane with Ulrich could prove lethal.

I looked at the clock. Just after six. Light through the office curtains said the sun had risen. If Milo had been up all night at the Glendale crime scene, he'd be home now, getting some well-deserved rest.

Some things could wait. I phoned him. Rick answered on the first ring. "Up early, Alex."

"Did I wake you?"

"Not hardly. I was just about to leave for the E.R. Milo's already gone."

"Gone where?"

"He didn't say. Probably back to Glendale, that double murder. He was out there until midnight, came home, slept for four hours, woke in a foul mood, showered without singing and left the house with his hair still wet."

"The joys of domestic life," I said.

"Oh yeah," he said. "Give me a nice freeway pileup and I know I'm being useful."

Milo picked up his mobile, barking, "Sturgis."

"It's me. Where are you?"

"Up on Mulholland," he said in an odd, detached voice. "Staring at dirt. Trying to figure out if I missed something."

"Son, I'm going to bring some joy into your wretched life." I told him about Ulrich.

I expected shock, profanity, but his voice remained remote. "Funny you should mention that."

"You figured it out?"

"No, but I was just wondering about Ulrich. Because I positioned my car where the van was, walked myself through the scene. When the sun came up it hit the rear window and gave off glare. Blinding glare, I couldn't see a thing inside. Ulrich claimed he and the girl discovered Mate right after sunrise, said he could see Mate's body through the rear window. Now that was a week ago, and the van's windows were higher than mine, but I don't calculate that much of a difference and I don't imagine the sun's angle has shifted that radically. I was waiting around to see if the visibility changed over the next quarter hour or so. By itself it wasn't any big deal, maybe the guy didn't remember every detail. But now you're telling me . . . Left the bastard's address back at the station, I'll run a DMV on him and Stratton girl. Time for a drop-in."

"The Stratton girl may be in danger." I told him why.

"Sick?" he said. "Yeah, she didn't look too healthy, did she? All the more reason to visit."

"How're you going to handle Ulrich?"

"I don't exactly have grounds for an arrest, Alex. At the moment, all I can do is scope him out in his natural habitat—my story will be that I'm dropping in for a follow-up, has he thought of anything else? 'Cause we're stumped—he'd like that, right? The cops being stupid, my coming to him for wisdom."

"He'd love it," I said. "If he believed it. But this is a

smart man. He'd have to wonder why, after Richard's arrest, you're knocking on his door on a Sunday morning."

Silence. "How about I imply there are complications with the current investigation—stuff I can't talk about. He'll know I mean Zoghbie, but I won't come out and say it. We'll tango around, I can watch his eyes and his feet. Maybe Stratton will give off some kind of vibe. Maybe I'll get her alone, later on in the day."

"Sounds good. Want me there?"

Silence. Static. Finally he said, "Yes."

When I walked into the bedroom, Robin was sitting up and rubbing her eyes.

"Morning." I kissed her forehead and began to get dressed.

"What time is it? How long have you been up?"

"Early. Just a bit. Have to run and meet Milo up on Mulholland."

"Oh," she said sleepily. "Something come up?"

"Maybe," I said.

That opened her eyes wide.

"A possible lead," I said. "Nothing dangerous. Brain work."

She held out her arms. We embraced.

"Take good care of it," she said. "Your brain. I love your brain."

33

Milo was parked on the road below the murder site, engine running, fingers tapping the steering wheel. I left the Seville a few yards away and got in the unmarked. He was wearing the same gray suit, but it looked ten years older. Driving east on Mulholland, he reached the Glen, headed north into the Valley.

"Where'd you get the address?" I said.

"DMV. No listings for Ulrich's BMW or any other vehicle in his name, but the Stratton girl owns a two-year-old Saturn, has an address on Milbank. Sherman Oaks, not Encino. Too far east by two blocks."

"Why tell the truth when you can lie?"

"Setting up the scene . . . He just loves this, doesn't he?"

"Every detail," I said. "Remember what you said about the only footprints being his and Stratton's? He cleaned up after himself, but just in case he missed something, he gave himself a legitimate reason to leave behind trace evidence."

"All these years . . . orchestrating . . . goddamn conductor." He took one hand off the wheel, raised it toward the roof. "Lord, grant me the opportunity to shove his baton up his ass . . . Anything else you think I should know before I approach him?"

"Act friendly but authoritative. Don't go overboard on either. While you're listening to him, let your eyes roam. Let him try to figure out if it's cop curiosity or you're looking for something. Let's see how he reacts to the uncertainty. Ask him lots of questions, but keep it general. Out-of-sequence questions, like you do so well. Dropping in on him without warning is good. You'll be the one orchestrating. If he gets nervous, he may do something impulsive. Like pack up and leave once he thinks you're gone, or try to hide something—a storage locker. He's likely to have one, can't afford to have Tanya come across his souvenirs."

"You're sure he keeps them?"

"I'll bet on it. Once you leave, can you get surveillance in place pretty quickly?"

"One way or the other, he'll be watched, Alex. If I have to do it myself, he'll be watched . . . Okay, so you're talking a one-man good-cop/bad-cop show. But keep it subtle. Yeah, I can do subtle. Even without the benefit of alcohol. What'll *you* be concentrating on?"

"Playing impassive shrink. If I can get Tanya alone, I'll take a closer look at her."

"Why, you suspect her, too?"

"No, but she's tiring of him. Maybe she'll say something revealing."

He bared his teeth in what I assumed was a smile. "Fine, we've got our plan. All that accomplished, *then* can I shove it up his ass?"

His gas foot was heavy and the ride took fifteen minutes, whipping us past canyon beauty and the barbered anxiety of hillside suburbia, accelerating into a too-fast left turn across Ventura. The Valley was ten degrees warmer. Encino appeared just past Sepulveda and the low-rise shops of Sherman Oaks gave way to mirrored office buildings and car lots. Very little traffic this early on a sleepy Sunday. The 405 freeway ribboned across the intersection, parallel with the western flank of the white carcass that had once been the Sherman Oaks Galleria. The shopping center was shuttered now, all the more pathetic in death because of its size. Someone had plans for the space. Someone always had plans.

Milo drove a block, turned right on Orion, stayed parallel with the freeway, headed west on Camarillo, circling around to the mouth of Milbank, a shady street with no sidewalks. Single-story houses, well-maintained, dimmed by the luxuriance of untrimmed camphor trees. Off to the east, the freeway thundered.

Tanya Stratton's address matched a white G.I.-bill dream box with blue trim. Carefully tended lawn, but less landscaping than its neighbors. No cars in the driveway, two throwaway papers on the oil spot. Shuttered windows, white-painted iron security grate across the front door, mailbox mounted on the steel mesh. Another white metal door blocked access to the rear yard.

"Someone likes their privacy," I said.

Milo frowned. We got out, walked to the security

door. A button was mounted on the front wall of the house, near the jamb of the security door. Milo pushed it and I could hear the buzzer sound inside the house. No answer. No barking.

I remarked on that, said, "Maybe they took Duchess on one of their early-morning walks."

"On Sunday?" he said.

"Hey, he's a fit guy."

He lifted the lid of the mailbox. Inside were four envelopes and two circulars from fast-food restaurants. He inspected the postmarks. "Yesterday's."

He toed the grate. I watched his lips form a silent curse as he stared at the jewel-bright brass dead bolt. "Who knows what the hell's in there, but Ulrich finding the body ain't exactly grounds for a warrant. Hell, I don't even exercise the warrants I do get."

"You didn't end up serving Richard?"

He shook his head. "So much for any future relationship with MacIntyre. Spent all night with my Glendale colleagues. Who, by the way, will not arrest you for trespassing a crime scene."

"They wouldn't know it was a crime scene unless I trespassed."

"Technicalities, technicalities." He punched the button again. Rubbed his face, loosened his tie, glanced over at the door barring the yard. "Let's go back to the car, try to figure something out. Meanwhile, I'll run searches on Ulrich's aliases. He repeated the hiker M.O., used Michigan twice, so maybe he's recycled an identity."

He tried DMV again, inquiring about Michael Ferris Burke, Grant Rushton, Huey Mitchell, Hank Spreen, with no success. We'd been sitting for a few minutes, alternating between silence and dead-end suggestions, when a small red car drove up and parked across the street.

Nissan Sentra, dark-haired woman at the wheel. She turned off her engine, started to get out when she saw us. Then she flashed a nervous stare and up went the driver's window.

Milo was out in a second, jogging over, flashing the badge. The Nissan's window stayed up. He produced his business card, I saw his lips move, finally the glass lowered. As if in appreciation, Milo backed away, gave the woman space. She exited the red car, looked at me, then at Milo. He had his hands in his pockets, was making himself a bit smaller, the way he does when he's trying to put someone at ease. I joined them.

The woman was in her thirties, slightly heavy, brown hair highlighted with rust, sooty shadows under her bright-blue eyes and a speck of mascara under one of them. She wore a bulky white cowl-neck T-shirt, black leggings, black flats. The rear of the car was filled with fabric samples in binders.

"What's wrong?" she said, eyeing the white house.

"Do you live in the neighborhood, ma'am?"

"My sister does. Across the street."

"Ms. Stratton?"

"Yes." Her voice strained half an octave higher. "What's going on?"

"We came to ask your sister and Mr. Ulrich some questions, ma'am."

"About what happened—about their finding Dr. Mate?"

"Your sister talked to you about that, Ms . . ."

"Lamplear. Kris Lamplear. Sure, we talked about it. It wasn't exactly an everyday thing. Not in detail, Tanya was grossed out. She called me to tell me they found it—him. Is there some problem? Tanya's already been through a lot."

"How so, ma'am?" said Milo.

"She was sick a year and a half ago. That's why I'm here. She was sick and I'm overprotective. She doesn't like me to be, but I can't help it. I try to give her space, usually we talk only two, three times a week. But I haven't heard from her in a few days, so I called her at work Friday and they said she'd taken some vacation time. I held off yesterday, but today . . ."

She frowned. "She's entitled to her vacation, but she should've told me where she was going."

"Does she usually?" I said.

Sheepish smile. "Honestly? Not always, but I don't let that stop me. What can I say? I decided to stop by this morning early, 'cause my kids have Little League in an hour. Just to make sure everything's okay. So there's no problem, you just want to talk to her?"

"Right, just following up, ma'am," said Milo. He eyed the fabric samples. "Interior-design work?"

"Fabric sales. I work for a jobber downtown." Another glance at the house.

Milo said, "Looks like they've been gone for only a day or so. Do they travel a lot?"

"From time to time." Kris Lamplear's eyes jumped around. "Paul probably took her somewhere on one of his impulsive *romantic* things."

"He's a romantic fellow?"

"He thinks he is." She rolled her eyes. "Mr. Sponta-neous. He'll come in and announce they're going to Arrowhead or Santa Barbara for a couple of days, tells Tanya to pack, call in sick. Tanya's ultraresponsible. She takes her job seriously. But she goes along with him, usually. He works for himself, so taking off like that's no big deal. He likes nature stuff, loves to drive."

"Nature stuff," said Milo.

"The great outdoors, he's a member of the Tree People, the Sierra Club, watches birds, actually reads the auto-club magazine. It was *his* idea to be up there on Mulholland at that hour. He's always pushing Tanya to rise and shine, exercise, all that stuff. As if that's going to do the trick."

"Do what trick?"

"Heal her up," she said. "Make sure she stays in remission—she had cancer. Hodgkin's disease. The doctors said it was curable, she's got a good chance of being cured. But the treatment knocked her out. Radia-tion, chemo, heavy-duty. The whole thing changed her. She *is* fine, I know she'll be okay, but I'm sorry, I'm still the protective older sister, so sue me. She should at least tell me where she's going, don't you think? Our parents are gone, the two of us are it, she knows I worry."

She tugged her shirt down, stared at the house. "I know I'm being neurotic. I'll get home and there'll be a message from her—don't tell her you met me here, okay? She'll get p.o.'d."

"Deal," said Milo. "So you don't keep a house key for her."

"You mean like some people do? That would be nice,

wouldn't it. But no, I'd never ask for one. Tanya wouldn't take well to that."

"Wanting to be independent."

Kris Lamplear nodded. "Her having a key to *my* house would be fine. And I'm married, have kids, I wouldn't mind. But she'd be all sensitive. Even when she was going through her treatments she was that way. Telling everyone she could do things for herself, not to treat her like a cripple."

"So Paul's a hands-off guy," I said.

"What do you mean?"

"To get along with Tanya he'd have to respect her independence."

"I guess," she said. "To be honest, I don't know *why* she stays with him. Maybe 'cause he was there for her when she was down."

"When she was sick?" I said.

She nodded. "That's how they met. Tanya was in the hospital for her chemo and he was volunteering there. He ended up spending a lot of time with her. When she couldn't hold food down, he'd be there, feeding her ice chips."

Describing an altruistic act, but she sounded disapproving. I said, "Nice guy."

"I guess—I used to wonder why he was doing all that. To be honest, he doesn't seem like the volunteering type—but what's the difference, she makes her own decisions."

"You don't like him," I said.

"If Tanya likes him . . . No, to be honest I think he's a pompous jerk. I think Tanya may be seeing it, too. Finally." Her smile was reluctant, mischievous. "Maybe it's wishful thinking, but she doesn't defend him as much when I tell her he's a pompous jerk."

I smiled back. "Which hospital did they meet at?"

"Valley Comprehensive over in Reseda. A dump as far as I'm concerned, but that's where her HMO said she had to go. Why all these questions about Paul?"

Milo said, "He and your sister are important witnesses. In a homicide case, we need to be extra thorough. Does Paul still volunteer at the hospital?"

"Nope. Soon as Tanya was discharged and they were dating, he quit. That's what made me wonder."

"About what?"

"About if it was just a technique to hit on women. She's recuperating, and all of a sudden they're dating. Couple of months later, both of them move out of their apartments and they rent this place."

"How long ago was that?"

"Over a year," she said. "I shouldn't put him down if she likes him. He treats her well enough. Does the cooking, the cleaning—*all* the cleaning, now *that's* a good deal. Doesn't leave clothes on the floor—he's real neat, a neat freak, I never saw Tanya live so organized. He even grooms Duchess—Tanya's dog—can spend a half hour brushing her. Duchess likes him now. At first she didn't, and I'm thinking, Yes, animals have a sense. But then she took to him and I'm thinking, What do *I* know? Or maybe dogs aren't that smart. After all, it was Duchess who got them into this mess by finding—but you know that, don't you."

"What else did Tanya tell you about finding Dr. Mate?"

"Not much. Like I said, she was grossed out—Tanya

isn't much of a talker anyway. *Paul* was really into it, though. I'm sure he'll be jazzed that you're back to ask him more questions."

"Why's that?" said Milo.

"He thought it was neat—*fascinating,* he called it. *Learning about police procedure.* After Tanya called me, I came over. To give her support. Paul had the TV on, waiting to see if he and Tanya would be on. So he'll be jazzed at more attention."

"Happy to oblige," said Milo. "Any idea where we can find him?"

"No, like I said, it could be anywhere. He announces to Tanya they're going somewhere and most of the time she agrees. He drives and she sleeps in the car."

"Most of the time?" I said.

"Sometimes she puts her foot down. She doesn't like it when her work piles up. When she turns him down, Paul gets all pouty and usually he stays home and keeps pouting. But sometimes he goes off by himself for a day or so . . . I have no idea where they are, but you could try Malibu. That's the one place Tanya likes to go."

"Where in Malibu?" said Milo, keeping his voice casual.

"Not the beach. We've got—Tanya and I own some land up in the Malibu mountains. Western Malibu, it's more like Agoura, across the Ventura County line and up into the hills. Five, six acres, I don't even know the exact size. Our parents bought it years ago, Dad was going to build a house, but he never got around to it. I never go there because there's really nothing there and it's kind of a mess—dinky little cabin, no phone, gross bathroom, tiny little septic tank. Half the time the electricity lines are down, the road's always washing out. My kids would go crazy from boredom there."

"But Tanya likes it."

"Tanya likes things quiet. When she was recuperating from chemo she went there. Or maybe it was to show she was tough. She can be stubborn. The place is probably worth some money now, I would've sold it a long time ago."

"Does Paul like it?" I said. "Being a Tree Person?"

"Probably. What Paul really likes is to drive, just for the sake of driving—like gas is free and he's got all the time in the world."

"Working for himself in real estate."

"I don't know what he does in real estate—he doesn't seem to work much, but he must be doing okay," she said. "He always has money. Isn't stingy with Tanya, I'll grant him that. Buys her jewelry, clothes, whatever. Plus he cooks and cleans, so what am I complaining about, right?"

Milo copied down directions to the cabin, promised to let her know if her sister was there.

"Great," she said. Then she frowned. "That means she'll know I was here, checking up on her. 'Cause I'm the only one who knows about Malibu."

"Do the people at her job know your number?" he said. "Maybe she listed you as her emergency contact."

Kris Lamplear brightened. "That's true, she did."

"Great. We'll just tell her that's how we reached you."

"Okay, thanks—there's nothing wrong, is there? With Tanya and Paul?"

"What would be wrong, ma'am?"

"I don't know. You just seem awfully eager to talk to them."

"Just what I said, ma'am. Follow-up. It's a high-profile case, we've got to do everything we can to avoid looking stupid."

"That I understand." She smiled. "No one likes looking stupid."

CHAPTER

34

He sped onto the 405. The intersection with the 101
West was nearly immediate, the heavy traffic was
flowing east, and soon we were sailing.

"Malibu," he said. "Sounds familiar."

"Oh yeah."

A few years ago, Robin and I had rented a beach
house just over the county line. The mouth of the canyon
road Kris Lamplear had described was less than a half
mile away. I'd gone hiking up there myself, passing
campgrounds, the occasional private property, mostly
state land walled by mountainside. I remembered long
stretches of solitude, silence broken by birdcalls, coyote
howls, the occasional roar of a too-fast truck. Brain-
feeding silence, but sometimes it had seemed too quiet
up there.

"'Paul likes to drive,'" he went on. "Your basic
prerequisite for Serial Killer School. A neat freak and the

bastard likes to drive. Now, why didn't I think of that? Could've arrested him the first time I met him, saved the city a lot of overtime."

"Tsk, tsk. And don't forget his generosity," I said. "Gives his girlfriend jewelry. I wonder how much of it was previously owned."

He gave a dispirited laugh. "Trophies . . . Lord knows what else he hangs on to."

He exited at Kanan, took it down to PCH and raced north along the beach. The Coast Highway was virtually empty past Trancas Canyon. The ocean was serene, low tide breaking lazily, too blue to be real. We crossed the county line at Mulholland Highway, just past Leo Carrillo Beach, where a handful of beachcombers walked the tide pools.

Back to Mulholland. End of the trail.

No way to travel Mulholland from start to finish. The road was thirty-plus miles of blacktop, girding L.A. from East Hollywood to the Pacific, choked off in several places by wilderness. Nothing important comes easy . . . Had Michael Burke/Paul Ulrich thought of that when selecting his kill-spot?

A mile into Ventura, Milo hooked right, veering toward the land side. I caught a peek of my rented house on the private beach just ahead, a wedge of weathered wood visible beyond a sharp curve of the highway. Robin and I had liked it out there, watching the pelicans and dolphins, not minding the rust that seemed to settle in daily. We'd stayed there nearly a year while our house in the Glen was being rebuilt. The moment the lease was up, the landlord had handed the place over to his brilliant aspiring-screenwriter son in hopes of spurring Junior to creativity. The only time I'd met Junior he'd been drunk. I'd never seen anything with his name on it at the multiplex. Kids today.

The car climbed into the mountains. Neither of us talked as we searched for the unmarked road that led to the property. Address on the mailbox, Kris Lamplear had said.

The first time, Milo overshot and had to circle back. Finally, we found it, nearly five miles from the ocean, well past its nearest neighbor, preceded by a good mile of state land.

The mailbox was ten feet up the entrance, concealed by a cloud of plumbago vine. Rusty box on a weathered post, its door missing. Most of the gold-foil address numerals gone, too. The three digits that remained were withered and curling.

Nothing in the box. The air was cool, sweet, and the unmarked's idling engine seemed deafening. Milo backed out, parked on the road, turned off the motor, and we returned to the mailbox on foot. Ahead of us, the dirt road—more of a path—swept to the left and flattened in an S that snaked through the greenery. Nothing in the immediate distance but more vines, shrubbery, trees. Lots of trees.

Milo said, "No sense announcing ourselves, giving him a chance to orchestrate. Let's see if we can get a view of the cabin, watch it for a while."

We walked a thousand feet before it came into view, graying clapboard barely discernible through a thickening colonnade of pine and gum trees and sycamores. Old, twisted sycamores, just like the one where Alice

Zoghbie and Roy Haiselden had been propped. Had Ulrich/Burke noticed that? I thought he had. He would have liked that, the symmetry, neatness. The irony. Frosting on the old murder cake.

If Milo was thinking that, he wasn't putting it into words. He trudged steadily but very slowly, mouth set, eyes swiveling from side to side, one arm loose, the other at his belt, inches from his service revolver. More tension than readiness for battle. He'd stashed his shotgun in the trunk of the unmarked.

The path finally ended at an egg-shaped parking area partially edged by large, circular rocks. The border looked like someone's primitive attempt at hardscape, long disrupted by the elements. Two cars: Ulrich's navy BMW and Tanya Stratton's copper-colored Saturn.

Ulrich had told us a tale of another dark BMW stationed on Mulholland.

BMW like ours.

I'd agonized over whether the car had been Richard's. Richard or Eric at the wheel. But it had existed only in Ulrich's lie.

Orchestrating.

The building was just beyond the cars, at the rear of the property, and we approached, trying to shield ourselves behind trees, straining for a better look. Finally, we had a view of the front door. Open, but blocked by a dirty-looking screen.

Ugly little thing, not much more than a shed, shoved up against a mountain wall and surrounded by brush. Tar-paper roof the brown-green of a stagnant pond, the clapboard, once white, now murky as laundry water. Nearly hidden by low branches—one bough swooped within a foot of the door—as if yielding itself to green strangulation.

Up above, barely visible through the sycamores, was a mountain ridge crowned by a thick black coiffure of pines. More state land. No prying neighbors.

We advanced to within twenty yards of the cabin before Milo stopped, ducked off the path and into the brush, motioning me quickly to do the same.

A second later, the screen door opened and Tanya Stratton stepped out, letting it slam shut with a snare-drum rattle.

She wore a long-sleeved tan shirt, blue jeans, white sneakers, had her hair tucked into a red bandanna. No dark glasses this time, but she was too far away for us to see her eyes.

She stretched, yawned, went to her car and popped the trunk.

The cabin door opened again, exposing a stretch of arm. Tan arm, male arm. But Ulrich didn't appear. Holding the screen ajar. A good-looking golden retriever bounded out and raced to Tanya Stratton's side.

Duchess. Great nose, thinks she's a drug dog.

"Great," Milo whispered. "So much for surveillance."

Speaking so softly I had to read his lips. But the dog's ears perked and she pivoted toward us, began nosing the ground. Walking. Picking up speed. Tanya Stratton said, "Duchess! Treat!" and the dog froze in her tracks, shook herself off. Turned and ran toward her mistress.

Stratton had pulled a bag out of the trunk. Now she opened it, reached inside, dangled something in front of Duchess's nose.

"Sit. Wait."

The dog settled on her haunches, watched the Milk-Bone that Tanya waved near her nose.

Tanya said, "Good girl," gave her the bone, ruffled the fur around the retriever's neck. Duchess stayed by Tanya's side, waited till Tanya let her back into the cabin.

"Good dog," muttered Milo. He looked at his Timex. "Separate cars. What do you make of that?"

"Maybe Tanya's planning on leaving before him. Work obligations, like her sister said."

He thought about that. Nodded. "Leaving him alone to do his thing. Which could be sticking close to base or taking another drive. Maybe he's got stuff stashed here. Buried here. Meaning I can't afford to mess up any of the search rules. Gonna have to coordinate with Malibu sheriffs to keep it kosher . . . Maybe the best thing is back off, find somewhere to watch the road. See if Tanya leaves, then what he does—if she's not in immediate danger."

"His pattern with his women friends is to wait until they've gotten ill again, minister to them, then take it all the way. Then again, he may have hastened the process along."

"Poison?"

"He'd know how."

"So what are you saying, forget waiting? Waltz right in?"

"Let me think."

I never got around to it.

The door opened yet again and this time Paul Ulrich showed himself. Fit and well-fed, in a white polo shirt, khaki pants, brown loafers, no socks. Muscular arms, ruddy complexion. Mug of something in one hand.

He drank, placed the cup on the ground, took a few steps forward.

Showed us his face.

Two alert, sparkling eyes, a smudge of rosy skin behind flaring mustaches.

Twin propellers of hair so huge, so flamboyant, that despite my attempt to get past them, to seize upon something—the merest grace note of recognition—that would tie his face into one of the photos in Leimert Fusco's file, my brain processed only *mustache*.

Facial hair could do that.

He retrieved his coffee, strutted around. Flexed a bicep and inspected the bulge of muscle.

Another sip. Big stretch.

So content. Top of the morning.

The mustache made him look like a Keystone Kop. Nothing funny about him.

Milo's hand was square on his gun, fingers white against the walnut grip, scrambling toward the trigger. Then, as if realizing what he was doing, he drew it away. Wiped his hand on his jacket. Rubbed his face. Stared at Ulrich.

Suddenly Ulrich dropped to the ground, as if avoiding gunfire. We watched him peel off fifty lightning push-ups. Perfect form. When he bounced back to his feet, he stretched again, showing no signs of exertion.

He ran a hand over his thinning hair, rotated his neck, flexed his arms, worked on the neck some more. Even killers get stiff . . . all those hours behind the wheel . . .

Smoothing one mustache, he reached behind and picked at his seat.

Even killers untangle their shorts.

Watching it—the banality—I felt let down. Human. They shouldn't be, but they always are.

Ulrich finished his coffee, placed the mug on the ground once more, walked to his own car. Popped his trunk. Out came something black. Small leather case, the polished surface reflected the filtered sunlight leaking down through the trees.

Doctor's bag. Ulrich stroked it.

I whispered, "There you go."

Milo said, "What the hell does he need *that* for right now?"

The cabin door opened again. As Tanya stepped outside, Ulrich moved quickly, shifting the bag behind his back, inching toward his car. She took only a few steps, was looking away from him, up at the treetops. Ulrich slipped the bag into the trunk, lowered the lid, sauntered over to Tanya.

Not acknowledging him, she started to turn, was about to reenter the cabin when he reached her. Slipping one hand around her waist, he kissed the back of her neck.

She was rigid, unresponsive.

Ulrich remained behind her, maintained his grip around her waist. Kissed her again and she twisted away from his lips. He stroked her cheek, but his face, unseen by her, bore no affection.

Immobile.

Eyes hard and focused. Face slightly flushed.

Tanya said something, broke away from him, disappeared back into the cabin.

Ulrich stroked his mustache. Spit in the dirt.

Walked back to the car. Quickly. Face still expressionless. Flushed scarlet. He popped the trunk and retrieved the black bag.

Milo said, "Not good."

His hand shot back to his gun and now he was stepping out from behind the tree. He'd barely taken a step when the shot rang out, hard and sharp, like hands clapping once.

From behind Ulrich. Above. The growth of pine at the ridge.

Milo ran back to his hiding spot. Gun out, but no one to shoot at.

Ulrich didn't drop. Not right away. He stood there as the red spot formed on his chest, got redder, larger, blossoming like a rose captured in time-lapse. Exit wound. Shot from the back. The leather bag remained in his hand, the mustache blocked out expression.

Another hand-clap sounded, then another, two more roses decorated Ulrich's white shirt. Red shirt, hard to believe it had ever been white . . .

Milo's gun hand was rigid, still, his eyes bounced from Ulrich to the pine ridge.

More applause.

When the fourth shot sheared off the top of Ulrich's head, he let the black bag drop to the ground.

Fell on top of it.

The whole thing had taken less than ten seconds.

Screams from inside the house, but no sign of Tanya.

Duchess was barking. Milo's gun was still out, aimed at the silence, the distance, the trees, that big mustache of trees.

35

It took a while for the sheriffs to arrive from the Malibu substation, even longer to assemble a squad to travel up to the ridge. A small army of nervous, itchy-fingered men in tan uniforms, each deputy assuming the shooter was still around, wouldn't hesitate to fire.

As we waited for the group to assemble, Milo hung out with the coroner, did his best to let the sheriffs feel they were in charge while managing to inspect everything. He asked me to comfort Tanya Stratton, but I ended up doing nothing of the sort. She shut me out, refused to talk, obtained whatever solace she desired by muttering to her sister over a cell phone and stroking her dog. I watched her from a distance. The deputies had shunted her away from the crime scene and she sat on the ground beneath a silver-dollar tree, knees drawn up, occasionally pummeling herself softly on the jaw. Her sunglasses were back on, so I couldn't read her eyes. The rest of her face said she was shocked, furious, wondering how many other mistakes she'd make over the rest of her life.

While we'd waited for sheriffs, Milo had inspected the cabin. No obvious trophies. Not much of anything in there. A careful search, carried out later in the day, revealed nothing of an evidentiary nature, other than the doctor's bag. Old, burnished leather, gold initials over the clasp: EHM.

Tanya Stratton claimed she'd never seen it. I believed her. Ulrich would have hidden it from her, produced it only when he was ready to use it. A while longer, and she might've lost the opportunity to make any mistakes at all.

Inside the bag were scalpels, scissors, other shiny things; a coil of I.V. tubing, sterile-packed hollow needles in various gauges. Rolls of gauze. Disposable hypodermic injectors, little ampules with small-print labels.

Thiopental. Potassium chloride.

The bag was taken into custody by a sheriff's detective, but he never bothered to ask what the gold initials stood for and Milo didn't volunteer the information. When the search party was ready, he and I rode along, sitting in back of a squad car, listening to nervous-talk from the two deputies in front.

The wounds—the way they'd passed through Ulrich at that distance, the size of the exits—indicated a high-velocity bullet, probably a military rifle, a good-quality scope. Someone who knew what he was doing.

How hard it would be to see the shooter if he'd chosen to barricade himself among the pines.

I knew he hadn't. He'd done his job, no reason to stick around.

• • •

Gaining access to the pines wasn't very difficult. The same road that had swept us past the property with the broken mailbox continued its climb for another mile before forking. The right fork reversed direction, descending back down toward the coast, but never completing the journey as it dead-ended at a forest preserve named after a long-dead California settler. A state-printed sign said scenic views were up ahead, but no path was provided, the curious were proceeding at their own risk.

The party fanned out, weapons ready. An hour later, it reconvened roadside. No sign of the shooter. One of the deputies, an experienced backpacker who let us know he'd walked the John Muir Trail twice and could navigate without a compass, estimated where the shooter had stationed himself, thought he probably had the exact spot.

We followed him to the far end of the forest, where the outermost trees, granted the best light, grew tallest and thickest. Nice clear view of the ugly little cabin and adjoining acreage. Nice view of the ocean, too. As the cops talked, my eyes drifted toward blue. I spotted a steamer gliding across the horizon, dust specks in the sky that were probably gulls.

Waiting up here wouldn't have been that bad. How long had the shooter been waiting?

How had he figured it out? Coming across the same detail I had? His copy of the file—the original file. The case of Marissa Bonpaine.

He'd claimed to be flying up to Seattle. Just a few hours ago, I'd taken him at his word, figured he wanted to review the details of Marissa's murder, cross-reference with Michael Burke's med-school schedule, what he knew about Mate's murder. Discovery by hikers.

Had he flown back to L.A. to trail the "hiker," gotten here a wee bit faster than Milo and me?

Or had Seattle been a lie and he'd never left. Figuring it out by doing exactly what I'd done: harnessing the power of obsession. Then watching, stalking, waiting . . . He was a patient man, had persisted so many years, another few days wouldn't matter.

Kill-spot with a view.

Had he laid his rifle down lovingly on a rectangle of oilcloth while he ate a sandwich? Drank something from a thermos? Made sure the lens of the scope was clean?

His own little picnic. The irony . . .

The cops kept talking, convincing themselves they needn't search any further, no one else was going to get shot today. I turned away from the ocean, looked down at the cabin, now fronted by coroner's vans and squad cars, tried to see it as Leimert Fusco had seen it.

"Yeah, this has got to be it, the angle's perfect," said the Muir walker. "Look how it gets flat, and there's that rock he could prop his gear against. Maybe he left some trace evidence, let's get the techies up here."

The techies came. Milo told me later they found nothing, not even a tire track.

That didn't surprise me. I knew Fusco couldn't have parked too far from his vantage point and been able to make his escape that quickly. Driving to the left-hand fork and disappearing into hills laced with side roads, most of which ended in box canyons, a few feeding to the Valley, the freeway, alleged civilization.

He'd known which road to take because he was a planner, too.

The main risk had been leaving his car at the side of the road. But even if someone had seen it, recorded the license plate for some reason, no big deal. It would end up traced back to a rented vehicle, hired with false I.D.

So, sure, he'd parked close.

No way he could've hiked far carrying all that gear— the military rifle, the high-grade scope.

Not with that limp.

"Easy shot," said another deputy. "Like picking off quail. Wonder what this guy did that pissed someone off so bad."

"Who says he did anything?" said another cop. "Nowadays, it doesn't take anything to get some nut going."

Milo laughed.

The men in tan stared at him.

He said, "Long day, fellows."

"It ain't over yet," said Muir-man. "We've still got to find the dude."

Milo laughed again.

36

November is L.A.'s most beautiful month. Temperatures get considerate, the air acquires the squeaky, scrubbed flavor of a world without hydrocarbons, the light's as sweet and golden as a caramel apple. In November, you can forget that the Chumash Indians called the basin L.A. sits in the Valley of Smoke.

Late in November, I drove out to Lancaster.

A month and a half after the slaughter of Eldon Mate. Weeks after Milo had finished cataloging the contents of four cardboard cartons located in a Panorama City storage locker rented by Paul Ulrich under the name Dr. L. Pasteur.

A key found in Ulrich's bedroom nightstand led to the locker. Nothing very interesting was found in the house itself. Tanya Stratton vacated the premises within days of the shooting in Malibu.

The cartons were beautifully organized.

The first contained newspaper clippings, neatly folded, filed in chronological order, tagged with the names of victims. The details of Roger Sharveneau's suicide had been preserved meticulously. So had the death of a teenage girl named Victoria Leigh Fusco.

Number two held meticulously pressed clothing— predominantly women's undergarments, but a few dresses, blouses and neckties, as well.

In the third box, Milo found over a hundred pieces of jewelry in plastic sandwich bags, most of it junk, a few vintage costume pieces. Some of the baubles could be traced back to dead people, others couldn't.

The fourth and largest carton held a styrofoam cooler. Layered within were parcels wrapped in butcher paper and preserved by dry ice. The attendant at the storage facility remembered Dr. Pasteur coming by every week or so. Nice man. Big mustache, one of those old-fashioned mustaches you see in silent movies. Pasteur had only spoken to offer pleasantries, talk about athletics, hiking, hunting. It had been a while since his last visit, and most of the dry ice had melted. The largest carton had started to reek. Milo left it up to the coroner to unwrap the packages.

In a corner of the storage locker were several rifles and handguns, each oiled and in perfect working order, boxes of bullets, one set of Japanese surgical tools, another made in the USA.

The papers presented it this way:

Victim in Police Shooting Believed Responsible for Eldon Mate's Murder

MALIBU. County Sheriff and Los Angeles Police sources report that a physician shot in a police-involved shooting in Malibu is the prime suspect in the murder of "death doctor" Eldon Mate.

Paul Nelson Ulrich, 40, was shot several times last week in circumstances that remain under investigation. Evidence recovered at the scene and in other locations, including surgical tools believed to be the murder weapons in the Mate case, indicate Ulrich acted alone.

No motive for the slaying of the man known as "Dr. Death" has been put forth by authorities yet, though the same sources indicate that Ulrich, a licensed physician in New York State under the name of Michael Ferris Burke, may have been mentally ill.

November found me thinking about how wrong I'd been on so many accounts. No doubt Rushton/Burke/Ulrich would've been amused by all my wrong guesses, but teaching me humility would've ranked low on his pleasure list.

I called Tanya Stratton once, got no answer, tried her sister. Kris Lamplear was more forthcoming. She didn't recognize my voice. No reason to, we'd exchanged only a few words when we'd met and she'd assumed I was a detective.

"How'd you know to call me, Doctor?"

"I consult to the police, was trying to follow up with Tanya. She hasn't called back. You're listed as next of kin."

"No, Tanya won't talk to you. Won't talk to anyone. She's pretty freaked out by all those things they're saying about Paul."

"She'd have to be," I said.

"It's—unbelievable. To be honest, I'm freaked, too. Been keeping it from my kids. They met him . . . I never liked him, but I never thought . . . Anyway, Tanya has a therapist. A social worker who helped her back when she was sick—last year. The main thing is she's still in remission. Just had a great checkup."

"Good to hear that."

"You bet. I just don't want the stress to . . . Anyway, thanks for trying. The police have really been okay through all this. Don't worry about Tanya. She'll go her own way, she always does."

November got busy, lots of new referrals, my service seemed to be ringing in constantly. I booked myself solid, reserved lunchtime for making calls.

Calls that didn't get answered. Messages left for Richard, Stacy, Judy Manitow. A try at Joe Safer's office elicited a written note from the attorney's secretary:

Dear Dr. Delaware:
Mr. Safer deeply appreciates your time. There are no new developments with regard to your common interests. Should Mr. Safer have anything to report, he'll definitely call.

I thought a lot about the trip to Lancaster, composed a mental list of reasons not to go, wrote it all down.

I sometimes prescribe that kind of thing for patients, but it rarely works for me. Putting it down on paper made me antsier, less and less capable of putting it to rest. Maybe it's a brain abnormality—some kind of chemical imbalance, Lord knows everything else gets blamed on that. Or perhaps it's just what my midwestern mother used to call "pigheadedness to the nth."

Whatever the diagnosis, I wasn't sleeping well.

Mornings presented me with headaches, and I found myself getting annoyed without good reason, working hard at staying pleasant.

By the twenty-third of November, I'd finished a host of court-assigned assessments—none referred by Judy Manitow. Placing the rest in the to-do box, I awoke on a particularly glorious morning and set out for the high desert.

Lancaster is sixty-five miles north of L.A. on three freeways: the 405, the 5, then over to the 14, where four lanes compress to three, then two, cutting through the Antelope Valley and feeding into the Mojave.

Just over an hour's ride, if you stick to the speed limit, the first half mostly arid foothills sparsely decorated with gas stations, truck stops, billboards, the red-tile roofs of low-cost housing developments. The rest of it's nothing but dirt and gravel till you hit Palmdale.

Motels in Palmdale, too, but that wouldn't have mattered for Joanne Doss, it had to be Lancaster.

She'd made the trip late at night, when the view from the car window would have been flat-black.

Nothing to look at, lots of time to think.

I pictured her, bloated, aching, a passenger in her own hearse, as someone else—probably Eric, it was Eric I couldn't stop thinking about—burned fuel on the empty road.

Riding.

Staring out at the black, knowing the expanse of nothingness would be among her final images.

Had she allowed herself to suffer doubt? Been mindlessly resolute?

Had the two of them talked?

What do you say to your mother when she's asked you to help her leave you?

Why had she set up her own execution?

I spotted a county sign advertising a regional airport in Palmdale. The strip where Richard's helicopter had landed on all those trips to oversee his construction projects.

He'd never been able to get Joanne to witness what he'd created. But on her last day on Earth, she'd endured an hour's trip, made sure she'd end up in the very spot she'd avoided.

Prolonging the agony so she could send him a message.

You condemn me. I spit in your face.

The Happy Trails Motel was easy to find. Just a quick turn onto Avenue J, then a half-mile drive past Tenth Street West. Lots of open space out here, but not due to any ecological wisdom. Vacant lots, whiskered by weeds, alternated with the kind of downscale businesses that doom small-town proprietors to anxiety in the age of mergers and acquisitions.

Bob's Battery Repair, Desert Clearance Furniture, Cleanrite Janitorial Supply, Yvonne's Quick 'n' Easy Haircutting.

I passed one new-looking strip mall, the usual beige texture coat and phony tile, some of the storefronts still vacant, a FOR LEASE sign prominent at the front of the commodious parking lot. One of Richard's projects? If I was right about Joanne's motives, just maybe, because the motel was in clear view across the street, sandwiched between a liquor store and a boarded-up bungalow that bore a faded, hand-painted sign: GOODFAITH INSURANCE.

The Happy Trails Motel was a single-story, U-shaped collection of a dozen or so rooms with a front office on the left-hand tip of the U and a dead neon sign that pleaded VACANCY. Red doors on each room, only two of them fronted by cars. The building had blue-gray walls and a low white gravel roof. Over the gravel, I saw coils of barbed wire. An alley ran along the west side of the motel and I drove around back to see what the wire was all about.

The coils sat atop a grape-stake fence that separated the motel from its rear neighbor: a trailer park. Old, sagging mobile homes, laundry on lines, TV antennae. As I cruised closer, a dog growled.

Returning to the street, I parked. Nothing crisp about the air here. High eighties, arid, dusty, and heavy as unresolved tension. I entered the office. No reception counter, just a card table in a corner, behind which sat an old man, hairless, corpulent, with very red lips and wet, subjugated eyes. He wore a baggy gray T-shirt and striped pants. In front of him was a stack of paperback spy novels. Off to the side sat a collection of medicine bottles, along with a loose eyedropper and an empty pill counter. The room was small, murky, paneled with pine boards long gone black. The air smelled like every kid's first booster shot. A comb dispenser hung on the rear wall, along with another small vending machine that sold maps and a third that offered condoms and the message *Be Healthy!*

To the old man's right was a glass display case filled with photos. Ten or so pictures of Marilyn Monroe in black-and-white. Scenes from her movies and cheese-cake shots. Below the montage and stretched across the center of the case, pinned in place like a butterfly, was a pink satin two-piece bathing suit. A typed paper label, also pinioned, said, CERTIFIED GENUINE M.M.'S SWIM-SUIT.

"It's for sale," said the hairless man wearily. His voice was half an octave below bassoon, clogged and wheezy.

"Interesting."

"If you meant that, you'd buy it. I got it from a guy used to work on her pictures. It's all bona fide."

I showed him my police consultant badge. The small print tells them I've got no real authority. When they're going to be helpful, they never bother to check. When they're not, a real badge wouldn't impress them.

The old man barely looked at it. His skin was pallid and dull, compressed in spots, lumped like cooling tallow. Licking his lips, he smiled. "Didn't think you were checking in for a room, not with that sport jacket. What is it, cashmere?"

He stretched a hand toward my sleeve and for a moment I thought he'd touch it. But he drew back.

"Just wool," I said.

"Just wool." He humphed. "Just money. So what can I do for you?"

"Several months ago a woman from L.A. checked in and—"

"Killed herself. So why're you here now? When it happened, the police didn't barely want to talk to me. Not that they should've, I wasn't working that night, my son was. And he didn't know much, either—you read the report, you know."

I didn't deny it. "Where is your son?"

"Florida. He was only visiting, doing me a favor 'cause I was indisposed." His fingers brushed against one of the medicine bottles. "Back in Tallahassee. Drives a truck for Anheuser-Busch. So what's up?"

"Just doing some follow-up," I said. "For the files. Did your son ever talk to you about who checked Ms. Doss in that night?"

"She checked herself in—the coward. Barnett said she didn't look too good, unsteady on her feet, but she did it all, paid with a credit card—you guys took the receipt." He smiled. "Not our usual clientele."

"How so?"

His laughter began somewhere in his belly. By the time it reached his mouth he was coughing. The paroxysm lasted too long to be trivial.

" 'Scuse me," he said, wiping his mouth with the back of a dimpled hand. "Like you don't know what I'm talking about."

He smiled again. I smiled back.

"Not poor, not horny, not drunk," he said, amused. "Just a rich coward."

"A coward because—"

"Because God grants you your particular share of years, you go and laugh in His face? *She* was like that, too." Pointing to the Monroe case. "Body like that and she wasted it on politicians and other scum. That bikini's worth something, you know. Big money, but no one around here appreciates memorabilia. I think I'm gonna get myself a computer, list it on the Internet."

"Did your son mention anyone with Ms. Doss?"

"Yeah, there was someone out in the car, waiting.

Behind the wheel. Barnett never looked to see who it was. We look too hard, we don't get business, right?"

"Right," I said. "Was there anyone else here who might've noticed?"

"Maybe Maribel, the cleaning girl. The one who found it. She came on at eleven at night, was working till seven. Asked for night work because she had a day job over at the Best Western in Palmdale. But you guys already talked to her. She didn't tell you much, huh?"

I shrugged. "Yeah, she was a little . . ."

"She was sick is what she was," he said. "Pregnant, ready to drop. Already had a miscarriage. After she found . . . what she found, she wouldn't stop crying, I thought we were gonna have one of those real-life video situations right out there in the parking lot—ever deliver a baby?"

I shook my head. "She end up delivering okay?"

"Yup, a boy."

"Healthy?"

"Seems to be."

"Any idea where can I find her?"

He crooked a thumb. "Out back, Unit Six, she's working days now. Someone had a party last night in Six. Longhair types, Nevada plates, paid cash. Should've known better than to give pigs like that a room. Maribel'll be cleaning that one for a while."

I thanked him and headed for the door.

"Here's a little secret," he said.

I stopped, turned my head.

He winked. "Got the Monroe *Playboy*, too. Don't keep it in the case, 'cause it's too valuable. One price gets you all of it. Tell all your friends."

"Will do."

"Sure you will."

Maribel was young, short, frail-looking, in a pink-and-white uniform that seemed incongruously proper for the pitted lot and the splintering red doors. She was gloved to the elbows. Her hair was tied back, but loose strands were sweat-glued to her forehead. A wheeled cart pulled up to Unit Six was piled with cleaning solvents and frayed towels. The trash bag slung from the side overflowed with filthy linens, empty bottles and stink. She gave the badge a bit more attention than her boss had.

"L.A.?" she said, with the faintest accent. "Why're you coming out here?"

"The woman who killed herself. Joanne Doss—"

Her face closed up tight. "No, forget it, I don't wanna talk about that."

"Don't blame you," I said. "And I'm not interested in making you go through it again."

Her gloves slammed onto her hips. "Then *what*?"

"I'd like to know anything you can remember about *before*. Once Ms. Doss went in the room, did she ever come out? Did she ask for food, drinks, do anything that caught your attention?"

"Nope, nothing. They went in after I got here—around midnight, I already told them that. I didn't see them until . . . you know."

"Them," I said. "Two people."

"Yup."

"How long did the other person stay?"

"Don't know," she said. "Probably a while. I was up at

the front desk, mostly, 'cause Barnett—Milton's son—
wanted to go out and party and not tell his dad."

"But the car wasn't there in the morning."

"Nope."

"Who was the other person?"

"Didn't get a good look."

"Tell me what you did see."

"Not much, I never saw the face." Her eyes filled
with tears. "It was disgusting—it's not fair bringing all
this up—"

"I'm sorry, Maribel. Just tell me what you saw and
we'll be finished."

"I don't wanna get anyone in trouble—I don't wanna
be on TV or nothing."

"You won't be."

She pulled at the finger of a glove.

Didn't speak. Then she did.

And suddenly, everything made sense.

37

Just wool again.

My best blue suit, a blue-and-white-striped shirt, yellow-print tie, shiny shoes.

Dressed for court.

I pushed open the double doors to Division 12 and walked right in. More often than not, family sessions are closed, witnesses kept out in the corridor, but this morning I got lucky. Judy was hearing motions from a pair of reasonable-sounding attorneys, scheduling hearings, bantering with her bailiff, a man named Leonard Stickney, who knew me.

I sat in the back row, the only spectator. Leonard Stickney noticed me first and gave a small salute.

A second later, Judy saw me and her eyes opened wide. Black-robed and regal behind the bench, she turned away, got businesslike, ordering the lawyers to do something within thirty days' time.

I sat there and waited. Ten minutes later, she dismissed both attorneys, called for recess, and motioned Leonard over. Covering her mike with one hand, she whispered to him behind the other, stepped off the bench and exited through the door that led to her chambers.

Leonard marched up to me. "Doctor, Her Honor requests your presence."

Soft lighting, carved desk and credenza, overstuffed chairs, certificates and award plaques on the walls, family photos in sterling silver frames.

I concentrated on one particular snapshot. Judy's younger daughter, Becky. The girl who'd gotten too thin, needed therapy, tried to play therapist with Stacy.

Becky, who'd been tutored by Joanne. Whose grades had dropped after the tutoring had stopped.

Becky, who'd gotten too thin as Joanne grew obese. Had severed her relationship with Stacy.

Judy slipped out of her robe and hung it on a mahogany rack. Today's suit was banana yellow, form-fitting, trimmed with sand-colored braiding. Big pearl earrings, small diamond brooch. Every blond hair in place.

Shiny hair.

She reclined in her desk chair. Glittery things occupied a good portion of the leather desktop. The picture frames, a crystal bud vase, an assortment of tiny bronze cats, millefleur paperweights, a walnut gavel with a bronze plate on the handle. Her bony hands found a weight and rubbed it.

"Alex. What a surprise. We don't have any cases pending, do we?"

"No," I said. "Don't imagine we ever will."

She squinted past me. "Now, why would you say that?"

"Because I know," I said.

"Know what?"

I didn't answer, not out of any psychological calculation. I'd thought about being here, rehearsed it mentally, had gotten the first words out.

I know.

But the rest of it choked in my chest.

"What is this, riddle time?" she said, trying to smile but managing only a peevish twist of her lipstick.

"You were there," I said. "At the motel with Joanne. Someone saw you. They don't know who you are, but they described you perfectly."

What Maribel had really seen was hair. Short yellow hair.

A skinny woman, no butt on her. I only saw the back of her, she was getting into the car when I came out to fill the ice machine.

She had this hair—real light, real shiny, a really good color job. That hair was shiny from across the parking lot.

"Mate had nothing to do with it," I said. "It was just you and Joanne."

Judy reclined a bit more. "You're talking nonsense, my dear."

"One way to look at it," I said, "was you were helping a friend. Joanne had made her decision, needed someone to be there with her at the end. You'd always been a good friend to her. The only problem is, that friendship had cooled. For good reason."

I waited. She wasn't moving. Then her right eyelid twitched. She pushed back from the desk another inch. "You're starting to sound like one of those psychic idiots—talking obliquely in the hope someone will take it for wisdom. Have you been under strain, Alex? Working too hard? I always thought you pushed yourself—"

"So friendship would be the charitable interpretation of what brought you out to Lancaster with Joanne, but unfortunately that wasn't it at all. Joanne's motivation for destroying herself was crushing guilt—some sin she couldn't forgive herself for. Richard never forgave her, either. And neither did you. So when she asked you to be there, I don't think you minded one bit about seeing her reach the end."

Her lips folded inward. Her hand reached out among the objects on her desk and found one. Walnut gavel. Brass plaque on the handle. An award. The walls were paneled with tributes.

"Having you there was part of the punishment," I said. "Like when family members of victims are invited to attend the execution."

"This is ridiculous," she said. "I don't know what's gotten into you, but you're talking gibberish—please leave."

"Judy—"

"This *minute*, Alex, or I'll call for Leonard."

"My leaving won't change things. Not for you, not for Becky. Does Bob know? Probably not all of it, I'd guess, because he would've expressed his anger more directly, immediately. Wouldn't have let it sit. But he's mad about something, so he must know something."

She took hold of the gavel, waved it at me. "Alex, I'm giving you one last chance to leave like a gentleman—"

"Joanne and Becky," I said. "When did it happen?"

She shot forward, half standing, and the gavel slammed down on the desk. But instead of making direct contact, the wood twisted, slipping out of her grip, skidding along the leather, pushing a paperweight to the carpet. The glass landed on the carpet with a feeble thump.

Pathetic sound. Maybe that's what did it, or maybe she really wanted to talk.

Her fingers curled into talons that she placed against her breast. As if ready to claw out her own heart. Suddenly they dropped and she sat back down and her hair was no longer in place. Hot eyes, wet eyes, a mouth that shook so badly it took a while for her to speak.

"You bastard," she said. "You goddamn, goddamn bastard. I'm calling Leonard."

But she didn't.

We sat staring at each other. I tried to look as sympathetic as I felt. I'd convinced myself this was all for the best, but now I wondered if it boiled down to feeding my own obsessiveness. A moment more and I might've gotten up and left. But she stood first, crossed the big, beautiful room, locked the door. When she sat back down, her eyes dropped to the gavel.

That's when she reminded me of my oath of confidentiality. Repeated the warning.

I told her of course I'd never talk.

Even then, she kept it theoretical, the way Richard

had, could barely stop herself from slapping me, kept drifting into corollary anger.

"What if you were a parent?" she said. "Why *aren't* you, anyway? I always meant to ask you that. Working with other people's kids, but you never had any of your own."

"Maybe one day," I said.

"So it's not a physical problem? Not shooting blanks?"

I smiled.

"Kind of arrogant, Alex. Preaching to other people about how to raise their kids when you don't have any direct experience."

"Maybe so."

"Sure, agree with me—you guys all do that, another one of those little tricks they teach you in shrink school. Did you know Becky wants to become a psychologist? What do you think of *that*?"

"I don't know Becky, but offhand it sounds fine."

"Why's it fine?" she demanded.

"Because people who've dealt with crisis can develop a special kind of empathy."

"Can?"

"Sometimes it goes the other way. I don't know Becky."

"Becky's beautiful—a beautiful person. If you'd bothered to father any of your own, maybe you'd have a clue."

"You're probably right," I said. "I mean that."

"Think of it," she said, as if talking to herself. "You carry this creature inside you for nine months, rip your body up pushing them out, and that's when the real work starts— Do you have any idea what it takes to nurture a child nowadays in this fucking urbanized, overfeeding, overstimulating world we've created? Do you have a *clue*?"

I kept quiet.

She said, "*Think* about it: you go through all that, feeding them with your body, waking up in the middle of the night, wiping their ass, getting them through all the tantrums and the hurt feelings and the bad habits, getting them past *puberty*, for Christ's sake, and someone comes along—someone you trust—and sabotages all that."

She sprang up, paced the space behind her desk.

"I'm not telling you a damn thing, even if I did you couldn't repeat a word of it—and believe me, if I pick up the merest hint you've let on to anyone—your wife, anyone—I'll make sure you lose that license of yours."

Race-walking the width of the room, back again, another circuit.

"Picture this, *Doctor:* you put all that into another human being, entrust them to someone they've known their whole life. Someone you've done favors for, and what are you asking? Tutoring, stupid *tutoring*, because the kid's smart but numbers have a way—math—just math, not another goddamn thing. And then you walk in and find that person with—with your treasure, this treasure you've wrought, and they've shattered it . . . by the pool, the goddamn pool. And where are the math books? Where's the tutoring? Getting wet on the deck next to the pool while they—wet swimsuits lying all wrinkled—oh that would be just great with you, wouldn't it? You'd let *that* pass, right?"

"Was it the first time?" I said.

"Joanne claimed it was—Becky did, too, but they were both lying. I can't blame Becky for that, she was ashamed—no, it wasn't the first time, I could tell it wasn't. Because it explained all sorts of things. A little girl who used to talk to me, who after she turned sixteen and started getting tutored didn't talk to me anymore. A little girl who'd suddenly cry for no good reason, leave the house, not tell us where she was going—her grades started to drop, even with the tutoring—she was *sixteen*, Alex, and that bitch *raped* her! For all I know it had gone on for years."

"After you found them you never talked to Becky about it?"

"No point. She needed to heal, not be shamed."

More pacing.

"And don't get that accusatory tone. I know the law and no, I didn't report it to the so-called *authorities*," she said. "What would *that* have accomplished? The law's an *ass*, believe me, I sit out there and listen to it bray every goddamn day."

"And Bob?"

"Bob hates Joanne because he thinks she refused to keep on tutoring Becky and that's why Becky flunked math and won't be able to get into a good college. If I'd told Bob, Joanne might've been dead sooner and that's all I'd need—my entire family destroyed."

"You did tell Richard," I said.

"Richard's a man of action."

Translation: Richard would punish her. Shutting her out, forever.

I said, "Joanne was a woman of action. Once

sentence had been passed, she carried out the punishment herself."

Killing herself slowly. Richard's contempt had been part of it—excommunicating her, letting her know he had nothing but contempt for her. Threatening to tell the children.

But there'd been more to the deterioration, force-feeding herself like a goose. Getting fat because Becky had gotten skinny.

Joanne had despised herself.

Stacy, the alleged problem child, had been kept out of the loop. Eric, dropping out to tend to his mother, had probably been privy to more. How much had Joanne told him? Not the essence of her sin, just that she'd done something for which Dad couldn't forgive her . . .

Judy said, "She finally did something right, goddamn her."

"She wanted you to see—her last chance at apology."

She shrugged. Drew her finger across her lips. "Leave now, Alex. I mean it."

I got up and headed for the door. "Despite all she did to your family, you cared about *hers*. That's why you referred Stacy to me."

"Talk about errors in judgment."

"Who else knows?" I said.

"No one."

"Not Becky's therapist?"

"No, Becky and I agreed she could get help without getting into it. And don't tell me I was wrong, because I wasn't. She's fine now. Planning to go to community college. Study psychology. We're back to where we were before, Alex. Becky will take strength from it—develop a higher level of empathy out of this. Be a *great* psychologist."

I turned toward the door.

"You don't know, either, Alex. This conversation never took place."

I reached for the doorknob.

"You're right," she said. "I don't ever want to see or hear from you again."

38

Two weeks before Christmas, I called FBI headquarters at the Federal Building and, not expecting any success, asked to speak with Special Agent Mary Donovan.

I was transferred to her immediately.

"Hello, Doctor. What can I do for you?"

"I was just wondering if you've had any success with Dr. Fusco."

"Success," she said. "As measured by?"

"Finding him. Helping him."

"You're serious."

"About what?"

"Helping him. As if we're a clinic or something."

"Well," I said, "there's always the issue of collegiality. And respect for what he once was. No sign of him, at all?"

Long silence.

She said, "Look, I took your call because I thought

you might've changed your mind, but this is a waste of time."

"Changed my mind in what way?"

"Being willing to cooperate. Helping us find him."

"Helping you?" I said. "As if I'm a clinic or something."

Another silence.

"I guess my question's been answered," I said.

"Have a nice day, Doctor."

Click.

I sat there holding the phone. Thinking about Alice Zoghbie's claim of being audited by the IRS because she'd rubbed important noses the wrong way. Probably a lie, covering for a call from Roy Haiselden.

But you never knew.

39

A week before Christmas, Stacy called.

"I'm so sorry," she said. "It was rude not answering, but things got really busy and . . ."

"Don't worry about it. How's everything going?"

"Actually, much better. Did pretty well on a bunch of A.P. exams, and I just found out I got in early to Cornell. I know it's far away and it gets cold, but they've got a veterinary school and I think I might want to do that."

"Congratulations, Stacy."

"Architecture seemed too . . . impersonal. Anyway, thanks for all your help. That's it."

"How's Eric?"

"He's okay. Dad's fine, too, busy all the time. He doesn't like visiting that probation officer, complains about it constantly, but he's lucky that's all he got, right? Eric changed his major. Psychology. So maybe you had an influence on him—I'm sorry about the way he treated you."

"That's okay."

She laughed. "That's what he says. Taking abuse is part of your job. Guilt's not a big part of Eric's life."

"Ah," I said, knowing how wrong she was.

"Did you hear about the Manitows?" she said.

"What about them?"

"They put their house up for sale and moved out of the Palisades. They're renting a place down in La Jolla. Judge Manitow's quitting and Dr. Manitow's trying to see if he can find work down there."

"No, I hadn't heard."

"They didn't exactly advertise it," she said. "One day I was seeing Dr. Manitow drive off to work, the next day the sign was up and the moving vans were there. Becky's moving with them. Going to some junior college in San Diego. Everyone else can't wait to get out of the house, but she's staying with her parents. Someone told me Becky said that she needs to stay close to home."

"Some people do need that," I said.

"Guess so. Anyway, thanks for all your help. Maybe one day I'll get my DVM and I'll get a chance to work with that cute little bulldog of yours. Pay you back."

"Maybe," I said.

She laughed. "That would be cool."

Positive Linking

Paul Ormerod is the author of *The Death of Economics*, *Butterfly Economics* and *Why Most Things Fail*. He studied economics at Cambridge and his career has spanned the academic and practical business worlds, including working at the *Economist* newspaper group and as a director of the Henley Centre for Forecasting. He is a Fellow of the British Academy of Social Science and has been awarded a DSc *honoris causa* for his contribution to economics by the University of Durham.

Further praise for Paul Ormerod:

'It is difficult to find a reflective economist who is happy with matters as they are. Professor Paul Ormerod has gone one step further . . .' Will Hutton, *Guardian*

'Mr Ormerod not only writes about capital, but also points to a way it may at last be understood.' *New York Times*

'Ormerod is on to something . . . The tools of economics are too useful to be squandered on shadow plays.' *Business Week*

'Ormerod wants economists to stop thinking about how the world ought to behave and start looking at how it does.' Robin Blake, *Independent*

'Interesting and entertaining . . . The scale and breadth of Ormerod's analysis deserves commendation.' Adrian Woolfson, *Nature*

Positive Linking

How Networks Are Revolutionising
Your World

Paul Ormerod

faber and faber

First published in 2012
by Faber and Faber Limited
Bloomsbury House
74–77 Great Russell Street
London WC1B 3DA
This paperback edition first published in 2013

Typeset by Faber and Faber Limited
Printed in the UK by CPI Group (UK) Ltd, Croydon, CR0 4YY

A CIP record for this book
is available from the British Library

ISBN 978-0-571-27921-0

2 4 6 8 10 9 7 5 3 1

Contents

Illustrations

Preface

My previous book, *Why Most Things Fail*, was published in the mid-2000s. I addressed what is probably *the* most fundamental feature of both biological and human social and economic systems. Species fail and become extinct, brands fail, companies fail, public policies fail. Despite the rather gloomy title, the book did well. It was a *Business Week* US Business Book of the Year.

The book built on general themes which I had already explored in my two previous books. In *The Death of Economics* in the mid-1990s I argued that conventional economics views the economy and society as machines, whose behaviour, no matter how complicated, is ultimately predictable and controllable. The financial crisis of the late 2000s showed only too clearly how deeply flawed is this view of the world, embraced enthusiastically by mainstream economists, international bodies such as the International Monetary Fund, central banks and politicians the world over. On the contrary, the economy is much more like a living organism.

In *Butterfly Economics* in the late 1990s, I developed this theme. I analysed a wide and seemingly disparate range of economic and social questions, seeing them as analogous to living creatures whose behaviour can be understood only by looking at the complex interactions of their individual parts.

Why Most Things Fail drew inspiration from the biological sciences even more, demonstrating close parallels between, for example, the extinction of biological species in the fossil record and the extinction of companies. The idea that economics should look to biology for intellectual inspiration is a long and distinguished one. Alfred Marshall, who founded the faculty of economics at Cambridge University around 1900, was the first major scholar to articulate this view.

Vernon Smith, in his economics Nobel Prize lecture in 2003, stated bluntly: 'I urge students to read narrowly within economics, but widely in science. Within economics there is essentially only one model to be adapted to every application . . . The economic literature is not the best place to find new inspiration beyond these traditional technical methods of modelling.' I have followed this precept in this book. In addition to biology, I draw on powerful insights from, amongst other disciplines, psychology and anthropology.

Both *Butterfly Economics* and *Why Most Things Fail* were fundamentally based on the concept of networks, the idea that individuals do not operate, as conventional economics assumes, in isolation, but are connected together in society. Both the theory and practice of networks is a rapidly developing area, and I make use of results at the forefront of knowledge in this book.

Viewed from a network perspective, many aspects of our social and economic world look completely different than they do from the conventional view of mainstream economics. The world is not by any means a machine whose behaviour is predictable and controllable by pulling a lever here, by pressing a button there. The individual components – people, firms, regulators, governments – interact with each other and each component has the capacity to change directly how other components behave.

In many ways, this makes successful policy making, whether in the public or private sectors, much harder. So much is contingent on who influences whom on a network and when. Simple causal relationships between a change in policy and any given outcome no longer exist – if they ever did!

At the same time, far more effective policy making becomes possible. It requires a fundamental change of mindset by policy makers. This does not mean no government, but it certainly means much more thoughtful government instead of the complacent, tick box mentality which currently dominates the public sector in the West. The positive aspects of the huge recent increase in knowledge about social and economic networks open up new possibilities for solving many long-standing problems. A lighter, smarter touch, one which exploits the positive linking aspects of our modern, networked world.

I am grateful to a large number of people for encouragement and discussions which have helped to develop the ideas of this book, and in particular to Alex Bentley, Greg Fisher and Bridget Rosewell. Julian Loose of Faber and Faber has once again proved to be a very helpful and inspirational editor.

Paul Ormerod
London, Wiltshire and Red Lumb, October 2011

Introduction

Modern economic theory was first set out on a formal basis in the late nineteenth century. There have certainly been developments since then, but at heart the basic view in economics of how the world operates remains the same. Economics is essentially a theory of how decisions are made by individuals, of what information is gathered and how it is used by the decision maker.

All scientific theories, even quantum physics, are approximations to reality. Theories involve making assumptions, simplifications, to enable us to understand problems better. A key feature of a good theory is that its assumptions are a reasonable description of the real world.

In the early twenty-first century, just as it did in the late nineteenth, economics in general makes the assumption that individuals operate autonomously, isolated from the direct influences of others. A person has a fixed set of tastes and preferences. When choosing amongst a set of alternatives, he or she compares the attributes of these alternatives and selects the one which most closely corresponds to his or her preferences.

At first sight, this may seem quite reasonable, indeed even 'rational', as economists choose to describe this theory of behaviour. But there is a serious problem with the assumption that individuals operate in isolation from each other, that their preferences are not affected directly by the decisions of others. The social and economic worlds of the twenty-first century are simply not like this at all. We are far more aware than ever before of the choices, decisions, behaviours and opinions of other people. In 1900, not much more than 10 per cent of the world's population lived in cities. Now, for the first time in human history, more than half of us live in cities, in close, everyday proximity to large numbers of other people. In the last decade or so, the internet has revolutionised communications in a manner not experienced since the invention of the printing press in the mid-fifteenth century.

The assumption that people make choices in isolation, that they do not adopt different tastes or opinions simply because other people have them, is no longer sustainable. Perhaps – perhaps, and it is a big 'perhaps' – over a hundred years ago this might not have been a bad assumption to make. But no longer.

The choices people make, their attitudes, their opinions, are influenced directly by other people. The medium via which this influence spreads is the social network. Often, social networks are thought of as purely a web-based phenomenon: sites such as Facebook. These can indeed influence behaviour. But it is real-life social networks – family, friends, colleagues – that are even more important in helping us shape our preferences and beliefs, what we like and what we do not like.

Network effects, the fact that a person can and often does decide to change his or her preferences simply on the basis of what others do, pervade the modern world. Throughout history, a crucial feature of human behaviour has been our propensity to copy or imitate the behaviours, choices, opinions of others. We can see it in the fashions in pottery in the Middle Eastern Hittite Empire of three and a half millennia ago. And we can see it today in the behaviour of traders on financial markets, where the propensity to follow the herd can lead all too easily to the booms and crashes we have lately experienced. Scientists such as Robin

Dunbar have argued that our anomalously large brain (compared to other mammals) evolved precisely because, from an evolutionary perspective, copying is a very successful strategy to follow.

This concept is just as crucial for companies and markets as it is for people. In September 2008 Lehman Brothers went bankrupt, precipitating a crisis which almost led to a total collapse of the world economy and a repeat of the Great Depression of the 1930s. It was precisely because Lehman was connected via a network to other banks that made the situation so serious. Lehman's failure could easily have led to a cascade of bankruptcies across the world financial network, first in those institutions to which Lehman owed money, then spreading wider and wider from these across the entire network. Incredibly, neither the systems of financial regulations which were in place, nor the thinking of mainstream economics which influenced policy so strongly, took any account of the possibility of such a network effect.

A world in which network effects are a driving force of behaviour is completely different from the world of conventional economics, in which isolated individuals carefully weigh up the costs and benefits of any particular course of action. A world in which network effects are important is a much more realistic description of the human social and economic realities which exist in the twenty-first century. It is the implications of this world which I explore in this book.

Incentives have not disappeared as a driver of human behaviour. It is still the case that if, say, Pepsi raises its price compared to Coke, more Coke and less Pepsi will be sold. This is the world which economic theory describes. It is not wrong. But it is often misleading, for it offers only a very partial account of how decisions are made in reality. Network effects can be far more powerful than incentives, and we will see many examples in which network effects have completely swamped the impact of incentives, leading to outcomes completely different from those intended by policy makers.

Network effects require policy makers, whether in the public or corporate spheres, to change radically their view of how the world operates. In part, they make policy much harder to implement successfully, and they help explain many of the failures of policies based on the assumption that incentives and not network effects are the key drivers of behaviour. But they open up the possibility of much more effective and successful policies, ones which harness our knowledge of network effects and how they work in practice. Hence the main title of this book: Positive Linking.

1

Unintended Consequences

On Wednesday 16 October 1555, two of the leading members of the reformed English Protestant Church, Hugh Latimer and Nicholas Ridley, were chained to a stake in the city of Oxford. They were then burned to death. By what amounted to a series of historical accidents a Catholic, Mary, had become Queen, the ruler of all England, scarcely two decades after the Church of England made its historic break with the papacy. She was attempting to re-impose Catholicism by a policy of publicly burning leading Protestants. If they renounced their faith, their lives would be spared and they might even continue to enjoy the power and trappings of high office. If not, they faced the fire.

But far from quailing at a terrible fate, Latimer and Ridley embraced it cheerfully. 'Be of good comfort, Master Ridley, and play the man; we shall this day light such a candle, by God's grace, in England, as I trust shall never be put out,' Latimer allegedly pronounced. They, along with other condemned Protestants, had formed a deliberate policy of facing death with equanimity, in order to make a positive impression on those who witnessed the burnings.

They believed that the story of their end would spread by word of mouth far beyond those present at the executions. Existing Protestants might be encouraged by their example to be steadfast in their faith, and new converts gained. And on this occasion, the martyrs were ultimately proved to be correct. On Mary's death, Protestantism was restored as England's religion.

Flash forward over 400 years to another event in English history, far less momentous, but one which offers a vignette of popular culture, not of the mid-sixteenth century but the late twentieth.

In Sardinia during the 1990 soccer World Cup, the English supporters were feared for their violent reputation. One evening in Cagliari, a large number gathered in the streets. Facing them were the police. As Bill Buford relates in his excellent book *Among the Thugs*, various individuals made attempts to stir the fans into collective action without success. Making himself conspicuous so that others could see his actions, one threw a metal object at the police. Another charged the police and yelled for others to follow. Further attempts were made by isolated fans to encourage the crowd into collective action, but none joined in.

Tiring of the whole situation, and in response to the actions of one particular youth, a police captain fired his pistol into the air in a signal for the potential mob to disperse. The reaction was unexpected. At the sound of live ammunition being discharged, the English supporters immediately began to destroy property and attack the police. The very action intended to subdue the fans into quiescence provoked exactly the opposite reaction. The individual supporters suddenly turned into a mob.

These two stories, disparate though they may seem, have a great deal in common. They illustrate the seemingly perverse and apparently irrational ways in which people can behave. Rather than sullenly dispersing back to the safety of their hotels or into bars when a firearm was discharged, the soccer fans ran at the police. Latimer and Ridley were offered the choice not just of their lives but their freedom if they embraced Catholicism. Rather than meekly agreeing, whatever private reservations might have remained, they chose to suffer an appalling death. Not just history but contemporary life is replete with examples of people behaving in seemingly inexplicable ways.

A key theme of this book is that these widespread forms of behaviour are explicable. They are illustrations of the power of social networks. Today, the phrase 'social networks' is often synonymous with networking across the web on sites such as Facebook. But this is just one, albeit new and important, aspect of a phenomenon that has existed for centuries. People do not live in isolation, but in society. Their lives are filled with interactions across social networks. The network of their families, the network of their work colleagues, the networks of their hobbies. Real-life social networks in which people meet, gossip, chat, argue. Networks in which people's choices, behaviour, opinions can be influenced, shaped, even altered dramatically by the process of social exchange with other people.

Within these social networks, people often copy or imitate what others do or think, for a variety of motives. An individual might have formed a private view on a matter, but might believe that others with a different opinion are better informed and so changes his or her mind as a result. Or someone may accept the behaviour of a particular social group simply from a desire to conform. More subtly, peer acceptance might give an individual permission to behave in a way that, in a different social context, would be unacceptable.

The idea that copying is an important aspect of behaviour does not mean that individuals operate as automatons, that they have surrendered control over their decision to others. People can copy and still retain a clear sense of agency, of purpose and intent over their own actions. So in a strange city, you may consciously decide to copy others, to go to the restaurant where there are lots of customers rather than to the one in the same street where there are few. Lacking any other reliable information, lacking local knowledge yourself, you decide to be influenced by the choices made by others. Even in the highly connected world of the twenty-first century, networks are not everything. People still retain their individuality, their capacity to decide actions and beliefs for themselves, despite what is popular, either in society as a whole or amongst their particular group of friends, family or work colleagues.

Most public policy on social and economic matters is based on the premise that people, or indeed companies, behave as individuals when they are making decisions. Like so many Robinson Crusoes, people exist in splendid isolation. And it is this view of the world that is epitomised by mainstream economic theory.

We explore in this book the connection between the impact of incentives, of the assessment of costs and benefits of different actions, on individuals, and the effect of social interaction across networks. When the power of the network takes over, people are no longer acting autonomously, but as part of a social group, and their behaviour and decisions are driven by the process of copying, of imitation.

Sometimes the initial impact of changes to incentives on the behaviour and decisions of a few individuals will be seen to be enhanced as the power of the social network takes over, and this effect can on occasion be dramatic. But, equally, there are times when the impact of copying behaviour across a social network, of imitating the behaviour of others, does not just offset the effect of incentives, but takes the system in the completely opposite direction to what was intended.

In recent decades, the discipline of economics has exhibited powerful tendencies of intellectual imperialism. Not content merely to analyse the familiar areas of firms, consumers, prices and markets, economists have turned their attention to a wide range of social issues, seemingly far away from the original scope of economics: the study of the allocation of scarce resources. The institution of marriage, crime, piracy, drug addiction – economists now focus on all of these and more.

Indeed, the two historical vignettes which opened this chapter can be translated into the context of economic theory. The popular image of economics is that it deals with 'big' things, national output (GDP), unemployment, inflation, interest rates. This is macroeconomics and these are the topics which appear in the newspapers and on our television screens and on which economists are regularly seen to pronounce.

But, in essence, economics is a theory about how individuals make decisions. About decisions made at the microeconomic level. The measure of the relative importance of microeconomics is indicated by the fact that, over the past two decades, the Nobel Prize in economics has been awarded for work which has been unequivocally 'macro' in character on only four occasions. Not all the others have gone to micro, for some of the Laureates have made advances in techniques of statistical analysis, but micro distinctly outweighs macro in these awards. At the core of microeconomics is a series of theoretical postulates about how the so-called 'rational' individual makes decisions. For example he or she has a well-defined and fixed set of preferences concerning the choices on offer. He or she gathers all available information when making a decision, matches it against his or her preferences, and then makes the best possible decision – the 'optimal' decision, as economists like to say to give it a more scientific air – given the information and the preferences.*

So the agent – the jargon phrase in economics for the person making the decision – may, if the products have the same price, prefer Pepsi to Coke. (It is in fact rather useful to use 'agent', rather than 'he or she', since the word subsumes the two genders and avoids having to repeat the two.) But if the price of Pepsi rises relative to Coke, at some point any given agent will

* I have discussed this model in more detail in previous books, such as *The Death of Economics*, a critique of free-market economic theory written in the mid-1990s.

switch and buy Coke instead. This is not because the agent's preferences have fundamentally altered, but because the money saved in buying Coke rather than Pepsi in this illustrative example can be used to buy more of other products. So, overall, the preferences of the agent might be more closely matched by switching to Coke.

Another example is the British savoury spread Marmite. The only other countries where I believe either it or a close variant are on general sale are Britain's closest cultural neighbours, Australia and New Zealand. Based as it is on the scrapings of the fermented residue at the bottom of beer barrels, agents' preferences on this tend to be sharply divided. I cannot abide it. My wife adores it. But there is some price at which I could be persuaded to eat it, probably a negative one in which the producer paid me rather than the other way round.

When making choices between fairly straightforward, inexpensive, well-established consumer products, the economist's view of 'rational' choice may be reasonable. Coke, Pepsi, Marmite have all been around for a long time and agents have formed their preferences. They are unlikely to suddenly alter them, at least in any appreciable numbers.

In making a decision about the choices on offer, only a relatively small amount of information needs to be gathered, mainly concerning price. This latter factor might not be completely obvious, because the price per unit of weight or volume may vary from store to store, by pack size, or because of special offers such as 'buy one, get one free' or 'three for the price of two'. The mathematical capabilities of many people are known to be low. For example on the very day I write these words, a TV advert to recruit teachers created by the Training and Development Agency for Schools has been exposed by a fifteen-year-old schoolboy as containing the wrong answer to a fairly straightforward question. But even making allowances for this, there is a limited amount of information for agents to gather before matching it to their preferences.

This model of rational behaviour is no longer relevant in many circumstances in the world of the twenty-first century. Agents face a vast proliferation of choice, massive information overload. Many of the products on offer are highly sophisticated, difficult to evaluate in terms of their attributes. And we live in a world which is far more connected, in which we are far more aware of the opinions and behaviour of others, than we were a hundred years ago when standard economic theory was first being formalised. In 1900, the clear majority of the population of the world lived in relatively isolated villages. In the twenty-first century, the majority lives in cities, in close proximity to large numbers of other people. And the revolution in communication technology brought about by the internet makes us dramatically more aware of the behaviour of others than at any time in the whole of human history.

We need a new model of rational behaviour, one which is empirically consistent with the real world, the world of the twenty-first century. The economist's definition of rational behaviour is only one possible way to define the concept of rationality. Behaviour which does not follow the precepts of economic rationality is *not* irrational, as economists would have us believe. Indeed, in the modern world in many contexts it is the economic definition of rationality which has become irrational!

The development of such a view of the world, a more realistic view of how agents actually behave in the social and economic contexts of the twenty-first century, is a main theme of the book. It has radical implications for the conduct of policy, both corporate and public. Potentially, its impact is very positive. Our knowledge of how networks influence behaviour in the social and economic worlds is growing rapidly, both theoretically and empirically. The opportunity both to exploit this knowledge and to develop it even further, for there is much still to be done, over the coming decades is enormous. Successful policy making in the highly connected, networked world of the 21st century will be impossible without understanding positive linking, how we can use what are often abstract and difficult concepts to help shape a better world.

*

How, then, might we think about the two historical episodes described above in the context of standard economic theory? The theory makes claim to be a general description of human behaviour, a general theory of how people make choices. These examples may seem outside the conventional areas of economics, but if a theory is claimed to be general, it ought to be able to illuminate these events. Besides, it is economists themselves who have pushed the theory into areas such as marriage and crime and claimed that it has strong explanatory power in what might more usually be thought of as social rather than economic settings. The Chicago economist Gary Becker received the Nobel Prize for exactly this kind of work.

The individual preferences of the soccer fans were to have some sort of riot in which property would be vandalised and innocent passers-by made to cower in fear or, even better, injured in some way or other. This is why they had assembled as they did. A message had been passed to meet at a particular time, six o'clock as it happens, in a particular square. The colloquial phrase used was 'it's going to go off', meaning that, for those interested, the gathering would offer an opportunity to participate in creating mayhem in the city of Cagliari.

The fans would derive 'utility', again using the jargon of economics, from rioting. But what were the related costs to set against these 'benefits', using the phrase in inverted commas on this occasion to emphasise that these were, of course, benefits only to those involved in trashing the city, not to those unfortunates on the receiving end. The most obvious cost was the phalanx of police standing in front of them. Heavily equipped with helmets, shields, truncheons and guns, they were clearly capable of inflicting costs, such as a beating or arrest and prison, on anyone foolish enough to provoke them.

Economic theory usually allows individuals to differ in their preferences. Incredibly, as we shall see later in the book, the trends in macro theory in recent decades have been to suppress this, trying to explain the economy as a whole in terms of a single 'representative agent'. But more of this later. For now, we remain firmly in the terrain of microeconomics, where agents can have different preferences. The youths gathered in the square would undoubtedly differ in the benefit each individual believed he would gain from having a riot compared to carrying out other activities, such as having a beer or reading a book on Einstein's theory of general relativity or Shakespearean sonnets. They would differ in the evaluation of the costs of any police action inflicted on them. And, according to standard economic theory, they would even be allowed to differ in their assessment of the probability of being the recipient of such action themselves (with the strict proviso, and I am not making this up, that over the course of a series of such riot events, each fan on average assesses the probability correctly).

On this view of the world, every single one of the fans who responded to the verbal message 'it's going to go off' derived utility from participating in hooliganism. On arriving in the square and seeing the police, at some point they must have formed the view that these benefits outweighed the likely costs, or the riot would not have happened. It is possible that a few crept discreetly away, having come to the opposite view, but Bill Buford's description of the events certainly suggests that almost all the English fans present participated in the subsequent vandalism and general criminal behaviour which occurred.

But this does not take us very far in understanding why the riot started when it did. The fans stand, confronting the police on a hot late afternoon. But at first, they are a collection of individuals and not a collective mob. They have the potential to become a mob, but nothing happens. Several fans try to incentivise them all to start behaving badly by carrying out prominent acts of bravery, or lunacy as most people would see it, against the police. We can in fact readily understand the behaviour of these particular individuals from the point of view of economic theory. Considerable status would be attached to being seen as a leader by the other fans, being seen as a Top Boy, to use the British colloquial expression for the leader of a gang of thugs or hooligans. The benefit from this would be perceived as outweighing the undoubted increase in the potential cost to the individual by identifying himself so prominently to the forces of law and order.

This whole rationale for the event, as described by conventional economic theory, may already seem somewhat convoluted, but it now becomes even more so. Why did the fans as a whole not respond to the actions of the individuals who deliberately tried to incite a riot by their provocative actions? According to this theory of how agents behave, we have to suppose that the responses to these by the police were such as to temporarily tip the balance between costs and benefits in the minds of all the would-be rioters. In other words, when a youth came forward and threw a metal object at the police, they perhaps brandished their truncheons more fiercely, and this signal increased the likely costs of a riot in the minds of the fans.

But then the police captain, tiring of confronting this unpleasant group of badly dressed, smelly individuals,* fired live ammunition into the air. He clearly believed that signalling this potential cost – the possibility they would be fired upon – would be a sufficiently large incentive to make them eschew the pleasures of a riot on this occasion. The cost of being the recipient of a bullet surely outweighs that of even a savage truncheoning, but the response of the fans suggests otherwise.

The fans immediately charged the police. A possible reconciliation with the core model of individual behaviour in economic theory is that the shot fired into the air was a sign of weakness on the part of the police, a sign that they would not actually open fire on the English, regardless of what they did. But this argument is now getting pretty tenuous. Ex post, economic theory can rationalise almost anything which has ever happened, but these attempts often amount to no more than a Just So story, as is certainly the case here. Their credibility gets stretched well beyond breaking point.

A much simpler explanation can be given in terms of networks. When the fans first gathered in the square, it is not implausible to interpret their behaviour in terms of individualistic economic theory. Each of them enjoyed a riot, they gained 'utility' from it, in the jargon of economics. As noted above, the strength of their individual preferences for participating in a riot compared to other activities undoubtedly varied, as did their assessments of the costs. The delay between the fans assembling and the riot starting, and the lack of collective response to the efforts of reckless individuals to incite them, suggest that almost all of the supporters had formed the view, given the serried ranks of the forces of law and order confronting them, that the potential costs involved outweighed the benefits.

---

* *Among the Thugs* graphically illustrates these qualities in a variety of contexts.

A shot was fired. The collection of individuals immediately became a mob. They lost their individual identities. And their preferences altered dramatically, so that when the gun went off they charged the police, acting as a single unit. They had arrived as individuals as part of a social network with a shared interest in hooliganism. Information about a potential outlet for this activity had been passed across this network. But the action of the unfortunate police captain altered qualitatively the structure of this network. The individuals became fused as one, with an overwhelming preference to riot almost regardless of costs to themselves as individuals.

What scientists call a 'phase transition' had taken place. When water is gradually cooled, it remains water as the temperature drops from ten to nine to eight degrees and so on. Then, suddenly, as it passes through zero, a phase transition occurs. Water becomes ice.

A simple example of this phenomenon which is almost certainly more familiar to most readers of this book than taking part in a public riot is a social gathering with friends, in a bar or perhaps at a party. Each individual present enjoys alcohol in moderation and dislikes hangovers. But the company is delightful, the wine flows. The collective mood temporarily overcomes the preferences of individuals. And the effect of the social network present in this particular milieu is that almost everyone is induced to drink more than he or she intended at the start of the evening, or would drink on their own or in a smaller or less congenial group. The next day, operating once more as individuals with their individual preferences restored, some will undoubtedly regret the collective set of preferences – to consume yet more alcohol – which spread across the social network. One or two may go so far as to pledge to themselves never to drink again. (Until the next time, of course!)

James Surowiecki wrote a very interesting book in 2004, *The Wisdom of Crowds*. This is essentially about the process of answering a question by taking into account the opinions of a large number of individuals rather than relying on just a few, no matter how expert these people might be. There are many practical examples where the 'crowd' certainly gives a more accurate estimate, such as the classic ones of guessing the number of sweets in a jar or the weight of a prize bull at a country fair. The word 'crowd' is put in inverted commas here, because the process only really works when the individuals participating in the process remain as individuals and not part of a crowd in the way the soccer vandals were.

The crucial assumption needed for the average of the collection of individual opinions to be more accurate than a single expert is that they do indeed form their views independently, without reference to those of others. Once this independence vanishes, once the agents become fused into a single whole, often the outcome is not so much the wisdom, more the 'madness of crowds', as it was described by Charles Mackay as long ago as 1841.

*

There is another very general point, and another key theme of this book, to take from the example of the English soccer fans and their rampage through the streets of Cagliari. The individuals received several attempts to incite them. But none of these worked. Then, completely unexpectedly, the one event which any detached observer might think would offer a clear deterrent, the firing of the gun, turned the group of individuals into an enraged crowd.

And this is the point. Most attempts to spread a choice, an opinion, a type of behaviour, across a network of individuals fail. The events in Sardinia are simply an example of this general point. And it is why we have to be very careful when designing public policy. Like the police captain, policy makers will often have little idea about the likely consequences of their attempts at nudging groups towards particular decisions or opinions. Duncan Watts, formerly Professor of Mathematical Sociology at Columbia, now director of the Human Social Dynamics group at Yahoo! and someone we will meet in much more detail later, used a phrase for this fundamental property of networks. They are 'robust yet fragile'.

The collection of individuals who make up a network will, most of the time, exhibit stability with respect to most of the 'shocks' which this particular system receives. The shock could be a piece of news in the context of financial markets, an advertising campaign in a consumer market, or, as here, attempts to incite a group of fans to alter their preferences and attack the police. The system is stable in the sense that most shocks make very little difference, they are absorbed, shrugged off, and few people change either their minds or their behaviour as a result. So the network is 'robust'.

But, every so often, a particular shock may have a dramatic effect. So the network is also 'fragile'. The behaviour of individuals across the whole, or almost the whole, of any particular network might be altered. Before the event, it can be very difficult if not impossible to discover what the eventual impact is going to be. A big shock, almost by definition, will have big consequences. So if the Italian police had opened up with machine-gun fire directly at the fans, we could reasonably conclude that in this particular instance a riot would not have taken place. But most events, most attempts to change behaviour, do not fall into this category. Most have very little impact. But occasionally, one does.

From these sordid events in Sardinia, we can now return to the altogether more dramatic happenings in Oxford over 450 years ago. Again, we can offer a partial explanation in terms of incentives, of costs and benefits, when people are acting as if they were isolated individuals. But, again, this kind of rationale soon becomes incomplete. Networks are needed to complete the picture.

Since time immemorial religion has been, and continues to be outside Western Europe, a major presence in human society. Yet mainstream economics has virtually ignored the topic, certainly in comparison to the enormous amount of work carried out in sociology, anthropology, psychology, history – disciplines considered 'soft' by most economists.

There has been some work on religion in economics. But when Laurence Iannaccone of George Mason University in Fairfax, Virginia, probably the leading modern economic scholar in this area, wrote an 'Introduction to the Economics of Religion' in the prestigious *Journal of Economic Literature* in 1998, he noted that 'the study of religion does not yet warrant a *JEL* classification number'. This simple observation is significant in revealing the amount of attention paid to religion by economists up to the late 1990s.

The example of the Oxford Martyrs is specifically religious, but the arguments being considered are relevant much more generally to all human belief systems where faith or ideology is important. In the decades around the middle of the twentieth century, why did highly placed individuals in both America and Britain decide to give their loyalties to the ideology of communism and betray their countries by revealing secrets to the Soviet Union? Neither Kim Philby nor Alger Hiss, two of the most notorious spies, appears to have been motivated by money, by the set of standard incentives in the economist's toolkit. They were motivated by faith, the wholly misplaced faith that the Soviets would create a better future for all humanity. They were utterly and completely wrong. But they believed.

History is replete with examples of ideological differences which cannot be accounted for on the basis of 'rational' economic decision making. Given the historical importance of religion, many such disputes involve this topic. But thinking still of the Soviet Union, after the collapse of tsarist rule in 1917, a vast proliferation of competing political ideologies bubbled to the surface. The Western liberalism of Kerensky, who formed a government for a few brief months in 1917. The several varieties of Whites, believers in monarchy, against whom the Bolsheviks fought a brutal and debilitating civil war. Within the revolutionaries themselves were differing ideological tendencies: anarchists, social revolutionaries, Mensheviks, Bolsheviks, to name but a few. And Bolshevism, the ultimately victorious faction embodied in the Communist Party of the Soviet Union, was notorious for vicious internal ideological disputes even when the key authority figure of Lenin was still alive.

There were undoubtedly many motives at work in each of the arguments and struggles. Personal ambition mixed with genuine belief that your opinions and those of your faction were the correct ones, the ones which would bring about Paradise on Earth. But all of them involved faith and ideology rather than rational, incentive-based decisions. So, although we now resume the discussion focused on religion, we should keep in mind that the points are relevant to any faith- or ideology-based dispute in human affairs.

*

All sciences classify the various aspects of their discipline. We earlier came across the basic distinction between micro- and macroeconomics. But the scientific classification goes into much finer detail than this. The *JEL* (*Journal of Economic Literature*) system is the one used by all economists. It divides the subject into well over 500 sub-categories. And in the late 1990s religion, one of the most fundamental features of human society, did not warrant a category of its own, so little work had been done on it. The situation has now changed. Religion does have its own economics sub-category. But, revealingly, it is allocated in section Z, 'Z12' no less, coming right at the end of the very long list, lower down even than the ten sub-categories in category Y, all of them 'Miscellaneous Categories'.

In some ways this is surprising, given that Adam Smith, the founding father of modern economics, wrote about the topic extensively in one of his two great books, the *Theory of Moral Sentiment*. He even analysed religious issues from the perspective of agents responding to incentives in his *Wealth of Nations*. He discussed how the clergy could be motivated by self-interest, how monopoly is as bad for religion as it is in other areas of human activity, arguing that competition – being able to choose between competing religions – is good.

Economics had to wait almost exactly 200 years before Smith's analysis was extended, in a model developed by Corry Azzi and Ronald Ehrenberg and published in the top-ranking *Journal of Political Economy*, based in the free market-oriented University of Chicago. A short summary gives a flavour of both this particular model and subsequent work by economists on the topic of religion.

Individuals allocate their time and money amongst religious and secular commodities with the aim of maximising lifetime *and* afterlife utility. 'Afterlife consumption', as Azzi and Ehrenberg describe it, is the primary goal of religious participation. Secular utility depends in the standard way on inputs of time (work) and the products which are purchased. Afterlife utility depends upon the entire effort devoted by the individual to religious activities over his or her lifetime.

The article is not a spoof, though it would be quite difficult to invent a more effective satire of the model of utility-maximising Rational Economic Man which dominates the entire literature of economics. So many points spring to mind. For example, on a purely technical point within the spirit of the literature itself, but one which is important empirically in some main religions, 'afterlife utility' does not vary continuously with the amount of effort devoted to religion during your lifetime. It is a simple binary outcome: either you are in Heaven, with boundless pleasure, or in Hell, with endless pain. And the outcome might very well not depend on the amount of time and effort which you devote to religious activity. Who will be saved in the well-known parable, the self-righteous Pharisee, obsessed not only with his own virtue but with the constant public display of it, or the sinful but repentant publican who devotes very little time and effort to religion? To be fair to the economics of religion, it has moved on to consider participation more as a group activity and to focus on institutions and their behaviour. But it has very little to say about the most fundamental question: why believe at all?

Despite all this, incentives were certainly at work in the religious world of England in the 1550s. Although there were many nuances within each religion, individuals faced a basic choice between being Catholic or Protestant. Queen Mary's father, Henry VIII, had broken with the Pope in the 1530s and established the Church of England. The institution had gradually come under the control of hard-line Protestants, a trend which accelerated during the short reign of his young son, Edward VI, in the years around 1550. Following Edward's premature death from tuberculosis, Mary – forever known in English iconography as 'Bloody Mary' because of her burning of the martyrs – had come to the throne determined to restore Catholicism.

There were some important directly economic issues to settle. Henry had carried out the biggest seizure of private property in English history, when the monasteries were dissolved and their lands confiscated by the Crown. Under Edward, the church leaders had gone even further, stripping and looting churches of the elaborate trappings and ornaments of Catholicism. How far should these measures be reversed? Mary's main adviser, Cardinal Pole, an Englishman who had almost become Pope in 1550, advocated a complete restoration. Mary had to balance the immediate benefits to her Church against the potentially destabilising political consequences and costs of expropriating the property which Henry had sold on almost immediately to wealthy noblemen and merchants.

But the main question facing her was how to restore the old religion of Catholicism, how to persuade people to re-embrace what she regarded as the true faith. It appears to be the case that the clear majority of the population in fact still adhered to Catholicism. Protestantism was the new brand, as it were, and was still some considerable distance from displacing the market leader. But it had achieved a strong market presence in London and its immediately surrounding areas, then as now the key focus of English political and economic power. Even more pertinently, the leaders of the Protestant Church were, in general, militants.

The bishops and other prominent churchmen could be, and were, removed from their formal positions by simple administrative acts and put in prison. A few were willing to adapt, presumably because they were attracted by the benefits of office and attached little weight to the potential afterlife costs of displaying devotion to possibly erroneous doctrines. The most notorious of these was the remarkable Anthony Kitchin, Bishop of Llandaff in Wales. He was the only person to serve as a bishop under all the various forms of religion embraced by Henry, Edward, Mary and her successor Elizabeth I and who would, in the words of one prominent historian of the time, have doubtless become a Hindu provided he could continue to remain Bishop of Llandaff. Behaviour such as this was satirised immortally in the eighteenth century popular song 'The Vicar of Bray', recounting the contortion of its eponymous subject in remaining in ecclesiastical office through the religious changes brought about by successive English monarchs. The chorus is a monument to placemen and timeservers everywhere:

> And this is Law, I will maintain,
> Until my Dying Day, Sir,
> That whatsoever King may reign,
> I will be the Vicar of Bray, Sir!

But the removal from office of most of Edward's leading clergy altered neither their beliefs nor those of lay believers in Protestantism. Mary and her advisers soon settled on a policy of terror to deal with this problem. Well-known Protestants would be given every opportunity to recant, but if they continued to refuse they would face the flames.

On the face of it, the strategy was a sensible one to follow from Mary's perspective. There had been many previous examples in human history of terror being successful in achieving its aim. And specifically in England, only 150 years previously, the Lollard heresy, an early form of Protestantism, had been suppressed effectively by a few selective burnings.

*

We might usefully pause to ask why this might be the case. The question of religious or ideological belief is enormously complicated, and one which is ultimately not susceptible to explanation by the model of 'Rational' Economic Man. In terms of this set of behavioural postulates, the agent has first of all to gather available information. But in this context, what is the relevant set of information? By definition, the existence of the afterlife can never be proved, no matter how much information we might gather. The information then has to be processed to come up with the best – sorry, the 'optimal' – choice.

The seventeenth-century French philosopher Blaise Pascal came up with his famous wager to claim that the best strategy is in fact to believe in God. Essentially, he argued that since we are incapable of knowing whether God exists or not, we have to wager on the outcome. In terms of the agent's overall happiness, the gains and losses of belief or non-belief have to be taken into account. In Pascal's own words, 'Let us weigh the gain and the loss in wagering that God is . . . If you gain, you gain all; if you lose, you lose nothing. Wager, then, without hesitation that He is.' In other words, if God exists and you believe, you gain an infinite amount of happiness but if He does not, you lose nothing. But equally if God does not exist, you lose very little either way.

Pascal was a highly original thinker, and his wager is one of the seminal contributions to modern theories of probability and decision making. Not surprisingly, there is a very large academic literature on his wager, a good introduction being in the online Stanford Encyclopedia of Philosophy.* The details need not concern us here, but suffice to say that even after thousands of academic articles, the outcome is unclear. We cannot establish an agreed basis on which an agent might use rational behaviour to believe in God, or a supreme being, or not.

Ultimately, religious or ideological belief for the individual is a matter of faith and not rational analysis. The social networks in which the person is embedded are also crucial in terms of cultural

* http://plato.stanford.edu/entries/pascal-wager/

norms and peer pressure and acceptance or otherwise of belief. 'Embedded' can mean far more than the current position. It can embrace the networks in which they grew up, for example, or which they have been part of previously and which helped shape their current beliefs. And in mid-sixteenth-century Europe, the question was: which variety of religious ideology to believe?

Even the most devout believer experiences doubt from time to time. Within Christianity, even the Apostles themselves experienced crises of faith in the immediate aftermath of the Resurrection. The two men on the road to Emmaus with Jesus were unable to recognise him, a scene given modern vibrancy in T. S. Eliot's memorable phrase in *The Waste Land*: 'who is the third who walks always beside you?' The phrase 'a doubting Thomas', meaning a sceptic, has its origin in the Apostle Thomas, who refused to believe until he had placed his hands in the Crucifixion wounds.

In any event, in the rapidly changing circumstances of sixteenth-century England, who could be really sure what was the true faith? Was the Pope the true Head of the Universal Church, or was he merely the Bishop of Rome, or even the Antichrist? The Bishop of Llandaff, whom we met above, would not have been alone in being able, if required, to subscribe to any one of these three distinct propositions.

In contrast, the prospect of being burned alive was only too real and certain. Sometimes, if the fire took hold well, death could be reasonably quick owing to oxygen deprivation, but it was an appalling end nonetheless. Equally, however, contemporary documents record examples of victims dying in prolonged agony, pleading for 'more fire' as a combination of damp wood and perverse winds slowly roasted them alive.

So Mary's policy had a definite incentive element, and agents did react. Some fled abroad. Others openly renounced

Protestantism. The most famous of all, Thomas Cranmer, Archbishop of Canterbury and head of the Anglican Church, recanted in prison no fewer than six times before finally summoning the courage to be led to the stake.

But we know from history that her policy failed. Even as Mary lay dying in the summer and autumn of 1558 after four years of terror, there was still a persistent supply of martyrs willing to be burned. And when her sister Elizabeth restored the Protestant faith, the nation embraced it with enthusiasm.

Networks were the reason for this failure. The negative incentive of the fear of the stake took her so far, but not far enough. It was overwhelmed in completely the opposite way by the power of networks. And networks were present in two separate but closely related ways.

The first was the very close network between the militant Protestants themselves, maintained even when they were in jail awaiting interrogation or execution itself. They sent messages, exchanged letters, a veritable torrent of encouragement to keep the faith and set an example to the population as a whole.

This latter, the entire people of England, constituted the second network. Much more loosely structured than the tight-knit religious one, information even in those days did pass pretty rapidly across communities. Most of the population of the country lived within three days' ride of London. The internet it was not, but news certainly travelled. And the burnings themselves were major public events, often attended by thousands of people. The Marian regime sometimes unwittingly contributed to the potential number of favourable message bearers. For the execution of Latimer and Ridley, for example, every household in Oxford was compelled to send at least one member to witness the event. The burnings were not just a deterrent. The authorities were in fact aware that they might also be a source of inspiration. So, leading

Catholic figures preached on pulpits specially constructed near the pyre, explaining the heresies of the condemned and expounding what they saw as the true faith. People could be either educated or frightened by the spectacle.

Much of our information on these events comes from a remarkable book, John Foxe's *Book of Martyrs*, first published very early in the reign of Queen Elizabeth I. The Protestant clerical elite were convinced from the outset that their deaths could cause the policy to rebound on the persecutors. They were well aware of the necessity of creating a good impression at the stake. Accounts of their behaviour would spread by word of mouth. Existing Protestants would be encouraged to keep the faith, and waverers influenced by their steadfastness.

To this end, then, they encouraged one another. On 8 February 1555, on the morning of his execution, Laurence Saunders, a noted Protestant preacher in London and the Midlands, wrote to his wife and supporters: 'God's people shall prevayle: yea our blood shal be their perdition, who do most triumphantly spill it.' He actively encouraged them to attend and enjoy the event: 'Make haste my deare brethren, to come unto me that we may be mery.'

In terms of dramatic impact, Saunders died embracing the stake. John Rogers, the first of the 300 or so martyrs to be burned, was seen to be washing his hands in the flames and Archbishop Cranmer signalled his adherence to the Protestant faith by thrusting into the fire the right hand which had previously signed his humiliating recantations. John Hooper, Bishop of Gloucester and a notoriously grumpy man, took the opportunity on his way to execution to bless a blind child and greet local dignitaries – for all the world like a modern politician out on the campaign trail for votes. Foxe put the crowd assembled to watch him burn at 7,000, 'for it was market-day and many also came to see his behaviour towards death'. Seven thousand may not seem a lot, but relative to the size of the population, it was the equivalent of around three quarters of a million in present-day America. In short, a massive crowd.

We know the outcome of this particular historical event. Incentives were put in place to persuade people to adopt one particular set of beliefs, and these had a certain amount of success. But their impact was completely offset and indeed dwarfed by the impact made by the martyrs across the network of the population as a whole. The deliberate policy of calm and even joyous acceptance of death made an impression across the land and people were influenced directly by this behaviour.

But there was no guarantee in advance that this would happen. Indeed, during the years of the Marian terror, there was evidence that the policy was working. As mentioned earlier, some leading Protestants left the country and others, from all walks and levels of life, recanted.

*

A contemporary example both of the potentially huge effect of networks and of the inherent uncertainty of outcome they create is the momentous events taking place in North Africa and the Middle East. I am writing these words in early April 2011, when neither I nor anyone else knows how they will unfold even in the (historically) short time between the writing and the publication of this book. And I am leaving the original words unchanged as the book itself is being revised during the summer and autumn of 2011. I want to capture on record how things stood in April of that year, to illustrate the uncertainties involved in such situations.

As I write, protests in some countries have already been followed by changes in regime. In Algeria, the government appears to have been able to defuse the tension. In Syria, the protests seem to be in the process of being ruthlessly suppressed. And the current situation in Libya is, to say the least, chaotic and uncertain.

The immediate catalyst to the events was Mohamed Bouazizi, a twenty-six-year-old Tunisian. Bouazizi was a university graduate living in a provincial town where he was unemployed and trying to find, but unable to get, work. He started selling fruit and vegetables in the street without a licence. The authorities put a stop to his activity, confiscated his goods and humiliated him. In response, he set himself alight and died in hospital on 4 January 2011. This sparked the riots which forced the President of Tunisia to flee the country, and was followed by similar uprisings in Egypt, Libya, Jordan, Yemen, Bahrain and Syria.

Clearly, the potential for social unrest was already in place in all these countries, ruled for decades by undemocratic regimes of various degrees of corruption and brutality, with large numbers of discontented young people. The incentives to replace the regimes were there. And doubtless, there had been many individual protests against the regimes, any one of which might have spread like wildfire across the latent network of the desire for change. But these protests have vanished into the mists of history. The network proved robust with respect to these now-unknown shocks. In the case of Bouazizi, however, the network responded in a fragile way.

Bouazizi's act of defiance was spectacular. Is this why it succeeded and others did not? Perhaps. Readers of a certain age will undoubtedly recall Jan Palach and his role in the events following the so-called 'Czech Spring' of 1968. Under the leadership of Alexander Dubček, the government of the then-Czechoslovakian state had carried out a series of liberalising measures which alarmed the Soviet leadership in the Kremlin. Czechoslovakia was part of the Warsaw Pact group of nominally independent countries, controlled in practice by the Soviet Union. In August 1968, Soviet military forces occupied the country and Dubček's government was removed from office.

A group of students made a pact to burn themselves to death in public as an act of protest against the Soviet invasion. Jan Palach actually carried it out, not in some remote provincial town but in the principal square of the Czech capital, Prague, on 16 January 1969. The event attracted widespread publicity world-wide, in contrast to the self-immolation of Bouazizi, with a leading British newspaper feeling able to write just four months after his death that 'the name of Mohamed Bouazizi has largely been lost in the unfolding story of the Arab Spring'.* Palach's self-immolation did trigger demonstrations, but these proved to be far from sufficient to bring about change and were suppressed by the security services. So in a network context, we cannot even say in advance whether or not a truly dramatic gesture such as being burned to death for your beliefs will be sufficient to persuade others and bring about change.

*

These rather disparate historical events have introduced the main themes of the book. Most policy, certainly public policy, is based upon the idea that people respond as rational individuals, in the sense in which economics uses this word, to incentives. If you fire a shot into the air as a sign to a group of football supporters to disperse, you believe they will be induced to regard the costs of a riot as being too high, and they will disperse. If you threaten to burn someone to death unless he or she changes their religious opinion or ideological belief, you think the negative incentive which such a death entails will be sufficient to achieve your aim, at least as far as most individuals are concerned. And if someone is sufficiently stubborn as to ignore the incentive and to undergo the dreadful ordeal, you think the public spectacle will act as a serious deterrent to others.

* *Daily Telegraph*, 2 April 2011.

In the main examples in this chapter, incentives have not worked in a way which has achieved the desired outcome. But quite often, they do. They even worked up to a point in the religious turmoil of mid-sixteenth-century England. So this approach to policy is not always without merit.

But the impact of networks can be considerably greater than that of incentives alone. If the two operate in conjunction, if we experience the phenomenon of positive linking, the changes to behaviour of a relatively small number of people which incentives might induce can spread across a larger group because of network effects. Equally, however, as we have seen, incentives can be swamped if behaviour across a network surges in a manner different from that intended by the policy makers applying the incentives.

Networks introduce an entirely different dimension into the policy picture. This argument is based on the truism that humans are social creatures. As mentioned earlier, in economic theory, individuals operate like multiple Robinson Crusoes, taking independent, autonomous decisions that are not directly influenced by the decisions or opinions of others. Network theory allows the social dimension of human activity to be taken into account when trying to understand how agents behave, and when thinking through the policy implications of their behaviour.

The examples used to illustrate this so far, those of rioting and being burned at the stake, are rather extreme events which relatively few people will ever encounter. But networks on which people copy or imitate the behaviour of others matter in many, more homely, everyday situations. Think of Crocs. For the few readers who have never come across the term, these are shoes which became very fashionable during the 2000s. Shaped like clogs, the upper material of the shoe is studded with holes. Shoes with holes? These may be perfectly functional in the arid climates of Adelaide or Arizona. But in rainy Seattle or Scotland? Yet the brand proliferated everywhere. And a key reason for the success of Crocs was precisely that they became fashionable in the first place.

A difficult problem, to which we will keep returning during the course of the book, is why something starts to become fashionable at all. Fashion seems to 'emerge' from nowhere in particular. Certainly, many companies, as we will see later in the book, are attempting to make use of the concept of positive linking to try to make their brands fashionable, to promote a cascade of sales. But for the moment we will park this issue safely, and simply note that once a brand, a concept, a way of behaving, starts to become fashionable, it becomes even more so simply because it is fashionable. People decide to buy something, to adopt an opinion, simply because others are doing so. It is this social dimension to choice and decision making which network theory captures. In turn, the increased demand sets up positive feedback on the supply side. More shops stock the item because it is becoming popular, which means that even more people become aware of it.

When network effects are present, people are using rules of behaviour which are quite different from those of the behavioural postulates of economics, in which individuals carefully gather information about alternative choices or courses of action and match them against their own fixed preferences. Instead, they may copy, they may imitate the behaviour of others.

And a key implication of basing your decision, at least in part, simply on what other people are doing or thinking is that your preferences are no longer fixed. Instead, they change and evolve over time, as the impact of people on your various social networks alters your own behaviour. Indeed, the preference of the English soccer followers changed in a matter of seconds once the shot was fired. In terms of fashion, you may be influenced by what you see other people wearing in the street – people you may never see again. In deciding whether to buy into a particular pension scheme, your network here is likely to be a very small number of individuals whose opinion in these matters you trust and value. But in each case, your own private opinion may be influenced and changed by what others are doing.

This is a fundamentally different view of the world from the one in which people are assumed to operate in isolation and to base their decisions on a fixed set of preferences. Even in the latter type of world, the world of standard economic theory, successful policy making might still be difficult. Discovering what people really do want might itself be a considerable challenge. But if their wants, their needs, their desires are fixed, in principle a smart policy maker, whether in the public or corporate sector, can discover them. And the right levers can be pulled, the correct buttons pressed, to change incentives in such a way that the desired outcome of the policy maker can be reliably achieved. In a world in which tastes change in response to the choices and actions of others, this model of policy can simply no longer be relied upon.

The problem for policy makers is even more complicated. Networks can appear in a variety of guises and be activated in a variety of ways. The soccer hooligans were connected by a network of shared interests such as violence and, in case we forget, the game of soccer itself. This is why they bonded together in this particular social network. The choices of individuals in this group on matters such as which brand of trainers to wear, or their opinions on which players should be selected for the team, would be influenced by the choices of others – exactly as they are in the wider, innocuous world of fashion and the purchase of items such as Crocs.

But with the vandals, the shot fired into the air was the signal for a qualitative change in the nature of this network to take place. From being a network of individuals connected in terms of shared interests but nevertheless capable of making decisions as individuals, it became fused into one. A particular mode of behaviour, involving the destruction of property and physical violence, flashed across the entire network. Everyone adopted and became consumed by the same mode of behaviour.

In the example of religious faith, a network of awareness was already in place across England. Many people knew of Cranmer, the Archbishop of Canterbury, and other nationally prominent church leaders such as Latimer and Ridley. At a more parochial level, people would be likely to know of the diocesan bishop, say, or a leading local preacher, even though people on the other side of the country might not have heard of them. So, the population of England was connected on a network which transmitted awareness of the existence of a range of Protestant leaders. The martyrs took the gamble that this pre-existing network, which essentially consisted of one in which information about them was exchanged, could be used by them to influence behaviour and opinions.

But the feature which all these examples have in common, in their widely different contexts and impacts, is that behaviour and opinions can be altered not just by individuals reacting to changes in incentives but directly by what others think, believe or do. The challenge for policy makers in the interconnected, networked world of the twenty-first century is to harness this positive power of networks and to use them in conjunction with incentives. We need networks both to make sense of the policy terrain and to design more effective policies, We need positive linking.

'Up to a point, Lord Copper!'

We have seen a range of examples, from harmless choices in foot-wear fashion to altogether more dramatic decisions on ideology, in which the effects of networks were much more powerful than those of incentives. One purpose of this chapter is to redress the balance somewhat by providing diverse examples of incentives having clear and identifiable impacts on behaviour. Successful policy making in the twenty-first century requires an understanding of *both* networks and incentives, a point which is illustrated again as we move through the chapter.

Incentives do matter. This is the one great insight into human behaviour which economics provides, an insight which is supported by an enormous amount of empirical evidence.

I should say immediately that this does not mean that free-market, equilibrium economics is correct. This latter sentence is so important that I will repeat it in bold type. **The fact that agents respond to incentives does not mean that free-market, equilibrium economics is correct**. It is not at all necessary to believe in the whole of the standard behavioural paradigm in economics in order to recognise that incentives matter. Indeed, in the centrally planned economies of the old Soviet bloc, incentives could take non-monetary forms such as social acclaim for meeting the production norm, or for being awarded a medal as a Socialist Hero of Labour.

We will see during the course of the chapter that the use of incentives to achieve aims or targets, perhaps changing tax rates or giving out subsidies or medals, is by no means a panacea for the policy maker. This is the case even when network effects are either weak or absent more or less altogether. Humans are inventive, innovative, and they may very well respond to changes in incentives in ways which are very hard to anticipate.

So incentives work only 'Up to a point, Lord Copper', as the editor of the *Daily Beast* in Evelyn Waugh's novel *Scoop* used to say when his titled proprietor asserted something which was at best only partly true and was often unequivocally wrong.

Sometimes, changing incentives does work out more or less as expected. This is certainly true in a qualitative sense, even if the exact quantitative predictions are not borne out. If Coca-Cola, say, puts the price of its products up and nothing else changes at the same time, to state that the sales of Pepsi will probably go up is perhaps merely stating the obvious. Agents who like this sort of fizzy drink are given an incentive to buy less Coca-Cola: its price has gone up. But incentives have been used in less expected ways, sometimes by the most unexpected people.

For example in 2003 Ken Livingstone, as mayor of London, introduced the 'congestion charge', a tax on vehicles entering central London during the day, in an effort to solve the problem of traffic congestion. Even the mayor's worst enemies could scarcely accuse him of being a gung-ho free-market economist. His political stance has always been firmly on the left.

Nevertheless, in a politically bold move, Livingstone attempted to deal with the traffic problem in a major world city by the use of incentives. There was great uncertainty in advance, which persisted even during the early months of the actual operation of the scheme, about how agents – motorists in this case – would respond. Many different forecasts were made. But the tax has worked *qualitatively* exactly as one would expect. Traffic flows into Central London are lower than they would have been without this charge. In other words, faced with an additional cost of driving into central London, some motorists have decided either to reduce their visits to the area, or to use alternative means of transport.

Livingstone made use of the reaction of agents to incentives to achieve a desirable social goal. It does not mean he had become a convert to the political ideology of Mrs Thatcher. Nor does it necessarily mean that motorists carried out a rational analysis of the costs and benefits of the scheme. But it worked.

Much more generally, the economics of the mainstream works up to a point exactly *because* it incorporates this fundamental insight into human behaviour, that changes to incentives alter it. But such insight is perceived as through a glass darkly. Except in certain limited circumstances, the rest of its theoretical constructs are at best shaky and often plain wrong. The core model of standard economics assumes that an agent gathers all the available information relevant to a decision, and is then able to process it in a way which enables the agent to arrive at the very best decision possible, given the tastes and preferences of the agent. These latter are assumed to be fixed and cannot be influenced by what other agents do. All theories are approximations to reality. The question is always: how good are the approximations?

Policy based on the use of incentives is mistrusted by many people, precisely because it has the image of being derived from the highly mathematical abstractions of economic theory. So, before going on to give examples of unintended consequences of changes in incentives, it is worth considering briefly whether the use of abstraction and maths can be justified in analysing social and economic problems. We are, after all, dealing with human behaviour.

I have no problem at all with abstraction, though I am mindful of the fact that this needs to be justified. Many scientific theories are highly abstract, far removed from everyday life. But this abstract quality is the very nature of the beast. From the myriad complicated details which surround many situations in reality, we are trying to distil a few key factors and to describe how their interactions help us to understand what is going on. Ideally, we would like this theoretical account not just to shed light on one particular problem, but to be capable of generalisation across many situations.

Ultimately of course, any theory, if it is to be regarded as being truly scientific, has to be tested by empirical evidence. It must be judged not by its abstract beauty, but by its ability to explain messy reality. This is how, for example, we are able to dismiss astrology as not being a science. For a number of years at the start of my career I was an economic forecaster, attempting to predict the future course of the British economy. Despite being equipped with the latest red-hot developments in both economic and statistical theory, the ability to achieve any degree of systematic accuracy proved elusive. Growing disillusioned with the whole process, for a short time I carried out a comparison between the accuracy of my macroeconomic forecasts and those of my daily horoscope. If anything, the latter had the edge!

But theoretical abstraction is both desirable and necessary for any sort of progress to be made in understanding the world, whether in the natural, biological or social sciences. So the abstract nature of much economic theory does not of itself make it a legitimate object of criticism. Even if the theory is misleading, or even plain wrong in many situations, this is not because of its abstract nature. It is because the assumptions, the simplifications which are needed to have any sort of theory, are not supported by the evidence.

*

It is rather harder to justify the use of mathematics in economics, especially the specific sort favoured by economists. Maths is pervasive in economics. It is an integral part of the self-image of the discipline. And it serves as a very distinct barrier to entry, a very clear 'Keep Out!' message to anyone who does not feel comfortable in this area. Given its importance, a fairly lengthy detour is warranted before we move back to an explicit discussion of incentives, the main theme of the chapter.

Maths can in fact be very useful, provided that we think of it as just a tool. Economists often make clever maths an end in itself, and in doing so overlook the fact that we are trying to understand and explain what happens in the real world. Elegant maths also often leads economists to make the mistake of confusing the model with reality. It is a tool which can assist logical thinking. It's like another language. It can help us find our way around and serve as a medium of communication amongst people discussing the same subject.

Here is a cautionary tale of how maths has become fetishised at the very highest levels of the discipline of economics. A friend of mine teaches economics at the University of Cambridge in England. Fairly recently, she had a first-year student who was very good indeed at maths. So much so that he complained there simply was not enough of it in his course. For his second year, he was sent on an exchange to the other Cambridge, to the Massachusetts Institute of Technology. Emails of an increasingly desperate nature began to whizz back to my friend across the Atlantic. The final one said simply: 'Help! Please let me back home. There isn't any economics in this course. It's *all* maths.'

Things are not quite as bad as that in most places, but the use of maths has become pervasive in economics. Just for the record, at the right time and amongst consenting adults, I, too, use maths extensively, albeit of a different kind from that which pervades economics. You can tell I am an economist myself when I say, on the one hand there are good reasons for the use of maths in economics, and on the other hand there are bad ones. So far, mainly the bad ones have prevailed.

It would not matter very much if economics was not taken so seriously by policy makers. Hardly anyone bothers about some of the lunacies in literary theory, for example. But economics matters. Why is it that maths came to be so pervasive in economics, when so much was achieved without it? The worst reason is that the use of maths makes economists feel that they are proper scientists. They suffer from deep physics-envy. Ironically, economists seem to envy the classical physics of a century and more ago. In many ways, physics itself has moved on to incorporate network-based ideas.

Physicists have to use maths – try doing quantum physics in words. And they are real scientists, who really have explained how lots of things really do work. So if we use maths, that makes us real scientists, does it not? The logical error in this last sentence is pretty obvious. But it does not stop the inner glow of satisfaction that most economists feel when they cover the page in mathematical symbols.

There is a more serious and more damaging reason why maths, or at least a particular kind of maths, is used in economics. This is inextricably linked with the concept of Rational Economic Man. In essence, as noted in the previous chapter, economics is a theory about how individuals behave. And in the standard theory, it is not just that people are assumed to be self-interested. Rational Economic Man acts like some sort of super-computer, always gathering every single bit of information which is relevant to a decision, and then making the best possible decision out of all the available options. Not just a good decision, or even a very good one, but the best. The 'optimal' decision.

Now there is a whole branch of maths devoted to 'optimal' solutions. This is differential calculus, which many readers will have come across at school. It is the ideal tool for a theory which says that individuals behave in a way which is optimal for them, given their tastes and preferences. So if you eat junk food and weigh 300 pounds as a result, or if you drink heavily and destroy your liver, or if you smoke and get cancer, if you riot when the police open fire, that is your choice. You must have been making what you believed to be the best possible lifestyle choice for you, and calculus can prove this.

This is still the basis for a lot of the economics which is taught today. Yet, paradoxically, it has been precisely the use of maths within economics itself which has exposed fundamental problems at the very heart of the model of the Rational Economic Man theory of behaviour.

Working out the full implications of these behavioural postulates proved an exceptionally demanding scientific task, which took a century to complete. By the mid-1970s, this programme of research was eventually finalised. There is nothing left to discover. It is a marvellous intellectual construct, but it turns out to be a scientifically empty box. It has no testable implications. In other words, there is no empirical test we can use with which the theory could be refuted. Such tests might be very hard to devise, but any true science has to be capable of being refuted empirically.

*

We might pause and offer some postulates which might be capable of being refuted by evidence. For example the familiar diagrams of basic Economics 1.01 show downward-sloping demand curves. This simply means that a lower amount of a product is demanded if its price goes up. A higher price means less sales by volume, and if we plot such a relationship in a simple chart, the relationship between sales and price will slope downwards. Figure 5.2, on page 151, illustrates the point. But we cannot deduce logically from the theory of Rational Economic Man behaviour that this key statement, widely used by economists, is true.

This result was established through pages of intricate maths. A translation into English could be carried out, but a full explanation would take many chapters. However, a useful insight into the proposition that we cannot deduce theoretically that market demand curves slope downwards, even if the demand curves for every single agent do slope down, is as follows. Suppose the price of a product is increased. The volume of sales will go down. The value, which is just price multiplied by quantity, may either rise or fall depending on how much the volume changes compared to the increase in price. If a 10 per cent price increase only reduces volume sales by 1 per cent, the value of sales will rise, but if it cuts volume by 20 per cent, value will fall as well. Either way, the income of the company making the product is changed. If the market for the product is tiny compared to the economy as a whole, we can reasonably stop our analysis of the implications of the price rise here.

But suppose we are thinking about the demand for labour, about how many workers firms want to employ. This market – or collection of markets – is typically enormous relative to any national economy. A persistent theme in economic discourse, and indeed policy, is the need to 'price people back into work'. In other words, to reduce wages so that more people are employed. A cynic might note in passing that the argument is usually applied to less skilled people, and few in the financial services sector have been suggesting that bankers take a salary cut in order to price them back into work after the financial crisis. However, this is indeed a point made in passing.

Suppose further that, by some means, a government succeeded

in cutting wages to increase the demand for labour. The potential problem here is that wages are not just the 'price' of employing someone to the company, they represent spending power across the whole range of goods and services. So a reduction in the price of labour might lead to *fewer* people being employed because consumption by the workers, the total amount they spend, may decline too. On the one hand, labour has become cheaper. On the other, workers have less to spend throughout the economy as a whole, so the demand for many products may fall, and fewer workers are needed to produce them. Of course, there could be an offsetting effect if firms spent any increase in profits resulting from the wage cut. This account, however, does give some insight into why it is not possible theoretically to prove that 'demand curves slope downwards'.

Despite the theoretical indeterminacy of the core model of conventional economics on this point, the idea that labour is too expensive, that it should be priced back into work, that real wages should be reduced, was a key ideological theme of the 1990s and 2000s in many Western countries.

Of course, the reality is that if the price of a product or service is increased then usually, but not always, its sales fall. In practice, and certainly when added up across any particular company, salaries cannot be significantly higher for a long period of time than the value of the contribution of the workforce. If they are, the firm will eventually fail. But these are empirical observations, which seem generally valid but which do not obtain on every occasion. The point about the theoretical model is that even if we observed the opposite, that, say, when the price of a product rises its sales increase, this would not be a refutation of the theory, because the theory allows the relationship between price and sales to take any shape whatsoever.

So, paradoxically, the use of maths in economic theory, and

more precisely the type of maths preferred by economists themselves, has provided some very powerful results which do much to undermine many of the policy-related claims it makes.

*

In practice, of course, returning directly to the main topic of the chapter, incentives often matter. To stress again, this statement does not necessarily imply that the theory of Rational Economic Man is correct. Further, when we speak of 'incentives', the usual concepts associated with the word are things like pay and prices. You may be offered a bonus at work in order to try and incentivise you, either to work hard or to stay loyal. A government may increase tax on fuel, say, to try to get people to use less of it, to respond to the negative incentive of the higher price. Yet as we have seen, incentives may often appear in an unconventional form, such as the 'price' of being burned to death.

It is not just that incentives may appear in odd or unexpected guises. Their effects may be hard to anticipate. This does not mean that they are not working at all. Nor does it mean that we have simply just not done enough careful statistical analysis of behaviour to be able to say that if, for example, we put the price of Coca-Cola up by 10p or 10 cents, sales will fall by x or y per cent. Rather, it can mean that agents *do* respond to changes in incentives, but the ways in which they respond may not be anticipated by the policy maker. Or it can mean that the incentives work in the way they were intended to, but that the wider consequences of this are not foreseen.

On the latter point, a few years ago, my wife telephoned to make an appointment with a doctor at our local National Health Service surgery. It was not urgent. Previously, she had been able to make such an appointment at her convenience several days in advance. But the rules had changed. Appointments could now only be made on the same day that the request was made. The government had brought in a target that a high percentage of patients had to be seen on the same day that they contacted the doctor. On the face of it, a perfectly desirable aim. Doctors received payments which were conditional on the target being met, so they were incentivised to do so.

But this led to great inconvenience. Working people cannot always guarantee to be free on any particular day, and even when they can, others may get in before them and take the slots. When she finally managed to get to see the doctor, many fruitless phone calls and over a week later, she raised this policy change with him. The doctor was most apologetic. It was not his fault. His funding depended in part on him meeting the government's new target. The doctor was responding to incentives in a perfectly sensible way from his point of view. The unintended consequence was that his unfortunate patients experienced considerable inconvenience in no longer being able to make appointments to suit their schedules.

The limitations of what we might term the 'clever regulator' approach to policy, using incentives to achieve specific targets, were also present during the UN Climate Change Conference in Copenhagen in 2009. This time, the authorities failed to grasp how agents might respond innovatively and imaginatively to the incentives put in place. The city's mayor, Ritt Bjerregaard, and the city council wanted to curb prostitution during the conference. They sent postcards to hotels and delegates to the conference urging them not to patronise the city's sex workers. The delegates were exhorted to 'Be sustainable – don't buy sex'. The hotels themselves were admonished: 'Dear hotel owner, we would like to urge you not to arrange contacts between hotel guests and prostitutes'. Here was a clear set of incentives placed in front of agents. The incentives were perhaps particularly strong for the hotels, for it is not in the interests of service providers such as these to incur the potential wrath of the local authority, equipped as it is with all kinds of powers which can make their lives difficult.

The response of the prostitutes shows how inventive humans can be. Members of the Sex Workers Interest Group simply offered free sex to anyone who could produce both their delegate credentials to the UN conference and one of the notices sent out by the mayor. Their incentive to maintain their business was sufficiently strong for them to introduce this innovative marketing arrangement. The choice they faced was between a much reduced income if the mayor's strategy was complied with, and a normal income reduced by the occasional free service.

A much more detailed example of unintended consequences, or, more precisely, consequences which are very hard to foresee because of the innovative responses of agents, is as follows. Jérôme Adda and Francesca Cornaglia of University College London published a study in 2006 in the top-ranking *American Economic Review*. The potentially detrimental effect of nicotine on smokers' health is well established. In recent decades, most Western governments have attempted to reduce cigarette consumption, and an important way of trying to achieve this aim has been by increasing excise duties – taxes – on cigarettes to make them more expensive.

The policies have undoubtedly been successful. A number of detailed academic studies have shown a distinct correlation between higher prices and reduced cigarette consumption. The initial impact of a tax increase tends to be diluted over time because of the addictive nature of the product, but it nevertheless persists.

In this context, we might usefully note that social networks have reinforced the impact of incentives, and in particular by their influence in persuading people to stop smoking altogether. The Framingham Heart Study is a unique database, monitoring the health of individuals over many decades in the eponymous town in Massachusetts. It is a rich source for medical research. But it also provides material for social scientists. Unusually for such medical surveys, the study contains information not just on the individuals but on their family and friends.

Nicholas Christakis and James Fowler of Harvard University analysed the data from a network perspective, publishing their findings in the *New England Journal of Medicine* in 2008. Their results were striking. The cessation of smoking by a co-worker in a small company decreased a person's chances of smoking by 34 per cent. If a friend gave up, the person was 36 per cent less likely to smoke, and the chances were 59 per cent less if a spouse stopped smoking. Their study does not identify the separate impact of incentives on individuals, such as price increase or the public information provided on the health risks of smoking. But once an individual makes the decision to stop, for whatever reason, the effect is potentially transmitted through his or her social networks – family, friends, work colleagues – to others, who might stop simply because of the example which has been set to them. So networks can operate *with* incentives, to reinforce and magnify the initial impact of the latter.

To return, however, to Adda and Cornaglia and the potential difficulties of anticipating the effects of changes in incentives. Their article is based on the so-called 'rational theory of addiction'. Full of heavy-duty maths, it is replete with phrases such as 'we assume a quadratic utility function' and 'the proof requires a second-order Taylor approximation'. But, to reflect on points made earlier in the chapter, we really do not need the assumption of rational behaviour at all. The empirical results of the study, based upon careful statistical analysis of the data, are clear.

They used the American National Health and Nutrition Examination Survey, a database of some 20,000 people across the United States, which contains information on the number of cigarettes smoked and their nicotine, tar and carbon monoxide concentration. Tax rates on cigarettes vary across states, providing plenty of variation with which to estimate their impact on behaviour. In common with many other studies, Adda and Cornaglia found that the higher the tax rate, the fewer cigarettes were smoked. So far, good and entirely expected news for the health-promoting policy maker. But they discovered that higher tax rates led smokers to switch to brands with a higher tar and nicotine yield. This was not in itself a novel finding, though it increased the credibility of the two previous research papers which had previously reported it. A large number of papers had been written on the impact of taxes and prices on the number of cigarettes smoked, but only two on this switching behaviour, so it was valuable confirmation of this effect, though nonetheless worrying.

The real originality of the research was the discovery that smokers also increased the intensity of their smoking by extracting more nicotine per cigarette, regardless of the brand which was consumed. Smokers become more inclined to smoke the cigarette right to the end, behaviour which not only increases tar and nicotine consumption, but also leads the smoker to inhale more dangerous chemicals, which in turn has been shown to cause cancer deeper into the lung. So, yes, higher taxes do reduce the sales of cigarettes. Incentives work as expected. But at the same time, smokers compensate by both switching to brands containing more tar and nicotine, and by consuming cigarettes in ways which are more dangerous to their health.

So, traffic in central London, the response of professional doctors to changes in payment structures, the supply of sexual services, nicotine consumption – a disparate range of circumstances in which incentives have altered behaviour. Sometimes in ways which the policy maker did not foresee and did not, in hindsight, desire. But incentives undoubtedly mattered.

Network effects have also been demonstrated to be important, reinforcing the impact of incentives, in at least one of these examples. And in general, as we saw in the opening chapter, in most real-world social and economic situations, we need to understand the potentially subtle and powerful interplay between the effects of incentives and the effects of networks.

*

So far in this chapter we have focused deliberately on incentives, on some of the strengths and weaknesses of the traditional tool of policy makers. It is time for a shift of gear. Time to discuss at some length an important policy area where both network effects and incentives are at work.

The complex relationship between incentives and networks to which I refer is that within the criminal justice system. A perennial question for policy makers is: does prison work? It is at this point that we put on our detached philosopher's hat and ask in turn what precisely this question means.

Even in the United States, where the rate of incarceration per 100,000 inhabitants is five or six times the average in the rest of the developed world, it is hard to get sent to prison. There are occasional highly publicised stories in which individuals leading hitherto blameless lives suddenly in a fit of rage murder their spouse, or even go on a killing spree. But the vast majority of people who get sent to prison have already had fairly extensive experience of crime and the criminal justice system. They are steeped in the culture of crime. Superb television series such as *The Sopranos* or *The Wire* hold our attention through the quality of their scripts and acting. But they also succeed because they are realistic. Almost like Dante's Circles of Hell, there are concentric rings of individuals, from the hard-core gang leaders out through people only peripherally engaged with them. But they are all engaged with the process of crime. And not surprisingly, once they become engaged in this way through their social networks, some of them end up in prison.

One thing we have observed empirically about crime is that once a person has been in prison, he (or, far less frequently, she) is very likely to commit a crime again. Recidivism rates are high, even though a vast range of policies have been tried in an attempt to get the rate down. In this sense, prison does not work.

Despite stories in the popular press about how criminals live a life of luxury in jail, in reality a prison term remains an unpleasant experience for most of those incarcerated. Apart from the loss of liberty, crime within prisons is often rampant, and many inmates live in fear of physical violence. Tom Wolfe's description in *A Man in Full* of the Californian prison in which one of the book's more sympathetic characters, Conrad Hensley, is incarcerated is awful, brutal – and entirely accurate. Yet the experience seems to provide scant deterrence against reoffending. Once someone is sent to prison, the influence of social networks on individual behaviour appears to dominate that of incentives. The social and cultural milieus of hard-core criminals, the social networks in which they are embedded, are ones in which crime is itself the norm.

A key fact is that most crime is committed by young men possessing little money or intelligence and few skills. And there does appear to be something inherently implausible about the idea that such individuals assess all the available information and choose the 'optimal' decision when they are contemplating breaking into a car or thinking about punching someone in a bar.

The standard response by economists to such points is to invoke the 'as if' argument. In other words, whilst it may not appear that agents go through the process of finding optimal decisions, they behave 'as if' they do. There are layers of subtleties to this argument which need not delay us. But even the simple statement of the point is not as foolish as it might first appear. Very few of us know how to solve the difficult non-linear differential equations which describe the flight of a thrown ball, yet most of us can predict its path well enough to catch one. It is 'as if' we had done the maths.

But, to repeat the point made at the start of the chapter, we do not need to invoke the idea that agents are responding in some optimal sense to incentives. People may be short-sighted in terms of the decisions they make, they may consistently make decisions whose outcomes go against their own self-interest. Yet they are still changing their behaviour in response to changes in incentives.

This is a point which most economists find hard to accept. Surely, the mainstream 'rational' agent argument goes, people do not necessarily always make the optimal choice, but rather over time they gradually learn to avoid decisions which are not in their own interests. This raises an issue of great importance to which the whole of the next chapter is devoted. In essence, in many situations, the best choice can *never* be identified, even after the event, no matter how smart we may be.

For now, however, in the spirit of empiricism, we simply note that, for most people, crime does not pay. Most of the young men who spend their days steeped in petty crime would actually be better off in straight money terms in low-paid legitimate employment. The proceeds from most crimes are very small. Criminals often act impulsively, paying less regard to the potential costs to them of committing a crime than the objective evidence indicates they should. For example, as known criminals in a locality, they have to endure the stress of frequent visits from the police, their own records making them natural suspects. So the benefits from crime are not as high as those from a regular job, and the costs – the stress of being known criminals, the court appearances, the fines, the frequent prison sentences – are much higher. Yet individuals persistently choose to follow a criminal life. In part, this can be explained by the culture in which they become involved, the social network of crime. But in part it can only be said that they are making a constant stream of decisions which, from the point of view of economic theory, are irrational, which go against their own self-interest.

However, this certainly does not mean that criminals fail to respond to incentives. True, they make decisions which, in terms of their own self-interest, are often not very sensible. True, they do not necessarily respond exactly along the lines of the theory of Rational Economic Man. But their behaviour can nevertheless be influenced by the various positive and negative incentives which criminals face.

An example of positive incentives occurred in April 1999, when Britain introduced for the first time a minimum wage, which provided pay increases for a large number of low-paid workers. Two London-based economists, Kirstine Hansen and Steve Machin, carried out a careful and very sophisticated statistical analysis of its impact across the forty-three police-force areas of the UK. They concluded unequivocally that 'altering wage incentives can affect crime and therefore that there exists a link between crime and the low wage labour market'. By making the alternative option of regular employment, albeit at the minimum wage, more lucrative, some potential criminals were incentivised to choose this rather than to 'earn' their living from crime. This does not mean that they had suddenly become rational agents in the economic sense of the term, able to assess costs and benefits more effectively. It simply means that incentives had changed and, however imperfectly, some agents responded.

*

Steve Levitt is famous for his blockbuster book *Freakonomics*. But he is also an extremely distinguished economist, winner in 2003 of the John Bates Clark Medal awarded to 'that American economist under the age of forty who is adjudged to have made a significant contribution to economic thought and knowledge'. One of his areas of interest is crime. And the discussion of why crime has fallen in America in his book is based in turn on an article he wrote in the prestigious *Journal of Economic Perspectives*, which in turn is based on a large number of technical academic articles.

One of his conclusions has struck a notable chord with many people, quite possibly because of the rather startling and unexpected nature of the topic: that one reason for crime falling sharply is a rise in the number of abortions. As noted, most crime is committed by poor, unskilled young men, and more abortions in their social group means that there are fewer of them around to commit crime.

But Levitt also concludes that prison is in part responsible for the dramatic reductions in crime, a finding often conveniently forgotten. Both Britain and America saw large increases in the prison population starting around twenty years ago, and in both countries there have been sharp subsequent falls in crime. Of course, simple correlation such as this does not prove causation, but Levitt's conclusions are based upon highly sophisticated statistical studies which readily encompass such issues.

One obvious factor is that people in prison cannot commit further crimes – at least against society in general. So, by simple arithmetic, a bigger prison population means smaller crime figures. But the more important impact arises from the deterrent effect, not on those who are actually serving sentences, but on those at liberty who are contemplating breaking the law.

A key step seems to be moving from a situation in which a young man has not committed a crime, to one in which he has. Although most crime is committed by poor, unskilled men, most such individuals remain law-abiding citizens. They will probably know who the criminals are in their neighbourhood, and may even socialise with them. But the main influence of their particular social networks, the main impact on what they regard as normal behaviour, remains people like themselves who live their lives within the law.

Of course, carrying out a single criminal act does not immediately lead to the destruction of an individual's existing social networks and to his re-embedding into a group of hardened career criminals. But it may begin to alter these relationships.

An elusive goal for criminologists is to identify individuals who are more likely to become prolific criminals (at some point in their lives) than others. The group of prolific criminals is usually thought to be some 5 or 10 per cent of the total population of offenders. Some progress has been made. Being born into a family where most members are criminals increases this probability substantially. And it is now clear that boys raised by single-parent, never-married mothers also exhibit a higher probability of being involved in crime than others with different family backgrounds. I should stress that it is not the case that boys from such backgrounds automatically become criminals. Indeed, most grow up to be perfectly respectable members of society. Nonetheless, the probability of them turning to crime is distinctly higher than it is for the population of boys as a whole, even taking into account factors such as family income. In general, the vast majority of offenders share the characteristics of the persistent offenders, making prior identification very difficult. Many such offenders abandon crime during their twenties and become productive, taxpaying citizens.

It is, of course, neither practical nor acceptable to incarcerate boys from criminal families as soon as they reach puberty, still less every boy from a poor, single-parent family. Could we not instead attempt to identify the much smaller number of those who are likely to commit large numbers of crimes and devote resources diverting them from such a path before it is too late?

If we could do so, there would be a double impact: first, fewer criminals would mean fewer crimes; second, the influence of criminality as a social norm amongst their peers would be weakened, since individuals known to have committed large numbers of crimes undoubtedly attract attention and gain influence in such social circles.

*

Surprisingly little systematic work has been done on the number of crimes committed by individuals, but there are two well-established databases which record criminality amongst a group of individuals over time. The first, the Cambridge Study in Delinquent Development, is a prospective longitudinal survey of 411 males in a working-class area of north London. Data collection began in 1961–2. The second, the Pittsburgh Youth Study, began in 1986 with a random sample of boys in the first, fourth, and seventh grades of the Pittsburgh public school system. The sample contains approximately 500 boys at each grade level, for a total of 1,517 boys.

The Cambridge data relates to the number of convictions for each boy over a period spanning the mid-1960s and 1970s. The Pittsburgh data describes self-reported acts of delinquency over short time intervals beginning in the late 1980s. In other words, the studies differ both in their time coverage and in the fact that the Cambridge study is based on convictions whilst the Pittsburgh one utilises self-reporting.

Despite these differences, there is a remarkable similarity between the two in the statistical distribution of the number of crimes committed. The 'statistical distribution' in this context describes how many individuals in each database commit (or record) zero crime, how many commit just one, how many commit two, and so on.*

There are two striking features of the results. First, a much better description of the number of crimes committed by individuals is given if we segment the number into two separate groups than if we analyse them all together. Specifically, the groups are 'the numbers who commit zero crimes' and 'the numbers who commit any crime'. In other words, the description of the data when the number of boys committing or reporting zero crimes are excluded is different from that when they are included.

Second, once this distinction is made, there is no 'typical' number of crimes which an individual commits. Once a boy has moved from committing no crime to committing just one crime, the scale of his resultant career in crime could turn out to be small, medium or large. Moreover, the number of crimes which any individual does in fact commit can be thought of as the outcome of a purely random process.

We see again, incidentally, the concept of 'robust and fragile'

---

* The actual analysis relies on a number of mathematical concepts which would take considerable time to describe in words. For those interested in the details, I have published the analysis as 'Scaling Behaviour in the Number of Criminal Acts Committed by Individuals', *Journal of Statistical Mechanics: Theory and Experiment*, July 2004. It may be thought unusual that a statistical physics journal would be interested in this analysis, but the statistical distribution which is identified is one of general interest to this particular research community.

networks introduced in the opening chapter, albeit in a slightly different guise. Here we have a network, in this case a population of young men, living on the same public housing scheme perhaps, who have not yet committed a crime. For whatever reason, one of them carries out a criminal act. Most of the time, he will never go on to commit more than a handful of crimes. Occasionally, he will graduate to a life involving numerous criminal acts spread over a period of years. The network is robust in the sense that most of the people in it carry out either no crimes at all or just a small number. And it is fragile because a small number do go on to be career criminals.

These abstract concepts have two important practical implications. First, the fact that the number of crimes committed by an individual is compatible with the outcome of a purely random process means that it is not possible to identify in advance, once a crime has been committed, how many crimes that individual will go on to commit. So we cannot hope to target *in advance* those boys who will have a highly prolific career in crime, and who may therefore exercise a strong influence over the behaviour of their peers. We may, as discussed above, be able to go some way in identifying those who are more likely to make the first crucial step from zero to one crime, but we cannot then go on to separate those who will commit many more crimes from those whose criminal career will involve only a small number.

The second is that the crucial step is indeed to make the transition from being law abiding to carrying out the first criminal act. In terms of the numbers of individuals committing different numbers of crimes, more commit just one crime than commit two, more commit two than three, and so on. But the largest and most important distinction by far is between zero and one.

Here is where we see an interplay between incentives and networks. Once a young man makes the initial transition to crime, his perception of himself starts to alter, as does the perception others have of him. He becomes potentially less acceptable to the members of his various social networks who do not commit crime, and, conversely, more in tune with the social values of those who do. He may himself accelerate the process of potential change, depending on how much his own self-image is altered as a result of his actions. His identity changes. Once a young man has carried out a few crimes, he is by no means predestined to become a career criminal. Indeed, most do not: the effect of the non-criminal social networks in which he has been involved as a non-criminal often draw a young man back into a law-abiding life.

Incentives, whether positive or negative, may influence either the crucial initial decision to commit the first crime, or, later, the decision to withdraw from a life of crime. But the influence of peer pressure, peer acceptance, the gradual increase in the relative importance of copying or imitative behaviour compared to that of incentives, increases the more a young man associates with criminals, and there is a chance that a criminal career has been born.

It is this which provides the intellectual basis for successful policies of containing crime. It is the positive use of networks of attitudes amongst the 'at risk' group, the search for the triggers which will generate positive linking across these networks, which will keep crime down. There is no check list of policies, each 'rationally' evaluated by teams of economists, which will guarantee success. Rather, it is the much more subtle concepts of social norms, of what constitutes reasonable behaviour in the relevant peer groups, which is the key. This is hard to achieve, not least because there is no readily specified tick-box approach to the problem. But positive linking has the potential to create massive changes for the better.

Yet a nagging question runs through this whole discussion of crime. Most criminals have backgrounds of poverty, they have low levels of conventional skills, and are often barely literate or numerate. It seems implausible that they behave as 'rational' economic agents, gathering information and meticulously processing it in order to arrive at the best possible decision, given their own tastes and preferences. Indeed, we have argued that this is *not* how we need to see them as behaving. Agents can still react to incentives even though they are not following the behavioural precepts of conventional economic theory.

The question is: does economics have anything to say about behavioural patterns which do not square with its core theoretical assumptions? Do we simply dismiss such behaviour as 'irrational', or is there something more useful we can say?

The concept of the rational agent does indeed remain very much alive and well within economics. But, as it happens, in recent decades, a whole new empirically driven field has developed within the subject itself, one which poses challenges to the mainstream view of how the world operates. This is known as 'behavioural economics', and it is to this which we now turn.

3

The Shoulders of Giants: Simon and Keynes

An innocuous pastime of sports fans is to discuss and debate an 'All-Time Team', the best players of all time, whether in the sport as a whole, be it soccer, basketball or whatever, or for the team they support.

One person who is at or very near the top of both my own and many other people's lists of the greatest ever team of social scientists is Herbert Simon. Born in 1916 to parents who moved to America at the start of the twentieth century, Simon's initial education and career was at the University of Chicago. In 1949 he became Professor of Industrial Management at Carnegie Mellon, and continued to teach in various departments until his death in 2001. He was awarded the most prestigious prizes in several disciplines. He received the Turing Award, named after the great Alan Turing, the father of modern computers, in 1975 for his contributions to artificial intelligence and the psychology of human cognition, and in 1978 he won the Nobel Prize in economics 'for his pioneering research into the decision-making process within economic organisations'. In 1993 the American Psychological Association conferred on him their Award for Outstanding Lifetime Contributions to Psychology.

He carried out outstanding original research in cognitive psychology, cognitive science, computer science, public administration, economics, management, the philosophy of science, sociology and political science. Simon often anticipated developments in a particular field years, and sometimes decades, ahead of the mainstream. In 1957 he predicted that computers would outplay the most proficient humans at chess within ten years. In this case he was wrong, but only on his time scale, for this did not happen until the 1990s. But remember that this was at a time when computing was in its infancy, when machines the size of a small house were nowhere near as powerful as the most basic laptop, or even smartphone, of today, and ideas such as this were the stuff of science fiction.

Perhaps his most significant intellectual contribution was in creating virtually single-handedly the field of what is today known as behavioural economics. Unlike most economists, certainly then and still to a large extent today, Simon took an active interest in how firms actually behaved. Companies are the foundation of the prosperity of the developed economies, and they are by a very considerable margin the most successful organisational innovation in the economic world over the past 200 years.

Simon's exceptionally innovative work on behavioural economics was carried out in the 1950s and, as we shall see, its main message is still very far from being accepted by the mainstream economics profession. We might reasonably ask, if his theories are as brilliant as I am painting them to be, why are these now not the accepted wisdom in economics? As we will shortly see, much of his work has indeed been incorporated in various ways, but his key, revolutionary message has been safely neutered by the mainstream. There are many reasons for this, but economics has a bad track record of either not rejecting its core theories when they are brought into serious doubt, or not accepting scientifically superior theories. So before examining Simon's theories, it is useful to spend a bit of time examining a key aspect of firm behaviour in economic theory, and showing how this had already been rejected empirically when Simon was writing, but that economists persisted with their incorrect assumptions nevertheless.

In much of economic theory, size is not just irrelevant but a definite handicap. A concept known as 'diminishing returns' prevails, so that as more labour and more capital are used in the process of producing any particular good or service, the extra output obtained from each additional unit inputted into the process eventually falls. This theoretical assumption is not made on the basis of empirical evidence. It is made because it makes the maths, hard enough as they are, much more tractable, easier to handle analytically. But in the real world, increasing returns are widespread. Companies often gain distinct advantages through utilising economies of scope and scale in their operations. As they get bigger, unit costs often fall, not rise.

Ironically, at the very same time that the concept of diminishing marginal returns was capturing the academic discipline of economics, the United States was moving towards world economic dominance by exploiting the unprecedented and massive increasing returns to scale of production and distribution which its rapidly expanding economy permitted. In other words, by taking advantage of the benefits of being big.

A large number of the companies which were to become household names in the United States in the twentieth century grew enormously and established their market strengths in the final decades of the nineteenth. Quaker Oats, Campbell's Soup, Heinz, Procter & Gamble, Schlitz and Anheuser Brewing, Eastman Kodak, American Telephone and Telegraph, Singer, Westinghouse, Union Carbide – all these are examples of companies which took advantage of increasing returns in production and distribution at that time to establish themselves on a national, and in some cases international, scale.

In 1870 the population of America was 39 million, not much more than that of Britain at 31 million. American income per head of the population was around 80 per cent of the British level, which was then the highest in the world. The combination of a larger population and a lower income per head meant that the size of the American domestic market was virtually identical to that of the British.

By the onset of the First World War, this had changed dramatically. America had overtaken Britain as the leading economy in terms of income per head. From being 20 per cent below the British figure in 1870, America was by then 20 per cent above. And whilst the population of Britain had grown by only 14 million over this period, in America the growth was 58 million. Indeed, the growth in the American population was of itself much bigger than the total size of Britain's population.

From a position of equality in 1870, by 1913 the American domestic market was over two and a half times that of its main European rival. Such a market was of a size entirely without precedent in world history. It offered tremendous opportunities for the exploitation of increasing returns to scale. Companies during this period found, contrary to the precepts of marginal economics, of which they were blissfully ignorant, that the bigger the scale of operations, the more could be produced, and the more profit could be made from the additional marginal unit of production.

Advances in technology made these leaps in economic progress possible, which in turn provided the finances not just for further investment in plant and machinery but for yet more research and development. Such positive feedback placed the Western economies, and particularly that of America, on a virtuous circle of growth.

So by the time Simon began his research in the 1940s, giant corporations had been in existence for half a century. The assump-

THE SHOULDERS OF GIANTS: SIMON AND KEYNES

tion in economic theory of diminishing returns in the process of production in these outfits had simply not been not borne out in practice. But, as already noted, economists continued to work with such assumptions in the core models of their theory.*

Simon's interest was in the validity of another concept, arguably even closer to the very core of economic theory, namely that agents – whether individuals, firms or governments – behave in a so-called 'rational' way. How did firms really behave, how did they actually make decisions? Remember that his initial Chair at Carnegie Mellon was not in economics, but in industrial management.

He published his reflections over the years on these matters in 1955 in a remarkable article in the *Quarterly Journal of Economics*, entitled 'A Behavioral Model of Rational Choice'. The article itself is theoretical, but throughout the paper Simon makes explicit the fact that his choices of assumptions are based upon what he considers to be empirical evidence which is both sound and extensive. This truly brilliant article, as already noted the basis for the whole field of behavioural economics, is worth quoting at some length.

Simon begins the paper with what by now will be familiar material:

Traditional economic theory postulates an 'economic man' who, in the course of being 'economic', is also 'rational'. This

* Allyn Young, a brilliant American economist who died relatively early through influenza, had illustrated the effects of the much more realistic assumption of increasing returns in an article in 1928 which was at least fifty years ahead of its time. Young had been head of the economics department at Stanford, had turned down the headship at Chicago, and held a chair at LSE when he died. So his work was very well known at the time – well known, but ignored.

man is assumed to have knowledge of the relevant aspects of his environment which, if not absolutely complete, is impressively clear and voluminous. He is assumed also to have a well-organized and stable system of preferences and a skill in computation that enables him to calculate, for the alternative courses of action available to him, which of these will permit him to reach the highest attainable point on his preference scale.

So far, all very relaxing and soothing to economists. But then comes his bombshell:

Recent developments in economics, and in particular in the theory of the business firm, have raised great doubts as to whether this schematized model of economic man provides a suitable foundation on which to erect a theory – whether it be a theory of how firms *do* behave, or how they 'should' rationally behave . . . [T]he task is to replace the global rationality of economic man with a kind of rational behavior which is compatible with the access to information and computational capacities that are actually possessed by organisms, including man, in the kinds of environments in which such organisms exist.

This latter quote essentially defines the research programmes carried out from the 1970s onwards by future Nobel Laureates such as Joe Stiglitz, Daniel Kahneman and Vernon Smith.

There are three distinct strands, to which each of these researchers is linked. First, the consequences for models based on the standard rational agent when either agents in general have incomplete information, or different agents or groups of agents have access to different amounts of information. With their predilection for grand phrases, economists refer to this latter as being a situation of 'asymmetric information'. Stiglitz has worked extensively in this area and is the source of much of its development. The other two strands blossomed into experimental economics and behavioural economics, inextricably linked to Smith and Kahneman, respectively. They overlap to a not inconsiderable degree and are often confused. Both relate to Simon's injunction to base theoretical models on agents which have 'computational capacities that are actually possessed by organisms'. In other words, to place realistic bounds on the ability of people to process the information which they have, regardless of whether it is complete. Again, the jargon phrase used by economists dresses this up as 'bounded rationality'.

The work on incomplete or asymmetrical information has been the easiest for mainstream economics to absorb, so much so that it is not only part of the standard toolkit of economists, but it has exercised powerful and pervasive influence on the conduct of economic policy. The seminal article, following Simon, and possibly the most brilliant single paper in the whole field of asymmetric information, is George Akerlof's 'Market for Lemons', published in the *Quarterly Journal of Economics* in 1970. 'Lemons' here does not refer to the fruit, but is used in the colloquial sense of a purchase that proves inferior to expectations. Akerlof illustrated his theoretical model with the example of the market in used cars, where the seller knows pretty well exactly how good the car actually is, whilst the buyer is less well informed. He deservedly shared the Nobel Prize in 2001 with two others: Michael Spence and Joe Stiglitz.

Stiglitz has become famous beyond the confines of economics for his espousal of what are often regarded as left-liberal positions on a range of important policy matters. The phrase 'left-liberal' does not imply that they are any more or any less correct, it simply describes the political views of many of the non-economists who follow his policy writings avidly. His distinguished work in economics rightly conveys status to his opinions. Fiscal deficits, globalisation, world poverty are all issues on which he has written extensively, and more recently he has supported the idea of the so-called 'Robin Hood' tax on every transaction carried out in financial markets.

Stiglitz is operating in the honourable tradition of political economy. The ultimate purpose of the study of economics is to gain a better understanding of the world, which might enable us to improve the human condition. It is desirable that its leading practitioners engage with policy debate rather than remaining cloistered in academia worrying about the role of the representative, rational agent in dynamic stochastic general equilibrium theory. I am not, incidentally, making this latter concept up, we will meet it in the next chapter. And we will see that this bizarre theory became very influential in central banks in the run-up to the financial crisis of the late 2000s.

Within economics, Stiglitz's major contribution has been to explore the implications of restricting the amount of information available to the rational agent of economic theory. To recap once more, this agent is postulated to have a fixed set of preferences, gather all information relevant to any particular choice, and then to make the best possible choice, the optimal choice, given his or her preferences. Again, all scientific theories are approximations to reality, and their usefulness depends strongly on how reasonable these approximations are.

The assumption that agents can gather all available information clearly restricts the empirical validity of the behavioural model of choice based on it. The realism of the rational economic agent is extended in its range once we allow imperfect information to be a part of the scientific model. Either when all agents have the same amount of imperfect information or, perhaps even more realistically, some have more than others, the so-called case of 'asymmetric information'. Imperfect information was one of the foundations which Simon laid for a new model of rationality. Stiglitz essentially erected the first proper building on these foundations, in the context of modern economic theory.

One brief but very important example will suffice to illustrate the concept, based essentially on the idea that there are two sets of agents: insiders, as we might term them, who have quite a lot of information in a given context, and outsiders, who have relatively little. The importance of this issue is shown by the fact that economists have a special jargon phrase to describe it, the so-called 'principal-agent problem'. The business firm based on the principle of limited liability of the shareholders has proved to be an enormously productive innovation. Companies have been and continue to be the key to the prosperity and the success of the developed economies. It is certainly possible to have large organisations able to benefit from economies of scale and scope in their operations which do not have shareholders – major accountancy and consultancy companies, for example, are often partnerships and not shareholder-based – but firms with shareholders are the dominant form of economic organisational structure in the Western economies.

Within these companies, there are two powerful groups, whose interests ought to work in synchrony but often do not. The shareholders own the organisation and they are the group which can exercise ultimate legal control over decisions. But, in outfits of any significant size, the owners – the shareholders – usually appoint professional managers to run them on a day-to-day basis. Again, there are exceptions, even in very large companies where the initial owner both continues to run the company and retains a substantial shareholding. Martin Sorrell of the multimedia conglomerate WPP is an example. Phillip Green of the UK retail giant Arcadia was another, although he transferred his shares to his wife based in Monaco, where in a single year she famously and entirely legally received a dividend of £1 billion.

The executives of a company are involved on a full-time basis with its operations and as a result acquire large amounts of information about its workings. Elaborate structures are put in place to ensure that such information is made available to shareholders as well, many of them with legal sanctions to back up any failures of disclosure. Yet, inevitably, it is simply not possible for the owners to be as well informed as the executive managers.

In the case of the aristocratic British bank Barings, the information asymmetry was dramatic. Nick Leeson, a trader based in Singapore, reported a consistent stream of large profits, from which the owners were only too pleased to draw their large dividends and the senior managers their bonuses. But it turned out eventually that the information was in general not only worthless – a fact very well known to Leeson, who was responsible for providing it – but to a large extent fraudulent, leading to the collapse and liquidation of the entire company. Bernie Madoff is an even more spectacular example of the asymmetrical distribution of information. Madoff knew that his scheme was based on a gigantic fraud. The unfortunate people who entrusted their money to him did not. This group includes not only individuals but professional fund managers such as Nicola Horlick of Bramdean Asset Management, based in Mayfair in the heart of London. Many clients were desperate to get their money into Madoff's funds, and it was regarded as a coup for Horlick when she was able to get such access.

More generally, in the run-up to the financial crisis of the late 2000s, there are numerous examples of cases where insiders – not in the narrow sense of illegal insider dealing but people who had a pretty good idea of what was really going on – were able to persuade outsiders, the shareholders, to adopt policies and follow strategies which turned out to serve their own short-term interests rather than those of the shareholders. To realise the scale of the problem we have only to recall a number of banks across the world such as Bear Stearns in which the shareholders lost all or almost all of their money but in which the executives were enriched. Most companies have a very distributed shareholder base, coordination amongst whom is very difficult to achieve and which therefore leads to a substantial weakening of the involvement of shareholders in company affairs.

Much of the current intense policy debate about appropriate structures and corporate governance of banks and other financial institutions centres on how best to handle this issue of the asymmetric information sets of executives and shareholders. There are other crucial issues as well, of course, but if their information could become more closely aligned, it is likely that their interests would converge as well.

*

The concept of asymmetrical information is a valuable one, but implicit in its workings is a related concept beloved of economists, namely that of 'market failure'. By this, the profession does not mean that markets fail in any way at all. Rather, the phrase describes situations where, for whatever reason, markets are unable to function as they would do if all the assumptions underlying the theory actually obtained: fully rational and fully informed agents and so on. A less snappy but more accurate alternative to the phrase 'market failure' would be along the lines of: 'in this particular context, there are factors which are preventing the market from operating as it should do'. Remember here Simon's phrase: 'how they [firms] "should" rationally behave'. The core model of mainstream economics does not purport to be merely descriptive – this is how the world works. It is prescriptive – this is how the world *ought* to work.

The theoretical world of general equilibrium is a seductive one. By a series of logical, mathematical steps, it can be demonstrated that such a world is perfectly efficient in the following sense. Prices are set so that supply and demand are exactly balanced in every single market. Everyone who wants to work has a job, for the supply of labour, the number people who want to work, is matched by an equal demand from employers. And there are neither unused resources nor shortages anywhere in the economy. It is perhaps not surprising that professional economists, after struggling in their graduate courses to master the fixed-point theorems needed to prove the existence of general equilibrium, often lose sight of the fact that this is merely a theory. And it is above all a theory of a static world, which tells us in principle how to achieve the best possible allocation of a given set of resources, of people, material, infrastructure and so forth. It does not tell us anything at all about how to create new, additional wealth and resources.

So economists have a description of the world which, if it obtained in reality, would possess a variety of apparently desirable characteristics. They slip rather easily into saying that this is how the world 'ought' to work. And if in practice that is not what is observed, there must be some 'market failure'. The world must be changed to make it conform to theory. So they devise schemes of various degrees of cleverness to eliminate such failures and enable the market to operate as it 'should', to allow rational agents to decide in a fully rational manner.

The concept of market failure has come to pervade policy making in the West over the past few decades, over a very wide range of policy questions. The role of the policy maker, in this vision of the world, is to ensure that conditions prevail which allow markets to work properly, and for equilibrium to be reached. Ironically, mainstream economics, with its idealisation of markets, now provides the intellectual underpinnings for government intervention in both social and economic issues on a vast scale.

In the UK, the Financial Services Authority is an example of a body created from exactly this mindset. Clever, rational people believed that other clever, rational people could devise written systems of rules, regulation and procedures which would ensure that situations could be created in which it would be as if markets were operating as they 'should'. In such circumstances, risks would be minimised, and possibly eliminated completely. The FSA was hailed at its launch in 1997 by Gordon Brown as 'a unique, twenty-first-century, one-stop centre, a single supervisor for all providers of financial services'. It has a staff of 2,500 people, is charged with enforcing no fewer than 8,500 pages of specific regulations,* and the direct costs of running it, excluding the costs to companies of complying with its myriad regulations, is now around £650 million (around $1 billion) a year.

As long as this rule book was followed by a financial company, the FSA was apparently satisfied. And despite its catastrophic failure to prevent the financial collapse of major banks such as RBS, this particular regulatory body in general continues to operate using exactly the same thinking: its purpose is to deal with market failure.

As an aside, illustrating the bureaucracy not in some Platonic ideal world where it is simply eliminating information asymmetries, but as it actually exists, readers will recall the terrifying month of September 2008 when the financial cataclysm burst. Lehman Brothers went bankrupt, and we seemed on the verge

---

* The new Conservative-led coalition government in the UK is committed to getting rid of the FSA, though whether this will change fundamentally the way in which any new regulatory bodies see the world remains to be seen.

of a repeat of the Great Depression of the 1930s. In October of that same year, barely a month after capitalism itself had returned from the brink of the abyss, a friend of mine at a hedge fund received a letter from the FSA. Its tone was stern. Indeed, its purpose was to issue a serious warning as to his future conduct. What had he done? Had he speculated irresponsibly to try to bring about the collapse of one of Britain's great banks? Had he sailed close to the wind and triggered concerns that he might be insider trading? Not at all. At the end of the month of September 2008, he had committed the grave offence of failing to send the Financial Services Authority the regular form in which he was required to document the activities he had carried out which had contributed to his professional development.

*

Simon raised the problem for the rational model of economic agents that they simply cannot gather all available information. The response from the profession has been to expand the theory to incorporate the concept, and to use it to justify massive interventions in the economy designed to eliminate 'market failure', to correct for the fact that agents may not have full information. But it is still fundamentally based on the idea that agents ought to behave as they do in a fully rational world. And, of course, these theoretical agents act entirely independently. Network effects are conspicuous by their complete absence.

Simon's second challenge was that, in many situations, agents lack the computational ability to work out what is the best choice to make, the optimal choice. Indeed, it may often not be possible to know what the optimal choice is, regardless of how we approach the decision.

The discipline of economics has responded to this in a way which is consistent with multiple personality disorder. At one level, and especially within macroeconomics, the problem raised by Simon for the economically rational agent has simply been ignored. It is 'as if', to use the favourite economic expression, the matter had never been raised. But at another level, within behavioural economics, some rather profound changes have taken place in how economists see decision makers, people, firms, governments making their choices. Agents are still presumed to be operating independently, but in ways which are markedly different from those of conventional economic rationality. As we shall see, there are some subtle differences between Simon's vision and the overall direction of this new research. But it represents progress nevertheless.

*

This aspect of Simon's vision has been taken forward by the two other Nobel Laureates, Vernon Smith and Daniel Kahneman, mentioned earlier in the chapter. As with asymmetric information, their work makes no use of the concept of networks and their impact on behaviour. But their empirical findings point the way to more realistic representations of how agents behave, albeit still as so many Robinson Crusoes, forming their opinions and making their decisions in splendid isolation.

Vernon Smith made the seminal contributions to the field of experimental economics. As the name implies, this is the study of economic situations using experimental methods, and during the course of which valuable data is gathered on how agents actually behave (as opposed to how they are posited to behave by mainstream theory).

Behavioural economics, linked irrevocably to Daniel Kahneman, is much more explicitly based upon experiments using methodologies developed in psychology to see how agents really do behave. And a key focus of such experiments is the actual rather than the theoretical cognitive capacity of agents. There is rather a fine line between this and experimental economics, and indeed in the rest of the book the distinctions will be ignored and the general phrase 'behavioural economics' will be used. Both provide valuable information on how people really do behave.

Like Herb Simon, Kahneman was not by training or profession an economist. Born in Israel in 1934, he obtained his degree in psychology from the Hebrew University of Jerusalem and he has made his academic career in the subject. He is currently attached to both the psychology and public and international affairs departments at Princeton, and in 2007 received the American Psychological Association's Award for Outstanding Lifetime Contributions to Psychology. Oh yes, and along the way he picked up the Nobel Prize in economics in 2002.

Kahneman's conclusions in his Nobel lecture are worth repeating here: 'The central characteristic of agents is not that they reason poorly, but that they often act intuitively. And the behaviour of these agents is not guided by what they are able to compute, but by what they happen to see at a given moment.'

*

There are many examples where people have been discovered to behave in ways which are pretty consistently different from the way the rational model of economics suggests that they should. The concept of 'framing' is one of them. This means that the choice a person makes can be heavily influenced by how it is presented. Volunteers in an experiment might be confronted with the following hypothetical situation and asked to choose between two alternatives. A disaster is unfolding, perhaps a stand is about to collapse in a soccer stadium and you have to decide how to handle it. Your experts tell you that 3,000 lives are at risk. If you take one course of action, you can save 1,000 people for certain, but the rest will definitely die. If you take the other, there is a chance that everyone will be saved. But it is risky, and your advisers tell you that it only has a one in three chance of working. If it doesn't, everyone will die. Simple arithmetic tells us that the expected loss of life in both choices is 2,000, for on the second option there is a two out of three chance that all 3,000 will be killed. When confronted with this, most people choose the first course of action.

The problem is then put in a different way, it is 'framed' differently. This time, you are told that the same first choice open to you will lead to 2,000 people being killed. The second will cause the deaths of 3,000 people with a chance of two out of three that this will happen, and one out of three that no one will die. The outcomes are identical to those set out above. Yet in this context, most people choose the second option.

Mainstream economists are often not persuaded by the results of experiments such as these. They are, after all, hypothetical situations and it is very unlikely that any of the participants would ever be called upon to make such a decision, or indeed anything remotely like it. There are many other aspects to this methodological debate, which is still ongoing between mainstreamers and experimental economists and which need not detain us.

For there are many real-life examples of the importance of framing. During the post-war period, trade unions in Britain gradually became more and more powerful, even bringing down Edward Heath's Tory government in early 1974 as a result of widespread industrial action. Heath's successor as Tory leader, Margaret Thatcher, was not only determined to change this when she came to office. She did. One of the ways by which she succeeded was by enabling an 'opt-in' rather than 'opt-out' method to be used as a way of deducting trade-union subscriptions from workers' wages. In some companies where trade unions were recognised by employers, everyone had to belong to the union, the so-called 'closed shop', and the company simply deducted the subscriptions and passed them on to the union. In others, membership wasn't compulsory, but it was assumed, and union dues were still automatically deducted unless the worker took the action of 'opting out', of filling in a form to say that he or she did not want to be in the union. 'Opting in' put the onus on workers to positively opt for union membership.

Almost exactly the same story is unfolding in Wisconsin and other American states as I write these words. Whether union dues are automatically deducted or whether workers have to opt voluntarily to pay and join is a very live political issue. The exact nuances vary from context to context, but the principle of framing is clearly at work here. How the choice is put can have a dramatic effect on the outcome, far greater than would be the case if it were a matter of 'rational' agents including the cost of the time spent filling in a simple form when assessing the various costs and benefits of trade-union membership. This might make a difference to a handful of people, those at the margin of joining or not. But in practice, the impact on the eventual outcome can be very strong.

Framing is just one of a number of concepts of behavioural economics which modify the standard way in which economists postulate that agents make 'rational' choices. In many ways, companies, and in particular their marketing departments, understood empirically the precepts of behavioural economics before academics got round to formalising the concept. They have always known that consumers often behave differently from the way that standard rational agent economic theory would have them behave.

Marketeers observed, for example, that discount offers such as 'buy one, get one free' or 'three for the price of two' – a concept

I am very keen on because this is how bookstores often package up their offers – tend to be more effective in boosting sales than the exact equivalent price reduction on a single purchase. The amount of money which is paid for the bundle of products is identical in each case, but more will usually be bought if they are packaged under an offer than if there is a simple equivalent reduction in the individual prices.

Marketing departments also understand that consumers can be very impatient and will pay to get something sooner rather than later. Turning to online shopping, the excellent range offered on Amazon makes the site extremely popular. The company offers an option to deliver for free within three to five working days. Alternatively, customers can pay to have their item delivered within two days, and even more to have it delivered the next day. Now, there will be circumstances in which the latter option is desirable, such as forgetting it is your wife's birthday until the very last minute. But many items – books, for one – are bought to be savoured, to last, and they may very well be re-read over a long period of time. So paying a premium, often a non-trivial percentage of its price, to have it the next day rather than just a few days later does not make 'rational' sense. But it is an option nevertheless routinely chosen by many consumers. Again, in practice it is often found that the introduction of a considerably more expensive option into a range often results in consumers switching from cheaper options to what is now the second most expensive brand. Few people will buy the newly introduced expensive product, but what was previously the most expensive is now perceived as somehow being better value than it was. The prices of all the previously available items remain unchanged, but people will switch away from cheap ones to the now second-most expensive.

These are all examples of how agents often behave differently from how the standard rational choice model would have them make choices, and give a flavour of the work of behavioural economists, which by now is voluminous.

*

Kahneman himself generously describes a 1980 article by the University of Chicago scholar Richard Thaler as the 'founding text in behavioural economics'. Thaler indeed is deservedly a major figure in behavioural economics. In 2009 he published a best-seller with Cass Sunstein entitled *Nudge: Improving Decisions About Health, Wealth and Happiness*. The dialogue with the authors on the amazon.com page for the book defines 'nudge' very clearly: 'By a nudge we mean anything that influences our choices'.

There are many examples, and here are just two. Two Yale academics, Dean Karlan and Ian Ayres, set up stickK.com, a website designed to help people reach their goals. So a person who wants to lose weight, say, makes a public commitment on the site to lose at least a specific amount by a specific date. He or she agrees a test to be carried out, such as being weighed in the presence of named witnesses, to verify whether or not the goal has been reached. But the person also puts up a sum of money, which is returned if the goal is met. If not, the money goes to charity. The second example is the 'dollar a day' plan in Greensboro, North Carolina, aimed at reducing further pregnancies in teenage girls under sixteen who have already had a baby. In addition to counselling and support, the girls in the pilot scheme were paid a dollar for each day in which they did not become pregnant again. Of the sixty-five girls in the scheme, only ten of them got pregnant again over the next five years. Of course, there are many criticisms of these and other such 'nudge' concepts. A persistent and strong one is that the people who really do want to lose weight are the ones who make the commitment, the girls who really do not want to get pregnant again are the ones who join the scheme. In other words, those who sign up to 'nudge' schemes are those who were likely to adopt this behaviour regardless. Nevertheless, 'nudge' remains an influential concept.

'Anything which influences our choices' is a definition which clearly includes the concept of incentives in the familiar guise of a monetary cost or benefit. But it also includes less obvious ones, such as making a public commitment to reach a goal. And we can even think of examples from the opening chapter as being examples of 'nudge', such as the 'price' of being burned to death or firing a shot in the air to signal a group of potential hooligans to disperse. But it is broader than that, as the example of framing suggests. It is not simply a question of incentives, but how they are presented.

These are all ways of extending the concept of incentives, which may or may not work in any given context, but which are nevertheless a useful intellectual construct. Less helpfully, it is claimed that 'nudge' appears to be able to solve almost any problem, certainly as far as policy makers of almost any description are concerned, as another exchange in the amazon.com interview makes clear.

Amazon: 'What are some of the situations where nudges can make a difference?'

Thaler and Sunstein: 'Well, to name just a few: better investments for everyone, more savings for retirement, less obesity, more charitable giving, a cleaner planet, and an improved educational system. We could easily make people both wealthier and healthier by devising friendlier choice environments, or architectures.'

The scene from the Monty Python film *Life of Brian* springs irresistibly to mind, when a member of the revolutionary People's Front of Judea haranguing a crowd asks rhetorically, 'What have the Romans ever done for us?' only to be provided in reply with a list including clean water, sanitation, roads, wine, education, peace. 'But apart from that?' he asks plaintively.

Incentives matter. Nudge widens the concept of how incentives operate, and Thaler has made a distinguished contribution to our scientific understanding. But might these claims be a little overstated? More wealth, more health, nicer people, a better environment, all can be achieved 'easily'. This has not so far, it should be said, been the experience of the Nudge team set up at the instigation of the current British Prime Minister, David Cameron, and advised by Richard Thaler himself, although to be fair it has only been in existence since 2010.

*

Behavioural economics advances our knowledge of how agents behave in practice. But in many ways it sidesteps the most fundamental challenge which Simon posed to rational economic behaviour. He argued that in many circumstances, we simply cannot compute the 'optimal' choice, or decide what constitutes the 'best' strategy. This is the case even if – especially if! – we have access to complete information in any particular situation. In many situations it is not just that the search for the optimal decision might be time consuming and expensive, it is that the optimal decision *cannot* be known, at least in the current state of knowledge and technology.

This is an absolutely fundamental challenge to the economic concept of rationality. Many economists nowadays choose to interpret Simon's work in ways which are compatible with their theories. Sure, they argue, there are often limits to the amount of information which people gather, the amount of time and effort they take in making a decision. But this is because they judge that the additional benefits which might be gained by being able to make an even better choice by gathering more information, spending more time contemplating, are offset by the costs of such activities. Agents may well use a restricted information set, and make an optimal decision on this basis. An even better choice might be made if more information were gathered, but not one sufficiently better to justify the additional time and effort required.

But this whole argument completely misses Simon's point. He believed that, in many real-life situations, the optimal choice can *never* be known. It is not just a question of being willing to spend more time and effort to acquire the information so that the truly optimal choice can be made. We simply cannot discover it.

A tragic, but nevertheless sadly rather routine, recent story from the north of England encapsulates this point. A ten-year-old boy drowned trying to save his step-sister who had fallen into a deep pond. Two police community officers who were present refused to enter the water, on the grounds that they had not been trained in water safety. Incredibly, at the inquest a detective chief inspector defended this behaviour. Given their lack of training it would, he explained sanctimoniously, have been 'inappropriate' for them to try to save the child's life.

But this was not the reaction of the human beings, in contrast to the tick-box robots, present at the scene. The brave young boy instinctively tried to save his sister. Two fishermen, both well into their sixties, leapt into the pond without thinking or training. They rescued the girl, but the boy died.

We can readily generalise from this single incident (although the true rational planner would dismiss it as 'anecdotal evidence'). Ex ante, there is usually no single best course of action to follow. Jumping into a pond of unknown depth risks your own life and in any case you may be too late. Standing by and doing nothing means the girl will die, but you will live. The future is fraught with both risk and uncertainty, inherent parts of the human condition, and therefore of our social and economic systems.

Incidents such as these occur on an almost everyday basis. But although there are always many self-righteous individuals willing to pontificate after the event on what 'appropriate' behaviour should have been, this does not mean that the 'optimal' behaviour can be identified even with the benefit of hindsight. The agents involved had to make a decision quickly, but they still had fairly complete information. Local knowledge meant that all the agents knew that the pond was deep and cold. The girl could not swim. What is the optimal course of action for anyone witnessing this unfolding tragedy? Even in a relatively simple situation such as this, there is too much chance and contingency involved to be confident of any analysis. Too many tiny details, whose interactions could lead to success or failure, for us to say what the best strategy of any of the agents involved would have been. The fishermen saved the girl, but, especially given their ages, the shock of plunging into the cold water may have induced cramp or even a mild heart attack, leading to the death of one or even both the brave rescuers. We simply cannot say.

In his 1955 paper, one of the illustrations which Simon used to make his point was the much more innocuous pastime of chess. There are very good reasons for his choice. In chess, agents do indeed have complete information. Not just a good selection of all the information which potentially exists, but literally all of it. The rules of the game are not only rather straightforward and few in number (around a dozen), but they are also fixed. So both players have total understanding of the rules. The game can be won in only one way, by capturing the opponent's king. The number and strength of each player's remaining pieces is irrelevant if one of them is able to checkmate. Indeed, many of the most brilliant games between grandmasters are based upon material sacrifice to achieve precisely that aim. So the purpose of the game is clear. And both players have complete information about what the other side has already done, the action is transparent.

But Simon points out that in the typical game, after fifteen to twenty moves or so on each side, a sequence of the next sixteen moves, eight by each side, might be expected to yield a stupendous total of permissible variations. He calculates the typical number of such variations in such positions as being approximately ten followed by twenty-four zeros. And this is just for the next eight moves on either side; often from these so-called 'middle-game' positions, in practice there will a further twenty moves each before the game is concluded, and sometimes many more. Clearly, it is literally impossible for any human, even aided by a computer, to work out so many variations. Left to our own devices, even at an average of one per second it would take longer than the lifetime of the universe.

Simon considered how players respond to such situations. Rather, he considered the much more general point of what the principle of rationality might look like in situations when the complications exceed the capacity of humans to compute all eventual outcomes. He simply used chess as a particular illustration of his thinking. And the game of chess is simplicity itself when we consider many of the decisions we all have to make on a more or less everyday basis. Choosing a partner, selecting a pension scheme, deciding whether to take another job, casting a vote in an important election, all these are clearly very complicated with potential consequences which last far into the future. Yet they occur with reasonable frequency. Even apparently much more simple situations are difficult to analyse in advance, as we saw above with the tragic incident of the boy who drowned in the pool.

When driving back to London, where I have lived for many years, from visiting my father in my home town I might equally well take one of three motorway routes. As I approach the motorway I face an immediate choice: turn left or turn right. Both are valid choices, involving completely different routes of approximately equal distance. Whichever I pick, on the approach to the vast London conurbation the number of potential routes proliferates rapidly. In common with most motorists, I use various satellite navigation aids to provide information. These, indeed, confirm the huge number of ways in which the journey can be made, well over 100,000 routes being examined by the machine when I set off. My choices through the journey are influenced by traffic information, but even this is not straightforward to interpret. I have to form a view on how long the delays have been in place, whether they will have cleared by the time I reach them and so on. And, of course, new delays may emerge after I have made any particular choice.

So how do I choose? Although I have made the journey many times, it has not been and never will be possible for me to sample more than a tiny fraction of the potential route combinations, and even if I did, the next time I chose a particular one the circumstances might have changed.

I use what as an economist I would describe as 'heuristics', but writing in English I call instead 'rules of thumb'. These are basic guidelines which an agent evolves, drawing on his or her experience over time, both particular to the choice in question and also possibly more widely. On any particular occasion, a given rule might not work in the sense that it leads to an undesirable outcome. I set off, and two hours later find myself in a major traffic jam owing to a serious accident which has only just happened. So the rules are not fixed, but might be modified over time.

A key feature of such rules is that they do enable me to scale down the problem of choice dramatically, to enable me to consider realistically no more than a dozen, or at the very most twenty, of the actual six-figure number of alternatives I face.

The overall trip is around 220 miles. But the shortest in terms of distance cuts around fifteen miles off this figure. It is a route I never use. Why? Because it involves crossing almost the whole of Greater Manchester, an urban area with a population of some 2.5 million. I know from my general experience that travel on such roads tends to be slow and that motorways are faster. There have been a number of memorable occasions over the years when it would almost certainly have been better to take this alternative, but these are few and far between and so I use this rule of thumb to discard not just this, but also other non-motorway routes over the course of almost the entire journey, until London itself is entered.

In terms of the first choice, left or right at the first motorway junction, encountered after a mere handful of miles, my rule of thumb has changed over time. Satellite navigation aids are not really helpful here, they indicate a right turn but in the absence of known traffic delays the left-turn journey is estimated to be only three minutes longer. I used to turn left and now turn right. This is because I began to encounter longer delays simply due to heavy traffic in the last thirty miles or so through London and its approaches. Just heavy traffic plain and simple, nothing which would show up as a delay on a Satnav system. It might now be quicker on average to use this route, but I don't. The right-turn route, despite problems, in general has given satisfactory outcomes.

And here is another essential feature of rules of thumb. Agents use them as long as they continue to deliver not optimal, but satisfactory outcomes. Indeed, even once I have arrived safely at home after completing one of these trips, I simply do not know which of the alternatives might have been the best, the 'optimal'. What I do know is whether the journey I have just experienced has been satisfactory.

These are exactly the processes which Simon described chess players using in his 1955 paper. They use rules of thumb to scale down dramatically the dimension, the scale of the number of possible alternatives to evaluate. And provided a rule of thumb continues to give reasonable results, they continue to use it. They realise that the search for the 'optimal' decision is very often completely pointless, and so settle for a viable decision which is likely to be satisfactory.

*

In principle, I suppose, the best route on the motorway could be calculated once the journey had been completed, but not before. Tracking by satellite of all the potential routes as I made my way back to London, and subsequent analysis of the data might be able to reveal what on this occasion would have been the optimal route. But this is a time-consuming process requiring very advanced technology. In many apparently simple situations, even the most advanced technology cannot compute the best decision. Think of the tragedy in the pond described above, and then try to think of the details of the information which would be required in order to decide what would have been the best course of action for everyone concerned.

This is why, again, Simon used the example of chess to illustrate the limits to knowledge. Chess is simple to describe, and players have complete information. But in a large proportion of all the stupendous number of potential positions, the optimal cannot be known, even using advanced technology in the form of computers. These are now very distinctly stronger than the best human players. Even the world champion now has no chance of winning if matched in a series of games against a computer.

In chess, even a beginner knows that the queen is by far the most powerful piece on the board in terms of its attacking powers, and the pawn the weakest. So sequences of moves which involve you obtaining an opponent's pawn at the cost of your own queen can be immediately discarded (unless, of course, there would be a consequential benefit such as checkmating your opponent's king). In most situations, there are many such possible sequences, less dramatic than this but which involve material loss with no apparent compensation.

But the use of rules of thumb goes much deeper than this in the game of chess. There are thirty-two pieces on the board at the start of the game. Computers have now solved completely all possible positions in the game – when there are only six pieces left on it! Some of these are far beyond the capacity of even the strongest human to compute, requiring sequences of over 200 moves, and at each stage in these cases literally the optimal move has to be selected. To put this in context, no more than a handful of games have ever been played between strong players which have 200 moves in total, and complete games over even 120 or 130 moves are rare. Some progress has been made by computers in solving positions with seven pieces, but the task is far from complete, even using very powerful machines.

In fact, between reasonably strong players operating at their best, differences in their abilities to calculate sequences of possible moves in any given position ought not to be that decisive in determining the outcome. Of course, in practice under competitive conditions, stress, nerves, or tiredness may often lead to mistakes, and some very strong players may indeed be able to 'see' a few moves further ahead in the sense that they can calculate all relevant sequences, and this can sometimes be a factor. But players at high levels differ more markedly in their ability to form a judgement on the likely result which will follow from a future sequence of moves, once the ability to calculate further moves through precise analysis is exhausted. Both players may 'see' a particular position after the next, say, ten possible moves perfectly. One may judge it a win for White, say, whilst the other may judge it a draw. Neither can possibly calculate such an outcome; both are relying on their experience and judgement to arrive at this view. So both sides readily obtain the resulting position, and the one with the superior judgement usually prevails (unless a significant error is made in the course of the rest of the game).

Indeed, in many positions in a game, there is little point in carrying out elaborate calculations on possible sequences of moves. Many famous positions, some of them decisive in world championship matches, have been extensively analysed by the very strongest players for decades after they were actually played. The results are published, available to everyone to scrutinise and to improve. But the best, the 'optimal' move in the crucial position remains unknown. Even Gary Kasparov, probably the strongest human player ever, equipped with modern computers, has been unable to solve some of these problems in his monumental five-volume series of books on all previous world champions, entitled *My Great Predecessors*. Incomprehensible to someone who has never played chess, they are nevertheless replete with practical illustrations of Herb Simon's concept of rationality.

Playing chess obsesses a small number of people, and interests a much larger number, but if chess disappeared tomorrow most of humanity would not notice. Selecting a route for a driving journey is a very humdrum, everyday task. Men of certain ages and predilections may enjoy fiddling with the technology, though for most people it is a tedious, routine activity. But, as we have seen, even in what we might describe as humble situations, far, far removed from complicated life-or-death decisions, it is often not possible to calculate the optimal choice. Agents use rules of thumb both to scale down the dimension of the problem and to select amongst alternatives.

It is always possible for true believers in the economic concept of rationality to describe any conceivable outcome, any conceivable apparent mode of behaviour, as being consistent with the postulates of the theory. It is, as they say, 'as if' I were choosing the optimal decision, given the various probabilities involved, in deciding my route, or 'as if' the world champion chess player were making the optimal move. The Communist Party of the Soviet Union made use of a marvellous phrase: 'it is apparent'. 'It is apparent that . . .', the Party would pronounce, before going on to assert something which was at best a half-truth and was often a downright lie. So, in this spirit, let us say that it is apparent that if an agent failed to take the optimal decision, he or she would eventually learn to take it.

*

We met circumstances in Chapter 1 – the behaviour of the mob, the courage of the martyrs – where ex post a story could always be told which would reconcile the outcomes and behaviour with economic rationality. But both these and the more everyday examples used here stretch the credibility of this way of thinking to breaking point. And especially when, applying Occam's razor, there is a simpler explanation available, which fits more comfortably with the empirical evidence. Agents often have imperfect information but, much more fundamentally, lack the computational capacity to calculate the optimal decision, even with the limited amount of information they do possess.

To emphasise again, this is really quite a different concept of rationality from the one defined by the postulates of conventional economics. The idea that there is only one definition of rationality, that of mainstream economic theory, has become firmly embedded in policy discourse. But it is completely wrong. If the assumptions, the simplifications, required by standard theory are reasonably congruent with any given empirical situation, then, yes, it is rational for agents to behave in this way. If they are not, we need a new definition of rationality, one which recognises not just the fact that not everyone has all relevant information at any point in time, but, more fundamentally, that many situations are so complex that, in the current state of scientific knowledge, the optimal decision cannot be computed by any conceivable agent. At some indeterminate point in the future, when they are incredibly more powerful than they are today, computers will eventually solve the game of chess completely. And maybe then we will be part of the way towards enabling agents to compute optimal decisions in everyday situations which, as we have seen, are often considerably more complicated than chess.

In other words, we need a definition of rationality which is consistent with the social and economic worlds of the twenty-first century, which accounts for the nature and limitations of human cognition, one which completes Simon's vision. Economics dismisses behaviour which does not conform to its precepts of what is rational as 'irrational'. But on the contrary, it is economic rationality which is itself irrational in many modern contexts.

We may note as an aside that very recent scientific developments go even further. Simon's concept of rationality is anathema to the believers in economically rational optimising behaviour. Fortunately for the blood pressure of the latter, such people are in general rather narrow minded and rarely read scientific material outside their own immediate field of interest. An article in the top journal *Science* in July 2010 by Dutch psychologists Ruud Custers and Henk Aarts would have burst more than a few blood vessels. The title – 'The Unconscious Will: How the Pursuit of Goals Operates Outside of Conscious Awareness' – gives a pretty good guide to its content.* The opening paragraph states boldly:

---

* This is often not the case at all. My old Cambridge tutor Christopher Bliss deservedly made his academic economics reputation with a paper entitled 'On Putty Clay'.

As humans, we generally have the feeling that we decide what we want and what we do. These self-reflections remind us that we are not bound to the present environment for our actions. We can envision ourselves in different places, in alternative futures, doing different things. We only have to decide to do so, and we can go and see a movie tonight or hang out with friends in a bar. It is up to us. Our behaviors seem to originate in our conscious decisions to pursue desired outcomes, or goals.

It goes on: 'Scientific research suggests otherwise', and concludes that 'the basic processes necessary for goal pursuit – preparing and directing instrumental actions and assessing the reward value of the goal – can operate outside conscious awareness'. The psychologists do, however, concede that 'it is too early to conclude that consciousness is redundant in the pursuit of goals'. But perhaps this line of thought is a little too radical even for the most iconoclastic economist. So let us proceed on more familiar ground.

The concept of limits to human computational abilities was not discovered by Simon. Indeed, we can trace it back at least as far as Aristotle, who wrote in the fourth century BC: 'It is the mark of the instructed mind to rest satisfied with the degree of precision to which the nature of the subject admits and not to seek exactness when only an approximation to the truth is possible.' It may not be possible to discover the best strategy, the optimal choice, because 'only an approximation to the truth is possible'. Not: 'only an approximation to the truth is used', as the modern economic distortions of Simon's key message would have us understand, that the best could be obtained but we just do not think it is worth it. But: 'only an approximation to the truth *is possible*'.

*

The same idea was expressed in modern economic terms by Keynes. His magnum opus, the *General Theory of Employment, Interest and Money*, was published in 1936, and immediately became the focus of intense theoretical controversy. It is the work for which Keynes is remembered. Much less well known is his 1937 article in the *Quarterly Journal of Economics* in which he set out to clarify aspects of his book.

Here is Keynes, anticipating Simon by nearly two decades: 'we have, as a rule, only the vaguest idea of any but the most direct consequences of our acts', he says. Only the vaguest idea! But Keynes was a practical man as much as a theorist, and he goes on: 'the necessity for action and for decision compels us as practical men to do our best to overlook this awkward fact and to behave exactly as we should if we had behind us a good calculation of a series of prospective advantages and disadvantages'.

He asks rhetorically: 'How do we manage in such circumstances to behave in a manner which saves our faces as rational economic men?' In other words, Keynes here opens the possibility of rational modes of behaviour which are quite different from those of the mainstream, equilibrium economic model.

And he answers his own question, describing what Simon would later call 'rules of thumb'. It is worth quoting this at some length:

We have devised for the purpose a variety of techniques, of which much the most important are the three following:

1   We assume that the present is a much more serviceable guide to the future than a candid examination of past experience would show it to have been hitherto. In other

words, we largely ignore the prospect of future changes about the actual character of which we know nothing.

2   We assume that the existing state of opinion as expressed in prices and the character of existing output is based on a correct summing up of future prospects, so that we can accept it as such unless and until something new and relevant comes into the picture.

3   Knowing that our individual judgement is worthless, we endeavour to fall back on the judgement of the rest of the world which is perhaps better informed. That is, we endeavour to conform with the behaviour of the majority or average. The psychology of a society of individuals each of whom is endeavouring to copy the others leads to what we may strictly call a conventional judgement.

So when agents have only the vaguest idea of the consequences of their decisions, when by implication they can never discover with any reasonable degree of accuracy what they might be, they adopt heuristics which scale down the dimension of the problem.

In his points 1 and 2, Keynes is essentially arguing that we give much greater weight to the current situation than is warranted when forming a view about the future. Certainly, the experience of the past few years supports this idea. During the financial and economic boom of the late 2000s, most people – regulators, governments, international bodies such as the International Monetary Fund (IMF) – thought it would go on for ever. When the bubble burst, everyone became plunged in gloom. The Nobel Prize-winning economist Robert Barro stated in the spring of 2009 that the prices prevailing on the various financial markets were signalling a 30 per cent chance of a repeat of the Great Depression of the 1930s. We might think the recent experience has been bad, but during it output (GDP) fell by only 3 per cent in America and by 5 to 6 per cent in the major European economies. In the 1930s, output fell by nearly 30 – thirty! – per cent in both Germany and the US. That is why it is called the Great Depression. And markets were indicating a 30 per cent chance of a repetition of that experience, which fortunately has not taken place.

It is Keynes's third point which is the most explosive, and which anticipates by many decades modern network theory, how agents are connected to each other, and how, where and when an agent bases its actions at least in part on the behaviour, opinions or decisions of others. In short, Keynes argues that copying the behaviour of others is in fact rational – the 'conventional judgement'.

Agents can rarely, if ever, know in advance with any reliable degree of accuracy the consequences of their actions. They have only the vaguest idea. This opinion fits in very well with Simon's radical and innovative concept of rationality. But it is still one whose explicit base is the autonomous agent, making decisions as an independent entity.

But Keynes gives a foretaste of the effect of introducing network effects into the principles of agent choice. It is in fact is a natural extension of Simon's principle of rationality. And at the same time it carries such radically different properties, such different implications, that it should be regarded as a separate definition in its own right.

Keynes argues that a good 'rule of thumb' on which to rely is to copy other people. In other words, to base your decisions (at least in part) on what other people do, other people to which you are connected and of whose actions and decision you are aware. In short, your network.

Effects, as we have seen, can spread across networks both for good and for ill. In the run up to the financial crisis, for example, the belief spread across networks of traders, networks of regulators, networks of politicians, that economics had finally solved our problems and the boom would go on forever. But it ended, as we shall see in the next chapter, with waves of doubt and pessimism percolating across a range of different networks. The trick for successful policy, for positive linking, is not which interest rate to try to manipulate, not whether to increase taxes or cut spending. It is the subtle but elusive goal of enabling the right frame of mind to spread across the networks which connect the relevant decision makers.

Herb Simon's programme for revolutionising the way we think about how people behave, how decisions are made, went deeper than just giving us a better way of thinking about how incentives operate, valuable though this may be. He argued that in many situations agents lack the ability to process the information, that our computational capacities are insufficient to deal with the complexities of the real world.

*

Most of the discussion in the book so far has been about what economists would call 'micro' issues. Some, such as the choice of a route to get from A to B or the playing of chess, have indeed been rather humdrum, everyday activities. Others, such as criminal activity, are of more substance and importance for society as a whole. Still others, such as the choice of religious faith or political ideology, have implications not just for society as a whole, but in the contexts in which we discussed them could literally be a matter of life and death for the relevant individuals.

We have already seen examples of where network effects can overwhelm the impact of incentives, however sophisticated or 'nudged' they may be. When people are influenced by networks, they are not just operating in a completely different way from that posited by rational economic theory, using rules of thumb rather than trying to optimise. People are operating in contexts where the capacities of even the most sophisticated policy maker to compute with a high degree of confidence the consequences of a decision are not just stretched to their utmost, but are inadequate for the task.

Of course, in practice, a mixture of incentives, whether conventional ones or in their more modern 'nudge' guise, and network effects will operate. But once network effects start to influence the outcome in any meaningful way then, as we have seen, the difficulties for the policy maker appear to increase considerably.

But we have not yet really touched on what economists call 'macro' issues, namely the behaviour of the economy at an overall, aggregate level. Keynes has now been mentioned, primarily for his insights into how people actually behave, how they act in a way which he describes as rational but which is utterly different from the rationality of the economics textbooks.

Keynes is mainly remembered as a macroeconomist, remembered for his great work the *General Theory*, in which he contemplated how it could be that the system of liberal capitalism, which he greatly admired, could have brought about a situation in which the total output of economies fell by nearly a third, and in which nearly one in four Americans were unemployed.

So in the next chapter, we look at some macroeconomic issues, and specifically the experience of the recent financial crisis. How did it come about? What was the role of rational agent economic theory? And what role was played by networks, of agents making decisions on the basis of how others behaved? The role played by what Keynes called 'the psychology of a society of individuals each of whom is endeavouring to copy the others'.

4

Did Economists Go Mad?

The conduct of economic policy making over the ten to fifteen years prior to the financial crisis of 2008–9 exemplifies the fundamental problems of the conventional mindset of economics. At the time, it seemed as though clever policy makers devising clever rules and regulations to set the right incentives, to which economically rational agents would respond appropriately, had indeed solved key problems of macroeconomic management. Economic growth in the West was strong and steady, and both unemployment and inflation everywhere remained low.

Networks were conspicuous by their complete absence from the intellectual framework of policy makers. Yet network effects were absolutely central to the causes of the crisis.

There had been a number of scares along the way. In 1997–8, the rapidly growing area of East Asia experienced a financial crisis, with huge falls in output and employment throughout the region in 1998. But very soon growth and rising prosperity were restored. Network effects featured strongly in both the crash and the recovery. The countries of the area were held up as shining examples of success, with rapidly rising prosperity and high levels of investment in education and infrastructure. Doubts began to emerge about the economy of Thailand. In particular, there were worries – harbinger of bigger things to come ten years later – about whether the country was experiencing an unsustainable real-estate bubble. The Thai currency came under attack, and the government cut its link, its fixed value, to the US dollar. This was the signal for massive speculation against the currency and a sharp fall in its value.

But the crisis then spread like wildfire across almost every single country in the region. Even China, then nowhere near as connected to the rest of the world as it is now, suffered from a loss of foreign confidence. The financial collapse led to dramatic falls in output in many of the countries, with soaring unemployment. In Indonesia, the thirty-year rule of the dictator Suharto collapsed after widespread rioting in protest. So events which were particular to Thailand cascaded across the networks which shaped opinion in financial markets, and the entire region came under speculative attack. In US dollar terms, the output of countries such as Thailand, Indonesia, Malaysia and South Korea fell by more in a single year than the worst affected economies in the Great Depression of the 1930s.

Then, almost as suddenly, confidence returned, across both the networks of financial markets and the networks which create business confidence, or lack of it, in the domestic economies of the region. Why? Well, as the old saying goes, success has many fathers and failure is an orphan. The IMF was widely blamed for its role during the crisis, but claimed credit for restoring stability and paving the way for recovery. Even now, despite over a decade of the most intensive study by economists, we do not have an agreed answer to the questions why the economies collapsed so spectacularly but then, very quickly, bounced back as though nothing had happened. Networks have played little part in any of this analysis, but were undoubtedly the key.

One of the most dramatic knock-on effects of the crisis in East Asia was on an economy outside the region: Russia. There were genuine reasons to be concerned about the financial health of the Russian economy. Taxes were not being collected, many state employees were not being paid for months at a time, and the government had already been forced to raise interest rates to an astronomical 150 per cent to try to stop even more money from fleeing the country. The East Asia crisis sparked even further doubts, if that were possible, about the Russian situation. In the late summer of 1998 the Russian government defaulted on its domestic debt and stopped paying interest on its foreign debt.

At around the same time, in the United States the collapse of Long-Term Capital Management, a hedge fund with two economics Nobel Prize winners in its luminaries, sparked a temporary panic. LTCM lost nearly $5 billion in less than four months and was forced to shut down completely in 2000. But the panic was temporary. The problem appeared solved and the world moved on. Exactly the same thing happened in the aftermath of the bursting of the dot.com bubble at the start of the new millennium.

So, a massive crisis in East Asia, a default on its debt by the Russian government, a huge failure of a speculative fund in America, the collapse of the dot.com bubble. Any single one of these might have triggered a worldwide crisis. But what might at any moment have turned into a bloodbath seemed to have been averted by the new-found skill and knowledge of policy makers, equipped not just with the longstanding tools of incentives but with the insights provided by the concept of 'market failure'.

The intellectual underpinnings for the apparent miracle were provided by economic theory. Olivier Blanchard is the chief economist of the IMF. Here is what he had to say in August 2008 in an MIT working paper entitled 'The State of Macro': 'For a long while after the explosion of macroeconomics in the 1970s, the field looked like a battlefield. Over time, however, largely because facts do not go away, a largely shared vision both of fluctuations and of methodology has emerged . . . The state of macro is good.' The state of macro is good! In August 2008!

A few weeks later Lehmans went bankrupt. Capitalism itself was on the brink of another Great Depression on the scale of the 1930s when unemployment in the USA reached nearly 25 per cent. The period which had been dubbed the Great Moderation, when policy makers seemed to have been granted the touch of King Midas,* in reality proved to be the Great Delusion.

*

One of Keynes's most well-known phrases refers to the power of ideas. In his *General Theory* he wrote, 'practical men, who believe themselves to be quite exempt from any intellectual influences, are usually the slave of some defunct economist. Madmen in authority who hear voices in the air are distilling their frenzy from some academic scribbler of years back.'

But in contrast to Keynes's view of the role of ideas in the crisis of the 1930s, the crisis of the late 2000s was grounded not in ideas which were advanced by academics 'years back'. It arose from ideas which play a prominent role in contemporary academic economics. Far from being 'defunct', these ideas became more and more important in the decade or so leading up to the crash in 2008.

There were two distinct strands to the intellectual mindset which believed that the right structures to correct market failure, the right incentives, the right appreciation of asymmetrical information, could solve all problems.

---

* Except of course the hapless British finance minister Gordon Brown who 'modernised' the UK's holdings of gold and foreign currencies by selling all the country's gold reserves when the price was at a near-record low. Why hold gold when all the uncertainties and problems of economic management have been solved? That was the thinking. At the time of writing, this decision has cost the British taxpayer at least $20 billion.

The first goes back about forty years, to a trio of American academics leading successful but blameless careers. The practical significance of their seemingly esoteric work has been immense. The intellectual impact of their findings was just as important, if by no means as obvious. But this, too, had huge practical significance in the policy stance which governments and regulators took towards financial markets. Fischer Black, described by one of his close friends as 'the strangest man I ever met', soon left academia to make millions at Goldman Sachs before his tragically early death. Robert C. Merton and Myron Scholes received the Nobel Prize in economics in 1997 for their findings.

These three discovered ways of applying concepts from statistical physics to financial markets. These concepts enabled prices – incentives – to be established in a vast number of markets which had scarcely existed before.

Their findings enabled the creation of today's industry of financial derivatives, worth over $500 *trillion*, according to the Bank for International Settlements. The basic idea of derivatives – so called because their value is derived from, or related to, that of an underlying asset – is very simple. Suppose an investor holds some Vodafone shares. He or she may worry that the price will fall. Someone else may think it will rise. A contract can be struck between them to trade the shares at a specified price at a date in the future. Its price will vary depending upon the price of Vodafone shares at any point between now and then.

The crucial feature of derivatives is that their price tends to fluctuate much more than that of the underlying share to which they are linked. The rewards of getting it right can be much bigger, but so too can the losses. Vodafone has traded for some time in the region of 150p a share, so suppose for illustration that this is the price today. If I feel optimistic about the company, I can buy the shares now. If in a month's time, say, they are 300p, I will have doubled my money. But I could instead buy *the right* to buy them at, say, 250p in a month from now for virtually nothing, 1p perhaps, since it is so unlikely that such a big increase will happen in such a short time. If I am proved right and the price really is 300p, I have the right to buy shares at 250p and can then sell them immediately for 300p. My 1p has turned into 50p, far, far more than doubling my money. But if I am wrong and the price stays below 250p, I will lose everything I put in.

In short, derivatives both satisfy and create an appetite for risk. They enable much riskier bets – sorry, considered investment judgements – to be made than if you can just trade in the underlying shares themselves.

As it happens, Merton and Scholes got their comeuppance when they totally misjudged some risks and their financial company, LTCM, mentioned above, collapsed in 1998 with a loss of nearly $5 billion, and had to be bailed out by the Federal Reserve. So today's problems are not exactly without precedent.

But Black, Merton and Scholes had initiated a period of stupendous innovation in financial markets. The introduction of incredibly high-powered mathematics into financial markets created all sorts of hitherto undreamt-of possibilities.

*

The major intellectual challenge in economic theory from the late nineteenth century for almost a hundred years was to specify as precisely as possible the conditions under which the operation of the free market could be guaranteed to be efficient, in the sense of establishing the theoretical existence of an equilibrium in which the price mechanism – incentives – would ensure that all markets in the economy cleared. That supply would equal demand in every market, and so no resources would be left unused. The details of this need not concern us here. Suffice that it is an exceptionally difficult intellectual problem, and no fewer than seven out of the first eleven Nobel Prize winners in economics received their award in whole or in part for their work on this problem. As we have seen, many economists have come to believe that this is a description of how the world *ought* to behave, and incentives and regulatory structures should be put in place to achieve this aim.

By the late 1960s, the problem – the existence of a so-called 'general equilibrium' – was essentially solved completely, with many of the necessary results having been established in the 1950s. However, there was a rather embarrassing implication which even economists of a high theoretical bent could not fail to notice. Essentially, for the existence of general equilibrium to be established, an assumption had to be made that there were complete markets.

'Complete markets'. Surely a rather obscure and innocuous phrase? But it means that a market must in principle exist for any transaction at any time. A price must in principle be able to be determined. So, to take two illustrative examples almost at random, a price has to be able to be set today for a purchase of sterling with dollars on 23 May 2041, and also for the purchase of the 1904 edition of Wright's *Grammar of the Gothic Language* on 15 September 2028. With a bit of scouting around, it may be possible to strike a deal on the former. But the latter? It is not even possible in practice to set a price for the weekly purchase of groceries in a month from now. All these are markets, and all require a price to be set.

The transparent lack of most such markets regarding future transactions led Kenneth Arrow, perhaps the single most distinguished contributor to the proof of existence of general equilibrium, to describe it in 1994 as being an 'empirical refutation' of the theory.

But here is where the academic trio rode to the rescue. One of the practical issues was that economists did not really know how prices should be established in this plethora of markets extending into the indefinite future which was required by the fundamental theory of free-market economics. Black, Merton and Scholes appeared to solve this problem. Their formula seemed to be able to determine what the price 'should' be for any transaction in any market in the future. Complete markets might not be observed in practice, but economists now seemed to know how to set prices in any market.

One of the products which could now, apparently, be priced 'optimally' was nothing other than risk itself. The markets would ensure that the right incentive, the right price, was in place to capture accurately the risk on any particular transaction, no matter how complicated.

One of these goes by the name 'securitisation'. The concept itself has been around for a long time. What was different in the run-up to 2008 was the use of risk pricing to cut up the securitised package into different packages and then create markets in which the packages could be bought and sold. It is this obscure and seemingly anodyne concept which made a major contribution to the subsequent financial crisis. A bank makes loans to a large number of individuals, the normal practice of banking since time immemorial. It collects fees for making the loans, and then, in the usual course of events, receives the interest due on them.

The innovation of securitisation involved bundling the loans up into a package, and selling the package on to a separate company, created by the bank itself. The risk was therefore taken off the bank, which still kept its fees. The separate company found the money to buy the package by issuing securities. These securities were bought by sophisticated financial market operators, who could then in turn sell them to someone else, almost like shares on the stock market. It was this latter operation, the creation of markets in securitised products, which was the real innovation. The value at any point in time would depend upon how the individual loans were performing and on how different people assessed the risks involved in buying the package. But this was now something which could safely be left to the market; everyone involved had the incentives to ensure that the risk was priced accurately.

The first real harbinger of the financial crisis occurred in the autumn of 2007, just a year before the real catastrophe took place. It led to the collapse of the British bank Northern Rock, a relatively small, geographically concentrated bank with a good reputation and an apparently sound business model. Yet its demise led to the sight on television of panicked savers queuing to try to get their monies out, the first time this had been seen in the UK since the nineteenth century.

The maths of pricing many of the individual parcel-passing trades is so hard that even the theoretical physicists doing it couldn't always be relied upon to get it right. It is certainly far beyond the capabilities of most board members in even the most august financial institutions.

This last point really gets to the nub of this first phase of the crisis. A system had been created which was so complicated, so convoluted, that even at the very highest levels in financial companies, no one really understood the level of risk which was being carried at any point in time. We might recognise the surroundings. They are none other than Herb Simon's strictures on the limits to human computational ability, and hence cognition. Literally no one had understood the full ramifications of the world which had been created. Gradually, doubts began to seep across the network of banks, doubts about whether it was possible to know the true potential extent of losses of another bank to which money had been lent. Once banks became uncertain about whether they understood the true financial positions of other banks, they became reluctant to lend to each other.

Indeed, in August 2007 they simply stopped doing so, more or less completely. A real, no-holds-barred credit crunch.

The problem was not specific to any one bank, not specific to any incentives, any specific pricing of risk which had been undertaken. It was a network effect. A network effect which gripped most of the world's banking system. One moment everything seemed fine and banks were happy to buy and sell these very complicated securitised bundles of loans. The next, almost in a twinkling of an eye, they were not. Indeed, they were extremely reluctant to carry out almost any sort of inter-bank trade, and specifically they stopped being willing to lend.

The price of each individual, isolated transaction had apparently been set optimally, the risk associated with it had been correctly assessed and taken into account. But banks had to believe that this was so. The belief had to be sustained across the networks on which the opinions and sentiments of bankers are formed. In Keynes's phrase, the bankers were 'a society of individuals each of whom is endeavouring to copy the others'. If they copied the opinion, the belief, that everything was fine, it would continue to be so.

But once they stopped believing, we had a credit crunch.

*

This was a decisive illustration in the run-up to the September 2008 crash of the robust yet fragile nature of networks which we encountered in the opening chapter. Banks, regulators, governments believed that the problem of pricing risk had been solved. Despite occasional doubts, occasional shocks, this belief persisted. Then, suddenly and dramatically, doubts about this spread like the Black Death across the networks of sentiment that run through financial institutions. And once this had happened, unlike Peter Pan exhorting the children to believe in fairies to save Tinkerbell from death, the authorities – regulators, governments, international institutions – found it impossible to exhort the banks to believe. Networks swamped all their efforts to restore confidence. Pessimism spread like wildfire.

To be fair, even though the authorities were not looking at the situation from a network perspective at all, there had been several prominent examples in the previous two decades of the robust nature of networks. Economies *can* withstand shocks and emerge relatively unscathed. Examples such as the East Asian crisis were mentioned at the start of this chapter. But there had been even more.

One Monday in October 1987, for instance, completely out of the blue, stock markets collapsed. In a single day, the value of the world's biggest companies fell by 20 per cent. But the sky didn't fall. Pessimism did not spread. Indeed, in Britain, the excesses of the boom of the late 1980s continued unchecked. House prices continued to soar, City traders continued to quaff champagne and collapse in stupefaction on their trains home. It was only two years later, for entirely unconnected reasons, that this particular party came to an end.

Even more telling is the experience of Japan over the past twenty years or so. By the late 1980s, Japan was *the* success story of the post-war era. Once derided for their cheap and nasty unreliable products, Japanese companies had come to bestride the globe. Visiting American bankers were obliged to overcome their squeamishness and consume live lobster sashimi in deference to their hosts.

Yet in 1990 pessimism suddenly infested the economy, and during the year the Nikkei share index lost 40 per cent of its value, bottoming out in 1993 at 80 per cent lower than its peak of just under 40,000. Even now it is only around 9,000, less than one-quarter its level of twenty years ago.

The collapse in land values was even more complete. In the late 1980s, rumours abounded that individual golf courses in Tokyo were worth more than the entire real estate of the state of California. But prices fell in large parts of the market by no less than 90 per cent.

Imagine. You are living in a house apparently worth half a million. You wake up the next day and find its value slashed to £50,000. Surely this would precipitate mass pessimism and a recession just as bad as the American one of the 1930s?

Logic says it would. But it didn't. In 2008 Britons and Americans were each, on average, about 40 per better off compared to the late 1980s, whereas in Japan the increase was just under 20 per cent. Not brilliant, but very far from being a disaster. Quite how the Japanese avoided catastrophe is still a bit of a mystery. Certainly, not just once but several times most of the major Japanese banks became technically bankrupt. With great aplomb, the Japanese central bank simply changed the rules and said they no longer were.

But the dramatic contrast between America and Japan shows that mass psychology, the percolation of pessimism or optimism across business and consumer networks, is almost impossible to judge in advance. In America in 1930, shocks in financial markets led to a stupendous collapse of the economy. In Japan in 1990, in apparently similar circumstances, things just bumbled along. Somehow, the authorities in Japan pulled off a very difficult feat of positive linking. They convinced everyone, financial markets, Japanese firms and consumers, that the spectacular collapse in land and equity prices were not about to plunge Japan into a repeat of the Great Depression of the 1930s.

Governments, central banks and international institutions like the IMF were bolstered in their Panglossian view of the world by intellectual developments within macroeconomics. We have seen above how the apparent ability to form complete markets and price the risk of each individual transaction 'optimally' proved seductive. Further enticement was provided by the concept of dynamic stochastic general equilibrium, or DSGE for short. Not perhaps the first phrase which sprang to the mind of the great seducer Lothario when in pursuit of one of his conquests, but one which proved just too beguiling for the authorities to resist.

The concept of the economically rational agent still has a firm grip on mainstream economics. But much of the exciting research in microeconomics, the study of individual agent behaviour, over the past three decades or so has distanced itself from this paradigm. As we have seen, Herb Simon's manifesto has by no means been carried out in full and has been the subject of attempts to neuter its most fundamental and radical message. But many economists now have a more realistic, more empirically grounded view of individual agent behaviour.

Incredibly, in macroeconomics the intellectual trend has been the complete opposite. The rational agent has emerged as the central character, the *only* character, in accounts of how the economy behaves at the overall, macro level. Imagine a *Macbeth* in which Shakespeare had fused Macbeth, his wife, Banquo and Duncan into a single character, and had written the play with no other characters at all. Imagine it? 'Rather tricky,' we Brits might say in British English, meaning 'almost impossible'. But this is exactly the sort of bizarre world in which modern macroeconomic theory invites us to believe.

Ideas such as these at the heart of modern macroeconomics have provided the intellectual justification of the economic policies of the past ten to fifteen years. And it is these ideas which the recent crisis has shown to be false. The dominant paradigm in macroeconomic theory over the past thirty years has been that of rational agents making optimal decisions under the assumption that they form their expectations about the future rationally – the rational agent using rational expectations.

Rational expectations do not require that an agent's predictions about the future are always correct. Indeed, such predictions may turn out to be incorrect in every single period, but still be rational. The requirement is that on average, over a long period of time, expectations are correct. Agents are assumed to take into account all relevant information, and to make predictions which are on average unbiased. Deviations from perfect foresight in any given period are an inherent feature of this behavioural postulate, but such deviations can only be random. If there were any systematic pattern to the deviations, the agent would be assumed to incorporate the pattern into his or her expectations. Again, on average over a long period, such expectations would be correct.

It will be apparent that the theory is difficult to falsify to someone who really believes in its validity. Even the most dramatic failure to predict the future, such as the 2008 financial crisis, can be explained away as a random error. A rational expectations enthusiast can continue to maintain the correctness of the theory by simply assuming that on average, over some (theoretically indeterminate) period of time, agents' expectations prove accurate.

An assumption of the theory is that, as part of the set of information being processed, the agent is in possession of *the* correct model of the economy. Indeed, on the logic of the theory itself, if the model being used to make predictions were not correct, the forecasts would exhibit some sort of bias, some systematic error, and agents would realise that it was wrong.

It might reasonably be argued that it is difficult to subscribe to the view that agents can even recognise the correct model of the economy, given that economists themselves differ in their views as to how the economy operates. In the autumn of 2008, many prominent American economists, including a number of Nobel Prize winners, vigorously opposed any form of bail-out of the financial system, arguing that it was better to let banks fail. Others, including decision makers at the Federal Reserve and Treasury, took a different view entirely.

The response of the academic mainstream has been to insist that there have been strong moves towards convergence within the profession on opinions about macroeconomic theory. By implication, anyone who takes a different view and is not part of this intellectual convergence is not really a proper economist.

A – possibly *the* – major project in macroeconomics over the past thirty-odd years has been to try to use equilibrium theory and the rational agent, rational expectations view of the world to explain the dynamic fluctuations in output which have been observed in the developed, market-oriented economies ever since the Industrial Revolution.

There are two aspects of this. First, the slow but steady growth in output over time, averaging around 3 per cent a year. It is this long-run growth which distinguishes capitalism from all other forms of social and economic organisation in human history. (This is a major topic in its own right, of course; I am merely mentioning it in passing here.)

The second is the persistent short-term fluctuations in output around this underlying slow growth. From time to time, these fluctuations are severe and output actually falls for a period of time, before growth is resumed. We in the West have just lived through one of these periods and, as I write, some people continue to believe another might well be imminent.

*

A theory based upon equilibrium appears to have an inherent problem when confronted with data such as that in Figure 4.1.

This shows annual percentage changes in total output in America from 1900 to 2010. It is entirely typical of the Western economies.

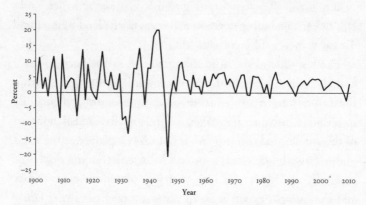

Figure 4.1 Annual percentage change in real US GDP, 1900–2010

Understanding why these fluctuations take place is very difficult. If they were understood in the same way as, say, building bridges is understood, we would have a pretty complete grasp as to why most of the world's developed economies are in their current predicament. But we do not. Given that these fluctuations are persistent both over time and across countries, they represent a serious challenge to a *Weltanschauung*, the framework through which the world is interpreted, based on the concept of equilibrium.

The first major attempt was 'real business cycle' (RBC) theory, developed in the 1980s by Finn Kydland and Edward Prescott. RBC has been very influential in mainstream economics, its originators receiving the Nobel Prize in 2004. According to this theory, periods of high or low growth – the booms and busts of everyday parlance – are initiated by random shocks to the economy. There are many problems with this theory, not least of which is the identification of what these shocks actually are, but the most widely used shock in RBC models is that of random changes in productivity.

In such models, recessions arise because of the rational response of individuals to adverse productivity shocks.* In a further illustration of the rather Orwellian use of words by mainstream economics, the 'real' of RBC signifies that recessions are caused by 'real' factors such as productivity and rational behaviour by agents. 'Real' is juxtaposed with 'nominal', nominal factors being such obviously irrelevant concepts as money, credit and debt!

Agents maximise utility over time, choosing between consumption and leisure. They have two decisions to make in every period. First, how much of their time to spend at work producing output (income) and how much to take in leisure. Second, how much of this output to allocate to investment, which will increase future levels of output, and how much to consume now.

Focusing just on the first of these may illustrate why even many fairly mainstream economists failed to be persuaded by the RBC approach. A temporary reduction in productivity today encourages people to work less now than in the future, because they will earn relatively more per hour in the future than they do today. So they choose to work less now. Some may work sufficiently less for it to seem as if they are unemployed, whereas according to RBC, they are actually rational agents maximising their expected lifetime utility by choosing to minimise their working hours. US Economist Paul Krugman famously noted that this account of the world suggests that the Great Depression, when nearly one in every four workers in America was unemployed, was essentially an extended voluntary holiday.

I have used the word 'agents' in the above description. But this is inaccurate. Strictly speaking, I should use it only in the

---

* All attempts to identify monetary factors as the source of shocks in this theory have failed.

singular, not the plural. For in these models, and their development into DSGE, as already mentioned above, there is only one agent. In the jargon, this is known as the 'representative agent'. I am not making this up. We are seriously invited to believe that the complicated workings of huge economies can be understood at the macro level by reference to a model containing only one agent, deemed to represent everybody, every firm, every government, every international body, every regulator. It is the complete antithesis of networks. They do not matter at all, because there is only one agent. Only one character in the play. Unless the agent started to trade with its counterpart on Mars – a hypothesis no less plausible than the concept of the representative agent itself – there is literally no one else with whom to form connections.

That aside, a rather glaring defect of the approach is that in financial crises, the responses of creditors and debtors may very well be, in fact almost invariably is, quite different. So just as a single-actor *Macbeth* is incomplete, as a very minimum any reasonable model needs two categories of agent: debtors and creditors.

Dynamic stochastic general equilibrium models are, just like RBC theory, based on the key microeconomic assumptions of orthodox economic theory. In other words, rational utility maximisation by consumers, rational value maximisation by firms, both operating under the assumption that they form expectations about the future rationally.

Essentially, DSGE models build on the RBC framework by trying to incorporate some features of the real world. So in RBC models, prices are very flexible and adjust rapidly to prevailing economic conditions. Under DSGE postulates, firms exercise some degree of market power and so prices may be more 'sticky' and take time to adjust to their new equilibrium levels following a shock to the system.

Although they are very complicated and difficult to construct, these models rapidly became very influential in academic economics.

These developments were not mere ivory tower musings. They rapidly gained influence with policy makers. Not of course that finance ministers themselves were intimately familiar with the nuances of DSGE models. But their advisers certainly were. As Olivier Blanchard of the IMF wrote just prior to the crash: 'DSGE models have become ubiquitous. Dozens of teams of researchers are involved in their construction. Nearly every central bank has one, or wants to have one. They are used to evaluate policy rules, to do conditional forecasting, or even sometimes to do actual forecasting.'

Note in particular the sentence 'Nearly every central bank has one, or wants to have one.' DSGE models became the central banker's fashion accessory of the moment – everyone else has one, so I must, too! Even within the rarefied portals of the world's central banks, network effects were present in terms of the fashion for copying such models.

So when politicians proclaimed the end to boom and bust, they had enormously powerful intellectual authority behind them, the models of the major central banks, the leading orthodox academic economists and the leading economic journals. They really did believe they had solved the macro problems of the Western world.

In the brave new world of DSGE, the possibility of a systemic collapse, of a cascade of defaults across networks connecting agents in the system, was never envisaged at all. Indeed, it is simply not possible in most such models, consisting as they do of just a single 'representative' agent. The models by their very nature ruled out the feature which distinguishes almost all financial crises in the history of the world: the loss of confidence which spreads rapidly across networks for bankers, traders, speculators.

*

Despite these apparent major intellectual advances, it should be said, forecasters continued to make exactly the same mistakes which they used to make when I started off as a macro modeller and forecaster way back in the 1970s. The problem was general amongst forecasters. Figure 4.2 is a chart from the October 2008 *Bank of England Quarterly Bulletin* about the revisions made to forecasts for GDP growth in 2009 as we progressed through 2008.

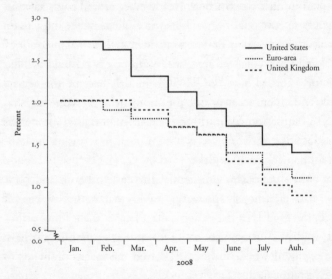

Figure 4.2 Predictions of real GDP growth for 2009 made during 2008. Source: Bank of England Quarterly Bulletin, October 2008

So at the start of 2008, decent growth was predicted for 2009. Even as late as August, the general view was that there would still be positive growth in 2009. But in fact, the West was already in recession in August 2008 and growth was already below zero! In actual fact, output fell by nearly 3 per cent in the US in 2009, by

5 per cent in the UK and by 6 per cent in the eurozone.

This was not simply a one-off error in an otherwise exemplary forecasting record. The major crisis in East Asia in the late 1990s was, as we have noted, completely unforeseen. Here are some figures to back up the assertion. In May 1997, the IMF predicted a continuation of the enormous growth rates which those economies had experienced for a number of years: 7 per cent growth was projected for Thailand in 1998, 7.5 per cent for Indonesia and 8 per cent for Malaysia. By October, these had been revised down to 3.5, 6 and 6.5 per cent, respectively. But by December the IMF was forecasting only 3 per cent growth for Malaysia and Indonesia, and zero for Thailand. Yet the actual outturns for 1998 for these countries were spectacularly worse, with output not growing but falling by large amounts. The fall in real GDP in 1998 was 10 per cent in Thailand, and 7 and 13 per cent in Malaysia and Indonesia, respectively.

So what happened next when the crisis struck? How was the world saved?

In the week of 15 September 2008 capitalism nearly ground to a halt. Share prices collapsed. Credit markets froze. And we were within hours of cash machines, ATMs, being closed to the public.

It was the American authorities who really saved the world in that terrifying week. And they did so not by the manipulation of elegant rational expectations models and theories, but by experiment and by relying on their knowledge of what had gone wrong in the Great Depression of the 1930s. Faced with a wholly uncertain immediate future, the authorities reacted by trying rules of thumb, by seeing what worked and what did not. They reacted exactly as Herb Simon said humans behaved all those years ago. They knew it was impossible to work out the optimal strategy. So they tried things which seemed reasonable and, quite literally, hoped for the best.

It was fortuitous – and an important illustration of the role of chance and contingency in human affairs – that the chairman of the Federal Reserve at the time, Ben Bernanke, was a leading academic authority on the Great Depression. He knew that, above all, the banks had to be protected. It may seem monstrously unfair that the bankers themselves escaped penalties – indeed, it *is* unfair – but the abiding lesson of the 1930s is that in a financial crisis the banks have to be defended. Money is the blood which flows through the economy to keep it alive. If the chairman instead had been, say, a world expert on dynamic stochastic general equilibrium models, we would almost certainly now be in the throes of the second Great Depression.

Bernanke had already restored a concept which is absent from the rational behaviour rule book, that of 'moral suasion'. Moral suasion, the central bank 'persuading' bankers to make particular decisions, is how central banks used to operate before the complicated, rule-based, hugely expensive bureaucratic control systems based on concepts of 'market failure' were introduced. Bear Stearns was a massive global investment bank which got into serious financial difficulties through massive losses on dealings in sub-prime mortgages. In March 2008, the company received an emergency loan from the Federal Reserve Bank of New York. It became apparent very quickly that this would not be sufficient to save the bank.

Using moral suasion, Ben Bernanke persuaded another bank, J. P. Morgan to take it over, with all its potential liabilities, in the course of a weekend. J. P. Morgan was under no legal or rule-based obligation to do so. But, somehow, they were persuaded, and also persuaded to pay $10 a share instead of the initial agreement to buy at just $2. (This, incidentally, is the same method used by the Bank of England to solve the previous banking crisis in the UK way back in the early 1970s.) The shareholders of Bear

Stearns still lost out dramatically, the peak share value over the previous twelve months having been over $130, but an immediate major financial collapse was avoided.

Of course, six months later the whole banking system was teetering on the edge. But why then and not previously? Why then and not even at all? Debt. That is the word that everyone began to worry about, and it is still an important source of concern in 2011. But why? Figure 4.3 charts debt in America from 1920 until immediately before the financial crisis in the autumn of 2008. Naturally, over such a long period the population grows, the economy grows, prices change. We cannot simply compare the amount of debt out there in mere money terms. What the chart does is divide the total amount of outstanding debt owed by people and companies, including financial ones, by the size of the economy.

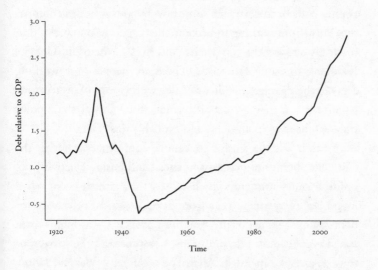

Figure 4.3 Total private debt in America compared to the size of the economy. Source: Steve Keen, University of Western Sydney

Shock, horror! Compared to the size of the economy, debt in 2008 was even higher than it was in 1929, the blip in the left-hand side of the chart, just before the Great Depression. The value of debt owed by individuals and companies is now nearly three times the size of the economy. Surely this meant that an economic collapse was inevitable?

The striking feature is the continuous rise in debt compared to the size of the economy over the entire post-war period. But the post-war period has been a time not of economic gloom but of entirely unprecedented rises in living standards. A willingness to take on debt can often be a sign of confidence about the future. For individuals, a confidence that things will get better and the debt be repaid.

Even more importantly, companies with new plans, new ideas, need loans in order to translate them into reality. These often fail, but when they succeed, the rewards can be spectacular. The last twenty years or so have seen some now famous American companies grow from nothing to become the biggest in the world, dramatically altering the way we live our lives – Microsoft, Google, Facebook to name but three. There are people now working away in their garages in Silicon Valley with visions of overturning Microsoft – if they are actually going to do this at some point they will need to incur debt, and probably lots of it.

Again, it was the elusive concept of confidence, or rather the complete absence of it, across financial and business networks of opinion and sentiment, which caused the crash to occur when it did. In every single year from 2000 onwards, private sector debt as a percentage of the American economy was higher than it had ever been. But despite scares along the way, the party continued, just like in Edgar Allan Poe's *Masque of the Red Death*. Then, suddenly, sentiment in financial markets became universally pessimistic.

Admittedly, the authorities did try the experiment of allowing Lehman's to fail. But it rapidly became evident that such a laissez-faire policy risked the collapse of the entire Western capitalist system. No monetary authority since has seen fit to repeat the experiment.

Much publicity and controversy surrounded the setting up of the resulting Troubled Asset Relief Program (TARP), a $700-billion bail-out fund which required political approval and so was played out in full light of the democratic process in America. But in many ways this was of second-order importance to the purely administrative actions of the American authorities, who:

* nationalised the main mortgage companies, Fannie Mae and Freddie Mac;
* effectively nationalised the gigantic insurance company AIG;
* eliminated investment banks;
* forced mergers of giant retail banks; and
* guaranteed money-market funds.

This last in particular has attracted very little attention, but was probably the single most important specific measure which was taken. The money-market funds hold very short-term assets, and are consequently obliged to hold highly liquid, high-quality assets. Indeed, the funds are essentially required to hold a dollar of assets for each dollar lent. But on 16 September, the Reserve Primary Fund* wrote off Lehman Brothers' stock, and the value of its shares fell below the critical dollar mark, to 97 cents. This almost triggered a massive run on the banking system as a whole. If this had happened, an immediate consequence would have been that ATM machines would have been closed and consumers would have had difficulties getting hold of cash. It is rumoured

* This was its name; it had no connection with the US Federal Reserve.

that the relevant sub-committee of the British Cabinet met to consider the risks of major public disorder if this actually happened. Companies would not have been able to roll over their short-term debt, and if they did not have cash in hand to cover what they owed, they would have had to file for bankruptcy.

In short, the default of money-market funds could easily have triggered by itself a massive recession. But on 19 September, the US Treasury announced that it would guarantee the holdings of any public money-market fund which participated (for a fee) in the programme.

The key point about all these actions is that the American authorities paid no attention to academic macroeconomic theory of the past thirty years. RBC theory, DSGE models, rational expectations – all the myriad erudite papers on these topics might just as well have never been written. Instead, the authorities acted. They acted imperfectly, in conditions of huge uncertainty, drawing on the lessons of the 1930s and hoping that the mistakes of that period could be avoided. It was not a grand plan, nor did one ever exist. This was a process of people responding to events on the basis of imperfect knowledge and experimenting to discover what did and did not seem to work, desperately trying to restore confidence across financial networks. And networks were important to the outcomes, to the decisions which were made, at a very detailed level.

Confidence across networks was key. Confidence across networks of financial institutions that the monies owed to them by others would be paid. Confidence across networks of commercial companies that output was not about to collapse like it did in the 1930s, so that they would then not act in ways which made this a self-fulfilling prophecy. And confidence across networks of individuals that their worlds were not about to fall apart.

*

The accounts of the seemingly perpetual meetings which took place between bankers, regulators and policy makers at the time make it clear that personal relationships, the interactions between the major players as human beings, also played a key role. If different people with different personalities had been involved, even if they too had thrown academic macro theory out of the window, the outcomes would have been different.

What they came up with worked. American GDP in 2009 fell by some 3 per cent compared to 2008, and by the autumn of 2011 the economy had not only stabilised but had grown for nine successive quarters. Indeed, by the third quarter of 2011, growth was sufficiently strong that the level of US GDP rose above its pre-crisis peak. (In contrast, between 1929 and 1930, the first year of the Great Depression, GDP fell by nearly 9 per cent, and the cumulative drop between 1929 and 1933 was 27 per cent.) Unemployment was still high, but employment had risen. The stabilisation programme worked, and a catastrophic collapse in output during 2009 was averted. It prevented pessimism and panic from percolating across networks.

It is a spectacular success of positive linking. The specific details of the measures which were taken were in general of second-order importance compared to the success in preventing the sentiment from spreading that America was about to suffer a re-run of the Great Depression of the 1930s.

The crisis in Europe during 2011 has mainly arisen through a failure of eurozone governments to generate anywhere near the same degree of positive linking of sentiment across financial networks. In late 2011, as the final revisions are being made to the book, it is still unclear as to what the eventual outcome will be. We can usefully think of much of the economic policy in Europe during 2011 as being not about specific measures in particular, the sort of thing which economists get excited about and whose impact they continue to believe they can measure, but about the desperate attempts by key policy makers to spread positive sentiment across the markets.

One thing is clear. Confidence is only weakly related to objective reality, to the actual facts. The principal concern is about public sector debt. In the case of Greece, the concern is entirely merited. Compared to the size of output in Greece (GDP), public sector debt is above 150 per cent, and there are few encouraging signs of a willingness to get to grips with the problem. With interest rates at around 7 per cent, this means that some 10 per cent (7 per cent of 150 per cent) of the total spending GDP Greece is going not on providing any form of services, but on paying the interest on its debt.

The comparable figure for Spain is only 60 per cent. Yet Spain, too, has experienced repeated crises of confidence in the markets, and its interest rates have hovered around 7 per cent. In contrast, the interest rates on government debt in both the UK and Germany are not much more than 2 per cent, even though public sector debt is 80 per cent of GDP in the UK and nearly 85 per cent in Germany. Obviously public debt is not the single cause of the lack of confidence, but the Japanese currency is perceived of as being strong despite a public debt ratio of nearly 200 per cent.

Policies which generate confidence are, once again, not so much the specific details, the economically 'rational' calculation of their potential consequences, but the creation of a positive mind set, a positive attitude on financial markets. Positive linking.

Such momentous events fully deserve the economists' description of 'macro', a prefix which is a straight transliteration of the Ancient Greek μακρο, meaning 'big'. Incentives were at work, in addition to network effects, not least because policy makers and regulators believed that they had put structures and incentives in place which would ensure that risk had been priced optimally and, in consequence, had been neutered. But, eventually, this belief was totally shattered by the impact of networks.

The world of the economically rational agent, forming expectations rationally, was both an intellectual and a practical mirage. The real world proved to be completely different. A world characterised by 'the psychology of a society of individuals each of whom is endeavouring to copy the others'. A world in which the optimal decision can never be known, where decision makers of all kinds fall back on Simon's rules of thumb. And a world in which the unexpected happens all the time.

But how far do these principles extend? As we have seen, they are certainly relevant not only to the economy at the macro level, but also to 'macro' issues which impact on many people, such as crime or ideological and religious beliefs. But do they only apply at the 'macro' level, using the word in its simple, original sense? We need to spend some time in the much more trivial, 'micro' world of popular culture to gauge how pervasive these factors might be. And the opening examples in the next chapter fit the description 'trivial' to perfection.

5

Lady Luck: The Goddess of Fortune

Ben Nevis is the highest mountain in the British Isles. Situated in the Highland region of Scotland, by world standards it is a mere pimple, standing at just 4,406 feet (1,344 metres). But even by the tourist path and the good track which it provides, hill walkers feel every single inch in the mere four miles it takes to get to the summit. And despite its modest height, the summit can be a brutal place. The mountain experiences the direct blast of the prevailing winds from the Atlantic, and gusts of 100mph are not uncommon. The mean average temperature is less than one degree above freezing. Snow can fall there on any day of the year, I have actually witnessed such a fall in August, at the height of so-called summer, from the comparative safety of a slightly lower hill where the precipitation merely fell as sleet.

The M1 in Britain is the main route out of London leading to the Midlands and the north of England. It was the first inter-city motorway to be completed in the UK, the main sections being built between 1959 and 1968, and carries a vast amount of traffic. Unusually, the traffic density reduces somewhat in the approaches to inner London, after the junction with London's orbital motorway, the M25, this extension having been opened in 1977. In April 2011, this part of the road was closed to all traffic for a few days because of a fire which had taken place immediately under one of the elevated sections.

These two seemingly disparate paragraphs, replete with details of wholly trivial facts, are connected. Videos of people doing their ironing on both sites were posted on YouTube in April 2011. One man struggled to the summit of Ben Nevis with an ironing board as well as a rucksack strapped to his back, the iron itself presumably being in the sack. Another man, unshaven and wearing a dressing gown, ironed a shirt over a period of three minutes on the closed lanes of the M1.

One of the videos received over 4,000 times as many hits on YouTube as the other. As the man in the more popular clip was reported as saying in a subsequent interview in a Sunday newspaper: 'I feel sorry for [him] . . . putting the video on YouTube only to receive forty-six hits. I climbed [. . .] and now my video has 204,000 hits. My story has been covered in Japan, America, Greece and Russia. People probably think I'm a mad Englishman, but I don't care.'

The missing words in the quote following 'I climbed' are 'through a gap in a fence and walked for two minutes to the motorway'. So it was the M1 ironer who experienced worldwide interest in his feat, if we might use this word to describe his doings, and the intrepid climber who disappeared into the mists of time.

The difference in the degrees of interest shown in these two events is very hard to explain in the framework of the isolated, rational agent reacting to incentives. As usual, we could in principle always tell a story after the event which purports to account for the much greater popularity of one video compared to another. But it is even harder to make up in this context than it was with the incident of the rioting soccer fans in Sardinia in the opening chapter. At least with the hooligans, the view of the world in which autonomous agents respond to incentives could offer a reasonable explanation for part of what happened, even though by no means the whole. Here, the imagination quails at even trying to offer a rationalisation in the incentives framework. Eccentric Englishmen iron clothes in unusual situations. The intrinsic similarities in the two events are profound. Yet one proves 4,000 times more popular than the other.

This is by no means an isolated example. On the contrary. In the world of popular culture, using this term in a broad sense, such massive discrepancies of outcome between virtually identical 'products' is quite literally an everyday occurrence. Most languish in obscurity, whilst a select few become very popular, for no obvious reason other than sheer good luck.

The most popular daily download on, say, Flickr or YouTube will usually be not just several thousand but several hundred thousand times more popular than most of the photos or videos which are uploaded on any given day. Occasionally, there will be an intrinsic, obvious reason for the most viewed or downloaded choices, such as footage of a tsunami taken by a lucky survivor. But most of the time, this is not the case.

I am writing this paragraph on Easter Monday. On the Flickr website today I see that 'Hot tags' in the last twenty-four hours include 'Easter', 'Easter morning', and '*resurrección*'. Not at all surprising. But there is also '*rund*', a tag of German origin containing photos of wholly disparate objects connected only by the quality of roundness, and 'Animal Collective'. The latter is not some modern communal or Soviet-style experiment in animal husbandry, but the word 'experiment' can indeed be used to describe what it actually refers to, for Wikipedia assures me that Animal Collective is an experimental rock band from Baltimore currently based in New York City. Another hot tag is 'specialty', which, on inspection, after the first few shots of various cakes, appears to consist of hundreds of photographs of an entirely ordinary dog doing entirely ordinary things.

The phenomenon of a lack of connection between any inherent, objective quality of an offer and its popularity relative to other, very similar things is not confined to leisure activities such as viewing and downloading from websites. It is increasingly widespread across markets where people pay real money, even for what we might in a Neanderthal kind of way call 'real' things.

A wide range of software programs, such as anti-virus tools and media players, can be downloaded from the CNET website. These have intrinsic technical features which can be measured and compared. Not quite the steel bars and lengths of cloth of the Industrial Revolution of the early nineteenth century, but their early twenty-first-century equivalents, which permit objective assessment of their relative quality. For anyone not inclined to carry out this task for themselves, there is plentiful and readily accessible information on the site in the form of both expert reviews of the different products and the opinions of ordinary users.

New Mexico-based researchers Rich Colbaugh and Kristin Glass did a study of real-life downloads of programs from the site to see if there was any way of predicting the daily totals for each of the different products, and presented their findings to a UCLA conference on complex systems in the agreeable setting of Lake Arrowhead in the San Bernardino mountains. They found that none of this information was of any use at all, whether it was a technical feature or the various reviews which were available. Colbaugh and Glass concluded that 'the average quality of the most popular software is not distinguishable from the average quality of all software available on site'.

A world in which the connection between the inherent characteristics of different choices and their popularity is broken is a completely different planet from the one the economically rational agent lives on, where incentives matter. In this rational world, we will try to sell more of our product by improving its quality and endeavouring to make its price more competitive.

We want to incentivise customers to buy more. But, it seems, in many modern contexts such a strategy may be pointless. A world in which network effects dominate incentive effects requires a radical reappraisal of how we behave.

In the software download study, at the start of each day we cannot predict using objective information which product in any particular software category will be the most popular download. All we know is that one of them will be the most popular (obviously), and that it will be downloaded many more times than the majority of similar products which are available.

The people who download a software product from the site during any given day will, in general, be completely unknown to each other. Yet they nevertheless make up a network. Users are given information on the number of downloads which have previously taken place during the course of that particular day. So a person choosing to download now may be influenced directly by the previous choices of others. He or she may download a particular program simply because it seems popular.

The precise composition of the network changes from day to day, in that the individuals downloading are not the same. But on each day, be it software downloads or YouTube hits or Flickr views, the structure of the network appears to encourage what we might term percolation across it. The choice of one or two programs, one or two videos, one or two collections of photographs, percolates across wide sections of the network. The most successful on any given day achieve huge popularity. The structure of the network seems to facilitate a small number of items – products, services, ideas, sites – receiving a great deal of attention.

*

A point discussed immediately below and to which we return at considerably greater length in Chapter 6, is that there are different kinds of networks, with radically different implications. Readers might usefully reflect at some point on the different networks in their own lives, of the different ways in which networks may influence their own decisions.

We can readily think of examples where networks are important in agents' decisions and where the networks, far from encouraging percolation, appear to be almost designed to resist the spread of different choices. Consider the world of economics textbooks.

Most students are fed not on esoteric maths but on the standard textbooks. But these have, if anything, gone backwards in recent years. Aimed at the mass market of US community college students, they have dumbed down the subject to a terrifying degree.

I have in front of me the 1967 edition of Richard Lipsey's *Introduction to Positive Economics*. This, along with Paul Samuelson's textbook, was the best-seller for many years. It is not aimed at geniuses, just ordinary, regular students, 'designed to be read as a first book in economics'. Of its 861 pages, only thirty-two contain any maths, and even that is of the simplest possible kind.

Yet it is full to bursting with really interesting examples of real-world behaviour. Yes, here is the basic model showing how in a simple market, price can adjust to bring supply and demand into balance. But here, too, is an immediate counter-example, of great practical importance, discussed at length. Indeed, it has its own separate chapter. What happens if supply can't be increased quickly, if it takes time to respond to price changes? (This is true of most agricultural markets: trees take time to grow, even chickens need five months before they can first start to lay eggs.)

Lipsey shows, simply and clearly, using only diagrams, how the free market might work very badly in this case. His chapter summary, printed in bold, states: 'in the unstable case, the operation of the competitive price system itself does not tend to remove any disequilibrium; it tends rather to accentuate it'. Careful, practical study is needed on a case-by-case basis to determine whether a free market is likely to lead to stable or unstable behaviour. The crude policy advice that markets always work is simply not given house room, even in a textbook for the ordinary first-year student.

So why are the textbooks not being rewritten, not just to bring back the insights of the word-rich, maths-poor texts of the 1960s, but to incorporate the advances which have been made in economics in recent decades, such as a more realistic, empirical view of how agents behave? Until I was drawn into the textbook world, this puzzled me.

A few years ago, I was approached by someone from a leading academic publisher. He was, he explained, their very top man across the whole of the sciences. His remit included economics. This sounded interesting. What did he have in mind?

What the commissioning editor had in mind was very exciting. He wanted an entirely new textbook, to incorporate not just the really interesting advances in the subject over the past twenty years or so but even to go beyond these into the world of networks. The editor already had a best-selling economics textbook of the standard kind in his stable. He understood that at some point in the future all existing textbooks will be redundant. The new generation of textbooks will contain the economics of the twenty-first century, not that of the twentieth (or even the nineteenth!), which the present ones do.

He was anxious that one of his rivals would get there before him, and bring out a textbook which would scoop the pool and be hard to dislodge from its number 1 slot. So he realised that his company would have to innovate and bring out a completely new text. Was I interested? It sounded like a dream. But like most dreams, it was too good to be true.

The editor faced a dilemma, which he articulated clearly. His problem was that the market – in this case the market for textbooks – is already occupied by the incumbents. They might ignore much of the interesting scientific work that has gone on in economics in the past twenty years, they might be guilty of dumbing down, but they are there. And their publishers and authors use every trick to make it stay that way. Top textbooks routinely have over 10,000 multiple choice questions helpfully provided on a web-linked site, for instance. So teachers don't even have to think about setting questions: they are all provided.

So we have a situation in which products with inferior qualities – containing lots of old-fashioned economics – are preventing products which are potentially superior from entering the market. The barriers to entry which they have erected are very hard to breach. In simple economics, this shouldn't happen. Consumers are supposed to have perfect information, so they should choose the new rather than the old. But the real world just doesn't work like this. Yet most students are now never told this, and they never get to choose – except by voting with their feet and dropping economics altogether.

And this was exactly the editor's dilemma. He knew that at some point the market will look completely different, that the new will eventually oust the old. But he had no way of knowing when this would be. In the meantime, any single attempt to enter the market with a new-style economics text would be likely to fail, unable to break the hold on the market which the current textbooks have.

We corresponded on this and talked. Eventually, the editor said he would go ahead on the basis that no more than 10 per cent of the total material could be the new economics, the other 90 per cent would be the old. But I just could not do it, I could not be part of disseminating a wrong-headed view of the world which leads to so much bad policy advice. I did not blame the man. He was thoughtful and anxious to do good, but faced commercial imperatives. Examples of textbooks which are trying to do twenty-first-century economics have since appeared, but their sales are very small regardless of their inherent quality.

In this example, it is the sheer density of the connections in the network which actively militates against change. Even the world of academic economics is not immune to innovation, far from it, and there is a chance, no matter how small, that their network would prove fragile. A completely new textbook could in principle see dramatic sales, as it cascaded across the network.

But each individual in a position to recommend adoption of the innovative text has so many strong connections which limit his or her powers to act. For lecturers there is the immediate pressure of being seen to act out of line with one's peers. There is the overarching network of the mainstream profession at the top level, which deems what is and what is not appropriate. There is the network which connects the lecturer to his or her students, who may or may not appreciate being taught differently from other economics students on their social networks. So it is very hard for any but the most determined to adopt the innovation. There are just too many connections which will not take the same decision, and the pressure to follow suit is very strong. Agents are more or less locked into a particular pattern of behaviour, which is hard to alter.

At the other extreme, we have the largely imaginary world of mainstream economic theory, in which individuals operate as entirely isolated agents. Choices cannot spread by contagion across the network, cannot cascade as a result of agents being influenced directly by the decisions of others, for the simple reason that there is no network at all.

In a universe such as this, we might start introducing a few connections, allowing at least some individuals to be affected directly by what others think and do. But, intuitively, when the agents remain only weakly connected in this way, the chances of a new idea, product, mode of behaviour, spreading across the network are limited. The potential for a cascade across most of the network is limited by the sparseness of the connections. Yet in the case of the economics textbooks given above, the potential is limited for quite the opposite reason, namely the sheer density and strength of the connections. These constrain any single agent from opting for a different choice from that made uniformly by its neighbours, using this latter word in the sense of the other agents to which it is connected. Everyone stays in line.

*

So, somewhat paradoxically, networked systems are resistant to change when they are either weakly or strongly connected. What happens when the degree of connectivity sits somewhere in between, when it is like Baby Bear's porridge, neither too hot nor too cold? It is in fact exactly the sort of mixture which is most likely to lead to positive linking.

Duncan Watts, whom we met briefly in the opening chapter, trained as a physicist at the University of New South Wales in Australia before moving to America, where he became Professor of Mathematical Sociology at Columbia University. More recently, Watts has moved to Yahoo! Research, where he directs the Human Social Dynamics Group. He explored the concept of cascades across networks in a brilliant paper published in the prestigious *Proceedings of the National Academy of Science* in 2002. The article has the austere and forbidding title of 'Global Cascades on Random Networks'. Although it is not exactly bedtime reading, it offers a simple but very powerful abstract model which tells us a great deal about the real world.

The description of his model, translating the maths into English, will take some time. But please be patient! The approach taken by Watts is similar to that used much more generally in network models. And the implications for policy are both surprising and profound.

Watts was interested in the question of what happens in a simple model in which, as a deliberate assumption, the *only* thing which affects how agents choose amongst alternatives is the choices which other agents have already made. In other words, in order to illustrate the potential impact of social influence, of choices being determined by what others do, he deliberately left out all other factors, such as price and quality.

Watts set up a computer model of individual agents who are connected to each other at random. We can usefully think of this as a game with some simple rules. One of the rules decides which agents are connected to each other. So we can choose to have, say, a hundred agents in the model* and decide that there is a 5 per cent chance of a given agent being connected to any other agent. On average, each agent will be connected to five others. This percentage can be varied each time the game is played.

In this context, the fact of being connected means that an agent to whom you are connected can potentially influence your behaviour. As we will see shortly, this does not mean that this agent will necessarily affect how you behave, but the small group to which you are connected are the only ones who have the potential to do so.

This way of connecting agents, by a purely random process, may seem entirely unrealistic but does in fact offer a reasonable approximation to many practical social and economic situations.

---

* In practice, there are usually a lot more agents in the model to avoid small sample problems, but a hundred is used to keep the arithmetic simple.

Epidemics are often spread by random contact. A person you do not know and will never see again sneezes on the train and you catch a cold. In a strange city, you choose the restaurant with more people in, even though you know none of them. In financial markets, a trader may very well monitor particularly closely the behaviour of a small number of others, but if the market starts to move strongly in one direction as a result of the decisions of many people entirely unknown to the trader, again a sensible decision might very well be to follow that trend, even if it is counter to what his 'control group' is doing.

Watts's game can be played with networks which have more explicit, much less random social structure to them, of which more later, but let us describe the rest of the rules of the game retaining the assumption of a random network. In this model, an agent has a choice between two alternatives. These could be a consumer deciding between two competing brands, a firm considering two different technologies, someone considering in the England of the 1550s whether to remain a Protestant or become a Catholic, to give just a few examples.

In reality, people will take into account a whole range of factors in making these decisions, but in all these cases, no matter how much information is used to make the choice, by assumption we are dealing with either/or. There may of course be more than two choices (including not choosing either of the alternatives on offer), but this can readily be accommodated in the model, and we concentrate on the simplest version of the model where the choice is between two alternatives and by assumption the agent chooses one or the other of them.

When the game starts, by assumption all agents have chosen alternative A. We need now to specify a rule of behaviour which determines whether they stay with A or switch to B.

We first of all make the entirely realistic assumption that each agent differs in his or her intrinsic willingness to switch. Take consumer products: some individuals are keen to try new products, whilst others have a preference for staying with what they already know and like. The more information we have about the persuadability of agents or their willingness to experiment, the more realistic the model can be made. But for the moment imagine we have no information on this at all. Lacking any better alternative, we can simply allocate at random to each agent a value between 0 and 1. Slightly confusingly, an agent allocated a number close to 1 is deemed to be *less* persuadable, *less* willing to switch than someone allocated a number close to 0. The reason for this will become clear. For purposes of description, we call this value the agent's *threshold*.

How, then, do agents decide whether to switch from A to B? In this game, by assumption the only information used by the agent in making this choice is the choices which the other agents to which he or she is connected have also made. Incentives do not enter the picture. If the agent is in state A and the proportion of these relevant agents who have chosen B is above the agent's threshold, the agent will also choose B instead of A. So if your threshold is 0.5, say, and three out of the five agents to which you are connected have chosen B, you will switch, because $3/5 = 0.6$, which is greater than 0.5. But if only two have chosen B, you stay with A. $2/5 = 0.4$, which is less than 0.5. It is apparent now why a higher threshold means that the agent is less persuadable than an agent with a lower threshold. Someone with a threshold above 0.8 will need all of his or her network to choose B before being persuaded to switch, whilst if it is less than 0.2, even just one person choosing B will lead the agent to also make this choice.

As noted above, there may be many factors which an agent takes into account in deciding between A and B. The choices made by those people whose opinion or behaviour he or she respects may very well be one of them, but not necessarily the only one. A simple example is if A and B are competing consumer brands, their prices may also be an element in the decision as well as what other people have chosen. But the essential features of Watts's model continue to be valid as long as the choices of others remain a key factor. Other things such as price can again be accommodated in the model; indeed, it is always easy, if not always edifying, to make models more and more complicated by bringing in more and more factors.

Besides, the assumption that the behaviour of others is the only factor may often be a reasonable approximation to reality. In the restaurant example above, you may have a guidebook to the city which has enabled you to filter down the options to just two, but the number of people in each may still be the decisive factor in your choice. In situations such as this, you have relatively small amounts of information on which to make a judgement, so relying on the choices made by others makes sense. In other situations, people may be able to acquire large amounts of information about products which are inherently difficult to understand. Processing and understanding the information available on, say, a choice of pension plans is a hard task. So a reasonable decision rule is to rely on the actions or recommendations of a small number of people whose judgement you trust.

*

Thomas Schelling is an American polymath who won the Nobel Prize in economics in 2005. His work ranges across not just economics but areas such as game theory, foreign affairs, conflict resolution and nuclear strategy. Back in 1973 he published an article in the rather obscure *Journal of Conflict Resolution*. The title of the paper is much more memorable, if somewhat bizarre: 'Hockey Helmets, Concealed Weapons and Daylight Saving'.

But that is not all, for it goes on to add, in smaller type, 'A Study of Binary Choices with Externalities'.

This latter phrase defines what has become a huge area of study in network theory, including Duncan Watts's illuminating model. What does it mean? 'Binary' means involving two things, so choices are situations such as those described above, where an agent faces a choice between two alternatives. 'Externalities', a very useful concept in economics, are situations where the decisions of any one agent can have consequences for others. For example, a factory which emits pollution creates a negative externality for inhabitants of the area. The factory produces goods which it sells, employs people in the process of doing so, but at the same time imposes costs on everyone else as a result of the pollution it creates. Unless there is some form of taxation on pollution in place, these costs are external to the firm itself, and have to be borne by other agents.

The concept has been an important one in economic theory for at least a hundred years, and there is a huge literature on the topic. Schelling incorporated the idea into networks for the first time. His inspiration was an event which took place in American ice hockey in 1969. A leading player, Ted Green of the Bruins, was not wearing a helmet and in a clash suffered a fractured skull. Schelling's paper begins with a quote from *Newsweek* on the incident: 'Players will not adopt helmets by individual choice for several reasons. Chicago star Bobby Hull sites the simplest factor "Vanity". But many players honestly believe that helmets will cut their efficiency and put them at a disadvantage, and others fear the ridicule of their opponents . . . One player summed up the feelings of many: "It's foolish not to wear a helmet. But I don't – because the other guys don't."'

I don't because the other guys don't! A short phrase which captures much of what modern network theory is about in social and economic situations. Here, the player actually *has* made an independent, 'rational' assessment of the costs and benefits of wearing a helmet and has concluded that it makes sense to do so. But the network effect, the impact of peers on the behaviour of individuals, trumps this calculation.

This unfortunate incident inspired Schelling to write the paper. As he points out 'the literature on externalities has mostly to do with how much of a good or a bad [e.g. pollution] should be produced, consumed or allowed. Here, I consider only the interconnectedness of choices to do or not to do, to join or not to join, to stay or to leave, to vote yes or no, to conform or not to conform to some agreement, rule or restriction'. Nearly three decades after the publication of the Thomas Schelling paper, Duncan Watts was inspired to formalise the concept of binary choice with externalities and to explore its implications more deeply.

*

So with all this in place, we are now in a position to play the game, or, more scientifically speaking, to run the model. Initially, remember, by assumption everyone has selected option A. The game is started by choosing a small number of agents at random to switch to B. Imagine that we have some sort of policy which induces this behaviour, some sort of nudge factor, some incentive, which succeeds initially in altering the behaviour of only a few people.

The purpose of the game is to see how many agents eventually end up selecting B rather than A. The process by which they do this is defined by the 'copying rules': who you are connected to (i.e. who can potentially influence your behaviour), how persuadable you are, and how many of your potential 'influencers' are making a choice different from your own. In turn, if you are persuaded to switch from A to B, you will potentially influence people who look to you as part of their decision-making processes to also switch.

The result of any particular 'play' of the game may be very sensitive to the particular circumstances. At one extreme, suppose the agents who were selected to make the initial switch from A to B were connected to agents who were very hard to persuade, who required almost everyone who might influence them to choose B before they themselves did. The 'cascade' – the spread across the network of people choosing B rather than A – may very well be stopped there and then. No one else chooses B at all beyond the small group assumed to do so as a result of the initial change in incentives which we might readily imagine in a real-life situation encouraged them to make this initial switch.

In practice, the more information we have about the agents, who they are connected to, how persuadable they are and so on, the more we can start calibrating the model to a real-life situation. But in the very general abstract way in which Watts played his game, such information is necessarily lacking. This, it must be stressed, is not a defect of his method but a strength. By exploring a wide range of initial choices, by having them connected to different sets of other agents, by giving these different levels of persuadability, we can start to understand the general properties of the model across a wide range of assumptions.

To do this in practice, the game is played many times under identical rules. The only difference in each solution of the model is the agents chosen at random to switch to B at the very start.* A crucial point is that the size of the initial disturbance, the initial shock to the system, is exactly the same in each solution. The same number of agents is selected to switch from A to B each time.

---

* Theoretically, of course, given that they are chosen at random, these could be identical in two separate solutions, but the chances of this are vanishingly small.

Examples have already been given of the sort of real-world settings which this model might help illuminate. There are others. The network might be the power grid of the United States, how power is transmitted across the country. State A means that each generator is working well, state B means that it has failed. A small number of outlets chosen at random experience a failure, the sort of thing which happens all the time. How far will this spread? In a different context, sentiment about the future, the degree of optimism or pessimism which firms feel at any point in time, is an important determinant of the boom and bust of the business cycle. Here, we are in Keynes's world from an earlier chapter, where we have 'a society of individuals each of whom is endeavouring to copy the others'. We can think of a firm in state A as being optimistic. The economy receives a small shock, a bit of bad news, and a few firms switch to state B, pessimistic. How many others will abandon their optimism? If enough do so, the economy will move from boom to bust. But by assumption, the economy in this case has received only a small adverse shock. Can this really be sufficient to precipitate a full-blown recession?

The answer is both yes and no! The same small initial disturbance can have dramatically different outcomes. Most of the time, the initial disturbance, the initial switch by a small number of agents from A to B, does not spread very far. But occasionally there will be a cascade across the system as a whole, and most agents will end up with B instead of A.

In the above few paragraphs we have fleshed out a feature of some networks highlighted in the first chapter – systems of interconnected agents whose behaviour influences each other are both *robust* and *fragile*. Most of the time, the system is robust to small disturbances, they do not spread very far. But occasionally, the system is fragile, vulnerable to exactly the same size of shock which it is usually able to contain. These properties present both difficulties and opportunities to policy makers.

Figure 5.1 shows the results of 1,000 separate trials of the model,* and the distribution of the proportion of all the 1,000 agents in each who eventually switch from A to B.

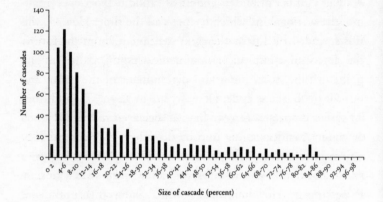

Figure 5.1 The size of cascade is the percentage of all agents eventually switching from A to B

Note: The data is grouped into bands of 2 percentage points, so the first bar on the bottom axis shows the range 0% to 2%, the next 2% to 4% and so on

Out of the total of 1,000 solutions, the vertical axis indicates how many of them were in a particular range and the horizontal axis shows the range. The largest bar shows that on some 120 occasions out of the total of 1,000, the percentage switching to B was small, in fact in the range of 4–6 per cent the way we have plotted the data. Next, we see around 100 solutions ending up in each of the ranges 2–4 and 6–8 per cent, and around 80 in the range 8–10 per cent. So most cascades are small, the initial

* Technically, this example is of a random network with the probability of connection set at 4 per cent, and ten initial seeds.

disturbance to the system when a few agents switch to B does not spread very far. The system is robust to shocks. But we also see a few occasions when there are very large cascades, over 80 per cent of all agents, in fact. It is therefore at the same time fragile. And, importantly, it is an entirely random process that 'decides' whether the *same network* is robust or fragile.

There are many subtleties even to this simplest version of the Watts model. But its implications for policy, in circumstances where network effects matter, are both disturbing and exciting.

*

If the world operates in anything like the same way as it does in the model, anticipating the impact of a change in policy becomes extremely difficult. The common-sense causal link between the size of an event and its eventual impact is broken. Of course, if a large shock were administered to the system so that, say, one half of all agents switched from A to B, by definition the eventual outcome would be large. But, equally, a small disturbance can have dramatic consequences.

However, by deliberate construction in Watts's model, *all* the shocks administered to the system – the number of agents selected to switch from A to B at the start of each solution – are the same. Yet the outcomes, the proportion who eventually switch to B, can be dramatically different.

This highly counterintuitive result is disturbing. How can it be that a small change can have a massive consequence? An initial reaction might well be that this is in some way an artefact of the model, which makes many abstractions, many simplifications from the real world. Surely human societies and economies simply do not operate like this?

But, as we have seen, they do. A man ironing clothes on a closed motorway gets 4,000 times more people watching his video than a man ironing clothes on the summit of Britain's highest peak. It is hard to see how there is anything intrinsically more interesting, more attractive in the former activity rather than the latter. With a dramatic switch in scale and scope, we can recall the 20 per cent collapse of stock market prices on that Black Monday in October 1987. Faced with a truly major event such as this, instinctively we look for the smoking gun, for the massive event which triggered it. An intensive hunt has been mounted, but the culprit has never been found. Traders on stock markets receive large numbers of potential shocks in the form of new information, whether about the overall economy, particular firms, or the actions of other traders. Each piece of new information has the potential to trigger a large cascade. Few do. For the most part, the disturbances are contained by the robustness of the network. Every so often, the system proves fragile.

In some ways, this is good news for policy makers. Suppose a desirable policy aim is selected, such as reducing the number of people who are obese. Policy instruments are chosen, which might include good old-fashioned incentives through tax increases on fatty foods, as well as less direct methods such as health education, restricting advertising, or whatever. Now, to achieve a big reduction in obesity, the use of incentives alone, no matter how smart or sophisticated, requires that the policy has a big effect, that it alters the behaviour of large numbers of people. Incentives plus networks means that, if you are lucky, the behaviour of only a small number of people needs to be changed, yet the number who eventually change their minds could be enormous.

This represents a potentially huge increase in the ability of policy to affect outcomes, to reap the benefits of positive linking. But in a networked world, things are rarely as clear cut as that. Suppose some individuals were indeed induced by a change in incentives, by a straightforward change in price or by some more subtle factor to alter their behaviour in the way intended.

However, the perception that the authorities were trying to influence people might induce others, through the network effect, to become more stubborn or even to adopt a completely contrary mode of behaviour. We have seen examples of this already, not least the experience of the Italian police captain confronting the English thugs and firing his pistol into the air.

Moreover, and more generally, networked systems bring problems to policy makers trying to evaluate the effects of previous policies. What worked and what did not work? A great deal of policy evaluation is carried out paying little or no attention to the potential impact of network effects.

But if these are important in any particular context, studies which ignore them can generate quite misleading results. A successful outcome may arise, not principally because of a partial, initial success with a change to incentives which leads a few agents to alter their behaviour, but because of the impact of imitation across the network. In such a case, the success would be mistakenly attributed to the incentive factor, and policy makers would be puzzled when a similar policy led to an apparent failure in a different context. In the marketing world, for example, successful viral marketing campaigns, whose specific purpose is to spread across a network, are notoriously difficult to repeat. The creators of rather spectacular successes find them hard to replicate.

The difficulties in identifying whether incentives have worked in the past, and to what extent, can be seen in an example that might be found in any basic introductory course in economic theory. We have a group of individuals contemplating whether or not to buy a particular product. Each individual has his or her own intrinsic preference for what is on offer, so each will decide to buy at a different price. Some are strongly attracted and will pay a high price, others will buy only if the item is perceived as cheap.

The usual interpretation of price is, of course, exactly that.

So we might examine a brand of shampoo and see how its price affects sales. But as we have seen, 'price' can have a much wider, multidimensional interpretation. It essentially summarises the costs associated, or thought to be associated, with any particular course of action. So, yes, it can just be the price of your favourite shampoo. But it could be the perceived costs associated with, say, being a petty criminal, taking drugs, or being burned to death.

*

From the individual preferences, the prices at which different people will buy the product (carry out the activity), we can easily obtain a 'market' demand curve. In other words, we add up the individual decisions and see how much is bought, how much of the activity is carried out, at different prices.*

With Amy Heineike, then of George Mason University, I investigated what happens to the very simple demand curves of economic theory when network effects are present in the system. In this very basic model, the top left-hand chart in Figure 5.2 represents the classic market demand curve. As price increases, demand falls, exactly as expected. If we can discover the shape of this curve by, say, some smart statistical analysis of the data, we can change incentives – the price – to change the amount people buy.

We then introduce into this elementary model what in this context we term the 'bandwagon' effect, so that the more people buy the product at any given price, the more likely any given individual is to buy it as well. The additional charts show the overall demand for the product (degree of participation in the activity) with different strengths of the bandwagon effect. The stronger this effect, the less price matters.

* For economic theorists, I am ignoring here any Sonnenschein–Mantel–Debreu effects which cause such fundamental problems in principle for the scientific nature of general equilibrium theory.

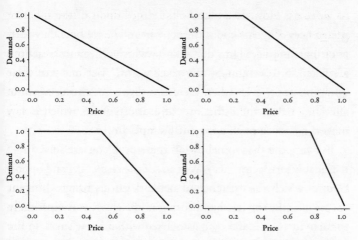

Figure 5.2 Simple market demand curve with price and 'bandwagon' effects. In the top left-hand chart there is no bandwagon effect, and demand simply depends upon price. The other three charts show the impact on demand of introducing stronger and stronger bandwagon effects.

Again, to repeat for explanation, the top left-hand chart shows the standard demand curve of the economics textbooks. As price increases, less of the product is bought. On the left-hand axis, labelled 'demand', we are plotting the proportion of the total number of people who are both interested in the product and actually buy it. So at a very low price, the proportion is close to 1, in other words almost everyone who might want to buy it, does buy it. As the price increases, the proportion falls, until eventually, when the price is sufficiently high, no one buys it at all.*

There are many questions from a policy perspective even with this simple chart. How do we know what the relevant measure

* The scale for price, between 0 and 1, is quite arbitrary for this illustrative example. Readers can imagine for themselves the actual price range over which either everyone or no one who might be interested would actually buy a product.

of 'price' is? How do we know the distribution of the inherent preferences of agents about the activity and hence how they react to changes in price? How do we know which other agents' actions are taken into account by any given agent?* But many of these questions apply even when there is no network effect present at all. They reflect the difficulties and uncertainties which policy makers face even in an apparently simple world.

But suppose that somehow all these problems are solved in a reasonably satisfactory way. We can see the challenges and opportunities which the existence of network effects brings. Imagine we are near the top left-hand corner of the chart. Participation in the activity is high, the costs associated with it being small. Policy makers want to discourage this form of activity and so increase the price, again using 'price' in the general sense of the term. It could, for example, refer to a more punitive criminal justice system in which the 'price' to the individual of breaking the law is the increased probability of being sent to prison for a longer period.

In a non-networked world, in the top left-hand chart, it is easy to see whether or not the policy is working. Put the price up, and demand falls. But if agents base their actions in part on the actions of others, increasing the price initially has no effect. Then suddenly, as can be seen in the other three charts, we get not just a reduction, but for any further small increase in price, we get a bigger change in demand than would take place in the absence of network effects. By this stage, however, the authorities might easily have concluded that the policy of increasing the price had not worked well before this critical point was reached.

Studies of past changes in prices which attempted to estimate

* This chart assumes agents know and react to the actions of all other agents, so the analysis retains an important feature of conventional economic theory with respect to the information set available to agents.

the impact of price on demand without taking into account network effects might also provide very different stories to policy makers, depending upon the part of the chart from which the evidence was taken. Often, with evidence taken from only a limited range on the chart, the policy would show no effect at all.

But the reverse starting point, near the bottom-right corner of the bottom-right chart, shows the huge potential gains to policy makers in trying to encourage certain types of behaviour – buying the product – if network effects are strong. Even a small reduction in price might have a powerful effect.

*

The crucial challenge for policy makers is to understand and take account of the fact that networks are becoming more and more important in the social and economic world. The internet revolution in communications technology is obviously a key factor. But the entire second half of the twentieth century featured the massive rise of globalisation, a huge increase in travel, and a greater and greater proportion of the world's population living in cities, exposed to many more people, many more networks than they would be in the confines of the village. The model described above is almost as simple as you can get, but it creates both opportunities and problems for policy, for positive linking.

The first problem for policy makers is simple: how do we know whether network effects are important in any given context? Do we have to spend a huge amount of time and resources investigating this issue, do we need more-or-less complete information, before we can even start to think about the policy implications? Or is there a Herb Simon-like rule of thumb which enables us to detect the presence of network effects without too much effort?

The second problem relates directly to the elementary market demand curves described above. Even if somehow we know that

POSITIVE LINKING

networks matter when we are considering a particular issue, they seem to introduce layers of additional uncertainty into trying to work out in advance what the effect of any given policy change might be. Gathering accurate information on the demand curve might be difficult in practice, even without network effects being present, and assessing the impact of changing incentives may often be hard, as we have seen in many examples. But in principle these problems can be overcome.

Networks appear to make things even more difficult, even more challenging for the policy maker. So much seems to be due to chance and contingency. To what we call in plain English, 'luck'. Are there ways of trying to reduce this uncertainty, of formulating new guidelines to offer policy makers to enable them to benefit from the new insights, the positive linking, which networks provide? These are the questions we consider in the next chapter.

6

The World Is Not Normal

Standard economics has demonstrated the importance of incentives. Behavioural economics establishes that these operate rather more subtly than conventional theory suggests, but still remains an analysis of incentives, from which network effects are notable by their absence.

We have already seen practical examples of the effects of networks, which alter the impact of incentives, whether standard ones such as price or the wider set identified by behavioural economics. And we have seen that where they are important, they introduce even more potential uncertainty into the outcome of any particular policy change than already exists when we think just about incentives and the ways they might work. Networks, in which agents copy or imitate the behaviour of others, can either enhance the effects of incentives, in whatever form, or completely swamp them. Positive linking is a very powerful force. This uncertainty is an inherent feature of the world, which no amount of cleverness will eliminate. But there are ways of getting to grips with this uncertainty, of obtaining practical guidance on what to do, on what might work, in situations where network effects matter.

But first of all, we need to ask: is there some way of knowing whether network effects are important in any particular situation? Fortunately, there is. We are not left completely floundering in the dark. There is a readily identifiable piece of evidence to be found wherever network effects are important. Decision makers can be alerted to the fact that the opportunities exist for positive linking.

A great deal of quantitative work in economics is based on a concept developed over 200 years ago by Carl Friedrich Gauss, one of the greatest mathematicians of all time. Statisticians are very interested in how the members of any particular group of objects, for example the population of cities in the United States, are distributed. In this context, 'distribution' does not mean the physical location of the cities. Rather it refers to how the sizes of the various cities are spread across the group as a whole. How many have a population greater than a million, how many between half a million and a million, or whatever bands of size we choose to select.

Gauss worked out the properties of a particular kind of distribution. It is often described, not surprisingly, as Gaussian. But, just like New York City, it is so good that it has been named twice. Its other name is 'normal'. An everyday illustration is the heights of individuals. The average height of American adult men is 5 feet 10 inches. It is also true that more men are of this particular height than any other. There are similar, though slightly smaller, numbers close to the average on either side, who measure 5 feet 9 or 5 feet 11 inches. The number of men we observe who are of any particular height will be less and less the further we move from the average. The resulting distribution looks like the one in the upper panel of Figure 6.1 on p. 160. This is just one example of many such distributions that exist in reality, and because it is common in nature, we call it 'normal'.*

The normal pattern we observe in the heights of American

---

* There are subtle arguments about whether this height distribution is exactly Gaussian, but everyone agrees that it either is, or is very close to being so.

men has two features. First, it is symmetric around the average. The number of men who are 5 feet 9 inches is very similar to the number who are 5 foot 11 inches, and so on. Second, and crucially in this context, in a normal distribution very large differences from the average are never observed in practice. No one has ever been found to be 10 feet tall, or 3 inches.

The measure statisticians use to describe how the numbers fall away as we move further and further from the mean is something called standard deviation (signified by the Greek letter sigma (σ), as readers familiar with statistical theory will know). Two-thirds of all the observations of data that follows the normal distribution will lie within one sigma of the average. In the case of American males, a so-called 'one sigma' event is just three inches. So two-thirds of American men are between 5 foot 7 inches and 6 foot 1 inch tall. That is a lot of people: roughly 80 million, to be slightly more precise. But in a normal distribution, these numbers drop very rapidly as we move further away from the average. Michael Jordan, probably the greatest basketball player of all time, at 6 foot 6 inches, is a 'three sigma event', and only 0.15 per cent of American men are taller. A very small percentage, but still a sizeable absolute number, some 150,000. Yao Ming, a contemporary star, at 7 foot 6 inches is a 'six sigma' event, and people of this height are so rare that he had to be imported from China.

*

The normal distribution underpins almost all the technical statistical analysis carried out by economists. Herb Simon, the great polymath we met at length in Chapter 3, looked at the world, and noticed that across a very wide range of examples, data was distributed in a completely different way. Simon was not the first person to notice that each of these examples were very definitely not normal distributions. But he was the first to pull together quite disparate examples of the same phenomenon.

He noted that 'its appearance is so frequent, and the phenomena in which it appears are so diverse, that one is led to the conjecture that if these phenomena have any property in common it can only be a similarity in the underlying probability mechanisms'. His examples were: distributions of words in English prose by the frequency of their appearance; distributions of scientists by numbers of papers published; distributions of cities by populations; distributions of incomes by size; distributions of biological genera by numbers of species. A diverse set indeed.

A key difference between Simon's data and data distributed in a Gaussian, or normal, way is the huge degree of inequality of outcomes which we observe. Unlike in the normal distribution, there are massive deviations from the average.

Such deviations are described by the word 'skew'. This was a key word in the enticing (!) title of Simon's path-breaking article on the topic, published in *Biometrika* in 1955: 'On a Class of Skew Distribution Functions'. The basic concept may seem austere, but it features in the opening sequences to one of the Monty Python sketches on the Spanish Inquisition. Set in the early years of the Industrial Revolution, the elegant daughter of the factory owner is sat quietly in the luxurious family home. Her obviously upper-crust fiancé bursts in with disturbing news from the factory. 'One o't crossbeams gone askew on't treadle', he pronounces in a broad northern accent, faithfully reproducing the mill-worker's report of the incident. Despite repeating the phrase, this time in his usual upper-class accent, neither of the pair has the slightest idea what it means. We can assist. A piece of machinery has 'gone askew', meaning it has become heavily displaced. In skewed distributions, there are observations which are heavily displaced – a long way away – from the average value. The greater the skew, the more extreme the biggest values will be.

Here is a more everyday example of skew. The first three sites to come up on a Google search attract 98 per cent – ninety-eight per cent! – of all subsequent hits from the search. *All* other sites popping up in the search get just two per cent of the traffic. This is a truly massively skewed distribution. Even within the top three, there is striking inequality, with the number one site receiving 60 per cent of all hits. The typical household income in Britain is some £25,000 a year. In America it is around $50,000. But there appears to be almost no limit to the amount by which some people's incomes exceed the average. Hedge fund owners will often pay themselves annual incomes in the tens of millions, whether pounds or dollars, and there are several examples of individuals who have been paid – I do not use the word 'earned' here – more than a billion dollars in a single year. A billion dollars!

Before going on to give examples of non-normal outcomes in a very wide range of human social and economic activities, a chart might be useful to bring out the differences. Figure 6.1 illustrates a normal and a typical non-normal distribution of data. The charts do not represent any particular examples, but the scale of the data in each chart is directly comparable. In both the charts, the *average* value of the data is the same. But the ways in which the values are spread around the average are completely different.

In both cases, there are 10,000 data points, with an average value of 7.5. We divide the data up into small ranges, and see how many of the data points lie within each range. So in the first chart, the tallest bar in the chart – just – sits exactly round the average value of the data. This shows how many of the data points in a normal distribution with an average value of 7.5 lie in the range 7.45–7.55. Reading across to the left hand side, we can see that there are just over 400 of them. Close to the average, there are also lots of other data points. But as we move further away from the average, on either side, we can readily see that the

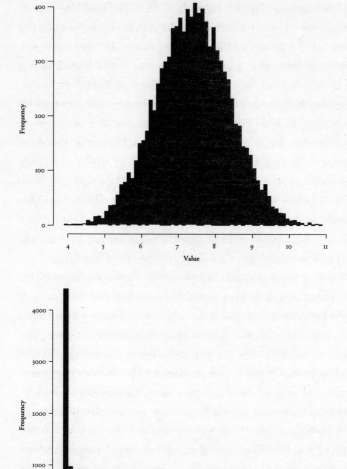

Figure 6.1 Typical examples of normal and non-normal distributions. By construction, the average value of the data is the same in both panels.

number of times we observe data with such values falls away quite rapidly. There are very few data points with a value of less than 4.5, and a similarly small number which take a value of more than 10.5.

The non-normal distribution is very different. It is not even apparent that the average value of the data is 7.5, although readers can be assured that it is. What we see here is a huge number of data points, well over 4,000, which take a value of close to 0. And we see a small number which have values of more than 50. So it is not just the shape of the distribution which is different, but the spread, or skew, of the data. In the normal distribution, most observations are confined to a narrow range around the average, and there are no really large deviations from this. The ratio of the highest value to the lowest is around three. In the non-normal, there is a massive spread, with the ratio of the highest (a value over 50) and the lowest (close to 0) being around 1,000!

Most urban agglomerations, be they towns or cities, are relatively small in terms of their populations. Tertius Chandler has compiled a marvellous book, *Four Thousand Years of Urban Growth: An Historical Census*. The contents are exactly what it says on the label. Estimates are given of the population of a large number of cities across the world over a period of four millennia. So we learn, for example, that in 612 BC Babylon was not only the largest city in the world, but was the first to ever have a population of over 200,000. And this was at a time when most human settlements were tiny, with populations probably numbered in single figures. Babylon dwarfed them, but there was only one Babylon. There are of course all sorts of arguments as to where exactly a city's boundaries lie. On the old city limits, the current population of Tokyo is only (!) around 9 million, but the urban mass which constitutes the Greater Tokyo area has a population of 35 million. Either way, the figures overwhelm the large number of towns around the world with populations of, say, 10–20,000. There are a few very large cities, and lots and lots of very much smaller ones.

In the last decade or so, many more examples of this kind of skewed distribution have been discovered. For example:

* downloads on YouTube
* film producers' earnings
* the number of sexual partners people have
* the size of price changes in financial assets
* crowds at soccer matches
* firm sizes
* the size and length of economic recessions
* the frequency of different types of endgames in chess
* the ratings of American football coaches in *USA Today*
* the distribution of £1 million homes across London boroughs
* unemployment rates by county in America
* deaths in wars
* the number of churches per county in William the Conqueror's Domesday Book survey of England in the late eleventh century.

There are arcane disputes about which variety of 'skew distribution' best describes each of these examples – remember the words in the title of Simon's article: a class of skew distributions, meaning not symmetric at all, heavily skewed in one direction or the other – but they all exhibit very marked degrees of inequality of outcome.

*

The idea that highly unequal outcomes are pervasive in the human social and economic worlds is interesting in its own right. But such outcomes are also of great practical importance for the policy maker. When we observe them, we know that network effects are almost certain to be present in the behaviour of the agents who constitute the system in which we are interested. As we will see below, the basic mathematics of how network effects operate enable us to make this statement. The agents are not merely reacting to incentives. They are changing their behaviour directly in response to others. They are copying, imitating the opinions, choices, behaviour of other agents. Incentives may also still matter, but network effects dominate their impact.

Non-Gaussian outcomes are the classic signature of network effects. This is obviously a very useful piece of knowledge for policy makers. Wherever we see such outcomes, the possibility of taking advantage of positive linking also exists. We do not need to invest huge amounts of time and resources in discovering whether network effects are present. We simply look at – more likely, get one of our advisers to look at! – the distribution of outcomes. This is a powerful rule of thumb with which to detect the presence of network effects. Unfortunately, most policy makers with training in the social sciences, notably in economics, have been taught to assume the Gaussian distribution.

Of course, it is one thing to make this point, another to demonstrate why this should be the case. To do this, we will have to delve in some detail into Simon's skew distribution paper. But before girding our loins for these rigours, we might usefully reflect on many of the examples we have encountered and ask how these might arise in a world where only incentives mattered, a world in which network effects were absent.

Remember the eccentric Englishmen featured on YouTube videos, one of them ironing on the top of a Scottish mountain, the other ironing on a temporarily closed section of motorway. One proved 4,000 times more popular than the other. It is very hard to imagine that the inherent preferences of those who viewed these videos were skewed in this dramatic way. Indeed, we can get a rough estimate of the relative inherent interest in the two by doing a search on the Google UK site. The word 'motorway' is used in British English to describe roads built specifically for higher-speed traffic. In other languages, or other variants of English, it is known as 'freeway, autoroute, Autobahn, autostrada' and so on. The point here is that 'motorway' is a specifically British way of describing this type of road, so a search on the UK Google site is the relevant one. If we search 'motorway', we get 30.2 million sites, and 'Ben Nevis', the mountain where the ironing was done, yields 2.9 million sites. So, as an approximation, 'motorway' has ten times the level of inherent interest as 'Ben Nevis'. But the former video attracted 4,000 times as many hits as the latter.

Another internet-related statistic was cited above. The first three sites to come up in a Google search typically attract 98 per cent of the subsequent hits by the searcher on that topic. The principle of behaviour which underlies these examples is not in any way confined to the internet, it is present in every single one of the examples quoted and discussed in the book. But the internet examples are both everyday ones, and enable us to focus on what this process, this principle, is.

Once a site, a video, a photograph starts to become popular on the internet, it becomes more popular simply because it has already become popular. A site gets enough hits for its head to start to poke out above the parapet, to impinge on the consciousness of users of the internet. And it is then very likely to get even more hits, purely because people have become aware of it, rather than the huge number of other sites which exist, even when a particular topic is being searched for. Almost every single reader of this book will be familiar with the behaviour being described here. You might open a page of a newspaper early in the day, or visit one of your favourite sites before getting down to work. An item catches your eye in the 'trending now' category. You had absolutely no intention of looking at anything to do with this particular issue when you opened the site, you may even not have been aware of its existence. Yet you may click on it – not the same at all as saying you *will* definitely click on it – simply because it is 'trending', because at that moment it is popular.

It may not be immediately obvious that when you are distracted in this way, you are being influenced by a network. But it is indeed a network which is the main driver of your behaviour when you make that click on to the 'trending' item.

It is the network of all the people who have previously clicked on the item. For the most part, any single individual who has done so will be and will remain completely unknown to everyone who subsequently clicks on the same thing. But he or she is part of the network. The network which influences you, in your turn, to investigate the same item. Your behaviour has been directly affected by the decisions of others, even though in this example they are anonymous to you. They, and now you and others who in the next few hours may be influenced by your own decision to make the click, are temporarily connected on a network, the network of those who clicked on the same site.

The network here is temporary. It will evaporate as other items take its place. But in other instances which we have seen, networks may last much longer, such as the network across which the Protestant martyrs of England influenced people's behaviour. Again, the internet examples are used for illustration here because they are such familiar occurrences. It is not every day that you reflect on changing your political ideology or religious belief. But lots of people use the internet on a regular basis for much less momentous purposes.

We can now return to Herb Simon and his 1955 paper in

Biometrika. Simon did not discover the empirical examples about which he wrote, which showed that non-Gaussian outcomes of human social and economic processes are so widespread that these, and not the so-called 'normal' distribution, appear to be typical of our world. The originality of his paper was in the fact that he articulated effectively an underlying mathematical process by which such outcomes can be generated.

The process was rediscovered in the 1990s by physicists such as Albert-László Barabási of the University of Notre Dame, who gave it the name of 'preferential attachment'. As we have seen above, it is based on the principle of 'to him that hath, more shall be given'. The twist is to add a few words: 'to him that hath, it is likely that more shall be given'. This is the fundamental building block of behaviour which underpins positive linking.

All scientific theories involve making dramatic simplifications and, especially in the social sciences, they are approximations to reality, not the same as reality itself. This point cannot be stated too frequently. So Simon's process is not intended to be a complete description, the whole story, of why we observe some particular outcome. But it is a mechanism which gives us an insight into many qualitatively similar outcomes from widely different fields.

Simon did not say that someone making a choice would necessarily choose the most popular item, opinion or whatever. But that it is more likely that an agent will choose this than a less popular alternative. The basic idea is straightforward. Suppose there are just three choices available to you, whatever these may be, and you are wondering which one to select yourself. One has been already chosen 6,000 times, one 3,000 and the final one just 1,000 times, making a total of 10,000 altogether. If we assume for purposes of illustration that the only rule of behaviour you are using when making your choice is that of preferential attachment, the rule says the following. You may actually choose any one of the three alternatives. But you are twice as likely to select the most popular rather than the second most popular, and six times as likely to choose this as the least popular. The most popular has been already selected 6,000 times compared to the second most popular, twice as many, so you are twice as likely to select it. And it has been selected six times more often than the least popular.

At first sight, this may seem a strange way of behaving. You are paying no attention to the attributes, to the features of the three alternatives. But the top three sites which are followed up on a Google search typically reflect exactly this pattern. The three of them get almost 100 per cent of the subsequent hits after the search, and the top one of them all gets 60 per cent of the total. Again, scientific theories are approximations to reality, but as a description of behaviour in a complex environment, preferential attachment seems to have something going for it.

*

This long discussion has been trying to put substance on the assertion made above that there is a typical 'signature' of social and economic outcomes in which network effects have an important influence on how agents behave. We simply inspect whether the various choices – whether opinions, consumer goods, types of behaviour or whatever – are selected in numbers which are 'skewed' or whether they are more like a Gaussian distribution. If we see a few choices being selected in relatively large numbers and most choices being made by few, we know in all likelihood we are in a networked world.

Network effects, as we have seen, introduce even more uncertainty for the policy maker in terms of assessing in advance – or even after the event – what the impact of any particular policy might be. But at least we have a straightforward way of knowing whether network effects are important in any given context. At least we can alert the policy makers to both the potential difficulties these create, and the benefits of positive linking which can be potentially exploited.

We can do even more. So far, we have simply spoken of 'networks' in a generic sense. But there are different types of networks, in the same way that there are, say, different types of mammals. We can think about 'mammals' in general, or we can think specifically of, say, rabbits or lions. And the more specific we can make the description, the more useful it is. Each individual rabbit or lion will differ in various ways from others of the same species. But the similarities between the individuals in a group of rabbits are sufficiently strong for us to be able to place them all in the species called 'rabbit'. This is now trivially obvious, but it was not always the case. The classification of species was a major achievement of the eighteenth-century Swedish scientist Carl Linnaeus.

Networks, too, can be classified into various types. And the way the classification is done is in terms of features of their deep, mathematical structure. I can offer immediate reassurance that there is no maths in this chapter, or indeed in the entire book, just descriptions of the features of networks which matter to us.

There are numerous types of network. But most of those which have been found in the social and economic worlds fall, rather fortunately, into one of just three different categories. When we are looking for real-life networks, we do not have to worry about whether an actual network is one of a hundred different potential types, but most of the time only whether it is one of the three pervasive network 'species'.

And from the perspective of the policy maker, each of these three network types requires a different approach, a different strategy in terms of trying either to generate or to stop a cascade of behavioural change, of positive linking, across the agents in the network. This does not solve the problem of the uncertainties facing policy makers in a networked world – the real world of the twenty-first century. But it helps to reduce the dimension of the problem they face. If we can obtain both a good indication that network effects are important, and also a reasonable approximation to the structure of the relevant network in any given context, we can identify its type and offer guidance on what kinds of strategies are most likely to work.

What, then, are these types? Simon's *Biometrika* concept is in fact the fundamental basis for one of the three varieties of network, and it is of considerable practical importance in human affairs. In its modern guise, this genre of network is known as 'scale-free', for reasons which need not detain us.* It has a particular mathematical structure which is of great interest to natural scientists and especially to physicists.

In a scale-free network most agents have only a small number of connections to others, whilst in turn a small number of agents are connected to very many others. There is a precise mathematical relationship which describes, in an idealised scale-free network, the probability of an agent having a given number of connections, and how this probability declines as the number of connections rises. Lots of people with a few links, a few people with lots of links. The process of preferential attachment describes how such a network evolves, and how its structure is then reinforced.

This structure is important, because it means that the highly connected agents, the 'hubs', may exercise a powerful influence on the behaviour of other agents on the network. This could, of course, be because they are important people of stature, power, prestige. They exercise potential influence over others and have

* The Wikipedia entry is helpful on this topic.

so many connections precisely because of their social standing.

A simple, stylised example of a scale-free network is plotted in Figure 6.2. Let me say straightaway that there are subtle nuances across different kinds of scale-free networks, but this is a complication which we can leave aside for the moment. The chart is not intended to represent any actual network, but to give a simple portrait of what a scale-free network looks like.

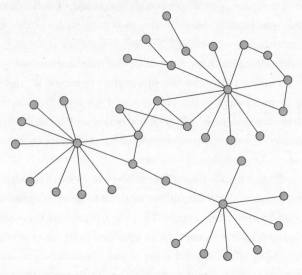

Figure 6.2 Stylised representation of a scale-free network

The circles represent the agents, whoever or whatever they may be, and the lines indicate whether a pair of agents is connected. We can easily see in this chart three 'hubs', which have lots of connections, and in contrast most other agents in the network are linked to only a small number of others, in many cases they have just a single link. Again, for emphasis, this is not meant to be a real-life network of an actual situation, it illustrates the principles.

We have come across an example of a scale-free network in

the England of the 1550s. A scale-free network of latent, potential influence was already in place. Many people would have heard of the Archbishop of Canterbury, the head of the Church of England, and other prominent clerics, bishops, preachers would also have been well known, some on a regional rather than a national scale, but famous nevertheless. The English martyrs took the gamble that they could convert, as it were, this latent network, one in which many people had heard of them, into a network which really did influence the opinions and behaviour of others.

In such circumstances, we speak of a 'weighted' network, in which a person who is well known carries more influence over someone to whom he or she is connected than an individual with few connections. But a key feature of scale-free networks is that the hubs are important even when the network is unweighted. In other words, even when an individual does not have any special power or prestige but is nevertheless well connected, he or she can exercise a strong influence on outcomes simply because of their sheer number of connections. Even if the agent has only a small probability of altering the behaviour, choice or opinion of each of the other agents to which it is connected, its influence may be strong simply because it has so many connections. A small number – the probability of influencing any given agent – multiplied by a large one – the number of connections – is still pretty big. And, crucially, in relative terms it is much bigger than two small numbers multiplied together.

Gene Stanley, a professor of physics at Boston University and editor of *Physica A*, gave a practical illustration of the influence of hubs in unweighted scale-free networks when he and colleagues discovered in 1996 that the distribution of the number of sexual partners across a sample of individuals essentially had this structure. Most people had relatively few, and a small number had very many indeed. These latter were in other respects perfectly ordinary individuals, without the prestige of, say, the Archbishop of Canterbury or even, more plausibly in this context, a film star or a famous rock singer. They were part of an unweighted network.

The implications for public health are quite disturbing. If just one of the hubs in any particular social network is carrying a sexually transmitted disease, the best way to contain the spread on the network is to identify and cure that particular hub. We can test and, if necessary, cure large numbers of less well-connected agents, but if that hub is still out there, our efforts will be in vain. Successful policy in this context requires very precise identification and targeting of a small number of individuals.

In practice, of course, we do not observe the perfect Platonic idea of a scale-free network. But, as ever, the question is whether empirically observed networks are sufficiently similar to warrant the description 'scale-free'. The formal mathematics of this gets pretty hard pretty quickly, but we can safely put to one side the various subtleties involved. Broadly speaking, however, there is a range of social and economic networks which can be approximated by this concept. This idea is already of considerable practical significance. Malcolm Gladwell's book *The Tipping Point*, published in 2000, has deservedly been a huge best-seller. Gladwell conveyed to a wider public the essential idea that, in many contexts, a relatively small number of people can exercise a decisive influence on the eventual outcome.

Marketing departments of global consumer goods companies have seized upon the idea, and very substantial amounts of money are spent on trying to identify the small number of people in any particular market who are believed to exercise undue influence on whether or not a brand or product is successful. They are making deliberate use of the concept of positive linking. If they can target and persuade the hubs, their product is likely to be very successful. As we shall soon see, the world is not always like this, and much of this expenditure may very well be completely wasted.

Gladwell identified three key ways in which individuals might be important in any particular social or economic network. He termed one group of such individuals 'mavens'. These are the people others rely upon to provide them with new information. Gladwell argues that mavens are crucial to behaviour spreading across a network by word of mouth, due to their knowledge and skills and the fact that other people regard them as having such qualities. Allied to these are the 'salesmen', who are subtly different in that they are uncannily influential in persuading others to adopt their particular buying habits or opinions.

We can usefully regard such agents as being the hubs in a scale-free network, if indeed the relevant network is of this particular kind. Gladwell's third set of potential influencers are rather more general, those he called 'connectors'. These are people with a 'truly extraordinary knack of making friends and acquaintances'. So at its most basic, they have many connections, exactly like the hubs in a scale-free network.

But the concept blurs into an entirely different one, a type of network where 'hubs' as such do not exist. A popular rendition of this is the Kevin Bacon 'six degrees of separation', the basis of a popular trivia game in which players are required to calculate the shortest number of links between two separate actors, or indeed any two individuals. The basic idea is that suppose A knows B and B knows C but C does not know A, nevertheless C is connected to A by only one degree of separation. So if B is persuaded by C to change his or her behaviour or opinions, then there is a much higher chance that A will also change than if A were not linked to B at all.

The idea that individuals can be connected in at most six

degrees of separation is an extraordinarily powerful one. A colleague of mine was recently reading a biography of Sir Roger Casement. Casement was born into a military Protestant family in Dublin, and became a quintessential member of the British establishment. However, his longstanding interest in what we now term human rights led him first of all into opposition to existing colonial empires, and eventually into active membership of the Irish Republican Army, at a time when what is now the Republic of Ireland was part of the United Kingdom. Casement tried to get German support for what proved to be the abortive republican uprising in Dublin at Easter 1916. However, Britain happened to be fighting the First World War with Germany, so Casement was tried and executed for treason.

Now, I have only three degrees of separation from Casement. My grandfather, sadly long dead now, often drank as a young man in the Jolly Gardeners public house in Rochdale, which was the preferred pub of one Jack Ellis. Although Ellis was considerably older, in the tight local community of the time, almost everyone in it knew everyone else. Ellis was a barber but also the public hangman in Britain. Casement was executed almost one hundred years ago by Ellis.*

This may seem a freak, a curiosity, but such strange connections are entirely typical. J. V. Stalin requires much less introduction than Roger Casement. With Stalin, my degree of separation is four. In the 1990s, my wife spent some time at a research institute in Stockholm. The father of one of her colleagues had been a prominent member of the Social Democrat party in Sweden from the 1930s, when that party was starting its very long reign in power in that country. However, he was a political defector,

---

* Incidentally, his immediate successor, by pure coincidence, came from the neighbouring town of Oldham, where he ran, without any apparently intended irony, a pub called Help the Poor Struggler.

having been general secretary of the Swedish Communist Party in the 1920s. In that role, he had visited Moscow several times, where he met not only Stalin but doomed Politburo colleagues of his such as Bukharin and Kamenev, executed in the 1930s purges. The Swede only escaped the same fate himself by seeing the light and becoming a social democrat, for a very large proportion of foreign Communists visiting Moscow in the 1930s finished up either in the execution cellars or being worked to death in the labour camps.

*

This feature of scale-free networks, that most agents in the network are typically linked by only a small series of connections, is shared by another type of network which is often found in social and economic situations. But the implications of the network for policy are fundamentally different. This is the 'small-world' network, discovered by Duncan Watts and Steve Strogatz of Cornell University in 1998. Their paper, entitled 'Collective Dynamics of Small World Networks', was published in the leading scientific journal *Nature*, and its importance is shown by the fact that over the next decade it proved to be the single most cited article of the thousands which were written on the new and rapidly expanding science of networks.

The many subtleties of the differences and similarities between small-world and scale-free networks need not concern us here, and there is a large technical, mathematical literature on them for anyone interested. But as noted already, they have the property that moving around the network, as it were, is usually pretty easy. Not many links need to be accessed for any pair of agents to be connected. Yet the two types of network are at the same time profoundly different.

Scale-free networks are distinguished by a small number of highly connected, potentially highly influential, individuals. There are no such people in a small-world network. Most individuals tend to have relatively small numbers of connections, which do not vary a great deal across the population. In other words, in a scale-free system people are characterised by the huge differences between the numbers of connections they have. In a small world, the striking feature is not the differences but the similarities.

The basic social structure of the two is radically different. Small-world systems are essentially overlapping groups of 'friends of friends'. So if X knows Y and Y knows Z, we have seen that X has the potential to influence Z's behaviour through their mutual contact Y. But in a small-world network, the contact may not need to go through Y at all. For the chances that X and Z also know each other, that they are directly connected, is high. It is by no means a certainty, but two agents who share a mutual connection are themselves likely to be directly connected.

So at a local level, when we zoom in on any particular part of it, this type of network will look pretty dense, with lots of direct connections between the agents under our focus. How can things travel across this sort of architecture, this sort of structure? To get to another part of the network altogether, it seems that many links might be required to be traversed. We have to go through successive groups of friends of friends to reach distant parts of the system. And by the time we have got there, the chances of exercising influence on the behaviour of people will be very small. So many connections have to be brought into play, and at each stage there is always the chance that our friend might just say 'no', might just persist with his or her previous choice, his or her existing opinion, rather than be influenced by us.

The feature which brings the agents much closer together, which enables this type of network to be described as a *small* world, is that a few people will have long-range connections across different groups. An individual might be an active member of a local running club, and at the same time be involved with a more sedentary hobby group, such as stamp collectors or model railway enthusiasts. Few people will be members of both. But the ones who are have the potential to spread ideas, choices, opinions, across disparate groups, sections of the network which appear, and indeed are, in other respects quite distant from each other. The word 'potential' must be emphasised. It does not mean that these 'long-range connectors' will automatically persuade people to adopt different opinions, to make different choices. In fact, they need be no more or no less persuasive than the typical agent in the population as a whole. But they have the potential to transmit behaviour across distant sections of the network.

Figure 6.3 shows a stylised small-world network with its local, overlapping connections and a few 'long-distance' connections. Again, this is not meant to be a representation of any actually existing network, but a simplified version to illustrate the key features.

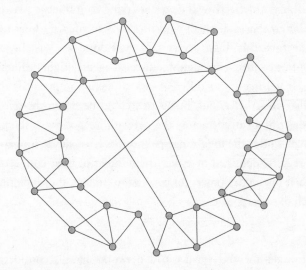

Figure 6.3 Stylised representation of a small-world network

An example of the small-world concept, where no single agent plays the role of the highly connected hubs in scale-free networks, is the network which is at work in the final chapter of Jennifer Egan's 2011 Pulitzer Prize-winning novel *A Visit from the Goon Squad*. The book is set in the future of a New York which differs in some key respects from the present-day city. Not only is energy running low, but it is socially unacceptable to use your social networks to make money. An ageing rock star is giving a concert. The promoter hires a well-connected person – a hub in network jargon – to pass on the details of the concert to his friends. He is somewhat ashamed of agreeing to do this and does not even tell his wife. Instead, he recruits a couple of much less well-connected sub-agents. The hub person is astounded when his wife suggests they go to the concert, which she has heard about from two or three people, who have all suggested it will be an exciting and novel event. Tens of thousands of people turn up and the concert is a wild success.

Clearly, an effective strategy for trying to influence networks similar to the ideal small-world form is to identify long-range connectors. But this is easier said than done. At least in some scale-free contexts, the highly connected agents might be identifiable. It is, of course, a different task altogether to persuade these to alter their behaviour, but if this could be done, there is the prospect of a cascade across the network, of positive linking. In a small world, the long-range connectors have subtle properties, not readily identified by either the number of their connections or their distinctive powers of persuasion. In fact, they look pretty much like everyone else.

*

Both scale-free and small-world networks have a considerable degree of structure which in each case corresponds to recognisable social situations. One in which there are a few highly connected agents, and the other which has an 'overlapping friends of friends' structure. But there is a third network category of practical importance which has none at all. Indeed, this lack of structure is reflected in the name: random networks. Such networks began to be investigated by mathematicians such as Paul Erdös in the late 1950s and 1960s. Erdös is well-known in mathematical circles for the fact that other mathematicians boast when they have a low 'Erdös number', the mathematicians' equivalent of degrees of separation. He was so enormously productive and collaborated with so many of his colleagues that many have an Erdös number of one.

It may seem strange that, in human social and economic contexts, the concept of random connections makes any sense at all. But it does. We have already mentioned the example of the common cold. You are travelling to work on the subway. The person next to you sneezes. Unfortunately, his cold is at the infectious stage. You have never met your temporary travelling companion, have no idea who he is, and may very well never see him again. But you have caught his cold.

Epidemiologists have analysed the spread of diseases for many years. Their basic model, developed as long ago as the 1920s, is so often used that it has its own name, the SIR model. The relevant population at any point in time can be allocated into one of three groups. Those who are susceptible to a particular disease, but have not yet caught it are in category S, those who are infected are Is and those who have been infected but are no longer so are the Rs. With infections that do not confer immunity, such as the common cold, R stands for 'recovered'. Because Rs are susceptible to reinfection, they can move back to the S category. In other cases, recovered individuals will almost certainly be immune to reinfection, so that R here stands for 'removed', a description which also applies more literally to altogether more sinister infections such as the Black Death.

So at any point in time, there is a proportion of the population which is susceptible, a proportion infected, and a proportion which has recovered. The mathematical models used in epidemiology describe how these proportions change over time. At its simplest, any individual is assumed to have the same chance of contracting the disease upon coming into contact with an infected person. So the chances of any individual flowing, as it were, from S to I depends upon this and the number of infected people he or she comes into contact with. Equally, everyone who is infected is assumed to have the same chance of recovery in any given period, of leaving the I category and moving into the R.

The above paragraph actually describes a system of differential equations. To be more precise, a system of non-linear differential equations. As these things go, it is just about as simple as you can get. But even so, it has proved to be an extraordinarily powerful scientific tool. Of course, there are many much more complicated variants, but the basic principles remain the same.

It also contains a hidden network. Can you see it? It is the contacts between an S and members of the I group. These links constitute the relevant network. No particular social structure is assumed. In fact, there is none. Susceptibles just encounter infected people at random. Purely chance encounters, like sitting next to a stranger with a cold, are the basic way in which infections spread in the fundamental model of the whole science of epidemiology.

But how does this relate to wider social and economic issues? Fashion – indeed, many aspects of popular culture – might reasonably be regarded as spreading (or not, as the case may be) across a network in which individuals are connected purely at random. Of course, to state yet again, all scientific theories are approximations to reality, and whether they are any good depends to a large extent on how reasonable their approximations are. So, yes, other factors, other types of network might impinge on the story, but an awful lot about the spread of fashion can be explained by random networks. The blurb for a contemporary fashion site called Fashion Indie makes this admirably clear: 'Fashion Indie is a collection of all things related to fashion, from news and notes on models and designers to a section called "random cool shit" that highlights, well, pictures of random stuff that's awesome.' Random stuff that's awesome!

The SIR model discussed above has been developed in more modern, networked-based versions. Individuals can be allowed to have different degrees of susceptibility, but the basic principle of a random social network is retained. From the longstanding work of epidemiologists, we know a key feature of such networks. Specifically, we know the things we need to know – the 'knowable knowns' – in order to work out whether an infection has the potential to spread across the network as a whole. From a policy perspective, this tells us the specific goals we have to achieve if we want an idea or mode of behaviour to percolate across a random network (or, conversely, what we need to do to prevent something spreading).

We have already encountered the idea that social and economic networks are 'robust yet fragile'. In other words, most of the time, most new events, shocks, new ideas, new choices do not percolate very far across them. But, occasionally, one event which is otherwise indistinguishable from those that fail encounters success. The network proves 'fragile', and the small initial change spreads through it. In random networks, we know that there is a distinct boundary between fragile and robust. Unless something gets enough traction within the network, enough people either catch or adopt it, it has literally zero chance of spreading on a substantial scale. Indeed, it will simply fade away and disappear altogether. Calculating where a particular infection is in relation to this boundary might be difficult in practice, but we know how to do it. The precise calculation will vary from context to context, but in principle we know how to calculate it.*

So, if we are faced with a random network and want to encourage the spread of a product or a mode of behaviour, we basically have to get enough people to buy into it to get over a critical mass, otherwise our efforts are wasted. Small-world networks are more complicated, though they often resemble random ones in this respect. The same is not true of scale-free networks. Although the probability of a large cascade may be very small, even if just a few people adopt a new fashion, a new behaviour, a new idea, there is still a chance that it will spread across the network as a whole. Obviously, it would be desirable to persuade more people rather than fewer in the first wave of marketing, but even if it does not go well, we can still cross our fingers and hope. All is not lost. It almost certainly is, but we might still succeed.

Here, then, is a way in which network structure might influence the strategy of someone wanting to influence the whole network in some way, including a policy maker or a marketing department. Facing a random network, or one which is more similar to this than any other kind, we just have to have a blitz, to try to persuade enough people so our offer leaps over the critical mass. Strategies on other networks might have to be more subtle. In other words, where networks are important, generalised statements about policy effectiveness across different policy domains lack validity because of the different natures of the different types of network which predominate in the social and economic worlds. The effectiveness of a policy will be contingent on the type of network upon which it is being enacted.

* A clear illustration of this in the basic SIR model is given at:
 http://en.wikipedia.org/wiki/Compartmental_models_in_epidemiology

THE WORLD IS NOT NORMAL

*

Inspired by Malcolm Gladwell, many marketing departments
have strategies that concentrate on finding the hubs of the network, the 'influentials' who are believed to be the key to success.
The concept has many followers. A Google search on 'influentials' comes up with 220,000 sites. The technical phrase 'discovering influentials viral marketing' yields no fewer than 55,000. Viral
marketing is a relatively new concept that takes its name from
the spread of viruses in epidemiology. How can we get awareness
of our brand, and then hopefully the sales of it, to percolate, to
cascade across pre-existing social networks? Word of mouth is
one answer, text messages another, and web-based tools include
techniques such as video clips and interactive Flash games.

The idea of influentials has a much broader scientific base,
and essentially goes back to the work of Paul Lazarsfeld in the
1940s. Born in Vienna in 1901, Lazarsfeld was one of the many
Jewish people welcomed by America in the 1930s and who did so
much to enrich intellectual life in their new country. He founded
Columbia's Bureau of Applied Social Research, and was a towering figure in twentieth-century sociology in America.

The 1940s was the decade when the mass media which dominated the second half of the twentieth century really came into
effect. Newspapers had existed for many years, had been more
recently augmented by radio and were now being massively
enhanced by the new medium of television. For an internet-ori-
ented population, it is hard to remember and grasp the truly dramatic impact of television. For the first time in human history,
millions of people could not just listen to but actually see those
who were trying to entertain, amuse or persuade them.

The latter possibility, that the media might influence people's
choices and behaviour, soon became a matter of serious concern.

Vance Packard published a stupendous best-seller entitled the *Hidden Persuaders*, allegedly exposing how advertisers and politicians manipulated public opinion subliminally through the mass media. Such worries persist to this day. In Britain we had in the spring of 2011 one of our very rare referendums. This was on whether to change the first-past-the-post system of voting, which has existed in Britain since elections began, in favour of some newfangled alternative. The change was rejected decisively by a majority of more than two to one. Yet this did not deter vociferous denunciations of the impact of the 'Murdoch press' on the result.* The electorate, it was claimed, were prevented from having a 'proper conversation' on the matter by the wicked media. In America, criticisms of the influence of both the liberal press and right-wing radio talk-show hosts are a routine feature of the broader political discourse.

Lazarsfeld articulated a sophisticated theory of how such influence might be exercised. He proposed a concept known as the 'two-step flow of communication'. On this hypothesis, individuals were not so much influenced directly by what they read, heard or saw in the mass media. Rather, the flow was mediated by influentials. Ideas, choices, behaviour go first from the media to influential individuals, who in turn then spread their own interpretation across the population as a whole. These influentials need not occupy prominent positions or be in any way obviously remarkable. Indeed, they are very similar to their peers in terms of interests and socio-economic characteristics. In the context of modern network theory, we have seen that the hubs of the network, the agents with large numbers of connections, may indeed exercise strong influence simply because they have so many connections.

* In the run-up to the referendum, the several right-of-centre UK newspapers owned by Rupert Murdoch all vigorously opposed the proposed change in their opinion columns.

They do not need to be especially knowledgeable or persuasive; they just know a lot of people.

The theory was seen as a way of explaining why some advertising campaigns, some political messages, succeeded whilst others failed. If, as was asserted to be the case, the mass media and the advertising budgets of giant firms now controlled people's choices, the fact that many such campaigns failed needed to be explained away. And the two-step theory formed the basis for this rationalisation. It wasn't so much that the influence of the media was uncertain, but the fact that the influentials it influenced might in some cases distort the message in ways that would render it less palatable. As a result, the concept, argument or product involved would not be widely adopted.

Like any seminal concept, the two-step flow of communication theory has generated a large literature, some of which puts forward supporting evidence, some of which is critical. It is useful to reflect, however, on Lazarsfeld's original article, a study carried out with Bernard Berelson, and Hazel Gaudet. This focused on how people decided how to vote during the 1944 US Presidential campaign. The research team came to the project with the hypothesis that the media would exercise a direct influence on the views and decisions of the electorate. To their surprise, informal, personal contacts were mentioned far more frequently as the source of influence on voting behaviour than exposure to the mass media. It seems to have been more or less axiomatic that the mass media did in principle exercise a powerful influence. So the direct contradiction of this hypothesis by the empirical evidence led to a theory which retained the concept of media power, but which at the same time accounted for the fact that it might not always be influential.

Echoes here of rational agent economic theory, but at least Lazarsfeld saw the need to confront his theory with empirical evidence. When the evidence failed to support the theory, just as the Ptolemaic epicycles could always account for observed deviations from the theory that the sun went round the earth by adding another complication to the model, a pretty spectacular addition was made, namely two-step communication flow.

Lazarsfeld went on to develop and examine this theory further with Elihu Katz, who published his reflections in the *International Journal of Public Opinion Research* in 2001. Katz noted that most of the work in the field confirmed Lazarsfeld's original finding that the media exercised mild influence on public opinion, but that interpersonal transmission was in general much more important.

For many sociologists and media-studies academics, the idea that the mass media lack this power is unacceptable, regardless of the fact that the empirical evidence points towards it. As Katz points out, one of the attacks is based on the view that the media generate a false consciousness of reality amongst the broad masses. How can it possibly be that people in general do not subscribe to the views of the liberal elite, which are so self-evidently correct? They must obviously have been brainwashed.

Despite the evidence, the idea that a small number of individuals are responsible for the spread of ideas, opinions, choices, behaviour, has become very widespread. Even by the mid-1990s, the two-step theory of communication and the concept of influentials had generated more than 4,000 academic articles, and the number has grown dramatically since then. The diffusion of technological innovations, communications studies, marketing – all these areas of study were affected.

*

Network theory moves us completely beyond these concepts. The deep insight that social and economic networks have the property of being robust yet fragile tells us exactly why some campaigns, whether commercial or political, fail to spread, and why others have a dramatic impact. It is an uncomfortable insight. The element of chance and contingency is prominent in the story. We have *inherently* less control over situations in which network effects are important than we would like, no matter how clever we might be in trying to design policies to bring about desired outcomes.

We have also seen that if the network in any particular context is best approximated by a random or a small-world one, then the very concept of influentials is not terribly helpful. Of course, if the relevant network is similar to the scale-free template, there are certainly individuals who do have the capacity to exercise a strong influence. These hubs, even when they are otherwise ordinary, unremarkable people, are important simply because they have so many connections. Even if each of their links has only a small probability of being influenced by them, the fact that they have a large number of connections means they have a good chance of altering someone else's behaviour. And if the individuals themselves are seen as being important, figures of prestige, then their impact is doubly important.

Indeed, in this particular context, when we are operating with a weighted scale-free network, the role of influentials and the media in forming public opinion takes on an entirely different meaning from the one articulated by Lazarsfeld and Katz. Friedrich Hayek, in his 1949 essay 'The Intellectuals and Socialism', considered the question of how ideas of planning and socialism had come to a dominant position in the market-oriented economies of the West. He attributed this to the role of intellectuals. By the word 'intellectual' he did not mean an original thinker. Rather, for Hayek, intellectuals were 'professional second-hand dealers in ideas', such as journalists, commentators, teachers, lecturers, artists or cartoonists.

The opening paragraph of Hayek's essay reads:

In all democratic countries, a strong belief prevails that the influence of the intellectuals on politics is negligible. This is no doubt true of the power of intellectuals to make their peculiar opinions of the moment influence decisions, of the extent to which they can sway the popular vote on questions on which they differ from the current views of the masses. Yet over somewhat longer periods they have probably never exercised so great an influence as they do today in those countries. This power they wield by shaping public opinion.

During the second half of the twentieth century, the influence of the concept of socialism in the West weakened. The view that governments can plan, predict and control outcomes still pervades much political thinking, and the role of the state in the economy remains very much larger than it was in the first half of the twentieth century. But market-oriented thinking has become much more powerful. In part, this is due to a sustained effort within economics to create a powerful intellectual argument for this view, and in part due to the disastrous performances of planned economies, whether in the former Soviet bloc, Africa or elsewhere. Acute poverty is now a distinguishing feature of anti-capitalist regimes rather than the more market-oriented ones. However, despite the overwhelming evidence of the success of the market-oriented economies of the West based upon capitalist principles, it still attracts opposition, often virulent, from many intellectuals. The system is indeed prone to occasional crises, such as the financial one of 2008–9, but it has brought unprecedented prosperity to literally billions of people across the world.

The success of liberal intellectuals – using the word 'liberal' in the American sense – is much more complete in social and cultural policy and debate, a phenomenon which arose mainly during the final quarter of the twentieth century. Hayek had earlier noted that 'it is perhaps the most characteristic feature of the intellectual that he judges new ideas not by their specific merits but by the readiness with which they fit into his general conception, into the picture of the world which he regards as modern or advanced'. Just one example will suffice. The view that all types of family structure are equally valid has become an article of faith with the metropolitan liberal elite. Yet it is rejected decisively by all serious studies of the problem. Children brought up in households of never-married single mothers, for example, face a very much higher probability of being consigned to a life of poverty and crime than in stable two-parent households.

Hayek himself is very clear on how such a small minority can set so decisively the terms of debate on social and cultural matters. He writes: '[Socialists] have always directed their main effort towards gaining the support of this "elite" [of intellectuals], while the more conservative groups have acted, regularly but unsuccessfully, on a more naïve view of mass democracy and have usually vainly tried to reach and persuade the individual voter.' He goes on later in the essay to state, 'It is not an exaggeration to say that, once the more active part of the intellectuals has been converted to a set of beliefs, the process by which these become generally accepted is almost automatic and irreversible.'

Hayek did not articulate a formal model of how this process operated, for network theory scarcely existed at that time, and was in any event mainly confined to the abstract musings of high mathematics. But he was essentially articulating a quite different process from that of Lazarsfeld and Katz. First of all, the small minority of influentials – Hayek's intellectuals – are targeted. If successful, they then define the terms of the debate and influence the media. Initially, their impact is on the more elite outlets, which in turn affect how the media as a whole frame the arguments. So the intellectuals affect and determine mass opinion both themselves directly, through appearing in the media, and indirectly, by influencing the arguments and how they are presented.

Simple network models based on the principle of binary choice with externalities which we saw in the previous chapter illustrate clearly how Hayek's idea can work in practice. As before, we have a population of agents who face a choice between two alternatives, and each person has his or her own degree of persuadability. An agent switches behaviour if the proportion of all the others to which it pays attention – is connected, in other words – is above its persuadability threshold. Last time, this was a simple matter of counting heads. But this time round, each agent to which an individual is connected is weighted by the number of agents to which it is itself connected. People with lots of connections, known by many, have prestige in this version of the model, and the weight given to their choice reflects this.

So, putting the agents on a scale-free network, we can start off with, say, 20 per cent of the population holding liberal social views and 80 per cent conservative. If these same proportions are reflected in the hubs, the key influencers in the network, when we run the model many times, the proportion which ends up as liberal on average falls. Indeed, in more than half of the solutions, the proportion which is liberal eventually falls below 5 per cent. But suppose now that we start off with exactly the same overall proportion, but specify that the most connected 2 per cent of the population, a tiny minority, start as liberals. It is then conservatism which ends up close to elimination most of the time. By making this initial percentage smaller we can of course get more mixed results. But the message is clear. In situations where highly connected people carry special influence because of the number of their connections, they can indeed be as decisive as Hayek intuitively believed them to be.

Networks are clearly very important in determining the outcomes of many social and economic processes. As we have seen, they introduce new levels of uncertainties for policy makers, a feature not just of network models themselves but, far more significantly, of the real world. We have begun in this chapter the task of trying to scale down these uncertainties. Scaling them down by finding ways which will not only help us to understand whether network effects are present in any particular situation, but which offer practical advice to policy makers depending on the particular type of network which is relevant. The theme of policy making in a networked world is one to which we return at greater length in the final chapter.

A disturbing feature of many of the examples which have been given is that, when network effects are present, it is the networks which are more important in determining outcomes than the objective attributes of the various choices and courses of action on offer. This is virtually a complete reversal of the principles of the rational model of behaviour according to economists. There, the qualities and features of the alternatives are crucial to their success or failure. If our world is like this, the phrase attributed to Ralph Waldo Emerson has distinct resonance: 'Build a better mousetrap and the world will beat a path to your door'. In a world where network effects are important, this appears to be by no means guaranteed. The mathematics of the network models suggest that almost any brand of mousetrap could end up being the market leader, with more and more people beating a path to the door of the producer, almost without regard to its efficacy if it is fortunate enough to be the recipient of the benefits of positive linking.

The maths certainly gives these results. But are we simply falling into the trap of mainstream economists, of reifying abstract mathematical approaches, albeit of a completely different, much more modern variety than the ones which economists use? Maths is all very well, but what evidence, what actual human behaviour, can be shown to be compatible not only with how these models work, but with their results, which seem to defy, if not common sense, then at least conventional wisdom? These questions are the focus of the next chapter.

7

Copying Is the Best Policy

Herb Simon's revolutionary insight for economics was that, in most situations, agents are unable, literally unable, ever to compute the optimal decision. It is not a question of placing constraints on their behaviour, such as the costs of gathering and processing information, and then assuming that they make the best possible decision in the light of these constraints. It is that they can never know what the best decision is, not just before but even after the event.

In Simon's theory, agents are still evaluating alternatives, but they decide amongst them on the basis of the features, the attributes, of the choices they consider. The model of behaviour outlined in the previous chapter takes us even further away from the model of rational choice in economics. It suggests that the actual benefits offered by a product, service, idea, lifestyle choice, etc. over those of its competitors are of little relevance to the outcome. Once something starts to become a little bit more popular than its rivals, for whatever reason, a feedback mechanism is set up. Its popularity makes it even more popular. It is positively linked.

All theories are approximations to reality, a familiar mantra by now. One theory about how an agent makes decisions postulates that it obtains all the information relevant to that decision, that it is capable of interpreting and processing this information so that it makes the best choice for itself, and that it operates independently, not being influenced directly by other agents, with fixed tastes and preferences.

This is, of course, the theory of Rational Economic Man. And it was being formalised and developed for the first time during the final quarter of the nineteenth century and the early years of the twentieth. Even then, its assumptions were not completely true. But perhaps they were not too bad; reasonable enough approximations to form a working model which revealed something about how the world worked.

I have a cherished copy of the April 1910 edition of *Bradshaw's*. Very few readers will know what *Bradshaw's* is. And when I explain that it is a timetable of all the trains which ran in Britain and Ireland in that month in that year, you may feel that a lack of acquaintance with this volume may be an advantage rather than a handicap. Yet it is a fascinating social document. Railways made journeys very much faster than they had ever been. The London to Edinburgh stagecoach even with the new turnpike roads of the late eighteenth century and better technical design of the coaches, could not reduce the journey time to less than thirty-six hours. By rail in 1910, the journey could be accomplished in a mere eight. On the other hand, when connections had to be made, perhaps from the main line to a branch, railway companies thought nothing of keeping passengers waiting for two or three hours for no apparent reason. Even on today's overcrowded roads, these journeys can be accomplished more quickly by car.

But the real interest in the present context is the advertisements that appear throughout the timetable. Not surprisingly, there are details of many hotels that the upper- and wealthier middle-class readers of *Bradshaw's* in 1910 might be drawn to. (One boasts that 'staff in full livery greet the train and carry your luggage'.) Other adverts are for quite simple, straightforward products. We read that 'Keating's Powder Kills Beetles', over a graphic picture of several dead beetles and another crying into a handkerchief. Apart from the prices of the variously sized tins in which it is sold, that is the entire content of the advert. Another boasts that 'Eux-E-Sis' is a 'delightful cream for shaving, no soap, no brush, no jug', though it is also careful – perhaps in an early example of today's paranoia that inadequate instruction might result in litigation – to specify that 'a razor is needed'. One of the most sophisticated products on offer is Benson's gold watch bracelets, which are described as containing 'lever movements' and to be 'warranted timekeepers'.

In short, the adverts essentially described what the products did. And they had limited functions which would be easy to evaluate. There was no promise of a fulfilled lifestyle, of sexual ecstasy, of the whole gamut of human emotions which twenty-first-century advertising evokes. We are simply told that Keating's Powder kills beetles and that Benson's watches tell the time.

*

Branded products were relatively new in Edwardian Britain. Of course, what we can think of as brands had existed almost as long as humanity. At a time when most people were illiterate, the Red Lion pub might have a sign outside painted with an image of that mythical beast. The sign both informed potential consumers that alcohol could be obtained there, and served as an indicator of the quality and reliability of the offer. In the great fourteenth-century allegorical poem *Piers Plowman*, in which the Deadly Sins are personified, Glutton is on his way to church to confess. He is waylaid by none other than Betty the Brewster herself, standing outside her premises delivering personalised messages to her potential customers, almost in the manner of recommender emails in our own times. She targets Glutton for his fondness for 'hotte spyces', and he succumbs, imbibing no less than a 'galloun and a gyll' (about five litres) of strong ale.

Products designed to be sold to a mass market were essentially an innovative feature of the nineteenth century and in particular the final quarter of that century. The Industrial Revolution ushered in for the first time a social and economic system in which sustained long-term growth was a fundamental feature. Ironically, it was none other than Karl Marx who was the first economist to understand that this was a permanent feature of the new capitalist system. Times were hard for the emerging industrial working class, with punishing hours and meagre wages. But gradually the benefits of growth seeped through. Millions of people began to have that little bit extra to spend over and above what was required for mere subsistence. Branded products were developed, designed to be sold to a new mass market, and corporate structures and technologies evolved to enable them to be produced and delivered.

Alongside them, the new profession of advertising sprang up. N. W. Ayer and Son opened in Philadelphia in 1869, and were the first company to perform what is now the central offer of advertising: the design of promotional messages for clients. In common with other agencies, they brokered the rates for advertising space in newspapers, but Ayer's were the first to take charge of the content. From these modest beginnings, advertising now operates on a massive scale. Estimates of the current global size of the industry vary, but its turnover is not far short of a trillion dollars. Initially, consumer choice and awareness remained relatively limited. Mass markets were in their infancy. Moreover, the products themselves tended to be uncomplicated, their qualities both few and obvious and readily evaluated. Fashions, of course, existed, as they have done throughout human history. But awareness of the choices made by other people and of the detailed events in the wider world was, by today's standards, limited. Things had moved on since 1840, when the inhabitants of the remote Atlantic archipelago of St Kilda, the farthest-flung part of the British Isles, were still offering prayers to the health of His Majesty King William IV three years after his death. But the instant access to what others are doing and thinking, which is now taken for granted, simply did not exist.

*

So perhaps a century ago, the assumptions of the rational choice theory of economics might not have been – how shall I put it? – completely unreasonable ones to make. This is not to say that they were necessarily good ones, just that they described a theoretical world which at least bore some tenuous connection to reality. But what does the world of the twenty-first century look like?

First of all, and most obviously, the speed and scale of communication of the opinions and decisions of others changed dramatically during the twentieth century. And in particular, the internet over the most recent ten to fifteen years has revolutionised these features of the world. The technological innovation of the internet certainly makes feasible an entirely different model of behavioural decision making, in which people take into account directly the choices and opinions of others.

This development was foreseen in the remarkable work of Marshall McLuhan, a Canadian Professor of English and a communications theorist based at the University of Toronto in the 1950s and 1960s. He became well known to the general public through his 1967 book *The Medium is the Massage*. The word 'massage' is correct, though the phrase was subsequently adapted to 'the medium is the message'. McLuhan believed that each technological medium of communication 'massaged' the way in which agents viewed the world. Behaviour itself was altered by revolutions in communications technology. The medium affects society and how people behave not by its content but by its characteristics. So for McLuhan, the actual content of what was broadcast on television did not matter.

Regardless of the validity of McLuhan's theories, in a very practical sense both twentieth-century technology and now the internet have completely transformed our ability to discover the choices of others. We are faced with a vast explosion of such information compared to the world of a century ago. We also have stupendously more products available to us from which to choose. Eric Beinhocker, in his excellent book *The Origin of Wealth*, considers the number of choices available to someone in New York alone: 'The number of economic choices the average New Yorker has is staggering. The Wal-Mart near JFK Airport has over 100,000 different items in stock, there are over 200 television channels offered on cable TV, Barnes & Noble lists over 8 million titles, the local supermarket has 275 varieties of breakfast cereal, the typical department store offers 150 types of lipstick, and there are over 50,000 restaurants in New York City alone.'

He goes on to discuss stock-keeping units – SKUs – which are the level of brands, pack sizes and so on which retail firms themselves use in re-ordering and stocking their stores. So a particular brand of beer, say, might be available in a single tin, a single bottle, both in various sizes, or it might be offered in a pack of six or twelve. Each of these offers is an SKU. Beinhocker states, 'The number of SKUs in the New Yorker's economy is not precisely known, but using a variety of data sources, I very roughly estimate that it is on the order of tens of billions.' Tens of billions! Tens of billions of alternatives from which a customer can choose.

So, compared to the world of 1900, the early twenty-first

century has seen quantum leaps in both the accessibility of the behaviour, actions and opinions of others, and in the number of choices available. Either of these developments would be sufficient on its own to invalidate the economist's concept of 'rational' behaviour. The assumptions of the theory bear no resemblance to the world they purport to describe. But the discrepancy between theory and reality goes even further.

Many of the products available in the twenty-first century are highly sophisticated, and are hard to evaluate even when information on their qualities is provided. Mobile (or cell) phones have rapidly become an established, very widely used technology (despite the inability of different branches of the English language to agree on what they should be called). Google searches on 'cell phone choices' and 'mobile phone choices' reveal, respectively, 34,300,000 and 27,200,000 sites from which to make your choice. And how many people can honestly say they have any more than a rough idea of the maze of alternative tariffs which are available on these phones?

So here we have a dramatic contrast between the consumer worlds of the late nineteenth and early twenty-first centuries. Branded products and mass markets exist in both, but in one the range of choice is rather limited. In the other, a stupendous cornucopia is presented, far beyond the wildest dreams of even the most utopian social reformers of a century ago. An enormous gulf separates the complicated nature of many modern offers from the more straightforward consumer products of a mere hundred years ago. And, of course, we are now far more aware of the opinions and choices of others.

*

There is very strong evidence from the discipline of psychology that, in a world such as this, the assumptions made by the rational choice theory of economics do not make much sense. William Hick was a British academic psychologist who spent most of his working life at Cambridge. In 1952 he published a paper in the *Quarterly Journal of Experimental Psychology* entitled 'On the Rate of Gain in Information'. It made him famous, at least within the world of psychology, and its results became immortalised in Hick's Law.

Hick carried out an experiment involving semaphore lamps and their corresponding Morse code keys. (More irreverent readers may recall the Monty Python sketch in which Heathcliff and Cathy enact *Wuthering Heights* by semaphore, to be followed by Wyatt Earp and Doc Holliday in *Gunfight at the OK Corral* in Morse code. But this code, in which each letter of the alphabet is represented by a combination of short and long clicks, was widely used for open communication, not least within the military during the Second World War.) Hick had lamps lighting at random every five seconds. The reaction time to choose the corresponding key was recorded, with the number of choices ranging from two to ten lamps. Hick's Law essentially describes the time it takes for a person to make a decision amongst the possible choices he or she has. Technically, given a number of equally probable choices, the average time required to choose amongst them increases with the value of log base 2 of the number of choices.*

But what does this mean? Rather obviously, it suggests that the time taken to evaluate and choose rises with the number of choices. It also tells us that the amount of time required rises more slowly than the number of alternatives. The value of 'log base 2' of any number is simply the number of times 2 has to be multiplied by itself to get that number. So the log base 2 of 2 itself is just one, the number of times 2 is multiplied by itself to get the

---

* Plus one, to be accurate, and with an empirically determined constant multiplicative factor.

COPYING IS THE BEST POLICY

value 2. Log base 2 of 4 takes the value 2, for 4 is 2 multiplied by itself two times, and so on.

Now, the value of this formula when applied to the number 1,000 is just under 10. Hick's Law suggests that if it takes me one unit of time, whatever that might be, to decide between two alternatives, it will take me ten times as long to pick one from 1,000. Log base 2 of 27,200,000 is nearly 25. So I Google 'mobile phone choices' and get 27,200,000 sites from which to choose just to find out more about the choices open to me. The one unit of time it would take me to decide in the extremely unlikely event of only two sites popping up in a search, expands by a factor of 25 to decide amongst all the alternatives, even if in some miraculous way they could all be presented to me on the same page. And moving between pages just to find out what the choices are is itself time consuming.

Not surprisingly, most people in this situation simply do not bother even to try to look at all the alternatives. Indeed, as we have seen, on average in such searches, 98 per cent of all searchers just hit one of the top three results. And no fewer than 60 per cent select the number one. They behave in exactly the way postulated by Simon, by trying to strip down the vast dimension of the choices which faces them and use instead a simple rule of thumb: hit one of the first three sites in the list.

In so doing, as we have already seen, their choices are influenced by a network. The random network of other people who previously selected the sites which have become the three most popular relating to that particular search. Before I typed 'mobile phone choices' into my search engine, I may not even have had a preference at all for the site I would investigate in more detail, may not even have known it existed. But now I do. My preference has not just been altered, but it has been defined by the previous selections made by agents on a random network.

This is a key reason that 'copying' has become the rational way to behave, the rational way to make choices in the twenty-first century. The range and complexity of choice are so vast that the only way in which agents can cope is by adopting behavioural rules which spectacularly reduce the dimension of the scale and scope of the choices available to them. The word 'copying' is, I should stress, being used as a shorthand description of the mode of behaviour in which your choice is influenced, altered, directly by the behaviour of others. Lying behind the actions may be several different motives.

An important one relates to the problem posed by Herb Simon back in the 1950s, when he argued that humans simply cannot gather and process information on the scale required by the standard economic model of rational behaviour. He suggested that in most situations we simply cannot compute the optimal decision, so instead we rely on rules of thumb. And we recall that in the late 1930s Keynes concluded that 'we have, as a rule, only the vaguest idea of any but the most direct consequences of our acts'. Keynes's response was the same as Simon's. In such circumstances, both these great thinkers argued that we need a new definition of rational behaviour. The economic definition of 'rational' is no longer relevant. Recall Keynes's explicit statement that copying is a key element of rationality: 'Knowing that our individual judgement is worthless, we endeavour to fall back on the judgement of the rest of the world which is perhaps better informed.' So, in many situations, relying at least in part on the actions and opinions of others is entirely rational. Copying makes sense.

*

Fashion is another reason, more basic somehow, and easier to understand. It seems to be a deep-seated human instinct to like to buy, wear or choose the things which lots of other people find popular. Of course, there can be reactions in the opposite direction. Thorstein Veblen's fame rests on his 1899 classic *Theory of the Leisure Class* and the phrase 'conspicuous consumption' which has become associated with it. In economics, there is even a special class of products which go by the name 'Veblen goods'. Their characteristic is that the demand for them increases as the price rises, as a higher price signals greater status. We might, of course, see this form of behaviour as itself a fashion, albeit one confined to those with sufficient income and wealth with which to follow it. Veblen's snobs adamantly refuse to buy or adopt any form of behaviour which is remotely popular with the broad masses.

On the day I wrote the first draft of this chapter, I saw in a popular newspaper a piece on the ultra-high-heeled shoes designed and marketed, at ultra-high prices, by Christian Louboutin. The journalist points out that 'price, not taste, is the only thing that matters to the rich and famous' before going on to administer a stern warning: 'But Mr Louboutin needs to beware. If you make a brand too popular and ubiquitous, allow it to be worn by the super-tanned rather than supermodels, you are in danger of devaluing it. Remember when Daniella Westbrook was seen dressed head-to-toe in Burberry check? This British brand's credibility plummeted overnight and it took years of clever marketing, a new creative director and pushing the brand ever more crazily towards so-called "luxury" to leave its less desirable customers floundering.' Purely by coincidence, when revising the draft, I read that Michael Sorrentino, famous for appearing in MTV's pseudo-reality TV series *Jersey Shore*, has been offered money by Abercrombie and Fitch *not* to wear their clothes on the programme. Sorrentino has a lack of discernible qualifications, talent or even good looks, and indulges in behaviour which might be regarded as hedonistic or even irresponsible. The company said:

'We are deeply concerned that Mr Sorrentino's association with our brand could cause significant damage to our image.'

But fashion seems eternal. The Hittite empire reached its peak in Anatolia in the fourteenth century BC, nearly 3,500 years ago. Even here, at this immense distance of time, we can find evidence of the fashion motive at work in the decisions people made. Archaeologists have put together, in a painstaking and thorough way a database of ceramic bowls from two successive phases of occupation of Boğazköy-Hattusa, capital of the Hittite empire and the largest Bronze Age settlement in Turkey. The bowls differ in features such as size and the materials used.

James Steele and his colleagues Claudia Gatz and Anne Kandler, of University College London, published an article in the *Journal of Archaeological Science* in 2010. They asked the question: to what extent are the observed frequencies of the different types of bowl due either to pure fashion, to people simply copying designs which were already popular, or to the inherent functional characteristics of the bowls? The latter case is an example of incentives at work, of rational choice in the economic sense. Agents consciously select amongst alternatives after considering the attributes of each of the potential choices.

Using some advanced mathematical techniques, related to the discussion on preferential attachment in the previous chapter, they concluded that the pure fashion hypothesis goes a long way in being able to account for the frequency with which different types of ceramic bowls are observed in Hittite culture 3,500 years ago. However, they also found that incentives, as it were, also played a part. Rational choice, conscious selection on the basis of the features of the bowls, also had to be invoked to give a more complete understanding. But fashion explained the most.

*

So far we have invoked two motivational factors which can underpin the theory of copying as the new rational mode of behaviour. One of these, fashion, is almost as old as humanity itself. The other is much newer, but equally fundamental in the modern world. This is the need to dramatically scale down the dimension of choice in the face of both the vast array of products and services that modern capitalism provides and the knowledge which communications technology makes available to us in terms of the decisions and opinions of others.

But there are further important behavioural principles which justify the concept of copying as the new rationality. Solomon Asch was born in Warsaw and in 1920 moved to America, where he carried out pioneering work in social psychology. His most famous experiments, like those of Hick, were done in the early 1950s. The participants were asked to compare the length of a line with other everyday objects. One such task was to compare a line with three others and say which one of the three was the same as the given line. Visually, the answer was obvious. It was not a matter of careful judgement, of close inspection and calibration. One of the three was obviously the longest.

Each group of players was seated in a room, and asked to announce their opinion out loud and in turn. In the control groups, in which everyone involved was giving their own independent opinion, almost everyone gave the correct answer. Asch then repeated the experiment with people planted to give an incorrect response. And these were seated so that they would be the first to speak. The 'real' participants, as opposed to Asch's people, were put at ease by carrying out two sets of comparisons in which all the plants gave the correct answer. On the third and subsequent trials, however, all the plants gave the same wrong one. To Asch's surprise, no less than three-quarters of the genuine responders repeated the incorrect answer at least once. And around a third almost always did so.

Asch then carried out modifications of the experiments. One was to discover how many plants were needed to make the real participants reply incorrectly. If there were only one or two, they were almost always ignored, but three was the critical number. Once three gave the incorrect answer, at least one real participant would follow their line.

There have been many subsequent variants of the Asch experiments. One was carried out by the French-Romanian psychologist Serge Moscovici in the 1970s. Groups of six were formed comprising four participants and two plants. They were all shown thirty-six slides, each slide a shade of blue, and asked to state the colour out loud. There were two groups in the experiment. In the first group the plants were consistent and answered green for every slide. In the second group they were inconsistent and answered green twenty-four times and blue twelve times. Moscovici found that when the plants answered consistently, the influence of the minority in inducing incorrect responses from the honest participants was distinctly stronger.

A number of criteria have been determined to judge the potential influence of a dissenting minority in more general situations, such as when discussion is permitted. Perhaps unsurprisingly, it is stronger when the minority is consistent, when it is perceived by others to be competent, and when the majority genuinely feels uncertain. Again, not surprisingly, if it is the majority which dissents from the correct answer, the impact is more powerful still. What *is* surprising is that even a minority can induce people to give a response which is obviously incorrect.

It is certainly surprising in the context of the rational agent model, where, once again, the agent is postulated to gather all information and to make the best choice, operating independently. How hard can it be to say whether lines are longer or shorter than another when the answer is clear from simple inspection? Well, it certainly appears to be too hard for many people when confronted with dissent from the correct opinion. The result has been obtained so often that it seems to be established beyond reasonable doubt.

There are two potential reasons why people behave in this way. First, someone may genuinely believe that the group – other people – have better information and so decide that it makes sense to copy their decisions. In the classic example of going to eat in a strange city, the rational choice is to select the restaurant which looks busy rather than its empty near neighbour. The diners may very well have information that it is indeed the better of the two. But, as we have already seen and will revisit below, there is no guarantee that this is necessarily true. The second motive is that people might well have a simple desire to conform, especially when the incorrect view is expressed firmly and consistently by the majority.

Copying the majority is certainly a strategy widely adopted in non-human worlds. Think of fish. Juicy fish such as herrings, which large predators relish. Such creatures have evolved the shoal or swarm as the natural way of moving around. One potential reason for this is the so-called confusion effect. A predator confronted by a large number of prey may experience sensory overload and so be less able to single out a single victim to gobble up.

*

Copying as a strategy can certainly have its drawbacks. Dirk Helbing of ETH Zürich is an intellectual leader of the social physics community – scholars trained as physicists who have turned their attention to such social and economic questions as how to evacuate a sports stadium safely in an emergency. Helbing and his colleagues have shown that simply providing more exits at regular intervals, a common-sense approach, may not necessarily work. And the reason for this is the principle of copying. In an emergency situation, an individual usually cannot gather much information, and so may believe that the group is better informed. But it is precisely this which leads to the phenomenon of flocking, so that large numbers may all try to use a single exit, whilst others may remain at best only sparsely used.

A completely different example, this time of successful copying, is provided by the rice farmers of Bali. The Indonesian island is far more than a resort for sun-worshipping Westerners. It sustains an exceptionally productive rice-farming industry. Essentially, Bali is a large extinct volcano with a lake in the crater that provides much of the water used to irrigate the crop.

For centuries, the rice growers of Bali have been engaged in agricultural practices which have proved highly successful. Without centralised control, the farmers have evolved a carefully coordinated system which allows productive farming in an ecosystem rife with water scarcity, pests and diseases, and apparent conflicts of interest between different groups of farmers. No one has planned this system. And farmers operating at different levels of the mountain have potentially conflicting interests about the control of water, the timing of rice planting, when fields should lie fallow and so on. Yet a highly productive, successful and sustainable system has evolved.

There are two key reasons why this has happened. First, the farmers simply copy the good behaviour they observe in others. Second, they place great emphasis on purely voluntary structures which promote and reinforce this cooperative pattern of behaviour and prevent less desirable patterns of individual behaviour from cascading across their social networks.

Top anthropologist Steve Lansing of the University of Arizona and the Santa Fe Institute has a very neat model which accounts for the key empirical features of Balinese agriculture. A crucial reason for the success of the system is that the pattern over the course of the year in terms of which fields lie fallow is very effective in controlling pests. This pattern can be explained almost entirely by a very simple model. Farmers operate in small units called subaks. Suppose we start the model off with each subak being allocated at random a particular month of the year for cropping. Bali lies almost on the equator, and its climate is very stable, enabling rice to be planted in every month of the year. At the end of the year, each subak simply observes the crops of its four nearest neighbours. If one of these has a better crop, the subak copies the timing of that neighbour for next year's cropping. The model rapidly converges on an overall pattern which is very similar to that which is actually observed. The subaks do not have masses of quantitative data, they do not perform the complicated mathematical 'optimising' procedures of economics, they do not rely on government officials and rules and regulations. They simply copy the good behaviour of their neighbours. Copying, simple imitation, works.

The second key reason for Bali's success is the strong emphasis placed on mechanisms for promoting cooperation. Within each subak, an individual farmer has incentives to free ride on any group arrangements. To share in the group's rewards without making a contribution. Pure short-term individual profit maximising suggests that individuals *should* behave in this way. But they don't. Great emphasis is placed on the social structure, on reinforcing the idea of individuals belonging to the subak. In other words, social conventions have evolved to try to restrain the human urge, the instinct, to react to incentives. Within the subak, of course, social sanctions could ultimately be taken against a non-cooperative individual. Outside the subak, this is not possible. Instead, an elaborate system of 'water temples' has evolved, which facilitate voluntary coordination and cooperation. The purpose is to make the social network robust, to prevent cascades of non-cooperative behaviour from spreading.

In the 1970s, the modern planner stepped into this world. On the advice of the Asian Development Bank, the government of Bali legally mandated the introduction of new, high-yielding varieties of rice. Armed with the modern panoply of mathematical models and plans, the government brought explicit regulation into this voluntary system. It was a disaster. The existing coordination mechanisms amongst farmers broke down and pests proliferated. Attempts to control pests by introducing yet further new varieties of rice resulted in the emergence of new pests. The whole planned, regulated experiment failed. It had the best of intentions, but the outcome proved dramatically different from these intentions. The idea was, fortunately, abandoned and agriculture on Bali reverted to the voluntary, unplanned but very successful system which had evolved over centuries.

*

In general, copying is usually a very good strategy to adopt. Kevin Laland, an evolutionary biologist at the University of St Andrews, posted a question on a website in 2007 and emailed it to academic departments around the world: 'Suppose you find yourself in an unfamiliar environment where you don't know how to get food, or travel from A to B. Would you invest time working out what to do on your own, or observe other individuals and copy them? If you copy, who would you copy? The first individual you see? The most common behaviour? Do you always copy or do you do so selectively? What would you do?'

In essence these are the questions posed by this entire book. Do we act as an economic rational agent and work things out by responding to the pay-offs yielded by different strategies, different choices? Or do we just copy other people? But not just this. Who do we copy and when? We have already seen examples where people copy others seemingly at random, and where, as in the case of the Protestant martyrs, the prestige of the individual is a key factor in whether or not they are copied.

The eventual outcome of the question posed by Laland was a paper published in the world's top scientific journal, *Science*, in April 2010, with nine co-authors, including UCLA's Rob Boyd, perhaps the world's greatest authority on cultural evolution. The article reports the results of a 'social learning' tournament – social learning being essentially the jargon in these particular academic areas for copying – in which entrants submitted strategies speci-fying rules of behaviour on how and when to use either social learning or individual trial-and-error learning to acquire success-ful behaviour in a complex environment. More than a hundred teams from around the world competed and submitted strategies in this computer-based tournament.

The problem the strategies – let us think of them as players, even though the 'player' here is lines of code specifying how to make choices – were confronted with is the so-called 'restless multi-armed bandit'. The idea is based on the one-armed bandit slot machine, in which pulling a lever sets off a game of chance with outcomes which yield different pay-offs. The pay-offs them-selves change randomly over time, hence the word 'restless' in the description. The winner would be the player acquiring most points from these pay-offs over a long period of time.

Each player has three options in every round: *observe*, which simply means watching another individual and the pay-off this agent obtains; *innovate*, which involves developing a behaviour of its own; or *exploit*, which involves actually invoking one of the strategies it has acquired and pulling the arms of the bandit. Only by exploiting can players acquire points. So an important decision for players is whether to stick with the strategies already acquired and 'exploit' on every round, or whether to invest time in learning a new behaviour which may or may not be better than the ones it already has.

As noted above, the tournament was made even more realistic by the fact that the pay-off point associated with each behaviour was not fixed, but varied over the course of the tournament. Strategies which had yielded lots of points might suddenly yield many fewer. This is a key element of the real world. Companies innovate all the time to try to outperform their rivals, so the competitive environment is constantly changing. For example the printed book revolutionised the world when it first appeared over 500 years ago. The skills of those involved in transcribing the written word by hand, the previous dominant technology, soon became redundant. And now the printed book itself faces serious competition from electronic media.

The design, testing and refinement of the tournament took eighteen months. The play took over a year, and was only feasible thanks to no less than 65,000 hours of free computing time being provided by National Grid, the company which owns the British gas and electricity transmission systems. The experts involved in designing the tournament had clear views in advance as to the type of strategy which would succeed. As the abstract of the *Science* paper states: 'Most current theory predicts the emergence of mixed strategies that rely on some combination of the two types of learning.' In other words, players would use a mixture of gathering private information by trying out their own strategies and seeing what pay-off they got and using public information by copying the behaviour of other players.

To their astonishment, a very simple strategy devised by two Canadian post-graduate students, Timothy Lillicrap and Daniel Cownden, proved the outright winner. And this strategy relied almost exclusively on copying. To quote again from the heavy-duty paper: 'This outcome was not anticipated by the tournament organisers, nor by the committee of experts established to oversee the tournament, nor . . . by most of the tournament entrants.' At one level, copying may seem advantageous because agents can avoid the costs of trying to work things out for themselves by rational learning. However, it may result in the acquisition of an inappropriate or outdated strategy, and for this reason the expert view was that it would be used sparingly by the tournament winner.

A common feature of the most successful strategies as a group was the emphasis which they placed on copying. But not only that. They spent as much time as possible 'exploiting', acquiring points, rather than searching and investing time in acquiring even better strategies. So they did not attempt to acquire an 'optimal' strategy, in so far as this word has meaning in the context of a changing environment. They found something which gave them points and used it. In other words, they took advantage of positive linking. The network in this case was the other strategies whose behaviour and success they observed. They copied, and they won.

Social learning – 'copying', in our terms – appears to be a very deep-seated aspect of human behaviour. Evolutionary anthropologists and psychologists have argued persuasively that the anomalously large brain (neocortex) size in humans, compared to other mammals, evolved primarily for social-learning purposes. As Robin Dunbar and Susanne Shultz of Oxford University's Institute of Cognitive and Evolutionary Anthropology stated in a paper in *Science* in 2007: 'The evolution of unusually large brains in some groups of animals, notably primates, has long been a puzzle. Although early explanations tended to emphasise the brain's role in sensory or technical competence (foraging skills, innovations, and way-finding), the balance of evidence now clearly favors the suggestion that it was the computational demands of living in large, complex societies that selected for large brains.' So the skills required for positive linking may even be hardwired into the human brain.

Of course, true believers in economic rationality have no real difficulty in reconciling the outcomes of the tournament with their view of the world. *Any* mode of behaviour which proves the best is obviously optimal and therefore would be learned by an economically rational agent. We might even say, invoking the old Soviet phrase again, that it is apparent that this is indeed the case. However – and this point is crucial – using copying as the main way of making choices can lead to outcomes which are so radically different from those predicted by rational economic behaviour that it really does not make sense to describe the former as 'rational' in the economic sense of the word at all.

The social-learning experiment introduced yet another, even more realistic aspect of the real world. The network which any given agent used to help make decisions was not fixed in structure, it was not static. It evolved over time. The group of individuals being monitored for their performance varied over time. The dynamic nature of the network is yet another way in which network approaches are in general much better approximations of reality than the models of orthodox economics. And in such worlds – both model worlds in the computer and the real human world – our understanding of what it is to be rational changes completely.

Incentives matter in the experiment; indeed, they are a key feature. You win the game by acquiring more points than anyone else, and you acquire points by making a series of decisions over time. But there is no meaningful sense in which we can say that even the strategy of the winning algorithm, the winning player, was 'optimal'. It was the best at exploiting the information provided by the networks of other agents, but that is the limit of what we can say, even ex post, after the experiment has been carried out. And ex ante, before the event, the most successful strategy in the experiment was extremely difficult to identify, a fact attested by the failure of some of the world's leading experts involved with the design of the experiment to anticipate that copying strategies would prevail.

So, yes, incentives still feature. But whether they are the conventional incentives of price – points in the experiment equate to price in the real world – or the more sophisticated range of incentives falling under the banner of 'nudge', the economic concept of rational behaviour, of responding to situations in this way, really makes little or no sense in this evolutionary, network context. Behaviour based on copying is the rational way to behave, a mode of behaviour with dramatically different implications from those of conventional economic rationality.

*

How much difference can the copying motive make to the outcome? When an important determinant of agents' choices is simply the proportion in which other agents have already selected the various offers, what happens compared to when they act 'rationally' in an economic sense?

Duncan Watts, the Columbia professor who moved to Yahoo! and whom we have already met, and his colleagues Matt Salganik and Peter Dodds carried out an intriguing experiment on this, which they published in *Science* in 2006. They created an artificial music market comprising 14,341 real participants, recruited mostly from a teen-interest website, who were shown a list of previously unknown songs from unknown bands. On arriving to take part in the live experiment, the young people were divided into one of two groups. The groups differed only in the amount of information provided to them when they were making their selections. In each case, each individual made choices on his or her own, without any others being present. A choice in this context was defined as being the decision to download a particular track.

Given the name of the song and the band, one group were allowed to listen if they wished, and were asked to assign a rating from one star (hate it) to five stars (love it). There were forty-eight songs in total from which to choose. Once someone had listened to a song and rated it, he or she was given a chance to download it, though this was entirely optional.

This part of the experiment essentially corresponds to the world of economic rationality. Individuals are choosing quite independently. They are given complete information, the names of the songs and the bands, and can listen to the songs before deciding whether or not to download. The amount of choice is not excessive, and the products are easy to evaluate. The teenage participants were not asked to decide on the relative merits of different renditions of Brünnhilde's great final aria in Wagner's *Götterdämmerung*, but to choose from a genre of music with which they were very familiar. Of course, the tastes of the participants may very well have been shaped prior to the experiment by the preferences and choices of their peers. But within the strict confines of the experiment, we can take their tastes as being fixed.

The number of individuals involved in each experiment varied, but it was usually between 500 and 1,000. At the end of each experiment, the numbers of downloads of each song were totalled. This distribution can plausibly be regarded as the independent preferences of the members of the group. Figure 7.1 plots the relative popularity of the forty-eight songs in a typical experiment. It shows how many times each song was downloaded, the totals across the individuals who took part. The only twist in the chart is that, in order to make comparison easier with the Figure 7.2, the actual numbers of downloads are not shown. Rather, the chart shows the number of downloads compared to the average number across all forty-eight songs. For simplicity, the average is set equal to 100.

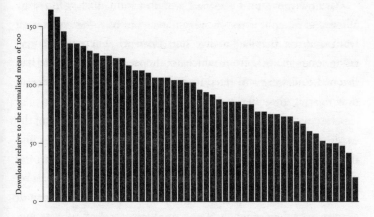

Figure 7.1 Typical outcome of the music download experiments; number of times each of forty-eight songs is downloaded over the course of an experiment, participants know only the names of the song and band and can listen to songs before deciding whether or not to download

Note: The average number of downloads is set equal to 100 for comparative purposes

The advantage of comparing everything to an average set at 100 might now be clearer. We can see that the least popular song got only about twenty-five downloads, or a quarter of the average. This stands out, however, and we can see that apart from this there are several in the 'least popular group', as it were, with around fifty downloads each, or around one half of the average. In contrast, the most popular get just over one and a half times the average number.

So there are genuine differences in popularity of the forty-eight songs, which can be reasonably seen as reflecting the individual preferences of the agents in the experiment, because each person's preference was recorded in isolation. Broadly speaking, the most popular are around three times as popular as the least.

We now move to the second group of individuals selected by Watts and his colleagues. In every respect but one, the experiment was exactly as described above. The difference was that each participant could see how many times any particular song had been downloaded already. At the start of each experiment, the clock was reset to zero, so people could only see the choices in their particular experiment, and not those of any other experiment. In some of the experiments, the songs were simply listed in alphabetical order, and the previous downloads set against the name. In others, the songs were listed in order of popularity, a hit parade with the existing number one at the top. Figure 7.2 shows the results of a typical experiment when agents have this one extra piece of information, with the songs listed in order of popularity.

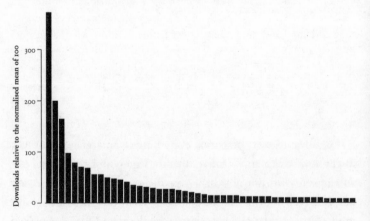

Figure 7.2 Exactly as Figure 7.1, except the participants know the number of previous downloads of each of the songs before they decide themselves

We do not need arcane statistical theory to know that the distribution of outcomes is completely different in the two figures. In the second case, most songs end up with very few downloads. The most popular gets around 350, the second most popular 200. The ratio between the most popular few and the least popular song is not just three to one. It is at least thirty to one. As Watts and his colleagues point out, the experiment by its very nature limits the degree of inequality of outcome which can emerge. The number of choices is very limited, for one thing – forty-eight to be precise. And participants could not meet or otherwise confer about the songs as they would be able to do in real life. They just had a single piece of information, no more and no less, about the choices which other people had made. But even so, compared to the outcomes under independent preferences, there was a very marked increase in the inequality of the various downloads.

But the results are even more dramatically different than this once we lift up the lid. The most popular are considerably more popular than those in Figure 7.1. But they are not the same! The most popular song in each of these two charts is different.

Giving people this one extra piece of information, on how fashionable each track is, does not make already popular ones more popular, and those which are less liked to be chosen even less. It alters spectacularly which songs end up as the most or least popular. Duncan Watts and his colleagues concluded that there was some relationship between the relative popularities of songs in the two types of experiment. But it was very weak. 'The best songs rarely did poorly, and the worst rarely did well, but any other result was possible.' So songs on the far right of Figure 7.1 did not end upon the far left of 7.2, and vice versa. But any other result was possible! A song in the middle of Figure 7.1 could end up in 7.2 either being wildly popular or, more likely, getting almost no downloads at all.

Where fashion matters, it affects the outcomes dramatically. Is it possible to use this knowledge to create self-fulfilling prophecies? Watts and Salganik went on to consider this question in *Social Psychology Quarterly* in 2008. They note an intriguing real-life example reported by American economist Alan Sorensen. He noticed that there were occasional errors in the construction of the *New York Times* best-seller list, and found that books mistakenly omitted from the list had fewer subsequent sales than a matched set of books that correctly appeared on the list.

But the main point of their paper essentially replicated their earlier experiment. With one difference. During the course of any particular experiment, at some point the relative ranking of popularity settles down, certainly as far as the most popular are concerned. A sufficient gap emerges between the number of downloads of the number one and two, two and three and so on, to make it difficult for the order to subsequently change.

At this point, Watts and Salganik gave false information to subsequent participants in the experiment. And the information really was false. They did nothing other than to completely reverse the rankings which had emerged. So the next player was told that what had actually been number 1 was number 48, number 2 was number 47, and so on. Most songs did in fact experience self-fulfilling prophecies, so that previously unpopular songs went on to become popular. The inversion did not hold true completely, for the songs which genuinely were the most popular in the independent-agent version of the experiments did gradually regain popularity if they were falsely reported as being way down the list. And participants tended to make fewer overall downloads when they were told that unpopular songs were popular. But false information on fashion still made a difference, even when it was by deliberate design the complete opposite of the truth.

*

Enormous resources are devoted to the task of predicting the outcome of social processes in domains such as economics, public policy, and popular culture. But these predictions are often woefully inaccurate. Two striking characteristics of popular cultural markets are, first, inequality (hit songs, books, and films are many times more popular than the average) and, second, unpredictability. In the original Watts experiment, songs which were well regarded by the players of the game when choosing independently rarely came near the bottom when the network of the choices of others was allowed to operate, and poor songs rarely came near the top. But, and this remarkable phrase certainly bears repeating, any other result was possible.

Imagine, then, that we are in the marketing department of a large corporation, developing a new variant of an existing brand. Let us say, fruit-coated Mars bars (which have never existed, as far as I know). The process would follow the same course as a political party or a pressure group testing out different nuances of a potential policy change. We experiment with a number of different alternatives – cherry, banana, gooseberry – and carry out extensive testing of the products with consumer groups. This may enable us to screen out fruits which nobody seems to like and allow us to settle on a smaller group, each of which resonates to some extent with potential consumers. Which of them to launch? If our market research has been mainly focused on consumers operating as individuals, the Watts experiment tells us that, if network effects matter in this market, then we cannot predict ex ante, before the launch, how well the new variant will actually perform. Most new products fail. And networks are the key reason why.

However, there is some hope. The future is not completely impenetrable. Before a product or policy or campaign is launched on the public, the curtain does remain firmly drawn. But chinks of light soon begin to appear. An important feature of such fash-ion-driven processes is that the choices which eventually prove to be the most popular seem to emerge at a very early stage of the process.

The 2010 conference on Social Computing, Behavioral Modeling and Prediction held in Maryland attracted a bevy of illustrious sponsors, such as the National Institutes of Health, the Office of Naval Research and Air Force Research Laboratories. All these outfits are aware of the inherent difficulties of predic-tion in a networked world. I published a paper in the proceedings of the conference which examines the data set from the original experiment carried out by Watts and his colleagues.* The ques-tion was: can a simple rule be devised which will enable early detection of the song which eventually ends up as number one in each particular experiment?

The answer is unequivocally 'yes'. And, paradoxically, the stronger the potential effect of the random network which con-nects you to the previous choices of others, the more likely it is that the winner can be identified. Recall Watts's three types of world: independent choice; previous choices known and ordered alphabetically; and previous choices known and ordered by pop-ularity. Before the start of each experiment, predicting the win-ner, even with the knowledge of the outcomes of the independ-ent preference experiments, is virtually impossible. We can make some very tentative remarks about a few songs which are unlikely to succeed and about a few which might. But that it is all.

The situation alters completely once the experiment starts. The trick is not to examine any of the inherent qualities of any of the songs, the way which economic rational choice would point

* The detailed description of the available data is available at http://opr. princeton.edu/archive/

the enquirer. It is to discover which sort of world we are operating in, how powerful are the network effects. Once enough steps have been taken, enough downloads made, for us to know that we are in the 'strong' network effect version of the experiment, the song which is the current number one has a very good chance of remaining there. And the identification can be made when the number of downloads of each song is still in single figures!

An appreciation of how this can be the case is as follows. (For interested readers, the technical paper is cited in the short list of further reading at the back of the book.) In Chapter 6 we met the great mathematician Carl Friedrich Gauss, and the so-called Gaussian, or normal, statistical distribution. It is the favourite distribution of economists, with much of their statistical analysis resting on the assumption that this is how the world is. But Herb Simon noticed that in a wide range of contexts, the outcomes of economic and social processes looked completely different. In particular, they were 'skewed'. In other words, they exhibited a high degree of inequality of outcomes, with the biggest, the most popular, being many times larger than the average in ways which the Gaussian does not really permit. Such outcomes arise precisely in systems where the component parts interact with each other, where the behaviour of any given agent can be influenced directly by the behaviour of others. So if we see in practice a distribution across a set of choices which looks like this, we know we are looking at a world where networks and copying are important.

The idea that in a networked world the early stages of any evolutionary process, such as how the popularities of different choices evolves over time, are decisive was shown very neatly by Brian Arthur, a highly innovative British economist who has been based for many years in New Mexico and California. Arthur's original work on this was carried out in the 1980s, well before the explosion of network science, so it is not formulated explicitly in these terms. But it has the advantage over the kind of rule of thumb described above because he obtained analytical results for a particular type of process, one which is often found in the real world.

Arthur's initial work was on a highly abstract concept in non-linear probability theory, something called Polya urns. Several rather obscure journals have already been mentioned in this book, but perhaps the one where this work first appeared is a candidate for the most otherworldly. He wrote a paper in 1983 with two Russian mathematicians, Ermoliev and Kaniovski, in a journal with the Russian title *Kybernetica*. Imagine we have a very large urn containing an equal number of red and black balls. (The colours are immaterial.) A ball is chosen at random, and is replaced into the urn along with an additional ball of the same colour. The same process is repeatedly endlessly. Within this enormous urn, can we say anything about the eventual proportions of red and black balls which will emerge? They start off with a 50/50 split. Can we say how this split will evolve?

Indeed we can. Arthur and his colleagues showed that as the process of choice and replacement unfolds, eventually the proportion of the two different colours will always – always – approach a split of 100/0. It will never quite get there, because at the start there are balls of each colour, but the urn will get closer and closer to containing balls all the same colour. The trouble is, we simply cannot say in advance whether this will be red or black. Just as in Duncan Watts's experiments, predicting the eventual winner before the process starts is extremely difficult. Except that in this context, the formal solutions to Arthur's equations show that it is literally impossible to do any better than a pure 50/50 guess. They also show that the winner emerges at a very early stage of the whole process. Once one of the balls, by the random process of selection and replacement, gets ahead, it is very difficult to reverse. The abstract nature of the analysis does not enable us to say what exactly constitutes 'very early', as we can do with rules of thumb in empirical contexts. But it establishes the principle unequivocally.

What has all this to do with the price of fish (or anything else, come to that)? Concepts of balls being drawn and replaced at random from an infinite-sized urn do seem rather abstract. We can usefully think of the balls as being connected on a network, one which evolves over time. As soon as the first ball is replaced, the chances of drawing one of the same colour on the next draw have become ever so slightly better than 50/50. We might need a large number of decimal places to say how much better, but better it has certainly become. It is as if a consumer is choosing between two complex alternatives, and is paying no attention to the inherent qualities of the balls, their colour, but just to how popular they were. The distribution of balls when *you* come to choose reflects the random networks which connect the people who have already chosen.

Brian Arthur explained the practical significance of his results in an article for the *Economic Journal* in 1989. Suppose a new technology emerges – internet search engines, to use a post-Arthurian example – and consumers have two alternative versions of the technology from which to choose. Arthur used the example of video recorders, the Sky+ box of the 1980s. The technology is entirely new, so no one really knows how to evaluate the various products associated with it. The principle of copying seems entirely rational. Someone makes a choice. In the abstract model, this is the extraction at random of a ball from the urn. The fact that brand A has been chosen rather than brand B tilts ever so slightly the possibility that the next choice will also be A rather than B – this is the replacement rule in Arthur's model. And so the process unfolds.

In practice, of course, as one of the brands gains a lead over its rival, factors other than consumer copying will come into play and reinforce its dominance. There will be positive feedback, positive linking, so that success breeds further success. The more successful brand may be able to advertise more, for instance. Retailers will give more shelf space to it, and may even, in the splendid language of retailers, delist its rival, so that it becomes harder and harder to obtain. Technologies and offers which piggyback on the brands – think of apps and iPhones here – become increasingly designed to be compatible with the number-one brand.

An important implication of all this, again completely consistent with Watts's experiments, is that success is not necessarily related to quality. In the traditional model of rationality, provided that the information can be supplied to consumers (or voters), they can be relied upon to select consciously, to choose the alternative which is best for them. In a world where the principle of copying is rational, for whatever underlying motive, this no longer holds.

*

We are beginning to get the pieces of the jigsaw assembled for a model of rational agent behaviour which is relevant to the world of the twenty-first century. Incentives still play a role, but the most important aspect is what we describe in shorthand as 'copying' the behaviour of other agents in a network. The mathematical features of networks and how they can impact behaviour were discussed in the previous chapter. In this chapter, we have fleshed out the concept. Psychological evidence suggests that copying is a very sensible mode of behaviour to adopt in the modern world. The amount of choice is enormous, the products and services available are often complex and difficult to evaluate, and giant leaps in communications technology mean that we are much more aware than ever before about what other people are doing, thinking and buying. The concept of Rational Economic Man has become largely irrelevant. Instead, we have Rational Copying Person.

This model of behaviour, which is able to explain a wide range of features in human social and economic systems, has quite different implications from those of the economic model of rationality. And these implications are often disturbing. Unequal outcomes – skewed distributions – appear to be an inherent feature whenever network effects are important. Network effects seriously weaken the connection between the qualities, the attributes, of any set of alternative choices and the relative frequency with which people make these choices. And network effects increase the uncertainty policy makers face when addressing any given problem.

But we have also seen some pointers which can help rather than hinder policy makers. When network effects are important, even small changes brought about by changes in incentives can be magnified dramatically. Networks can make policy more rather than less effective. Positive linking has the potential to transform the world for the better.

There is a rule of thumb which is a pretty good indicator of whether network effects are present in any particular situation. The structure of the network, its type, offers good guidelines to policy makers on how to encourage or prevent the spread of particular behaviours, the cascades, across networks of agents. And there may very well be reasonable early warning signs in any situation in which network effects are important on whether a policy change is likely to succeed or fail.

These are all points to which we return in the final chapter. But first there is one outstanding point to address, one issue to examine, in this twenty-first-century approach to rational agent behaviour. As we have seen, network effects give rise to unequal outcomes. A particularly disturbing feature of such a world is the self-reinforcing nature of the processes at work. This seems not only to ensure great inequalities of outcome, but outcomes in which the number one stays there for ever. And, by implication, those choices, whether of products, ideas, lifestyles, which are doing less well at any given time appear condemned to have no chance at all of ever succeeding in the future. Are there more subtle versions of the rational copying model, versions which both enhance its empirical realism and perhaps qualify some of its very stark implications? It is to this which we now turn.

8

All Good Things Must Come to an End

Network effects take us into territory where outcomes are distinctly unequal. Herb Simon's article on skewness, as we have seen, languished relatively unread for many years. But we now see it as a most prescient paper, decades ahead of its time, describing the basic mechanism which underlies the emergence of the unequal outcomes we observe in the real world of human social and economic systems in a wide range of disparate settings.

Rational behaviour in the twenty-first century is essentially based on this approach, on 'copying' the decisions of other agents. The word 'copying' is again put in quotation marks, to remind us that it is a shorthand description of a range of plausible and realistic motivations for such behaviour. This approach enables us to account for a wide range of real-world outcomes.

But, as discussed at the end of the previous chapter, the approach implies that we get locked into these unequal outcomes. Once the differences between choices, between alternatives, starts to widen there is no mechanism for reversing the trend. The rich get richer, more popular choices become even more popular, and those left behind appear to have no prospect of future success. They seem condemned to failure. Yet this does not seem to be what actually happens. Yes, we see inequalities in outcomes, which require us to invoke network effects rather than incentives in order to be able to understand them properly. But there does seem to be turnover in the outcomes over time. The most popular, the most successful, the biggest, does not stay there for ever.

Consider a major contemporary problem: unemployment. As I write these words in the summer of 2011, after the unemployment rate in America has experienced a small but nevertheless distinct fall from its peak level of 10.1 per cent in October 2009. But the rate is still high, and it is a big political issue. This figure measures the percentage of the people in the labour pool who are registered as unemployed. But the true proportion of those excluded from work is even higher. Almost all Western countries operate welfare systems in which out-of-work individuals are not classified as unemployed if they are in receipt of certain other benefits, such as disability benefit, irrespective of whether they are capable of work. Some may regard this state of affairs as merely a cynical attempt by governments of all persuasions to try to disguise the true total of unemployment, others may regard it as socially beneficial.

Regardless of what interpretation we place on this, and regardless of whether we focus on the registered unemployed or the wider population of adults of working age not in work and on some sort of benefit, we observe very wide disparities of outcomes at local levels. This is the case regardless of the overall state of the economy and the overall level of unemployment. In good years, the average number of those not in work is lower than in bad years, but we still see great inequalities in local outcomes.

A social housing scheme in the town where I was born attracted national notoriety in the UK in 2010, when it was discovered that a whopping 84 per cent of all adults of working age living on it were not in work and drawing some sort of benefit. Yet there were almost identical schemes in the town that had much lower rates. The rates were still high, both because there had just been a major recession and because a large proportion of the relevant populations were unskilled, but they were 20 or 30 per cent rather than 84. It should be said that the entrepreneurial spirit in the area is not entirely dead. A cafe on the scheme promoted on its outside board an 'All-day full English breakfast for £4.50 – with a can of Stella'. Even without the lager it wasn't bad value.

We see unequal outcomes in unemployment rates at local levels, but we also see turnover in the relative performance over time. The basic unit of local government in America is the county, of which there are just over 3,000 in total. Their sizes depend on local political factors and vary enormously, from the giant Los Angeles County to tiny rural ones with mere hundreds of people. On average, an American county is of similar population to the average local authority in the UK. But their size is not the immediate topic; rather it is the distribution of their unemployment rates. The rates tell us the number of unemployed, as a percentage, compared to the total workforce.

If we go back twenty years to 1990, the economy was pretty sluggish, heading into the mild recession of 1991. The average unemployment rate across the counties as a whole was 6.2 per cent.* But the lowest unemployment rate in an American county was just 0.5 per cent, in Grant County, Nebraska. In case this might just be a fluke because the county itself is tiny, there were no fewer than 205 counties where less than 2.5 per cent of the labour force was unemployed, the lowest rate ever recorded at the national level, way back in 1953. In contrast, the highest was an enormous 40.8 per cent, in Starr County, Texas. There were 265 counties with rates above 10 per cent, the peak reached in the most recent recession in 2009.

Flash forward now to 2010. The average rate of 9.4 per cent

---

* This is the average across the counties, regardless of their size, so it is not exactly the same as the unemployment rate across America as a whole.

across the counties was higher than in 1995 because of the impact of the financial crisis. But there was still a wide disparity of outcomes. The lowest, 1.6 per cent, was Slope County, North Dakota, where it seems like the recession never happened. In 115 counties the rate remained below 4 per cent, the forty-year national low observed at the height of the dot.com boom. The highest was 27.6 per cent, in Imperial County, California, and in 2010 the rate was above 15 per cent in no fewer than 128 counties.

There was certainly a fairly strong tendency of counties with relatively high or low unemployment rates in 1990 to also have high or low rates, compared to the average, in 2010. For those of a statistical bent, the simple rank correlation was 0.60. But, clearly, the rankings do not stay fixed. There is turnover. So, just looking at counties with substantial labour forces rather than the tiny rural ones where small changes in jobs can generate big changes in unemployment rates, examples more or less at random are Union County, New Jersey, with a workforce of over 250,000, which fell from rank 1,365 in 1990 to 1,775 in 2010 and Du Page, Illinois, with more than half a million workers, which moved from rank 664 to rank 1,238. Big counties which improved their relative positions include Plymouth County, Massachusetts, with over 200,000 workers, which rose from 2,200 to 1,560, and Bexar County, Texas, with more than half a million workers, which improved dramatically from rank 2,279 to 879. Even the oft-derided Baltimore City improved its relative position, moving from 2,436 to rank 2,262, still a bad rank to have but nevertheless moving in the right direction.

A clear example from the British labour market is provided by the local areas in the UK where coal mining used to be important. For many years regarded as the elite of the British industrial working class, the miners were treated with kid gloves by successive governments. Harold Macmillan, a Conservative Prime

Minister in the 1950s, once said that there were three bodies which no sensible politician would ever challenge: the Catholic Church, the Brigade of Guards and the National Union of Mineworkers.

All this changed in the early 1970s. The country had another Conservative Prime Minister, Edward Heath. The miners were becoming more and more militant, symbolised by the rapid rise of a charismatic hard-line left-wing union leader, Arthur Scargill. Unlike Macmillan, whose social roots were firmly in the upper class and the tradition of noblesse oblige, Heath had risen from the petit bourgeoisie, with its rather more Poujadist attitude towards the workers. He decided to teach the miners a lesson. The outcome was Heath's total humiliation. The miners physically overwhelmed a large force of police who were trying to keep open supplies to a major coal-fired power station. Industrial disputes escalated. Heath called a general election on the platform that it was the elected government which ran the country and not the NUM. This time, Macmillan was proved right. Heath was summarily ejected from office by the voters.

It is 1979, and Mrs Thatcher enters the scene, determined to crush the union once and for all. She waits patiently and chooses her moment carefully. Coal stocks are gradually built up during the next five years before a series of provocations are launched against the miners. They take the bait and go on strike. But this time, their enemy is far more determined and there is no hint even of compromise, let alone surrender. The strike is broken in the winter of 1984–5. A short while later a major programme of pit closures is introduced, and by the end of the decade there are hardly any mines, or miners, left.

In the year prior to the fatal strike, 1983, there were twenty-nine local authority areas in the UK, out of a total of 459, where coal mining accounted for more than 10 per cent of total employment. How did these areas react to these massive shocks on employment loss and what was the outcome? Twenty years seems a sufficient period for the various feedbacks to work their way through and out of the system. So we can compare total employment in each of these areas in 2002, twenty years on, to what it was in 1983.

Across the mining areas as a whole, the effects of the shock of the pit closures persisted. In Britain as whole, employment grew by 23 per cent, but by only 9 per cent in the former coal-producing regions. But the striking feature is the sheer diversity of experience in the seemingly devastated areas. In no fewer than ten out of the twenty-nine, employment in 2002 continued to be lower than twenty years previously. In three, Wansbeck and Easington in the north-east of England and Cumnock and Doon valley in the west of Scotland, the fall was nearly 20 per cent. Yet in others, employment grew faster than the national average, with one, South Staffordshire, posting a rise of no less than 45 per cent.

We have here what we might usefully think of as dynamic tension. Tension between the self-reinforcing factors which keep a local area trapped with high unemployment, and those which might help it escape and move up the rankings. Imagine an area where there is a substantial employer. We do not have to go so far as to imagine the classic 'company town', such as Consett in the north of England, once dominated by its steel works, or Winston-Salem in North Carolina, where much of R. J. Reynolds's output was located. It is enough to have a reasonably sized employer close down, for whatever reason.

There is clearly an immediate knock-on effect on other businesses located in the immediate area as the now-unemployed workers have less money to spend. But there are more subtle signals which can reinforce even more strongly the negative feedbacks on the area. The culture of not working may spread locally, and people on low wages may gradually manoeuvre themselves into a situation where they have lots of leisure. In other words, out of work with not much income, but plenty of free time. The more people there are in this situation, the more acceptable it becomes to their immediate peers on their social networks. Social values evolve, so that being out of work may even become the new social norm. Some of the more dynamic individuals may move out and seek prosperity elsewhere. Indeed, entire firms may relocate. And once an area gets a reputation for high unemployment and lack of initiative, its image spreads across networks of companies, and it becomes less attractive for them to either expand within or move into the area.

The network approaches we have seen in previous chapters help to explain this process of self-reinforcing lock-in. They are abstract models, designed to give a general insight into these processes, and lack the richness of detail of any specific example. But both Brian Arthur's model and Herb Simon's preferential attachment describe how network effects help us understand the deep reasons why some local areas remain relatively poor over long periods of time. Through the spread of both perceptions and behaviour on the relevant networks, feedbacks are set in train which make it difficult for the area, once set onto the path of high unemployment, to escape.

Yet it is not at all inevitable that areas of relative poverty remain in this position for ever. There is turnover in the rankings. Yes, there is a strong tendency for the relative rankings of performance, on whatever context, to become fixed. But, somehow, they are not fixed. There is persistent turnover.

We see exactly the same phenomenon across almost all the wide range of examples we have encountered so far. The most popular video on YouTube today is rarely the most popular tomorrow. The song which is at number 1 this week does not usually stay very long in this position. Over the entire period from 1952 to

2006, no fewer than 29,056 songs appeared in the Top 100 chart in the UK. Of these, 5,141 were in the chart for just a single week. Almost exactly a half stayed in for less than a month, so four weeks was the typical life span, as it were, of a song in the Top 100. In contrast, fifty-nine remained popular for more than six months, and one, 'My Way' by Frank Sinatra, spent an incredible 122 weeks in the chart.* The typical life span at number 1 was just two weeks, the longest unbroken reign being sixteen weeks ('(Everything I Do) I Do It For You', by Bryan Adams in 1991). In popular cultural markets such as these, turnover is rapid.

At the other extreme is the ranking of the world's largest cities. Mike Batty, a distinguished spatial geographer at University College London, published an analysis of this in *Nature* in 2005. He begins his work with the largest US cities from 1790 to 2000. At any point in time, a snapshot of the relative sizes of these urban areas reveals a considerable degree of stability. The absolute sizes of the populations grew enormously over time as the US itself expanded, but the skewed nature of the plot stayed remarkably similar.

Such apparent stability disguises substantial turnover. Over the 210-year period, 266 cities were at some stage in the top hundred. From 1840, when the number of cities first reached one hundred, only twenty-one remain in the top hundred of 2000. On average, it takes 105 years for 50 per cent of cities to appear or disappear from the top hundred, whilst the average change in rank order for a typical city in each ten-year period is seven ranks. This latter point means that if a city is, say, number 50 in size now, on average in ten years' time it will either be number 43, seven places higher, or number 57. It may of course be neither; this is the typical experience.

In terms of world cities, using the data from 430 BC mentioned

---

* I absolutely prefer the Sid Vicious version, it has more zest.

a couple of chapters ago, the turnover in the top fifty is slow-er, but it is still there. Naturally, the period since the Industrial Revolution, almost a blink of an eye in the overall context, is a period of rapid transition, but other periods saw distinct changes. The pace of change has itself been variable, but it has always been there. Who would guess the longest period a city has spent in the world's top fifty or, even harder, the name of the city itself? Suzhou in China records 2,158 years in the biggest fifty cities of the world, closely followed by Nanking with 2,080 years. No city in the top fifty in 430 BC survives in the list in 2000, but of the fifty biggest at the time of the Fall of Constantinople in 1453, a major event in world history, six are still there.

Team sports is another area where unequal outcomes combined with persistent turnover is observed. In American football, the champions of the two major conferences, the NFL and the AFL, play each other for the Super Bowl. These are the elite teams of all those who play the sport. In the forty-five seasons of its existence, the Super Bowl has been won by no fewer than eighteen teams. But just four of them – Pittsburgh Steelers, Dallas Cowboys, San Francisco 49ers and Green Bay Packers – account for twenty of the victories, so there are unequal outcomes. And even though a team like the Steelers in the mid-seventies or the Cowboys in the early nineties may appear near-invincible, eventually they drop down the rankings.

American football at its highest levels has rules designed to try to promote turnover in success. The weaker teams in any particular season get priority in signing the star college play-ers who want to turn professional. There is a strict salary cap per team, based on the revenues of the league as a whole rather than on those of the individual teams. This further restricts the ability of the most successful sides to consolidate their success by paying their players more money than is available at the less successful outfits. Even so, there is rather marked inequality of outcome in terms of the teams which have won the Super Bowl.

Salary caps, which help promote turnover in success, are prevalent in the major American professional sports leagues. The National Basketball Association, the National Hockey League, and even Major League Soccer all have them. Baseball has its own variant, the so-called 'luxury tax'.

Somewhat paradoxically, Europe, often viewed as a hotbed of socialism from across the Atlantic, places virtually no restrictions on the ability of successful soccer teams to reinforce their success by spending more on players.* The European Champions League Final of 2011 was played between Barcelona and Manchester United, not only two of the most famous clubs in world soccer but two of the wealthiest. A pan-European club competition was first contested in 1956. There are several thousand professional soccer clubs across Europe, any of whom could in theory be crowned champions of Europe. Yet in fifty-six seasons, only twenty-one teams have ever held that title, less than 1 per cent of the total number of professional teams on the continent. And by now you will not be at all surprised to learn that there is a heavy concentration even within that small group of victors, with just six clubs winning a total of thirty-three times between them, the other twenty-three championships being distributed amongst fifteen other teams.

For long periods, teams appear unbeatable. The European competition was won by Real Madrid in each of the first five seasons, but eventually they were dethroned. The current Barcelona side are being eulogised as the greatest ever, but they, too, will eventually lose their number-one spot.**

* Restrictions have been discussed on and off for years, and it appears that some may soon be introduced. But these relate to the financial viability of clubs rather than the absolute amounts they spend. So teams with a lot of money who are viable can continue to spend.
** Indeed, at the final proof stage of the book, they were in fact knocked out of the 2012 competition in the semi-finals.

*

Soccer, and in particular what has today evolved into the European Champions League, can illustrate some important themes in the 'copying' process, the process in which success breeds further success. Although the particular points are specific to soccer, the principles involved have far more general applicability. Most situations in the human social and economic worlds will have their own nuances, their own details, which are required for a more complete explanation of the outcome. But the basic driving force is the principle of copying, the principle of preferential attachment.

We could illustrate these ideas instead with the far more momentous question of why the continent of Europe, and more specifically a small number of countries in Western Europe, came to dominate the globe in a way wholly without precedent in human history. With the benefit of hindsight, we can advance several plausible, powerful reasons why this happened. But in, say, the middle of the fourteenth century, how could this have possibly have been foreseen? Ravaged by the Black Death, suffering military defeats at the hands of the Muslim Ottoman Empire, technologically inferior to China, who could have said with any confidence that this relatively small land area would achieve world domination? But this is a massive topic in its own right. The soccer story we are about to read is much more containable, much easier to comprehend, but the principles it illustrates are very general.

Yes, success is self-reinforcing. But it is often very hard to predict in advance, and so by implication it is very hard to predict exactly when a very successful agent, be it a team, company, idea, individual city, website or whatever, will cease to be successful. The example I have chosen to use is the soccer team of the town where I was born, Rochdale. Why have they never been champions of Europe? In fact, their record as a professional team has been the complete antithesis of such success, having spent all but eight seasons of their entire existence in the lowest division of the English professional game and never having won even the humblest domestic trophy, let alone the most prestigious one in Europe.

It is easy to point now and explain why. Their total annual income, for example, is not much more than £2 million, a sum which would scarcely pay the wages of a single player even in one of the more run-of-the-mill teams in the highest division, the Premier League. So they cannot attract very good players. This may seem not only trivially obvious, but of no interest to anyone without personal links to the town. It is the dramatic contrast with a nearby rival which is of interest. For barely a dozen miles away from the comparatively humble, windswept Spotland stadium where Rochdale play sits the 'Theatre of Dreams': Old Trafford, the home of Manchester United, the most successful side in the history of the English game with a turnover well over a hundred times that of Rochdale, and possessing worldwide brand recognition.

It's easy to see now why they have finished in the top three for each of the past twenty seasons, on sixteen occasions in the top two, but both teams had equally humble origins. Manchester United started life as essentially the works team of the Lancashire and Yorkshire Railway company, based in – and called – Newton Heath, then as now a poor district in the eastern part of the city. Rochdale AFC was formed somewhat later but this team, too, began life in a heavily industrial town which was also part of the Manchester urban conurbation. And just five years prior to the emergence of Rochdale, Newton Heath had been served with a winding-up order. A consortium of local businessmen paid what in today's money is around £750,000 to rescue the club, and changed its name to Manchester United. Despite some fleeting success, the club languished, spending a good number of years in the division only just above Rochdale. In 1931 they were effectively bankrupt again and were rescued even more cheaply than before: for some £400,000 in today's money. Yet in 2011, the value of Manchester United is of the order of £1 billion!

So, in 1931, the clubs were not dissimilar. Both were based in undiluted working-class areas in the north of England, in fact in the same conurbation. One was placed a division above the other, but it was about to fold in bankruptcy. United's great rivals, Manchester City, appeared more likely to be destined for success, and indeed they won both the League and the Cup in the 1930s. Only two random events – twice being able to secure the help of local businessmen to rescue the team financially – had prevented the disappearance of Manchester United, perhaps for ever. It was not predestined that this should happen. The club did not have special qualities which led these individuals to make their investments in those desperate days during the Great Depression, but they did.

Having said this, particular factors do seem to have played a role in United's subsequent success. Just before the end of the Second World War, the club offered the position of manager to Matt Busby, a man who built not one, not two, but three extremely successful teams during the course of his career. His third squad became the first English side to win the European Champions Club trophy. But many soccer judges regard his greatest team to be the very young one which was effectively destroyed in an air crash in Munich in 1958, returning from a successful game which had progressed them to the next stage of the competition.

Once a team starts to be successful in this way, factors come into play which reinforce, though do not guarantee, its further success. It attracts more fans, more sponsors, in short more money, so it can buy better players, give them better treatment, better physiotherapy, and so on. But Busby's appointment itself was to a considerable degree one of chance. Thirty miles to the west of Manchester lies its great rival, the city of Liverpool. The antipathy between Manchester United and Liverpool FC, the second most successful English team ever, is intense. No player has been transferred directly between the two since 1964. Yet Busby almost joined Liverpool, who had been courting him for some time. The clincher appears to have been that Busby was friendly with a member of the United board through their membership of the Manchester Catholic Sportsman's Club.

Rochdale, too, following the mass migration from Ireland in the nineteenth century, has a large Catholic population. Suppose that in 1944 one of them had, in the local jargon, 'made a bit of money' and had known Sir Matt through Catholic social circles . . . Ah well, Rochdalians, whether at home or in exile, can only dream of what might have been.

The points in this story are far more general than the actual examples of the two teams. It is easy now to say why United are so successful and Rochdale less so. But, from the perspective of 1931, who could ever have predicted the stupendous success which one of these clubs would eventually enjoy? At the time, it had only just been prevented from disappearing from the face of the earth.

*

The rational model of 'copying' which we have illuminates the process by which success emerges and evolves. But it does not yet encompass why things eventually fail, or at least cease to be as successful as they previously were. Mike Batty reflects on this point from the elevated pages of *Nature* when discussing his results on the turnover in city sizes over the whole of human history. He draws an important conclusion from his analysis, couched in cryptic scientific jargon: 'The conventional model . . . cannot replicate these micro-dynamics, suggesting that such models and explanations are considerably less general than has hitherto been assumed.' What does this mean? Batty's 'conventional model' is not the conventional economic model of rational choice, but the preferential attachment model of Herb Simon, the model of twenty-first-century rational behaviour we have described. His 'micro-dynamics' refer to the persistent turnover in the rankings of cities by size. Far from converging on a stable outcome, in which the biggest just keeps getting bigger and bigger and, importantly, stays the biggest, in practice this is not true. Yes, we see a non-Gaussian outcome in terms of the size distribution at any point in time. But when we delve into the details, the micro-dynamics, we observe lots and lots of changes in an overall outcome which appears stable.

And wherever we see such non-Gaussian outcomes, we know that networks matter. We know that the potential for positive linking exists. We know that agents are taking decisions which are based, at least in part, directly on what they see or know about what other agents are doing, thinking, deciding. So unless we grasp this fundamental point, and unless we try and get some idea of what type of network it is and how it is influencing events, we will simply not have a proper appreciation of what is going on. Even a crude network-based approach is likely to give us more insight than a highly sophisticated one from which network effects are absent.

The Polya urn-based model of Brian Arthur, the preferential attachment of Herb Simon and the binary choice with externalities of Nobel Laureate Thomas Schelling and Duncan Watts – each of these models is highly illuminating when applied in the right situations. They are all based on the principle of copying rather than conscious, rational selection in the economic sense. And, as we have seen, copying is the rational way to behave in the twenty-first century. However, the outcomes of the dynamic processes at work in these models are, paradoxically, eventually static. Yes, they lead to distributions of outcomes which look like those of the real world at any point in time, but they cannot explain why there is persistent turnover *within* these outcomes over time.

Attempts have been made to modify these approaches, especially the one of preferential attachment which was rediscovered in the late 1990s by the leading physicist Albert-László Barabási, to try to take account of the universal phenomenon of turnover in rankings. So, suppose we assume that the probability of the next person choosing a particular location, brand, idea, etc., declines with the age of the object being chosen, whatever it might be. This is sufficient to introduce turnover in relative popularity of choices over time. In some contexts, this may seem reasonable, but it is a rather ad hoc extension of the basic model. Besides, ideas do not become extinct because they are old. They become extinct because no one uses them any more. Christianity is two millennia old, but it continues to flourish everywhere outside of Western Europe. Confucianism and Taoism are even older. And in many cases, the opposite is true. Some of the most frequently used words in the English lexicon are also some of the oldest.

How can we expand the behavioural model based on copying rather than rational selection to explain not only the ubiquitous right-skewed outcomes we observe, but also the persistent turnover within the rankings? We will certainly not find inspiration within economics. As Vernon Smith, economics Nobel Laureate in 2002, said in his Prize lecture: 'I urge students to read narrowly within economics, but widely in science. Within economics there is essentially only one model to be adapted to every application: optimisation subject to constraints . . . The economic literature is not the best place to find new inspiration beyond these traditional technical methods of modelling.'

I am not arguing that such a model, if it exists, would offer a complete explanation of human social and economic systems. Far from it. Not least because in many situations, as we have seen, conventional incentives play a role along with what we describe in shorthand as the copying motive. Rather, it is to establish the basis for a fundamental model of rational agent behaviour which is relevant to the twenty-first century. The traditional rational agent model of economics, with its assumptions of full information and always making the best possible choice, has partly been made more relevant by introducing limited information. In the same way, we need a behavioural model which is the new benchmark, the new basic tool we use to see how far any particular situation can be explained by it. If necessary, its assumptions can be relaxed, other factors such as incentives added to it, but it would be our first port of call in any situation which bears the hallmarks of network effects being present.

Smith enjoins us to seek inspiration not within economics itself, but from the much wider body of science. A fertile field from which to draw ideas is the work of the ecologist Stephen Hubbell, based at the University of California at Los Angeles and recipient of many honours. The biodiversity of natural systems, the focus of Hubbell's work, may seem remote from the study of social and economic issues. But there is a very good reason for asking what this can tell us. The biodiversity of natural systems has several key empirical features which should by now be familiar from the numerous examples given from a wide variety of social and economic contexts. First, a small number of species account for a substantial fraction of the total number of individuals, whatever they might be, in the system as a whole. Second, most species are represented by very few individuals. In other words, we observe the sort of skewed, non-Gaussian outcomes in biological systems that we see in profusion in the human social and economic worlds. In any given context, a few species account for most of the individuals, and most species are represented by only a few.

We can add the third key feature of such biological systems, that the rankings of the frequencies with which different species are observed changes over time. The pace of change is often very slow, because the environment in which biological evolution takes place alters much more slowly than does the social and economic environment in which humans operate. But the same principle is observed, namely that the dominant species at any point in time does not remain so for ever.

These are precisely the phenomena which we observe in the wide variety of human social and economic systems we have already seen.

*

In its modern guise, economic theory is not just remote from evolutionary, biological systems, but operates as if it were on a different planet altogether. But this was not always the case. Alfred Marshall held the principal Chair in Economics in Cambridge in the decades around 1900. As a student, he was a formidable mathematician, being placed second overall in the entire university in the final-year examinations. At his peak, Marshall dominated the discipline of economics, not just within imperial Britain, but across the world. His *Principles of Economics* became and remained the major textbook for students for much of the first half of the twentieth century.

Marshall played a central role in formalising the basic models of supply and demand within economics. But he was far from being an ivory-tower theorist. Marshall was an acute observer of contemporary economic and business life. His *Principles* are littered with insights, some elaborated at length, others merely mentioned in passing, which remain interesting and thought provoking even today. He held a persistent belief that 'the Mecca of the economist lies in economic biology'. In other words, that the economy is essentially based on evolutionary principles, rather than in the much more mechanistic concepts of standard theory, concepts which have remained in place to this day. The tools for formalising evolutionary models did not really exist in Marshall's day, nor would they for some considerable time. But he left little doubt that this is where he saw the eventual future of economics, a vision which was eliminated from mainstream thinking by the middle of the twentieth century. So, in seeking inspiration from evolution and biology, we are in distinguished company.

Hubbell developed the so-called 'neutral theory' to explain these phenomena. The theory is not without controversy but it is very influential in its field. All scientific disciplines have their own jargon, and the word 'neutral' will be decoded shortly. But, first, how does the theory work?

The basic principle on which the theory is built will by now be familiar. Imagine one of Brian Arthur's urns, but this time filled with lots of different coloured balls, where each ball is a species. The process is not quite the same as Arthur's model, not just because there are many rather than just two colours. Take one out at random, and put it back in, exactly as in the Arthur urn. But we do not add another individual of the same colour. Instead, we change an existing individual at random to be the same colour. If a species is drawn, its number increases and that of another species falls,* which makes it

---

* Unless, of course, the individual drawn at random to be changed is already the same species.

slightly more likely to be drawn again the next period.

There is an even more dramatic twist, which gives the model the ability to generate turnover. The preferential attachment rule is the fundamental one by which the system evolves. But it does not apply every single time a draw is made. Each time, there is a small probability that a different rule will be used. Namely, the individual which is drawn at random is replaced by one of an entirely new species. Essentially, both the distribution of the numbers of individuals in each species *and* how the relative frequencies change over time are described by this, the neutral theory. To repeat, because it is important, the description of the process: there is a fixed (large) number of balls of a wide variety of colours. One is drawn at random. With a given (small) probability, it is put back in, not in its existing colour, but in a colour which is not represented at all in the balls in the urn, a new colour entirely. The rest of the time, it is put back in and another ball in the urn is changed at random to have the same colour. (Alternatively but equivalently, we can think of both the ball itself and another one of the same colour being put back in, and at the same time another ball being taken out for ever.)

So, what does the word 'neutral' in Hubbell's theory mean? First consider two other words: 'rare' and 'abundant'. A plausible hypothesis is that rare species are rare because, for whatever reason, they have not adapted well to their environment. Similarly, abundant species must have particular attributes which enable them to flourish. But the word 'neutral' in this context means that *no* species has any special qualities or characteristics which make it more or less suitable to operate in its given environment. Their relative success or failure is 'neutral' to their attributes. In other words, how a species behaves, what it can and cannot do, is irrelevant to whether or not at any point in time its numbers are small or large. The outcomes which we observe are the result of purely random processes. First, the random draw of any given individual. Second, the random draw as to whether to replace another agent with one of the same kind to the one which is drawn, or whether to replace it with an entirely new species.

Of course, and this should be by now another familiar mantra, all scientific theories are approximations to reality. The neutral theory is not claimed to be accurate all the time, to explain everything. Nor is it claimed that its assumptions are necessarily completely true. But its assumptions are often sufficiently good explanations as to justify its status as a genuine scientific theory. It helps us understand the world. In any specific situation, we can always add bits of information to calibrate the model more closely to the key features we are trying to understand. But the core model, without any tweaks or add-ons, applies across a very wide range of situations.

Despite the simplicity, indeed frugality, of its assumptions, this model of twenty-first-century rational behaviour does give a good explanation of a very wide range of the social and economic outcomes we observe in the real world, from the size of the world's largest cities to downloads of popular culture such as videos on YouTube, to give two examples which both exhibit non-Gaussian distributions at any point in time, but which exhibit persistent turnover of rankings, albeit on completely different time scales.

The idea that the qualities of a species are irrelevant to its success or failure appears to strike against common sense. We might note, however, that common sense is not always a good guide to how the world actually is. It seems common sense that the earth stands still – we don't feel it moving – and the sun moves across the sky round the earth. But we know that both these common-sense perceptions are profoundly wrong.

After the process has unfolded, exactly as with the rational choice theory of economics, when we observe abundant and rare species, it is possible to tell stories about why there are lots of one and hardly any of the other. So we can describe why Manchester United is now the most famous soccer club in the world, and why Rochdale remains virtually unknown. We can give an account of why unemployment is high in one area and low in another, of why one city is successful and grows to a large size, whilst another does not. It gets much harder in many other of the examples we have seen, such as the ironing videos on YouTube. One man climbs Ben Nevis and irons. The other irons on a temporarily closed section of a motorway. One attracts more than 4,000 times as many downloads as the other, and this intrepid ironer becomes, albeit briefly, known around the world. Both at a very similar time were introduced into the YouTube ecosystem as innovations, as new species. One was much more successful than the other, for reasons which it is hard to account for in terms of rational selection.

*

Even in the much more serious context of religious faith, as we saw in the opening chapter, the eventual triumph of Protestantism over Catholicism in England in the mid-sixteenth century owed a great deal to mere chance and contingency. Queen Mary gambled that a policy of terror, of burning those who ultimately refused to reconvert to Catholicism, would succeed. The experience of the fifteenth-century Lollard heresy in England suggested it would work, and it almost did. The hard-line Protestant leaders gambled that by behaving with stoicism in the face of a terrible death, the population would be inspired by their examples, their faith would reap the benefits of positive linking. But, as we have seen, there was a strong element of chance and contingency, of randomness, in the eventual outcome. The outcomes of processes which involve copying across networks are intrinsically difficult to predict.

It is hard to argue that the Protestant success was due to the inherently superior qualities of the faith compared with Catholicism. Indeed, there were other areas of Europe in the second half of the sixteenth century where the Counter Reformation did prove to be successful, and allegiance to the Pope restored. It can, in fact, be argued plausibly that the qualities of the version of Protestantism which prevailed in England at the end of the 1550s were *less* attractive than the alternatives on offer. For this particular brand succeeded not just in undermining Catholicism, but in driving out of existence other varieties of Protestantism which were on offer at the same time. Following Luther's first defiant stand in 1517, a dazzling array of different strands of Protestantism burst out across Europe over the next few decades. Some were truly exotic, such as the Anabaptist sect under John of Leiden which established a polygamous theocracy in the German city of Munster for eighteen months in 1534–5. Communal living was a key element of the teaching, as was the use of the death penalty for almost every conceivable offence, John himself personally beheading at least one of his sixteen wives.

Most such variants sprung up, only to wither and disappear just as rapidly. But a genuine rival in England to the views of the established Protestant Church were the so-called Freewillers. The religion of the English martyrs, Cranmer, Ridley, Latimer and the rest was both sparse and terrifying. The first Prayer Book published under the young King Edward VI in 1549, for example, still contains a considerable liturgy in the funeral service, the Order for the Burial of the Dead. But by the 1552 edition, this has largely disappeared and the content is perfunctory in the extreme. Very few words of comfort are offered to the grieving relatives and friends of the deceased. This is because the then leaders of the Church of England believed firmly in the doctrine of predestination. God decided at the beginning of the world who would be saved and who was to be damned for all eternity. We might even regard this as an early articulation of the neutral theory of biodiversity! The behaviour, the qualities, exhibited by an individual in his or her lifetime are of no consequence in terms of the soul's salvation. All that matters is whether God allocated you at the beginning of time into the company of the elect. Naturally, this was a very disturbing doctrine to its followers, causing much anxiety in trying to work out into which category they had been allocated.

The Freewillers rejected the authority of the Pope and denied the corporeal presence at the Communion service. The bread and wine were, quite literally, just that; Christ's body and blood were not present. In short, they were good Protestants. But they also believed that what individuals did during their lives affected what would happen to them after death. They believed in free will, in the capacity of individuals to decide how to act. We have to be careful in assigning to people living in the sixteenth century the views of the early twenty-first century, when free will is much more closely aligned with our individualistic view of the world. But there is ample contemporary evidence which shows the anguish created by the doctrine of predestination compared with Protestant alternatives.

The Freewillers were of sufficient concern to the established Protestant leaders that, even in their prison cells under Mary, they wrote to each other about the threat posed by what a Leninist in the modern era would call an ideological deviation. John Bradford, shortly before his execution, wrote that 'more hurt will come by them, than ever came by the papists, inasmuch as their life commendeth them to the world more than papists'. In other words, the predestinarians knew that their doctrine was not attractive and that free will 'commendeth' itself much more to ordinary people.

But despite its apparently more attractive qualities, Freewill Protestantism was not the brand which was selected. The inspiration of the martyrs led to conversions not just from Catholicism but from this Protestant rival. Network effects, positive linking, offset and dominated the attributes of the two offers, and by 1560 the Freewill variant had essentially been driven into extinction.

*

So, we have a model of behaviour which assumes that people make decisions in the following way. They look at the choices which others have made and copy them, in proportion to the relative popularities of the various choices. This is the basic principle. But, in addition, they may also, with a small probability, make a choice at random. In particular, they may make an entirely new choice which no one has selected before.

To conventional thinking, it seems strange. Strange, because it makes no reference to the qualities of the choices which are available. Decisions are made without conscious consideration of the attributes of the alternatives. Instead, a deliberate decision is made to use copying. Agents are not acting in some moronic fashion, dumbly imitating the actions of choices of others. They appreciate that in complex situations, copying is the rational way to behave. It is the complete antithesis of the building block of orthodox economics, the so-called rational agent model.

But it works empirically. Most outcomes of most social and economic processes in the twenty-first century are unequal, a few alternatives are chosen many times, most are chosen infrequently. And within these outcomes, over time, relative popularities are not constant but evolve. This basic model of human behaviour is able to offer a good account of what actually happens in the real world today.

One area where this behaviour seems very applicable is in the choice of baby names. This topic may seem rather trivial, but it is a very important aspect of the culture of a society. For linguist Steven Pinker, the choice of a name 'connects us to society in a way that encapsulates the great contradiction in human social life: between the desire to fit in and the desire to be unique'. First names reveal much about a culture, including kinship patterns, popular culture trends and social values. They are found throughout time and space and are easily measured and counted. Indeed, the choices of first names reflect three principles of collective behaviour that apply to popular culture much more generally. They involve a number of people carrying out the same or similar actions at a point in time. The behaviour exhibited is transient or continually changing. And there is some kind of dependency amongst the actions; individuals are not acting independently.

The United States Social Administration provides a database on baby names that has been extensively studied in a variety of ways because of its exceptionally deep and chronologically resolved records. The data includes the top hundred baby names by US state since 1960, and, for the US as a whole, all names with at least five occurrences in each year since 1879. There have been some fascinating developments. In 1960 the most popular name for girls was Mary in most US states, except for Susan in the north-west and north-east, and some variety in the western states. This homogeneity in 1960 is also reflected in boys' names, when the five that were locally most popular (David, James, Michael, John, Robert) comprised the top five for most states, and none was lower than eighth place in any state. By 2009, this had all changed. No fewer than thirteen names were the most popular in at least one state, only one of which (Michael) had been number one anywhere in 1960. A boy's name such as Logan – the most popular name in Minnesota, Idaho and New Hampshire – was not amongst the top thirty in New Jersey or California. The same turnover and rise in heterogeneity is observed in girls' names as well. None of the 1960 names survived as 'winners' by 2009, when some of the names most popular in at least one state were not even in the top hundred in 1960, such as Madison in South Carolina and Ava in Iowa.

Anthropologists such as Alex Bentley at Bristol University in the UK and Stephen Shennan at University College London have shown that the basic 'neutral' evolutionary model of choice gives a very plausible account of how the relative popularity of baby names evolves over time. For good measure, the same article also uses it to explain archaeological pottery and applications for technology patents. With the same two authors, I have also shown, in the same journal, how the same model can explain three fundamental features of the evolution of languages. One mark of a good scientific theory is that it should be able to explain a wide variety of phenomena. Well, baby names, ancient pottery, modern technology patents and linguistic laws seem to get this one into the starting blocks!

But there are simple ways of making the approach even more powerful. In this evolutionary theory of choice and behaviour, agents look at the relative popularities of the choices already made by other agents. There is a dog here which has not barked. How far back do people look when they are making decisions? A teenager wondering what music track or YouTube video to download is not usually interested in what was popular ten years ago. Indeed, not even ten months and quite possibly not even ten days. What matters is what is trending right here and now. In contrast, a firm considering locations in which to start or develop its business often needs to take into account choices made over many years. Typically, this is the time scale on which the distinguishing characteristics of a city emerge and evolve.

The technical details need not concern us, but two quite different versions of 'memory', of how far back into the past previous decisions matter, have been developed. One assumes that only the immediately preceding period is relevant. This might be likened to genetics, in which either an existing gene is copied or a mutation happens. The system does not look back beyond the range of genes on offer right now to be copied. The other variant postulates, in complete contrast, that all previous time steps, all previous periods, are relevant. So if a variant, in whatever context we are operating, was selected even just once in the dim and distant past, it forms part of the choice set available in the present. The chances of it being chosen again are very small, but in principle this remains a possibility.

More realistically, we can allow the time scale over which previous choices have been made to vary according to the particular context. For the YouTube teenager, a short trip into the past is enough, maybe even just today's choices, and for the firm looking to expand, a much longer period. But we could select the time frame and make it relevant to any given situation rather than being required to say 'only the absolutely immediate past' or 'all previous periods' are relevant.

With anthropologist Alex Bentley and spatial geographer Mike Batty I explored the consequences of what happens when we take this realistic step.* It makes the copying approach, the model of twenty-first-century rational behaviour, even more powerful. *Any* of the skewed outcomes we observe in human social and economic systems can be captured by suitable tweaks of the two controls of the model: how often people innovate and whether they make choices other than by the principle of preferential attachment. And, when using the latter principle in order to choose, how far back do they look?

* The technical details are in *Behavioural Ecology and Sociobiology*, vol. 65 (2011).

The outcomes of many human social and economic systems reveal the characteristic footprint which networks invariably leave. Whenever these effects are present, whenever people make decisions, adopt behaviours, take up ideas, at least in part, by copying what others have, we know that there is a network lurking. 'Copying' is of course a shorthand description of a whole range of plausible motivations. The twenty-first-century model of behaviour explains many very diverse outcomes in the human social and economic worlds. And in our complex modern world, it is in general the rational way to behave.

We know that the effects of policies designed to influence and control such systems become much more uncertain, much more difficult to predict in advance, than in a world where most of the time people operate independently, making choices on the nineteenth-century principle of economically rational choice. In a world where there is a cornucopia of choice, of products, of lifestyles, of ideas, where many of these are complex and hard to evaluate, and where we are all increasingly aware of what other people are doing – in such a world, rational behaviour involves a strong element of copying. The outcomes and consequences of this twenty-first-century rationality are quite different.

We are at least in a better position than Aeneas in the opening book of Virgil's *Aeneid*. There, the Trojan hero encounters his own mother, Venus, disguised as a Carthaginian huntress. 'O quam te memoram, virgo?' he cries, quite unable to recognise her. 'By what name shall I call thee?' In contrast, we know the tell-tale marks of any system in which network effects operate; we know them for what they are. But does this make us any better able to control the outcomes than Aeneas himself could, to take advantage of the potential benefits of positive linking?

9

What Can Be Done

The conduct of business and policy decisions of all kinds must take account of the fact that the fundamental features of our social and economic worlds have been qualitatively transformed over the course of the past century. The word 'must' is used here with its full imperative force. Network effects are the driving force of behaviour.

The transformation has been particularly rapid during the second half of the twentieth century and in the opening decade of our current one. There is now a stupendous proliferation of goods and services available to consumers with, as we have seen, over 10 *billion* varieties on offer in New York City alone. Many of these are complex and sophisticated, difficult to evaluate even when plentiful information about them is provided. Choice is available on a hitherto undreamt-of scale, and selection amongst the choices is a challenging task.

Fashion and fads are phenomena in which something becomes even more popular simply because it has already become popular. Such patterns have existed since time immemorial. We have seen evidence of ceramic bowls being the subject of fashion in the Hittite empire, three and a half millennia ago. Success breeds success. Agents copy the choices made by other people.

The second half of the twentieth century saw a huge rise in globalisation, with the world becoming more and more open. Thirty years ago both the entire Soviet bloc of countries and

China were more or less closed to Westerners. Today, whilst Russia itself remains relatively isolated, many of its former satellites are fully integrated into the European Union, and the huge population of China is increasingly connected with the rest of the world. The same period experienced a dramatic rise in urban living. It is estimated that in 1800 a mere 3 per cent or so of the world's population lived in cities. By 1950 this had risen to around 30 per cent. It is now believed that more than half of all humanity lives in cities. In urban environments, we are far more exposed to a wide range of opinions, behaviours and choices than we are when confined to life in the village, the lot of most of humanity for most of our existence.

Developments in communications technology, based around the internet, reinforce this tendency very strongly. The internet is revolutionising communications in an equivalent way to the impact of the printing press over 500 years ago.

All scientific theories are approximations to reality. The usefulness of a theory depends upon how well its assumptions, the simplifications which any theory has to make, approximate what happens in the real world. The above description of the world of the twenty-first century is the background against which we have assessed the validity of the model of how a 'rational' agent behaves. According to this theory, agents gather available information about an issue, process it to arrive at the best possible decision given their fixed tastes and preferences, and do so in isolation from other agents. In other words, their preferences are not affected in any way by what other agents do. Neither do they change in any way over time.

Clearly, this is not how the world works. (Readers of a certain age might reflect on their youth to compare their tastes and behaviour with those they exhibit today.) To be fair, the theory may – may – have been a reasonable approximation to reality in the late nineteenth century, when it was first being formalised. But in general it does not fit with the world in which we live now. There are many reasons for this, but the principal one is the fact that our individual tastes and preferences are not at all fixed and independent of the preferences of others. They evolve over time. And a key factor in their evolution is that we often copy the opinions, actions and choices of others.

The word 'copy', as has been stressed, is a shorthand way of describing a range of motivations for an agent changing behaviour as a direct result of the influence of other agents. The fashion motive is one. Peer pressure is another, as is the related but subtly different concept of peer acceptance. For example the more people who are obese in your social circles, your networks, the more acceptable it is for you to be obese also. People do not decide to copy others deliberately and become obese themselves, but the social pressures and influences on them not to become obese are relaxed when other people in their networks are already obese.

Even in the 1930s, as we have seen, Keynes believed that the world was sufficiently complex, sufficiently difficult to interpret, that 'we have, as a rule, only the vaguest idea of any but the most direct consequences of our acts'. Keynes argued that the very concept of rationality needed to be redefined in such a world. Copying other agents often makes sense because they might be – it does not mean that they necessarily are – better informed than we are as individuals. In the 1950s, Simon again raised the need to reassess the definition of what constitutes rational behaviour: '[T]he task is to replace the global rationality of economic man with a kind of rational behaviour which is compatible with the access to information and computational capacities that are actually possessed by organisms, including man, in the kinds of environments in which such organisms exist.' In the complex situations which characterise much of our lives, copying is a powerful way of solving this problem, of scaling down the vast dimension of choice and its subsequent consequences into a manageable rule of behaviour. We might copy different agents for different reasons on different networks, but we copy nevertheless.

We have seen in Chapter 6 that when network effects matter, the outcomes we observe have a marked degree of inequality. Positive linking can generate success on a spectacular scale. The most popular downloads on YouTube or Flickr are often literally millions of times more popular than the huge number of videos or photos which receive hardly any hits. A few large cities are very much larger than the much greater number of modestly sized ones. At any point in time, the outcomes are unequal. But we also see persistent turnover in the rankings, so that the most popular, the biggest, do not stay in that position for ever. The time scales on which turnover takes place differ considerably between popular culture and, say, the evolution of the sizes of cities. Yet turnover is always present.

At this point, we might usefully pause for reflection: this is all very well, but look how much better off we are now than in, say, 1950. Since then we have had a great deal of state activity, of public policy interventions in both social and economic problems. And these interventions have been based on the model of economically rational agents, on the assumption that agents respond solely to incentives. Network effects and copying are entirely absent from this model. Surely we have done rather well using rational theory, especially when boosted by the addition of the late-twentieth-century insights into asymmetric information and the principle of 'market failure'. Why do we need a new, positive linking perspective on policy at all?

The stark fact is that the combination of large-scale state activity and a mechanistic intellectual approach to policy making has simply not delivered anything like the success which the founding fathers of the post-Second World War social settlement imagined would be the case. Serious economic and social problems persist.

A distinguishing feature of the social and economic history of the second half of the twentieth century is the enormous rise in the role of the state throughout the Western world. Gradually, many of the functions previously within the domain of the third or private sector have been embraced within the public sector. Roosevelt's New Deal in America in the 1930s was bitterly denounced by critics at the time as being nothing less than socialism. But the percentage share of the whole economy accounted for by the spending of the Federal government was not much more than half of what it was under Ronald Reagan. The most avowedly socialist government in the history of the UK was that of Clement Attlee from 1945 to 1951. Yet the share of the public sector in the economy as a whole under Attlee was less than it was during the government of Mrs Thatcher, renowned for her robust approach to the privatisation of state activities.

Within this framework, generations of policy makers have been raised to have a mechanistic view of the world, and a checklist mentality: all that is necessary to achieve a particular set of aims is to draw up a list of policies and simply tick them off. Such an apparently dependable, predictable and controllable environment is a comforting one in which to live.

The intellectual underpinning of the burgeoning activity of the state has been provided by mainstream economics. Paradoxically, a theoretical construct which purports to establish the efficiency of the free market has justified an enormously enhanced role for the state. It is not just the sheer size of the public sector but the range of private activities which governments now try to influence or control, either through direct regulation or through exhortations to avoid behaviour deemed inappropriate by bureaucrats, such as becoming obese or drinking more alcohol than we are told is good for us.

We have seen in Chapter 3 how the concept of 'market failure', at first sight a critique of free-market economics, has provided powerful backing to state intervention. If markets, for whatever reason, are unable to function in practice as the theory suggests they should, then regulation, taxes and/or incentives of all shapes and forms are justified. They are justified in order to make the imperfect world conform to the perfect one of economic theory. Economists, have we have seen, slip all too easily into the attitude that their core theory does not merely purport to describe how the world actually is, it is a prescription for how the world *ought* to be.

The world view of free-market economic theory is precisely one in which rational agents are able to make optimal decisions and achieve the best possible outcome in any particular set of circumstances. And so behaviour can be influenced by the appropriate set of incentives selected by the authorities. Indeed, we see a vast array of taxes, subsidies, benefits, all aimed at achieving precise, detailed outcomes. And where there are obstacles to agents making the best choice, where there is 'market failure', the clever, rational planner can intervene to ensure that the world works as the theory deems it ought.

I use the word 'planner' deliberately. In the 1940s and early 1950s, at the frontiers of high economic theory, it was demonstrated that an omniscient socialist planner, by using the price mechanism as a way of deciding how resources should be allocated, could achieve results identical to those of an idealised free-market economy, but with a more egalitarian distribution of income and wealth.

There was a great deal of practical interest in planned economies at the time. Western economies had been subject to rigid restrictions and controls during the Second World War. The planned economy of the Soviet Union not only seemed to have escaped the economic crash of the 1930s, but had been instrumental in defeating Nazi Germany, the most titanic land battles of all time taking place on the Eastern Front. Socialist planning was shown – theoretically – to be just as efficient as free enterprise, and at the same time more equitable. Of course, the discrepancy between theory and practice in the planned economies of the Soviet bloc was plain for all who chose to see. But even so, as the problems of the actually existing planned economies of the Soviet bloc became more and more apparent, the intellectual belief in the ability of clever, rational planners to control social and economic outcomes remained strong in the West. Mainstream economic theory, rooted in its particular vision of rational behaviour, provided the required intellectual framework.

We have now had over sixty years of this vision of the state. It is fundamentally different from anything that preceded it in the Western world, except during the two world wars. Yet those deep social and economic problems remain. For example in the six decades since the Second World War both the average rate of unemployment and the range within which it varies are scarcely different from those in the six decades preceding it, and, of course, in 2011 the number out of work stands at a high level in most countries. If the policy planners were supposed to achieve anything, then surely it was full employment. Joblessness on a grand scale was the scourge of the West in the early 1930s. To be fair, the maximum rates of unemployment have never again reached those of the Great Depression, but taking a longer view, averaging over decades, the rates are very similar in the pre- and post-Second World War periods. In America, the pre-war average was 7 per cent compared to just under 6 per cent post-war, in the UK the two averages are virtually identical at about 5.5 per cent, whilst in Germany the average unemployment rate since the Second World War, at just over 5 per cent, is around 1 per cent *higher* than the pre-war average.

Comparing crime rates over time is difficult, but despite sharp falls since the mid-1990s in both America and Britain, crime is everywhere much higher now than it was in 1950. Income and wealth might have increased overall, but their distribution has widened dramatically. Rational planning and clever regulation designed to cope with 'market failure' did not prevent the biggest economic recession since the 1930s from taking place in 2008–9.

*

The principal cause of the failure of what we might describe as the social democratic model to achieve its objectives is not the size of the state but the intellectual framework in which it operates. At heart, from this perspective the world is seen as a machine, admittedly a complicated one, but one which can be controlled with the right pressure on this button, just the right amount of pull on that lever. It is a world in which everything can be quantified and targets can be not only set but also achieved, thanks to the cleverness of experts.

The world is simply not like this. It is much more complex, much less controllable than 'rational' planners believe. Policy is very difficult to get right.

The main reason for this is that both Keynes's and Simon's insights into the limits to computational ability apply not just to people and companies but, equally, to what we might term the agents of the state, the public servants, the regulators, the planners. They are not specially privileged in this respect, and may very well be unable to decide, even in principle, the 'optimal' strategy to achieve any particular goal. Simon demonstrated the limits to human competence in this respect even in the humble setting of the game of chess. And most social and economic problems are considerably more complicated than chess. So, even when agents are presumed to be acting autonomously, without direct reference to the behaviour of others, when they are confronted by different information, by a different set of incentives as a result of a change in policy, their responses may be hard to anticipate. Agents may react in innovative ways, unanticipated by the planner. Or there may be entirely unintended and unforeseen adverse consequences of a change in incentives.

The problem of gauging in advance the reaction of agents to changes becomes even more difficult in situations where they base their actions, choices, opinions in part on those of others on the relevant network. So even if we know for certain how any given agent will react to a policy change now, there is no guarantee that the response will be the same tomorrow, next week, or in six months' time. The response will depend to a greater or lesser extent on how others react. This may seem obvious. But these things are not taken into account either in many ex-ante assessments of the policy terrain, or in the ex-post analysis of the impact of policies. The introduction of these fundamental features of reality into the picture rapidly leads to great uncertainty about the consequences of any given action.

At heart, policy in the West, both social and economic, rests on the framework of the economically rational agent. Agents who respond to incentives in entirely predictable ways. But unfortunately, they don't. Incentives still matter, of course, but network effects often matter even more, and in such cases they can either swamp or enhance incentive effects. We have seen, with the example of the simple market demand curve in Chapter 5 and Figure 5.2, how network effects make the evaluation of policy much more difficult than if incentives alone are operating.

Ignoring network effects when they are present can lead to seriously misleading interpretations of how things work.

Policy, whether corporate or public, needs to be looked at through the lens of the twenty-first-century model of rational agent behaviour outlined in this book. In its essentials, this is based on the principle of copying. The theory recognises that agents can innovate, make choices that have never been made before. But the guiding principle of behaviour is that agents copy the actions, opinions, choices of others according to the principle of preferential attachment. This, recall from Chapter 6, was the concept articulated by Herb Simon in his *Biometrika* article. The more an alternative is selected, the more likely it is to be selected by the next agent confronted by the choice. This, almost paradoxically, both introduces much more ex-ante uncertainty into the outcome of any given policy measure, and at the same time potentially enormously increases its potential impact through the power of positive linking.

This new model of rational behaviour is able, as we have seen, to account for two fundamental empirical features of many modern social and economic outcomes: the unequal distribution of the outcome at any point in time, and turnover within the outcome over time. It is this latter property, the ability to account in a perfectly natural way for the ubiquitous phenomenon of turnover, of popular things becoming less popular and vice versa, which is the real innovation and which previous theories are either unable to explain, or can do so only in artificial ways. In addition, it simplifies dramatically the scale of choices which agents face in the modern world. The model is an example of Simon's rules of thumb which he believed guided agent behaviour, and which he regarded as being the rational way to behave in situations of any degree of complexity.

The model of twenty-first-century rationality satisfies the basic scientific requirement of being able to explain key features of the real world. Karl Marx famously wrote, 'The philosophers have only interpreted the world, in various ways; the point is to change it.' He was completely wrong. Without a reasonably scientific way of interpreting the world, it will be very hard to change it. But it is essential that we do not fall into the trap of confusing the model *with* the world. The model of rational behaviour is merely a tool for thinking about how the world works. Like any model, it makes simplifying assumptions. It offers a way of interpreting social and economic issues which is more realistic than the economic model of rational behaviour.

*

One objection to this way of thinking is that it suggests that policy is very hard to get right. Uncertainty is a key feature of the model of twenty-first-century rationality. However, uncertainty is also a key feature of reality. Certainly, this is true ex ante, before any decision is taken. And even after the event, as the simple market demand curve in Figure 5.2 shows, network effects make evaluation of the effects difficult. This is disconcerting to many people, especially those trained in the social sciences, and in particular economics, in recent decades. The belief that clever people, with sufficient thought, really can be social engineers and design the perfect society is very deeply embedded. Real engineers really can design bridges that really work exactly as intended. The vision of society and the economy as machines encourages policy makers to take the same view of their ability to design human behaviour. But it is no longer relevant, if it ever were, to most aspects of human social and economic behaviour.

This is why the network effects view of behaviour is so challenging. I have heard frequent arguments along the lines: this is all very well, these networks may seem very clever, but they lack clear guidelines about what we should actually *do* to solve a problem. If we used the economically rational approach, we would know what to do.

The first of these points is serious and valid, and is the subject of much of the rest of this chapter. The second is an obvious non sequitur. The economic rational agent model is indeed capable of providing policy makers with an exact answer to a question: in order to achieve X, do Y. But all too often, doing Y leads to Z, or even to what we might call minus X, the complete opposite of what was intended! Recall the example of the police captain in Chapter 1. One of the most frequent and conspicuous instances of outcomes such as these is provided by financial markets. During the summer of 2011, for example, there has been constant concern about the state of Europe's economies, and the future of both the euro and the eurozone. Periodically, the French president or the German chancellor or the head of the European Commission will make a statement intended to calm the markets, or the European Central Bank will intervene in the bond market with the same intention in mind. But instead of recovering, the markets often fall further.

This way of thinking about policy does not provide control, merely the illusion of control. The twenty-first-century rational behaviour model gives a good description of how the world is. Rejecting the model as a policy tool because it may not give unequivocal recommendations is wholly invalid. The model describes how the real world actually operates, and a failure to take this into account really does mean that the success or failure of any given policy becomes a random, hit-or-miss affair.

There are other, rather more philosophical objections to a model of rational behaviour based on the principle of copying as explained by Keynes: 'Knowing that our individual judgement is worthless, we endeavour to fall back on the judgement of the rest of the world which is perhaps better informed.' At first sight, the approach seems to deny the existence of individual agency, of deliberate purpose and intent when an agent is making a decision. At a deeper level, it may even be argued that it is denying the existence of free will, the capacity of individuals to choose between right and wrong. If agents simply copy the decisions of others according to some set formula, the choice dictated by the principle of preferential attachment, then are they not merely acting as automatons?

The answer to this was implicitly provided by Keynes himself. Remember that he started his analysis from the precept that 'we have, as a rule, only the vaguest idea of any but the most direct consequences of our acts'. However, he recognised immediately that 'the necessity for action and for decision compels us as practical men to do our best to overlook this awkward fact'. Keynes argued that, to cope with situations in which we may only have a vague idea of the consequences of our acts and yet at the same time are obliged to take some decision, 'we have devised for the purpose a variety of techniques'. And the main technique, as Keynes recognised only too well, is to copy the group because the group is probably better informed than we are. We have noted a wide variety of motives which can underpin the principle of copying in addition to the one described by Keynes. But the point here, in answer to the charge that the model of behaviour based on copying denies free will and agency, is that *agents consciously choose to copy* as the basic principle of their behaviour in many situations. It is entirely rational for them to do so. They may appear to be surrendering their capacity to act as individuals, but they are deciding for themselves that this is the most sensible course to take.

A related but different criticism is that an approach to policy based upon recognising the importance of network effects will lead to companies or governments obtaining so much knowledge about individuals that they will be able to control our behaviour as never before. The terrifying vision of the world which George Orwell set out in his novel *1984*, when the citizen is powerless before the all-seeing Big Brother, is the inevitable consequence of this view of the world. Some background explanation seems necessary.

Ironically, it is the vision of the world based upon free markets and the economically rational agent to which this criticism is more pertinently applied. As we saw above, in theoretical terms, the Platonic ideas of a free-market economy and of a centrally planned economy are identical. Given sufficient information on the tastes and preferences of agents, in principle the central planner could set prices to ensure that supply and demand balanced in all markets, that the economy was in 'general equilibrium'. And so by implication, by altering prices, the planner could bring about a different equilibrium in line with his or her policy aims, or the aims of the Politburo or whatever. Agents, with their fixed tastes and preferences, can in principle be manipulated by the use of prices – incentives – to achieve any desired outcome. Of course, the contrast between the theory and the practice of the centrally planned economies was dramatic. Far from being efficient, almost to the very last days the old Soviet Union was scarcely able to feed its own population.

The revolution in communications technology does not only mean that agents are much more aware than ever before of the choices and opinions of others. It supplies companies and governments with stupendous amounts of information on how people actually behave. Some readers of this book may have bought it after being told about it by a recommender system. Such systems hold information on your previous online purchases – of books in this case – and then let you know when a book comes out which appears to fit in with your tastes. Recommender systems themselves are pretty big business. Teams of high-powered mathematicians* are competing to find better and better ways of discovering the tastes and preferences of agents based upon their previous purchases, or even previous search behaviour. The more they can discover, the better able are companies to make recommendations which are even more closely in line with an individual's tastes, and so the more likely he or she is to purchase the recommended product.

So far, all this is compatible with the view of the world encapsulated by the economically rational agent, operating in isolation from others. In such a world, recommender algorithms may indeed be able to discover over time the complete preferences of an agent, assuming these remain fixed. However, the mathematicians who devise these algorithms are also perfectly aware of the principle of copying, of the fact that a product can experience positive feedback. Once it achieves a certain level of popularity, a product, a service, an idea, may become even more popular simply because it is popular. Sophisticated strategies are developed to try to ensure that, say, a particular website comes high in the list of searches – remember that the top three sites on a Google search typically get 98 per cent of the hits. Equally, the search engines attempt to prevent their sites being gamed in this way. Behind the innocuous facade of internet searches and recommendations, teams of some of the world's best young mathematicians are pitted in a relentless struggle against each other.

Attempts to sway opinions, and possibly as a result subsequent behaviour, are by no means confined to sophisticated mathematical

---

* The maths of this is pretty hair raising. 'Quantum state diffusion', for example, is one of the concepts used in some approaches. A flavour of the difficulties can be obtained by following up some of the technical papers cited on the Wikipedia entry for 'recommender algorithms'.

manipulations. Hoteliers, restaurant owners, authors, are frequently exposed as having either posted numerous favourable reviews of their own products on internet comparison sites, or, in some cases, concocting highly unflattering reviews of their rivals. Rather like Eliza Doolittle in George Bernard Shaw's play Pygmalion, who had been speaking grammar for years without knowing what it was, these characters, too, in their own rather haphazard way, have discovered the potential of positive linking without knowing anything at all about the underlying theory.

The same techniques of discovery, of monitoring individuals and their tastes and preferences, are, of course, available to governments. The fears associated with the view that we are now in a world where companies may know more about an individual's preferences than the individual can articulate are magnified many fold when the potential powers of government are considered. And might governments in some way use the power of networks, the tendency for positive feedback to spread ideas or behaviour through a network, for sinister purposes of control?

Again, these issues are features of the real world. The twenty-first-century model of rational behaviour simply tells us, as a good initial approximation, how agents behave in such a world. It does not create the world, it describes how the world operates. Any worries which we have are caused not by the model, but by reality. But increased information about agents, whether in the hands of firms or of governments, can actually be beneficial. Alerting agents to products which they might like can be seen as a dangerous form of manipulation, but it can also be regarded as reducing the costs to the individual of discovering such things for themselves.

For example a better understanding of vehicle movements might enable traffic systems to be designed more effectively to deliver more efficient flows. As we saw previously, Dirk Helbing has increased dramatically our understanding of pedestrian flows, and provided insights into how to reduce the chances of people being crushed in panics. In normal circumstances, people exiting a stadium or a theatre do so in an orderly fashion, leaving adequate space between themselves and their neighbours, but in a panic, people both collide, slowing progress, and also exhibit strong flocking behaviour, copying what other people are doing. Even if there are exits spaced at regular intervals, there is still an inherent tendency for many people to attempt to escape by the same one. So, even in the hands of companies or governments, an increase in information about individuals can have beneficial effects.

*

Despite the masses of information that can be gleaned from technological advances in communications and electronic payment systems, there are formidable practical difficulties in the way of any attempt to organise the world in a way which matches the design of the policy maker. The challenges include knowing, or at least having some idea of, the structure of the network across which agents are influenced in the given context. We remember from Chapter 6 that there are different types of network in the social and economic worlds, and the kinds of approaches which might work on one may have little impact on another. So although we do not need complete knowledge of the network, we need to have a reasonable approximation to its basic structure.

It might reasonably be suggested that modern communications technology would allow policy makers to obtain a complete picture of a network: the mobile phone records of an individual, for example, can be known perfectly. However, such a network is, most emphatically, not much use in general in policy contexts. We need to know not the complete list of people with whom an agent is in contact, but who on this network might actually influence the agent's behaviour, might induce him or her to copy, might trigger the phenomenon of positive linking. And, of course, the most influential people might not be the ones the agent phones most often. It is the relevant social network which is of interest, not the readily mapped networks of phone connections or emails. In short, a lot of important, and in particular qualitative, information concerning networks is effectively impossible to know in many practical situations.

In addition to the structure of the social network, who copies from whom, we need evidence on the willingness of agents to be persuaded, to copy the opinions, behaviours or choices of others. In practical terms, these are formidable obstacles. But if we do obtain at least some information on such matters, as we can recall from Chapter 6, network theory itself gives us useful guides to the conduct of policy, on which strategies are more likely to work than others.

In a scale-free network, we know that we need to identify the well-connected individuals and to try by some means to induce them to change their behaviours. In a random network, we know that there is a critical value of the proportion of agents we need to influence in order to encourage or mitigate the spread of a particular mode of behaviour or opinion across the network. This at least gives us an idea of the scale of the effort required, and tells us that money and time which is unlikely to generate the critical mass is money and time wasted. In a small-world context, targeting our efforts is more difficult, but at least we know that it is the long-range connectors, the agents with links across different parts of the network, or who have connections into several relevant networks, who are the most fruitful to target.

A key point here is that when network effects are present, the most effective policies are unlikely to be generic, across-the-board changes to incentives. Careful prior analysis and thoughtful targeting become the order of the day. If we can get it right, or even approximately right, less can be more. Fewer resources used more intelligently can potentially lead to much more effective strategies. To positive linking.

Altering the structure of the network might itself also become a policy target, and one which could have powerful effects. We discussed in the previous chapter the problems of local areas where unemployment was not just high but practically endemic. At a very local level, even in poor towns, different public housing schemes, with residents from essentially identical socio-economic backgrounds, can exhibit quite different levels of worklessness. A culture can readily evolve in which an income from benefits supplemented by petty crime and casual labour becomes the social norm. In short, it is essential to take into account the fact that people live in a social context, and the particular circumstances of their various social networks can have a decisive influence on their decisions.

The most important way in which people find jobs is through personal contact. A vacancy is heard about through a friend, a family member, a neighbour. In turn, the fact that such individuals are the source of your information may send a signal to the prospective employer, especially from your informant who already works there. In an informal way, you are being recommended.

For professionals, the idea of networking – making personal contact as a key way of advancement – is second nature. But the same effect occurs at all levels of skill and qualification. Social networks are the single most important avenue for the individual to discover that a job vacancy exists. They are much more important than formal channels such as newspapers, the internet, recruitment agencies or public employment services. And from the point of view of the employer, the grapevine is less risky than recruiting from the open market, because they have additional information about the recruit.

Some public housing schemes may indeed have evolved as their social norm a network in which most adults of working age receive some form of state handout. Equally, however, the network of connections of the residents to the world of employment may just be too sparse. They simply do not hear about vacancies because not enough of them are in the loop, as it were. And we have seen in Chapter 5 that if a network has few connections, few links, then percolation across it is likely to be very limited. So policy in this instance should be directed towards increasing the social connections of the residents with the world of work, of altering the structure of the network so that it is easier for information about job vacancies to spread amongst the workless residents. And at the same time, the stronger these connections become, the greater the chance that a different social norm, that of being in work, even if it is low paid, will spread. Exactly how this is achieved, or attempted, will depend a great deal upon the purely local circumstances, of particular knowledge of the area – a theme of localisation, of devolving decisions as far as possible, which will be taken up again later in the chapter.

*

We do have the great advantage of a reliable indicator of whether network effects are present in any given situation. They leave their distinct, characteristic footprint. Namely, we observe unequal outcomes. This is a sure sign that feedbacks are operating, that factors are at work which can readily intensify the initial impact of any change in the relevant system. So we can be alerted to the presence of network effects. And we know that the type of network will influence the approach to policy which we take in any particular context. We might try to alter the network, or we might attempt to exploit its particular features once we have an approximation to its structure, its type. But how do we obtain the latter?

In many situations, simple old-fashioned survey data can do the trick, can help us approximate the type of network we are dealing with. The results need to be used in conjunction with network theory, but survey evidence can tell us a lot. This is just one illustration of how progress is being made in understanding network effects, but it is perhaps worth looking at a particular example. Social problems in particular are amenable to this way of identifying network effects and the type of network which is operating. The technique discussed in this example could be applied in a wide variety of situations.

The example I would like to focus on is a contemporary problem in British towns and cities, especially on Friday and Saturday nights: binge drinking. This involves the rapid consumption of almost unbelievable amounts of alcohol, such as a half-litre of vodka to start the evening off before getting down to more serious drinking. The results are entirely predictable. Young people – and a new aspect of this is that women are involved just as much as men – collapse incapable into the gutter, get into fights, require hospital treatment, stomachs pumped, wounds stitched, to say nothing of the inconvenience and distress this causes to respectable citizens on a night out.

Many incentive-based policies are suggested to try to deal with this problem, such as putting up the price of strong drink and restricting 'happy hours' when alcohol is served cheaply. There has always been a small percentage of young men who get into such a state, but it has become much more widespread in recent years and, as noted already, young women have become eager participants. There is no obvious correlation between the rise of this type of behaviour and factors such as the price of alcohol, which has certainly not become dramatically cheaper. So it seems very likely that a network effect is present. Binge drinking started to become that bit more popular. As a result the behaviour was copied even more, and instead of being frowned upon, it gained peer acceptance.

A survey was carried out by the marketing survey company FDS in which young people were asked to categorise themselves as binge drinkers or not. Getting people to reveal their drinking patterns is notoriously difficult, so there were plenty of cross-checks in the questionnaire, my personal favourite being the question: 'Have you ever woken up next to someone you did not recognise?' – a pretty reliable guide to alcoholic excess the night before! Nearly 20 per cent of young British adults were classified as regular binge drinkers in the survey. More interesting, however, was the way in which the participants classified their family members, work colleagues and friends. Table 9.1 shows the results of one such question: 'Are your friends binge drinkers?' We do not need statistical theory to tell us that there is a great deal of difference between the behaviour of the friends of binge drinkers and the friends of non-binge drinkers. Far more of the former themselves participate in the activity.

Proportion of friends thought to be binge drinkers	Proportion (%) for binge drinkers	Proportion (%) for non-binge drinkers
All or almost all of them	54	17
Most of them	31	24
Some of them	12	36
Hardly any or none of them	3	22

Table 9.1 Binge drinking habits of friends of binge and non-binge drinkers

The table certainly suggests the existence of network effects, of binge drinkers being influenced by the behaviour of their friends, and the non-binge drinkers being restrained by their set of friends. Of course, there are qualifications to this. We have no direct evidence on the behaviour of the binge drinkers' friends, but rely on the perceptions which the drinkers themselves have about them. There is therefore a risk that the respondents exhibit a certain amount of cognitive dissonance about their own behaviour in order to rationalise it and to protect their self-image. That said, the results do have a basic plausibility, since drinking, after all, is in general a social activity. Further, it is possible that friendship groups are formed on the basis of attitudes towards drinking. But it would be curious, to say the least, if large numbers of young people had suddenly decided quite independently of each other to binge drink, and then had happened to congregate together in friendship networks. So whilst the existence of a copying effect amongst friendship networks is not technically proved by these results, it seems a far more likely explanation than the alternative.

The results in Table 9.1 are interesting in their own right. But we can make even more use of them to obtain an approximation to the type of network structure which is operating in this particular context. Essentially, we set up mathematical models populated by agents who potentially copy each other's behaviour, and use them to see which type of network is best able to approximate the friendship structures of the two groups described in Table 9.1. We start the model off with everyone being a non-binge drinker, exactly as Duncan Watts did in his model described in Chapter 5. A few agents are chosen at random to become binge drinkers, and we follow the percolation of behaviour across the network and examine the match between the friendship patterns in Table 9.1 and what happens in the model with different networks.

I developed this methodology for a conference organised by

the US Office of Naval Research, and used data on individuals with and without bank accounts to illustrate the approach. Most people without access to financial services were receiving some form of benefit, but otherwise were very hard to distinguish in terms of their socio-economic characteristics from apparently similar people who did have bank accounts. But whether members of their friends or family did or did not have bank accounts gave a powerful explanation of whether or not any given individual would do so. Other social phenomena such as child obesity can be analysed using the same method. This description is rather cryptic, almost out of necessity, but technical details are provided in the articles referred to in the 'Further Reading' appendix.

Our analysis indicated that the network structure which best accounts for the binge-drinking phenomenon is that of the small world, or overlapping 'friends of friends', which is perhaps not surprising in this particular context. Now, the knowledge of this does not tell the policy maker exactly what to do to get a grip on this unpleasant problem, to solve it through positive linking, but it sets the parameters within which policy needs to be made. We know that we are facing a problem where network effects are important, and we have a good approximation to the type of network which is involved. If we are in some way able to penetrate the network, policy can be highly effective in reducing dramatically the scale of the problem. If we understand neither of these things, we are simply looking through a glass darkly, scarecely aware of the way in which the issue has arisen.

*

So, we have some good ways of knowing whether network effects are present in any particular situation. We have methods to approximate the network structure, the type of network which appears to be operating. We have guidelines for policy approaches once we know the nature of the network. What else do we have to help the policy maker across this difficult and challenging terrain? Again, just to repeat for emphasis, it is not the network approach to modelling which makes life problematic for policy makers, but reality itself. The network approach best describes the real world.

Importantly, network analysis is a scientific discipline which is still in its infancy. It is only in the past ten or fifteen years that the concept has really taken off and been applied to real-world systems, in both the natural and social sciences. So there is a great deal we do not yet know. We do, however, now have glimpses into two key aspects of network effects in addition to the general concepts and guidelines summarised in the previous paragraph.

The one about which least is known is the question of ex-ante prediction of percolation across a network. In other words, imagine that we are in a situation where we know that network effects are important. We believe we have a policy, perhaps a change in incentives, which might persuade a few agents to alter their behaviour or opinion; how far will this spread across the network? Will it remain confined to a relatively small number, perhaps those who are initially persuaded and a handful of agents who are very close to them, or will it cascade across the network as a whole and lead to radical alterations in the behaviour of the group of agents in the network, to positive linking?

Any attempt to give a precise answer to this question encounters a deep-seated problem. Namely, the robust yet fragile nature of networks, one of the concepts we came across in the opening chapter. We saw an application of the idea in Duncan Watts's simple but profound model, with the results plotted in Figure 5.1. The collection of individuals who make up a network will, most of the time, exhibit stability with respect to most of the 'shocks' the network receives when a few agents change their opinion or their behaviour. The system is stable in the sense that most shocks make very little difference, they are absorbed, shrugged off, and few other agents change either their minds or their behaviour as a result. So the network is 'robust'. But, every so often, a particular shock may have a dramatic effect. So the network is also 'fragile'. The behaviour of individuals across the whole, or almost the whole, of any particular network might be altered.

Of course, if we had complete information about the structure of the network, exactly who had the potential to influence whom, and exactly how persuadable each agent was, we would be able to give an exact answer to the following question: If we get a few people to change their behaviour, how far will this change spread? But then we would no longer have a model, but reality itself. It would be as if we were on a mountain, and our map was on a scale of 1:1, showing every single detail of the terrain. Obviously, even if such a map could be constructed, it would be wholly useless in practice. Imagine trying to open it to find directions struggling in a gale on top of a mist-shrouded peak! Moreover, and importantly, unlike the hills, human networks can change over time. A map that is completely accurate one year may be out of date the next.

The more information we have, the better. But in practical circumstances, what do we need to know and how much can it tell us? It seems to be the case – and this is about as much as we can say in the present state of scientific knowledge – that what really matters is how persuadable are the agents who are directly connected to the agents who initially alter their behaviour. In general, it is not so much how many agents are potentially influenced by members of this initial group, although this can be a significant factor in scale-free networks with their highly connected hubs. It is more a matter of how easy it is for the initial group to persuade the agents to whom they are connected to change their minds as well. If these are firm minded individuals, much less inclined to copy than the average person, then the change in behaviour will fizzle out, the change will not percolate across the network. But if they are keen to experiment, easily persuaded to try something different, then the behavioural change starts to spread out across the network. There is no guarantee that it will get very much beyond this second tier of agents, as it were, but it at least it has a chance.

Very recent work also suggests that the positioning in the network of the agents who initially change their minds is important. If they are either very close to each other or widely scattered, there is more chance of the initial impact spreading throughout the network. But these are rather esoteric concepts, and translating them into positive linking practice will be far from straightforward. We do know that if we can somehow acquire information on that 'second tier', the agents who are potentially influenced directly by the initial group we manage to persuade by a change in policy, we will be getting some way towards understanding how far the change is likely to spread. But even this kind of information may not be easy to obtain in practice.

We are on somewhat firmer ground in predicting the eventual outcome once an initial change has taken place in agent behaviour, as discussed in Chapter 7. Somewhat paradoxically, the very network effects which make purely ex-ante prediction difficult increase our chances of predicting how far the change will spread once we have some initial evidence on the early effects of the change. The trick is not to look for any inherent qualities or attributes of the change in which we are interested; it is rather to interrogate the data and see how strong the network effects are. This would apply equally whether we were marketing a new variety of chocolate bar or trying to get people in social housing schemes off benefit and back into work.

In a world in which network effects are important, the early stages of any evolutionary process, such as how the popularities of different choices evolve over time, are often decisive. So we can obtain a pretty good reading on where to concentrate our future resources, where to reinforce potential success in order to amplify it, once we have some initial evidence on where a change in behaviour is beginning to gain traction.

This certainly has a practical policy implication in terms of tapping into the potential of positive linking. Rather than putting all our eggs in one basket, with the misplaced confidence of the central planner, and declaring that one size fits all, we should instead experiment with lots of variants around any particular theme. Companies in fast-moving consumer goods markets such as confectionery already implement this kind of strategy intuitively. The challenge is how to go about this with public policy, a theme to which I return below. But the inescapable fact about social and economic systems in which network effects are important is that there is inherent uncertainty. Uncertainty about the future course of the economy or a social issue, and uncertainty about the impact of any policy change designed to alter the future. Even with the vast proliferation of information from the new communications technologies, and even with the advances which are being made in understanding the mathematical properties of networks, these uncertainties will remain.

An important reason was anticipated by science-fiction author Isaac Asimov in his great 1950s *Foundation* series. Asimov imagined the development of a science which combined history, sociology and maths to make general predictions about the future behaviour of large groups of people – almost exactly the challenge which now faces the social sciences when we start to incorporate network effects into our thinking. Asimov called his invention 'psychohistory', designed by the character Hari Seldon, who predicted the collapse of his civilisation, the Galactic Empire. The intricate details of the subsequent plot need not concern us, but Asimov stated that a necessary condition for Seldon's equations to work is that the population should remain in ignorance of the results of the application of psychohistorical analyses.

Here, in a nutshell, is a fundamental issue confronting any attempt to exercise precise control over the behaviour of human beings. If people become aware that attempts are being made to manipulate them, they have the capacity to alter their behaviour. And the collective imagination, the creativity of a group of humans, exceeds the ability of the would-be planner to anticipate how their behaviour might change. So, in the examples of the opening chapter, the police captain firing his gun into the air imagined that this would disperse the crowd of would-be rioters. Queen Mary thought that a policy of burning recalcitrant Protestants to death would persuade them to either flee the country or recant. Both were perfectly reasonable views to hold ex ante, but both incorrectly anticipated how people would actually react.

As we have seen, great social scientists in the past emphasised the inherent limits to our knowledge of human systems. Simon argued that the number of future paths open to us at any point in time was so vast that it made no sense at all to speak of the best, the optimal, decision. Keynes, as we have seen, stated that 'we have, as a rule, only the vaguest idea of any but the most direct consequences of our acts'. Hayek, whom we met in Chapter 6, was another great polymath social scientist who, like Simon, received the Nobel Prize in economics. Although he and Keynes clashed on specific issues of economic policy, they shared the vision of the limits to knowledge. Indeed, his Nobel lecture was entitled 'The Pretence of Knowledge'. Hayek is often seen as a free-market economist. But he was deeply critical of mainstream economics, precisely because its fundamental building block, the rational economic agent, was assumed to possess knowledge and capabilities which Hayek regarded as absurd.

A crucial point is that these limits apply to everyone. They apply to politicians, to government officials, to central bankers, to national and international regulators, to everyone. This is a very difficult point for policy makers to accept. The mentality of the central planner remains pervasive across the governments of the West, the belief that the bureaucrat is able to draw on special knowledge, special information, maybe even special gifts and talents – certainly many of them think they possess these! That, ultimately, the bureaucrat knows considerably better than the ordinary person what does and does not work.

Our current political institutions are to a large extent based on the vision of society and the economy operating like machines, populated by economically rational agents. This view of the world leads to centralised bureaucracies and centralised decision making. We live in a society where decisions are made through several layers of bureaucracy, in both the public and private sectors. On the whole, this leads to decisions that are insensitive to local (micro) conditions, and which are insensitive to society as it changes.

A lack of both resilience and robustness is a characteristic feature of such approaches to both social and economic management. Structures, rules, regulations, incentives are put in place in the belief that a desired outcome can be achieved, that a potential crisis can be predicted and forestalled by such policies. As the financial crisis from 2007 onwards illustrates only too well, this view of the world is ill suited to creating systems which are resilient when unexpected shocks occur, and which exhibit robustness in their ability to recover from the shock. The focus of policy needs to shift away from prediction and control. We can never predict the unpredictable. Instead, we need systems which exhibit resilience and robustness, which can respond well to unpredictable future events, which can recover through the strengths of positive linking.

*

Policy decisions – both in the political and corporate worlds – are largely based on thinking that emerged out of the European Enlightenment. Social sciences have been heavily influenced (understandably) by the scientific method and the tools and techniques developed in classical physics during the nineteenth and early twentieth centuries. The Enlightenment was essentially about the application of rational analysis to a sophisticated machine, in order to bring about a better world. This cognitive framework might not only have been necessary but could even have been essential to create the world in which we now live, a world of wholly unprecedented prosperity. But, as we have seen, the basic assumptions behind the social science which underpinned this vision, that of the economically rational agent, are out of date in the context of the globally integrated world of the twenty-first century.

Almost paradoxically, the global and networked society of the twenty-first century requires an emphasis on devolving decision-making power as far as is practical, a concept often referred to as 'subsidiarity'. Much tacit knowledge, knowledge derived from experience which is hard if not impossible to codify systematically, rests with individuals at a local decision-making level. Even in a large, mass-production factory, the individual workers know things about their particular task which are hard to write down. And, when telephoning a company to make a complaint, would you rather deal with a complicated rule-based system which requires you to press a sequence of digits to get a response, or would you rather speak directly to a real person, someone who might actually understand what your complaint is about? As we have seen, network effects require as much knowledge as we can possibly gather as we struggle with the uncertainties they bring and attempt to generate the benefits of positive linking.

This concept applies both within and outside any institutional structure. Take banking: most lenders apply rigid, centrally determined rules as to whether a loan can be granted, or whether an existing one is running into problems and should be called in. In contrast, Svenska Handelsbanken, Sweden's largest bank, devolves a great deal of autonomy right down to the individual officer in the local branch. In turn, these officials have an informal network across which they consult and seek advice about the creditworthiness of a company, the prospects for an industrial sector. In the early 1990s Sweden experienced a localised economic recession which was even more severe than that of the Great Depression of the 1930s. Corporate loan defaults rose sharply, but nowhere near as sharply amongst Handelsbanken borrowers as in the rest of the Swedish banking sector. The recession of 2008–9 led to exactly the same experience. One set of good results could be down to chance. Two, and it looks as if they have their devolved system and the use of informal, tacit knowledge to thank.

The devolution of decision making is also more likely to convey legitimacy on whatever decisions are made. As we have seen, agents are capable of responding in seemingly perverse ways – perverse, that is, when viewed from the perspective of economic rationality – to policy changes. Occasionally such perversity is deliberate, and intended to frustrate the intention of the policy maker. But the greater the local involvement, the greater the legitimacy is likely to be, and the more likely people will respond favourably to some policy change.

Whilst subsidiarity is usually thought of as a question of

decision-making power, there is an equivalent question about responsibility. Many believe that 'something should be done about social problem X, and since the national government is very powerful and is supposed to represent us, it should be responsible for sorting X out'. The machine metaphor approach means we have tended to think the state does have significant power – buttons, levers, the full panoply of control. This has increasingly encouraged a moral hazard-type effect, with people ceding a lot of individual and group responsibility to the state. Our understanding of networks allows us to see that the state is less powerful than we had thought. This in turn raises the question of distribution of responsibility in society. Communities ought to take more responsibility for outcomes, for their own benefit, rather than relying upon some external, magical power to solve the problem. They themselves are in a much better position to realise the benefits of positive linking that some remote, would-be bureaucrat still burdened with the mind-set of a central planner.

This is not an argument for no government, it is an argument for different government. A recurring and legitimate question posed by policy makers who have been exposed to network-type approaches is, 'Where is the silver bullet?' In other words, what is the action, the crucial decision, which will penetrate to the heart of whatever problem is being considered? The silver bullet of twenty-first-century networked reality is simple: it is to realise that there is no silver bullet. Devolution of decisions, experimentation and, yes, the recognition that many of these experiments will fail, will not deliver in terms of value for money. But experiment will discover the approach which really does work, which kicks in the network effects to deliver changes which are far more substantial than could be achieved by incentives alone, which delivers positive linking. It is a totally different approach to public policy from the one that has been in almost exclusive use throughout the West since the Second World War.

Think of some of the major challenges facing the world at present, and then think how successful the rational, central planning approach to public policy has been. Let us take as an example the management of economic crises. The rational paradigm has spectacularly failed to explain and predict not just how the present crisis emerged, but how it spread and burgeoned, initially starting with a relatively small US mortgage crisis, quickly developing into a credit and banking crisis, leading to a worldwide financial crisis, a global debt crisis for small and then big countries such as Italy, and finally, at the time of writing, into a general political crisis that is threatening the economic stability of the entire planet and the welfare of everyone on it.

Inequality is a major concern across several dimensions of the concept. The most obvious is the increase in inequalities of wealth and income in the West in recent decades. But there is also the fact that outcomes in health care from hospitals, for example, or in education from schools are 'unequal' in the key sense that they differ at any point in time. But how does inequality arise? Is some degree of inequality inevitable in a complex world of networked agents, and, if so, what can be done to mitigate it?

Inadequate supplies of food, water and energy have led to social, economic and security-related problems in many parts of the world. One crucial issue here is what economists call the 'tragedy of the commons'. If everyone has access to a particular resource how do we prevent it from being exploited to the point of exhaustion? We saw in Chapter 7 anthropologist Steve Lansing's demonstration of how Balinese rice farmers created structures and institutions at the local level to produce viable solutions. Political scientist Elinor Ostrom has showed more generally how societies evolve ways of dealing with the 'tragedy of the commons' to give outcomes which are quite different from those predicted by economic theory. Her economics Nobel Prize awarded in 2009 was the subject of many vituperative attacks from economists unable to escape the constraints of their own model of so-called rational behaviour – 'She is not even an economist!' was a cry repeated many times.

We do not yet have the answers to such shortages, or to many other major problems, but an approach to them based on an intellectual framework which recognises the paramount importance and influence of network effects is at least in tune with the real world as it exists today. It is the one which is more likely to deliver success – to discover what works in the twenty-first century and to deliver the benefits of positive linking.

Suggestions for Further Reading

This is not intended to be a comprehensive set of references covering every single point made in the text. Rather, it is a mixture, documenting in more detail some of the works mentioned in the main body of the book, and giving suggestions for interested readers to pursue. By the very nature of the subject, a substantial part of the material is not readily accessible to readers lacking some familiarity with mathematics. But the level of difficulty varies, and the fact that part of an article contains maths should not always act as a deterrent.

Contrary to the bad press it often receives, Wikipedia is in general very good in this area. The site both helps visitors discover more about a particular concept or topic, and also usually provides fairly extensive lists of further reading, of varying degrees of technicality. I have referred to Wikipedia at various points in the text, and I definitely encourage its use. Not least, the entry 'Social network' opens up a wide range of interesting material.

My own website, www.paulormerod.com, contains a considerable amount of work I have drawn on for this book. Even for academic journals, I endeavour to write in as clear and accessible way as possible, although there is often an inevitable level of technicality involved.

In terms of further web-based sources, the Cornell University Library site http://arxiv.org/ is a very extensive archive of e-prints of scientific papers. The section 'Physics and Society' lists a large number of interesting articles, although the mathematical level is in general very high and prior familiarity with the material is an advantage. The papers on the site are at the very forefront of our scientific knowledge about networks in society.

There are many books on networks, but Duncan Watts's latest, *Everything is Obvious: Once You Know the Answer* (Crown Publishing Group, 2011) is written in English and is definitely recommended. Two good sources of more technical material are Mark Newman and Duncan Watts's *The Structure and Dynamics of Networks* (Princeton University Press, 2006), which contains some classic articles, and Newman's own *Networks: An Introduction* (Oxford University Press, 2010) which is perhaps as close as you can get to a textbook in this field.

Many of the references below are to academic papers, and a judicious search of the web should enable them to be accessed for free. For example academics often post on their home pages earlier versions of the papers which are eventually accepted for publication, and so it is not always necessary to download the article exactly as published, for which many journals charge a fee. The example of the soccer hooligans in Chapter 1 is amplified in a very interesting and at the same time amusing way by Bill Buford in his book *Among the Thugs: The Experience, and the Seduction, of Crowd Violence* (W. W. Norton, 1992). There is a vast amount of material on the burnings carried out under Queen Mary. Eamon Duffy's *Fires of Faith: Catholic England Under Mary Tudor* (Yale University Press, 2009) is a well-written account by a leading historian, particularly interesting in this context because the author gives a sympathetic rationale for Mary's policy. With the historian Andrew Roach, I wrote a network-based analysis of the policy 'Emergent Scale-free Social Networks in History: Burning and the Rise of English Protestantism', published in 2008 in the web-based journal *Cultural Science* (http://culturalscience.org/journal/index.php/culturalscience/issue/view/1). We also traced how the original Inquisition gradually learned how to use networks to suppress the Cathar heresy in the thirteenth century, the first major challenge to Catholic orthodoxy in almost 1,000 years, in 'The Medieval Inquisition: Scale-free Networks and the Suppression of Heresy', *Physica A*, vol. 339 (2004), pp. 645–52. The more technical sources used in Chapter 2 are J. Adda and F. Cornaglia, 'Taxes, Cigarette Consumption and Smoking Intensity', *American Economic Review*, vol. 96 (2006), pp. 1013–28; N. A. Christakis and J. H. Fowler, 'The Spread of Obesity in a Large Social Network over 32 years', *New England Journal of Medicine*, vol. 357 (2007), pp. 370–9; and N. A. Christakis and J. H. Fowler, 'The Collective Dynamics of Smoking in a Large Social Network', *New England Journal of Medicine*, vol. 358 (2008), pp. 2249–58. The paper on crime by Steve Levitt, although it appears in a top economics journal, is very accessible to the general reader. It refers to evidence on why crime fell in America in the 1990s, although its main points remain directly relevant to crime since then. It is available in the *Journal of Economic Perspectives*, Winter 2004.

George Akerlof and Joe Stiglitz were instrumental in introducing the concept of imperfect information into modern economic theory. The seminal article is probably Akerlof's 'The Market for "Lemons": Quality Uncertainty and the Market Mechanism', *Quarterly Journal of Economics*, vol. 84 (1970), pp. 488–500, and an example of Stiglitz's work in this area is his article with Steven Salop, 'Bargains and Ripoffs: A Model of Monopolistically Competitive Price Dispersion', *Review of Economic Studies*, vol. 44 (1977), pp. 493–510.

The experimental and behavioural economists Vernon Smith and Daniel Kahneman each wrote very accessible lectures when receiving their Nobel Prizes. These were both published in vol.

93 of the *American Economic Review* (2003): Smith's is entitled 'Constructivist and Ecological Rationality in Economics' (pp. 465–508) and Kahneman's is 'Maps of Bounded Rationality: Psychology for Behavioral Economics' (pp. 1449–75). As discussed in the text, in my view possibly the most important article published in the social sciences in the second half of the twentieth century is Herbert Simon's 'A Behavioral Model of Rational Choice', in the *Quarterly Journal of Economics*, vol. 69 (1955), pp. 99–118. It is quite intricate in places, but much of the paper is in English and not maths. Friedrich Hayek does not feature as prominently in this particular book as does Simon, but his 1974 Noble lecture, 'The Pretence to Knowledge' (www.nobelprize.org/nobel_prizes/economics/laureates/1974/hayek-lecture.html), is also a seminal paper.

It is worth reading Keynes's reflections on his great book from 1936, *The General Theory of Interest, Employment and Money*, in the following year's *Quarterly Journal of Economics*, especially in the light of the economic crisis of 2007 onwards. A huge amount has been written about this, and an expanded version of Chapter 4 is in my article 'The Current Crisis and the Culpability of Macroeconomic Theory', *Journal of the British Academy of Social Sciences*, vol. 5 (2010), pp. 5–19. The other key article referred to by Simon – he wrote many more – is densely mathematical, and can be found in *Biometrika* (1955), entitled 'On a Class of Skew Distribution Functions'. This sets out a mathematical basis for the concept of copying and derives some implications. Classic psychological references to why people copy are much more accessible and include Solomon Asch, 'Opinions and Social Pressure', in *Scientific American*, coincidentally also in 1955, and S. Moscovici, E. Lage and M. Naffrechoux, 'Influences of a Consistent Minority on the Responses of a Majority in a Colour Perception Task', *Sociometry*, vol. 32 (1969), pp. 365–80. An important recent article on the effectiveness of copying is in the austere journal *Science* of 9 April 2010. Although the text is dense, it is in English and can be understood by non-specialists. As is often the case with such articles, there are many authors, but the first two named are Rendell and Boyd and it is called 'Why Copy Others? Insights from the Social Learning Strategies Tournament'. The anthropologist Steve Lansing's *Perfect Order: A Thousand Years in Bali* (Princeton University Press, 2006) offers very interesting reflections on copying and how to sustain cooperation.

Duncan Watts has done a great deal of interesting and original work on networks and copying, and the two articles discussed at some length in the text are M. J. Salganik, P. S. Dodds, and D. J. Watts, 'Experimental Study of Inequality and Unpredictability in an Artificial Cultural Market', *Science*, vol. 331, no. 5762 (2006), pp. 854–6, and D. J. Watts, 'A Simple Model of Global Cascades on Random Networks', *Proceedings of the National Academy of Science*, vol. 99, no. 9 (2002), pp. 5766–71.

Finally, a selection of my own articles on networks. One of the first I wrote which established the empirical importance of networks in people's choices was on why some people in the UK did not have bank accounts, and was written with my wife Pamela Meadows. It is 'Social Networks: Their Role in Access to Financial Services in Britain', *National Institute Economic Review*, July 2004. I formalised the procedure for approximating network structure from very limited information in 'Extracting Deep Knowledge from Limited Information', *Physica A*, vol. 378 (2007), pp. 48–52. Three more recent articles are one with Greg Wiltshire, 'Binge Drinking in the UK: A Social Network Phenomenon', *Mind and Society*, vol. 8 (2009), pp. 135–52; R. A. Bentley, P. Ormerod and M. Batty, 'Evolving Social Influence in Large Populations', *Behavioral Ecology and Sociobiology*, vol. 65 (2011), pp. 537–46; and R. A. Bentley, P. Ormerod and S. J. Shennan, 'Population-level Neutral Model Already Explains Linguistic Patterns', *Proceedings of the Royal Society B*, vol. 278, no. 1713 (2011), pp. 1770–2.

Index